AUNTIE CLEM'S BAKERY

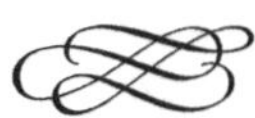

ISBN: 9781774680773 (KDP Paperback)

ISBN: 9781774680759 (Ingram Paperback)

ISBN: 9781774680766 (Ingram Hardcover)

ISBN: 9781989415009 (Kindle)

ISBN: 9781989415016 (ePub)

pdworkman

AUNTIE CLEM'S BAKERY

BOOKS # 1 - 3

P.D. WORKMAN

Delusions of the Past

Fairy Blade Unmade

Web of Nightmares

A Whisker's Breadth

Skunk Man Swamp (Coming Soon)

Magic Ain't A Game (Coming Soon)

Without Foresight (Coming Soon)

Zachary Goldman Mysteries

She Wore Mourning

His Hands Were Quiet

She Was Dying Anyway

He Was Walking Alone

They Thought He was Safe

He Was Not There

Her Work Was Everything

She Told a Lie

He Never Forgot

She Was At Risk

Kenzie Kirsch Medical Thrillers

Unlawful Harvest

Doctored Death (Coming soon)

Dosed to Death (Coming soon)

Gentle Angel (Coming soon)

AND MORE AT PDWORKMAN.COM

GLUTEN-FREE MURDER

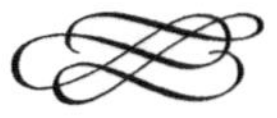

AUNTIE CLEM'S BAKERY 1

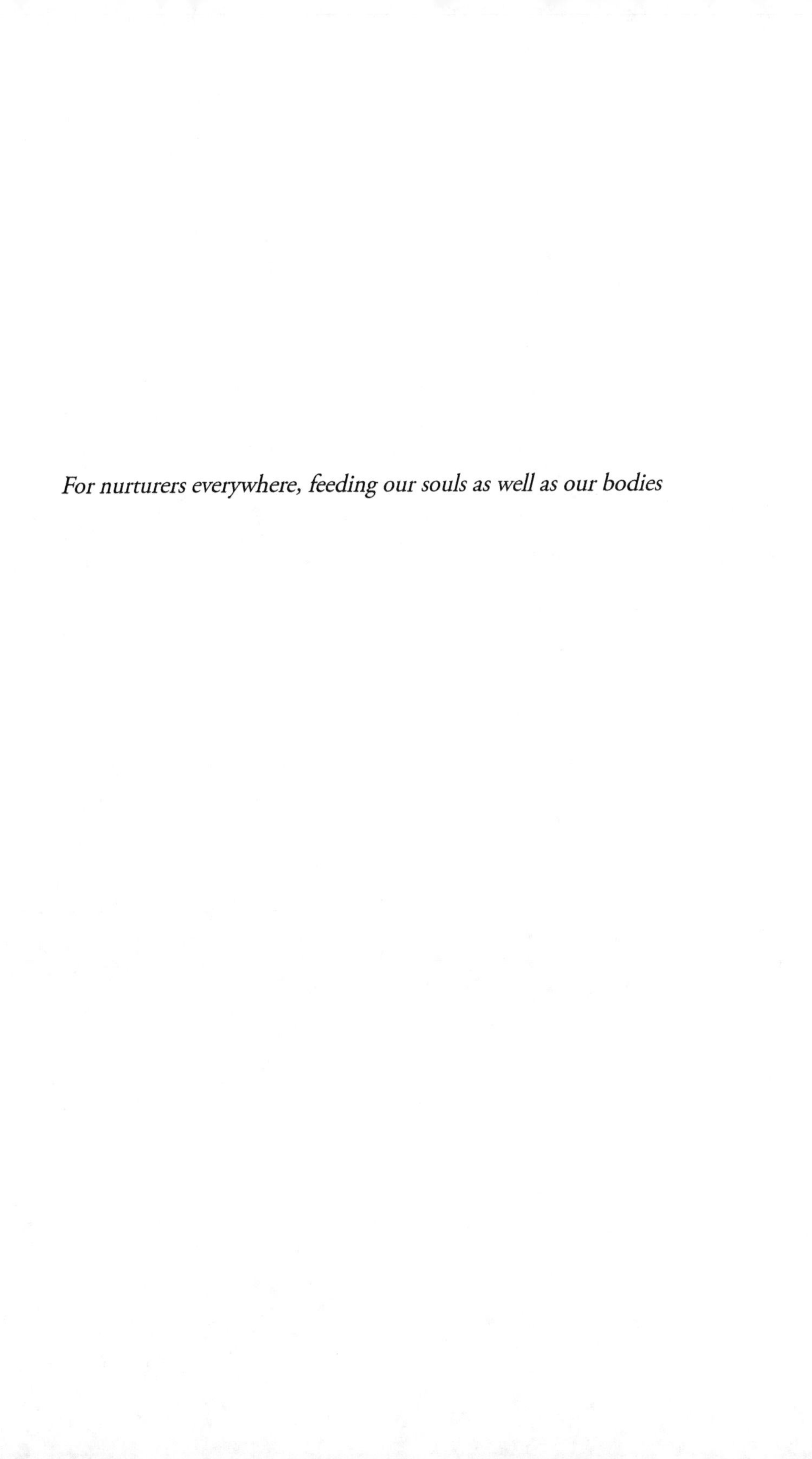

For nurturers everywhere, feeding our souls as well as our bodies

CHAPTER 1

*E*rin Price pulled up in front of the shop and shut off her loudly-knocking engine. She took a few deep breaths and stared at the street-side view. She hadn't seen it since her childhood, but it looked just the same as she remembered it. Maybe a little smaller and shabbier, like most of the things from her childhood that she re-encountered, but still the same shop.

Main Street of Bald Eagle Falls was lined with red brick buildings, pasted shoulder-to-shoulder to each other, in varying, incongruous styles. Each one had a roofed-in front sidewalk to protect shoppers and diners from the blazing Tennessee sun they would face in the coming summer. All different colors. Some of them lined with gingerbread edges or whimsical paint jobs. Or both. Some of the stores appeared to have residences on the second floor, white lacy curtains drawn in windows that looked down at the vehicles, mostly trucks, nose-in in the parking spaces. There was no residence above Clementine's shop. She had lived in a small house a few blocks away that Erin had no memory of. She had spent most of her time at the shop and did not remember sleeping over at her aunt's when her parents had brought her for a visit.

A US flag hung proudly on a flagpole in front of the stores, just fluttering slightly in the breeze. It was starting to get dark and she knew she'd have to find the house in the dark if she were going to stop and take the time to explore the shop.

With another calming breath, Erin unbuckled her seatbelt, unlocked the door, and levered herself out of the seat. She felt like she'd been pasted into the bucket seat of the Challenger for three days straight. She had been pasted into the bucket seat for three days straight, other than pit-stops and layovers. She wasn't tall, so she wasn't crammed into the small car, but she'd been in there long enough to want to get out and straighten her body and stretch her legs. And to go to bed, but bed was still a long way off.

Erin walked up to the shop and put her key into the lock. It ground a little, like it hadn't been used for a long time. Maybe it needed a little bit of lubrication to loosen it up.

The air inside the shop was too still and too warm. She remembered when the little shop had been filled with the smells of exotic teas and fresh-baked goods, but Clementine had retired and closed it years ago. It had been a long time since anything had been baked there. It just smelled like dust and stale air. Erin left the front door open to let some fresh air circulate while she took a look around. There wasn't much space to explore in front of the counter. She would need a couple little tables, with a limited number of chairs, for the few people who wanted to eat in. Most of her business would just be stopping in to pick up their orders. She walked behind the counter. Everything seemed to be in good shape. A good wipe-down and some fresh baked goods in the display case and she'd be ready to go. Maybe a fresh coat of paint on the wall and a chalk board listing the daily specials and prices.

She walked into the back. A kitchen with little storage and a microscopic office that might once have been a closet. The back stairs led to a larger storage area downstairs, she remembered. And what Clementine had always called the commode. There was a second set of stairs from the store front down to the commode for customers. Not exactly convenient, but it was a small, old building. The arrangement had worked okay for Clementine. As a girl, Erin had always been a little afraid of the basement. She would creep down the stairs to use the bathroom and then race back up again, always drawing a warning from Clementine to slow down or she would trip and catch her death on those stairs.

All the old appliances were still there in the kitchen. Even a decades-old industrial fridge stood unplugged and propped open. There was no microwave and Erin was going to need a fancier coffee machine, but everything else looked usable.

~

"What are you doing here?"

Erin turned around and saw a looming figure in the kitchen doorway at the same time as the clipped male voice interrupted her thoughts. She just about jumped out of her skin.

She put her hand on her thumping chest and breathed out a sigh of relief when she saw that it was a uniformed police officer. But he wasn't looking terribly welcoming, jaw tight and one hand on his sidearm. There was a German Shepherd at his side.

"Oh, you scared me. I'm Erin Price," she introduced herself, reaching out her hand and stepping toward him, "and I'm—"

"I asked you what you're doing here."

Erin stopped. He made no move to close the distance between them and shake her hand, but remained standing there in a closed, authoritative stance. His tone brooked no nonsense. Erin couldn't imagine that she looked anything like a burglar. A little rumpled from the car, maybe, but she hadn't been sleeping in it. Was a slim, white, young woman really the profile of a burglar in Bald Eagle Falls?

"I own this shop."

He raised an eyebrow in disbelief, but he did let his hand slide away from the weapon and adopted a more casual stance. Erin allowed herself just one instant to admire his fit physique and his face. He was roguish, with what was either heavy five o'clock shadow or three days' growth, but his face was also round, giving him an aura of boyishness and charm.

"You own the shop. And you are…?"

"Erin Price. Clementine's niece."

"If you're Clementine's niece, why haven't we ever seen you around here?"

"It's been years since I've seen her. My parents died and I lost all my family connections years ago, living in foster care. A private detective tracked me down."

He considered this and took a walk around the kitchen, looking things over. His eyes were dark and intense. "You'll be selling the place, then? Why didn't you just hire a real estate agent?"

"No, I'm not selling," Erin said firmly. "I'm reopening."

The eyebrows went up again. "This place has been sitting empty for ten years or more. You're reopening Clementine's Tea Room?"

"No, I'll be opening a specialty bakery, once I get everything whipped into shape." She folded her arms across her chest, looking at him challengingly. "I assume you don't have a problem with that?"

"No, ma'am."

But he didn't give any indication of leaving. Erin swept back a few tendrils of dark hair that had slipped from her braid, aware that she was probably looking travel-worn after several days in the car. She had put on mascara and dusty rose lipstick before getting on her way that morning, but she felt gritty and sweaty from travel and would have preferred a shower before having met anyone in her new hometown.

Erin strode toward the front of the store and the policeman moved out of the doorway and then back around the counter toward the front door.

"You shouldn't leave the door wide open."

"I wanted some air in here. I've only been here five minutes. Do the police always show up that fast in Bald Eagle Falls?"

"I just happened by. Thought it was strange to see Clementine's door hanging open. Didn't recognize the car."

"Well, thank you for looking into it." Erin waited until he stepped out onto the sidewalk and then followed, pulling the door shut behind her. He watched as she locked it again. "You see? I have the keys."

"Where did this detective find you?"

"Maine."

"Is that where you're from?"

"I'm from a lot of places. Now I'm looking at settling back down here."

Erin looked at the German Shepherd, doing the doggie equivalent of standing at attention.

"I've never heard of a small town like this having a K9 unit."

"Well," he looked down at the dog, chewing on his words, "this is the extent of our K9 contingent."

"He looks... very well-trained. What's his name?"

"K9."

Erin cracked a smile. "Seriously?"

He kept a serious face, nodding once.

"Okay. Well, again, thank you for checking in on my store, Officer…?"

"Terry Piper."

"Erin Price." Erin offered her hand and this time Piper took it, giving her hand a brief squeeze as if he were afraid of crushing it.

"Pleased to meet you, Miss Price. Or is it missus?"

"It's Miss."

"Keep safe. Give us a call if you need anything." He produced a business card with a blue and yellow crest on it. "We don't exactly have 9-1-1 service but there's always someone on call."

Erin nodded her thanks. "I'll keep it handy. A lot of crime in Bald Eagle Falls?"

"No. It's a sleepy little town. Not too much excitement. Rowdy teenagers. Some of the drug trade trickling down from the city. The occasional domestic."

"Not a lot of break-and-enters?" she teased.

He didn't look amused. "You can't be too careful. Where are you headed now? There's a motel down the way…"

"No. I got the house too. I'll be staying there."

"You can't sleep there tonight. Won't be any water or power."

"They've been turned on. Thanks for your concern."

He looked for something else to say, then apparently couldn't find anything, so he nodded and walked down the sidewalk with his faithful companion.

Erin kept one eye on the GPS and the other on her rearview mirror to see if Officer Piper had any ideas about hopping into his car and following her home to make sure that she was properly situated. But apparently, he couldn't think of any laws she had broken and he never appeared behind her. Clementine's house was only a few blocks away. Erin parked on the street in front of it and took it in. It was a pretty little house with white siding and green shutters, roof peaks, and accents. The living room had big windows to let in the light and a window up at the top peak hinted at an attic bedroom or study. Beside and behind the house, beyond the fence line, were shimmering green, dense woods.

Erin got out of the car and grabbed her suitcase before walking up to the heavy paneled door and inserting her key in the lock. This one didn't stick, but turned smoothly like it was welcoming her home. Erin lugged her suitcase into the front entryway and closed and locked the door behind her. No point in inviting more visitors. She really didn't want to have to deal with anyone else until morning.

The AC was on, so the house wasn't stifling like the shop had been. Erin hadn't been sure what to expect. Burgener, the lawyer, had informed her that the house was furnished, but she hadn't known what kind of state it would be in. But it was neat and tidy. Furnished, but not cluttered. There were a couple of magazines on the coffee table in the living room that were months old, but other than that, Clementine might have just left it a few days before. Or still be in the other room just awaiting Erin's arrival.

She wasn't a believer in ghosts or restless spirits, but Clementine's smell and flavor still clung to the place.

Erin left her suitcase at the door and explored the house slowly. Living room, small dining room, kitchen, Clementine's bedroom, a guest room, and what Erin thought she might call a sewing room. There was fabric, rolls of wrapping paper, partially finished crafts, and post-bound books of genealogy, painstakingly written in longhand.

There were pull-down steps to the attic. If there had only been a ladder, Erin probably wouldn't have explored any further, but the stairs were well-made and modern and raised her hopes that the attic had been properly developed and wasn't just a storage space full of boxes, bags, cobwebs, and dust.

She mounted the stairs. At the top, there was enough light from below to find a light switch. Erin switched it on and had a look around.

It was a beautiful, bright room. Erin knew she was going to be spending a lot of her free time up there. White paneling and built-in cabinetry, soft, natural-looking lighting; it consisted of a reading nook, a writing desk, a comfy-looking couch, and various other touches that would make it a paradisiacal oasis at the end of a tiring day of baking.

Or driving.

After exploring the attic, Erin shut off the light, descended, and pushed the stairs up until the counterbalance took over and raised them to snick softly into place in the ceiling.

Erin returned to the kitchen for a glass of water, not looking forward to the fact that she was going to have to go out and pick up groceries if she wanted anything to eat. She found a sticky note on the fridge on notepaper preprinted with the lawyer's logo and phone number.

Welcome home. You'll find some basic supplies in the fridge. JRB

Erin opened the fridge door and sighed. Milk, juice, eggs, bagels, jam, and some precut fruit and vegetable packs. That and the coffee maker on the counter would do just fine. If James Burgener had been there, she would have hugged him.

A quick snack and then she would be off to the guest room for some shut-eye. Ghosts or not, she wasn't going to be sleeping in the master bedroom until she had made it her own.

Never one to let moss grow, Erin set to work immediately the next morning. She found a sort of a general store which carried both the small appliances she needed and painting supplies. With the back seats folded down, she filled the cargo area of the Challenger with as much as it would hold. She went back to the shop, opened the windows, and prepped the walls to start painting. Best to get a fresh coat of paint on before installing anything new.

"Knock, knock?"

Erin was startled out of her thoughts. She yanked the earbuds out of her ears and turned to face the woman who was trying to get her attention.

"I'm sorry," the woman said, giving her a tentative smile. She had a pleasant face; a middle-aged woman with ash blond hair. Either she had the perfect figure, or her clothes were hand-tailored. "I didn't want to startle you, but you were pretty engrossed…"

Erin wiped her forehead with the back of her hand. "Yeah. A little caught up in my music and my work."

"My name is Mary Lou Cox. I heard a rumor that you were here. So, I just had to come over and extend a good old Bald Eagle Falls welcome."

"Erin Price. I, uh… Clementine was my aunt."

"Well, if you're kin to Clementine, you're kin to half the mountain. Welcome home."

Erin nodded awkwardly. "Thank you. That's very kind of you."

"So…" Mary Lou took a look around the kitchen. "A fresh coat of paint and then I hear you're opening up Clementine's Tea Room again? I'll tell you, this town has surely missed the tea room."

"Uh. No. I'm not reopening the tea room." Erin enjoyed a cup of tea at the end of the day as much as anyone, but she was much more interested in baking. The groove she got into while painting was nothing compared with the nirvana she would achieve while baking. "I'm opening a specialty bakery."

Mary Lou patted her hair. "We already have a bakery in Bald Eagle Falls."

Erin ran the roller down the wall, watching carefully for seams or drips.

"I'm sure the town can support more than one bakery."

"But we already have The Bake Shoppe. We don't need another bakery."

Erin gave her a determined smile. "I'm opening a bakery."

"Angela Plaint owns The Bake Shoppe and does a really nice business, I'm not sure any of us would go to another bakery. It wouldn't be a very loyal thing to do."

"You could go to The Bake Shoppe for… whatever Angela Plaint is best at and then come to my bakery for gluten-free muffins."

"Gluten-free?" Mary Lou echoed.

"I assume you don't already have a gluten-free bakery."

"No, we do not. If you want that kind of baking, you have to drive into the city."

"Well, now you'll be able to get them in town."

"There aren't that many people that want that gluten-free stuff in Bald Eagle Falls. I don't see how you could make a living off it."

"We'll just have to see. I do other specialty baking as well. Dairy-free, allergy-free, vegan."

"We don't have a lot of *those* kind of people here. We like our meat. Whoever put meat in muffins anyway?"

Erin studied Mary Lou for a moment, trying to divine whether she was teasing or being sarcastic. "You might not put meat in a muffin, but you would probably put eggs and dairy."

"And you could make it without all those things? Who would eat such a thing? It would be like eating cardboard."

"Not when I make it."

"I guess we'll just have to see," Mary Lou said. "I sure don't cotton to the idea of you trying to take Angela's business."

"I guess we'll just have to see," Erin echoed.

Mary Lou was the first citizen of Bald Eagle Falls to express her opinion and welcome Erin to town, but she wasn't the last. Next came Melissa Lee, a woman with curly dark hair and a wide, even smile. And then Gema Reed, with her long, steel gray locks and a girlish complexion.

Erin did her best to explain to them that she wasn't there to horn in on Angela's business and take money out of her pocket, but to offer a new service that hadn't previously been available. But it was like talking to the wall. Or yelling at an avalanche. It didn't stop them from dumping advice all over her, while smiling and telling her she was welcome in town.

She didn't feel welcome.

At least Terry Piper did not show up with his K9 to give his input on the matter.

It was a long day and Erin never did meet Angela, her competition. The end of the day, the walls were freshly painted. Everything looked fresh and new. Exhausted though she was, Erin spent a few more minutes in the tiny office, going through the papers and plans in the folders she had brought with her from Maine.

Then she locked everything up tight and headed back home.

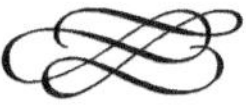

The day dawned bright and clear. Erin woke up earlier than she expected after her hard work of the day before. She was looking forward to each new day, rather than dreading another day of work.

Starting the day in her attic study, Erin wrote up lists of things she would need to get in the city. Not only did Bald Eagle Falls not have a specialty bakery, the general store did not carry any of the specialized flours or other ingredients that she would need. Erin had no intention of taking months getting outfitted. The store and the appliances were on hand and ready for use, so why wait?

It was late when Erin returned to the shop at the end of the day. Darkness was settling over Main Street and the streetlights were few and far between. As she juggled her first armload of goods while trying to unlock the front door, chiding herself for using the front door instead of the back—even though she would have had the same problem at the back—a voice spoke in her ear.

"Can I help you with those?"

The bag of flour she was pressing against the door with her body in an effort to hang on to it while unlocking the bolt was removed from its position. Erin laughed a little and unlocked the door, turning to get the bag of flour back from him.

She froze, looking into the dirty, sweaty face of a man she had never met before. He was white, though the word white did nothing to convey the color of his skin, dirt ground into it as if he had been working in a coal mine or living on the street for weeks. He had a fringe of a mustache and a few bristles on his chin, looking more like he was careless with his shaving than that he had intentionally trimmed his facial hair in a particular style. He had a filthy, army-green cap pulled down low so she could just make out his dark eyes.

"I can take this in for you," he offered. His voice was gravelly and low, but polite. He didn't have the drawl that would indicate he was native to the area.

"Oh, no, let me take it back," Erin said, encircling the bag with her arm and taking its weight.

He looked at her with a sullen expression that told Erin he understood that she didn't want him in her store. She turned her back on him to take the supplies into the kitchen, mentally sorting out possible weapons and escape routes. She was sure he was going to follow her in. Would a scream bring Officer Terry Piper or whoever else might be on shift?

When she went back out to her car for the next load, the man was still hanging around, as she had expected. He took bags out of her car and handed them to her.

"Really," Erin told him politely, "I'm okay. I don't need any help."

He didn't react with anger or violence, but his dark eyes glittered under the bill of his cap. "Just trying to be neighborly."

"I appreciate it. You're very kind. But you're making me nervous."

She surprised herself by telling him that. Was she acting like a victim? Encouraging him to menace her further? She knew from self-defense classes that predators looked for shyness and low self-esteem. Did she sound weak saying he was making her nervous?

But the man immediately backed off, shaking his head. "Not trying to make anyone nervous, miss."

"Then please leave me alone."

He stood there looking at her for a minute, then turned without a word and walked away. Erin blew out her breath, relieved. Here she had thought that moving to a small town in the South, she would be safe from crime and unwanted attention, but obviously nowhere was completely safe. She needed to be realistic instead of idealizing small-town living as being something it wasn't. Next time, she would not be unloading her car after dark. She would plan ahead and be better prepared.

Erin took the rest of the supplies into the kitchen and put them away. She stopped in the office to pick up one of her folders, frowning. She had a strange feeling of vertigo, like everything was slightly out of place. She couldn't identify any one thing that would make her feel that way, but couldn't help feeling like her things had been touched and moved around. She found the folder she was looking for on signage and took it home with her, locking up carefully.

Traffic was even quieter than usual in the sleepy town when Erin got to the shop to finish organizing her ingredients and to make plans for what she would make to kick off her opening and really wow her customers.

She was sitting at her desk in the tiny office, scribbling away and flipping back and forth between recipes when she heard the bells over the front door jingle. She didn't want anyone sneaking up on her today.

Erin reluctantly stood up from her work and went out to the front of the shop. It was Gema Reed, the beautiful gray-haired woman.

"I thought I saw your car outside," Gema declared. She couldn't very well have missed it. It wasn't exactly camouflaged. And it was one of the only vehicles parked on sleepy Main Street. "So, I thought I would drop in and make sure everything was okay?"

Erin tilted her head slightly, trying to figure out where Gema was going with the inquiry.

"Umm, yes. Everything is fine. Why wouldn't it be?"

"Well, being as it's the *Sabbath* and you're at work. I was worried maybe you had a water main break or vandals. Maybe even a fire. You never know what's going to happen."

"No, there's nothing wrong. I just wanted to get some work done. There's lots to do before I open."

They stood there looking at each other awkwardly for a few moments. Erin knew she was moving into the Bible belt, but she hadn't expected things to be that different from the way they had been in the North. Some people were religious and some people were not and everybody observed their beliefs as they wished. But apparently, things were not quite so straightforward in the South.

"Well, maybe no one invited you to Sunday morning services. You probably don't even know the schedule!" Gema proclaimed. "Now there are lots of churches to choose from, of course, but if you want to join us at First Baptist, just down at the end of Main Street and Garity, why, we'd *love* to have you!"

"I'm going to have to pass..." Erin said slowly, feeling her way through. "I'm not really the churchgoing type."

"Not the type? Why, bless your heart, dear, you don't have to be a type to join your fellow Christians at worship on Sunday! You... *are* a Christian, aren't you? Not one of these... other sects? I don't mean to put down Jews or Muslims or anyone else, but here in Bald Eagle Falls, we're Christian. Baptists, Catholics, Protestants, it doesn't matter, as long as you're Christian!"

Erin cleared her throat. She wished she had brought a cloth with her out to the front, so she could occupy herself with polishing the glass and chrome display case and counter. Just to have something to do with her hands and somewhere to look other than Gema Reed's benevolent Christian face. "Actually, Mrs. Reed. I'm not."

"You're not... what? You don't look like a Jew or one of those... pagan people. Not everyone goes to church every Sunday, but..."

"I'm... not Christian. I'm atheist."

"Atheist!" Gema was aghast. She held her hand dramatically at her throat, halfway to covering her mouth in horror. She stared at Erin pleadingly, as if she thought it might just be a clumsy joke and Erin would change her tune. "You're not! Really?"

"Yes. I am. I'm sorry if that upsets you..."

"Well, Jesus loves every humble seeker of the truth. You are a seeker, aren't you? Not everyone can be converted, but as long as you're looking for the truth, you will find it in the end..."

Erin took a deep breath and let it back out again. As much as she wanted to smooth Gema's ruffled feathers, to just reassure her and send her on her way, she wanted to get it out in the open. Her real beliefs, not just rumors or half-baked explanations.

"Mrs. Reed—"

"Gema, sugar..."

"Gema. I am an atheist. Not an agnostic. Not an investigator or a seeker. An atheist. I'm not looking for something to believe in. I already have a belief system. And it doesn't include God."

Gema gasped audibly and this time she did cover up her mouth. "Oh, my dear…"

Erin forced a smile. "I'm not a witch or a devil-worshiper. And I won't try to talk you out of your beliefs. But I, myself, do not believe in God. Not a god of any sort. Not the universe, or Mother Nature, or a higher power, or Jesus. I'm sorry."

"Well." Gema looked for a moment as if she would flee without another word. Instead, she smoothed her waves of silver, took a calming breath and gave a polite nod. "Everybody is entitled to their own opinion, no matter how wrong. I'd better get on my way, or I'll be walking into service late. I just hope… that you won't be encouraging others to break the Sabbath by your blatant disregard for it. You won't have your bakery open on Sunday, will you?"

Erin gave a little shrug. "Didn't my Aunt Clementine have it open after services on Sunday?" she asked tentatively. Her memories of Clementine's Tea Room were startlingly clear in some respects and shrouded by fog in others. She was sure she remembered helping to serve the church ladies after Sunday services. They had all thought her such a cute, pretty young thing. She remembered her resentment over being treated like a puppy or a baby instead of a person with a mind of her own. She loved helping Clementine in the tea room, but she didn't like that part of it.

Gema made a noise of indecision, not wanting to admit that Erin was right and yet compelled by her Christian morals not to tell a lie. "Mmmmm… yes, it is true that she opened up for an hour or two after services on Sunday, so the ladies would have somewhere to go to discuss Christian services required in the upcoming week…"

"So, it would be okay, as long as I waited until after your worship services?"

"As an atheist, I'm not sure it would be the same…"

"I would be shunned for opening my restaurant, but a Christian would not? When it's against a Christian's beliefs, but not mine? Wouldn't it be worse for a Christian to do it?"

"I just don't know," Gema snapped, shaking her head in confusion. "I must get on now, but I'll… I'll think it over."

"Okay…" Erin gave her a little wave. "You be sure to let me know what you ladies decide. Someone mentioned that Clementine's Tea Room had been sorely missed and I thought that if I could provide a similar service…"

Gema Reed gulped. She shook her head and retreated. The bells tinkled behind her and Erin stood there, watching her get into her big red truck and pull out into the street. Then she was gone.

Erin went back to her office to continue working on her opening and marketing strategy. She added 'Sunday social tea' to her list with a wry smile and continued to look through her recipes.

After Erin finished her plans, she carefully filed her folders in the cabinet beside the desk. There was no reason to leave her lists scattered all over her desk and take the chance of losing something when she had a perfectly functional file drawer to put everything neatly away. She emptied the dregs of her cold coffee from her mug and washed it out, leaving it upside down on a towel to dry.

When she stepped out of the shop onto the sidewalk, she nearly collided with a woman coming the other direction. Sunday had been so quiet, she hadn't expected any foot traffic and hadn't even looked before stepping out the door.

"Oh, I'm sorry!" she apologized.

The other woman was ruddy, a redhead, on the plumpish side. Her hair fell in waves around her head, partially obscuring her face. She stepped back from Erin, folding her arms across her chest and staring at Erin as if she had just committed a mortal sin. Which, given Gema's reaction to Erin working on a Sunday, was probably the case.

"I didn't see you coming," Erin apologized. "That was my fault. I'm sorry."

The woman ignored the apology. "You're Clementine's niece."

"Yes, I am."

"You don't favor her, do you?"

"I don't remember her too clearly," Erin admitted. "And I don't really know what she looked like in later years."

"If you don't remember her, then what are you doing here? Why come to Bald Eagle Falls?"

Erin's mouth was dry. She tried to put together words that made sense, flummoxed by the woman's attack.

"I inherited the store and the house. I wanted to reopen the shop."

"Only you're not," the redhead hissed. "You're not reopening the tea room, you're opening a bakery."

"Well, yes. That's what I do, I bake. I'm still planning on serving tea after Sunday services each week, so the women can get together…"

"We don't need another bakery."

Erin sighed and shook her head. "It's a specialty bakery. It means people won't have to go into the city to get gluten-free or allergy-friendly baking. It doesn't directly compete with the other bakery."

"You are competing, little Miss Out-of-Towner. And you're not going to last a week!"

With that, the redhead marched on, shouldering past Erin with a force that staggered her and made her catch herself on the side of the building.

Looking across Main Street, she saw Officer Terry Piper watching her, K9 at his side. She considered calling him over to vent about the rude woman, but decided that would just be sour grapes. She didn't really want to charge the woman. There was no point in reporting the encounter to the police.

Erin yawned as she pushed open her door, sending the little bells tinkling in welcome. She was going to have to get used to getting up early if she were going to be running a bakery. She was going to have to get up while it was still dark and everyone else was sleeping in order to have freshly baked goods in the display cases when people started walking in for a little something to go with their coffees or office meetings.

Her day would start way before anyone else's and, if she were going to stay open past afternoon, she was going to need to find an assistant to split shifts with. It wouldn't have to be another baker, just someone who could answer questions about ingredients and work the cash register.

Taking into account the not-so-warm reaction she was getting from the women of the town, she might have to go to the city to find someone willing to work the bakery.

Erin juggled her keys and her bag of groceries to turn on the kitchen light and put her bag on the counter.

Her coffee mug lay on the floor, shattered. Erin frowned and looked around. A shiver ran down her spine. Had someone been there? Had her shop been broken into?

For a few moments, she just stood there, frozen, listening for any movement.

There was only silence. She considered the situation. Had she put the mug too close to the edge of the counter and it had fallen off by itself? Were there earthquakes in Tennessee?

The imprint of the mug was still in the towel she had left it sitting on. Close to the edge of the counter, but not over it.

She heard the bells on the front door ring and hurried out to see whether someone was leaving the shop. Had she actually walked right past an intruder? Maybe hiding behind the counter, below her eye level while she yawned and juggled her groceries in the morning dimness?

She stopped stock-still. Nobody had left the shop; wild-haired Melissa Lee had come in. She was all smiles and sweetness, launching into a long-winded description of some fundraiser that she and some of the other women were running. She cut herself off abruptly.

"My dear, you look like you've just seen a ghost. Are you okay?"

"I… I think someone has been in here."

"What do you mean, in here?" she asked doubtfully.

"I think someone broke in…"

"You have been burgled?" Melissa's voice rose, a mixture of disbelief and alarm. Such things were probably unheard of in sleepy little Bald Eagle Falls. "Honey, you stay right there while I get the police."

Melissa hurried back out the front door and, without a clue what else to do, Erin obeyed, standing there like a statue. It was only a few minutes before Melissa returned, Officer Terry Piper in tow with his K9. Melissa was babbling on about crime rates and burglaries. Piper ignored her and focused on Erin.

"The place was broken into?" he demanded.

"I don't know. I think someone has been here."

Feeling embarrassed that she might be overreacting, Erin took him into the kitchen and showed him the broken mug and where it had been sitting on the counter. Piper nodded and looked around, his brows drawn down.

"Anyone else have a key?" he asked.

K9 sniffed at the broken mug with interest, but didn't lead his master along a scent trail. He just sat back on his haunches and panted.

"No. I haven't given anyone else a key."

Piper looked into the small office. "Anything been touched in here? Anything missing?"

Erin hadn't yet had a chance to look. She gave a little laugh and slipped by him to see. The room looked untouched. Erin checked her file drawers.

"There was one other time… when I thought things had been moved in here. I put everything away in my drawers, this time…"

"Do you have petty cash in here? A safe?"

"No. Nothing like that. And no cash in the register yet, either. I haven't opened for business yet." She knew she didn't really need to add that part. Terry Piper was undoubtedly aware that she hadn't yet opened to the public. If there had been any doubt, the fact that there were no baked goods in the display case or in the oven would pretty much be a giveaway.

"When are you opening?" he asked. "Assuming you still are?"

"Yes, of course. I'm just putting together my plans for a small opening celebration right now. A few days…"

He raised an eyebrow. "That quickly? I thought it would take longer to get things up and running."

"Everything is already in place. I've bought supplies. I am still waiting on signage and a few little things like that, but for the time being, I'll just put a handmade sign in the window."

He pursed his lips and nodded. He and K9 went to the back door and examined it to confirm it was still locked and had not been tampered with. He looked at the steep stairs to the basement.

"What have you got downstairs?"

"Storage and the commode. I haven't been down there yet this morning…"

K9's ears pointed down the stairs curiously.

"Does he hear something?" Erin asked.

"No… not yet. Come on, K9. Let's go investigate."

The dog eagerly led the way down the stairs. Erin realized she was holding herself tense and she tried to relax. There wasn't anything downstairs. She already knew it. There had been no sign of forced entry at either door. No open windows somebody might have crawled in through.

She was going to have to accept that there had been a tremor or something else that had made the counter shake and caused her coffee mug to go crashing to the floor. The shops were all connected; perhaps someone had dropped a pallet of books with enough force in the bookstore next door that it had shaken the shared wall and sent her mug on its kamikaze journey.

There were no sounds of conflict downstairs. No sign that the officer had found anyone lurking below them. He was back up the stairs in a minute.

"All clear."

They went back out to the front, where Melissa was anxiously waiting. Piper examined the front door and frame.

"There aren't any signs of forced entry," he said with a shrug. "Is it possible you left it unlocked last night?"

"No, I'm sure I…" Erin remembered colliding with the woman on the sidewalk as she left. Had she locked the door afterward? Erin knew she had unlocked the door in the morning. And it could only be locked from the outside. If she'd had to unlock it in the morning, then she had locked it the night before. "Yes. I'm sure I locked it. It was locked when I came in this morning."

"Maybe you knocked the mug down without realizing it, last night or this morning. Or maybe a crosswind or the building shaking for some reason?" Piper shrugged.

"It's a mystery!" Melissa said in dramatic tones.

Piper gave her a tolerant smile. "Yes, Mrs. Lee. It surely is."

"Maybe it's a ghost! The tea shop is haunted."

"Bakery," Erin corrected, aware she was nitpicking, but irritated about the community's opposition to a second bakery opening.

"We haven't had a ghost here before," Melissa enthused. "I wonder who it could be. There are a lot of civil war ghosts in the area. We have a rich civil war history, you know. Why, the library is practically famous in these parts. There are so many legends of lost and buried treasure in the hills around here, a person can hardly go for a hike without tripping over one!" She laughed.

"If there hasn't been a ghost here before," Piper said gravely, "then the ghost must be of a more recent vintage, wouldn't you say?"

Melissa stopped and considered. "Well, yes, I suppose. Unless you've somehow awoken a restless spirit. You haven't been digging down there in your basement? Or in the back?"

"No," Erin assured her. "The basement floor is concrete and so is the parking lot in back."

"Then we need to think of who might have died recently that would have a reason to haunt the store." Melissa pondered the problem.

Erin exchanged looks with Piper. He appeared to be suppressing a smile.

"Maybe… the owner?" he suggested.

"Erin?" Melissa said blankly.

"The… previous owner…?" Piper prompted.

"Oh, Clementine! Why, of course it would be Clementine! Silly old me!" She put her hand on Erin's arm. Her dark curls quivered with her movement. "You are being haunted by your Aunt Clementine. Did you have any unfinished business with her? Something that she would be expecting from you?"

"Just opening the bakery. And why, if there was such a thing as ghosts, would my aunt's restless spirit want to break my coffee mug?"

"She's trying to reach you, dear. Ghosts are very limited in what they can do. Move things, appear to you, maybe make noises. It's not like on TV, where they can just walk up and talk to you and explain themselves in words. All she can do to reach you is to move things around."

Erin nodded. "I see. Well, I don't believe in ghosts, so I'm going to look for more earthly explanations. You can… believe what you like."

"Oh, I do," Melissa agreed. "I am going to talk to the others and we'll see if we can sort this out. After all, we all knew Clementine. I knew her my whole life. We'll figure out what it is that she wants to reach you for. Mary Lou's sister-in-law, she's very good with spirits. We'll see if she can come here and make contact with your poor dead auntie."

Erin glanced over at Piper, widening her eyes, sure she was being played. But Piper gave no sign that Melissa was joking. And Melissa continued to look earnest and excited about the whole ghost business.

"Isn't contacting ghosts considered sorcery in Christian circles?" Erin suggested.

"No, no! Mary Lou's sister-in-law won't be using a Ouija board or any other devil's tool. She just uses prayer. There's nothing wrong with that."

"Ah." Erin nodded. She looked at her watch as obviously as possible. Time was trickling by and she had work to do. "Did you want to leave me a flyer about your fundraiser, Melissa?" At Melissa's blank look, she indicated the woman's clipboard. "That was why you came in here, wasn't it?"

"Oh, yes!" Melissa pulled a fuchsia-colored page from her clipboard and handed it to Erin. "Of course, no one is required to donate or put time into it, but every little bit is appreciated! I'd better get on my way! If I stop to yap at every store, it's going to take me all day! I'm already busier than a one-armed paper hanger."

Erin nodded and gave a little wave, and Melissa went on her way. Erin sighed and looked at Officer Piper. He had a gorgeous smile, when he let it show.

"Miss Price, I'm sorry I couldn't be of more assistance. You feel free to call on me if you have any more troubles. Hopefully, your ghost won't cause any more trouble."

"Thanks," Erin said dryly. "Just tell me... everyone in town doesn't believe that, do they? In the existence of ghosts, I mean? And that they can just... be contacted?"

"Not everyone is quite as literal as Mrs. Lee, but... I do imagine most of them will agree that your shop might be haunted. They might not be willing to say that it is, but they won't say that it isn't..."

Erin shook her head. "I suppose it's harmless, as long as they aren't demanding to hold séances in here."

CHAPTER 3

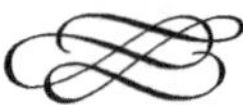

*E*rin had done everything she could to prepare for opening. She had taken out an ad in the Pennysaver, had delivered flyers to all the surrounding businesses, had put her handlettered 'Auntie Clem's Bakery' sign up in the window. She was up at three in the morning to start baking. Some of her batters and breads had been prepared and chilled or frozen ahead of time, but it still took time to bake a wide enough variety of treats to interest a new clientele.

The kitchen smells were heavenly and she was looking forward to propping open the front door to get some cross-ventilation, which would also help to spread the delicious scents and bring in walk-by traffic.

Wiping her forehead with the back of her forearm, Erin paused for a moment before taking out a batch of blueberry muffins. Her stomach was growling and it was time to sample some of her own goods. Blueberries were always a favorite of hers. Even better than chocolate chips.

After putting a variety of goods in the display case, Erin went to the front door. She was ten minutes early, but there were people hovering around the door. She took a calming breath and arranged a smile on her face. Then she opened the door.

She had been afraid that no one would come after all the remonstrations that the town didn't need another bakery. How many people with special diets were there in the population? Would people who didn't have any special needs still come by to check it out? But there were a couple of businessmen with tall cups of coffee, and a mother with four children of varying sizes, both sophisticated Mary Lou and sturdy, gray-haired Gema Reed, and a few faces Erin didn't know. She let the fresh air breeze in, displacing the warm, fragrant air.

"Ooooh," the children sighed as they smelled all the baked goods.

One little boy of six or seven tugged on Erin's apron. "We get a free cookie?"

"Yes! A free cookie or a muffin. A special opening-day treat!"

He darted over to the display case and pressed his hands and face against the glass, peering in at the cookies.

"Which ones don't have wheat?" he demanded. "My tummy can't have wheat."

"None of them have wheat," Erin told him.

The boy's mouth dropped open. "Are you *sure?*"

"I'm sure. I made them myself."

He studied her seriously, his brows drawing down. "Do they have white flour? White flour is still wheat."

"No, they have superfine rice flour and cornstarch. Or other flours. And some of them have oats. I know oats still bother some people, so those ones are all marked."

"Certified gluten-free oats? Or oats from the grocery store?" he interrogated.

"Certified gluten-free."

The boy looked at his mother. Erin looked at her as well. "He knows his stuff, doesn't he?"

"We've had plenty of experience. He's learned how to advocate for himself." She beamed with pride, jiggling a pink-cheeked baby tied to her in a sling.

The boy went back to peering at the cookies, considering his options. He had probably never had a choice of bakery-fresh cookies before.

Erin went back behind the counter and started to serve up the complimentary cookies and muffins. The mother of the little boy bought a couple of loaves of bread and some muffins for breakfast the next day. The little boy, whose name was Peter Foster, settled on a chocolate chip oatmeal cookie, the chips still warm and gooey. At Peter's suggestion, his sisters chose a gingersnap and a macaroon, so that each could have a taste of three different kinds of cookies and decide which kind they liked best.

Erin was waving goodbye to Peter and his family when the angry redhead came in through the door. Erin froze there with her hand up like an idiot, wondering what the woman was doing coming into the store. The other ladies greeted her, but she didn't smile and make nice. She seemed to have a permanent scowl. She made her way to the display case and looked down at the baked goods.

"Everything here is gluten-free?"

"Yes. It's all gluten-free."

"So, you don't even have any wheat or other gluten flour in the kitchen?"

"No. Completely clean. All gluten-free."

She scowled down at the cookies.

"There is a free cookie or muffin for every customer today," Erin offered, forcing a smile. It felt plastic and unnatural. Like it belonged on someone else's face.

"I am highly allergic to wheat. If you use any in the kitchen, I will know it."

"I don't. And none of the pans or implements have been used for anything but gluten-free cooking. There is no chance of cross-contamination."

The other ladies were watching the redhead, no longer pretending to have their own conversations. It was just Mary Lou, Melissa, and Gema. Everyone else had eaten their free treat, placed their orders, and gone.

The redhead turned around and looked at the women, giving them a glare that made them huddle around their treats and giggle nervously, hiding their mouths behind their hands.

"I'll have a chocolate muffin," the woman announced, turning back to Erin so suddenly that she just about dropped her tongs.

"Oh. Okay," Erin agreed. She selected one of the chocolate muffins and passed it across the counter. "My name is Erin Price."

"I know who you are." The redhead took a bite of the chocolate muffin and chewed slowly. "Not bad," she admitted. "I'm Angela Plaint."

"You're Angela Plaint?" Erin was floored. This was the owner of The Bake Shoppe? Highly allergic to wheat and running a traditional bakery? No wonder the woman was bitter.

"Yes."

"Oh…" Erin spluttered, looking for something to say. "Well… I'm glad you came to my opening. Would you like anything to take home?"

"Six of these."

Erin packed up six chocolate muffins and took Angela's money, feeling unaccountably guilty. Why should she feel bad about selling to the competition? It wasn't like Angela was going to resell them in her own bakery for a profit. She just wanted something for later. If she were the only one in her family who was allergic, she would probably freeze the muffins individually to keep them fresh, thawing out one at a time as she needed them.

Erin couldn't think of anything else to say to Angela. She realized belatedly that Angela was talking to her. Asking a question.

"I'm sorry, what?"

"Is this the commode?" Angela pointed to the door to the stairs. She could see the ladies'/men's placard, so Erin wasn't sure why she was asking.

"Yes. Down the stairs. I'm sorry about that, it's not very accessible."

"No," Angela sneered. "It's not."

She opened the door and headed down the stairs. There was no one else at the counter, so Erin went over to talk to Mary Lou, Melissa, and Gema.

"That's my competition?" she asked in a whisper. "Why didn't anyone tell me she was allergic to wheat? Doesn't she sell any gluten-free products?"

"No, no," Melissa shook her head, eyes wide, curls bouncing wildly. "She doesn't do the baking anymore, because the flour in the air would make her sick. She just owns the place. And if they made gluten-free goods, they would be contaminated with the flour in the air and on the same equipment. She wouldn't be able to eat them."

"I guess not," Erin admitted. "Why on earth does she own a bakery?"

"She used to be a wonderful baker," Gema said, eyes distant. "She loved to bake and she was at it sun-up to sun-down. And then one day… she just started to get sick. She couldn't eat wheat, or breathe it, or touch it. There was no way she could keep it up. She had to hire bakers and can't even go into the bakery while they are cooking. If no one is baking, she can go in for a few minutes, as long as she doesn't touch anything."

"I can't imagine. Why didn't she just sell the business and start something else?"

Mary Lou smoothed her pastel pant suit and gave a wide shrug. "Angela Plaint is as stubborn as a mule. She doesn't want to give up what she loves, even if she can't literally have her hands in the business anymore. Nothing is going to keep her from the baking business."

Erin shook her head slowly. She looked toward the door to the stairs and retreated to the serving counter, not wanting Angela to find Erin gossiping about her when she returned.

An older couple came in the front door, moving slowly, the husband with a walker and the wife with a cane. Both had to talk over all the options in the display case, going over them several times, asking Erin for her advice, and bouncing ideas back and forth.

"Where is your rice flour from?" wondered the elderly woman, who had introduced herself as Betty. "Is it from California rice or Chinese rice?"

Erin blinked. "I honestly have no idea."

"Maybe you could go and look? See what is says on the package? I worry about all the arsenic, you know."

"Uh, right," Erin agreed. "If you can wait just a minute… I'll go check."

She took a glance toward the door to make sure no one else was getting impatient with the elderly couple dithering about and then ducked into the kitchen. She scrutinized the various labels on the rice flour, then returned to the front of the store.

"It looks like it's domestic," she said. "Not from China."

"Hmm… maybe we should go with something with oats in it, so it's not *all* rice flour," Betty suggested, looking at her husband.

"They are actually all blends of flours," Erin explained. Not just rice, but sorghum, corn, millet, buckwheat… and some of them have oats, like you said…"

More discussion and interrogation ensued, and two more trips to the kitchen to scrutinize labels.

At last, their bag full of gluten-free goods of varying types, they toddled off again. When she looked around the front of the store, she saw that only Mary Lou remained, savoring a blueberry muffin with a takeout cup of tea, looking though her agenda.

"Blueberry is my favorite," Erin told her.

Mary Lou looked up from her agenda, giving Erin a reserved smile. "Mine too. And I would never guess that it was gluten-free. Most of the gluten-free baking that I've tasted is either gritty or like cardboard. Or it's full of kale or some other weird superfood that nobody in their right mind would put in a dessert."

"Blueberries are a superfood. I'd much rather have blueberries in a muffin than kale!"

"Me too!"

Mary Lou looked down at her agenda for another minute, writing something down. She looked up.

"Do you think you should check on Angela? She's been an awfully long time."

Erin's stomach clenched. She looked toward the stairs. "Didn't she come back up? I just assumed I missed her leaving while that lovely couple was here…"

"No. Not unless she went the back way."

"I have the other door locked. Can't have customers marching through the kitchen."

Mary Lou looked at the closed stairway door. Erin went around the counter and opened it. She peeked down the stairs, afraid she was going to find Angela sprawled there with a head injury or a broken leg. How would a major insurance claim on her first day of business go over? And what would that do to her sales?

"Uh… Angela? Are you okay?" she called down.

There was no response. But if Angela was in the bathroom with the door shut, or had just flushed the commode or was running water, she wouldn't be able to hear a thing. Erin felt like she was being intrusive going down the stairs to check on Angela, but if Mary Lou was right and Angela had not slipped past without either of them seeing her, something could be really wrong.

"Angela?" Erin started down the stairs.

Behind her, Mary Lou got up from her table and walked to the doorway, looking down.

"Is she there?"

"I don't know yet…"

Erin turned the corner and stopped.

It was worse than she had imagined. Worse than her worst nightmares of all the things that might go wrong on opening day. *What if nobody came? What if someone complained about the baking? What if she didn't sell a thing?*

It was worse than all of that.

CHAPTER 4

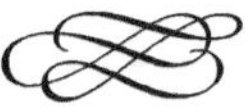

"Are you okay, Miss Price?"

Erin took another sip of her water and nodded.

"Do you think you can answer some questions now?"

"I—I don't know. I—it was so awful!"

"I need you to tell me step-by-step what you saw. Everything. Every impression."

Erin took a deep breath. Her head was still whirling. She wasn't sure how she had ended up sitting in the chair Mary Lou had previously occupied, by the front window of the shop. She wasn't sure at all that she'd climbed the stairs of her own accord. Officer Terry Piper, hovering over her now, might have carried her, or helped her get up the stairs again. She wasn't really sure.

"Where's Mary Lou? Is she okay?" Erin asked.

"Mary Lou is just fine. You will be able to talk to her later. For now, we need to keep the two of you apart."

"Why?"

Piper just looked at her and didn't answer her question. "Tell me what happened."

"I just went downstairs. It had been too long. I thought she might have fallen and hit her head. I was worried about insurance."

"Start at the beginning. What made you go downstairs?"

"Mary Lou. She said that Angela hadn't come back up. Angela went down to use the commode… and she never came back up again."

"What did Mary Lou have to do with it?"

"Nothing. She was just there. She just noticed that Angela hadn't come back out. We decided I should go down and see. Make sure she wasn't sick or hurt."

"Why did you think she might be sick or hurt? Why were you worried about your insurance?"

"I didn't have any reason. Just that she hadn't come back up. The most logical reason was that she was sick. Or hurt. She'd had an accident, hit her head, maybe. And so I just needed to go check, make sure."

"It was Mary Lou's suggestion?"

"Yes."

"You never heard Mrs. Plaint call out? There was no noise from downstairs?"

"No. Nothing. I was serving customers up here. There wasn't any noise from downstairs."

"Did you call down to her?"

"Yes."

"Why? Why didn't you just go down?"

"It just seemed… intrusive. I didn't want her to think that I was checking up on her, if she was just stuck in the commode for longer than usual. I didn't want to embarrass her."

"Okay. Go on. So, you called her and then you went down the stairs."

"I called her again, partway down, in case she just didn't hear me the first time. Flushing the toilet or something."

"And still, no answer."

Erin gave him a look. He knew very well that Angela couldn't have answered. "No. No answer. Not a sound."

"And what did you see when you got to the bottom of the stairs?"

"I went around the corner and there she was…"

"Describe what you found." His pen hovered over his notebook, waiting.

"You know what I found, because it's exactly the same thing as you found when you went down there."

"Please tell me what you saw."

"I saw Angela Plaint. On the floor. Dead."

CHAPTER 5

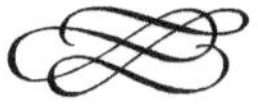

"What do you think Mrs. Plaint died of?" Piper asked.

Erin took another sip of her water. It all seemed so strange. She felt removed from the situation. Like Piper was questioning someone else. Time was elastic, stretching out forever, and then snapping back into place, propelling her forward much too fast. She rubbed her temples.

"I guess… she choked or had an allergic reaction?"

"Why do you think that?"

"Her face was all… purple. And swollen. And her skin… she had welts. Wheals. Hives. She must have eaten something she was allergic to. She wouldn't get hives from choking."

"Uh-huh…"

"But the only thing she ate was one of the chocolate muffins. And they don't have any wheat in them. She told me she was deathly allergic to wheat, but there is no wheat in the place. None at all."

"She didn't tell you if she had any other allergies?"

"No, nothing. Wheat was all that she mentioned."

"And the muffin couldn't have been contaminated from something else? Or she ran across something downstairs that was contaminated?"

"No. Not unless it was contaminated at the factory before I bought it. That's the only possibility I can think of… accidental cross-contamination at the factory. I haven't brought anything with wheat in it into the building."

Piper wrote a few words down. "What was it that made you decide to open a gluten-free bakery? Are you allergic to gluten yourself?"

"No… one of my foster sisters was gluten intolerant… I was really good at cooking up things she could eat. Back then, there wasn't much available commercially. You had to improvise. Experiment with different ingredients. Pick up alternate flours at import stores. It wasn't like it is now, with so much available in grocery stores and health food stores."

"What happened to your foster sister?"

There was an iron knot in Erin's stomach. "What…?"

"You said your foster sister *was* gluten intolerant. That could mean a lot of different things. It could mean that you were only foster sisters for a short period of time and then you were separated and didn't keep in touch. Or…"

Erin seriously considered lying. What were the odds that Piper would actually check her answer? Erin had been through lots of foster sisters in her lifetime. There were plenty of them she no longer kept in touch with. It was such an easy answer. She *was* my sister, she isn't anymore.

"No. She died."

"She died. Was it related to her gluten allergy?"

"Intolerance. Yes, it was."

"How did that happen?"

"She didn't stay compliant. She didn't like having to eat gluten-free all the time and she cheated. She couldn't stick to the diet."

"And that could kill someone who was just gluten-intolerant? She didn't actually have an allergy, so how could it kill her?"

Erin took a deep breath. It was easier to answer an academic question than it was to talk about finding Angela's body, or explaining what had happened to Carolyn.

"A lot of people think that allergy means you have a bad reaction and intolerant means you have a mild reaction. But that's not the difference. An allergy means you have a histamine reaction. An intolerance means that you have another kind of reaction. You can have a mild allergy, maybe a bit of itching or a stomachache, or you can have a severe allergy that causes anaphylaxis and is life-threatening. You can have a minor intolerance, where you can eat a certain amount of a substance without reacting, or where you don't even realize you are having a reaction because there is no pain or discomfort, or you can have an intolerance that is life-threatening."

She stopped and took a sip of water.

"My foster sister kept cheating on her diet and that caused damage to her intestinal tract. They tried to repair it, tried to keep her on a strict gluten-free diet, but she wouldn't comply and nothing they did helped. She lost weight, couldn't absorb nutrients from anything she ate… until she just wasted away."

Erin blinked her eyes rapidly and wiped away tears. "But that was Carolyn. That's not the same as what happened to Angela."

"So, you decided to do something for others who had gluten intolerance. You went into specialty baking."

"Not right away. It was just a hobby. Something I did on the side, for friends who were intolerant or on special diets. Just because it was something I enjoyed doing, and they appreciated it so much, and… it did help me to feel better about Carolyn. Like maybe I could help someone else stay on a gluten-free diet and save their life like no one had been able to do for Carolyn."

"When did it become a business?"

Erin sighed. "Today. Today was the first day that I was a professional gluten-free baker. The first day that it wasn't just a hobby, but my job."

"I see. So you don't have any professional experience."

"No. Plenty of experience, but not professional until today."

"And you haven't run a bakery or eatery before."

"I've worked at restaurants before. I even helped Clementine with the tea room when I was just a little child. I've always been interested in the food industry."

"You've run a restaurant before? Or a bakery?"

"No. Just worked at one."

"And what was your profession in Maine? You were a food service worker?"

"No," Erin admitted reluctantly, "I was a bookkeeper."

"I see." Piper made a few additional notes in his notepad.

Erin shifted uncomfortably in her chair and held her glass against her forehead. "I know what I'm doing," she told him. "Just because I haven't run a bakery before, that doesn't mean that I don't understand the rules and laws involved. And I know more about cross-contamination and how sick gluten or allergies can make someone than anyone. I didn't make a mistake and… kill Angela."

"As far as you know."

Erin looked for a way to argue with the statement. "Well… no," she agreed finally. She obviously couldn't say that she knew more than she knew. "As far as I know."

He turned the page on his notepad. "What was the beef between you and Mrs. Plaint?"

"I… beg your pardon?"

"Easy enough question. The two of you didn't get along. Why not?"

"I didn't even know her."

He stared at her for a few seconds, impassive. That smile that had peeked out when he was discussing ghosts with Melissa Lee was nowhere in evidence. He was on the job. Dead serious.

"I witnessed an altercation between you and Mrs. Plaint myself."

A wave of nausea washed over Erin as the images of her collision with Angela on the sidewalk in front of the store flashed through her mind.

"That wasn't an altercation. I just bumped into her as I left the store. I'd never even met her before that and I didn't know who she was at the time. She didn't tell me her name until today."

"The two of you had a very… intense conversation, for two people who didn't know each other."

"I…" Erin stared out the window at the place where she and Angela had stood on the sidewalk, replaying what she could remember of the conversation. "I didn't know who she was, but she knew who I was. Started up on the same old nonsense about how Bald Eagle Falls already had a bakery and didn't need another one. I didn't even know that she was the owner. She just started in on me, saying that I shouldn't compete with The Bake Shoppe."

He scratched down a few notes. Erin's face was warm.

"The 'same old nonsense,'" Piper repeated slowly, as he wrote the phrase down. "So, you had discussed this with Mrs. Plaint before."

"No! Not with her. Just with the other ladies. Everyone thought I should reopen as Clementine's Tea Room, not as a business in competition with the bakery. When Clementine was running the tea room, she did very little of her own baking. Most of what she sold here, she bought. I don't know if it was from Angela Plaint's bakery, or if that even existed when I was a little girl. Everybody kept saying that I shouldn't compete with Angela."

"And now you won't have to. Now we'll be down to one bakery again."

Erin's stomach twisted and gurgled. "Are you implying that I deliberately killed Angela Plaint with contaminated muffins?" she demanded. "Maybe I should be calling a lawyer."

"No one is making any accusations right now. This is a routine investigation. Of course, you have the right to have your lawyer present during any questioning."

"I don't know what happened to Angela Plaint. But I didn't have anything to do with it. I think we're done here."

"Okay. Thank you for your cooperation." Piper snapped his notepad shut. But he gave no indication he intended to leave.

"I'll call you if I think of anything else," Erin told him, looking significantly toward the door.

"I'll just supervise while you lock up. The business will be off-limits during our investigation. I'll let you know when we release the scene."

"This is my shop!"

"Yes, ma'am. And this is an investigation into a sudden, unexpected death. I will be sealing the doors and you will not be allowed back in until the police department releases it to you. You won't be able to take anything from the scene."

"She died from an allergic reaction! You can't possibly be implying there was foul play involved."

"We will need to make that determination. We don't have Cause of Death yet."

"I have a business to run! How long will this take?"

"I'll let you know when we're finished processing all the evidence."

It took Erin a long time to get to sleep. She felt sick and run down by the end of the day and thought that after getting home, she would just fall into bed and sleep for twelve hours. After all, she had been up since three o'clock, had run her grand opening, and had found a body and dealt with a police investigation. It was enough to wipe anyone out. But when she got home, she didn't climb into bed. She was so angry and worked up, she couldn't even look at her bed.

She rummaged through the fridge for something nourishing to eat. She had planned to bring home a loaf of bread and some muffins from the bakery for her supper and breakfast, but Officer Terry Piper had advised her that she wasn't allowed to take anything home, not even a crumb of bread. It would all have to be tested, he said, to see if any of it was contaminated with wheat or any other substance that might account for Angela's sudden demise. She was left with the fruits and vegetables in the fridge, some cold cereal, and coffee. Whatever was left of the bagels. Not the best dinner.

Of course, she could have gone out to eat. There was a family restaurant in town that boasted 'meat plus three' on the big sign with removable letters outside the building. There was a BBQ place with a special on hot chicken. There was even a little Chinese restaurant that always seemed to have a full parking lot. But Erin wasn't up to appearing in public or dealing with anyone over the phone for takeout. She couldn't stand to think of the management of those places whispering behind her back about her. *Do you know who just ordered the baby back ribs? That woman who murdered Angela Plaint!*

After her unsatisfying meal—what she really wanted was a pint of Ben and Jerry's—she went up to the attic with a cup of coffee. She had a few notes on her plan for the grand opening on her writing desk, though most of her papers were at the office, inaccessible during the police investigation into Angela's death. Even though she had been writing down her lists and plans less than twenty-four hours before, Erin felt like years had passed. Had she really been that excited about opening up? Naive enough to believe everything would go off without a hitch? She had been worried about what she should bake and how she should display it. Worried that no one would show up at the opening. It had never occurred to her that one of her customers would be so inconsiderate as to die on the premises, immediately after eating Erin's baked goods. Erin had been a naive little girl, acting no older than the five-year-old who had helped Auntie Clementine serve the church ladies their tea and cookies.

She tried reading in her little nook, but couldn't focus on the page. Couldn't find anything that interested her. She found herself staring at the wall, going over and over the events of that day and the discussion with Piper. She hadn't made herself look good. Piper thought she was an irresponsible, inexperienced girl pretending she knew what she was doing, a hazard to all her customers.

She paced back and forth across the attic for long hours before she was tired enough to go to bed, almost twenty-four hours after she had gotten up to bake for the opening. And then, even when she lay down, the events of the day kept playing over and over again.

Erin slept fitfully, tossing and turning all night long. Despite the fact that she didn't have to get up to run Auntie Clem's, her brain wouldn't shut off and let her sleep even long after the sun was up.

She dragged herself out of bed and wandered out to the kitchen, looking sadly through the cupboards. She didn't even have any baking supplies at home. Everything was at Auntie Clem's.

The doorbell rang. Erin looked at the cat clock with a swinging tail on the kitchen wall. It was too early for visitors. She felt sick as she considered whether it might be Officer Piper, there to ask her more questions or charge her with something in connection with Angela's death. What would she do? Who would she call? Surely he wouldn't put her in jail. Not over an accident.

With a feeling of dread and her heart pounding, Erin went to the door. It wasn't Officer Piper, but Gema Reed. Erin swung the door open wide.

"Gema?" She stopped herself from asking what she was doing there. Gema held a cardboard tray with two cups of takeout coffee and a brown paper bag.

"I figured you could use some company and a real breakfast this morning," Gema said. "Did I wake you up?"

Erin smoothed her messy bedhead. Gema's gray hair was pulled into a neat ponytail and she looked polished and professional and there Erin was in her ratty housecoat, hair a mess, makeup-less. She guessed by the scratchiness of her eyeballs that they were probably bloodshot.

"You'll feel more human once you've had some java and fuel," Gema assured her. She entered and Erin ushered Gema into the kitchen to sit at the table.

Gema looked around. "You haven't changed anything."

"No. Not yet. I'll add my own touches… sometime."

Gema nodded understandingly. "When you're more comfortable with it being your own."

Erin shrugged. Gema passed her one of the tall coffees and indicated the sugar and creamer packets. "I don't know how you take it." She opened the paper bag and pulled out a couple of chocolate chip muffins that looked suspiciously like Erin's own. "I didn't know what you could eat, so I thought I was best going with something you had made," Gema said with a laugh.

Erin smiled. "I actually don't have any special dietary needs. It's a passion, not a necessity. But I do enjoy the fruits of my labor. Thank you, this was really thoughtful of you. I'm feeling a little… off-kilter this morning. I just don't know what to do with myself."

Gema took a sip of her coffee, her eyes wide. "Wasn't that just the craziest thing you've ever heard? Fancy Angela dying like that, right in your bakery! After all the close calls she has had, she dies in the one place that should have been safe." She covered her mouth. "I don't mean it was your fault, of course, or that your bakery wasn't safe, except… it wasn't!"

"She'd had a lot of close calls?"

"Oh, Dinah! Had she! Why, everyone in town knew about her allergy and about her carrying one of those pen-needles? If she ever had an attack, she said, just pull off the cap and jab it straight into her leg and hold it in there a while. I don't know if I ever could have done it myself. I cringe over popping balloons!"

"I wish someone had been there to do it. When I think about her down in the basement, all alone, with no one to help her…" Erin trailed off. Gema's expression sobered and she looked down.

They both picked at their muffins for a few minutes, thinking over it.

"Such a tragedy," Gema said. "Always sad to see a life cut short."

But Erin thought she seemed just a little too philosophical over it. She had thought that they were friends, that all the women who had visited her and declared their loyalty to the established bakery were friends of Angela's. But Gema wasn't with her church friends, mourning the loss together. She was breaking bread—or muffins—with Erin, the instrument of Angela's death.

"Had you known Angela for long?" Erin asked.

"Well, now, she's not my generation, but I reckon I've known of her since she was born. I can't say we spent a lot of time together, but I knew who she was and I was at the bakery every week. Everyone was."

"Only she hasn't been at the bakery, because of her allergy."

"No, you're right. Not since she developed the allergy. But before that, she was there every week for years. I got accustomed to her."

It was awkward phrasing. They hadn't become friends. Gema had gotten accustomed to Angela.

"You weren't close, then."

"No…" Gema considered her words carefully. "Angela was a hard woman to know. She'd led a hard life. She could come across as… unfriendly. But she was an excellent businesswoman. She had a real knack for it. Not a lot of women do. Not naturally."

"Just the bakery, or other businesses as well?"

Gema scraped her thumbnail along the waxy coating of the coffee cup, looking intent.

"Seems like she always had something on the go. Investments, promotions, new ideas of things that needed to be done around the town or to make a little extra money. She had her finger in a lot of pies."

Erin attempted a joke. "But not literally."

Gema stared at her with wide, surprised eyes and Erin suddenly had a sinking feeling that she had misjudged the situation and it was too soon after Angela's death to joke. She was about to apologize when Gema burst into laughter. Wide, open-mouthed, side-splitting laughter. "Not literally!" she repeated, barely able to catch her breath. "No, definitely not literally!"

Erin was feeling a lot better after Gema's visit. The coffee, baked goods, and companionable conversation had soothed her soul, and she was feeling less out of sorts and more like herself. She had the energy to take a shower and get dressed, deciding she would try reading in the nook in the attic again. Having had a chance to rest and to talk about the accident, maybe she would be less distracted and would be able to concentrate on it.

She was just about to climb the stairs to the little attic retreat when the doorbell rang. Another of the town's women come to chew the fat? Erin had heard stories about the nosy, gossipy women in small towns, but she had never really believed them. Not the more extreme ones, anyway. She'd seen enough gossip in small communities and school to know that it wasn't out of the realm of possibility, but she thought the stories were exaggerations. Maybe the women of Bald Eagle Falls were the ones the stories were all about.

As she composed herself and moved toward the door to answer it, the doorbell rang again, followed by a hard rap of knuckles. Someone was certainly impatient to talk to her!

Erin opened the door and found herself face-to-face with Officer Terry Piper. For a moment, she was disoriented. She had only ever seen him downtown at the shop, so it seemed out of character for him to come to her house. But of course, they were only a few blocks apart and the police department for Bald Eagle Falls probably covered a wide geographic area, expanding outward to include the more rural homes around the town as well.

"Officer Piper. I didn't know you were coming."

He nodded. K9 panted at his side. Erin just looked back at him.

"Can I come in, ma'am? I have some more questions for you."

"I was hoping… that you were just here to tell me that I could go back to my bakery. Have the police released the scene?"

"Not yet, I'm afraid. Probably by the end of the day. It's not a big area, there's not that much to search."

Erin reluctantly stepped back to let him in. What else could he have to ask her about? She had already told him everything she could think of with regard to finding Angela's body. As he'd said, it was a small area. There wasn't that much to tell. She went down the stairs, turned the corner, saw the body. By that time, it was too late to do anything for Angela. The opportunity for intervention was long gone.

Piper came in, wiping his feet on the mat. The dog was quiet at his side, well-behaved, though looking around and sniffing the air eagerly, gathering information about the unfamiliar surroundings. Piper raised his eyebrows and Erin directed him to the couch, sitting across from him in a Queen Anne chair.

"Have you found anything?" she asked. "I mean, it's probably too early to have tested any of the food for wheat ingredients, if they were contaminated at the warehouse."

K9 made a grumbling noise as he lay down at Piper's feet. He would, Erin was sure, much rather have done some further investigating, sniffing out all her secrets.

"Yes, they have to be sent to a lab in Memphis. They've all been bagged and tagged and sent over on a rush. But it will be a few days before we hear anything back."

"You have a courier to Memphis?" Erin hadn't seen any courier companies around town, though she supposed one of them might have a drop box somewhere. Or would they make a special trip to pick something up for the police department?

"We sent a contractor with all the evidence that needed to be tested. You don't need to worry, everything is sealed. It can't be tampered with."

Erin hadn't even thought of that. She gave it a little consideration before she decided that it really was nothing to worry about. They had special procedures and protocols. Ways to ensure that the chain of evidence was maintained.

"So… what did you want to ask me about? I haven't thought of anything else that would be helpful to you."

"How much did you know about Mrs. Plaint's allergy?"

"Nothing. I didn't know anything about it until she told me at the counter that day."

"Exactly what did she say to you?"

"Exactly?" Erin closed her eyes and tried to conjure it up. "She said… she had a very severe allergy to wheat. She was worried about if I used any wheat at all in the bakery. She said she would know if I did. She'd be able to tell." Erin opened her eyes and looked at him. "She was sort of intimidating. But I know how it is with people with severe reactions… they have to stand up for themselves and sometimes act like a bit of a bully… because people don't understand or won't believe that they have a life-threatening condition."

"Why wouldn't they?"

"Because other people adopt special diets as fads and they don't really keep them, or are casual about them. Someone who says they are allergic to gluten and then picks at the pasta on the plate of the person next to them. Or order beer. People who think that it will help them to lose weight. Or just that it's a healthy thing to do for one reason or another, but they're willing to bend the rules. So then servers and restaurant owners think it doesn't really matter. They think that everyone who comes into the store with 'allergies' is just being a pain in the neck and they won't react if there's a questionable ingredient or cross-contamination."

"Did Mrs. Plaint tell you that she had an…" Piper pulled out his notepad and referred to it. "An autoinjector?"

"No… not that I recall. Gema Reed was by here earlier and she said that

Angela had one. She said that everyone knew about it, that Angela told them how to use it if she had an attack."

Piper gazed at her for a moment, considering this, then made an additional note in his pad. "It's interesting that you would offer that information."

Erin shifted uncomfortably. "What do you mean? You asked me about her autoinjector. That's all that I know about it. I didn't hear anything from Angela. Just from Gema, today."

He rubbed the space between his lip and his nose.

"Why didn't Angela use her autoinjector?" Erin said with sudden realization. "Didn't she have time to realize that she was having a reaction? Or was it faulty? Did she use it and it didn't help?"

He held up his hands to stop her from asking further questions. "She didn't have an autoinjector on her person."

"What? But Gema said that she had one. That she told people how to use it."

"And when she needed it, not only was there no one there to help her, but she didn't even have it with her."

"But that doesn't make sense. Gema said that Angela has had a number of close calls. If she knew she was that sensitive and she had had close calls in the past, why wouldn't she have it on her?"

"We've looked for it. We've checked every inch of the bakery, in case she dropped it and it rolled under something. But no luck. It isn't there."

Erin covered her mouth, horrified. Angela wouldn't have left it in her other purse or pants. She wouldn't have left it at home just once. Or in her car. She knew she was going into a bakery, potentially a hot zone for contamination. Surely she wouldn't have walked into a bakery without making sure her autoinjector was handy. Or two. A lot of people carried two, in case the first wore off before an ambulance could get there. With how far Bald Eagle Falls was from a major hospital, she might have even had a stockpile of them, to last her however long it would take to get her to proper medical care.

"She wouldn't have gone anywhere without an autoinjector. Especially not into a bakery."

"You said that you didn't know her that well and had never talked to her about her autoinjector."

"And that's all true. But would you? If you knew you were deathly allergic to wheat, would you walk into a bakery without one?"

"Maybe into a gluten-free bakery. It was supposed to be safe."

"But she didn't know that beforehand. She didn't know whether I catered to multiple special diets—like I do—and only some of the product was gluten-free. She could have been walking into a cloud of flour dust hanging in the air."

"And that would have been enough to trigger her allergy?"

"From what everybody has said, it would have."

K9 let out a big sigh, breaking the tense atmosphere. Erin laughed and Piper allowed a tiny crack in his facade, one corner of his mouth curling into a dimple. He nudged K9 with his toe.

"Decorum, partner. Maintain an appearance." He looked at Erin. "He prefers foot patrol to the cerebral stuff."

"I can understand his point. He doesn't know why he has to come sit here and listen to us talk. He doesn't understand what happened to Angela."

Piper nodded. He rose to his feet, tugging his heavy belt up a little. K9 jumped eagerly to his feet.

"You'll let me know when I can go back to my shop?" Erin asked. "I'm really anxious about having to stay closed today. The day after opening… it's not good for business. And I'll have a ton of baking to do before I can open tomorrow, if it's been cleared. I can't just open without anything to sell."

He nodded. "You do all the baking yourself? No assistant?"

"I'll need to get someone before too long. Even if it's just an after-school student to take care of the till. Otherwise, I'll burn out."

As soon as Officer Piper told her she could go back to the shop, Erin was there. Almost before she even got off the phone with him. He rolled his eyes when she arrived there before he was finished removing the police tape from the front and back doors.

"Ready to get cookin'?" he inquired.

"More than ready." Erin looked at her watch. "But only for a couple of hours, because I have to be up early in the morning. That's assuming that everything was left clean in here?" She unlocked the front door of the shop.

"There may be some fingerprint powder to wipe down, I don't think there's anything else to worry about."

"And what was removed from the scene, other than samples of my baking?"

"Small amounts of ingredients. We didn't take the whole bags, just a sample to test for contamination."

"Okay. Thanks."

She hurried into the shop and locked the door behind her, not wanting Piper or anyone else to interrupt her. She didn't have a lot of time and she didn't want to talk to anyone.

Her sensitive nose picked up on a chemical smell that still hung in the air. She wondered what they had used and what they had been testing for. She was pretty sure that fingerprint powder wouldn't leave any detectable scent. She remembered K9 sniffing the air at her house. Would it be a blessing or a curse to have a nose as sensitive as a dog's? She always regretted hers when there was something noxious in the air. Other people seemed to be able to ignore it, but Erin would have to leave the room gagging. She'd always been that way. Probably no one else would even notice the chemical odor. The chemical smell would be gone by morning, replaced by the smells of chocolate, vanilla, and fresh-baked bread. There could be nothing better.

The fingerprint powder was all over everything. The display case where little Peter had pressed his hands and face into the glass to look at the baked goods. The wall. The chrome around the glass case. The steel countertop. The door handles. Everything. Deciding she didn't have the time to go downstairs to see what state the basement had been left in, Erin just locked the door and took down the placard. If anyone wanted to use the facilities, they would have to try a different store. She didn't need any ghouls snooping around in the basement, trying to identify the exact spot Angela had died in. She would keep public access to the stairs locked until interest had petered out and she'd had a chance to do a thorough cleaning.

There were a couple of muffin batters in the fridge, so Erin started by pouring those into paper liners and throwing them in the oven. She had a sourdough as well and took a portion to shape into loaves, getting those started. While the muffins baked, she quickly wiped down all the fingerprints she could find and then started on some cookie dough. She would use the same base mixed with several different add-ins to cut down on the prep time required for a variety of cookies.

She hadn't put her earbuds in, working too quickly to even stop to do that, so she heard the noise at the back door, quiet though it was. Erin froze, elbow deep in a vat of bread dough, and listened.

It was just a tree branch rubbing against the outside of the building.

Or something equally innocuous.

Though she tried to make herself get back to work, she couldn't focus on her work, trying to hear what was going on. *Was somebody trying to pick the lock of the back door?* They had to be able to see the lights on in the bakery and know that someone was there.

Or was that part of the plan? Maybe it was someone who wanted her to be there. Someone who wanted her out of the way. She had thought that Angela was her only real antagonist. The competition. But what if there was someone else? Someone who had previously picked the lock or used some other method to get into her bakery. The entity who had broken her mug and shifted the papers in her office.

It was just paranoia. Anxiety. Because Erin was tired and because she was involved in a police investigation of an unexpected death. Her imagination was getting away from her.

Erin determinedly went back to kneading her bread. Though, since gluten-free bread doughs were more liquid than gluten bread dough, it was really just mixing rather than kneading.

The noise continued. Eventually, Erin's anxiety subsided. No one was going to take fifteen minutes to pick the lock of an occupied shop and keep at it. It had to be a branch rubbing against the building, like she had initially thought. Or just the building itself making noises.

After it ceased to be anxiety-producing, it became an irritant. She should just put her earphones in and keep working, but she would know, even with music on, that the noise was still there. She'd have to keep taking the earphones out to check one more time whether it was still there.

She hadn't heard the noise other days that she had been there.

And there hadn't been a wind when she had arrived at the shop.

With an angry breath out, Erin extricated herself from the dough, scraped it off of her hands and arms, and washed up. She wiped sweat from her forehead and went to the back door. The door to the stairs was open. She closed it, irritated that the police had left it sitting open. She didn't want to have her attention drawn to the basement.

The scratching at the door resumed. Erin stood there for a moment, breathing shallowly and staring at the back door. It was low on the door. Animal-like. She was sure it would just be a branch.

She unlocked the door and tentatively pushed the door open a few inches to have a look.

There was a movement, a silhouetted shape in the dimness, that made Erin gasp and jump back.

And then a dirty little head thrust through the door, and a slim, lithe shape followed it into the shop.

A cat.

A little, bedraggled, mostly-orange kitten.

"Oh, my goodness." Erin let out another breath. "Where did you come from?"

The kitten looked up at her and meowed silently. Something too ultra-sonic for her to hear.

"You must be a stray. It doesn't look like anyone has been taking care of you."

The little cat rubbed against her legs, but when Erin moved toward it, it took off, streaking away from her.

"No you don't! I don't want a cat in here. Come on. Out you go." She pushed the door open wider and went after the cat, trying to shoo it back out of the shop. "Out, out, out! No animals in my bakery."

The cat avoided her, moving much faster than she would have thought possible, and wedged itself back behind the fridge. Erin was afraid to move the fridge in case she hurt it. After considering the situation for a few minutes, she decided to leave the door open, and the cat would eventually wander out and leave the shop once she was occupied with something else. It was only afraid of her because she had chased it.

She went back to work, keeping an eye out for the kitten. It stubbornly stayed out of sight. Erin looked at her watch. It was getting late and she knew she had to be heading home. She covered up the loaves of bread and cleaned up the various mixing bowls. As she put away milk and eggs, a little head poked out inquisitively from under the fridge.

"Well, hello," Erin murmured to it.

The kitten mewed and came out from under the fridge. It again rubbed against her legs and this time Erin did not try to pet it. She continued to put things away, ignoring the kitten. It became gradually bolder, not flinching away whenever she moved. Erin took the garbage out to the back lane, expecting the kitten to follow her out the door. But the perverse little creature didn't. It just sat in the kitchen waiting for her to come back.

"It's time for you to go," Erin told the cat firmly.

The cat tilted its head and looked at her.

Erin went to the fridge and looked over the contents. The cat watched as she got the carton of eggs back out again, then got out a saucer and cracked the egg into it. It meowed and wound itself around her ankles.

Erin whisked the egg with a fork and bent over to hold it close to the kitten. "You see that?" she asked. "You smell that? You're hungry, aren't you?"

The cat meowed eagerly, following the saucer. Erin moved slowly, not wanting to scare it away. It followed the saucer closely, sniffing at the air and occasionally standing up on its hind legs to try to get a better look. She walked out the back door. For a moment, the kitten stayed inside the warmth and shelter of the kitchen, but it was drawn by the smell of the egg and eventually followed her out. Erin put down the saucer. The kitten hovered close by, not approaching while she was still too close. Erin moved back to the door of the shop and the kitten closed in on the saucer, bending down to sniff and then to lap at the raw egg. Erin stepped back into the shop and closed the door.

Erin unlocked the front door of the bakery, her stomach tied in knots with her anxiety that she wasn't going to get any business. The lost day meant that she didn't have any momentum. People would be afraid her goods were contaminated. Or they wouldn't want to eat somewhere that someone had died. Or they would decide not to frequent her establishment out of loyalty to the deceased. There were so many reasons for people to avoid going to Auntie Clem's and few she could think of for them to go.

But there were already a few people waiting outside the door. Erin smiled and greeted them and went back behind the counter to serve them.

"I just can't believe about Angela," Melissa said, after Erin had served the first two customers, who had been tactful enough to avoid the topic. "Who would ever have thought that such a thing could happen?"

"I'm told she had had several bad reactions before," Erin offered, trying to keep her face pleasant and not rise to Melissa's tendency toward drama.

"Well, I know, but here, of all places!"

"It's possible that she had developed a new allergy. That happens some-times, you know, especially once you have one severe reaction. She might have been allergic to something she had never had a reaction to before. Another ingredient in the muffins, or something in the air or something she touched. It could have been nothing to do with the muffins or the shop. Maybe she took a cough drop or some other medication. We don't know anything yet about what she actually reacted to."

"That's a very positive way to look at it, I'm sure." Melissa looked around at the other customers and leaned closer to Erin. "Have you seen the paper this morning?"

"No. I thought the paper came out Thursdays?"

"They did a special print run today. Because of breaking news."

Erin wasn't so sure she wanted to know what the breaking news was. In fact, she was sure she didn't want to know.

"Did you want a muffin this morning?" she asked Melissa. "Maybe some rustic bread for supper tonight?"

But Melissa wasn't even looking at the baked goods in the display case or at the price board. She was digging around in her oversized shoulder bag. The businessman behind her was shifting impatiently and Erin made a show of looking around Melissa at him.

"Could I help you, sir?"

He smiled and stepped forward beside Melissa to make his breakfast selection. Erin rang up his order, ignoring Melissa, and looked to the next person in line. She saw Peter and his mother. She had the baby in a sling again, but the two little girls were not with them. Peter eagerly stepped forward to point out which muffin he wanted. His mother bent in close to Erin.

"Peter didn't have any reactions," she said.

Erin blinked at her. She smiled tentatively. "That's good," she said. "I'm glad to be able to provide products that he can eat…"

"What I mean is… there couldn't have been any gluten in the cookies or bread, or Peter would have had a reaction. I don't think any of your food is contaminated."

Erin breathed out in relief and gave her a more genuine smile. "Thank you for that. I've been worried about what people would think. I'm sure there are all kinds of rumors going around about what happened and the people who really need the bakery will end up avoiding it."

The bells over the front door jingled several times. Erin looked up. The bakery was getting rather busy. Even busier than on opening day, when she had offered complimentary cookies and muffins. She didn't recognize all the faces as people who had been there before. A lot of people who normally went to Angela's bakery must have decided to try out Auntie Clem's instead. Gema had said that Erin no longer had any competition. Angela's bakery must have closed with her death, which was odd if she was the owner but didn't actually work out of the bakery herself. Wouldn't her business keep operating until it was transitioned to a new owner?

Erin settled up with Peter's mother, her mind elsewhere. Then Melissa had finally sorted out what she was looking for in her bag and thrust the slim little town newspaper in front of Erin's face.

"There! That's what I'm talking about."

Erin pulled back slightly to look at the big black headline.

POLICE DETERMINE ANGELA PLAINT'S DEATH A HOMICIDE.

*E*rin's mind immediately flashed back to the questioning by Piper about what Erin knew of Angela's allergies and autoinjector.

Auntie Clem's no longer had any competition.

Did Piper really think that Erin would murder the competition? What kind of person would jump from having a discussion about the competition between the two bakeries to murdering her opposition? Even if Piper interpreted the sidewalk collision between the two women as a physical altercation, what would make him think Erin was capable of murder?

"Are you okay?" Melissa asked.

Erin blinked. She had customers. She didn't have time to be panicking about Terry Piper's speculations. She smiled at the next person in line behind Melissa.

"Can I help you?"

Melissa still didn't move away from the counter or choose a muffin. Erin continued to serve customers while Melissa tried to engage her in conversation.

"Can you believe it? Murder?"

"No," Erin snapped. "I can't believe it. Why would he think it was murder? It was obviously just an allergic reaction. An allergy. No one could have predicted it."

"Someone could have caused it," Melissa countered. "It could have been malevolent. Contaminate something that Angela had with wheat. Steal her autoinjector. It would kill her as surely as a bullet between the eyes. In fact, it did."

Erin counted cookies into a bag, and then had to go back and count them again to be sure she had the right number.

"But why? If it was murder, then someone had to have motive. Who had motive to kill her? And who could have gotten close enough to her to steal her autoinjector? I don't see how it could be anything other than a tragic accident. She left her autoinjector at home. She ended up reacting to something she didn't know she was allergic to. End of story."

"It was the end of the story for Angela," Melissa agreed, her dark eyes glittering. She folded the paper and put it back into her bag. "And the police determined that she did not leave her autoinjector at home. Or in her car. It is missing."

"Officer Piper told the newspaper that it wasn't at her house?"

"Officer Piper wrote it in his official report. The report that he gave to the coroner in the city."

"How would you know that?"

"Because I do transcription for the police department."

Erin closed her mouth before she could blurt out a comment about police reports being confidential. That would be shooting herself in the foot if she wanted Melissa's insight into the investigation. Erin rang up the next order and collected the customer's money.

"She could have dropped the autoinjector somewhere. Officer Piper can't search the entire town."

"He doesn't think so. He thinks it was intentionally taken from her to prevent her from saving herself from a fatal reaction." Melissa looked at Erin expectantly.

Erin sighed. "I could never do something like that. It would take someone pretty sadistic to take away her autoinjector and just watch her choke to death."

Melissa looked thoughtful. "They didn't necessarily watch her," she pointed out. "They could have taken it before she had a reaction. Or left before she died."

"This is morbid." Erin took a breather while the next customer stared at the display case, mulling over her choices. "If he thinks it's murder, he doesn't think someone just happened to take her autoinjector and then she just happened to have a reaction and needed it. He thinks…" Erin swallowed. "He thinks that someone intentionally took her autoinjector and caused a reaction. Or caused a reaction and took her autoinjector."

"You?"

"Did he… name me in his report? As a suspect?"

"Not in the report to the coroner."

Erin let out a sigh of relief. She put blueberry muffins in a box, smiling at her customer, a wrinkled little Asian woman with cherry cheeks and sparkling eyes. The sweet vanilla smell of the muffin filled her nose.

"But he *does* name you in his report to the Sheriff." Melissa smiled broadly, as if Erin should be proud of herself for being a prime murder suspect.

"How could he think I had anything to do with it? I can understand him thinking that she was the victim of accidental cross-contamination of something she bought here. But murder? I don't have a motive, I only just met the woman!"

"You are competitors for the town's business."

"Competitors don't kill each other!"

The next customer in line was Mary Lou Cox, looking as coiffed and put-together as always. "I gather you've heard the news," she said in a low, sympathetic voice.

"I was just filling her in." Melissa gave Mary Lou's arm a conspiratorial nudge. "Isn't it awful news about Angela?"

"Worse news for Erin than for Angela. Angela is dead whether it was an accident or homicide. But for Erin to be implicated in the crime…" Mary Lou tsked and shook her head. "You're the one I feel sorry for."

"I can't believe anyone could think I would kill her!"

"How about a dozen assorted cookies?" Mary Lou suggested, peering into the display case. "That would be a nice treat for a couple of hard-working boys, don't you think?"

Erin nodded and started putting cookies into a bag.

"Only don't give me a baker's dozen. Just twelve. Thirteen doesn't split evenly and they'll give me all kinds of grief."

Erin smiled. "You could eat the thirteenth and they wouldn't know any better."

"Oh, no." Mary Lou smoothed her pantsuit. "Straight to the hips! I have to watch so carefully."

"How are the boys?" Melissa asked. "And Roger?"

"Just about the same." Mary Lou gave a tranquil smile. "You know, every day above ground is a good one."

Erin realized that she knew little or nothing about the families of the women she had met. As a businessperson, she would do well to learn about their families and their tastes, so she could make recommendations and build a close working relationship. It sounded mercenary, but she needed to get out of her comfort zone and ask people about themselves and their loved ones if she wanted to grow her business.

"How old are your boys?" she asked, unintentionally cutting Melissa off.

"Teenagers, fifteen and seventeen. They both have part-time jobs and work hard to contribute to the household. And working keeps them out of trouble."

"Great!" Erin too had started working young. She had known that she was going to have to support herself once she aged out of foster care, so she started earning her own income as soon as she could. "And your husband? Roger, is it? What does he do?"

Mary Lou and Melissa exchanged glances.

"He's... not been well," Mary Lou said eventually. "But we're hoping he's on the upward climb."

"I'm sorry to hear that." Erin waited, unsure of whether Mary Lou wanted to share what illness her husband was suffering from, but Mary Lou didn't say and Erin was afraid to ask. "I hope he gets better soon."

Both ladies nodded.

"Did you get anything?" Mary Lou asked Melissa, taking a step toward the door. It was plainly her intention to walk Melissa out. Erin could have hugged her.

Melissa scanned the display. Erin was pretty sure by now that Melissa had never planned to buy anything. She had just come in to gossip and see what Erin's reaction would be to the news that she was a murder suspect. "How about one of those trail mix muffins. They look good." Melissa examined her muffin while Erin rang up the purchase. "Does it have nuts in it? It seems like everyone is allergic to nuts these days."

"No, no tree nuts, no peanuts. A few kinds of seeds, dried fruit, and chocolate chips. Very power-packed, great for hikes or a post work-out meal."

Melissa patted her belly. She wasn't fat, but she wasn't as slim as Mary

Lou or Erin. "I won't be hiking anytime soon. I apologize to my body in advance."

Mary Lou chuckled and the two of them left together. Erin turned her attention to the next customer in line. It was shaping up to be a busy day.

~

At the end of the day, Erin went out her back door to the little two-stall employee parking pad. She usually parked in front of the store, but she supposed she should start parking in back instead, leaving the space in front open for customers. There wasn't a lot of parking on Main and sometimes people had to walk a few blocks to get where they were going. And what was pleasant on a winter day would become unbearable in the summer. Though, at least, the sidewalk was shaded by the little roofs extending from the storefronts.

But would she still be there when summer came around? With the position she was in, was it wise to be planning that far ahead?

Surely nothing could come from Officer Piper's suspicions. They were baseless. He would have to come up with some proof before they were in any position to arrest Erin, let alone find her guilty in a trial.

It was bound to just fade away. She shouldn't pay it any mind. Officer Piper and Melissa could think what they liked. Erin knew she hadn't done anything wrong and anyone who knew her would know she hadn't done anything wrong.

Except, no one in town knew her at all.

She looked down at the empty saucer her little furry visitor had licked clean. She looked around, but couldn't see any sign of the kitten. She stopped herself from calling out to it. She didn't want a kitten. Especially not anywhere near the store and the baking. It was a health hazard. And someone might be allergic, reacting if they were even in the same room as the little ragamuffin. She didn't want a cat at the bakery. Someone else could take care of the stray.

She went back into the kitchen with the saucer, shutting the back door firmly behind her.

Five minutes later, she was back in the parking lot, a little kitten kibble in the saucer. She had noticed it in Clementine's pantry—in her pantry—

after breakfast that morning. What would it hurt to feed the cat outside? Just to make sure that it had some source of healthy food?

She just wouldn't let it into the shop.

"Kitty, kitty, kitty?" she called softly. What was the point in calling the cat? Cats never came when they were called and this one was a stray, maybe feral. It didn't have any idea why she was making those funny noises. She shook the saucer, hoping the cat would be able to interpret the sound as food.

She had just about given up when she saw a little orange and white face peer around the corner of the fence.

"Kitty, kitty?" She shook the dish again.

The cat slunk around the yard, close to the fence, not approaching her directly across open ground. It watched her, slowing its approach as it got closer. Erin stepped back, giving it a little more space.

"Kitty, kitty? Come on little kitty. Aren't you hungry?"

It shied away at her voice, but when Erin didn't do anything threatening, it approached the saucer. It sat down and looked at the food from a few feet away. The kitten looked at Erin and mewed softly.

"It's okay. I'm not going to do anything to hurt you. Have something to eat, little fella. You must be starving. You're so skinny."

The cat watched her for a few more minutes, then covered the rest of the ground to the bowl and sniffed at the food. It started to eat.

Erin wondered if the chunks of kibble would be too big for the little cat. It was really no more than a kitten. Probably barely weaned. Or maybe the mama cat was still around somewhere, but not feeding it as often, pushing it to go out into the world to fend for itself.

But it seemed to be managing the adult cat food just fine.

"Miss Price?"

Erin looked up from the cat. Officer Piper was coming down the back lane.

"I knocked on your front door, but I couldn't get your attention. I thought something might be wrong…"

As he came to the end of the short fence, Erin saw K9 at his side. Before she could anticipate it, K9 saw the kitten and lunged, letting out a volley of barks. The kitten ran straight up Erin's pant leg, its little claws piercing and scratching through her clothes like needles. Piper reacted quickly and was able to catch K9's collar to restrain him, but the cat was already on the move.

"Ow, ow, ow!" Erin tried to catch the kitten to pull it off, but it went behind her back and, the harder she tried to reach it, the more it dug in its claws, ripping up the skin on her back and shoulders. "Oh, ow! Settle down, kitten. It's okay, he won't hurt you. He can't get you. Ow!"

Piper looked suspiciously like he was suppressing a smile. "Can I help you, Miss Price?"

"Just get that dog out of here!" Erin snapped "Get him away! It's not going to relax until the dog is gone."

"I could catch it and get it off…" He took a step forward to help.

K9 growled and pulled to get closer to the tasty morsel.

"He just wants to say 'hi,'" Piper said. "He likes other animals."

"For dinner? Don't come any closer. Take him out of here."

Piper stood there for a moment, looking for another solution. Then he shrugged. He walked away, hauling on K9's collar, and was soon out of sight and earshot.

"Okay, little guy," Erin coaxed. "He's gone now. Big mean doggie is gone. You can let go. Come on…"

No matter how she twisted and squirmed, she couldn't get her hands behind her back to capture the frightened kitten. It nimbly avoided every effort.

"Big mean doggie?" Piper repeated.

Erin turned to see him return, without the dog this time. He held up his hands.

"No big mean doggie," he assured her. "Now can I help you?"

Erin suppressed the desire to snap at him and remind him that it was his fault she was in the situation in the first place. But he was trying to help. He was trying to make up for it. She turned her back to him and held still while he approached and unstuck the kitten one claw at a time. Once she felt herself free, Erin turned back to face him.

Piper stood there, a slight dimple in one cheek, holding the terrified kitten to his chest, stroking it gently to calm it. The combination of the handsome officer in uniform and his gentleness with the helpless ball of fur just about melted Erin into a puddle right there.

"Thank you."

"To serve and protect. That's my job."

"Well, I doubt you spend all day rescuing kittens. Or maidens in distress."

"That wouldn't be half bad."

Erin took a deep breath and let it out again in a sigh.

"I didn't know you had a cat," Piper said.

"Well, I don't. Not really."

He raised an eyebrow questioningly.

"Say hello to my ghost," Erin explained. "I think it must have gotten into my bakery one night and knocked the coffee mug off the counter."

"It?" Piper repeated. "Ginger cats are usually male." He drew the kitten away from his chest for a moment, peeled back the tail for a look, and nodded. "Male."

"*He*, then," Erin amended. "I apologize for disparaging his manhood. He must have gotten into my shop."

"You know if you feed him, he'll just keep coming back. You'll never be rid of him."

"The poor thing is starving. I'll feed him until he's tamer and then… I don't know. Find a home for him."

"We've got him now. No point in waiting until he's been tamed. You want me to take him to the pound?"

"Bald Eagle Falls has a pound?"

"Well, it's really just Doc Edmunds, the vet. If he has an empty kennel or two. He'll keep it—him—for a few days, see if anyone wants him."

"And then what?"

Piper raised both eyebrows and sighed. "Not much market for stray kittens in a town like Bald Eagle Falls. Everybody who wants one has one and the rest end up prey or motor vehicle statistics. Doc Edmunds' way is kinder."

"No, I couldn't do that," Erin protested. She reached for the kitten. "Give him to me. I'll find him a home."

He didn't relinquish the kitten. "What are you going to do? If I give him to you and you take him back into your bakery, you have to put him down to get ready to go home. Then you can't catch him again."

"I tempted him out with an egg yesterday… but he still wouldn't let me touch him."

"Go get your stuff together. Lock up. Meet me at your car with a towel."

"A towel?"

"You have one, don't you? A dishtowel?"

"Yes…"

He headed out of the yard with the kitten.

"You can just walk through the bakery, you don't have to take the long way around."

"If I go inside, he's going to try to get away again. Trust me. Right now I'm the only protection he can see. Inside, there's lots of places to hide. He'll go nuts trying to escape."

"Okay… I'll see you in a minute."

Erin obeyed his instructions, gathering together what she needed and locking up. She met Piper beside her car with the dishtowel.

"Now what am I supposed to do with this?"

"Give it to me."

Erin handed him the towel. He put it over the kitten, still held at his chest. Then, as Erin watched, he began to wrap it around the kitten, until it was swaddled, little face peering out at them, all cozy and protected and unable to move.

"Did you hypnotize him?" Erin asked, looking at the motionless cat. She expected it to be frantic all wound up like that, trapped. He should be frantic, squirming and trying to wriggle free. Erin didn't have a lot of experience with cats, but she knew they could wriggle free of just about anything. "I've heard some people can hypnotize them."

"No special powers," Piper assured her. He handed her the wrapped bundle. "Just put him on your seat for the drive home. It isn't far, he'll be okay. Don't unwrap him until you're in your house. In the room you want to release him in. You might want to put him in the bathroom with a litter box, until you're sure he has the hang of it."

"You seem to know a lot about kittens."

"We always had cats around growing up. It was always a lot easier to take them to the vet wrapped in a towel than in a cage. Have you ever tried to put a cat in a cage?"

"No."

His expression was deadpan. "I wouldn't recommend it."

Erin laughed. She sat down in her car and put the kitten on the other bucket seat. "Well, thank you for rescuing me, Officer Piper. And our little friend. That really was above and beyond."

His expression became sober. He leaned in to talk to her. "I still need to talk to you. There's no point in trying to do it now, you'll just be distracted by the little furball. Could I arrange a time for you to come in to the police department for a chat?"

Erin didn't answer right away. She looked at the kitten. "Am I really a suspect, then? In Angela's murder?"

"We have some more questions."

"You really think it was murder?"

"Everyone who knew Mrs. Plaint agrees that she wouldn't go anywhere without her autoinjector. She kept it secure and on her at all times. There is no way it was an accident. Someone took that autoinjector from her. And there was only one reason anyone would take it away."

His eyes were hard, intense. All hint of amusement, tenderness, and friendliness were gone. Officer Piper was back on the job and Erin was his prime suspect in a homicide.

"When do you want me at the police station?" Erin's own voice sounded small and far away to her.

"This time tomorrow? After work? I know you're up late, so I don't want to impose on your evening. You're probably to bed right after dinner."

"If I manage to stay up long enough for dinner."

"Tomorrow then? This time?"

"Okay. I'll see you then."

If there was a good time to be saddled with a stray kitten, it was in the middle of a police investigation when Erin was badly in need of a distraction. Without the ginger kitten, she would have been left with her own thoughts all night, worrying about what was going to happen at her police interview the next day. As it was, she seemed to fly from one kitten exploit to another.

Was it any wonder that 'catastrophe' started with 'cat'?

She decided to take Officer Piper's recommendation and release the kitten in the bathroom. There, he decided to go straight up the plastic curtain. She was still wondering how he had managed to get his claws into the plastic when it became obvious that he couldn't get them back out. Just over her head, the cat was stuck, struggling mightily to free himself. She was afraid he was going to fall and wrench the leg that was stuck in the plastic out of joint. But he wasn't too keen to let her free him, biting and slashing when she tried to pull his tiny claws free.

He fell from above her head into the bathtub with a thud and she was sure he had knocked himself out or broken something, but he was up again almost immediately, trying to get a purchase on the curved porcelain sides of the tub to get out. He jumped, he cried, he scrabbled frantically without success. But he avoided her hands, whirling around and around the tub like an Indy 500 racer. Erin tried to pincer him from both sides at the same time or to throw a towel over him to try Officer Piper's trick, all without success.

But the thrown towel did succeed on one count. It was draped over the edge of the tub within the kitten's reach and he used it to climb out of the tub so that he was once more free. He squirmed back behind the commode and hid there, peering out at Erin, squished into such a tiny ball she could barely see him. Erin decided he was safe there and left him alone. She left the towel draped over the edge of the tub so that the kitten would be able to get in and out without mishap, and pulled the door shut behind her.

Of course, she didn't have any cat things prepared and that meant she would have to go back into the bathroom, risking letting him out if he didn't stay put behind the commode. But it couldn't be helped. It was the easiest place to clean up after him if he didn't use the litter box.

Since there was cat food in the pantry, Erin had to assume that Clementine had once had a cat and that she hadn't gotten rid of all her supplies. Perhaps she had intended to get another cat, but had ended up being too sick to take care of one. So, Erin went hunting. She didn't find any food dishes, so she just went with a couple of heavier bowls from the cupboard for food and water. Kitty litter sand was behind the door in the garage. There was a covered litter box in another corner of the garage. Erin decided to leave the cover off of it to make it easier for the kitten to get in and out of to encourage him to use it. She grabbed an old newspaper to put down on the floor around the kitty litter box to catch any sand that got kicked out. She considered covering the entire floor with paper to catch any accidents, but that was how you trained a dog, not a cat. A cat should instinctively go in the litter box.

Erin inched the door open, ready for an escape attempt. But the kitten did not try to get out and Erin was able to get in with the litter box and put it down, kicking the door shut behind her. There was still no sign of the kitten. Bending down to look, she saw that he was still squished behind the porcelain, watching her with concerned eyes. Erin left again to get the food and water dishes. His ears did perk up when he smelled the cat kibble. He watched her intently. Erin filled the water bowl and put it down.

"How about that, little guy?" Erin whispered. "Still hungry? Thirsty? You're safe here. You can come out and eat."

But she knew he wouldn't venture out. Not while she was there. It was going to take a while before he was used to her.

"Okay. See you later."

She hesitated as she left. Shut off the light or leave it on? Would he be scared of the dark? Would the light keep him awake? He didn't need the light on to see his food or the litter box, did he? Cats could see in the dark. Eventually, she decided to turn it off.

"Goodnight, kitty."

CHAPTER 7

*I*f she thought that the kitten would give her a peaceful night's sleep, she had another think coming. She forewent her usual bedtime bath, deciding that might be traumatic to the kitten. She instead put on fuzzy pajamas, had a cup of tea, read a few pages in her book, and slid into bed. As soon as she closed her eyes, her thoughts went immediately to Officer Piper. And not in a good way.

But before she could worry about how anxiety was going to keep her awake all night, she was faced with a new concern.

At first she thought it was a baby crying or someone having a fight outside. But as she tried to sort out the wails, she realized that the caterwauling was, in fact, a cat. Her cat.

And it was loud enough that she was sure the neighbors could probably hear it. How could such a little animal make such a horrible racket? Erin went to the bathroom door and banged on it.

"Quiet down!"

The noise stopped.

Erin went back to her bed. Just as she was pulling up the covers, it started again. Erin listened for a moment, thinking maybe it was just one last hurrah, the kitten getting in the last word, and then he would stop.

He did not.

Erin went back to the bathroom. She opened the door and turned on the light, wondering if she would find that he was again hanging from the curtains or had gotten himself into some other fix. But he was standing in the middle of the bathroom. He immediately scooted backward and again hid behind the toilet.

"What's wrong with you?" Erin murmured to him. "Don't you know it's time to go to bed? Kittens need their sleep."

He stared up at her.

Erin reconsidered turning the light off. Cats were nocturnal, so maybe leaving the light on would signal to him that it was time to go to sleep. Or maybe if he was frightened, the light would be soothing. He was just a weanling, she reminded herself. It was probably the first night he'd been away from his mother and littermates.

Deciding that maybe he needed something comforting, Erin went to the sewing room and started looking through the fabric and craft supplies for inspiration. She cut a couple of yards of penguin-patterned fleece from a bolt and grabbed a couple of scraps of leopard-spotted faux fur. She put them into a wicker basket that was much too big for the kitten, but would be cozy when he was full-grown.

She returned to the bathroom, still opening the door with great care in case the little cat was getting more bold with all of the coming and going. He was still hiding behind the commode. With the litterbox and the food dishes, the small room was already crowded. The basket was going to make it unnavigable if she had to get up in the middle of the night. But she couldn't think of another solution.

Hoping to reduce the likelihood of a nocturnal adventure—she certainly didn't want to be chasing a kitten through the house in the middle of the night—Erin used the facility.

"Sorry," she murmured to the kitten before flushing. She was afraid he would go rocketing around the room when his hiding place was suddenly filled with the sounds of rushing water, maybe even climb her like he had when K9 put on an appearance, but he stayed put. Erin washed and dried her hands.

She crouched down and reached around the toilet. Not to get the kitten out, just to stroke him for a moment. To try to connect with the little furball and reassure him. He didn't slash at her, bite her, or back away, all of which she considered good signs.

"There, see? Everything is okay. You're safe here. No need to cry. Okay?"

She settled the basket as close to his hiding place as possible to encourage him to investigate it, left the light on for him, and headed back to bed.

All chance of sleep seemed to have fled. Her brain was in high gear. Her thoughts went again to the upcoming police interview. Surely Piper wouldn't arrest her. If they'd had anything they considered proof of her guilt, he would have arrested her that evening, not helped her to rescue the kitten. After all, she couldn't take care of a kitten while in jail.

The crying started up again. Erin looked at her clock. She would give him fifteen minutes to settle down. The neighbors couldn't report her for fifteen minutes of noise. If he continued after that, she would… check on him again and try to calm him down. It was worse than having a baby. She really didn't have any idea what to do to calm down a lonely kitten.

She lasted five minutes. Five minutes of torture. When she couldn't stand it anymore, she threw herself out of bed and stalked to the bathroom. She opened the door.

"Stop crying!"

The kitten froze in the middle of the floor, staring at her with big, liquid eyes, then all four feet were scrabbling for purchase on the slick tile floor before he managed to get moving and again dashed behind the commode. After making sure the door was shut securely behind her, Erin followed the kitten. She reached behind the toilet and got her hand around his belly. He scratched and bit, which hurt, but Erin wasn't letting him go. She carried him to the basket and put him down, holding him there firmly.

"This is where you go to sleep. You can't be up crying all night. See how nice and comfy cozy it is? Feel the fur." She stroked it with the other hand. "Just like your mama. I know it's scary, but you can be warm and safe here. You're okay. Just snuggle into this little nest and you can curl up and go to sleep."

She gradually released the pressure on the kitten's body. Once he was free, he squirmed away from her, around the side of the basket, burrowing down under the fleece. Then he hid there, turning his body in a circle so he could look up out of his burrow at her.

"That's right," Erin whispered. "Isn't that so much more comfy than hiding behind the commode? Silly kitty. Now go to sleep."

She crept out of the bathroom, watching to make sure the little kitten didn't make a break for the door. She tiptoed down the hall. Maybe if he didn't hear her walk away, he'd think she was still outside the door and wouldn't be so lonely. *Sleep, kitten.* Erin needed her sleep or it was going to be impossible to get up in the early hours to bake. She really did need to find an assistant. It wouldn't pay much, but if she could get a student to work a few hours before and after school…

She slid into bed as quiet as a mouse. But the kitten seemed to know exactly when she got herself situated. She closed her eyes and he immediately started howling again. Erin muttered a few choice words under her breath about kittens who keep people awake at night and went back down the hall.

This time she didn't open the door and go in. She just stood outside, making calming, soothing noises. The kitten quieted. Erin waited. Just as she was about to head back to her bedroom, the noise started again.

"Shh, kitty. Go to sleep. Curl up in a little furball and go to sleep in your basket…"

The noise stopped. Erin waited. She looked at her wrist, even though she wasn't wearing a watch.

She was starting to feel weepy.

She was a murder suspect.

She had to get up early in the morning. And that blasted little kitten wasn't going to let her get a wink of sleep.

She opened the door. The kitten was in the middle of the floor. He completed his skittering run behind the commode. Erin scooped him up and put him in the basket. He burrowed down under the blanket.

Erin picked up the basket and took it out of the bathroom. She considered putting it in the garage, but that would be cruel. The concrete floor was cold and there were all kinds of tools and maybe pesticides or other poisons that could kill a curious kitten. She wouldn't be able to catch him again and she was afraid she would still be able to hear him crying even all the way back in the house. She went instead back to her bedroom. She shut the door and put down the basket. Then she climbed into bed.

It was a few minutes before she could hear the kitten moving around, climbing back out of the basket. He started to cry.

"Shh, go to sleep."

He stopped. There was silence for a few more minutes. He started to cry again.

"Shh, kitty. Enough crying. You're not alone. Now go to sleep."

He quieted again. Erin listened for him. He was quiet, kitten soft paws on plush carpet. But she could still hear him every now and then as he sniffed and sneezed at various items around the room or pushed against things with his face or body. Listening to his explorations, Erin started to drift. She wasn't thinking about her police interview because she was listening too closely to the tiny noises of the kitten. She was almost asleep when he climbed up the sheets onto the bed. He crept around the bed, exploring. Erin kept absolutely still, not wanting to scare him away or to have him start chasing her wiggling toes under the bedding. If she just stayed still, he would settle in and let her sleep.

Eventually, she felt the kitten squeeze up against her back, kneading the bed with his little paws. He started to purr, a tiny, old-man grumble. His purrs and the warmth of his body lulled her to sleep.

When Erin's alarm went off in the morning, she reached over to slap it off, then lay there in the bed trying to rouse herself enough to get up and go to work. As she lay there, her mind started to work, reminding her with a sick feeling of dread of her upcoming interview with Officer Piper after work. Maybe she would stay home sick. He couldn't complain if she were too sick to make the appointment.

But she couldn't stay sick forever and, sooner or later, she would have to talk to him. It might as well be sooner. She had learned, over the years, that if she were in trouble, it was best to get it over with. Half the suffering was in avoiding punishment.

Then she remembered the kitten. She didn't move, trying to locate the critter before moving. He was so small, she didn't want to crush him rolling over.

"Kitty, kitty, kitty?" she called softly.

The pillow she was lying on shifted. Erin moved her hand up and found the kitten, his body soft and warm, lying on her pillow curled around her head.

"You silly cat!"

Erin sat up. She turned on the lamp next to the bed and looked at him. He sat up and yawned, a wide pink-tongued yawn with his eyes closed and his ears quivering back.

"You're just the cutest thing."

He didn't run away at the sound of her voice. He just sat there, looking at her. Erin reached a tentative hand out toward him, expecting him to rocket away. But he just sniffed. Not getting any closer, not backing away, just getting her scent.

"Are you actually going to let me pat you?"

She inched closer. He touched his little pink nose to her fingers and didn't pull away. Erin stroked him gently. He started to purr, pushing his head into her hand. She rubbed his head and ears and ran her fingers along his back. He stretched out on the bed and turned over, showing his belly. Erin scratched his belly and he was suddenly all claws, grabbing her hand.

"Ouch!" Erin jerked her hand back and this time he did jump away from her, scampering off the bed and hiding in the open closet. Erin sucked on one of her knuckles, bleeding from his needle-sharp kitten claws. "Ow, what did you do that for? I thought you wanted me to scratch your belly!"

He peered at her from the depths of the closet.

Erin caught sight of her clock and realized she'd better get moving. She was normally much more efficient about getting ready in the morning. Kittens slowed things down significantly.

"You can hide there all you like," she told the kitten. "As long as you find your litter box when you need it!" She headed off for the bathroom herself. Time to shower and get ready to go.

When she stepped out of the shower, the kitten was there, in the middle of the bathroom floor. He sat there staring up at her, unafraid. She was glad he hadn't held her outburst against her. As she toweled off, he rubbed against her legs, getting his fur damp. He sat and tongue-washed while she quickly combed out her hair and put on a touch of makeup. The ladies in Bald Eagle Falls did not go out in public without makeup on. But she would probably need to reapply it after working over the stove for a couple of hours.

"You're going to need a name."

He stopped licking for a moment and looked at her. Then he went back to work. She wondered whether she was going to have to give him a real bath to get all the dust and dirt out of his fur. Or whether he had fleas or mites or some other parasite. She hadn't even thought of that before letting him sleep on the bed with her. She'd been so tired she hadn't thought any of it through.

"Well, time to eat. You're going to need some breakfast too, aren't you?"

She picked up his dishes and carried them with her to the kitchen. The cat followed close behind her.

He sat in the middle of the floor and continued his grooming regimen. Any time she made an unexpected movement, whether across the kitchen to the fridge, or getting a mug out of the cupboard, or closing the door on the toaster oven to warm her bagel, he stopped what he was doing and looked at her. But he didn't run away.

Erin tended to the kitty, giving him a fresh bowl of water and putting kibble into the dish. As soon as she put the dishes on the floor, he sauntered over to have a look, as if he'd been a house pet his whole life. Erin smiled and watched him for a moment before grabbing her coffee and bagel and sitting down at the table for a quick repast before heading over to the bakery.

She was a little worried about leaving the kitten all alone in the house. She hoped that he wouldn't yowl while she was gone. Since it was daytime, he should be more interested in sleeping and, hopefully, wouldn't be looking for company. And she didn't yet know whether he would use the litter box, but didn't dare shut him in the bathroom. His cries would have the neighbors on the warpath, at the very least, if not the police called, thinking there was a baby left in the house alone. But the cat had eaten and found a patch of sunshine to lie down in. He didn't appear to be worried about her leaving. Hopefully the house would be intact when she returned at the end of the day.

Her mind was still on the kitten when she pulled into the parking lot behind the store. And on the baking she was going to need to get done before opening in a few hours. And, niggling at the back of her mind, the interview with Officer Terry Piper when she closed the shop for the day. She wondered what had really happened to Angela. How she had really ended up dead in Erin's basement.

She was not thinking about the ghost. That mystery had already been solved.

She immediately got to work on the batters she had left in the fridge. The muffins could bake while she got the ingredients for the next treat assembled. But as she started the big mixer, which ground and grumbled like the bearings were going to pop out, she caught a movement out of the corner of her eye.

She turned her head to see what it was, even though she knew it was just a shadow or a trick of a light and there was nothing to see.

But there was.

The girl froze, her eyes wild.

"Who are you? What are you doing in my store? Where did you come from?" The words tumbled out of Erin's mouth without a thought and she moved toward the girl to prevent her from leaving. Who was this, appearing in the middle of her store with both of the doors locked?

The girl was worn and rumpled. She had stringy blond hair that reached her shoulders. Erin put her at seventeen or eighteen. She looked frightened. Lost and homeless.

"I—I'm sorry." The girl attempted to navigate around Erin, heading for the door. Erin put out her arms, making herself big and preventing the girl from going around her.

"Stop. You stay there and answer my questions, or I'll call the police."

The girl stopped. Her jaw jutted and she put on a tough front. "The police in this hole? I'd be miles away before they showed up." Her voice was a little hoarse, like she had a cold. But despite the words, she didn't try to get by Erin again. Erin was sure that she could run if she really wanted to. She could shove Erin down and make a run for it. She was right, Erin probably wouldn't be able to get Piper in there until the girl was long gone. It seemed like he was always right outside her door, though, so the girl might just as easily be wrong. And it didn't look like she wanted to take the chance to find out. Better to answer questions and get out than to take a chance and not be able to escape.

"I'm… I'm Vic. Vicky. Victoria. I just… I stayed here when you were gone, to stay safe at night. It used to be empty." She looked around, giving a shrug. "Usually, you come in the front door. The bell rings. Why didn't you come in the front door this time?"

"I parked in the back. Decided to use the employee parking space. How long have you been staying here? Since before I got to town?"

Vic nodded, watching Erin carefully for her reaction. "Yeah, sorry…"

"You broke my mug, not the cat."

"The cat?" Vic shook her head. "I knocked it off in the dark getting a drink of water. I didn't mean to. I've tried to keep everything tidy, but some-times… you notice."

"Yes. Sometimes I do. You had Melissa convinced that the bakery was haunted by my Aunt Clementine's ghost."

The girl smiled slightly at this. "I wish I was a ghost and could go through walls."

"But you can't," Erin said. "So, how did you get in here?"

She hesitated, weighing her answer. "I might have… had a key."

"A key? How did you get a key to my shop? No one else has a key."

"My aunt was friends with yours, I guess. She had a spare key."

"And you made yourself at home, camping out in my store."

"Yes."

Erin pointed at a step-stool. "Sit down."

Vic looked like she would rather run, but after a delay of a few seconds, she obeyed and sat down. She was a tall girl, slim. She perched on the chair, looking at Erin and waiting for her to say what she was going to do about Vic's breaking and entering. Or entering, anyway. Trespassing.

"You've been staying here every night. Running out the back door when you hear me come in the front."

"Yes. You get here really early."

"A baker has to be up early."

Erin attended to her ingredients. First a stray cat and now a stray girl. The world was determined to make her open late. She wouldn't have time to replace all the day-old baking. It would still be fresh enough; she'd just mark it down. People would be happy to get specialty foods at a discount. Maybe she would start a kids' cookie club. Children could have a free cookie once a day? Once a week? How often would she need to clear out old stock? She hated to have to throw anything out. Maybe a seniors' muffin club too.

"Where are you from?" she asked Vic.

"Mmm… north…" Vic temporized. She didn't offer any more details. Didn't want to be tracked down for some reason. Had she been in trouble? Were there warrants out for her arrest? She was homeless, a burglar, was it possible she was a murderer? Had she been in the bakery when Angela had died? Without meaning to, had she contaminated something in the kitchen? Batters sitting in the fridge? Flour containers sitting open? Or had she been in the basement when Angela had died? If she had her own key, she could have let herself in and hidden in the basement, thinking she was perfectly safe, since Erin was upstairs serving customers. Until Angela discovered her.

"You're not being very helpful."

"I'm sorry… I just don't want to talk about it. I wasn't… things weren't good before I got here."

"Victoria what? What is your last name?"

"Uh, Webster. Victoria Webster."

Erin went to her office and pulled out a notepad. She wrote down the name. "Is that your real name?"

Vic didn't offer a response.

"Why did you come to Bald Eagle Falls?"

"To see my aunt."

"Who is your aunt?"

But Erin already knew before Vic could answer.

"Angela Plaint." Vic's voice was quiet, almost inaudible.

"Angela Plaint is your aunt?" Erin repeated, flabbergasted.

"Yes. Well, she was. Though… she wasn't exactly friendly when I went to see her. I thought… she would help me out. But she wouldn't have anything to do with me. Wouldn't give me so much as a glass of water or put me up for the night."

"So, you decided to stay here instead."

Vic looked down. "Yeah. I'm sorry. I thought… I don't know what I thought. It was just the only place I had to go. Aunt Angela had a spare key. I thought the place was standing empty… at least I could be indoors, off of the street. Then when you brought stuff in and opened up… I was only using it at night, when you weren't here."

"Well, you can't do that. I can't have people wandering through here. Everything in the kitchen has to be kept clean and free of cross-contamination. If you brought anything with wheat in here…"

"I didn't eat anything in here," Vic promised. "I only came here to sleep and use the commode. I didn't touch anything."

"You broke my mug. You touched my papers."

"Only to see what was going on. Whether you were starting up a business or selling the place. That's all, I swear."

Erin studied the girl's flaming red cheeks. She looked terrified. And Erin understood why, too. Vic knew that anyone with sense would immediately turn her over to the police. She had motive, means, and opportunity.

Tears glistening in Vic's eyes. "I didn't do anything to hurt Aunt Angela. She was my favorite aunt. Even if she did turn me out. I know she's had a tough life. It made her a hard person. She didn't understand my—why I went to her. I guess it was a stupid thing to do. But I didn't hurt her. I'd never hurt anyone, especially not someone in my family."

"Why don't you go home?" Erin asked gently. "Why did you run away?"

If anyone could understand running away, it was Erin. How many times had she run away from her foster families? How many times, as an adult, had she just left when a situation became fraught? Just packed up her bags and left town?

"I didn't run away. They kicked me out. I'm eighteen, they don't have to look after me anymore. And they don't want me around. I'm... a black mark against their name."

Erin gazed at the young blond. She had obviously been living rough, but she had a pretty face. She couldn't understand how anyone could turn another person out on the streets, but especially someone so obviously young and vulnerable. Didn't they know the kind of life she would be forced to live on the streets with no lifeline?

"How would you like to earn some money?"

Vic's mouth dropped open. "What?"

"Help me out today. Help me get the baking done and set up and then you can assist behind the counter. I can't pay you much, but I have some start-up capital. Tonight you can come home with me. Have a shower and sleep in a bed for once."

Vic shook her head. "Why on earth would you do that?"

"Call me crazy," Erin said with a shrug. "I've been left with nothing too many times. I'm not going to be the cause of someone else getting turned out in the street."

"Thank you. But you don't have to do that. I can... I don't know, I can work something else out."

"You don't want the job?"

Vic stared at her, her eyes still round and disbelieving. "You really want me to work for you?"

"Let's start with a day. See how it goes."

"Okay," Vic finally agreed, her voice low and hoarse. "Yeah. I'll help you."

"Good. We'd better get to work, because I'm already behind. We can talk while we work."

She got Vic to wash up and don an apron and cap and they worked side-by-side, Erin showing Vic what she needed to do so that she could get everything into the oven on schedule.

"What are you going to tell people?" Vic asked anxiously. "Please don't tell them I'm Angela's niece."

"People won't know you? You haven't visited her before?"

"No... it's been a while, I've changed a lot. I don't think anyone will recognize me. If you tell them I'm Angela's niece, they're going to think that I killed her!"

"No one is going to think that," Erin soothed. Though she knew it was probably true. People would jump all over the disaffected relative. They'd say it was because Angela had refused to help Vic, or because Vic thought she would get Angela's money. The girl wouldn't have a chance. "If you don't want me to, I won't tell. We can just let people think that you're a friend of mine from out of town."

"Yeah." Vic blew out a breath of relief. "That would be really good. Thanks."

~

Gema stared at Vic and shook her gray head. "Where did she come from? I haven't seen you around here before."

"This is Vic, she's helping me today," Erin said, smiling steadily.

"North," Vic offered, again providing no further detail. Erin knew what it was like not to be from anywhere particular. People didn't like it. That was one of the reasons she always added 'Maine' when people asked. People liked to have something more. They liked something identifiable, classifiable. 'North' was just too amorphous.

"She's new in town," Erin said.

Vic was looking put-together in a crisp white apron and server's hat, her hair combed and pulled back into a sleek ponytail. She had borrowed Erin's makeup to do her face before opening, Erin keeping a close eye out while she was in the commode to make sure she didn't bolt. Vic was much more polished and relaxed, looking like she was actually enjoying herself.

A breakfast of muffins and milk hadn't hurt, either.

Vic made Erin think of the cat; homeless, in need of love and nurturing, but skittish and not sure that she was safe there.

Erin walked her through the various products on offer. "If someone wants to know about ingredients, just ask me. I haven't printed up information lists yet." Erin made a mental note that she would need to do that.

It was much easier to work the counter with two people. She really should have hired an assistant before opening in the first place. She and Vic fell into a routine. Vic smiled brightly and was enthusiastic about the food. Erin felt like she had been there right from the start. And she had been, in a way.

They grabbed an early lunch when the morning rush calmed. There was plenty of bread and fixings for sandwiches.

"This is really nice," Vic said, as they both rested their feet and munched on sandwiches, the 'back at 11:30' sign up in the door. "And the food doesn't even taste like it's gluten-free. It's real good."

"Gluten-free doesn't mean it has to suck," Erin said.

"No. I guess not. All the stuff I've had before, it's always gritty and falls apart. Or it tastes like cardboard. Your baking is real nice."

"That's the rice flour. If you're going to use rice flour, it should be superfine. You should let your batters soak. And you should combine it with other, softer flours."

"Huh." Vic took another bite of her sandwich. "You can't just substitute rice flour for wheat flour?"

"No. It would be pretty horrible."

Vic was quiet, staring out the window. She had smiled a lot while serving the customers, but now her face was solemn and contemplative.

"What are you going to do?"

"About you?"

Vic nodded.

"I don't know." Erin sighed. "I don't want to get you in any trouble. I'd like to help you out. You seem like a really nice kid. But there is a police investigation going on. They're going to need to know that you were around. They'll need your statement."

"She really died right here in the building?"

"She really did. You must have known that, you would have seen the police tape up when you came back here that night. I don't know where you were when it happened, but the police will need your alibi."

"What if I don't have one?"

"That doesn't mean you did it. It just means you can't prove where you were. It's not like you had a motive." Erin bit off the words.

Vic shook her head. Erin knew it looked bad. If Piper thought Erin was suspect, he was going to be doubly suspicious about Vic.

"We have to come clean. If it comes to light that you withheld information, they won't believe anything you say."

"What are you going to do with me?"

"I think you should come to the police station with me. After closing today."

"Or else?"

"I think you should come, Vic. Don't you?"

Vic chewed slowly. Erin knew how she felt. Or she thought she did. She wasn't any too excited about going to see Officer Piper herself. Vic was just a kid, without a friend or relative to help her through. Erin knew what it was like to be all alone.

"Yeah," Vic said finally. "I guess I better. Can't run away from it."

Erin nodded. She was relieved that Vic had agreed to go on her own. She did not want to have to turn Vic in to the authorities. It was better if it was voluntary.

Piper wouldn't throw her in jail, would he? He'd see that she couldn't be responsible for Angela's death.

❧

Erin and Vic were both slow about closing up and cleaning up, preparing the bakery for the next day. Neither one wanted to be done and on their way to the police station.

Erin told Vic about the cat and his antics of the night before, laughing at how loud he was and how worried she had been of waking the neighbors.

"He couldn't be that loud," Vic protested.

"He was! I swear, he was like a fire alarm!"

"Are you sure it wasn't a mountain lion?"

"Just an itty bitty kitten," Erin held her hands out to demonstrate the size. "Barely old enough to be on his own."

"Let me see your hands," Vic said, looking at them. Erin held her hands

79

out tentatively, showing Vic the palms, then the backs, not sure what Vic wanted. Vic shook her head. "He sure clawed you up."

Erin looked at the scratches, nodding ruefully. "I know. Stings like heck. But he's so cute, I can't blame him for it."

They looked around the kitchen, but there was nothing left to do. It was time to go see Officer Piper.

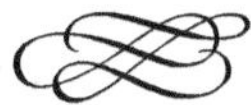

The police station was no more than a couple of offices at the Town Hall, which was a store front just a couple of blocks down from the bakery. A receptionist for the entire Town Hall had them sit down in a couple of straight-backed chairs to wait. It was only a few minutes before Officer Piper was there to usher Erin into the office. He looked at Erin and then looked at Vic, frowning.

"What's all this?"

"This is Vic. She needs to talk to you as well."

"Vic." He studied her with his brows drawn down. "I don't know you."

"No, sir." Vic looked at the floor.

"She's been… she's…" Erin stumbled over her words. "Can we talk to you in private? I'd rather the whole town didn't know everything."

Piper looked around. The only other person there was the receptionist. But after dealing with Melissa's gossip over what was in official police reports, Erin wasn't trusting that any of the administrative staff would be any better. Piper nodded and motioned for them both to go with him. He took them into a jumbled office, shut the door, and sat down. K9 lay down at his side, grumbling just as he had when they had come to Clementine's house. Vic snickered.

"Okay," Piper said. "Explain to me who you are."

Vic looked at Erin. She licked her lips, but couldn't seem to get started.

Erin felt sorry for the girl. "She's apparently been sleeping at the bakery," she said. "She had a key and let herself in and out."

"You told me that no one else had a key."

"I didn't know that anyone did. I guess Clementine had given out at least one copy."

"You'd better get the locks changed if you don't know how many copies are floating around. That should have been your first order of business when you took possession. Always change the locks on a house or a business when you take possession. Helps to prevent... unexpected guests."

"I guess I should have. I never thought of it. And I never suspected that anyone was sleeping there."

"You knew someone had been there, though. I take it Vic is your ghost."

Vic nodded. "I broke the mug," she said hoarsely.

"Well, that's one mystery solved. But not the one I would really like to be solved."

Erin nodded. "You wanted me here to talk to me about... Angela's death."

"Yes. And I expected you to be alone. I don't conduct interviews in pairs. You find more out if you interview... witnesses... separately."

"I know you just asked for me. But you didn't know about Vic. No one did."

"Exactly how long have you been in town?" Piper asked Vic.

"A few weeks."

"You were here before Miss Price."

"Yes."

"Squatting at the shop before she was even in town."

"Yes."

Piper chewed the inside of his lip, studying her. Eventually, he looked at Erin.

"I know it's a lot to ask, but could I get you to wait while I interview Vic? You probably just want to go home and to bed, but I'm going to need to get her story without you in the room. And vice versa."

"Sure, yeah. Understood."

"You're okay to wait for a while? Have you had supper?"

"I can wait. But no, I haven't had supper."

"The Chinese place across the street is good. Then you're not just sitting around waiting and won't have low blood sugar when I'm ready to talk to you."

Erin thought about it. He was probably right, and she hadn't had a really good dinner for a week, always just grabbing something quick on the way to bed.

"Okay," she agreed. "You know where to find me if I'm not back when you're ready for me."

Piper looked across the desk at Vic. "We're going to be a while."

Erin felt a lot calmer after dinner at the Chinese restaurant. Piper was right about her being in better shape for a police interview once her blood sugar was stable. She had been letting herself get run down with the launch of the bakery. If she didn't eat right and take care of herself, she wouldn't be able to keep it up.

She again took her seat outside of the police department offices. Vic and Piper were still behind closed doors. Another three quarters of an hour passed before the door opened and Piper escorted Vic out. Erin smiled at Vic, who was looking tired and red-eyed.

"Okay?" she asked, putting a hand on Vic's arm.

"Yeah." Vic sniffled. "I'm fine."

Erin looked at Piper, looking for some sign of how much trouble Vic was in. Did Piper suspect her now? And if he did, that would be good for Erin. If Vic had taken Erin's place as the prime suspect, she should be happy. But she wasn't. Her strongest instinct was to protect Vic. Just like the kitten.

"You go get something to eat now," Erin suggested, pulling her wallet out of her purse to give Vic some cash. "I'll look for you over there, or back here. Okay?" She tried to meet Vic's eyes. "You're not going to run off on me, right? You need a bed for the night; I'll help you out. Introduce you to the kitten."

Vic brightened a little at this. "Yeah, I want to see him," she agreed.

"Good. Then I'll see you back here, or across the street at the Chinese place."

Vic nodded and took the money Erin offered. Piper and Erin both watched her walk out of the building and head across the street.

"You think she'll be back?" Piper asked. "You don't think she'll run?"

"I don't know. You?"

They headed back to Piper's office and sat down.

"Hard to say. I've called Tom to keep an eye on her. He'll pick her up over there. But our resources are pretty thin. Tom's not an experienced tail."

"I'm glad you didn't arrest her."

"All I have right now are suspicions. I haven't caught her breaking any laws or even caught her in a lie. You're not charging her with trespass. There's no evidence that she had anything to do with Mrs. Plaint's death. Yet."

"You don't really think she did it, do you? It wasn't like she had a motive to murder her own aunt."

"Did she talk to you about Mrs. Plaint?"

"No, not much…" Erin shook her head. "What did she say?"

"See if she'll talk to you about it. I only have the bare bones… she wouldn't say anything more to me than she had to. But it doesn't look good."

"She couldn't have intentionally killed Angela. Not that little girl."

"She's not a little girl. She's an adult. You don't know anything about her. And what you do know should be a warning to you."

Erin knew he was right logically. But her heart was overriding her head. Yes, Vic had effectively broken into her shop and squatted there without her permission. She knew the victim and they were apparently not on the best of terms. But the girl didn't seem to harbor any grudge against her aunt. She seemed open and friendly and she had a knack for customer service.

"There's more to that girl than meets the eye," Piper warned. "You're offering to take her into your home when you know next to nothing about her… not the smartest idea."

"She needs a place to stay. You don't have any shelters in Bald Eagle Falls, do you?"

"No. But we could figure something out. Have someone take her into the city. Book a room at the motel. There's no need to put yourself in a vulnerable situation. She could steal from you and disappear in the night in your car. She could slit your throat in your sleep. There are a hundred other ways she could damage or endanger you."

"Well, she's not going to, knowing that the police are already onto her, is she?"

"There's no guarantee of that."

Erin sighed. "I trust her. I know, I'm naive to do it, but I have to. I've been Vic too many times before. I know what it's like not to have anyone or to have anywhere to go. I know what it's like to be discriminated against for being homeless, alone, or destitute. To have to rely on little kindnesses from people who don't know anything about you. People have helped me to get where I am. I have to help Vic. I have to."

Piper stared across the desk at her, his eyes narrow, dissecting her like a scalpel, trying to uncover all the secrets she kept hidden under the surface.

"You have an interesting past, Miss Price."

She wondered how much he'd been able to find out about her. She had dropped below the radar for long periods of time. Had he been able to fill in those gaps? Or was he still looking for answers and trying to figure out what kind of a person she really was?

"There are lots of people with interesting histories."

"Did you come here because you were in trouble?"

"I came here because my aunt left me a house and a store. I've never had an opportunity like that before. I decided to take advantage of it."

"This detective who tracked you down in Maine. What did you say his name was?"

They both knew very well that she had never told him any details about the detective. "His name was Alton Summers."

"Did he get a finder's fee for tracking you down?"

"I don't know what arrangements he had with the Estate. Of course he was paid to find me. Detectives don't work for free."

"But you don't know what kind of financial arrangements were made."

"No. Why would I?"

"What proof did you give him that you were Erin Price?"

"What do you mean? I have ID."

"ID can be faked. And even if it is real, I'm sure there is more than one Erin Price in the country. In fact, I know there are, because there were other hits on the name when I looked into your background. What proof do you have that you are Clementine's niece? Or did you and the detective just decide that you would step into the role and split the profit between you?"

"I am Clementine's niece. There was no need for any subterfuge. He got paid whatever he had arranged with the estate. I presented myself and confirmed that I was the Erin Price they were looking for. That's it. That's what happened."

Piper leaned back in his chair, making it creak in protest. K9 raised his head to look at his master, then put it down again with an irritated huff.

"You weren't even going by the name Erin Price when the detective found you."

"No," Erin admitted reluctantly. He'd done his homework. How much did he know about her past? She couldn't be easy to track.

"In fact, you've gone by a number of assumed names."

"Yes. But not because I'm a criminal. I took the names of my foster parents, when I could. But my birth name is Erin Price. That's what's on all my papers."

"Still, I find it troubling. You're a drifter. A con artist. Moving from place to place, operating under different names, staying around for a few months, and then going on somewhere else."

"I'm not a con. I haven't conned anyone. I have moved around. But that's not a crime."

"You're not from Maine."

"I don't think I said I was. I never misled you. I lived in Maine before I came here."

He considered that for a moment, then shrugged. She searched his face for some sign of the friendliness and good humor she had seen when he had helped her with the kitten. But his face was an impassive mask. He was the police. He had a job. And it wasn't his job to befriend her.

"Tell me again about the day that Mrs. Plaint died."

Erin rolled her eyes and groaned. "I've gone over it before. Why do you need me to tell it again? You're trying to see if I'll tell the same story? If you can trip me up?"

"No. I have new information. I need to hear your story again, fit it all together."

Erin shook her head. "What new information?"

"There was someone else in the bakery the day of the murder. It changes everything. I need to review everything again."

"Because of Vic? But she says she wasn't there. She left when I arrived and stayed away until after you left."

"And that may or may not be true. It colors everything. I can't verify where she was. I need to work on the assumption that she was still in the building. I need to look at the whole sequence of events again."

"Okay. Fine." Erin started to outline her day, telling Piper everything she could remember.

"When did you unlock the back stairs?" he interrupted.

Erin cut herself off and let the question sink in.

"I kept the back stairs locked. I could go through the door from the kitchen to the basement while it was locked, because it wasn't a bolt, just the door handle. But to come back up from the basement to the kitchen, I needed the key. I didn't leave it unlocked, though, just opened it with the key. I kept it locked so that customers using the commode couldn't come back up through the kitchen. No traffic through the kitchen. Just me."

"So as far as you are concerned, it was locked the whole day."

"Yes. It was."

Piper said nothing. Erin thought back. She had been through that door several times. She had used her key to reenter the kitchen every time. But had it been locked, or had she only assumed that it was?

"I never unlocked it."

"But you weren't the only one with a key."

"Did Vic say she unlocked it? Why would she do that?"

"She didn't say she did. But did she? If she was going to come and go without being discovered, wouldn't it make sense to be able to get through that door quickly? Another escape route?"

"If she had a key, she could get through it. And no one could follow her unless they had a key. It would make more sense to leave it locked. A trap."

Piper nodded slowly. He made several lines of notes on the ruled yellow pad on his desk. He shuffled papers so that a sketched floor plan was in front of him. Erin watched his eyes as he studied it. Tracing possible routes through the shop. Testing her theory.

"Vic wouldn't have unlocked that door," she told him.

"If Vic didn't unlock it, and you didn't unlock it, then who did?"

Erin blinked at him. "What makes you think someone did?"

He stared at her and didn't answer for several beats. "Because it was unlocked when I arrived on the scene."

"What?" Erin frowned and shook her head. "How? Who could have unlocked it, and how? Why?"

"There are apparently more keys around than you are aware of. And you didn't change the locks when you took possession. I've been focused on who was in the bakery. Who could have gone down to the basement while Angela was there. That meant you and any customers who were there between the time Angela went down to use the facilities. Mary Lou Cox. Melissa Lee. Gema Reed. The Potters, who you were assisting—"

"The senior couple?" Erin asked. "They couldn't have gone down and up the stairs. Especially not in the time that I went back to the kitchen to check ingredients. They both had mobility issues. They couldn't have."

"As I was going to say."

"Oh. Right."

"Glad that we're agreed on that point. So the suspect pool was limited to you and the three other ladies eating at the table."

"And now Vic," Erin said.

"Yes. The back door was bolted. The back stairs were unlocked. You could have gone into the kitchen and downstairs. Any of the three ladies could have gone down the front stairs while you were in the kitchen. They all alibi each other, but people sometimes make mistakes. Remember things differently. Or collude to keep something from the police, out of ignorance or misguided loyalty."

"But now, you think there are other suspects?"

"Who else has a key?"

"I don't know. I wasn't in contact with Clementine. So it could be..." Erin trailed off, seeing the answer in Piper's eyes. "It could be anyone."

"Exactly. If you didn't unlock the back stairs, because you didn't want customers wandering into the kitchen, and Vic didn't unlock the door, because she wanted to keep open an escape route that she could prevent anyone else from taking, then who unlocked that door and neglected to lock it again? If nobody came through the kitchen to go out through the front door, then it had to be someone with a key. The back door was bolted. Not just a spring lock. It could be opened from the inside by someone who came up the back stairs, but that person could not bolt it again. Not without a key."

Erin supposed she should be happy the suspect pool had opened up. That took some of the police suspicion off of her. With everyone who might have had a key having had opportunity to sneak down the stairs to murder Angela, Piper would have to focus his attention on those who had motive to harm her. Which put the focus back on Erin. Or maybe on Vic.

"Have you found anything out about the food that was tested?" Erin asked. "Was there any cross-contamination? It's still possible that it was just a tragic accident. Angela might have forgotten her autoinjector. Or used it and not gotten a new one yet."

"So far, nothing from the bakery has tested positive for wheat."

"Well, that's good! I mean, for my business. You can confirm that my products aren't unsafe. So the public won't avoid buying from me for fear of contamination."

"That also means it was intentional poisoning. If the wheat didn't come from the muffins, where did it come from?"

"I was wondering if she might have another allergy she didn't know about. To… chocolate, or eggs, or something else in the muffin. Or even something in the air down there. Dust or spores. Fumes from the paint thinner I used to clean the brushes."

"How likely is that?"

"You'd have to ask the coroner, I guess… I don't know if they have any way of telling whether it was wheat or some other allergen. I don't even know if they can tell the difference between something that was ingested and something that was inhaled."

"You really want this to be an accident."

"Well… yes. Of course. I don't want to be the suspect in a murder investigation. I just want to run the bakery."

He gave a thin smile. Not the kind that made the dimple appear in his cheek. No real humor behind it.

"Like I told Vic. Don't leave town."

"I don't intend to." Erin looked at her watch. "I'd really like to get home and get to bed. After making sure the kitten hasn't destroyed the house, of course."

She gave a little laugh and waited for him to join in and ask her how the kitten was and how it had settled in. But he didn't. He looked through his notes, mouth pulling down.

"Keep yourself available for further questions. I'm not done with you, but I'm going to need to go through everything again. There is still the possibility that Vic was still in the shop at the time that Mrs. Plaint was killed. And relatives… it's a fact that family is more likely to have killed her than a near-stranger."

"So, she's a better suspect than I am."

"That should make you happy."

"It should, but it doesn't. I feel bad for Vic. She didn't do it."

"You leave that to me."

❧

She walked out of Officer Piper's office feeling disappointed and depressed. A lot of it was probably just attributable to being tired. She always got more emotional when she was tired. 'Things will look better in the morning' had long been a late-night mantra for her. And things always did look better once she was rested.

She should have been happy there was a better suspect than she was. She should have been happy that Piper was considering outsiders. Anyone else who might have a key to the bakery. And she should have been happy that he hadn't arrested her for anything.

But she didn't feel better. Just glad that the interview was over.

Vic was sitting on the chair outside the police department that she had previously occupied. She was sitting ramrod straight, not slouched over. If she was guilty, she wouldn't be there. She would have taken Erin's twenty dollars and found the quickest way she could out of town.

Unless she knew she was being tailed and was waiting for the right opportunity to present itself.

Vic gave her a tired smile. "All done? I feel like I've been up since three o'clock."

"Maybe because you have been."

Vic stood up. She looked a little awkward, as if she didn't know what to do with herself.

"You're coming home with me," Erin said. "We'll both get a good sleep, and…"

"Everything will look better in the morning?"

Erin laughed.

"My mom always used to say that," Vic said apologetically. "I know, it's sort of lame…"

"It's exactly what I was just thinking. It's always been true for me."

Vic sighed and gave Erin a sideways look. "I hope it's true this time."

❧

Erin walked in the front door with a sigh of relief. It was good to be back in the familiar surroundings. It was becoming her sanctum. Starting to feel just a little like home. Vic entered behind her. They were both careful, looking down, watching for the kitten. He might want to run free after being cooped up all day, so they opened the door no farther than they had to in order to slip through the opening, and then shut it quickly behind them.

"Doesn't look like it's been destroyed," Vic observed.

"No. Everything looks fine out here."

She led the way into the house. "Here, kitty, kitty…"

When they went into the kitchen, she heard the skittering of claws and turned to see the orange kitten running toward them. He stopped and sat down, smelling the air. Vic cooed.

"Oh, isn't he just the cutest little thing!" She reached to pick him up. "You aren't big enough to keep someone up at night, are you?"

He tried to avoid her hand, but Vic was too quick and in a minute had the kitten snuggled to her chest and was stroking him and scratching his ears. The kitten started a loud, motorcycle purr.

"Awww…"

"You've got the touch," Erin said. "I couldn't catch him."

"Well, here," Vic handed the kitten to her. "You should hold him, then. Get him used to you."

"He slept on top of my head last night."

Vic giggled. "He's just so precious. I can't believe he's big enough to leave his mama."

"He seems to be able to manage the dry cat food, so that's a good sign. He won't starve and doesn't have to be bottle fed."

Vic patted him with one finger while Erin held him.

"Yeah. That's good."

"Do you want the bathtub first? You probably need it the most."

Vic sniffed at her shirt. "I'm not that bad, am I? I tried to sponge off every day. You know, at the sink. The bathroom one, not the kitchen."

"No, you're not bad at all. I just know it's been a while since you had access to a tub or shower. Do you want it?"

"Yes, yes," Vic said quickly. "I do!"

"Help yourself. Grab a towel from the linen closet at the end of the hall and I'll get you something to change into. I'm shorter than you, so the pants will be too short, but it's just for bed. We'll wash your clothes so that they're fresh for the morning. Do you have other clothes… somewhere?"

"I have a few things stashed," Vic admitted.

"Okay, good. You can bring them back here so that you have what you need for a few days."

Vic stood there looking at Erin.

Erin swallowed and looked away. "What…?"

"Why are you being so nice to me? I mean… my own aunt wouldn't have anything to do with me. You could have told the cops all kinds of things to implicate me and instead you're telling him you don't think I did it. You're a stranger to me."

"That doesn't mean I shouldn't care about you. I think… people should take care of each other."

Vic's eyes glistened. "Maybe you wouldn't say that if you knew more about me."

"I've been where you are… You're right, I don't know your past. But I know what you need."

Vic moved suddenly away from Erin. She left the kitchen and went down the hall to the linen closet. Erin heard her open the bathroom door and turn on the water. Erin looked down at the kitten.

"Okay, then. Vic can have the first bath and I'll get you your dinner. Have you been waiting patiently all day?"

The kitten purred and kneaded Erin with sharp claws. Erin quickly detached him and put him down on the kitchen floor again. The kitten looked up at her towering over him. She must be like a monster to him.

"It's okay," Erin said softly. "Let's get you some food."

She felt bad about only having the hard kibble intended for adult cats and looked through the pantry for something else appropriate. There was no canned cat food, but there was tuna. Erin grabbed it and picked up the cat's dish. As soon as she had the can open, the fishy smell flooded the room and the kitten was rubbing around her ankles, making excited little mrrrow noises. He obviously liked what he was smelling. Erin liked a tuna sandwich now and then, but the smell was so strong she had to breathe through her mouth to avoid gagging. Erin started with half the can of tuna and sprinkled in some of the dry kibble. She added a splash of water and stirred it, leaving it on the counter for a minute to soften. She refreshed the water dish, which the kitten sniffed at. He took a couple of laps, as if to show his gratitude, but then went back to trying to climb straight up the cupboards to sink his teeth into the good stuff. At least he wasn't trying to climb her leg.

In a couple more minutes, the kitten was gobbling down his gourmet supper. Erin went to her room to get some clothes for Vic, and then to Clementine's room to prepare it for company. It only took a couple of minutes to change the sheets.

"Clothes for you," Erin announced as she poked her head into the bathroom and put the clothes down on the counter. Vic jumped and instinctively turned away from her. But with the shower curtain pulled shut, Vic's modesty was protected. Erin chuckled. "See you in a few minutes."

"I won't be long," Vic promised, her voice sounding strange in the enclosed space of the bathroom. "I won't use up all the water."

Erin went up to the attic room to read for a few minutes while she waited for Vic to get out. She was finally able to focus on her book, relaxed, but not too sleepy. Or maybe it was just the sound of the shower below her, and having someone else in the house, so it didn't seem so quiet and lonely.

She always told herself that she didn't get lonely. She had lived on her own for so long, how could she? She liked to be independent and have her own space. But her little family had grown from one to three and she liked the feeling of having others around her. Her life felt more... cushioned. Like she was safely in a nest instead of rattling around the empty house, all hard surfaces and sharp edges.

"Erin?"

Erin startled at Vic's voice somewhere close at hand. She had been engrossed in her book and hadn't noticed the shower turning off.

"I'm up here." Erin got up and went to the top of the stairs. Vic was peering up at her. "Come on up."

Vic hesitated. She put her foot on the bottom step. "Are you sure? I thought this might be your... retreat. Maybe you don't want other people in your space?"

"No, come have a look."

Vic ascended the stairs without any more persuasion. She looked around the attic room.

"This is awesome! Really! I love it."

"Me too. Come up here to read, write, or just chill out. No distractions. It's so restful."

"You have the perfect little house. You're so lucky!" Vic covered her mouth and reddened. "Sorry. I mean… it's not lucky when someone dies. That's not the right word."

"It's okay," Erin assured her. "It was a great opportunity for me. I never had anything like this before. I never thought I would. I was just living day to day, trying to make ends meet. Trying to keep myself from going crazy. And then suddenly… I had this. It still hasn't really sunk in. I keep think-ing… someone will come and tell me it was all a joke. Or a mistake. That it isn't really mine and I don't have any rights to any of it."

Vic nodded. "Yeah. I can understand that."

Erin stood up and stretched. "But… no point in stressing out over these things. Whatever happens, happens. We have to enjoy what we have right now, because no one knows what we might or might not have tomorrow. It could all be gone in a day."

She went over to the stairs and paused.

"Do you want to stay up here, or do you want me to show you your bedroom?"

"I'm ready for bed. It's been a long day."

"Come on, then. Light switch is here, just hit it before you come down."

Erin waited at the bottom of the stairs, then showed Vic how to fold them back up to the ceiling. Vic stared up at them.

"That's just really cool."

"It is." Erin agreed. She went to Clementine's room and indicated it. "This one is yours. There are fresh sheets on the bed. We'll clear out some closet space after you retrieve your things."

Vic looked at the room, her mouth falling open. "But… this is the master bedroom, isn't it? This is your room."

"I'm in the next one down. I wasn't comfortable with this one. So, you'll have to deal with it. This was my aunt's room. I don't think I could sleep in here, thinking about her. But you didn't know her. You should be fine."

"You don't want this one?"

"Nope."

"Well… you'll let me know if you change your mind? Because it's your room. You should be able to sleep in your own room."

"I'll let you know if I change my mind. But that's not going to happen in the near future."

Vic tiptoed into the room. Erin giggled at the sweat pants which climbed almost to her knees. Vic looked down at her legs and shook her head. "You're right about them being too short. But they're fine for sleep."

"Good. I'll say goodnight now and see you in the morning. We'll need to be up bright and early."

"That's the plan. Thanks so much, for everything. You've done more than anyone could be expected to."

Erin patted her on the arm and headed back to the bathroom. There was a moment of silence, and then Vic closed her bedroom door.

CHAPTER 10

*E*rin woke up in the morning with the kitten sleeping on the pillow against her cheek. Erin's nose tickled and she sneezed, making the kitten jump up and stare at her indignantly. Erin laughed.

"Serves you right for sleeping against my nose! I can't help it, you know. You got your fluff up my nasal passages!" She sneezed again and the kitten jumped down from the bed. He made a little noise as he exited the room.

After getting dressed, Erin pulled Vic's clothes out of the dryer and knocked on the door.

"Got your clothes."

She just about walked into the door when the knob didn't turn in her hand. It was locked. Erin stared at the door for a moment, surprised, then knocked again.

"Vic? It's time to get up, Vic. Rise and shine! I'll leave your clothes here outside the door."

There was a groan from within, which Erin took as acknowledgment. She went into the kitchen to feed the kitten and have a quick bite to eat before heading to the bakery. And coffee. She needed coffee.

Mrrrow, mrrrow! The kitten rubbed against her legs, making excited noises.

"Yes, you can have the rest of the tuna this morning. Just wait a minute while I get it ready for you."

The cat continued to chirrup and patted at the cupboards, trying to climb up to where Erin was working. Erin did not enjoy the smell of tuna first thing in the morning.

Erin heard Vic open her door and head across the hall to the commode. In a few more minutes, she was in the kitchen, sniffing at the air like the cat.

"Coffee?"

"Over there," Erin indicated the machine. "Grab a to-go cup, because we need to be on our way soon." Erin bent down to put down the cat's dish. "I'm going to put some fresh papers down in the bathroom, just in case. Do you need anything else?"

Vic shook her head. "No, I think I'm good."

"There are bagels. Or—"

"I'm not the kind of person who can eat first thing in the morning. I'll have something at the bakery later, once my stomach wakes up."

"Okay." Erin nodded. "No problem."

She went to the back door where the newspapers and other recycling were stored. She took the top newspaper from the pile. It was a few months old. Erin picked it up and glanced over the headlines.

Sleepy little town. Not much happened there.

But under the newspaper was another kind of paper. This one oversize, the paper yellow, brown at the edges, and crumbly. Erin picked it up. She carried it back to the kitchen with the newspaper, studying it.

"Vic, look at this."

"What is it?"

"It's a map."

Vic leaned over her shoulder, looking at it. "A map of what?" She frowned. "That's out on the mountain somewhere? It looks really old."

"Yeah. It does." Erin studied it. "I think it's a mining survey." She glanced at her watch. "We'll have to look at it tonight. Got to get in to the bakery now."

~

Erin had awoken that day with new resolve. If she wanted to prove her and Vic's innocence, she needed to find other suspects for Officer Piper to focus on.

The question that loomed up before her to begin with was who had a key. Someone had unlocked the back stairway door and probably relocked the back door to the parking lot. She just needed to find out who had keys.

"How's your new little assistant working out?" Mary Lou asked, putting down her tall coffee cup to pay for her muffin. She straightened her blouse and smiled in Vic's direction.

"Vic is really a help. I don't know how I thought I was going to run the place by myself. I could even use a third person, someone in the kitchen, to keep things running and make sure we don't let something burn in the oven."

Erin was keeping her ears open for the timer, but was afraid that she would miss it with the conversation and the noise of the till. She really should bring her timer to the front to keep an eye on it instead of leaving it in the back. That would make a lot more sense.

"It's a lot of fun," Vic said.

"I'm glad you think so." Erin didn't hand Mary Lou her money right away. "Mary Lou… you knew my Aunt Clementine, didn't you?"

"Everyone knew Clementine, dear. Well, maybe not so much the last few years, with her being mostly housebound and new people moving into town, but before that, when she was running the tea room, everybody knew who she was."

"Yes, but I'm wondering who was particular friends with her."

Mary Lou held her hand out for her change and Erin handed it over. "Well, Clementine was very well-liked. She had a smile and a kind word for everyone. Like you and Vic. Unlike some recently deceased who went around sour-pussed all the time, acting like the world owed her something."

"I thought you were friends with Angela."

"As close as anyone. Which is to say, not very close at all. We were on speaking terms. Of course we would talk, exchange pleasantries. But Angela wasn't an easy person to know. She was angry and pushed people away. She got people involved in… questionable business dealings. She was… self-righteous and closed-minded…" Mary Lou gave a sweet smile. "Not to speak ill of the dead."

"No… I didn't realize. I thought she was just like that toward me, because of the bakery. I thought you were all friends. You didn't think I should start a bakery either. Why would you be loyal to Angela's bakery if you didn't like her?"

"My loyalty does not require that I like her, my dear."

Erin realized she had let herself get diverted from her initial question and there were other customers waiting while she talked with Mary Lou. "I was just wondering about Clementine. About who she was friends with. I'm… trying to find a key."

"A key?" Mary Lou looked mystified. She stepped aside so that Erin could run the next couple of customers' orders through the till, but stayed close enough to talk. "What key are you looking for?"

Erin hadn't prepared a lie. Which, of course, she should have done, since she couldn't tell the holders of the store keys that they were suspects in the murder investigation. She deliberately ran into difficulty with the next couple of orders, trying to come up with a good explanation for Mary Lou.

"There's a locked cabinet in the storeroom downstairs," she explained, dropping her voice confidentially and leaning toward Mary Lou. "I didn't really think anything of it before, but this morning Vic and I found an old map hidden at Clementine's house. A really old map. Civil War era, maybe. It wasn't until then that I remembered Clementine told me years ago, when I was just a little girl, that there was a secret in the old cabinet. A clue to find a treasure. So, now I'm wondering," Erin cut her eyes left and right as if to make sure no one but Mary Lou was listening, "if it's something to do with this map."

Mary Lou's eyes were wide. "But why would someone else have the key to Clementine's locked cabinet? What happened to her key?"

There was a lull in the line of customers while a young lady in a suit looked over the goods, trying to make a decision.

"I thought maybe she gave the key to the cabinet to someone with the spare key to the store. Maybe she got her key chains mixed up and gave the one with the cabinet to someone to hold on to when she closed up the store. She might not have even remembered about the cabinet, after she got frail…"

"How fascinating. But I don't remember Clementine ever mentioning anything like that. About a treasure or a map."

"She said it was a family secret. I don't know, maybe it was ill-gotten gains from some ancestor. You know how some of those Civil War villains were…"

"Every family has got some bad ones," Mary Lou agreed.

"And you heard about my ghost, didn't you?"

"Melissa did mention something about that! But this shop has never had a ghost before. I would have known. Clementine would have told us." Mary Lou shook her head slightly.

"Maybe the ghost is Clementine. That's what Officer Piper thought. Or maybe Clementine or I somehow disrupted a ghost that hadn't been active before." Erin tried to remember what Melissa had suggested. She hoped she didn't sound too flippant. How would she talk if she believed in ghosts? "Maybe someone… disturbed it."

"By taking the map home?" Mary Lou suggested. "Maybe it was the map that was in the cabinet. Are you sure there is still something in there? I can't imagine her closing up the shop and leaving something that was potentially valuable behind."

"Maybe," Erin agreed. "But why lock the cabinet again if it was empty?"

Mary Lou withdrew slowly, turning toward the door. "Well, you just let me think on it. I'll see what I can come up with."

~

"Do you really think that map is to a buried treasure?" Vic asked when they closed up to have their lunches. Obviously, she had heard at least part of Erin's conversation with Mary Lou.

"No, of course not. Why would she put a treasure map in the recycling? It wasn't something valuable to her. I just thought… I needed an excuse to be asking around for keys to the bakery. And I already had the map on my mind, I guess, so I just concocted a story around that."

"Oh." Vic nodded. Erin wondered if she detected disappointment in the girl's expression.

"Sorry. Were you all ready to go hunting treasure?"

"Yeah, kinda. It sounds like fun."

"Well, according to that map, there are all kinds of caves and mines around here. There must be a few places where a person could go exploring."

"Spelunking."

"What?"

"Exploring caves? It's called spelunking."

Erin gave a shiver. "That makes it sound creepy. I have visions of slimy cave walls and white fish in a pitch-black underground lake."

Vic nodded. "Exactly."

"Ew. I'm not sure I'd be up for that. But we should ask around, there are probably a few caves that a novice could explore without a bunch of expensive equipment… and blind white fish."

"Maybe there are cave paintings. I've always wanted to see some real cave paintings."

Erin nodded, chewing her sandwich. Cave paintings would be near the surface. Easily accessible. And they would probably be a really popular place to visit, so there would be guides and lights and railings to prevent people from falling over underground cliffs. Or into underground lakes full of blind, white fish.

"Maybe we could do that some Sunday afternoon, after the church ladies are done their tea."

"We're open on Sunday? Here?"

"Just for the after-church social. Then we can close the doors and go exploring."

"I don't think they'll like that." Vic shook her head slowly, dubious.

"You don't think they'll like what? Us being open after church?"

"Us going cave exploring on a Sunday."

"Why would they care about that?"

"Because of the Sabbath," Vic pointed out. "They don't like people doing… secular stuff on Sunday."

"But it wouldn't have anything to do with them."

Vic continued to shake her head. Erin studied her.

"Do you believe in God?" she asked. "And the Sabbath and all that?"

Vic was hesitant. She looked toward the front door, as if hoping someone would stop by and save her from answering the question.

"You don't have to answer," Erin said. "Sorry. That's a really personal thing to ask. I don't care whether you do or don't believe in God. I was just curious. Wondering how you felt about it."

"I believe in God," Vic said. "I just don't know… what kind of God. I don't like the idea of a God that punishes people for… I don't know, breaking the Sabbath or some other commandment. I'm not too sure about Jesus being a god on earth, but I like his ideas about loving people, even the sinners. I've looked a little bit into other religions, Buddhism and so on. But I haven't really made up my mind… what it is I believe. I guess I'm still Christian… for now."

Erin got up to pour herself a glass of milk. She held it up. "You want one?"

"Yeah, sure."

"Were you raised religious? Christian?"

"Yeah. Pretty much. I mean, we didn't really go to church except maybe sometimes at Christmas, which was kind of neat. But my parents taught me right and wrong... from that perspective."

"Meaning they punished you for breaking the rules they cared about?"

"They weren't really bad. I mean, a lot of kids are abused, physically beaten really bad by their parents, or one of them. I wasn't punished like that. It was more... emotional... psychological. And then when I... strayed too far... they kicked me out. But I was old enough to be on my own. It wasn't like I was fourteen or something. I'm an adult..."

She trailed off and Erin wondered how close that was to the truth. It seemed like there was an 'almost' at the end of that sentence.

"You're eighteen?"

"Uh, yeah. So, I'm an adult and it's okay that I'm on my own."

"Except that you didn't have anywhere to go. No job, no home, no prospects. You might be an adult, but you're still pretty young. Pretty tough to be trying to start out all on your own when you're that young."

"I guess. It's been hard. I came here, thinking that Aunt Angela would let me stay with her until I got onto my feet. Maybe even offer me a job at her bakery. I always liked it here."

"I don't understand anyone who turns a kid out on the street. Not your parents, not your Aunt Angela... I just can't understand it. People should help each other. Especially young people."

"I sure appreciate the way you're helping me out," Vic spoke around a mouthful of sandwich. Then, realizing what she had done, she covered her mouth as she finished chewing and swallowing it. "Sorry. I'm going to pay you back for everything you've done for me, as soon as I can. Except I guess it's all going to come out of your pocket, since you're the one paying me. Kind of hard to pay you back for letting me work by giving you back the money you gave me..."

"There's got to be a tax advantage there somewhere. Don't worry about paying me back. People have helped me from time to time... I just want to do the same for someone else."

"You've done more than anyone else, even the people who are supposed to know and love me." She grinned. "And after I broke into your store and smashed your coffee mug."

"The coffee mug I expect you to replace!" Erin said severely, wagging her finger at the girl. Then she giggled. "We'd better open back up. I can see people gathering out there."

"It seems like a strange time for a rush." Vic looked at the clock on the wall. "It shouldn't be the lunch rush yet."

"Maybe everyone is hungry early."

Erin went up to the door, flipped the sign, and unlocked the door. She smiled at Melissa and Gema, but she felt uneasy about them both showing up at once and at such an odd time.

"What can I get for you ladies today?"

They walked up to the display case and alternated between looking at the products and at the board on the wall, neither one in a particular hurry.

"I hear you're trying to find some keys," Gema said casually.

"Yes, I am," Erin agreed. She pointed to the chocolate chip cookies. "I know you're probably just here for an early lunch, but those are fresh out of the oven."

"Oooh... those do look good," Gema admitted. She pushed her hair back behind her ear. "I'll take a dozen."

"Do you want twelve or thirteen?"

Gema raised her brows. "Is there a price point difference? Usually a baker's dozen is just an extra cookie for the same price."

"Same price," Erin confirmed. "But Mary Lou, when she bought some the other day, didn't want thirteen because her family can't split them up evenly."

Gema laughed. "That sounds just like Mary Lou. No, thirteen is fine with me. My husband will eat most of them, but no one keeps track."

Erin started counting them out. "Is it just you and your husband at home, then? I don't really know about anyone's families."

"Yes. Kids are grown and gone, so it's just me and Fred now."

"Empty nesters."

"We're quite happy to have the nest to ourselves, truth be told. No boomerang kids, if we can help it."

Erin nodded. "Boys or girls?"

"Three boys. I always wanted a little girl, but... Fred and I only ever had boys..."

"Maybe you could adopt or foster a girl. An older child."

"I'll bet you didn't go back to your parents after you left the nest." Gema changed the subject abruptly.

"Umm… no. My parents are dead. I didn't have anyone to go back to. Once I hit eighteen, I was on my own. No safety net."

"Oh, my! Well, that's the way the birds do it. And you seem like you turned out okay. A responsible young woman. Owner of your own baking establishment."

Erin handed her the bag of cookies and waited for payment. Gema poked around in her wallet, laying down bills and coins one at a time. Eventually, she had the right amount and pushed it over to Erin.

"Except I didn't exactly earn this place," Erin reminded her. "It was left to me by Clementine. So, I guess… there was a safety net. Eventually. But it took a few years to find it."

"You could very well have just liquidated everything and blown the cash on drugs or an exotic vacation. But you didn't. You started a business. And not Clementine's business," Gema held up a finger. "Your own business. What you wanted to do. No matter what anyone said."

"I guess I'm past needing anyone's approval." Erin turned to Melissa. "And what would you like?"

"Getting back to the keys…"

Erin had been enjoying Gema's and Melissa's looks of frustration as she led the topic away from the treasure hunt.

"The keys?"

"You were looking for a lost key? To something Clementine had?"

"Right. I guess Mary Lou must have told you about it. So far, no one has come forward with any keys. Clementine must have been the only one who had keys to this store. Just the ones I got from the lawyer."

"Clementine had more keys than that," Melissa protested. "Everyone around here has everyone else's keys. I look at the keys on my rack at home and I don't even know which ones belong to who anymore. A lot of good that does!"

"Everyone has everyone else's keys? Why even have keys, then? Why not just leave the door open for whoever comes by?"

"You couldn't do that!" Gema protested, jumping back into the conversation. "We may not have a lot of crime in Bald Eagle Falls, but there are still robberies. Drug addicts who drift through. Things… could still happen.

But sharing your keys with your friends, that's just neighborly and good policy."

"So, did you have any of Clementine's keys?" Erin looked from one to the other.

"Why, I'd have to know what I was looking for, like I said," Melissa reminded her. "I wouldn't recognize them myself. Can you describe the key that you're looking for?"

"You don't put tags on the keys? Clementine's Tea Room? Something like that?"

"I guess that would be the smart thing to do. Everybody just hands you whatever they've got on hand. Then you put it on your peg board, or in your junk drawer, and in six months, you can't remember where they came from." She gave a laugh.

"Huh." Erin turned to the next woman in line, a large woman in a red blazer who Erin thought might have been there opening day.

Melissa and Gema waited impatiently while Erin served her.

"You don't know if you had any of her keys?" Erin asked.

"What did this key look like?" Melissa persisted. "This key to a cabinet. How big? What do you think is in the cabinet?"

"How would that help you find the key? It's just a little one, I guess. Half the size of a door key. Probably a little brass key. Old."

"Old? How old?"

"I don't know. The cabinet has been there as long as I can remember. But if Clementine never gave you any keys, there's no point in worrying about it."

"And what do you think is in the cabinet? Mary Lou said something about a treasure map?" Gema asked.

"It's not a treasure map. Just an old map. And I'm sure it's nothing important. Maybe it was just something to do with her genealogy, or a cave she wanted to explore when she had the time." Erin thought she'd better play down the treasure angle. It was just a little too fanciful for anyone to believe. But minimizing it only seemed to encourage the women.

"But the cabinet is locked. Like something was left there. Forgotten, all this time."

"Do you have any of Clementine's keys?" Erin demanded. "There's no point in even talking about it unless you have Clementine's keys."

Gema and Melissa exchanged looks. They weren't, Erin thought, rolling their eyes at her demand, or exchanging a knowing look. Instead, they looked like they were sizing each other up. Weighing what they wanted to say in front of the other.

If they had something to hide, they shouldn't have come in together. Had they just been swept up in the excitement of a mysterious treasure map and hadn't thought of the consequences? Mary Lou had been a lot more wary about buying into the idea of a secret to a treasure hunt.

"I'm sure Clementine did give me keys at one time," Melissa admitted slowly. "But I'll have to look for them. I just thought if you could describe the one you were looking for, it would make it a lot faster."

"Would you mind returning any of Clementine's keys to me? Even if it's not the key to the cabinet, I'm supposed to be inventorying them and getting the locks changed."

It was Gema who narrowed her eyes at this statement. "Why do you need to inventory the keys if you're getting the locks changed?"

"Well… that's what the lawyer told me I needed to do. I guess maybe in case there are keys to other things that we don't know about, like the cabinet. Maybe… a safety deposit box or storage locker somewhere. Or a safe at the house. They weren't sure they had identified all her assets and there could be something else."

"She wouldn't have given anyone her safety deposit key or anything like that. They would be on her own key chain. She would have wanted to keep them safe."

Erin gave a shrug. Maybe she wasn't as good of a liar as she thought she was. Her stories kept unraveling on examination. "That's what the lawyer said. I wouldn't want to get cross-threaded with him."

"I'll have to look through what I've got," Melissa said. She looked at Gema. "You don't think *you* had anything like that, do you?"

"No. I don't know if there ever was a key to that cabinet. I never heard Clementine say anything about it. Maybe it's just a cabinet with a stuck door. Are you sure it's locked? Is it one of those flimsy sheet-iron things? You can generally pop one of those right open with a crowbar."

"I didn't think of that."

Both women looked toward the door that led down to the basement. Each eyed the other.

"Sorry, it's closed," Erin said. "I'm not supposed to let anyone down there until the police have cleared it. You know, in case there's still evidence... some evidence as to who it was that killed Angela."

Gema shook her head. "That's so ridiculous. I can't believe little Terry Piper would go so far as to claim that it was murder. It was obviously just an accident. Angela had severe, life-threatening allergies. She got exposed to something. And she died. It wasn't anyone's fault and it certainly wasn't murder. That's ridiculous."

Erin smiled at Gema calling the policeman 'little Terry Piper.' She obviously remembered him from his younger days, before he was the law in Bald Eagle Falls. She imagined Piper trying to give her a ticket and Gema waving her finger at him, telling him that he needed to do more research, or go home and practice his piano, or something from whatever other role she had played in his past. Gema worked at one of the stores in town. Maybe she had caught Piper shoplifting once as a child.

"Well, if either of you can return Clementine's keys to me, and let me know if you can think of anyone else she might have given a key to..."

"I'll look through my keys," Melissa agreed. She turned and looked at the silent Gema. "And what about you, Gema? You have a set of Clementine's keys, don't you?"

"I would have to look. I got rid of a lot of old stuff. I doubt I do anymore."

And if she had used them to commit the murder, she wouldn't be handing them over to Erin any time soon. Anyone who turned keys over to Erin was unlikely to be the murderer. It would be someone who claimed not to have keys.

"What about Mary Lou? Would she have had keys?"

"Didn't you ask her?"

"She didn't say she did. I'm just wondering... I mean. She might have forgotten."

"If anyone had a key, it would be Mary Lou," Gema said. "She was the closest one to Clementine. Her or Angela."

"You think Angela might have had a key?" Erin asked, surprised at Gema's guess. Hadn't Mary Lou said that no one really liked Angela? "Why would she have had one?"

"They were friendly. Clementine made a little bit of baking, but mostly she bought from Angela. They were probably back and forth to each other's shops all the time. It would make sense for them to have a way to get in and out. Angela would be up before the birds to bake bread and she could put it in Clementine's shop before opening up her own store. Or if Clementine ran out of something, she could run over and get it, and they would settle up over it later."

Erin avoided looking at Vic. She was sure Vic was straining her ears to hear every word she could. Funny how their lives were mirrors of each other. Their aunts friends together, running their businesses with each other. The aunts both eventually dying, and now their nieces, side by side, trying to unravel the threads of what had happened before Clementine shut down her business. Before Angela was murdered.

Was the secret to the murder in the recent past? Or years ago? Was one of the three ladies responsible for what had happened to her? Or did they know something that would identify the killer? The threads of their lives had obviously all been intertwined.

Before she could think of anything else to ask, both women were saying goodbye and heading out the door. Erin watched them go and sighed, turning to look at Vic.

Vic gave a little shrug and they continued to work together without comment until the lunch rush was over and the shop was empty again for a few minutes. Erin put some more muffins in the oven for the after-school crowd. Kids and teachers looking for something sweet at the end of the day. Parents wanting dessert to go with supper or breakfast for their children the next day. She was starting to get a feeling for the ebb and flow of the people going through the shop.

Erin was rearranging the products in the display case when she saw a man walk by the big window. At first, she saw just a dark and threatening shadow, then realized she had seen him somewhere before. But where? She hadn't been to that many places in town. He could have been working or shopping at one of the stores she had been to.

But even through the window, he seemed grimy and work worn. Not like someone who worked in a shop or at a desk. Someone who belonged on an oil rig or down a mineshaft. Maybe a welder.

"What...?" Vic followed her gaze.

"That man out there. Do you know him?" It was probably silly to ask

Vic. Vic had been there a little longer than Erin, but she had been hiding out, not out meeting people.

"Uh, yeah. William something. Willie… William… is it Anthony? Something like that. William Anthony. No. Andrews. William Andrews." Vic nodded, sure she had hit on it. "Yes. William Andrews."

"How do you know him? What exactly does he do?"

"Drifter. Lazy good-for-nothing," Vic said. When Erin looked at her in astonishment, open-mouthed, Vic grinned. "Aunt Angela's words, not mine. I don't think he's a lazy good-for-nothing. I've always seen him working. Odd jobs. Maybe that's why Aunt Angela thought he was lazy. Because he didn't have one steady job. But he's always doing something. Not begging or living off of anyone else."

"How do you know that? I thought your aunt wouldn't let you stay around. It didn't sound like you sat down to discuss the pros and cons of each of the town's residents."

"No." Vic laughed. "Other years. I used to come here to do work for Aunt Angela sometimes. Just give her a hand with whatever she needed done around the store. And she talked about people. More than she should."

Erin nodded, accepting this. Though Vic's words niggled at her. If Vic had come to Bald Eagle Falls in past years, why didn't people know her? Everyone seemed to accept that she was a friend of Erin's, an outsider they had never met before.

"So, William Andrews has been around for a few years. He's not someone who just drifted into town recently."

"No. I don't think he's from here originally, so that makes him a drifter as far as Aunt Angela is concerned. Not Bald Eagle Falls prime stock."

"That's a pretty narrow view."

"Aunt Angela had a lot of narrow views. I didn't really understand that until I came back here. She was the aunt who always had something in the cookie jar. And who paid me to do jobs for her. I thought she was a pretty good person. I didn't understand that she… she was really prejudiced against all kinds of people."

"Prejudiced?" Erin's mind had been wandering and the word drew her back. "What kind of people was she prejudiced against?"

That was just the type of insider information Erin needed. Anyone

Angela was prejudiced against would be a prime suspect. She had been unfair to them, they had retaliated…

"Everyone," Vic said. "I didn't realize how she found fault with everyone. It wasn't just the people who didn't follow the rules of her house. William Andrews was a drifter, because he wasn't born here. He was a good-for-nothing because he didn't have one job. She always had something to say about Blacks or immigrants. People who weren't educated, or who were too educated and thought they were better than she was. People who wouldn't get involved in investments or another one of her schemes, they were scared rabbits. Gutless. But the people who did get involved and complained about her losing their money were just whiners. Worthless, no-account people who didn't know what they were talking about or how risky the market was." Vic shrugged. She shook her head, as if reliving a private hurt that she couldn't tell Erin about. Something worse. Erin wondered what it was.

"Did she say who had invested and lost money?"

"I don't know. I suppose. But I kind of got the feeling that it was everyone, at one time or another. She acted like the whole town was against her."

"And yet, she wouldn't take in one person who wasn't against her," Erin observed.

Vic turned her back to take some dishes to the sink, sliding them carefully into the soapy water.

"What kind of odd jobs does William Andrews do?" Erin asked, when Vic returned to the front of the shop.

"I'm not sure. He drives things around. Like a courier or hot shot service. He does yard work. Painting. Cleaning. Lots of different things."

Then Erin remembered where she knew him from. He had been the man who had helped her—or tried to help her—to unload groceries when she was first stocking up the bakery. She'd had to chase him off, because he was being so persistent and making her uncomfortable. Maybe he had just wanted to help. Maybe he had expected a couple of dollars by way of tip for having helped her out. If the poor man was destitute, surviving on odd jobs, maybe it had been wrong of her to chase him away like that. He had said that he only wanted to help.

"Oh, yeah," she said. "I remember him."

Had Andrews known who Erin was and what she was doing, opening up the specialty bakery? He had been the one person who had gotten close to her flours and other baking supplies. Was it possible he had tampered with something? If Angela had bullied him for not having a job, maybe he had decided to take his revenge. And the missing autoinjector was just a coincidence. The icing on the cake. Or maybe he had done a job for her and picked her pocket.

"Was he here on opening day?"

"I don't know," Vic reminded her. "I wasn't around on opening day."

"Oh, that's right. I'm sure I would have noticed him." Erin remembered how busy opening day had been. "Maybe. But not if he had a key and came through the back. If he did odd jobs for Clementine, maybe he had a key. It doesn't seem like he could have contaminated one of the ingredients… No one else reported reacting to any of the baking. It seems like Angela was the only one. Like it was targeted."

Vic raised an eyebrow, listening with interest to Erin rambling on. "So, is he another suspect?"

"Maybe. But it is a reach. I'll have to mention him to Officer Piper."

She watched him out the window for a minute. He was putting flyers on cars. Was he being paid by someone else, or trying to drum up for business for himself? He was younger than she remembered from that night. Older than she was, but not by so much. Not a grizzled old man. Handsome, in a way, if it hadn't been for the dirt that seemed to be ingrained in his skin.

Vic caught her staring at the man and raised her brows.

CHAPTER 11

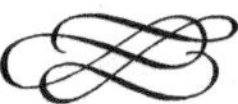

Somehow, word that Erin had gotten her hands on a Civil War era treasure map seemed to have spread through the town like wildfire. Bald Eagle Falls might have only had a weekly newspaper, but news obviously traveled much faster through other means. Everyone seemed to have something to say about it, even Peter's mother, when she stopped in to pick up some bread and some cookies. Erin reminded herself that she had been planning to start up a kids' club. She just needed to sit down at the computer and design some kind of membership and point-tracking card. In the meantime, she offered the Foster children each a free cookie.

"I've heard there's all kinds of treasure in the hills," Mrs. Foster said. "Gold for soldiers' payrolls, or valuables stashed away by rich families who didn't want to be pillaged. Some of the rumors go back even further than that. To pirate gold or valuables the early settlers hid from the natives. Or sacred artifacts that natives hid from the settlers!"

"Pirate gold?" Vic echoed. "In Bald Eagle Falls?"

"Pirates!" Peter exclaimed, brandishing an imaginary sword while he munched on a cookie in the other hand. "We should search for pirate gold!"

"No, not right in Bald Eagle Falls," Mrs. Foster said. "In the hills. Hidden in caves. The map Erin found, it's a map of the caves, isn't it?"

Erin smiled as she rang up the bill. "I really don't know how much the map would help anyone searching for treasure. It is old, but I don't think any of the information is secret. It's just a mining survey or something, not a pirate's map."

"No one knows where all the caves are around here. There are all kinds of stories about lost caves and mines. The hills are riddled with them. Like Swiss cheese."

"Can we search for gold?" one of Peter's sisters begged. "Can we go to a cave?"

"We're not going to a cave," Mrs. Foster told her. "That's all I need. My children getting lost in a cave."

"We wouldn't get lost!" Peter objected.

"Yes, you would. You get lost at the grocery store. What would I do? Go home without all of my children?"

"We don't get lost," Peter said. "Just separated. That's different. We could find our way home."

"From the grocery store, maybe. Not from a cave, deep down in the ground."

The littler girl started to cry and Mrs. Foster rolled her eyes. "What's the matter, Jody?"

"I don't want to get lost in a cave in the ground!"

Mrs. Foster pulled her close. "You are not going to get lost in a cave, Jody. No one is going to get lost in a cave."

As they left the store, Jody continued to whine and snivel, while the others made their plans to go searching for pirate gold.

"Pirate gold?" Erin said to Vic, laughing.

"Never get between a southerner and rumors of treasure!"

"You still want to explore caves?"

"I promise I won't get lost!"

It felt good to go home at the end of a busy day, back to the comfort and familiarity of the house, to pat her furry little fuzzball and just relax. It was nice to have someone else there and not just be knocking around by herself through the empty house.

As she sat on the couch and patted the snoozing kitten, Erin reminded herself that she needed to take care of the household chores, too. Kitty kibble crunched under her feet in the kitchen and the litter box needed to be looked after. She should do some grocery shopping so there was some real food in the kitchen and they could have a substantial supper without having to order in.

But she was so tired after her work days that she just didn't have the energy to do much else.

Vic was sitting across from her, poring over the map like she was looking for Blackbeard's treasure. Erin smiled and looked down at the slim weekly paper that she still hadn't finished reading. Her eyelids were heavy and, by the time she finished reading it, the next one would be out. Aside from an article recapping the news of Angela's murder, there were only a few articles, a couple of weekly columns, and several large blocks of advertising. It shouldn't take her a week to read that much.

But she was still so new in town that she read through each of the advertisements carefully to learn all she could about the other businesses in town. What services they offered, what methods they used to attract business, keywords in their advertising copy. She even studied the graphics and pictures they used to figure out what resonated with the readership base. She would need to start advertising as well. Using the wrong picture or words in her ads would be like flushing her hard-earned money down the toilet.

Erin turned the page and closed her eyes for a moment to rest them. She needed to get herself bathed and off to bed, or she was going to be falling asleep on the couch. She didn't want to end up with a crick in her neck for the next week.

"Can we really go to one of these caves on Sunday?" Vic asked.

Erin startled slightly and opened her eyes. Even after telling herself she couldn't go to sleep on the couch, she was dozing instead of reading the weekly.

"Sure, I don't see why not," she said, rubbing her eyes. "We need to do something to relax. We've been working hard. We should pick up some groceries too. And…" Erin stifled a yawn, but couldn't stop it, and covered the view of her tonsils as best she could. "And I need to do some cleaning and sorting through some of Clementine's things."

"You won't throw anything out, will you?"

"I don't know yet. I don't know what there is. I certainly don't need to keep all her clothes. And I don't think you want them, do you?"

"She wasn't exactly my size," Vic admitted. Clementine had been a tiny woman. Her pants would be as short on Erin as Erin's were on Vic. "But there are some things that might work okay. Scarves and accessories. You might be able to wear some of her shirts or blazers."

"I don't think so. But I'll see if there's anything either of us wants to keep before I give them away. We're both going to need closet space. We can't just keep living out of boxes and bags."

Vic nodded. "I suppose."

"Just let me know if you want something. I don't mind."

"It's really nice of you letting me live here—"

"Don't start that again. I need you. I had no idea how much I was going to need someone else to help me run the bakery. Even now… I think we could still use another person. What do you think?"

"Maybe," Vic agreed slowly, "but I don't like the idea of having someone else in our space."

Funny how quickly Vic had adopted it as her space.

"We'll work it out. I don't have anyone to hire right away anyway, just thinking about what we're going to need if we're going to stay afloat. If we both run ourselves into the ground, we won't be doing ourselves any favors."

"Yeah."

The kitten stretched and readjusted itself in Erin's lap. He needed a name. She scanned for name ideas on the newspaper page. James? Terrence? The General? She blinked drowsily.

"I think I found the one I want to go to," Vic said.

Erin opened her eyes again. She was going to have to get up; if she sat on the couch any longer, she was going to be asleep for sure. She looked down at the newspaper and saw Vic's picture.

Erin frowned. She rubbed her eyes and looked at the photograph again. It wasn't Vic. It was a boy. A teenager, around Vic's age, but a boy, not a girl. There were similarities between their features. If Angela were Vic's aunt, then maybe she had cousins around as well. Erin studied the words around the photo. A missing boy, several towns away. James. Erin stared at his eyes, fringed with long lashes that would have been the envy of any girl.

She had seen those eyes before and she knew where.

"Vic…?"

Vic looked up from the map, her excited smile fading as she took in Erin's expression. She got up and went to see what Erin was looking at in the paper. Her face lost the pink flush in her cheeks.

"Oh."

"Vic, is this… your twin?"

Vic scratched the back of her neck. "Uh… no."

Erin looked again at the name of the boy. The full name. James Victor Jackson. Vic. "Then… is this you?"

Vic sighed. "Yeah."

Erin tried to process it. To make sense of what was going on. "Did you… dress as a girl so that no one would find you?"

"No." Vic sat down and Erin could see that she was shaking. "I'm sorry. I'll leave if you want me to. I know you probably don't want… someone like me staying in your house."

"Explain it to me. I'm confused."

"I am a girl," Vic asserted. "But… I'm transgender. I was raised as a boy, but my gender identity is female."

"And that's why your parents kicked you out."

"Yes."

"And that's why Angela wouldn't have anything to do with you when you went to her for help."

"She was always nice to me when I presented as a boy. I did work for her during summers and school breaks. Helped around the bakery or her yard or whatever she needed done. She was always really good, paid me, looked after me while I was staying with her. I just thought… that was the logical place to go."

"But when you went to her as a girl, that all changed."

"I've been called names before. I always stood out, even trying my best to be masculine. But Aunt Angela… she was so cruel!" Vic's voice broke. She wiped at her eyes, trying to keep the tears at bay. "And then I didn't know where to go. I didn't know what to do. I knew where she kept the key to Clementine's and I thought I would just stay there a night or two, while I figured out what to do."

Erin was no longer sleepy. She put her arm around Vic's shoulders and gave her a squeeze. Then she rubbed the girl's back.

"I'm so sorry your aunt treated you that way. And your parents. That's not right. Even if they don't agree with your… gender identity… that's not what they should have done. They should have… shown you love and support."

"It goes totally against the way I was raised." Vic sniffled and tried to stop the tears. "I get that. I was raised that there are only two sexes, male and female, and that's it, and whatever parts you're born with, that's what you're stuck as. That God decides, and that's what he makes you, and it's a sin to feel different. So, I get it… they think it's breaking a commandment, just like stealing or murder… But…" her voice broke.

"I know." Erin gave Vic another squeeze. "It's okay."

The kitten was disturbed and got up, climbing from Erin's lap to Vic's.

"Oh! Ow, he's got claws!" Vic picked the kitten up, detaching him carefully from her pants. She held him to her chest to stroke him, bowing her head close to him. He wriggled around, getting fur up her nose. When Vic sneezed, the kitten jumped away, landing on the floor and looking at the two of them as if offended.

Erin laughed. The kitten stalked away. He disappeared into the kitchen.

"We need a name for him," Erin said, wiping the corners of her own eyes. "I mean, kitty is fine, but he should have a name."

Vic got a couple of tissues from a box in a crocheted cover on one of the side tables. She blew her nose. "I have a name for him."

Erin smiled. "What's your idea?"

"Well, he's orange."

"Yes."

"I thought… Orange Blossom."

Erin raised her brows. "Orange Blossom? Kind of a funny name for a cat, don't you think? Especially for a boy cat?"

"People name their cats all kinds of things. And as far as it being too feminine… don't forget who you're talking to."

That made Erin laugh in surprise. "Well, okay, consider the source," she agreed. "I don't know. I'll think about it. We'll see if it sticks, shall we?"

"Okay," Vic agreed.

"And now, I think it's time to get ready for bed. I was falling asleep sitting here reading the paper."

Vic nodded her agreement. Erin got up and headed toward the bathroom.

"Erin…?"

"Yes?"

"You won't tell anyone, will you?"

"That you picked the cat's name? I'm not taking the blame if people think it's weird."

Vic giggled. "No… about me. People here, they're not very open-minded."

"You might find that more people are accepting of you than you think." At Vic's stricken look, she continued. "But I won't out you to anyone. It's up to you to tell people or not. You're really lucky that no one else has matched that picture up with you."

"I know… but if they do, I'll just say he's my twin, or something. Like you thought."

"Okay. That's up to you. Won't folks around here remember you, though? And that you didn't have a twin, when you used to come work for your aunt?"

"I'll just say… we were raised by different parents, or something. Like in that Disney show where the identical twins were raised apart."

"Whatever you want. It's your choice."

Vic let out her breath. "Thanks. And what about… the policeman? Officer Piper. You won't tell him?"

Erin considered that, closing her eyes to focus on the question and imagine the scenarios in which she might have to tell Officer Piper about Vic's situation.

"If he asked me directly, I'm not going to lie to him," she said. "That might get me in deeper water than I'm already in as a murder suspect. And get you in deeper trouble too, if he figures you have something to hide."

"You can't tell him."

"If he asks me something… that leads to me having to tell him about you or else lie, then I will ask him to talk to you about it. That's the most I can do. Let you decide what you want to say. But if I tell him to talk to you about it… you're going to have to tell him."

"Yeah, I know. But you won't bring it up?"

"No. Why would I?"

"Because you would be a lot better off if he put me in jail. We're his two best suspects, so it's better for you if he picks me."

"I'm not throwing you to the wolves, Vic." Erin held Vic's gaze. "I'm not that kind of person. I'm not going to do that to you."

"Okay." Vic breathed out. "You're crazy not to. But okay."

～

Morning came too quickly. Erin and Vic were at the bakery before dawn to get the day's baking done and rearrange the products in the display case. Erin discovered that Vic had beautiful penmanship and had her write up the labels and the changes to the chalk board.

Officer Piper showed up partway through the morning, after the rush when things had quieted down. He had a cup of coffee and K9 stood alertly at his side, nose quivering as he took in all the scents of the bakery.

"What can I get for you today?" Erin asked, as if he were in there every day and it wasn't startling or worrisome for him to just show up out of the blue.

"Well… what's good? What would you recommend?"

"It's all good. Some people are worried that it's going to taste really weird, have a bad texture or an aftertaste. But it doesn't. It's all pretty much like you would expect baking made with wheat flour to taste like."

Piper nodded, but looked doubtful.

"I've heard that gluten can be bad for some dogs," Erin offered. "Maybe I should carry a few doggie biscuits too. Do you think K9 would like that?"

The dog looked at her, ears pricking up at his name.

"Are you trying to bribe an officer of the law?" Piper asked, his face and voice serious. But she could see by the beginnings of the dimple in his cheek and the sparkle in his eye that he was teasing.

"No, I would never do that!" Erin declared, drawing out her vowels and forcing her eyes wide open. Then she fluttered her lashes at him.

She became aware that her heart was racing. Not because she was anxious about him showing up there, but because she was enjoying the attention of the handsome officer. Disconcerted, she looked over the display case to see what product she should be trying to move. But even looking away from him, she was still aware of him. The scent of his aftershave tickled her nose.

"Let's see, the chocolate chip zucchini loaf is a hot seller," she said, even though it wasn't, and that was why she wanted to sell it to him. "Or if you prefer a savory bread for sandwiches or to be paired with soup, this jalapeño cheese bread is just to die for!" She covered her mouth, realizing what she had said. "I mean… it's really good. If you like a little bit of a kick. Do you like things… uh… spicy?"

She could feel rather than hear Vic laughing beside her. Erin's face got hot as she grew more flustered. Piper just stood there looking at her, the corner of his mouth twitching.

"So, chocolate chip zucchini bread, or jalapeño cheese bread?" she asked briskly.

"Well, I do like spicy…" Piper trailed off, considering. His eyes twinkled. "But I also like sweet."

Erin used the tongs to grab a slice of the zucchini bread and put it into a paper snack bag. Then she selected a small loaf of the jalapeño cheese bread and put it into a longer sleeve.

"Something for now, and something for later," she announced. "If you don't use the cheese bread tonight, wrap it in plastic to keep it from drying out too much. Then just warm it in the oven for a few minutes before eating to crisp it up a bit." Erin watched Vic ring it up on the register and complete the transaction with Officer Piper.

"Be sure to come back in a couple of days," Erin told him. "I'll be sure to have some biscuits ready for K9."

Piper nodded. "I'll be back," he agreed.

And he walked back out without a single question about the murder.

"You and the cop?" Vic demanded, after the door had closed behind Officer Piper. "Holy cow! And you the prime murder suspect? Or one of them?"

"I don't know what you're talking about," Erin said. "I just sold the man a few baked goods."

Vic flapped her hand at her throat, fanning herself. "Is it hot in here, or is it just you? Just selling him a few baked goods? I don't think so!"

"He paid for them."

"Yeah. He did. And he'll be back for more."

"Well then, that's just good business, isn't it?" Erin said brightly, with an innocent smile.

"He's good for what ails you, all right."

"I don't know what you mean."

Erin ran into Melissa at the grocery store and took the opportunity to chat with her for a few minutes to get her views on Angela Plaint and her murder. She wasn't investigating, exactly. Just getting to know one of her clients better. Getting a bit more background on Vic's aunt. Definitely not investigating.

"So, what did you think about Angela?" Erin asked, as they both considered the various yogurts, sour cream, and soft cheeses in the dairy case.

"What did I think of her?" Melissa let the question hang for a few minutes, then gave a little shrug. "I don't know. What am I supposed to think of her? She was a fixture here. The owner of the bakery and all. And now she's dead. I don't know anything about it. Not sure what you're looking for from me."

"Nothing special," Erin said. "I just never really got a chance to know her. And I'm wondering now… what she was like. Were the two of you friends?"

"We were all friendly with each other," Melissa deflected. "Me and Angela, Gema, Mary Lou, other ladies from the church. We all did things together. Worshiped. Had some fun. Gossiped and commiserated. Everybody knew everybody else."

"You knew each other for a long time?"

"Not as long as Gema, maybe. I'm quite a bit younger than either of them. But yeah, we all knew each other. It was nice now and then, to get together to do something."

"Birthdays, weddings, bridge night…"

"Yes. Like that. Just the girls getting together for a little relaxation. Nothing unusual about that."

"So, you would consider Angela a good friend."

"No… a… friend. An acquaintance. Someone familiar."

"Did you… like her…?" Erin asked tentatively. They were up to the beverages aisle and Erin picked up some club soda. She considered the big display of RC cola, remembering how much she had enjoyed it as a girl when she had come to visit Clementine. But she couldn't drink her calories anymore as an adult. She needed to be disciplined and stick to healthy food and drink. An RC might get her engine going in the morning, but in the evening, it would either keep her up all night, or she would crash and wouldn't be able to get up in the morning. Erin walked on by the display with an iron determination. Melissa reached over and grabbed a big bottle, which she put in her cart. Erin eyed it.

"Do you have children?"

"No, I'm just on my own." She caught the direction of Erin's eyes. "It's for bridge night," she said. "I'm not drinking the whole thing. You wouldn't begrudge me one drink of RC, would you?"

"No, of course not. What you eat is your business. I wouldn't want anyone judging me by what I put in my cart." Erin looked down at several pounds of butter, cream cheese, and sour cream.

"Yes, but everyone knows you run the bakery. It's not like you're eating it all by yourself."

"You can't run a bakery without tasting some of the goods," Erin said. Then she remembered Angela. "Well… I couldn't anyway."

Melissa nodded. "It was hard for Angela. Giving up everything she loved. Not just eating, but baking. It really was her calling."

"Is that why she was so angry?"

"When?"

"All the time, from what I could tell. Wasn't she?"

"Mmm…" Melissa considered. "I wouldn't want to speak ill of the dead."

"No, of course not…"

"It wasn't just not being able to eat things or bake anymore. She was… not a nice person before that, either."

Erin looked at her. Melissa's face was flushed. She turned away from Erin, pretending to be studying the prices on the cold cereal. It wasn't like the specials weren't marked with bright red signage.

"Was she mean to you?" Erin asked. "Is that what you're saying?"

"She was mean to everyone. Not just me. Everybody was afraid of her."

"What did she do to you?"

"I didn't say she did anything to me. Just that she was a mean person. To everyone."

"Okay." Erin pushed her cart down the aisle and let silence do its work. People didn't like silence. They tried to fill the vacuum.

"I went to school with Angela's kids," Melissa offered. Her face was getting redder.

"Did you?"

"Do you know what that was like? She was horrible to her kids."

That hadn't been what Erin had been expecting. "Was she? What happened?"

"Can you imagine having a mother like that? Who would intentionally humiliate you in front of your friends? Punish you? Call you out? With no regard for your privacy at all?"

"That must have been pretty tough on them. Were you… good friends?"

"No!" Melissa's eyes widened and she shook her head. "She wouldn't have let them be friends with me anyway. She never thought anyone was good enough for them, even though she acted like they were worthless. Why do you think none of her kids live in Bald Eagle Falls anymore? They all got out as soon as they could."

"That's pretty sad. Is she married, then? I never heard anyone mention her husband…?"

"No, there hasn't been a man around for a long time."

"Did they divorce or separate? Or did he die?"

"I don't know."

Erin frowned. "How could you not know? I thought everyone knew everyone's business in a town like this."

"She made it this big mystery. She would refer to him all the time, try to intimidate people. 'When I got rid of my husband…' It was actually really creepy."

"So, she… implied that she killed him? Or ran him off?" Erin shook her head. "Or what?"

"That's just it. She never said. Just let everyone draw their own conclusions and wonder what had happened. I expect that he just left her one day. Got tired of all the nagging and complaining and berating him in front of his own children and ran away. I would have, if I'd been living in that house."

"Someone must know."

"I don't know. It's a small town, but when someone just up and disappears without a trace… I'm telling you. No one knows what happened."

"What did the kids say? You said you went to school with them."

"They didn't know. She just told them he was gone and he wasn't coming back."

"And his work? His boss and his coworkers would have reported him missing, wouldn't they?"

"Angela and he worked together. Family business. It started out as his inheritance. The store. The business. But she squeezed him out… until there wasn't anything left of him, financially or physically."

Erin stopped walking and just looked at Melissa. "The business? The bakery was his business?"

"Initially, yes. But she just sort of… took over."

"And nobody looked for him when he disappeared?"

"He didn't disappear. Well, he did, but nobody reported him missing. That was up to Angela. She said he wasn't missing, so what was anyone else to do?"

"That's just bizarre."

"That's Angela."

"And the kids, they didn't try to track him down after they left home?"

Melissa added a couple of 'slim' soups to her basket. "The kids are all train wrecks. Davis is an addict. In Seattle, last I heard. Sophie committed suicide. I don't know what happened to Trenton. Like his dad, he just… walked out of Bald Eagle Falls one day and was never heard from again."

"Walked out of Bald Eagle Falls?" Erin repeated. "How could anyone walk out of Bald Eagle Falls? It's in the middle of nowhere."

"He didn't take a car. Didn't get on the bus. Must have walked out and hitched a ride. There was no sign of what had happened to him."

"Two disappearances? And nobody thought anything of it?"

"Trenton *was* reported missing. But the police never turned up a trail. I don't think they tried all that hard. They just figured that he'd gone off like his dad. Turned tail and ran."

"Those poor kids," Erin said, shaking her head. "What a toxic place that must have been."

"I hated that whole family," Melissa said vehemently. Her coy 'I would never speak ill of the dead' manner was gone. The emotion she radiated was raw, almost palpable. Erin saw one of the clerks looking nervously in Melissa's direction. Erin was sure she couldn't have actually heard what Melissa was saying. She could just see or feel the anger and outrage Melissa was giving off. "The whole flippin' family. They were sickos raised by a sicko. Or a psycho. Everyone pussyfooted around here, pretending that Angela was a pillar of the community. She wasn't any pillar, they were just afraid of setting her off. Afraid of what she would do to them if they ever crossed her. They were the most dysfunctional family you ever saw, putting on masks and pretending that they were perfectly normal."

"Did they bully you?" Erin guessed. The anger had to be coming from somewhere. It had to stem from something. Not just a dysfunctional family in the community, but one that had done her wrong. One that had done something that hurt her so badly she couldn't forgive it decades later. It was still an angry, raw wound.

"That Trenton was in my grade. It was a small school, we only had one class per grade. He was always in my class. I could never get away from him. He was always so smarmy and respectful in front of the teacher, they all loved him and thought he was the greatest thing on earth. But when their backs were turned… it was hell. He wasn't an angel; he was a demon. I was glad when he was gone. Glad that he disappeared and never showed his face here again."

"How long ago was that? Did he disappear while you were still in school?"

"He was eighteen. Just barely. Hadn't graduated yet, but was on track to be the class valedictorian or prom king. Or both. He was so smart and the teachers all thought he was so wonderful."

"Then it must have been really strange for him to disappear so suddenly."

"The whole town wanted to know what had happened to him. All the adults, anyway. Not the kids. We were just glad he was gone."

"Do you think…" Erin's mind was racing, trying to make sense of all of the new information. "Do you think that he just took off, ran away, or do you think… someone did something to him? If all the kids hated him so much, do you think there was foul play?"

"I don't know. No one ever said who it was. No one spilled it. If someone did something, they kept quiet about it. Never bragged about it."

"And his family? How did Angela and his siblings react?"

"Just like with his dad. After the initial investigation, they never talked about it again. Angela acted like he hadn't even existed. No pictures up. Never talked about how he had done so well at school or anything like that. She didn't talk about him at all, positive or negative. Just wiped him out."

"Everybody mourns differently," Erin allowed, feeling like she should say something to defend Angela. Surely the woman couldn't have lost her son without feeling something, as Melissa implied. One woman sets up a shrine to her child, and another, unable to bear thinking of him or referring to him again, wipes out everything that would remind her of him.

Melissa just looked at Erin. Erin forced herself to push on, getting some freezer meals so that she and Vic would have something that wouldn't take any energy at the end of a long day. Frozen dinners weren't a great choice, but they would be better than takeout or just eating nothing because no one had the energy to cook.

"So, if Angela was so difficult to get along with," she circled back to the initial topic. "Then there must be a lot of people who were bitter about her."

"A lot of people who wanted to kill her, you mean?"

"Well…" Erin couldn't think of a tactful way to put it. "I suppose, yes. Do you think there were a lot of people who would have wanted to harm her?"

"I don't think anyone was too broken up about it."

"Do the police know all of this stuff about her past? Are they looking into any connections?"

"Officer Piper was younger than us. He would have heard about it when Trenton disappeared. I would guess those old files are around somewhere. Unless they were part of the batch of files we had to destroy that had that dangerous black mold on it. I don't know if Trenton's missing persons file would have been in that batch."

"But he knows about it. Piper. He must be considering any suspects in Trenton's disappearance."

"I guess." Melissa's shoulders rose and fell like it made no difference to her. And maybe it didn't. Maybe she didn't realize that having a key to the shop and being there around the time that Angela was killed made her a suspect. Maybe she didn't think Piper was looking at her and would be looking for any connections to Trenton's disappearance. Like the fact that they had been in the same class at school at the time that Trenton had disappeared. And that she had been one of Trenton's victims.

Had Melissa harbored bitter feelings toward Angela for all those years? Pretending to be friendly with her, playing bridge with her and going to church with her, all the while believing that Angela had made her sadistic son what he was and had been the ultimate cause of Melissa's pain?

Erin gave a shiver, even though they were well past the freezers.

CHAPTER 12

$\mathcal{E}$rin sat in her car for a few minutes in the parking lot of the grocery store, scribbling down lists. She didn't want to forget any of the details of what Melissa had said. If any of it was motive for Angela's murder, she wanted to make sure she had it all down.

After she had recorded everything she could think of, she glanced at the back of the car where the groceries were stacked. She had both groceries needed for the bakery and groceries to be taken home. She knew that she should go back to the shop and put all of her supplies there before going home. She wouldn't want to go out again once she was home. But maybe she could save herself time by just taking everything home with her and then taking it in to the bakery with her the next morning. Instead of having to go two separate places.

But she knew from the start that was a bad idea. That would mean putting things in the fridge at the house and then getting them back out to take with her to the bakery. It meant putting things away twice, which was a waste of time. And she really needed to be efficient with her time.

With a sigh, Erin pulled out and headed over to the bakery. Just a few minutes there to get everything put away, then she could go home and relax. And put away the groceries. And warm up something for supper. And she should do a little cleaning, so that it wouldn't all be piled up for her to do on Sunday after she and Vic got back from their exploring.

She pulled into her parking space behind the store, grabbed a couple of the bags of groceries earmarked for the bakery and hurried to the back door. If she were quick, it wouldn't take so much energy. She had already taken too long at the grocery shopping, listening to Melissa's recollections.

Erin opened the back door and shouldered her way through it before realizing that she had not unlocked it. She knew she had locked it before dropping Vic at home and going grocery shopping. She locked it every day. And Vic would have noticed and reminded her if she had somehow forgotten.

Erin stood just inside the back entrance, holding the groceries, trying to decide what to do.

"Hello? Anybody here?"

She knew that they had keys. The other murder suspects had keys to the shop. She had put in a work order to have the locks on the shop changed out, but the locksmith was apparently on a fishing vacation and could not be talked into coming back to do an emergency job. If she were that desperate, she could get a locksmith from the city. But none of the locksmiths from the city were willing to make the trip out. It wasn't even the money, they just didn't want to make the trip.

So, the shop sat there without the locks being changed. For at least another week.

She thought she heard a noise in the distance. The clink of a tool. Outside? Downstairs?

"Is there somebody here?" Erin called down the stairs.

Was she really expecting someone to answer her? A silly excuse, 'oh, I was just here because I thought I left something incriminating in the bathroom when I murdered Angela.' Or, 'I just wanted a look at that locked cabinet,' or, 'I was just testing to see if these were the keys you were looking for.'

But there was no answer. Erin put down her groceries. She couldn't take them down to the storeroom if there were someone else in the store. Unless...

"Vic, is that you?" Maybe Vic had forgotten one of her possessions there and had walked back over from the house. She might have had something stashed away. Or had left her favorite lipstick in the bathroom by accident.

But there was no reply from Vic.

Erin pulled out her phone and searched for Officer Piper's number. Had she remembered to enter it? She remembered him giving her his card, telling her that there was an after-hours line that was manned twenty-four hours a day, even though there was no 9-1-1 service in Bald Eagle Falls. But she didn't know whether she had put the number into her contacts or not.

There was only one number listed for Officer Piper and she hadn't noted whether it was his office number or the 24-hour number. She pressed 'call' anyway and waited while the phone took its own sweet time connecting. She had two bars, so it should go through. Finally, she heard the ring tone and waited a bit more for the dispatcher to answer the call.

"Piper."

"Oh… is this your personal cell phone?" Erin was flummoxed and didn't know what to say.

"Yes. Who is this?"

"It's Erin Price. I meant to call the emergency number, but I must not have written it down. Can you tell me what it is?"

"They're just going to turn around and call me, I'm on call tonight. What's wrong?" His voice had taken on an edge.

"I'm at the bakery and I think… I think there's someone here. In the basement. The back door was open. Someone must have picked it or used an extra set of keys to get in."

"I told you to change the locks."

"I know, but the guy is on vacation…"

"Michael Fletcher is about as useful as a steering wheel on a mule. You should have called me, I would have lit a fire under him. I'll be at your store within five minutes. Don't go down to investigate. Go back outside to your car. Are you parked behind or in front?"

"Behind."

"Just wait for me. Don't try to do anything yourself. Even if the burglar comes back out, just stay in your car with the doors locked."

"Okay." Erin slipped back out the door. "I called out to them. That was probably a stupid thing to do. I was startled, it was just my first reaction."

"I'm hanging up so I can get over there. Just get in your car and wait."

"Okay."

Piper terminated the call and Erin slid the phone back into her purse. She got into the car and locked the doors, then sat looking at the back door, waiting for the intruder to come back out.

She didn't even see Piper at first. He had a dark car and crept down the back lane with no lights on. He pulled in behind her car. He and K9 got out and headed for the back door. Erin unlocked her door to get out and talk to him, but he motioned for her to stay put and entered the bakery, weapon drawn. It was like watching a TV drama with the sound off. Except that once he entered the building, there were no cameras following him, so she was left to imagine what was going on.

It had to be at least ten minutes before Piper returned to the car. He motioned for her to roll down her window. Erin did.

"Was there anyone there? Did you find anyone?"

"They were gone by the time I arrived. Out the front door. I'm sure it wasn't their preferred exit route, because they could have been seen out on the street, but knowing that you were at the back door, they didn't have much choice."

"Did you see them? Do you know who it was?"

"No." He frowned at her. "Why would someone be breaking into your store? We already searched it for evidence in Mrs. Plaint's murder. I can't think of a reason for anyone to be there, other than the thrill of visiting the site of a murder."

"Well..." Erin trailed off, trying to think of how to avoid telling him about her amateur investigation. "It could be that."

"Or...?"

"It could be the ghost. Seeing if they can catch a glimpse of my ghost."

"We both know that your ghost was Vic."

"But everybody in town doesn't know that. Just the three of us. We couldn't very well go around telling everyone that she'd been hiding out in my bakery."

"What else?" He was staring at her. As if he could see right into her brain and tell if she was lying.

"I might have said that there was a locked cabinet down there," Erin said slowly. "A mysterious locked cabinet that might hold the secret to a buried treasure. Or something."

"And why would you have said that?"

"I was trying to find out who might have keys from when Clementine was here. She apparently gave out a few of them and I wanted to track them all down. To help you out."

"So, you told people there was a locked cabinet."

"I thought if I said that I didn't have a key to it, but Clementine might have given a copy to someone with keys to the bakery… I might be able to find out who had keys to the bakery." It all sounded pretty lame to Erin when it came out of her mouth.

"And it didn't occur to you that people might want to investigate this mysterious cabinet with its clue to a buried treasure on their own? To beat you to the punch?"

"I didn't think it through. It was just spur of the moment."

"Why don't you leave the investigating to me?"

"Yeah. Sorry. It turns out there were a lot of keys floating around, though. If that helps you. Probably Mary Lou, and Melissa, and Gema. Angela herself. Maybe some of the other church ladies."

"We may never be able to trace them all. It seems like she gave out her keys pretty indiscriminately. The killer isn't going to tell us they have keys."

"No. I guess not. Did you find anything down there? Any clue as to who it was?"

"A crowbar. Like someone might use to pry open a locked cabinet."

"Oh." Erin remembered that Gema had suggested something like that. Which didn't mean it was Gema, of course. Melissa might have taken up her suggestion. Or someone else might have overheard, or had the same idea. It wasn't exactly proprietary technology.

"I'll need you to write up a statement. I'll get you the forms."

Erin nodded. Her evening wasn't over yet.

Piper went back to his car and returned with the statement forms for her to fill out.

"Are you actually after a buried treasure?" he inquired.

"Uh… no. Vic and I found a map at the house, to some caves and mines in the area, so that's why it was on my mind."

"Really." His lips pressed together grimly and Erin wondered what he was thinking.

"Yes… you sound like you don't believe me."

"You haven't exactly been forthcoming."

Erin thought she had been pretty up-front with him, so she wasn't sure what omission he was talking about. And she wasn't sure she wanted to know.

"We found an old map at Clementine's house. That's all."

"A geological map. What would she have a geological map for? She wasn't exactly in a business that required it. She didn't hike or climb. It's curious."

"Well, curious, yes. But not suspicious."

"I didn't say it was suspicious."

His expression and body language certainly had. But Erin couldn't argue with what he said. She turned on the car's dome light and bent over the witness statement to start filling it out.

"You're not planning on exploring any caves or mines?" Piper said, watching her.

"Uh… Vic wanted to go see a cave. She's picked one out on the map. We're not going to do anything adventurous. Just have a look around. Nothing that's too deep or requires special equipment."

He shook his head. "I wouldn't advise it. Some of those caves look perfectly safe, but have hidden hazards. If you want to see a cave, go see one of the touristy ones with guides and barriers. Not a random cave from the map."

"We'll be careful. I won't let Vic go into anything that I'm not sure of. And we'll be together, if something happens."

"You'll have to make sure it's on public land. You don't want to run afoul of some moonshiner with a shotgun because you've trespassed on his land."

Erin laughed, but then realized he was serious. "Are there really moon-shiners around here still? I mean, prohibition ended long ago."

"Alcohol is regulated and there are unregulated stills operating in the mountains around here. You want to stay away from anything like that, because moonshiners can be very touchy about strangers."

"Okay. I'm not going to mess with anyone's still or trespass on private land. And we're not going to do anything dangerous."

Erin went back to writing her statement. But she gathered from the way Piper was hovering over her that he wasn't finished. She looked up at him.

"There are other things going on in the hills too. This may be the back country, but that doesn't mean there's no crime. The drug trade makes use of those large tracts of unmanaged land. There are growing fields, drug labs, stashes. It's not really safe to go poking around."

"You make it sound like the wild west. Or some ghetto. It's not really that bad, is it?"

"It's bad enough that I'm warning you."

"Okay... well... noted. I'll talk to Vic about it. Maybe I can convince her to go to a public admission cave instead."

He nodded. "Good."

Erin scratched out a few more words on the witness statement. "I was going to ask you about William Andrews."

"What about him?"

"Is he... okay? Is he a suspect?"

"Everyone is a suspect. Why William Andrews?"

"He was hanging around when I unloaded groceries before Angela died. He seems like sort of a shady character and I just wondered... it's possible he could have tampered with something. I can't imagine why or that Angela would have been his target, but it's a possibility."

"Hanging around how?"

"He was trying to help me carry things in. Grabbed one bag of flour when I asked him not to. He was still trying to help out after I told him not to. I eventually had to chase him off by threatening to call you."

"Did he have the opportunity to put something in the flour or any of the other ingredients?"

"I... don't think so. He'd have had to be quick and have planned ahead. But it was dark and my back was to him, and I was out of sight in the bakery for a few minutes. So, it is conceivable."

"But not likely."

"No... I don't see how he could have targeted Angela. But maybe it wasn't just targeted at her... do we know for sure now that it was an allergic reaction and not a poison?"

"That's what the coroner says," Piper said with a nod.

"So, it wasn't just a general toxin. Unless it's something that everyone is allergic to, like poison ivy."

"If it was poison ivy, everyone would have had a reaction. Not just Mrs. Plaint."

"Yeah... you're right. But even if he didn't contaminate something then, when he was trying to take my groceries in, that could have just been his first attempt. He could have tried and succeeded with something else later on."

"It's possible. Is there any indication that he might have had a key?"

"No. Just... I understand he does odd jobs around here. It's possible that he did some work for Clementine and had a key. Or was hired to maintain the place after she died."

"I'll have to make inquiries. I don't know if your aunt kept any financial records at home, but if she did, you could look through them and see if there were any check stubs to Mr. Andrews."

"Okay. I'll do that." Erin smothered a big yawn. "I'm beat. Can I finish this statement in the morning? I can barely put two thoughts together."

"Sure. Just drop it by the office." Piper gave a little frown, as if troubled.

"What is it? What are you thinking about?"

"Mm. Nothing. Just that Mr. Andrews is the courier we use to send evidence to the coroner."

"He has access to the evidence in this case?" Erin was horrified at the thought.

"No. Not access, exactly. Everything is sealed and the coroner would let me know if anything had been tampered with. But I might just ask them to do a full inventory, to make sure that all evidence was accounted for. It would be risky for Mr. Andrews to 'lose' anything along the way. Chances are the coroner would notice it was missing when comparing the log in sheet with the inventory sheet that was sent over. But sometimes, when there's a load of exhibits, it's easy to miss one and things do go missing."

"Why would you use someone like that as a courier?"

His brows drew down. "Someone like what?"

"Someone so…" Erin trailed off, realizing that she had adopted Angela's opinion of the man, as someone shiftless and lazy, a drifter. Someone to be suspicious of. But when she compared what she knew of the man firsthand, she realized there was nothing to back the opinion up. The man had volunteered to help her with her groceries, not asking for anything for doing it. She had seen him doing work for others. The police department used him as a courier. Every indication was that he was a busy, productive member of the community. "I don't know what I was thinking. I don't really know anything about him."

Piper nodded. "You can't judge people by their appearances," he reminded her.

And she was. "No. I'm sorry. I didn't even realize I was doing it."

He looked mollified by her apology.

"What exactly *does* he do?" Erin asked. "I mean other than acting as a courier and doing odd jobs? His skin… he looks like he does welding."

"He's a prospector of some sort. He keeps himself to himself, so I don't know the details. Some kind of mining out in the hills."

"Gold?"

"I said I don't know. He doesn't trade it in town. Whatever he digs out of the mountain he takes elsewhere for processing or sale."

Erin thought about his warnings about drug dealers working in the area. Could William Andrews be one of those drug dealers? If he were doing so many other odd jobs, it wasn't beyond the realm of possibility that he was involved in some stage of the drug trade.

Erin rubbed her forehead. "I'd better be going. Sorry to keep you. I feel sort of silly about calling you when I'd already scared the burglar off."

"Don't say that," Piper ordered. "You did the right thing. You never go into the building when you think there's been a break-in. These heroines on TV who just go waltzing in to investigate for themselves or confront a burglar, in real life they would be dead. You let me deal with it."

Erin gave him a little smile. "Okay, Officer Piper," she agreed. "I don't feel so bad, then."

"Bring that by the police department in the morning. Or when you take a break."

"I hear you had a burglar," Mary Lou said, startling Erin when she fell into step beside her on her way to the police department the next morning.

Erin put her hand over her heart to calm its rapid beating. "How did you hear that so soon?"

"Word spreads fast in a small town," Mary Lou said. "I think your young Vicky mentioned it to Mrs. Foster."

"Oh. Sure. Well, yes, somebody was in the basement when I went by to drop off some supplies."

Mary Lou shook her head, smiling. "That's what happens when you start spreading rumors of treasure maps and such. Best you keep your mouth shut about things you don't want anyone to know."

"Yes," Erin agreed. "You're right, of course. It was pretty stupid of me."

"Is that your report?" Mary Lou nodded to the pink form that Erin held clutched in her hand.

"Yes."

Mary Lou lifted her brows and made a small motion with her hand as if she expected Erin to hand it to her. Erin resisted her automatic impulse to hand it to her.

"Nothing too interesting, I'm afraid. I never saw who it was. They were out of there before I could see who it was."

Mary Lou's shoulders dipped a little. There was a slight relaxation of the muscles around her eyes. Erin tried not to react to these small indications. They didn't qualify as proof that Mary Lou had anything to do with the burglary and was relieved to find that she was not suspected. There might have been something else on her mind, or Erin might be completely misreading the signs, just seeing what she wanted to.

It was unnerving having the store broken into, even though nothing was damaged or stolen. Erin wanted to know who had done it. She felt vulnerable and angry at the same time.

"You don't have any idea who it could be?" she asked Mary Lou.

"Goodness, how would I? Everyone was talking about your treasure map and the missing key. It could have been anyone. Even someone from out of town."

"Not just anyone. Someone who had a key. The back door was unlocked."

Mary Lou's eyes flickered. "You might have left it unlocked by mistake."

"No, I didn't. Whoever broke in let themselves in with a key. Which means it was someone from town."

"I suppose it does. You didn't have any luck finding out who your aunt gave keys to…?"

"Some," Erin said. "But no one who has actually turned them in."

"I saw Fletcher on Main Street. I assume he's there to change out your locks?"

"Yes. I tried to get him to do it last week, but apparently he needs an order from the police to get into action."

Mary Lou gave a low chuckle. "He does sometimes need a little encouragement to get out to a job."

"We might have been able to avoid the burglary if he'd done it when I asked him to."

"Or if you hadn't spread the rumor that there was a mysterious locked cabinet in your basement."

Erin met Mary Lou's eyes. It was obvious Mary Lou knew that there was no locked cabinet. Was it because she had been there and seen for herself? Or had the burglar then spread the word that there was no such cabinet? Or maybe Mary Lou had been down in the basement before and knew it didn't exist? It was pretty obvious to anyone who had been downstairs that it held no secrets. There was no cabinet, no safe, no mysterious locked door. Just a small bathroom and storeroom.

"If you want to keep a secret in Bald Eagle Falls, you have to be pretty savvy," Mary Lou offered. "There aren't a lot of secrets here."

Erin chewed on the inside of her lip. It seemed to her that there were a lot of secrets in Bald Eagle Falls. A lot of things that were kept secret from Erin, at any rate. Maybe to a long-time resident like Mary Lou, it was different. She would know who to talk to and would have the trust of the gossip-mongers. But they were more likely to talk *about* Erin than *to* her.

"Secrets like what happened to Angela's husband and son?" she suggested.

Mary Lou's eyes widened. She put her hand on Erin's arm, stopping her. They were only a few steps from the civic center. Mary Lou obviously wanted to continue the conversation beyond what they could discuss before reaching Officer Piper's door.

"How did you hear about that?" she demanded in a hushed tone.

"Someone was telling me how Angela's husband disappeared without a trace. And then later, in his graduating year, her son. Same thing. Just disappeared into thin air."

"Nobody disappears into thin air."

"Does that mean someone knows something about it?"

Mary Lou considered this for some time. "Somebody always knows something. And in a little town like this, probably more people than you would expect know something."

"Does that mean you know what happened to them?"

Mary Lou's hand dropped away from Erin's arm.

"I do not." Her voice was crisp and firm, devoid of emotion. "I know nothing about what happened to them and I don't want to know. The family was apparently much more dysfunctional than it appeared to be in public. Angela always appeared to have things in control. But there are some things you just can't hold on to. The harder you try, the more they squirm away."

"Like secrets?"

"Like I said, secrets are hard to keep in a small town like this. Even if you lie to cover them up, people still figure it out. You try to cover it up, but someone sees. Someone hears. Someone knows."

Erin gave a little shiver in spite of the heat of the day.

"*Who* knows?" she asked. Was Mary Lou trying to give her a warning? Or a clue?

There was a period of silence from Mary Lou while she considered her answer. Erin had decided that she wasn't going to answer, and then Mary Lou spoke. Her voice was low.

"Angela was the type of person who always knew. Always figured things out. Trying to keep a secret around her was like… trying to hold on to the wind. Somehow, she always knew things that were best left alone."

"Did she know things about you?"

"Honey, I don't have any secrets. It's all out there. Everybody knows my business. I don't try to cover it up. But other people. Most people have something they would rather keep private. An indiscretion. A secret addiction. A mask that they wear…"

Erin thought of the people around her and, in particular, the suspects in Angela's murder. If Angela was someone who collected other people's secrets, that made her a target to a lot more people than just Erin or Vic. Erin's and Vic's motives were tiny in comparison to secrets that other people might be desperate to keep from public view.

"Was Angela a blackmailer? Is that what you mean? Did she make people pay her to keep quiet?"

"Of course not. Nothing so crass. But she had other ways of manipulating people. Getting what she wanted from them. A little twist here, a nudge there. A word or two dropped at a time when only her target would understand. You can understand how someone who wanted to protect their reputation could become… hostile."

"Do you know who wanted to hurt her?"

Mary Lou looked back the direction they had come. "I shouldn't have said anything."

"Do you? Do you know who wanted to hurt her? Who would want to kill her?"

There was only silence for a reply.

"Mary Lou!"

"A lot of people wanted to put a stop to what Angela was doing."

"You?" Erin could hear the malice in Mary Lou's normally calm, cultured voice. "What did she do to you?"

Mary Lou looked down at her watch, then ran her hand over her hair, smoothing it. "I'm afraid I can't chat any longer. You can get my story from anyone in town. Like I said, it's all out there. I don't have any secrets."

Erin reached out to delay Mary Lou, but the gesture was pointless; Mary Lou had already turned away from her and was walking away at a quick pace, her heels clicking down the sidewalk. Erin watched her go. There was so much hate and anger toward Angela; it seemed that the surprise wasn't that she had died, but that she had survived for so long in the first place.

She went on to the police department and looked in on the offices where she had previously met Terry Piper. He was not there, but there was an unfamiliar woman typing at one of the computers. She looked up and nodded at the form clutched in Erin's hand.

"Witness statement?" she asked briskly. "In the bin over there." She nodded to a tray on the corner of the desk that was neatly labeled 'forms to be processed' and contained a few other varicolored papers waiting to be dealt with.

"Thank you." Erin put it down and looked at the woman, awkward and unsure what else to say.

"You must be Erin Price."

"Yes. I don't think we've met?"

"Nope. Clara Jones."

"Uh… nice to meet you."

"So, you run the new bakery." Clara was a middle-aged woman with brassy red hair and large earrings. She seemed out of place in a police department, but seemed to be comfortable there and acted as if she knew what she was doing. Erin remembered that Melissa had said she worked there as well, transcribing reports for Officer Piper.

"Yes. I hope you'll stop by. You missed opening day, but I'll give you a free muffin."

"I'm sure they're good for gluten-free. But I don't eat that kind of crap."

"Uh…" Erin wasn't sure whether it was 'crap' because it was gluten-free or because it was full of processed flour and sugar, and decided that either way, she didn't want to take it up with Clara. "Sure. Well, any time."

"I don't know what you're still doing in town," Clara said, pausing in her typing to pick up her mug and take a sip of coffee. "If it was me, and I was accused of murder, I wouldn't be sticking around for them to pin it on me. Nobody wanted another bakery in town, and with Angela Plaint's murder… if it was me, I'd sell the business and pack up."

"I can't really leave," Erin protested. "Not while it's still being investigated."

"You stay around here stirring up trouble like you have been and you'll be the next one on a slab in the city. Don't you know how you're upsetting people?"

"Stirring up trouble? What did I do?"

"Asking questions. Stirring up the past that is best left undisturbed. What business is it of yours?"

"It's my business because I'm the one who's been accused of murder! You expect me to just tuck my tail between my legs and run away? Maybe that's how people handle things here in Bald Eagle Falls, but like you say, I'm not from around here. And that's not how I'm going to act. I'm not going to pull a disappearing act. I have just as much of a right to live here and to run my business as anyone else."

"Sometimes people don't leave of their own free choice," Clara said cryptically.

"Clara." Terry Piper's voice came from behind Erin, making her jump.

Clara had been looking at her computer screen and obviously hadn't seen Piper approaching. She took another sip of her coffee, hiding her face behind the big mug. "Miss Price brought in her witness statement," she said, indicating the pink page at the top of the basket to be processed. "About the *alleged* burglary of her shop by someone looking for an *alleged* buried treasure."

Erin opened her mouth to retort, but Piper spoke over her.

"Good. We need to get that into the computer as soon as possible. It's important to stay on top of these reports."

"Yes, sir," Clara agreed, her voice light and unconcerned.

"Anything else?"

"No, it's been pretty quiet. Barking dog complaint from Mrs. Snell. Mr. Timon asking for the latest on the Plaint murder for an update in the paper."

"I'll deal with those later." Piper motioned to Erin. "I'll walk you back to the bakery."

"I think I'm pretty safe," Erin retorted. She looked at Clara. "It isn't like anyone is trying to kill me."

"Come." He grasped her upper arm lightly and steered her back out of the office. He didn't speak until they got out to the sidewalk and started heading back to the bakery. K9 kept pace at Piper's side. "Too many loose lips in Bald Eagle Falls," he said. "I wish we had a bigger pool to draw on for administrative help at the office. But there really aren't that many people who are interested. The help that we do get is too... undisciplined."

"It's a bit of a shock living in such a small town. I thought I had lived in some little places before, but by Bald Eagle Falls standards, they were huge. Here... everybody really does know everybody else's business, don't they?"

"There are plenty of people who are happy to spread it."

They walked for a couple of minutes in silence. "I hear that Angela was someone who knew everyone's business," Erin ventured.

"I don't know that she was any worse than anyone else."

"From what I've heard... it sounds like she was blackmailing half the town."

Piper chuckled. "Now that she's not around to defend herself. That's pretty blatant gossip. I don't have any evidence she was blackmailing anyone."

"Maybe not blackmailing," Erin said, "I don't mean she was demanding to be paid. But... manipulating people, threatening to expose them."

Piper frowned, shaking his head. "I haven't heard anything like that. I'm not sure how to prove something like that."

"Maybe she had pictures of people, or recordings or letters..."

"Nothing in her possessions. We've already searched through them." He caught her glance at him. "What?"

"Who is *we*? You and K9?"

K9 looked up when he heard his name. He let out a whine.

"I'm not the only person in the police department. We have the Sheriff. And Tom Banks is the other officer, but he is only part time, called in as we need him. All three of us searched Mrs. Plaint's house. I can assure you, there was no evidence she was keeping dirt on anyone."

Erin sighed and nodded.

"I am investigating Mrs. Plaint's death, Miss Price. You seem to think that I'm just a country bumpkin and don't have any idea what to do with a murder investigation, but I can assure you I'm fully qualified and I have federal resources to draw upon."

"You could call me Erin."

He gazed at her for a moment, his eyes deep, dark pools. "No. I don't think I can. I need to maintain a certain level of professionalism."

Erin thought about what he had said. "I believe that you're investigating," she said. "It just seems backward that you're focusing on the two people who are from out of town, when it seems more likely someone who knew her well would have a motive to harm her. What motive would I have? You really think I would kill someone because they were a competitor?"

"People have killed for less."

"I didn't kill Angela Plaint because I want a monopoly on Bald Eagle Falls's bakery business."

He shrugged. "Okay."

"Okay?"

"You had the best means and opportunity. But I admit that your motive is not as strong as others'. Vic's, for instance."

"Vic didn't kill Angela."

"How much do you really know about Vic?"

He turned his gaze on her. Erin looked away uncomfortably, not wanting to give anything away.

"I know she didn't kill Angela."

"You hope she didn't. You don't *know* anything about her."

"I know what kind of person she is. She's been living and working with me. I know she's not a killer." She turned back toward Piper and stared at his nose. She couldn't meet his eyes, but she knew he wouldn't be able to tell the difference as long as she was close. She had promised Vic she wouldn't tell him about her past unless asked directly and she intended to keep that promise. She needed to give him the impression that she had told him everything she knew. That she was trustworthy. "I'm a good judge of character."

Piper continued to look at her. "Do you know that's not her real name?"

Erin swallowed. "Yes."

"Really. What is her real name?"

"You'd have to ask her."

"Did you know she's not Angela Plaint's niece?"

"Angela was her aunt," Erin said firmly.

He considered this, then shrugged. Aunt could mean different things to different people. It didn't always mean there was a blood or legal connection. Sometimes an aunt was your mother's best friend, or a godmother or cherished babysitter. Or a cousin who happened to be a generation older.

"You can let her know that I need to talk to her again. Go over a few things in her statement." He looked at his watch. "I know you're getting ready for the lunch rush, so I won't expect to see her right now. But I'd like to talk to her again soon."

Knowing that they were going to be working Sunday morning and that they were going to need a little bit of equipment for their trip to the cave after the women's tea, Vic and Erin closed up shop early Saturday afternoon and took Erin's car to the city.

Vic seemed much more anxious in the city than in Bald Eagle Falls. Erin caught her looking around the camping gear store nervously, as if she were expecting to be attacked or accused of something.

"What's wrong?" Erin asked. "Did Officer Piper tell you not to leave town?" she teased.

"Well, he did, but I told him we'd be coming here. He said that was okay, as long as I was going to be around and would make myself available for questioning."

"It was a joke. I didn't know he had really told you that."

"I know." Vic turned all the way around, like a searchlight sweeping the darkness for some hidden danger. "I know you like him, but I don't like having to answer all his questions. He's nice enough about it, but I know he suspects me. He thinks I killed Aunt Angela."

"We'll have to just keep asking questions and pushing him to look in other directions. As long as he keeps looking, he'll find out who it was sooner or later."

But she knew that the disappearances of Angela's husband and son had never been solved. Who had the police been at that point? It would have been too long ago for it to have been Officer Piper. Then again, Melissa wouldn't necessarily have had all the details. She hadn't been transcribing police reports back then. She had only been seventeen when Angela's son disappeared. And younger when Angela's husband left. The police might have tracked both of them down. Might have satisfied themselves that there was nothing to be concerned about, that they simply hadn't wanted to be with Angela anymore. A man was entitled to leave if he wanted to. Plenty of men did, and never contacted their families again.

Still, it worried her. Maybe crimes weren't so easily solved in Bald Eagle Falls.

"What are you so nervous about?" she asked Vic, getting back around to the original question.

"I don't want anyone to see me who might know me. From before. I don't want to run into any old friends or neighbors. Or worse, family. Or somebody who knows my mom and is going to run back and tell her all about seeing me here. Like this." Vic slid her fingers through her smooth blond ponytail, frowning.

"You look lovely," Erin assured her. "If anyone recognizes you… well, we'll just deal with that. What's your mom going to do? She already kicked you out. You're not in contact with her. What does it matter what she hears or thinks?"

"Yeah." Vic bit her lip. "You're right. I just can't help feeling…"

"It will be okay. We'll handle it. Nothing bad is going to happen."

"Okay."

They went on with their shopping, referring to the equipment list that Vic had compiled. Erin couldn't believe how eager the girl was to explore some caves. Erin felt anxious just thinking about it, but Vic was all-in. She wanted to be crawling through dark tunnels, miles underground, where there was no telling when you might fall off of a cliff, into an underground lake, or just asphyxiate from lack of oxygen.

"We're not going anywhere dangerous," Erin said. "Nothing that's really far underground. We're both just beginners."

"I know." Vic gave her a grin, laughing at Erin's anxiety now. "But even beginners need flashlights and safety equipment. Just the basics."

"It seems like an awfully long list for just the basics."

"That's all it is. I just went by beginner lists."

"What else?"

"Uh…" Vic looked down at her neat, concise printing. "Rope."

"Rope? Why do we need rope? We're not going to fall down anywhere."

"Just to be safe. Just for emergencies."

"No emergencies. I'm not going to any caves if we're going to have emergencies."

"We won't. It's just on the list. So, we get it."

Erin grumbled while Vic searched through the spools of rope to find the kind that she wanted. An employee cut it to the specified length and finished the ends. Vic added it to the shopping cart.

"Oh, look who it is!"

Vic's head whipped around and she followed Erin's pointing finger to see Gema. She breathed a sigh of relief. "Don't scare me like that!"

"I'm sorry. I wouldn't know any of your family or friends anyway. The only people I know around here are from Bald Eagle Falls."

"Oh. Right."

They were both watching as Gema spoke to another woman, a little younger than she was. She was closer to Erin in size and body shape and, unlike Gema's iron-gray waves, she had close-cropped, spiky red hair. The two women were too far away for Erin and Vic to hear what they were saying. The other woman had on the green vest of a store employee, but Gema didn't seem to be looking for anything. They were just having a friendly conversation. Gema's fingertips rested on the clerk's arm, as if stopping her from leaving.

"These little towns," Vic said. "You can never go anywhere without running into someone you know. Even when you go into the city."

"I suppose. I haven't lived anywhere as small as Bald Eagle Falls before."

"Compasses."

"What?" Erin looked down at the shelf display of compasses. "Do we need anything special? Maybe we should get a GPS. Do they make GPSs for caving? They make those little fish radar things for fishing, is there anything like that for mapping out the tunnels in case you get lost?"

Vic rolled her eyes. "There is no GPS or radar for caving. You need a compass."

"You're the one who has been doing the research. You pick one out."

As Vic looked through the compasses and compared features and prices and how they felt in her hand, Erin watched Gema and the store clerk. Eventually, they said their goodbyes and gave each other a hug. They separated to go their different directions. Erin waved to catch Gema's attention.

"Gema! Over here!"

Gema turned her head, obviously catching Erin's voice. Then Gema spotted her. She looked hesitant at first, looking toward the exit doors of the camping store as if she had to leave. Then she turned back toward Erin and moved toward them, smiling.

"What are you guys doing here?" she asked. "Doing some camping?"

"Spelunking," Vic declared, at the same time as Erin said, "Caving."

Erin shook her head. "Fine. Spelunking," she agreed. "But no underground lakes."

"That sounds like fun," Gema said. "Where are you going? There are some nice ones around here."

"Erin found a map—"

"Oh, yes. Your map." Gema laughed. "Treasure hunting, then?"

"I wouldn't mind if we found some treasure," Vic said.

"We're not looking for treasure," Erin disagreed. "We're just going to look at a couple of caves. Nothing too remote or scary. Just some well-traveled, safe caves."

"I looked at the map and picked a couple out," Vic contributed, ignoring Erin. "And I looked them up on Google Maps and made sure that none of them are big commercial places. There are a couple of small ones that I couldn't even find on Google Maps, so I don't know if they've had a cave-in, or what—"

"Cave-in?" Erin echoed weakly. It was sounding like a worse and worse idea. What were they thinking, going to explore caves where there was no one else to help them? Two inexperienced women, alone. Probably GPS and cell phones wouldn't even work out there in the sticks. They could be lost for days.

"We won't go into one that has had a cave-in," Vic assured her. But that wasn't what Erin wanted to hear. She wanted to hear that they wouldn't go anywhere near any of the remote, non-tourist caves.

Erin looked at Gema for help. "Have you ever done this? Explored a cave?"

"Sure. I grew up in the area. I've been in a lot of caves around here. Even used to take my boys to some of them. Boys love exploring caves."

"Maybe we should get Gema to go with us," Erin suggested to Vic. "That would be okay, wouldn't it?"

Vic's face fell. "I wanted it to be just the two of us." She looked at Gema. "I don't mean anything by it, I just wanted to do something ourselves."

"Of course I'm not offended. If you want to explore caves together, that's what you should do. People should do what makes them happy." She looked wistful. Erin wondered if she was thinking about her family and how they used to explore together. Now it was just Gema and her husband. Erin had seen the two of them together, but Gema's husband didn't match her for vibrancy. He looked more like the type of husband to fall asleep with a beer in front of the TV than someone who would go on adventures with her. And maybe that was fine with Gema. But she did look like she was missing the fun they had had when they were raising their boys together.

"So, what brings you here?" Erin asked. She made a motion to where Gema had been talking with her friend. "Was that—"

"A young cousin of mine. I always see how she's doing when I'm in the area."

On considering, Erin thought there had been similarities in their features.

Gema looked at the compasses on the shelf. "Do these ever bring back memories." She tapped one. "Did you know that Mary Lou and I were in Girl Guides together? A coon's age ago, to be sure. Can you believe we've known each other for that long?"

"Wow," Vic said. "I haven't known anyone that long."

"You haven't been alive that long!" Erin laughed. "I haven't either, though. I moved around so much... I haven't known anyone more than a couple of years."

"Really?" Gema shook her head. "That would be very strange to me. I've lived in Bald Eagle Falls all my life. I'm practically a fixture."

Vic finally picked out a couple of compasses and showed them to Gema, the experienced one. "These ones? Do you think they're good?"

"Those ones will be just fine."

"Mary Lou said something funny the other day," Erin said, thinking back.

"What was she talking about?"

"She was talking about Angela." Erin glanced at Vic to make sure she didn't mind Erin talking about her aunt in front of her. Vic gave a little nod. "She was saying that Angela was the type of person who knew everything about everyone. Even the things they wanted to keep secret."

Gema raised her brows.

"And she would hold what she knew over people to make them do what she wanted them to. Like… emotional blackmail."

"I wouldn't know anything about that," Gema said. She gave a little laugh and swept her hair back behind her head with both hands, looking like she was going to scrunch it all together into a ponytail. Then she released it. "What exactly was Mary Lou talking about?"

"I don't know. She didn't give any specific examples. She just said that everyone had secrets… and Angela knew them all."

"I see."

"But she said she didn't have any," Erin continued. "She said her life is an open book; she doesn't hide anything. When I asked her about what happened between her and Angela, she said I should ask someone else about it. Why it was Mary Lou didn't like her."

Gema shook her head. "That's a long story. Well, not so much a long story as a sad one. A tragedy."

"Really?" Erin added the compasses to the shopping cart. She was hoping they were at the end of Vic's list and could start to head for the check-out. Vic folded the list up, which Erin took as a signal they were done. She turned the cart around and pointed it toward the check out lines. "So, what happened?"

"Angela was always involved in these new businesses and ideas. She was a good businessperson, she always made back her investment. She was very sharp."

"I heard that."

"That is, she always made her investment back… until she didn't."

"What does that mean?"

"She got Mary Lou and half the town involved in some scheme. One of these things where everyone is supposed to get back ten times what they put into it. If it sounds too good to be true, it probably is. That's what I always said."

"How did Angela get Mary Lou into something so risky? She seems so level-headed."

"I don't know. Just because Angela was Angela. It always worked out.

So, why wouldn't it work out again? It was more risky, but that just meant that it was going to bring in a better return."

They waited in line for a cashier. Erin could already see how the story was going to end.

"She always made her investment back. Until she didn't."

Gema nodded. "Mary Lou went all-in. She put everything she had into the scheme. And more. She borrowed."

"Oh, no…"

"Yes. When everything came crashing down… Angela had only invested modestly. Some people had been careful and some had risked more. But Mary Lou… she had been sure it was her chance to put away enough for retirement. Maybe even an early retirement. They had never been wealthy. Her husband, Roger, he was a plodder."

"She must have been crushed."

"Mary Lou is made of pretty stern stuff. She declared bankruptcy. Promised all her creditors that she was still going to pay them back, no matter how long it took. Started working, which she hadn't done since before the boys were born. But Roger couldn't handle it. The way that he'd been embarrassed in front of everyone he knew. Losing the house and his car. The way that people talked about them."

"What did he do?"

"He tried to take his own life, of course. And failed at that too."

Erin swallowed and nodded. She didn't know what else to say, or if it were acceptable to ask for more information.

"He has a brain injury from going without oxygen," Gema said matter-of-factly. "And, of course, he still suffers from depression. Not just over the money, but now about what he's done to himself and his family, too. He completely failed them. And he put all of that burden on his wife and sons."

Her words made Erin feel the horrible bleakness herself. They had lost everything. And his attempt to escape it all had just made it that much worse.

"Mary Lou is always so cheerful," she said in amazement. "You'd never guess by looking at her that any of this had happened! And she doesn't look…" Erin struggled for a tactful way to say it and failed, "…poor. She always looks so perfectly turned-out."

"And those boys are the same way. You'd never guess there was anything wrong at home. They're all-stars at school. They work part time to help support the family. And they're like her, always cheerful and not letting anyone feel sorry for them."

"That's amazing. It really is."

Vic had been silent throughout the story. After the cashier finished ringing everything through, Erin paid with her credit card. She'd always done her best to master the situation and pull herself out of the holes she ended up in. But Mary Lou reached a whole new level with the way she dealt with her troubles.

Gema smiled a polite goodbye. "I still have some errands to run before going back to Bald Eagle Falls. I'm sure I'll see you girls there."

"You're coming by for tea after church tomorrow, right?" Erin verified.

"Yes. I'll be there. We'll all be there."

Vic helped Erin to load their gear into the car, quiet and contemplative. Erin looked at her as they sat down in front and put their seat-belts on.

"Are you okay?"

"Just thinking."

"About Mary Lou?"

"I thought I had things tough. You know, I get myself down and sit around feeling sorry for what I've been through. And then I hear something like this… and I realize, I'm still such a baby. Not because I'm young, but because… what I've gone through is nothing compared to what someone like Mary Lou had been through. Losing everything, including her house. Her husband. His wage-earning ability. It's just… it's so sad. What happened to me? I got called names. I got kicked out. So, what? I still have the ability to make money and learn to support myself. I have a friend who gave me work and a place to live until I get on my feet. I really have everything I could want."

Erin nodded her agreement. "Same for me. I mope around about how I didn't have any parents. Had to grow up in foster homes. Had to fend for myself when I was eighteen, and pretty much for a couple of years before that. I was working as soon as I was old enough to get a job, because I knew I was going to have to look after myself. And… so what? Now I'm independent. I'm strong. I have my own business and an employee. And a cat. I'm not tied down to a disabled husband and two children. I don't have thousands of dollars in debt to pay back. Mary Lou would probably love to have all the advantages that I do."

"Yeah."

Erin blew out her breath in a sigh. "It just puts everything in perspective."

"Even being a murder suspect. It isn't like they've arrested me and put me behind bars. Things could be a lot worse."

"Just be glad we didn't live back in the days when they would just string you up. No judge or jury, no investigation or human rights. Someone thinks you did it, and they hang you."

They drove in silence for a while.

"We're still going to the caves, right?"

Erin laughed. "We're still going to the caves. But you better make sure I don't die there."

~

Sunday morning they slept in, and it was heavenly. God or no god, Erin awoke with a prayer of thanks in her heart for the extra hours of sleep. And that Orange Blossom had let them sleep in and not started howling for his breakfast.

Since all they were doing was tea and not opening up the bakery for a full shopping day, they just had a few items to put in the oven and had prepared it all ahead of time so that all they needed was a couple of hours before church let out. Then the church ladies made their way down Main Street and set the front door bell ringing as they gathered in the chairs to gossip and relax. Erin had tea steeping—several varieties, in fact. The smells threw her back into the past, to Clementine's Tea Room. The smells and flavors of the teas that Clementine had carried were so familiar. Erin remembered all the old boxes and wrappers. And the women chattering away happily while little Erin carefully carried cookies and other treats to the tables.

"Erin, this is lovely," Mary Lou said, taking one slim biscotti biscuit from her tray. "Just like when Clementine was around. I hadn't even realized how much I have *missed* it. She was forced to retire because of her health. Certainly none of us ever held that against her. She just did what she had to do. But I have missed this."

There were nods from the other women and choruses of agreement from the sipping and munching clientele.

"There's nothing like sisterhood," Gema declared. She had a blueberry muffin with her tea, light-colored with the addition of plenty of cream. Erin didn't know all of the women well, but the faces were familiar and Erin had to agree with what Gema said about sisterhood. She felt warm and comfortable and secure. All her anxiety evaporated with the steam from the tea.

"You really should join us at church too," Melissa said. "We had a really nice service today."

The other ladies quieted, looking at each other and looking at Erin out the corners of their eyes, not daring to meet her gaze.

"Thank you," Erin said. "But I don't have any plans to go to church in the near future."

"And… what about you, Vic?" Melissa asked. "You're not an atheist too, are you? Did the two of you *not go* to the same church back in Maine?" She laughed at her own joke.

"No, I'm Christian… but God and I aren't exactly on good terms these days," Vic said haltingly.

There were a few minutes of awkward silence. Vic hovered, offering treats and coffee refills to anyone who appeared to be getting low. Erin didn't know what to do with her hands or how to get the conversation flowing smoothly again. If she bombed the first ladies' tea, there wouldn't be any point in trying it again. She could forget about bringing in any business on a Sunday.

"We're going exploring this afternoon," Vic offered brightly.

"Exploring? Exploring what?" One of the ladies immediately took up the thread.

"Caves. I have a map and I picked out a couple near here that look like they could be interesting. We picked up some gear yesterday and we're going to explore this afternoon!"

"How adventurous," Mary Lou said. She looked off into the distance. "We had some wonderful adventures when the boys were young. There was always somewhere new to explore. Now with the new geocaching, it seems like the young people are staying closer to home, picking out the easy walks instead of delving into the unexplored."

"Geocaching? They even do that in the city," Erin said. "There are a lot of urban caches; I had friends who did that."

"It's a great way to get out and be active," Melissa declared.

"But at the expense of *real* treasure hunting and exercise," Mary Lou pointed out.

"Maybe it's just one step along the way. Maybe if they start with geocaching, they'll get into more challenging stuff later."

Mary Lou sniffed. "I doubt it. People are happier to play games in front of the computer these days."

"What cave you going to?" Gema asked.

Erin looked at Vic, who was the one in charge of their adventure. She didn't know where the caves were that Vic had picked out. But Vic didn't answer.

"It's kind of… a secret," she said.

There were some giggles from the ladies, but they looked at Vic indulgently.

"Well… let me give you some advice." Gema said. "There are a couple of caves about ten miles north of town, near Beaver Creek."

Vic nodded, blinking. "Yeah, I saw those."

"Stay away from them."

Vic looked at Erin, then back at Gema. "They looked like they would be good."

"I've seen that shiftless William Andrews out there, messing around."

"He's just prospecting, isn't he?" Erin asked. "That's what Officer Piper said."

"Terry Piper doesn't know what's going on under his own nose."

"I hear he's a treasure hunter," Melissa said.

"Officer Piper?"

"No, William Andrews. He's searching those caves for Confederate gold."

"He's not looking for ore or for treasure," Gema disagreed, shaking her head at both of them. "He's a drug runner. He's got a stash out there."

Just like Officer Piper had warned Erin about. Despite what Gema thought, Piper did know there were drug runners using the caves. Not the specifics, maybe, but generally speaking.

"How do you know William Andrews is using the caves by Beaver Creek?" Erin asked Gema.

"I told you, I've seen him."

"Did you report it to the police department? I would think that if they knew something that specific, they would arrest him."

Gema laughed. "They have to catch him in the act and he's too canny for that. And those caves are like a labyrinth, you could wander down there for days and not find where he had hidden the drugs. And that's if you knew they were down there. A police investigation won't do much more than look in the mouth of the cave, or maybe a couple of the nearby passages if he's feeling adventurous. Searching every little crack and crevice? Not likely."

Erin didn't like the sound of labyrinthine caves, even if William Andrews wasn't using those caves for his nefarious business. "We'll find another cave to explore," she said to Vic. "Okay?"

Vic didn't look happy about it, but she nodded. "I have another one in mind."

CHAPTER 14

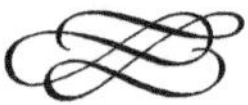

$\mathcal{E}$rin woke up in blackness. Her head was pounding and when she shifted her position, a wave of nausea washed over her. She tried to force her way through the fog in her brain to remember where she was or how she had gotten there. She was lying on her back.

Was it time to get up and start her baking?

She couldn't hear her alarm or see her clock, so she decided it was not.

She wanted to put her hand up to rub her head, but she couldn't seem to control her hand properly so she gave up

She wasn't sure if her eyes were open or closed. Everything hurt. It was quiet and dark, so she went to sleep.

The next time she awoke, she knew she had been lying there for a long time. It had to be time to get up. She tried to turn her head to look at the clock. The pain that ripped through her head like a knife left her gasping with shock and pain.

What had happened?

She was cold down to her bones.

The darkness hadn't lifted at all.

Without moving again, she evaluated her position. She wasn't lying in bed, like she had initially assumed. She was lying on something hard and gravelly. Had she slipped and fallen in the back alley?

Without turning her head, she tried to open her eyes and look around her. But her eyes were already open and she couldn't see a spark of light. No streetlights, no stars, nothing.

She was blind, then.

The pain in her head and the blindness meant that she had fallen and hit her head. She'd hurt herself badly.

Had she left the shop to put out the garbage, and had slipped and fallen?

Erin floated in and out of consciousness, unable to focus on a single thought.

She couldn't have slipped and fallen at the store. If she had, then Vic would have come looking for her.

She could kill you in your sleep.

Piper had warned her more than once.

You don't know anything about her.

Vic was the prime suspect in a murder investigation. There was a reason for that. Rejected by her favorite aunt because of her gender identity, Vic had retaliated. She had plotted to kill her aunt or had been surprised by her while hiding in the basement and somehow been able to trigger an allergic reaction. She had taken away Angela's autoinjector. The tall, strong girl would have easily overpowered her older, unwell aunt, either before or after an allergic reaction.

Erin could hear Vic's words in her head. *It was easy.*

It wasn't Vic. Erin's brain rebelled against the idea. Vic was a gentle, nonviolent person. Whenever she had spoken about Angela, it had been with sadness, not anger. The voice in her head could not be Vic's. It was someone else.

Because she *had* heard those words.

It was easy.

She was becoming more convinced that she had not fallen down outside of the shop. She had been hit. But it didn't feel like she was lying in the parking lot. She lay on a surface that was as hard as rock, but not as flat as the parking lot behind her building. There were loose bits of rock on top of the surface.

But the air was too still. And it was too dark. She had to be inside.

Why would there be rocks inside?

Erin tried to wet her lips, but her mouth was as dry as cotton and she couldn't work up any spit. Her lips were sore and cracked. She tried calling out anyway.

"Hello? Is there anybody there?"

Her voice was weak and odd in her own ears. Why did she sound like that?

The room was large, like a cathedral. Her voice, as quiet as it was, echoed off of the hard walls. Was it possible she was in a church? Paved inside with large flagstones, built out of rock? Why would she be in such a place?

Her face felt like a mask. Like it was made of thin plastic pulled taut. She could feel a pull on her skin whenever she moved her mouth.

There was a warm, foul smell in the still air.

"Hello?" she tried again.

There was no answering voice. All she could hear was her own trembling words and the voice in her head. The one who said it had been easy. Killing Angela had been easy, like squashing a particularly disgusting bug.

Erin tried again to move. Not her head, because that was too painful. Not her hands, since they didn't seem to follow her instructions properly. She stretched out one booted toe to prod first at the air and then at the wall beside her, trying to sense what she could about its shape.

It was rough and irregular. But she could tell little more through her boot.

Why was she wearing boots?

The darkness again became overwhelming. She had to fight back the urge to throw up. There was a dizzying swirl of vertigo and she passed out again.

~

She was in a cave.

That was what came to her the next time she surfaced. It was cold and dark and hard with vaulted ceilings. A cave. Buried somewhere underground.

She couldn't remember how she had gotten there.

Where was Vic? If Erin was there, Vic must also be there, somewhere beside her in the darkness.

"Vic? Vic, are you there?"

Her voice echoed again. But there was no answer. Erin squirmed around, looking for some sign of light. Listening for Vic's breath in the darkness.

Nothing.

How could she be there without Vic?

They had become separated. Had they made different turns down a labyrinthine tunnel? Had Erin fallen over a cliff and Vic had gone back for help?

Vic couldn't have hurt Erin. She was sure of that. The voice still buzzed in her head. *It was easy.* But it wasn't Vic's voice. Erin couldn't be sure whose it was. She had met so many new people since arriving at Bald Eagle Falls. She couldn't recognize all their voices.

"Vic? Victoria? Are you there? Can you hear me?"

Shouting took a lot of effort and Erin was left panting afterward. Was she low on oxygen? Were there heavy gases in the chamber, replacing the oxygen in her lungs with something her body couldn't use? Erin moved her shoulders, feeling for a backpack of equipment. She couldn't remember whether they had agreed to get small oxygen canisters or not. Vic had wanted to be prepared, but Erin had insisted that they'd better not be going anywhere dangerous. They didn't need oxygen if they were sticking close to the surface in well-ventilated caves. Who had won? Had Erin given in and paid for oxygen, just in case?

It didn't matter, because she didn't seem to have any gear. If she'd had a backpack when she entered the cave, she had somehow become separated from it. Lost it going over that cliff, maybe. Or maybe she had put it down while they had a snack and something had happened to distract her from putting it back on again.

Erin blinked her eyes, trying to keep herself awake. But it was impossible. The periods of sleep or unconsciousness were frequent, her periods of consciousness brief. She bit the inside of her cheek. She could barely feel it. She tried to pinch herself, but her hands were not working.

~

When she awoke again, Erin concentrated on her hands. Why were they not working? Had she put them out to catch herself when she fell, breaking her arms? It didn't seem likely. The worst pain in her head was in the back, not the top or the front. Surely if she landed on her hands, she would have broken her nose. But the goose-egg was on the back.

She had movement. Left, right, up, down, in, out. Her fingers seemed to be opening and shutting, though they were numb with cold, so she couldn't be one hundred percent sure.

"Then what's wrong?" Erin demanded out loud, trying to force her brain to process the problem and come up with a solution.

She moved them again. Left, right, up, down, in, out, wiggle.

She tried moving just her right hand, but her left stayed with it. She tried moving just her left, but her right moved in parallel. When she tried to pull them apart, she only got resistance and she couldn't separate them.

Erin closed her eyes. What did that mean? What did it mean if her hands would only move together, never apart?

It took a long time for the answer to make its way to the surface.

Her hands were tied together.

And that couldn't be an accident. She hadn't fallen over a cliff and tied her hands together. Somebody else had tied her hands together. They weren't splinted. It wasn't because she was injured. Someone had tied her up.

Erin tried moving her feet. Similar to her arms, she had a range of motion, but they stuck stubbornly together. Her ankles were also tied together.

Erin swore. It sounded funny, her little voice in all of that empty space, swearing. As if there were someone to hear her or care. Nobody was there. Nobody cared what happened to her.

The only person who cared what happened wanted her to die.

Erin couldn't think of any other reason she would be tied up and left in a dark cave with no equipment. Someone wanted to kill her.

Not a person like William Andrews, who did things with his hands. Someone who didn't want to stab or shoot or throttle her. The kind of person who would rather just stand by and watch her die. Or leave her there without waiting to see how long it took.

The kind of person who had taken Angela's autoinjector and left her there to choke to death in the cool basement of the bakery.

Erin's brain moved creakily. Each thought and deduction was an effort of will, not the effortless flow that she normally experienced.

Not Vic. It hadn't been Vic who had killed Angela. It wasn't Vic's voice she could remember hearing. Someone else.

~

Erin groaned.

Every time she awoke, she had to remember again. She had to force herself to remember where she was and why, and to try to sort out who had done this to her and how she was going to get out of it. And by the time she could get that far, she had started to fade again, her body and her brain in too advanced a state of shock to do anything about it.

She tried to raise her head. It was excruciating.

There was a fine balance between forcing herself to move in order to wake up and pushing herself so hard that she blacked out again. She had to move only a fraction of an inch at a time, then wait for the pain to subside to a more bearable level, and then make another infinitesimal movement.

She swore again, with the pain this time.

She wasn't going to save herself lying on the hard ground trying to make sense of what had happened to her. It didn't matter whether or not she could solve Angela's murder and figure out who had hurt her and left her there to die.

What mattered was moving. Finding some way to get herself out of there. Underground, she was just going to freeze to death. Shock would kill her. Or the swelling of her brain inside her skull. Was that what was making it difficult to breathe?

She had raised her head just enough to know that she still couldn't see anything. And as long as she was lying on her back, she was not going to be able to move. She needed to change her orientation, not just move her head.

Easier said than done.

She felt a little more awake and alert with her head raised. But moving her whole body was going to take a lot of work.

Her hands and her feet were each tied together, but she was not hog-tied. And her hands were tied in front of her body, not behind. That meant

161

it was conceivable that she could crawl, hitching forward on hands and knees, if she could slither onto her belly.

Conceivable, but maybe not possible.

She tried to turn over, but her body didn't follow the instructions from her mind.

Erin stretched her arms out in front of her, then let them drop slowly to the side, trying to use the pull of gravity to help inch her body over. Her shoulder lifted off of the rocky ground, but she needed more.

She'd participated in yoga and workout classes before. How many times had she performed boat pose without worrying about anything but how long she could keep her core tight and hold the pose without shaking? She'd never had to worry that she was going to pass out and let her head go crashing back to the solid rock beneath her. She'd never had to worry that her arms and legs wouldn't both obey her brain's instructions at the same time.

And her legs and arms had never been so heavy.

They didn't feel like her own arms and legs. They felt like they were tied, not just to each other, but to the ground. Pressing one shoulder into the ground, Erin managed to get her conjoined legs up off the ground, and then shifted them to allow them to lower to the ground, turning her body in the process.

She was sweating when she was finally lying on her side instead of on her back. Sweating, clammy, and shivering all at the same time.

Erin tried to control her breathing. She didn't like the raspy noise that was coming out of her. Her head was spinning again with the new orientation and she just wanted to put her head down and rest.

But she was afraid that if she did so, she would pass out again. And maybe she wouldn't wake back up. She needed to move.

Erin held her hands in front of her chest and tried to maneuver one leg around and to twist her body onto her belly. It took a few tries, ages and ages. But she was still awake and finally in a position to move away from the spot she'd been lying in. How long had she been there? Minutes or hours? Or days? There was no way to measure the passage of time.

She had pictured herself crawling on hands and knees. But the reality wasn't so pretty or well-coordinated. She was more like an inchworm or like a baby commando crawling. Unsteadily. She couldn't move her arms and legs in tandem. She couldn't get right up on her knees and elbows. She could just inch and squirm forward, listening to her breath rasp in the pitch blackness.

Erin had never seen such darkness before. It wasn't just the lack of moon or stars or any visible shapes around her. It was as if the world had ceased to exist at all. There were no shades of light or dark. It was as if her vision had been completely taken away from her. And with a head injury, that wasn't beyond the realm of possibility. Perhaps something in her eyes or brain had been damaged beyond repair.

She didn't know whether she could call it progress. She stayed against the wall, using it as a guide to keep her going in a straight line. She kept bumping into it with her body or shoulder, trying as hard as she could to keep from banging her head into it. If she banged her head, she wasn't sure she would ever wake up again.

It wasn't Vic. It wasn't Vic. The mantra kept running through her head as she wriggled and inched along.

Then where was Vic? Was she lying there somewhere in the darkness too? Erin couldn't hear Vic breathing. Did that mean she was dead, or in another cave? Or had she become separated from Erin and was looking for her? Or had she gone back to get help?

What if Vic were more badly hurt than Erin was and needed her help?

She had to keep pushing herself. No matter how exhausting it was and how impossible it seemed. She didn't know whether she had one hundred feet or several miles to crawl before she got out of the cave. She didn't know in what direction safety lay, but she put that out of her mind and just kept moving. If she stopped, she wouldn't get anywhere.

Then suddenly, there was nothing in front of her.

CHAPTER 15

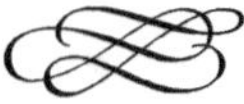

*E*rin's arms dangled in empty air and she took all of her weight suddenly on her chest and stomach, nearly knocking the wind out of her. She froze.

She swore.

She only had to move backward a bit. Readjust her direction and crawl along the edge of the precipice until she reached another wall. Or another precipice. Eventually, she would find solid ground that led away from the cliff edge.

For a few minutes, she lowered her head and tried to fight off the tears and fatigue.

She didn't have the time to feel sorry for herself. She didn't know how long it would be before her body succumbed to the shock or the concussion. She might have only minutes before her time was up. And Vic might need her.

It might be too late for both of them, but Erin had to believe that there was still some chance of survival. She couldn't just give up and let her life trickle away into nothingness. She hadn't had an easy life, but she wasn't ready for it to end. Not when she had just started up a new business. And made new friends.

And she had a cat.

What would happen to Orange Blossom if she never returned home?

There was no shelter, just the vet, who would give the cat a few days and then put him to sleep. Erin couldn't let that happen.

She crawled along the edge of the cliff, terrified she was going to overbalance and roll over it. She kept her body as flat to the ground as she could.

"Vic?" Would her voice carry all the way down to the bottom, if Vic had fallen or slid over that edge? How far down was it? A few feet or hundreds? "Vic, are you there?"

There was still no answer. Her voice sounded lost in the darkness, reaching far out before it was stopped by the walls of the cavern.

"Why did we have to go caving?" Erin muttered, as she squirmed along. "Spelunking, then. *It'll be fun, Erin.*" She affected a falsetto. "*It'll be an adventure.* Adventure, my foot! I could live without an adventure like this!"

She stopped for a moment to get her breath back. She could barely move an inch at a time and her breath was as labored as if she'd been sprinting. Another inch or two and she had reached another wall. Erin turned, following the wall, leaving the precipice behind her.

Erin muttered to herself, "Remind me never to go in another cave again."

She realized she had passed out again. How long this time? With no way to tell the time, she felt like it had been days. When had she last eaten? Her lips were cracked and her tongue swollen.

And when had she actually slept, rather than just passing out where she lay? She was worried she didn't have much time left.

It was so easy.

Erin heard the words as clear as a bell. Like the woman was still right there beside her.

You thought you were so clever, with all your ideas and questions. You could outsmart the police department and the killer. You could figure it all out on your own. No one would even know you were investigating it, with your innocuous little questions. Just getting to know people in Bald Eagle Falls. Just making friends and getting to know people.

And Erin couldn't really deny it was true. She had thought that if she just gave it a little time and engaged people, she could eventually sort out who it was that had killed Angela.

She had been naive. She obviously watched too many TV sleuths or read too many mystery books. It was always so easy in the fictional world. But she'd gotten too close to exposing the killer without even realizing what it was she knew. That never happened to Miss Marple.

Erin wiggled along. Her brain felt like it was sloshing around inside her head like a seasick turtle. Every movement brought pain. She thought she would get used to it, or it would subside once she got moving, but she was wrong. She hadn't thought it could feel any worse, but it could.

Seeing us together and then letting me know you intended to blackmail me. All the while pretending to be the sweet little baker. You know I actually felt bad when Terry Piper suspected you? I never thought he would pin it on you. And if you'd just left well enough alone, the case would have gone cold. He never would have had enough to arrest you. It wasn't like he wanted to.

The knot on the back of her head gave one particularly sharp, all-consuming throb and Erin's stomach erupted. She didn't know when she had last eaten, but apparently that didn't matter. The retching made the pain worse and the pain made the retching worse. She stayed there, frozen, trying to keep her body turned in such as way that she wouldn't drench herself with the vomit or end up having to squirm through the puddle. The acid sharp smell of bile filled her nose and she didn't suppose she'd managed to avoid getting it all down her shirt. She was already soaking wet with cold sweat from the effort of crawling along the floor.

She wanted nothing so much as to just lie down and rest.

But after the retching stopped, she forced herself to continue onward. She wouldn't get anywhere if she didn't move.

Blackmail? She hadn't threatened to blackmail anyone. Angela was the one who had been the blackmailer. She was the one who had hoarded all their secrets.

Had Mary Lou been lying when she said she had no secrets? Everybody had something to hide. Was she really the exception?

She had good reason to hate Angela, whether she had any secrets or not.

Gema? She seemed open and friendly, but appearances could be deceiving. If everyone had secrets, that meant that Gema did too. She hadn't invested with Angela, hadn't lost everything she ever had. But that didn't mean that she didn't have anything to hide.

Or was it Melissa? Had Melissa the gossip accidentally said something to

Angela that she shouldn't? Or had her involvement with Trenton been less innocent than she had let on? Maybe she had been involved in Trenton's disappearance. Or maybe she knew something about it, something that Angela had done. Had she confronted Angela? Had she just been unable to hold back her hate for the family another minute?

Why had any of them waited? They had all known Angela for years. And yet, something had changed recently. Something had triggered Angela's murder.

Erin breathed hard, swallowed, and breathed some more. It felt like she had been crawling for hours. The darkness obscured any landmarks and she could not see how far she had gone. A few feet? Had she made headway down a long corridor, or was she still only inches from where she had started, traveling in a U shape when she hit the precipice and ended up turning back the way she had come?

What was it about blackmail? Her attacker had said that Erin had tried to blackmail her. What had Erin discovered that was a secret from the rest of the town? How could she blackmail anyone? All that she knew she had been told by other townspeople.

Erin's mind was circling feverishly. She wasn't able to stay focused on the killer's words and sort them out. Instead, her mind went back to opening day. She tried to count each of the patrons who had come through the store to keep herself alert. The Fosters. The older couple who had taken so long to make their choice. The church ladies. Angela. There had been businessmen and other women from the town. Not Officer Piper, he hadn't come until later.

She should have listened to him and just let him investigate. She had been stupid to try to draw the killer out, asking questions about keys and blathering on about hidden treasure. Who would ever believe such a story?

Melissa had. The poor woman seemed to believe every story she was told hook, line, and sinker. Ghosts, Confederate treasure, everything. Or had it been Mary Lou? Pretending to be skeptical, but checking just to be sure.

"Just a little further," Erin said aloud. She didn't know how far it was. But she could feel how she was lagging. How her body was gradually shutting down, one muscle fiber at a time, until she would no longer be able to push and pull her body forward.

She had to believe that she had some chance of getting out.

Time stretched on. It seemed as if Erin had been crawling all night. Crawling for days, even. In spite of the numbness in her fingers and toes, she could still feel all of the exposed skin being scraped away. And her head continued to roil and throb with every movement. Still, she pushed on.

There was a noise far off in the distance.

At first, she thought it was just her brain. The murderer talking to her again in her brain.

Erin. Erin poking her nose into everything. Can't leave well enough alone. Erin. Erin.

But then Erin realized it wasn't the killer's voice. Someone *was* calling her name.

It was so faint that she could only hear it clearly when she held her breath. They were so far away, she knew they wouldn't be able to hear her weak voice if she tried to answer. Best to conserve what little voice she had left for when they got closer. And in the meantime, to try to get closer.

It was a male voice. Or several voices. She couldn't tell whether the overlapping words were separate voices or echoes.

But someone was there looking for her.

Someone would find her and help her, if she could just get close enough for him to find her.

She was so eager to reach the voices that she forgot to take care, and smashed her face into an outcropping rock.

Erin let out a yelp of pain and sucked in her breath over her teeth, trying to breathe through it and keep the pain under control.

Once steadied, she tried to feel in front of her with her hands. There as a wall in front of her. Not just a single outcropping. Erin searched for a hole, for a break, but there was none. How had she gotten into the cave if it was blocked on every side? Erin turned, following the wall around. She was crawling away from the voices, but was determined to get turned around again as soon as she could. The caves were a maze. But if she could just keep following the wall, keep it to her right, that was the way to get out of a labyrinth, wasn't it?

A fraction of an inch at a time. She didn't know how long it would take to get around the wall and facing the right direction again. Or maybe she never would. Maybe they'd just keep missing each other in the dark, moving along parallel tunnels, never meeting up.

"Hello?" Erin tried to call out. "Vic?"

It wasn't Vic looking for her. She knew that. But she was still missing the girl, hoping that she was okay, not lying dead in the darkness somewhere close by.

"Erin?"

The voices were still too far away. They couldn't hear her.

Erin's body shuddered. She was getting too weak. Too cold and weak to continue. Her traitorous body was getting ready to shut down.

"No. No, no, no. Keep going. Keep moving."

Then she spotted the twinkle of a light. At first, she thought it was just an image from her brain. Maybe that light that people claimed to see when they had near-death experiences. The scientists she had read about said they were just images thrown up by the oxygen-starved brain. They weren't really anything. Just hallucinations.

But she stayed focused on it and kept squirming toward it. She didn't care if it was a hallucination or not, it was a goal. And she sorely needed a goal to work toward.

"You see?" she told herself aloud. "Hang in there just a bit longer. I can get us out of here."

The light was getting bigger and brighter. Not very quickly, but it was definitely a light and not just a hallucination. It was more than just a twinkle or a flash.

Then it was gone. It just winked out and disappeared.

"No!" Erin shouted. "No, don't go!"

The words were so forceful they ripped her dry, raw throat. She heard them echo off of the hard stone walls. It didn't sound like her voice, but it was louder than any sound she had been able to make up until then.

A few more seconds passed in blackness and then the light reappeared.

"Yes," Erin whispered.

"Erin?" The searcher's voice was stronger now too, getting closer. "Erin, are you there? I'm coming."

"Yes."

Her brain was telling her that it was okay to stop and rest. Help was on the way and she could just wait for it. But she was afraid that if she stopped, her shocked body was going to shut down completely. It would be too late for them to do anything for her.

"You can't stop now," she said sternly. "You have to keep going. Keep pushing."

And she did. Each excruciating, infinitesimal inch at a time. Her hands and face and knees raw. Her head nauseated, alternating throbbing with a sharp, stabbing pain.

Something was approaching her in the darkness. The light hadn't yet reached her, it was still somewhere in the distance. A mile away? Closer? Farther? It was impossible to tell. But there was definitely something moving toward her, low to the ground, not a human footstep but some kind of animal.

"No! Get out of here!" Erin whispered sharply. She was too weak to defend herself from a predator. And so close to being found and rescued…! She puckered her lips and whistled, as high and loud as she could, trying to scare the creature away. Rat or coyote or whatever it was, surely it wouldn't like the unexpected noise. It would know that she wasn't yet weak enough to be taken.

"Erin?" came the distant call from the bobbing light.

The creature came at her then. But it wasn't growling or snarling. And when it approached, it didn't bite her. There was no attack.

It let out a bark.

Erin's brain scrambled to sort out the new information. A bark? A dog? It wasn't trying to avoid her rescuer, but to call him.

"K9?"

He nosed at her. He gave a little whine, snuffling and investigating. She couldn't take a full-on doggie greeting and was thankful he didn't jump on her or try to join in with this new, unfamiliar game. Instead, he lay down beside her, settling his long, warm body beside her torso. He barked again, a single time, encouraging the searcher to hurry up.

Erin stopped trying to crawl. She relaxed her body, melting into K9, trying to soak up his body's warmth.

The light was close enough that she could detect the dip of each individual step. Erin was breathing heavily through her mouth.

"Erin!" The man's pace redoubled. He must have been able to make something out in the darkness. Erin still couldn't see him, hidden in the darkness behind the light.

Then he was right there in front of her, the light shining full in Erin's face. Her eyes streamed and she couldn't open them.

Piper was swearing, the light moving around as he examined her without touching her. He clicked a walkie-talkie.

"She's here. We're going to need the stretcher."

There was a staticky, garbled response. The man was leaning over her.

"Erin, can you hear me?"

She avoided nodding. Moving her head would just make the pain and nausea worse.

"Yes," she whispered.

He swore again. "You're a mess. What can I do?"

Erin rasped for breath. "Air?"

"Yes. Yes, I have oxygen." He went to work. There was a thud and a clank as he put down his gear. Zippers buzzing and equipment being shifted around. "Can I turn you onto your back?"

"Okay... might pass out... hit on the head."

He bent close to examine her head and swore.

"I see it. I'll put a pad over it and try to cushion it."

He worked to secure a bandage over the bump without much success.

"That's not going to work," he said finally. He put a mask over her mouth and carefully worked the elastic around behind her head, doing his best to avoid the worst of the damage. He put something on the stone floor beneath her. Not a blanket. Maybe a balled-up rain poncho. "You can rest on that."

Erin lowered her head a hair's breadth at a time until her cheek was resting on the squeaky vinyl pillow. Piper checked the oxygen mask and opened the release valve on the small oxygen tank.

"That should help."

Erin tried to relax. She was safe now. Piper would get her out of the cave. They would tend to all her injuries. They would warm her up again.

Piper pulled out an emergency blanket, unfolded it, and laid it over her. His fingers found her wrist and stayed there for a minute, monitoring her pulse.

"Vic?" Erin asked. "Where's Vic?"

"What?"

Her voice was muffled by the oxygen mask. Erin tried to make her words as clear as possible. "Where... is... Vic?"

"Vic is fine."

"She's okay?"

"Yes. She came to get help. She did the right thing."

Erin sighed in relief. She waited for unconsciousness to take her away, but it didn't. She lay still there, listening to her own breathing. She was thankful for the heat of K9's body. He still lay against her, warming her up directly and heating the air trapped under the reflective blanket.

"Who was it?" Erin asked.

The light turned toward her. "You don't know?"

"I don't remember… I heard her voice…"

"Well, best if I don't tell you anything yet. I don't want to taint your testimony."

Erin thought about that. He was probably right.

She felt like she was floating up above them. The pain in her head wasn't going away. If anything, it was getting worse. She hoped that she could last until they got a stretcher in there and got her out. Was it far? It seemed like a long time since Piper had radioed that he wanted a stretcher.

He would feel so bad if he couldn't even get Erin out of the cave alive. She really didn't want to do that to him.

～

"Erin." There was a little nudge on her arm. "Erin, are you okay?"

Erin tried to rouse herself.

"Wha…?"

"Maybe you should keep talking to me. You have a head injury, I don't think I should let you go to sleep."

"Not sleeping."

"You're drifting."

"Uh-huh."

"Why don't you try to tell me what you remember? Do you remember how you got here?"

"No…"

He nudged her again. Erin was able to blink now and squint at him when his light wasn't shining right in her face. It was nice to be able to see again. She hadn't been blind after all. Just in total darkness.

"You're drifting again. Can you keep your eyes open?"

"Keep the light away."

"Oh. Sorry." He readjusted the headlamp so that it was pointing up instead of down at Erin. "There. How's that?"

"Better."

"What's the last thing you remember?"

Erin took a few deep breaths of the oxygen, hoping it would clear her muddled brain.

"Remember the tea."

"What tea?"

"At the bakery. After church."

"You went to church?" His tone was one of surprise.

"No. The ladies. The church ladies came… for tea. To Auntie Clem's."

"After *they* went to church."

"Yes."

"I didn't think you were a churchgoer."

"No." She wondered briefly what she had said or done that had clued him in to the fact. Or maybe he had just heard gossip around town. It did seem to be a little scandalous, the type of thing people loved to share around. In a Bible-belt town like Bald Eagle Falls, someone openly admitting to being an atheist was shocking.

"I'll let you in on a little secret." He leaned forward. His voice was low and confidential. She couldn't see more than the shadows of his face and had to picture the dimple in his cheek.

"What?"

"I'm not either."

"A Christian?"

"Well… I was raised Christian… so I guess I still am. But I don't go to church."

"Why not?"

"I say it's because of my work schedule. People are very understanding; they know emergency services still have to protect the public on Sundays."

"But…?"

"But… that's not why."

She waited for him to say more, but he didn't explain further.

"So, you had the church ladies over to the bakery for tea after their services? Clementine used to do that, didn't she?"

"Yes."

"I'll bet they all enjoyed that. Everything went off well? Without a hitch?"

"Yes." Erin's voice was tired and far away.

"Nothing that seemed… out of place? Or that indicated you were in any danger?"

"No. Nothing like that."

"You didn't feel threatened?"

"No."

There was a dragging noise, starting in the distance but getting gradually closer. Erin saw another light, twinkling off in the distance. Piper sighed.

"That will be the stretcher. Then we can get you out of this hole and to the hospital for proper care."

"Yeah. Good."

They were silent for a while, both watching and listening to the man approaching with the stretcher. It wasn't a wheeled gurney, which wouldn't have been able to roll over the uneven floor, but a stretcher that had to be carried between two people and was currently being dragged behind one.

Piper turned to look at the newcomer and the man's face was lit up by Piper's headlamp.

"Oh. It's *you*."

William Andrews looked down at Erin. His face, blackened as always, seemed both amused and concerned.

"We haven't exactly been introduced. My name is Willie. William Andrews."

"Hi," Erin greeted faintly. She looked at Piper, concerned. Hadn't he heard the rumors of William Andrews's supposed drug-running? What was he doing there?

Was Erin in one of his caves? One of the caves that Gema had said to stay away from? Had they gone straight to the caves that Gema had advised them to avoid?

"Mr. Andrews is something of an expert on the caves in the area," Piper said. "When I needed a guide to help me find you, I knew he was the one person I could trust."

Unless William Andrews had been somehow involved in Angela's murder. Or Erin's attack. Or drug-running and stashing drugs in remote caves where they could be hidden from prying eyes. Erin's heart sped and her breaths started to come in gasps again.

Piper put a hand on Erin's shoulder. It was very warm and had a much stronger calming effect than she would have expected. "Trust me," he said softly. And Erin did.

William Andrews put the stretcher down and he and Piper moved in concert to lay it down next to Erin. Once it was in place, Piper shooed K9 out of the way.

"Sorry, boy, can't carry you too!"

K9 obediently moved off to the side and waited.

"Do you think you have any back or neck injuries?" Piper asked. "Obviously, you have a head injury, and that could mean a neck injury as well. Do you have any numbness or tingling? Pain in your back?"

"Numb from the cold," Erin said.

William Andrews shone his headlamp along the floor of the passage, following Erin's trail. "She's already been moving around. I think we're fine lifting her onto the stretcher. It's less than she's done by herself already."

He walked a few feet along the passageway, then returned to Erin and Piper.

"We need to move her to get her out of here. We don't have a back board or collar. We can't wait for them to deploy a rescue team from Chattanooga; she's already in shock."

Piper nodded his agreement.

"I concur. Erin, do you want us to move you? Or call for help?"

"You do it."

"Okay. I want you to try to stay completely still. We'll do this as gently as we can, but it may still hurt."

"I know."

The two men got into position. Erin took a couple of deep breaths to try to calm and relax herself and prepare for the jolt she was going to get.

When she awoke, it took some time to swim through the fog of her brain and sort out the sensations. She was still face-down and still tied up. She was moving, rolling up and down or back and forth, she wasn't sure of the axis. Just the movement, like a ship rolling over waves on the ocean. It made her seasick, the nausea building up inside her.

She choked, trying not to vomit, but she knew she wouldn't be able to hold it back. The movement stopped and she was set down on a hard surface. Someone was holding her head, turning it to the side as she threw up again, foul, acidic bile burning her throat and nose.

Erin was pretty sure she had baptized her assistant. She realized she was no longer wearing the oxygen mask. Maybe it wasn't the first time she had thrown up. Or maybe it had been too awkward to keep the mask on her while she was on the stretcher.

"Okay?" he questioned.

In the light that moved around her, Erin saw that it was Piper. Officer Piper had rescued her. Was rescuing her. Soon they would be out of the darkness, able to see the light of day once more.

"Yeah. Thanks."

"You done?"

"Seasick."

He chuckled. "Sorry about that. We'll do our best to make it a smooth ride."

They again lifted the stretcher and resumed their walk down the twisting paths of the caves. Erin tried to focus her eyes on something to combat the nausea, but they were still surrounded by darkness. The light from the men's helmets was enough to illuminate the space for a few feet, but the little bubble of light didn't extend very far.

She tried to focus instead on her attacker. Did Piper already know who it was, or was he expecting her to supply the details? If Vic had gone to get help, then she must have been able to tell him something. They would have been at the cave together to explore. Vic had seen Erin attacked and had gone for help.

It was a woman's voice. Not William Andrews's. But she wasn't sure which of the women it belonged to.

Seeing us together and then letting me know you intended to blackmail me.

Who had she seen together? She had certainly never told anyone that she was going to blackmail them. The woman had killed Angela for threatening to reveal her secret. And she thought Erin knew and was doing the same thing. She was paranoid about having her secret revealed. That was what had driven her to action both times.

Mary Lou? She claimed to have no secrets. But everybody had secrets.

Melissa? Did she know where Trenton was? Did she know what had happened to him, or had she been involved? But that didn't fit the puzzle.

Seeing us together.

The clue was in those three words. Who had she seen together?

"Gema," Erin croaked.

The men heard her and again set down the stretcher so that Piper could talk to Erin face-to-face.

"What was that?" he asked.

"Gema. Was it Gema Reed?"

"What did you remember?" he asked, giving nothing away.

"I'm not sure… it could have been her voice… she said, 'you saw us together.'"

"Who did you see together? What was she talking about?"

"I saw her at the camping store… she said… it was her cousin."

"Her cousin?"

"She was talking to a woman…"

Piper shook his head. "So?"

"I don't know… she said it was her cousin."

"Why wouldn't it be?"

Erin tried to sort it out. She pictured their faces, thought about their expressions and body language as they had been talking together. As cousins, it made sense that they were close. That they were friendly.

If Gema had been upset by Erin seeing them together, though, then maybe she had something to hide and they weren't just cousins.

Erin licked her chapped lips. Both her tongue and her lips were like sandpaper. So dry, they just rasped against each other.

"Do you have water?"

"I do," William Andrews offered, standing close by. He put down his backpack and pulled out a water bottle.

"How long was it?" Erin whispered to Piper.

"How long… were you in here?"

"Yes."

"It's been…" he held his watch close to his eyes and twisted his wrist back and forth, trying to catch the light of his headlamp. "Just over twenty-four hours."

William Andrews crouched beside her, holding the water bottle sideways for Erin to drink from. She ended up with water down her face, trying to drink at such an odd angle, but she was glad to moisten her lips and mouth.

"Thank you."

He nodded. "Let's keep going," he told Piper. "The longer we stop to talk, the worse her condition is going to get."

Erin was impressed with the way William Andrews took over. In town, she had taken him to be an untrained laborer, someone who was only able to get odd jobs because he couldn't hold down anything permanent. But it was obvious from Piper's deference to him on matters caving and medical that there was more to William Andrews than there appeared.

They hoisted her up without any further discussion. Erin still wanted to talk to Officer Piper, to try to sort out the random bits of knowledge knocking around her brain. Somehow, she knew Gema's secret. Gema thought she was a threat.

Was it because of the woman at the store? Or something else?

They seemed to be on an uphill slope. Erin wished they had untied her wrists so that she could hold on to the edges of the stretcher, as she felt her body shifting down toward the end. There was light now, more than just what was coming from the two men's headlamps. Erin lay still and tried to see where it was coming from. It kept brightening the farther they went up. And then Erin was blinking, her eyes streaming, as they broke out of the cave into the light.

There were people there. She wasn't sure who, because the sun cut into her brain like a knife and forced her to squeeze her eyes shut in an effort to block it out. She was afraid she was going to throw up again and called for Piper to help her. They put down the stretcher, but the man who ministered to her was not Officer Piper. He was a doctor or paramedic, barking out orders like an army general.

Erin cowered there, overwhelmed by the noise and the light and the pain. They put a collar around her neck to hold it still and wrapped a bandage around and around her head before laying her down on a backboard. Once she was face-up, they finally cut away the ties that bound her arms and legs.

"I still don't want you to move," the doctor told her gruffly. "I'm going to immobilize your arms and legs. Don't be afraid, it's just to protect your spine until we know the extent of your injuries."

Erin didn't say anything as he proceeded to do so. Tears were streaming from her eyes. While mostly they were from the sun, Erin was also at the end of her rope. Far past the end of her rope, in fact.

"Where's Vic?" she asked, before they loaded her into the ambulance. "Is she okay?"

"I'm here!" It sounded like Vic was calling from far away. "I'm right here, Erin. I'm fine."

"Is she hurt? Vic? Are you hurt?"

"No. I'm okay. Not hurt."

"Good. Did you remember to feed Orange Blossom?"

Vic laughed. "The cat is taken care of, don't you worry! But he cried all night looking for you and kept the neighbors up!"

They slid her into the ambulance, away from the bright sunlight. Away from the crowds of people. "Terry? Is Officer Piper there…?"

"He can meet us at the hospital. Just rest, now."

Despite the layers of bandages wrapped around her head, every bump and bounce of the ambulance caused excruciating pain and made it feel like her brain was bouncing around the inside of her skull. She closed her eyes and tried to do as the doctor told her and rest.

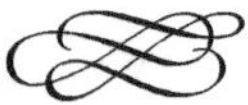

With Vic beside her, holding her hand, Erin was finally able to relax and believe that her young assistant was safe and well. For so many hours, she had been sure that Vic was lying in the cave somewhere, dead or dying. No matter how many times they told her Vic was okay, she couldn't really believe it until she could see and touch Vic for herself.

"How much do you remember?" Officer Terry Piper inquired, sitting in the other visitor chair observing the two of them.

"Most of it, I think," Erin said. "Some of it is still kind of foggy, but hopefully Vic can fill in those parts."

She glanced at Vic. The pretty blonde nodded.

The painkillers in Erin's IV kept her reasonably comfortable and she didn't have to move around anymore. They had operated, removing a piece of her skull to ease the pressure the swelling had caused, and cleaning up the wound and the fracture Gema had caused.

It was Gema. Erin could remember that much now.

"How did she know where we were going?" Erin asked Vic. "You didn't tell her which cave we were going to, did you?"

"No." Vic shook her head. "She must have guessed. She just told me not to go to the Beaver Creek caves. So that convinced me to go to the old mine."

"She knew we'd go one of those two places?"

"She knew we were beginners, but we didn't want a big commercial outfit. So… that only left a couple of choices nearby. I guess it was a good bet."

"I suppose if we'd gone somewhere else, she would have waited for another opportunity." Erin looked over at Officer Piper. "Seems like she was pretty good at waiting for the right opportunity."

He nodded. "So it would seem." He was being very careful not to tell her any of what he knew, which Erin found annoying. She knew it was the right thing for him to do. He couldn't plant information in her brain. But it was still annoying. She wanted to talk to him about what he knew, not drag the story out of her brain one thread at a time.

"So, we got there, got all our gear out and ready. And then… Vic had to… uh… do something."

"Do what?" Piper asked suspiciously.

"I had to pee!" Vic laughed. "So… I went into the trees to find a private spot…"

"It's not like you had to go far," Erin said. "I could have just turned my back."

Vic shrugged. "I'm shy. I had to be where I knew no one could see me."

"And that's when Gema showed up," Erin explained. "I don't know where she parked her car; I didn't see it. She just came… out of nowhere. She hit me with something before I even saw her."

"I think a shovel," Vic told her.

Erin reached up and touched her bandaged head. "A shovel," she echoed.

"Ouch."

"Yeah. She hit me and I just went over like a log. After that, I'm not sure of much. She tied my hands and feet, I guess, and dragged me into the cave."

"So that when I came back from the woods, Erin was nowhere to be seen," Vic contributed. "I thought maybe she decided to use the facilities before going down as well, so I waited." She looked at Erin. "But you never came back."

"You must have been scared," Erin empathized.

"Me? You must have been terrified! That woman dragging you down to the bowels of the earth! You didn't even want to go exploring to begin with.

I had to talk you into it. Being down there with your skull caved in and a homicidal woman railing away at you…!"

"It was scary," Erin admitted. "It was so dark. She had a light, but I could barely see anything. She didn't even let me walk, she just dragged me from one place to another. She must be really strong!"

"She used to do lots of exploring and climbing," Piper agreed. "She's quite athletic."

Erin looked back at Vic again. "Do you remember seeing Gema at the camping store?"

"Yes, of course."

"What do you remember about it?"

Vic thought back. "She helped me to pick out a compass. I don't know what else. She told us about Angela and how she had messed things up so badly for Mary Lou, when Mary Lou invested with her."

"Do you remember anything else?"

"Nnno…?"

Erin didn't say anything right away. Vic shook her head, looking bewildered. "What else? What am I missing?"

"She was talking to someone."

"Before she talked to us?" Vic shrugged. "One of the sales clerks."

"Yes."

"What about it?"

"Gema didn't look like she was there looking for something or getting help. She was having a friendly chat with her, not asking for advice."

"Right." Vic nodded her agreement. "And she said something. That she was just checking up on her cousin, or something like that."

"Yes. But when she was talking to me, when she took me down to that cave to leave me there… she said, 'you saw us.' Because I saw the two of them together."

"So, what? Why wouldn't she be talking to her cousin? Who cares if someone saw them together?"

"But she did care. So, it wasn't her cousin. It was somebody she didn't want to be seen with."

"Why not?"

"She'd already been blackmailed by Angela. She'd killed Angela to stop her from revealing Gema's secret. And when I said something, she thought it was starting all over again."

Vic looked puzzled. She shook her head slowly, not believing it.

"What did you say to her?" Officer Piper asked.

"I made a comment about her being there to see someone." Erin looked over at Vic, reminding her. "They'd been having a very close conversation and they hugged goodbye. Gema didn't see us until afterward; she didn't know she'd been seen until then. And then I brought up how Angela knew everyone's secrets and used those secrets to get her own way…"

Piper chuckled. Vic was a little slower to understand; then her face got a little pink.

"She thought you were telling her that you knew her secret now so you were going to blackmail her?"

"Yes. She thought I was just being subtle, in front of you. But I wasn't being subtle… I was completely clueless that I'd just seen her…"

"*You think they were lovers?*"

Erin shook her head. "Good guess, but I don't think so. I didn't think anything of it when she said the girl was her cousin, because they had similar features. So, I'm thinking she wasn't a cousin, but maybe… her daughter."

"But I thought Gema only had boys. Isn't that what she said?"

"That's what she said. *She and Fred* only had boys. She must have had the girl out of wedlock."

"And she went to church with those other Christian women. If they knew she'd had another child…"

"She was willing to kill to keep that secret from them."

"Oh, wow."

"Did she say anything to you about Mrs. Plaint's murder?" Piper inquired.

Erin sighed. She put her fingers over her ears for a minute, as if she could block out the words that kept replaying in her mind.

"She said it was so easy. That's what she kept saying. Angela's allergy made it a piece of cake." Erin laughed humorlessly at her turn of phrase. "Gema went down to the basement. She knew Angela would go down there because… she liked to snoop into other people's business. She'd go down there to have a look around. She'd go up to the kitchen, if the door was left unlocked, have a snoop around there too. But Angela never got that far. Because Gema was waiting for her."

"How would she poison Mrs. Plaint?" Piper asked. "How would she convince Mrs. Plaint to eat something that had been contaminated? I'd be pretty suspicious of someone who laid in wait for me and then offered me food. Especially if I was deathly allergic to something like wheat."

"She didn't convince Angela to eat anything." Erin swallowed her disgust. It was difficult to describe what Gema had told her. Gema had thought that Erin would die in that passageway. She was injured, already drifting in an out of consciousness, bound hand and foot. It wouldn't take her long to die in the cold, rarefied air of the deeper caves. No one would find Erin. She would die of exposure, if not from the head injury. "She was so proud of herself. She just put a little flour in her hand. And when Angela got close, blew it in her face. Angela gasped and breathed it in, straight into her lungs."

"And that is as effective as eating it?" Piper asked.

"Probably more so. She took Angela's purse when she started to react, saying that she would use an autoinjector to save her... and then just stole the autoinjectors. Wiped Angela's face so that she didn't have flour all over it. And walked back out. Left her there to die."

"What a horrible thing to do!" Vic said, outraged.

Erin nodded her head the tiniest bit. "I agree."

Officer Piper was writing notes in his notepad and didn't look up at them for a couple of minutes. Then he became aware of their attention and raised his brows.

"Now will you tell us what happened with Gema?" Erin asked. "Did you arrest her? Did she confess?"

Piper shifted to get more comfortable in his seat, giving Erin a little smile that showed the dimple in his cheek. "Vic was pretty quick about getting help, once she took a closer look around and saw the bloody shovel on the ground. She drove out to the highway and called me as soon as she could get a signal. I scrambled whatever help I could get from Bald Eagle Falls and the city and got out there. Gema was still in the caves when we got there. I arrested her in connection with your assault and kidnapping when she came out... but she wouldn't talk, wouldn't say where you were. Said that we were just mistaken; she was out there to explore just like any other day. If something had happened to you, she had no idea what it was. And the cave system is pretty complex... you can have several parties down there and never run into each other. We couldn't prove what she had done unless we could find you, get you out safely, and get your story."

"But now you can. Because I'm telling you she's the one who hit me and put me down there."

He nodded. "We'll proceed with formal charges. For that and Mrs. Plaint's murder."

"Thank goodness," Vic breathed.

"Thank you," Erin told them. "Without both of you, I don't think I would ever have gotten out of there alive."

"If it wasn't for me, you wouldn't have been there in the first place," Vic said miserably.

"Don't talk like that. If it hadn't been there, it would have been somewhere else. Maybe somewhere that she had to make sure I was dead right off, instead of just leaving me to die, which seems to be her first preference."

"She's got a point," Piper agreed. "As far as my part in this... I credit Willie and K9." The dog raised his head to look at his master, then put it back down when he decided he wasn't being addressed. "Willie knows those caves better than anyone and it was K9's nose that led us to you."

"I was so glad to see him," Erin said. "Or hear him." She was feeling drowsy again. Pleasantly tired though, rather than the crushing fatigue that had made her feel like she was never going to wake up again if she let herself succumb. She closed her eyes. "I thought he was a coyote."

"Well, be glad he wasn't. A coyote would have made short work of you in that condition."

"I am glad."

"I heard you," Piper said. "Just that one time. I took a turn down the wrong passage and I heard you call out."

"Your light disappeared. I was scared."

"Without you shouting, I don't know if we would have found you in time. So you saved yourself too."

"Hmm."

"I prayed that they would find you," Vic confessed.

Erin opened her eyes and looked at her employee. Vic ducked her head and swept her hair back over one shoulder, getting red.

"Well, I did," she said. "I know you don't believe in God, so I'm sorry, I know I probably shouldn't have, but... it was the only thing I could do."

"You can pray about whatever you like," Erin said. "Even if it's me. I would never dream of interfering."

"Okay." Vic scratched her jaw, still looking embarrassed, but giving Erin a smile. "Thanks."

"I thought you and God weren't on good terms, though."

"Well... that doesn't stop him from answering when I call. And I've decided... to give him the benefit of the doubt. Maybe just because people say that he hates me because of something they say is a sin... maybe he doesn't."

Erin shrugged. "You're okay in my book."

"Thanks." Vic looked down again. "I'm going to go look for coffee. Anyone else want one?"

"Sure," Piper agreed. "I could really use something."

Vic looked pleased. She left the room, giving Erin a wink.

After she was gone, Erin looked at Piper. "I guess you must be pretty tired too. You must have been searching for me for hours."

He nodded. "I'll get some sleep before long." He gazed at the door, checking to be sure Vic was gone. "So, your young friend... she seems to be coming to terms with her... transition?"

Erin's jaw dropped. "How long have you known about that?"

"It *is* my job to investigate a suspect's background."

"But you never said... she was so worried about you finding out."

"She obviously didn't want me to know, so I didn't feel the need to mention it. Once I figured out her identity, I knew why her aunt had turned her away. I wasn't sure if you knew..."

"No, not to start with. It took a few days."

They both just looked at each other for a minute.

"Well, she had the luck to find the two people in town who could keep a secret," Piper said. He straightened up and squared his shoulders. "She has to understand, though... she won't be able to keep her past a secret forever. Not here. It's easier for you, because you're from further away. But Vic's from just a couple of towns away. It won't be long before people start to figure it out."

"I know." Erin's eyes were drooping. She wasn't going to be able to stay awake much longer. She blinked, trying to stay awake just a few more minutes. "And for the record, I'm not trying to hide anything about my past. Just... trying to start fresh."

～

It was a few days before Erin was up to reopening the bakery. Even then, she had to allow Vic to help with more than usual. The girl was happy to have more of a hand in planning the specials and helping to pull them together. Erin needed to rest often. A high stool beside the counter helped her to keep up even when she was sitting, mixing batters and filling cupcake wrappers or forming cookies. When they opened, Erin found one of the wrought iron chairs normally at the customer tables waiting for her behind the register so that she could rest between orders. It wasn't quite tall enough for her to use while using the register and the stool in the kitchen was too tall, but she could at least stop to rest there as she needed to, and Vic could run a few of the orders through the till. Vic was flourishing under the increased responsibilities, looking for all the world like she was the owner of the shop rather than Erin.

"Will you be staying, then?" Mary Lou asked, as Erin rang up her order for a blueberry muffin. "I was worried that with all this business and your injuries, that you would decide Bald Eagle Falls wasn't for you."

Erin leaned against the counter. Was it madness to consider staying after she had been attacked and kidnapped? She had been the suspect in a murder investigation and she had nearly been killed. Was that really the kind of place she wanted to live? She could sell the business and the house and whatever else was of value in Clementine's house, move to another small town where the cost of living wasn't too high and start over.

But she wasn't sure she was ready to do that. She glanced over at Vic, who was watching her for her answer. Erin had an employee to consider, now her friend and housemate. And there was Orange Blossom. From what Erin understood, cats didn't like moving. He could run away at the first opportunity, if she tried to take him somewhere else and start anew.

"No," she said to Mary Lou. "I don't think I'm going anywhere. I like Bald Eagle Falls and Clementine's old shop… it's one of the only places I have any childhood memories of."

Mary Lou nodded, smiling. "I'm glad," she said. "Don't let all of this nastiness scare you off. There really are a lot of nice people here, once you get to know us."

"Besides," Vic contributed. "What are the chances that you would ever get caught in the middle of another murder in a little place like Bald Eagle Falls?"

CHAPTER 17

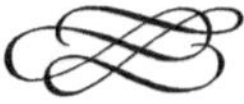

*E*rin took her time locking up.

The lock turned into place with a satisfying snick. All the locks had been replaced and she knew where all the keys were. There was no one squatting there at night and no ghost.

"What are you doing here?"

Officer Piper's question brought her back to the present. She turned to look at him, giving him and K9 a smile.

"Hi. On your rounds?"

"You should be home by now. Your doctor won't like you doing so much on your first day."

Erin was tired after a long day of work, but was still feeling steady on her feet.

"I'm on my way, as you can see. Vic's already gone to get dinner on, so I'm going to eat and hit the sack. If that meets with your approval."

"Are you okay to drive?" He nodded to the Challenger.

"Yes. The doctor said as long as I'm not feeling dizzy or lightheaded, I can drive."

"Okay."

He watched her walk from the door to her car.

"I'm okay, Officer Piper." She assured him, aware that he was watching her gait to make sure that she wasn't impaired by her concussion.

"Terry," he corrected.

A smile tugged at the corners of Erin's mouth. She ducked her head a little, self-conscious. He had called her Erin during the search, but he couldn't very well have called 'Miss Price' for hours on end. It just wasn't done that way.

"Terry. You don't need to worry about me. Thanks to you I'm just fine."

DAIRY-FREE DEATH

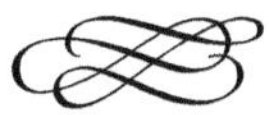

AUNTIE CLEM'S BAKERY 2

For those making homes for themselves and others

CHAPTER 1

Orange Blossom no longer howled at night, as long as Erin or Vic was around and the cat could snuggle with one of the two young women when they went to bed. Usually with Erin, but sometimes the traitorous feline chose Erin's eighteen-year-old housemate instead, for no discernible reason. Erin would lie awake, waiting for him to come in, and he simply wouldn't come. She would fall asleep eventually, but those were always restless nights. She got up very early to go to the bakery, and it was those mornings that it was hardest and felt like just throwing in the towel and finding some line of work that kept office hours of nine to five, so she could be a normal person instead of a zombie by evening and an early bird chasing down the worm in the morning.

Orange Blossom no longer kept the neighbors awake, but he still knew how to use his voice, and as soon as Erin stepped into the kitchen following her wake-up shower, he would immediately be winding himself around her ankles, meowing chattily, making sure she couldn't forget to feed him.

Vic laughed as she followed Erin and Orange Blossom into the kitchen. She hit the button on the coffee maker while Erin tripped three times over Orange Blossom trying to get to his food bin in the pantry. Victoria's pink flannel jammies were wrinkled, and she smelled warmly of sweat. Her hair was as blond as Erin's hair was dark. Erin's hair was not quite black, but as dark a brown as you could get without being black.

"Why does he still act like that?" Vic asked. "Like he's starving to death and you might forget to feed him? I mean, he's been fed every day. It's a routine now. Shouldn't he be settling down about it?"

Despite the facts that there were only ten years between them and Vic topped her by a head, Erin often felt like she was in a parental role to Vic. She emerged from the pantry with her scoop of kibble and filled Orange Blossom's bowl. Her kitten plunged his head into the bowl that was still too big for him, wolfing the food hungrily, making little yipping noises between gulps.

"I don't know, Vic. I assume that sooner or later… he'll at least dial it back a bit. But you have to remember, he's still just a kitten, and he was a starving street cat when I brought him home."

She remembered how hard he had been to catch, how skittish and slippery he had been. No problem with that now. He was always underfoot. And when she did pick him up, he immediately snuggled against her, purring warmly and bumping the top of his head under her chin. No one would ever guess that he'd once been such a frightened stray.

The first cup of coffee was done, and Vic handed it to Erin before putting the second pod in.

"You look tired this morning," she offered by way of explanation since the first cup was almost always for her.

"I didn't sleep very well. Where was that silly cat? In with you?"

"Yes." Vic giggled. "Right under my chin. Kept getting fur up my nose whenever either of us moved."

Erin shook her head and took a sip of the coffee. It was still too hot to drink, so she held it there, smelling the rich, dark, comforting scent. The smell itself was almost as good as the caffeine boost. She sighed and put it down on the counter to cool for a few minutes.

"I'd better grab a couple of things for lunch."

They usually had sandwiches for their early, pre-lunchtime-rush meal, a combination of the bakery bread or rolls and whatever fixings were in the fridge. And if they wanted more than tomatoes on toast, Erin needed to restock.

Vic picked up her coffee once the machine finished dripping and headed for the bathroom. By the time Erin was ready for her work day, all her lists prepared, Vic would be dressed for the day and ready to go. The coffee would hold them both over until the first batch of muffins was fresh out of the oven, and then they would take a break to each have one or two before continuing their preparations. Waking up so early and working through the breakfast and lunch rushes, they took their own meals at odd times.

"Book Club day?" Vic asked as she and Erin climbed into the Challenger to buzz over to the bakery. It was only a few blocks from the little green and white house, but they had things to carry, and they would be on their feet all day. It was still dark, a couple of hours before dawn.

"Yes," Erin agreed, mentally reviewing her lists for the day. Book Club Day was a big deal for the ladies, but it didn't really change Erin's product line-up. They enjoyed a cookie or two, but she didn't have to do anything special, just make sure there was a variety to choose from. Vic would make up a platter and take it over to The Book Nook next door after lunch. "And I need to do a cake for Peter Foster's birthday. His mom is so excited about being able to order a bakery cake instead of having to make one herself this year. 'Decorated and everything.'" Erin chuckled over how excited Mrs. Foster had been about it. "She's got her hands full with that little Traci. I honestly don't know how she gets anything done."

"What kind did Peter want?"

"Chocolate cake. Darth Vader. I have a pattern."

"That will be cool." Vic swept her blond hair over her shoulder and tucked stray strands behind her ears. "I wonder what Traci will want on her birthday."

"Anything she can get her hands—and mouth—on."

"I love the way she gets so excited whenever the Fosters come into the shop. When we started, she was just a nursing baby. Now, she wants her cook-kie!"

"Yes, she does!"

As she opened the back door to the bakery and stepped into the kitchen, Erin took a deep breath of the warm, yeasty air. It was like a drug. Or a perfume. Bottle that smell and she would have a better mate-catcher than any floral concoction. The caffeine of her morning coffee was kicking in, and Erin felt energized and excited to begin her day. She always felt like that. It was hard to wake up initially, but by the time she got to the bakery, she was raring and ready to go.

"You want to start with those maple-bacon muffins?" her young assistant suggested.

Vic had initially been disgusted by the idea, but once she tasted the perfect balance of sweet maple and salty, smoky bacon, she was a convert. Now they were one of her favorites, and were frequently her choice for breakfast.

"Sure," Erin agreed. "Maple-bacon it is."

They already had several batters mixed ahead of time, so Erin selected the maple-bacon muffins and put them on the counter while the oven preheated.

CHAPTER 2

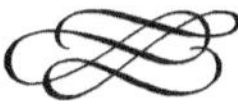

id you see?" Melissa asked as she paid for her muffins. Her dark, curly hair was looking a little windswept, even though it was a calm day. She looked back over her shoulder, but Erin had no idea what she was supposed to be looking at.

"Did I see… what?"

"There's somebody over at the bakery. Angela's old bakery," Melissa clarified, even though Erin had a pretty good idea that Melissa was talking about the only other bakery in town, which had been shut down after the death of Angela Plaint, the former owner.

"Who's at The Bake Shoppe?"

"I don't know. It's an out-of-state car. No one has any idea who it belongs to."

Erin wasn't sure who 'no one' was, other than Melissa herself, but Melissa looked over the people in line behind her, and a few of them nodded a little, verifying what she said. A strange car that no one knew.

"No one saw who got out or knocked on the bakery door to make sure they had a legitimate reason to be there?" Erin knew how things were handled in small-town Bald Eagle Falls. Everyone felt like they had the right to know. If an outsider was in Angela's bakery, then they'd better have a darn good reason to be there.

"No. No one saw them get out. The door's locked and no one is answering. But someone is there. The car had to come from somewhere."

"Maybe Officer Piper should have a look. Maybe somebody just dumped the car here. That happens, sometimes."

"In the big city, maybe. Where there are other places to go and ways to get out of town. But people don't do that here. You dump your car and you're stuck."

Erin motioned for Melissa to step back so that she could ring up the next customer.

"Maybe it's one of the employees," she said. "Just cleaning up or picking up personal items."

"They wouldn't have out-of-state plates. It's someone who doesn't live here."

"Angela's lawyer?" Erin suggested. "Realtor?"

"Neither are from out of town," Melissa insisted.

Erin exchanged a look with Vic. "It's a mystery, then," she said with a shrug.

Melissa nodded eagerly. "Exactly!" she said. "Maybe we'll have to put our local PI onto it." She gave Erin a wink.

"Whoa, Nelly." Erin held both hands up in a 'stop' motion. "I am not a private investigator. I'm a baker, and I've got plenty to keep me occupied without sticking my nose into someone else's business."

"But it is related to the bakery business," Melissa coaxed. "Since you are the only bakery in Bald Eagle Falls, and this person is in Angela's old bakery…"

"That doesn't make it anything to do with me. I'm not getting involved."

~

The door to Auntie Clem's Bakery opened with such a wild jangle of the entrance bells that everybody looked up or turned around to see who had just come in and what the big emergency was. No one hurried in Bald Eagle Falls.

It was Lottie, another of the First Baptist ladies that Erin knew from her Sunday post-service teas. Her face was red and she leaned back against the door, breathing out a puff of breath. She was not embarrassed by having the attention of everyone in the store on her. Rather, she seemed to expect it.

"It's Trenton," she burst out. "Trenton Plaint."

The blood drained from Melissa's face. She stared at Lottie in shock. "*What's* Trenton Plaint?" she said finally, forcing the words out and breaking the stunned silence.

"The out-of-state plates. The man at the bakery. It's Trenton Plaint."

"No." Melissa shook her head. She looked as if she had seen a ghost. "It can't be. This is a mistake."

"It is!" Lottie's voice went up a notch, petulant as a child's. "Come and see if you don't believe me."

But Melissa stayed exactly where she was, frozen to the floor. Erin looked at Vic, not sure what to do. She thought she ought to offer a hand. Or a coffee. Or a good stiff drink. But she wasn't sure. Vic, young as she was, always seemed to have a better knack for customer service than Erin did. Erin was good at the business. She was good at baking and at figuring out marketing and other things to do with the business. But it was Vic who added the warm human touch at Auntie Clem's Bakery.

Vic recognized the panic in Erin's eyes and touched her arm briefly as she walked by and out from behind the counter. Just that fleeting touch made Erin feel better. Vic really did know what to do. Vic took Melissa gently by the arm.

"Are you okay? Would you like to sit down?" She steered Melissa toward one of the chairs provided for customers. They were never all full except during the after-church service on Sunday when they had to bring in a few extra to round out the numbers.

Melissa let Vic guide her into a chair. She shook her head and whispered, "It can't be true."

"Can I get you a drink of water? Tea?"

Melissa gave a confused head-shake. Vic looked at Erin. "Why don't you get her a glass of ice-water anyway?"

Erin nodded and went into the kitchen. When she got back out to the front of the shop again, Vic was still hovering over Melissa, who was sitting in one of the wrought-iron chairs. And Lottie was still leaning against the door, entranced, as if she were watching a movie.

Erin handed Vic the glass and headed for the door.

"You need to get out of the doorway," she told Lottie firmly. You're blocking anybody from getting in or going out.

And maybe that had been Lottie's intention. To hold them all hostage there until she got the reaction she wanted. If that were the case, Erin wasn't sure what she was waiting for. Melissa's reaction must have been satisfying enough for anyone.

Lottie took a sulky step forward from the doorway, making it obvious that she wasn't waiting in line for service. Erin studied her for a moment. She'd never quite understood where Lottie fit in. She had girlish blond pigtails and a round, broad face, which made her look like she was stuck between forty and fourteen. Too girlish for a mature woman, too worn and experienced for a teenager.

"Are you going to come see?" she demanded from Melissa.

"No. No, I don't want to see him. I don't… I didn't think I would ever see him again in my lifetime."

"How about we give Melissa a little space to breathe and some time to calm down again?" Vic suggested, straightening up and moving toward Lottie. Vic was quite tall, and she moved confidently into Lottie's personal space, making Lottie instinctively pull away. "Melissa just needs—some— space." She repeated. Lottie took another step back.

Everyone was frozen for a minute, still watching the drama. Then people started to murmur to each other, acting like they hadn't seen and heard everything that had happened and were only interested in their bakery orders and settling up. Erin finished counting the cookies that Mrs. Potter had finally picked out and rang up the order on the register. Lottie sniffed and walked back out the door with a bang and another clash of bells.

Melissa eventually gathered her wits and left the bakery, giving Erin and Vic a half-hearted nod and heading out the door without further discussion or explanation. Erin retrieved her half-consumed glass of water from the table and put it in the sink in the kitchen. When the line of customers dried up, Erin flipped the sign on the window to "We'll be back…" and she and Vic retired to the kitchen to get off their feet and have their early lunches. Erin wriggled her toes, breathed in the savory scent of her grilled vegetable sand-wich, and took a big bite.

"So… what do you think is going on with Melissa and Trenton Plaint?" Vic asked, after swallowing her first bite.

"I don't think anything is going on with them. Trenton Plaint disappeared almost twenty years ago, the year they were both in twelfth grade. Melissa hasn't seen him since."

"There's something going on there," Vic said with certainty. "You don't act like that when you just hear that some guy you knew twenty years ago has returned to town. They were more to each other than just acquaintances."

"Maybe," Erin allowed. "But I don't think they were friends. From what Melissa has said about the Plaint boys… they were bullies. Nasty to people their age, even though the adults thought they were wonderful. I don't think that Trenton and Melissa were friends."

"Enemies?"

"That might be closer."

"She'd be pretty ticked about him showing up here again if they were enemies too, wouldn't she? It would make more sense that she didn't want to go see him."

Erin nodded. She took another bite of her sandwich and chewed it slowly, appreciating all of the tastes and textures. There was no point in rushing through lunch without enjoying it. She'd end up craving all the baked goods in front of her in the display case at the front of the store. No good if the baker is drooling over everyone else's purchases.

"Did you think Lottie came to tell anybody in particular that Trenton was back? Or just everyone in general?" she asked Vic.

"She wanted to tell Melissa. She didn't care about anyone else."

"Yeah." That was what Erin had sensed as well. Lottie barely even saw anyone else in the bakery. She only had eyes for Melissa. "But why? If they were enemies, why would she rush to tell Melissa that Trenton was back?"

"I don't know. Some people like to be the bearers of bad news. Or just to stir up trouble in general. She's more trouble than a nest of hornets."

Erin smiled. "I've met people like that. Melissa tends to be a bit dramatic herself. Maybe she and Lottie are used to winding each other up. They probably went to school together; they're around the same age."

Vic got up and made some tea. Erin could tell that Vic still had something on her mind. Vic liked to move around when she was thinking. To physically work her way through any knotty problems. When they each had a cup of tea, Erin stirring a little wild honey into hers, Vic looked away as if examining the baking schedule on the whiteboard.

"Are you worried about Trenton being back in town?" she asked.

"No! Why would I be?"

"Because… he's at The Bake Shoppe. He's Angela's heir, isn't he? Maybe he came back here to reopen the bakery."

Erin sipped her tea, frowning.

"I doubt that he is. Reopening the bakery. I mean, he's never had anything to do with it before. Why would he do that?"

"*You* did."

"Well… it's a little different…"

"How? Your aunt died and left you the shop, and you reopened it. His mother leaves him her bakery…"

"But I didn't reopen as the same business. I just used the building and equipment… and opened it as a bakery. It wasn't a bakery when Clementine ran it."

"She did some baking."

"Some," Erin allowed. "A few treats to go with the tea. But mostly she bought them at the bakery and just served them in the tea room."

"You don't think we need to worry about Trenton reopening The Bake Shoppe?"

"No." Erin shook her head, but there was a knot growing in her gut. Her business had been going quite well as the only bakery in town.

What if Trenton did reopen Angela's bakery? Was there enough business to go around and for both stores to be viable? And would people choose a gluten-free bakery over one that sold traditional bread, given the option? When Erin had first moved into town, everyone had said that there was only room for one bakery in Bald Eagle Falls.

"I don't think he's going to reopen," she told Vic. "And if he did, baking probably isn't his thing. He left his mom to run The Bake Shoppe and stayed away for twenty years. If he wanted to run a bakery… he would have come back at some point. Wouldn't he?"

Vic leaned back in her chair. Her shoulders lifted and fell.

"He's probably just having a look around to see how much he has to clean up," Erin said, "What he can sell. What the place is worth. If he's the heir, he'll need to take care of all of that."

"A lawyer and real estate agent could have taken care of all of that without him ever coming to town."

"Maybe he needed to prove his identity. Or do something in order to inherit. I don't know. Maybe he just wanted to come back to make sure that Angela was really dead."

"Yeah." Vic's tone was subdued. It wasn't until then that Erin remembered Angela was Vic's aunt.

"Do you remember Trenton? No, you wouldn't remember him, he left around the time you were born. But did you see pictures of him? Hear stories? Do you know any of the other kids? I think Melissa said... there were three children? Two boys and a girl?"

"Uh..." Vic rolled her eyes upward, trying to remember. "Trenton, Davis, and Sophie. But Sophie died, and Trenton disappeared. Davis... I don't think he disappeared, exactly. Not like Trenton did. I think Aunt Angela still knew where he was. But she didn't have anything to do with him. He was... you know... an addict. She was very... judgmental."

Vic herself had felt the sting of Angela's judgments due to her gender identity. Erin looked at Vic, hoping she hadn't made her assistant uncomfortable bringing up the subject.

"Are you okay?"

"Sure. Yeah. It doesn't matter to me."

"So, there are two heirs, Trenton and Davis. If she didn't write them both out of her will."

Vic nodded.

"And she must not have," Erin mused, "or Trenton wouldn't be here. If she just left everything to First Baptist, there wouldn't be any need for him to come to town to look The Bake Shoppe over."

"Could she do that?" Vic sounded surprised.

"Leave it all to the church? Of course. People leave money to churches or charities all the time. You're not actually required to give it to your family."

"Really? You can just leave it to whoever you want?"

"Yes. Sure."

"But what if her family objects? I mean, what if she did leave it to the church, and Trenton... didn't think the church deserved it?"

"I guess he'd have to take the estate to court over it... challenge the will..."

"Because he could be like you. He could want to take over the bakery. The church wouldn't have any use for it, and if he wanted to…"

"I… don't know," Erin admitted. "The sum of my knowledge of estate law is what I learned from Clementine's lawyer and popular TV. That doesn't exactly make me an expert."

CHAPTER 3

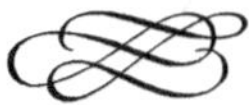

They heard more rumors about Trenton as the day wore on and customers drifted in and out with the latest gossip. The town's rumor mill was legendary. Internet social networks had nothing on the gossip network of a small town.

Trenton was opening the bakery. He was selling the bakery. He was opening the bakery as some other business, much as Erin had. It all sounded like speculation, the flavor changing every hour or two. If Trenton really were changing his mind that fast, it was no wonder the poor man had fled town decades before.

They stayed open long enough to catch the after-school crowd, the moms who got off work early to be home when their children arrived. The ones who wanted that last loaf of bread, pizza shell, or package of cookies for supper. Sometimes it was the children themselves who wandered in with a dollar or two for a cookie or muffin. By five o'clock, business had again slowed to a trickle and Erin and Vic were both yawning as they took turns prepping for the next morning and cleaning up the kitchen.

Erin served the last couple of customers, locked the door, and shut off the lights. She yawned her way back to the kitchen, dragging her feet a little.

"Well, I'm all in," she confessed. "Everything is set, here, right?" She looked at her list and checked the fridge, nodding.

"I think I got everything," Vic contributed.

"Looks like it. Let's head for home."

They locked the back door. Erin looked up and down the darkening back lane, a city habit of looking for danger even though she knew there was none in quiet little Bald Eagle Falls. There was a dark silhouette making its way down the alley toward them, a man-shape. Erin suspected it was Officer Terry Piper, who liked to chat for a minute and see her off at the end of the day. But as the figure drew closer, she realized it was not Terry. He was taller and heavier than the officer. Erin checked to make sure that Vic was getting into the car and tightened her grip around her keys.

"Who's there?" she called out.

Just a neighbor. Bald Eagle Falls was a neighborly place. People thought nothing of walking down alleys even after dark. There was little street crime, aside from the drug dealing that overflowed from the city. Maybe some teenage vandalism. Certainly, no violent crime.

There was no answer from the approaching man. Erin was torn between getting into the car and getting reassurance that it was just one of her friends, nobody of any danger to her.

"Hello?" she called again.

"Who are you?" The answer was not threatening, but it still made her uncomfortable. The voice was unfamiliar. And anyone who lived in Bald Eagle Falls knew who she was. She was in the parking lot behind her own bakery. Who else would be there?

"It's Erin Price," she said anyway. "Who's there?"

He was close enough that he was no longer silhouetted, but it wasn't light enough to make out the features of his face. Just the general lines, the nose and the chin, the close-cropped hair. Unfamiliar.

"My name is Trenton," he said, confirming what she had already guessed. "You're the bakery lady? Auntie Em or whatever?"

"Auntie Clem's Bakery," Erin corrected. "My name is Erin, though. It's named… after my aunt," she finished lamely.

"No kidding."

"My aunt knew your mother," Erin offered hesitantly. "I'm sorry, but I didn't know her…"

"You'd be sorry if you did." He sighed heavily. "Well, I guess that makes us competitors, then."

"You're… reopening The Bake Shoppe?"

"Don't know why the idiot estate lawyer shut it down in the first place. If you have a successful business, why would you shut it down and let your customers be poached by someone else? Why not keep it running until you know what the heirs of the estate want?"

"That would make more sense," Erin agreed. "I was surprised when they just shut it down."

"Everything is still in place, and it looks like I can get most of the staff back. Those I can't... I'll just have to replace. I figure I should be able to get it open again within a week."

"Well..." Erin's heart sank at the news. She had been happy with the amount of business Auntie Clem's Bakery had been getting. She was going to have to re-evaluate. Could she still be profitable with only half the clientele? She wouldn't need as much inventory. She wouldn't have to lay off any staff, as it was just her and Vic. They ran a pretty lean business, and Erin had been banking as much as she could. "Good luck. I'm sure there's enough business for us both in Bald Eagle Falls."

"You'll still have all of the gluten-free," Trenton offered, and Erin could just make out the curve of his contemptuous smile. "I'm not planning on offering anything like that at my place."

Erin nodded. "Sure, that's good," she agreed, trying to force cheer into her voice. "There will always be people that have special dietary needs. That's what I cater to."

"No need for normal people to be buying that crap, though. Without The Bake Shoppe, there's nowhere in town that people can go to just buy regular baking." He rolled his shoulders. Erin was struck by how tall he was. Had he played basketball in school? He appeared too heavy for a basketball player, but he might have been slim as a boy. "Other than the *grocery store*," he amended, sneering over the words. "But I mean... assembly-line bread..."

"Yeah. It's just not the same as handcrafted."

"Handcrafted," he repeated. "Yeah."

She could almost hear him making a mental note of the word to use in his own ad copy. It irked her. She turned away from him slightly.

"Well, I need to head for home," she told him. "You know how early a baker's day starts."

"I remember," Trenton agreed, his voice far away. He had lived at home before Angela had developed the allergies that prevented her from entering her own place of business. She had been the head baker, and Trenton could, presumably, remember how early she had had to get up to bake before the day started.

Erin meanly hoped that he didn't like to get up early. That that one thing might be enough to change his mind and make him decide that it wasn't worth his while to reopen the bakery. He could sell it instead. Just take the money and get back out of town. He had run away from Bald Eagle Falls before. He didn't want to live there. The place held bad memories for him. Melissa had told Erin what kind of a mother Angela was, always belittling her children, humiliating them. She had been a bully. Why would Trenton want to come back to Bald Eagle Falls and relive those memories? Why would he want to see the people he hadn't seen in twenty years, who would also remember those incidents and how ineffectual he had been back then?

Erin slid into the car. "I guess I'll see you around, then."

"I guess so."

Erin pulled her door shut with a bang and pulled back, leaving him there in the parking lot, watching her. Vic didn't say anything right away, so the inside of the car was silent, filled with just the noise of the Challenger's engine and air conditioning.

"Are you okay?" Vic asked eventually.

"Sure, I'm fine."

Vic didn't push it any further. Erin knew Vic didn't believe it. Erin didn't know exactly what it was she was feeling. She was okay; that hadn't been a lie. No matter what, she would find a way to continue. She'd been through a lot worse. She was adaptable.

When they pulled in front of the house, Vic looked at Erin again.

"You're okay? With Uncle Trent reopening The Bake Shoppe? Isn't that going to cause you problems?"

"We'll lose some of our customer base. But we'll figure it out. I'm sure we can keep things going."

Getting out of the car, Erin resolved to put the whole incident behind her and to think of other things. There was no need to mope around all evening being miserable about it. She would think things through later. Make a list.

As soon as she opened the door to the house, Orange Blossom was there, trying to tangle up her feet, making eager noises of greeting and yowling for her attention. No one had told him that cats were supposed to be laid-back and composed. She felt bad sometimes for leaving him alone all day. He clearly missed them. He was a good boy and didn't chew up her shoes or claw up the furniture while she was gone. But he made such a fuss when they got home. Erin put down her purse and a bag of day-old goods and scooped him up.

"Did you miss us, Blossom?" she crooned, holding him in her arms and pressing her face into his fur. Orange Blossom wriggled and bumped his head against her. His car-motor purr filled the room.

"I think that's a yes," Vic observed.

"Yeah. You did miss us, didn't you, baby?"

Vic stood close and scratched Orange Blossom's ears, getting in on all the loving.

"What's all this?" a deeper voice inquired.

Erin didn't need to turn around to see who was there. She knew that voice. But she did anyway, smiling at Terry, the handsome, dark-haired cop who stood looking in the door, which Vic hadn't pulled shut behind her.

"Come on in," Erin invited, swinging the door back open the rest of the way.

"You really shouldn't leave your door open," Terry teased. "Anyone could walk in off the street."

"Like Trenton Plaint? I already met him."

Terry and K9, his German Shepherd, entered and Terry pulled the door shut behind him. He gave Erin a quick little shoulder-squeeze in greeting.

"Ow, ow!" Erin tried to detach all of Orange Blossom's needle-sharp claws. "Calm down, you silly cat! You know K9."

But despite regular visits from Terry, the kitten still hadn't made friends with the dog. He writhed to be put down. Erin let him jump down to the rug and dash off. Erin shook her head.

"He just wants to be friends," Terry apologized, holding on to K9's collar to keep him from going after the cat. "Do you want me to leave him outside?"

"No. I know he'll behave himself. Orange Blossom is just going to have to get used to him coming with you to visit. He will sooner or later... won't he?"

Officer Piper was the one who actually had experience with cats. Erin had never had a pet before. Terry nodded.

"He'll come around sooner or later." He motioned toward the furniture grouping in the living room. "You want to put your feet up?"

"No. Food."

They all headed to the kitchen, where Orange Blossom sat by his food dish, staring into it intently.

"Now you're going to sulk?" Erin asked.

The cat didn't even flick an ear in her direction.

They all went in different directions, feeling at home in the kitchen. Erin went into the pantry to get fresh food for Orange Blossom's bowl. Vic went to the freezer for something to warm up for supper. Terry sat down at the table with K9 beside him. The dog stretched out on the floor with a snort and a deep sigh, his eyes on the cat.

Erin added fresh food to the kitten's bowl and he dug in, purring between gulps.

"How did you meet Trenton Plaint?" Terry asked, settling himself into the kitchen chair and readjusting his heavy equipment belt.

"Hmm? Oh… he caught me just now as we were leaving the shop."

"What did he want?"

"I guess just to tell me he was going to reopen The Bake Shoppe." Erin considered. "I'm not sure why he thought it necessary. But at least… now I know for sure instead of having to try to sort out the rumors."

Terry rubbed his chin, his whiskers rasping. "That's sort of an aggressive move. Why would he find it necessary to confront you about it?"

Vic had their dinners lined up at the microwave. "It was kind of weird. He didn't threaten her or anything, but… coming up on a woman, in the dark, and telling her you're taking half her business…"

Terry's mouth pulled down into a pronounced frown. "He didn't come into the bakery? He approached you outside in the dark?"

"Yes. But like Vic said, he wasn't threatening. Just…"

"Aggressive," Terry repeated the word he had used before.

"Yeah, I guess. Uncomfortable. A weird approach, when everyone around Bald Eagle Falls goes out of their way to be so nice. Having someone who doesn't even try to be pleasant about it."

She thought about how Angela had confronted her when she first moved into town.

"But then, maybe it's a family trait. Angela wasn't exactly welcoming either."

Terry let out a bark of laughter. "That's putting it mildly. No, I think you're right, The Plaint family just doesn't play by Bald Eagle Falls' social rules."

Both Terry and Erin glanced over at Vic, remembering belatedly that Vic was part of Angela's extended family as well.

"Not you," Erin said quickly. "I don't know anyone who is nicer than you."

Vic gave a little shrug like it didn't matter.

"Really," Erin pressed. "You're not just pretending to be nice, which is what I get from half the women in town. You really are genuinely nice and care about people, deep down. It's who you are."

Vic turned a little pink at that. "But I wasn't raised by Aunt Angela. Maybe things would be different if I had been."

Erin tried to picture a Vic who was as mean as Angela. She couldn't even imagine it.

"Then it must be learned," Terry contributed. "Either that, or you managed not to inherit the gene."

"Mmm," Vic made a noncommittal noise. She put the first of the frozen dinners into the microwave. "Do you want anything?"

"No, I'm fine." Terry waved his hand. "Nothing for me."

As Erin moved across the kitchen to get some iced tea from the fridge, she saw K9's head move sharply toward her, ears pricked. She stopped herself and opened the bone-shaped cookie jar on the counter. K9 sat up eagerly, nose and ears pointing at her.

"Are you waiting for one of these?" Erin asked, her voice pitched higher to the dog. "Did I forget to offer you any hospitality?"

K9 licked his chops. Erin reached into the cookie jar and took out a thick, homemade dog biscuit.

Terry and Vic were both smiling as Erin offered the cookie to the eager dog. He took it from her politely and lay back down on the floor with it between his paws to eat.

Orange Blossom left his bowl to slink around the kitchen and see what K9 was eating. Erin had noticed lately that if anyone else were eating, Orange Blossom found their food far more interesting than whatever was in his dish. No matter how good what she gave him was, he was always on the prowl for something better.

K9 wasn't paying any attention to the kitten, occupied instead with his treat. Orange Blossom snuck closer and closer, ears forward, nose quivering, belly to the floor.

"Look at the mighty hunter," Vic whispered. They all watched him get closer and closer until he was nose to nose with K9. K9 finished the cookie, but there were still crumbs on the floor between his paws. Orange Blossom's quick pink tongue rasped along the floor to clean them up. He raised his head to sniff at K9, and he licked up a crumb that clung to the dog's chin.

K9 sniffed the kitten with interest. Orange Blossom decided, now that all remnants of the cookie were gone, that he was once again enemies with the dog. He bristled and hissed and backed away, his fur all puffed out. Back at his own dish, he crouched and growled as if the dog were threatening to eat his food.

"Orange Blossom isn't very hospitable," Vic observed.

"He needs some training," Erin agreed.

The microwave beeped, and Vic pulled out the first dinner. "Do you want… Alfredo or primavera?"

"Whichever." Erin shrugged. "You take one, and I'll have the other."

Vic looked at them. "I'll have primavera," she decided. "More vegetables. Since I'm having pasta *and* a roll from the bakery!" She pulled one out of the bag Erin had brought home.

"I'll have one of those," Terry volunteered. He flushed a little. "If you have extra, that is."

"Sure," Erin assured him. "Even if we're too tired to cook at the end of the day, there's always plenty of baked goods on hand!" She patted her stomach. "Way too many baked goods!"

Terry eyed Erin's figure, a sparkle in his eye and that little bit of a dimple pocking his cheek. "You haven't put on any weight that I can tell."

In a few minutes, they were all sitting down at the table, Erin and Vic with their microwaved dinners and all of them with rolls also warm from the microwave. Erin had retrieved butter and jars of jam from the fridge.

"I got these from The General Store. Mary Lou said that they are really good. She wouldn't let me buy any of the commercial brands; she said these are made by a local lady and are to die for." She flicked a glance at Terry. "Her words."

Vic looked at the labels. "The Jam Lady. Doesn't give many clues of who it is, does it? Did she say who makes it?"

"Just somebody local. That's all she would tell me."

"How mysterious." Vic opened the jar and put it back down on the table. She dipped her knife into the deep purple jam. "I suppose everybody in town actually knows who it is." She looked at Terry and raised an eyebrow. He put up both hands.

"Don't look at me. I'm not hooked into the latest gossip on jams and preserves." He reached for an apricot jam and applied it assiduously to his roll.

"Doesn't sound like you're doing your job, then," Vic teased.

There was a period of silence in which they all applied themselves to their dinner. Erin didn't normally go back for seconds, but she had to have another roll with more jam.

"These jams really are delicious. I'm glad I let Mary Lou talk me into them."

Vic nodded, mouth full. She chewed and swallowed. "We should get some wholesale to sell at the bakery. It would be a good up-sell."

"You're right. I'll ask Mary Lou who to talk to."

"Are you sure that's not just a way to find out who makes them?" Terry asked. He licked off his fingers. K9 looked up at him.

"Maybe."

Vic pushed herself back from the table a few inches, distancing herself from the temptation of the rolls and jam.

"We're still going to the cave this weekend, right?" she asked Erin.

Erin shifted uncomfortably. "Uh… yes. That's the plan."

Terry's brows lowered. "What's this? Haven't you had enough of caves?"

Vic shook her head. "I still want to explore. I never got to."

But Terry wasn't looking at Vic; he was looking at Erin.

"Vic still wants to go," Erin repeated. "So, I agreed to go with her."

"I thought you never wanted to set eyes on another cave again."

"Well… I might have said that. But I had good reason."

"I still think you have good reason for not going back," he said. "Are you sure you really want to? What if something happens? What if one of you gets hurt or you have a panic attack?"

Normally, Erin would have been offended at the suggestion that she might have a panic attack. She had never had a panic attack in her life. She was made of sterner stuff than that. But after her last experience in a cave, she couldn't swear that she wouldn't. She remembered the darkness, the feeling of running into walls where she didn't expect them or suddenly finding no more cave floor in front of her. She had agreed to go with Vic, but she wasn't looking forward to it by any means.

"Willie is going to go with us as a guide, so we'll be perfectly fine."

"Oh," Terry nodded. "Good. That's sensible." But there was no dimple in his cheek when he said it. He kept his face expressionless. "Which one are you going to?"

"Do you want to go?" Vic asked. "You could come along with us if you want."

Erin blinked at Vic. She wasn't sure she wanted both Terry Piper and Willie Andrews there. They would be a crowd in the narrow passages of the cave systems. And it would look suspiciously like a double-date; two men and two women. It wasn't meant to be romantic. Just the two girls, along with a guide to direct them and make sure they didn't run into any trouble. She liked Willie. The guy had grown on her, despite her initial misgivings about him. He *had* helped to save her life, after all. Erin also liked Officer Terry Piper. But they had never gone out together. The most they had done was to start calling each other by their first names once Angela's murder investigation was finished, or to stop and chat at the bakery or at the house after work. Despite what Vic might say, there was no overt flirting. Just a friendly companionship.

Even as she thought it, though, Erin's face warmed. She *did* like Terry. And maybe they did flirt. Just a little. Subtly. Like grown-ups.

"I don't know," Terry said, his eyes going from one woman to the other. "It sounds like this is just a girl's day out… I don't want to interfere."

"No, no, you should come," Vic pressed. "It would be great. You like spelunking, don't you? And K9 can help."

K9's ears pricked up and he looked at Vic and then Terry. He put his head back down again and watched Orange Blossom having a post-prandial tongue-bath in the middle of the kitchen.

"Are you sure? You wouldn't mind?" Terry looked at Erin. "Really?"

Erin shrugged and forced a friendly smile. "Of course not, Terry. We'd be happy to have you along. The more, the merrier."

"Okay then. Sure. When are you going? I'll have to check my shift schedule."

"Sunday afternoon," Vic told him. "Two o'clock. I'll text you the coordinates."

Terry nodded, the dimple making a reappearance on his cheek.

Vic was impatient with Erin the next afternoon as they worked, a peeved "why aren't you more excited about going to the caves?" hanging in the air between them. "I thought you'd be happy about Officer Piper coming with us and not be so scared."

"I didn't want him to come," Erin told her. "You should have asked me before inviting anyone else." But she couldn't explain to Vic why it was that she didn't want both men there at the caves. Even when she tried to explain it to herself during a lull in customers, she couldn't quite connect everything up logically. It wasn't really logical, the feeling of not wanting Terry there. It was just emotion.

That was when the stranger walked in.

Erin was pretty sure she had never seen the woman before. A small, skinny, blond woman. Erin had seen lots of women like her during her time in New York. Dressed in form-fitting workout gear like she had just bustled over from the yoga studio. Designer handbag. Blond from a bottle. Fake bake tan. Showy jewelry that she couldn't possibly have worn while working out. Perpetually in a hurry because there were oh-so-many important things she had to stay on top of. But the type was rare in Tennessee and practically unheard of in Bald Eagle Falls. She was like a brilliant peacock that landed in the middle of the henhouse. And all the hens immediately started clucking.

"My, you do a lot of business in here!" the woman said in a high, stringy voice. "I've been watching for a break all day, and other than when you closed mid-morning before the lunch rush, there has been a steady stream of people in and out of here!"

"Yes, ma'am," Vic agreed, drawing it out like a true southerner faced with an impatient visitor. "We keep ourselves right busy."

"Well, it's good that you have so much business here. That means you should still be able to scrape up a living when The Bake Shoppe reopens, I imagine."

Vic and Erin just stared at her. Erin looked toward the door. Where had the woman come from? She had to be associated with Trenton Plaint some-how. If not his girlfriend, then his lawyer, real estate agent, or personal trainer.

But the woman, who seemed all skinny arms and legs like a spider, didn't jump in and introduce herself. She just smiled and preened, letting everyone admire her. Except that everyone was just Vic and Erin and neither one particularly admired the type. Vic was much prettier than the stranger, Erin decided. With a kind of friendliness and grace that the other woman would never learn in a million years.

"What can I help you with?" Erin asked, since Vic didn't jump in with the appropriate words.

The woman tip-toed up to the display case and peered in like she was afraid there was something in there that was going to bite. Or maybe some-thing gross and disgusting. Mold or slime rather than delicious fresh-baked goods.

"I'd like some cupcakes," she said slowly, an awkward pause between each word, like she wasn't sure if they would have cupcakes. When they were right in front of her face.

"Yes...?"

"But I know you specialize in gluten-free goods..."

"Yes..." Erin gave her an encouraging nod. "They're very good. You can try a sample if you're not sure if you'll like something."

"No, it's not that." The woman wrinkled her nose. "You see, I'm a vegan, and I'm sure everything here is just *laden* with animal products."

"I'm sure you are," Vic murmured. Meant for only Erin's ears, but she should have kept it to herself and just said it in her head. Because the woman heard her, or part of what she had said, and cocked her head, looking suddenly threatening.

"What was that, dear?"

"We do carry vegan goods," Erin offered, rushing in over anything that Vic might have to say. "Not everything is vegan, of course, but we do try to keep a few things dairy and egg free for those who are allergic or who... prefer not to eat them."

"Oh!" The stranger raised her eyebrows. "Really? I just assumed that since you were making gluten-free... well, gluten-free baking often relies on extra eggs and dairy. It's so hard to find anything that is really good that is both vegan and gluten-free."

"I do my best. Now the ones that are vegan that we have on today are the chocolate chip cupcakes, with all the icing and chocolate sprinkles over here… the ginger snaps on the bottom shelf there… and if you want something for dinner rather than dessert, these rosemary bread sticks over here."

"I'm not sure…" The woman peered through the glass at the various offerings. She had said she wanted cupcakes, so Erin wasn't sure why she didn't just go immediately for the cupcakes. But the odd woman looked dubious about them. "I'll need to see ingredients for everything. Are you sure there's no shellac in those sprinkles? Or cochineal food coloring? It's not just about eggs and dairy, you know. I want to be sure that no living creatures were harmed to make my food. You know a lot of people put honey in their baking because they say it's healthy. But honey is from bees. It's not vegan!"

"It's not like they kill the bees to get it," Vic said impatiently. "It's all natural. The bees don't need all of the honey they produce."

Erin made a small motion for Vic to be quiet. She knew that any reasoned argument would only get the woman more worked up. "I have ingredient sheets here." She reached under the cash register for the 'Bible,' her binder with all the ingredients to everything they baked. "Here are the cupcakes…" She flipped through the plastic sleeves to find the list. "And I'll get you the sprinkles label to double-check."

"And the chocolate chip label," the woman said, rising on tiptoes as Erin headed toward the kitchen door and raising her voice. "Even chocolate labeled 'dark' has milk in it most of the time…"

"Yes, ma'am," Erin agreed.

She made faces while she was in the kitchen. Just to get them out of her system and to ensure that she could keep a straight face while she served the woman. She grabbed the bags she needed and took them with her out to the front, running her eyes over them quickly as she did so. She was usually pretty careful when she bought ingredients, aware of red flags, but that didn't mean she couldn't make a mistake. One instance of shellac or red #4 could have snuck by her if she had been tired and not paying close enough attention. But she didn't see anything worrisome on either ingredients list.

The stranger perused ingredients lists like she was the lowest reader in her class, studying them and moving her lips. She murmured 'I just don't know,' several times. Erin looked toward the door, wishing someone else would show up and interrupt the little drama. Even the glacially slow Potters were preferable to the new out-of-towner.

"And the breadsticks…?" her customer asked. "You're sure that you used shortening in them and not lard? Around *these parts*," she looked around her in distaste, "I just imagine everyone uses lard around here."

"No. I used shortening," Erin promised. "I am very strict about following those recipes, so I can guarantee that I know every ingredient when a customer needs help sorting through multiple allergies."

Like Bertie Braceling. Erin was determined that one day she was going to be able to make something that Bertie Braceling could eat. Something other than a cold glass of water. But Bertie's multiple allergens had so far foiled all of Erin's attempts to feed him. They would discuss Bertie's needs at length, and then Erin would whip something up, only to be informed that one ingredient or another gave Bertie hives, or the runs, or made all the skin peel off of his hands. Just when she thought she had it all figured out, Bertie's body would stump her again. Bertie would laugh good-naturedly, remind Erin that, 'I told you not to even try feeding me,' and walk out the door until the next time.

"It is nice to see someone who is so thorough," the woman conceded. "You should hear some of the people I talk to. They have no idea what they're eating or putting into their food. So ignorant!"

"That must be frustrating," Erin soothed.

She looked at Vic to give her a sympathetic eye roll. After all, Vic was suffering through the whole production as well. But Vic's comical expression took Erin off guard, and she snorted back a laugh, then tried to cover it with a discreet cough into the crook of her elbow.

"I'm sorry," she said, mortified. "I just had a little tickle…"

The woman studied her for a moment, suspicious.

"You should try hot yoga," she said. "Nothing like it for working viruses and impurities out of your system. Sweating is very healthy, you know."

Erin nodded along with her.

"I don't imagine you even have a hot yoga studio in town."

"No… but Mrs. Leong leads tai chi in the park. And we sweat a lot here."

She could feel Vic trying not to laugh beside her. Erin gave her a glare and then looked away, not wanting to be infected herself.

"I think I will go with the cupcakes," the woman decided. "Six of those. And six of the red velvet ones?"

Erin froze. "The red velvet cupcakes are not vegan," she warned.

"Oh, I know. But they're not for me. They're for my boyfriend. Just so he has options. You know how childish men are about any of these alternative diets…"

So that clinched it. She *was* Trenton's girlfriend. Well, good for her. She could have him. Erin still hadn't seen Trenton in the light of day, but she had already decided that she didn't like him. She was rushing to judgment too quickly, she knew. The man had grown up in an extremely dysfunctional family. In a town that probably shunned psychology as witchcraft. How did she expect him to turn out? A perfect gentleman? Someone like Terry Piper?

Erin put the cupcakes into boxes one at a time, slow and deliberate, making the woman wait for Erin, since Erin had had to waste so much time on her. She put six cupcakes in each half-dozen-size box rather than all twelve in the same dozen-size box, so they wouldn't touch each other or breathe the same air. Vic rang them up at the cash register and waited. The woman paid by credit card, and finally wandered out of the store, without so much as a 'good-bye.'

Erin gave a sigh of relief.

"You're the one who wanted to cater to all the special diets," Vic reminded her.

"Ugh. I know. Usually, it's fun, but Miss Prissy Pants rubbed me the wrong way!"

"Those pants were so tight I could see her religion!" Vic snickered. "Joelle Biggs."

"What?"

"That was the name on her credit card. Joelle Biggs."

"Well!" Erin couldn't think of what to say to that. She was not going to be forgetting Miss Joelle Biggs anytime soon.

CHAPTER 4

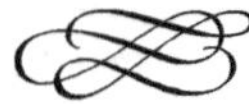

A couple of times during the day, Erin had seen the name 'Alton Summers' flash across the screen of her phone. She frowned and ignored it. She didn't have the time to talk during the work day. She knew who Alton Summers was, and knew he wasn't calling her to ask her about the ingredients in her red velvet cupcakes.

She wasn't sure why he was calling her, but she didn't like it. There was no reason, as far as she knew, for Detective Alton Summers to be calling her. They had concluded their business months before.

"Erin?"

Erin looked down the counter to Vic, completely blank about what Vic had just been talking about or what she had asked. Things were quiet, and Vic had obviously been trying to carry on a conversation.

"Umm… sorry…?"

"Mrs. Foster called. About the Darth Vader cake. She said that Peter practically swooned over it. It was perfect and really made his day."

Erin smiled. The biggest, most natural smile she'd had in days. She didn't get a lot of compliments in her life, and they always turned her to mush when they came out of nowhere.

"Aww… That's just the sweetest. It was so nice of her to call."

"That's not all. She said that Peter wanted to know whether you had made the cake. He said that the food you make never makes him sick, and he knew if the cake was from you, he would have a good birthday and not be sick at the end of it."

Erin blinked, trying to prevent hot tears from escaping her eyes. She smiled even harder.

"Don't you just love Peter? I think he's my favorite."

"Your favorite Foster?"

"My favorite everything. My favorite customer."

"Not Miss Joelle Biggs?"

"Argh! Not Miss Joelle Biggs. How could you even suggest it?"

Vic guffawed. "I'm just teasing. The woman could make a preacher cuss. So, Peter told all his friends that they should get their birthday cakes from you. Because it looked so awesome, and because then Peter would be able to have a piece of birthday cake whenever he went to a friend's party."

Erin nodded and tried to swallow the lump in her throat. "I remember what it was like for my foster sister, Carolyn. How she could never go to a friend's party and have a piece of cake or pizza or anything else. People would invite her and not even try to have something that she could eat. Our foster mom tried to send her with her own food so that she could eat and not be left out. But she hated to look different. She wanted so badly to fit in, and she felt like the only way to fit in was to eat what they were eating."

"So, she'd be sick?"

"Yeah. Sometimes she would sneak just a little, and our foster mom wouldn't find out, so she'd think it was okay... and then she'd end up having so much that she'd be sick for days. And eventually... her body just couldn't heal itself anymore."

Vic nodded solemnly. She'd heard Erin talk about Carolyn before, and Vic knew how her story had ended. Erin shook her head, depressed. She knew better than to talk about Carolyn; it always made her impotently angry. So furious that she hadn't been able to do anything for her sister. So angry that food, something that was supposed to nourish her and help keep her healthy and strong, had eventually killed her. Carolyn was Erin's inspiration for alternative baking. But Erin still felt so lost and useless at not having been able to help her. In the end, Carolyn had decided that fitting in and looking like everyone else was more important to her than anything else, including her health.

"Sorry," Vic said softly.

Erin nodded. The happy smile over Peter's sweet words was gone and she had to force a fake one for the next customer who came to the till. It just happened to be Mary Lou Cox. Erin dropped the plastic smile and sighed.

"Having a rough day?" Mary Lou sympathized. Like always, she looked like she had just stepped out of a salon. Perfectly fit and pressed clothes, not a hair of her blond bob out of place or a smudge in her makeup. But Erin knew that the small, slender woman had a tough life. With all her troubles at home, Mary Lou could have walked around town with a storm cloud hanging over her, but she never did. She was always pleasant and friendly.

"No, not really," Erin said. "Just feeling sorry for myself for a minute there."

"Don't I know what that's like!" Mary Lou said, opening her little clutch purse to carefully count out the money for her purchase. Erin was grateful for the small purchases Mary Lou made at the bakery every few days. She was cost-conscious and could have just gone to a warehouse store in the city to buy twenty-four jumbo cupcakes at a time and stick them in her freezer. But instead, she supported Auntie Clem's Bakery, paying for the slightly pricey handcrafted gluten-free muffins without complaint. Erin gave her a more genuine smile of gratitude. Mary Lou could sometimes seem distant, but she was a good friend. "Is it because of Trenton Plaint?" Mary Lou asked as Erin put the money into the till.

"No… not just him. I mean, that's on my mind, of course. Just other things. Life likes to throw you curveballs to keep things interesting."

"Yes, it does," Mary Lou agreed. "I sometimes think that it wouldn't be so bad to be bored every now and then. I really think I could manage without the interesting little plot twists."

Erin chuckled. "Amen to that."

Mary Lou gave her a surprised look, eyebrows raised and head cocked but didn't make any comment. Erin wondered belatedly if using 'amen' so frivolously was an insult to the church ladies. Or maybe just completely inappropriate for an atheist to say. She'd have to be more careful in the future.

"Oh," Erin remembered the entry on her task list suddenly. "I wanted to ask you about the Jam Lady. Vic and I were thinking it would be good to have some jars here to up-sell to customers. I wanted to get the contact from you, to get the wholesale price."

Mary Lou just looked at her for a moment, and Erin wondered whether she needed to repeat or reword something. Had Mary Lou just been thinking about something else? It hadn't been a complicated question.

"I'll find out the pricing for you," Mary Lou said slowly, "and I'll bring you an assorted case."

Erin didn't see any point in using Mary Lou as a middleman. "Just give me the name of who I should contact, and I'll buy direct."

"No, I can't do that. You know the Jam Lady wants to remain anonymous."

"But you know who she is. You have to."

"Yes, but I'm the only distributor. If you want to sell her jams here, you need to deal with me. You can't go to her directly."

"You are her distributor."

"Yes." Mary Lou nodded.

Vic looked over at Erin and Erin immediately knew what she was thinking. Mary Lou herself was the Jam Lady. She didn't want anyone to know, for some reason. Maybe building a bit of mystery was part of her marketing plan.

"I see. Okay, then. Can I come over to The General Store later? You can let me know what you find out on the wholesale price of a case, and I'll pick one up from you? Do you have a full case in the stockroom?"

"Certainly. That would be just fine. I just need enough time to put a call in to the Jam Lady and find out the details."

"Great. I'll come over sometime this afternoon, after the lunch rush.

"Perfect." Mary Lou waved, fingertips only. "Toodle-oo. Hope the rest of your day goes better."

Erin smiled and nodded. Beside the register, her phone buzzed, and she glanced down at it.

Alton Summers.

~

"I'm going to run over to The General Store to pick up that case of Jam Lady jams," Erin told Vic. "And I guess I'll stop in at The Book Nook and pick up our platters as well. You need anything?"

"No, I don't need anything. I'll hold down the fort."

"Won't be long, then."

As soon as she stepped out the door, Erin regretted her decision. It was the hottest part of the day, and stepping out of the air-conditioned bakery into the afternoon heat, she felt like a fish pulled out of the water. The air felt thin and oxygen-depleted. She felt like her skin was going to shrivel and bake like a turkey that had been in the oven too long. It was, as Vic would say, hotter than blue blazes.

Erin figured she would be fine as long as she stayed on the sidewalk, in the shade of the colorful sun-blocking roofs that extended from the shoulder-to-shoulder buildings out to the street. She would walk slowly. Then she could stay comfortable and not wear herself out too quickly.

It sounded good, but by the time Erin was a block down, she was sweating heavily. She stopped to rub her forehead and the corners of her eyes. She hadn't even put on sunglasses. The air in the street shimmered with heat. She hadn't taken off her apron, and all her clothes were pasted to her.

"I need help!" a shrill voice wailed nearby.

Erin looked around, startled. The street was nearly empty. No one else was stupid enough to be out walking in the heat of the day. They ducked from their air-conditioned cars into the air-conditioned buildings. They didn't walk a couple of blocks to run errands like a dumb tourist.

"Help me!"

Erin saw a familiar yoga-clothed figure across the street, looking around frantically. Erin did a quick check for traffic out of habit and crossed the empty street to see what was wrong.

"Miss Biggs? What is it? What's wrong?"

"I don't know! He's in there. I can see him. But he won't answer the door and let me in. I don't understand what's going on. Why won't he come get the door?"

Erin glanced at The Bake Shoppe. The interior windows were covered with brown paper, though there were a few cracks and rips.

"Who's in there? Trenton?"

Joelle nodded. "Trenton. Yes."

"He's probably just working in the back and can't hear you. Did you try the back door?"

"No, he's not at the back door. I can see him."

Erin took a step closer to The Bake Shoppe. "You can see him?"

"There, look!" Joelle pointed to one of the rips in the brown paper.

Erin peered into the shop, cupping her hands around her eyes to block the glare of the sun off the glass.

"I don't see anything…" The Bake Shoppe appeared to be empty. What was Joelle Biggs getting so hysterical about?

"Look behind the counter. On the floor."

Erin lowered her gaze, and Joelle was right. Erin could see a man's shoes just poking out from behind the counter. He was probably kneeling. He was using a power tool or had headphones on and couldn't hear his girlfriend knocking.

"Does he have a cell phone? Have you tried calling him? He probably just can't hear you knocking." Erin rapped as loudly as she could on the glass, but the noise was muted and probably didn't sound like much more than a tap from within.

Joelle took out her phone and fumbled with it. "He should be able to hear me. I've been knocking and knocking. He was expecting me."

"You know how men are. He just lost track of time."

Joelle managed to tap or swipe Trenton's number, and held the phone to her ear, jiggling impatiently. "Something is wrong," she insisted. "I know something is wrong. He never ignores me."

Erin suppressed the urge to roll her eyes. They must be pretty early in the honeymoon stage if Trenton never ignored his annoying girlfriend.

"I'll tell you what. I'll go around and see if the back door is unlocked. You can stay here and keep calling and knocking."

Joelle's eyes were so wide, Erin could see the whites of her eyes all around the iris. She looked like a deer, eyes wide, frozen in fear.

"I tried calling 9-1-1," she said, "but it doesn't work! It doesn't go through."

"There's no 9-1-1 service in Bald Eagle Falls."

"Well, what do you do if there's an emergency, then?" Joelle shrieked, grasping Erin's arm so tightly that her acrylic nails bit into Erin's flesh. "What the hell kind of backwater place is this?"

"Look. The police department is just down there." Erin pointed. "In the municipal building. A couple of blocks. You can hop in your car and get down there quicker than you can get ahold of someone on the phone. They'll dispatch Officer Piper or one of the others if you think this is an emergency. But I think you're overreacting."

Joelle pushed Erin aside to look in the window again, pounding her phone against the glass. Erin winced, but neither the glass nor the phone broke.

"You go around back," Joelle ordered. "I'll get the cops!"

"Okay."

Erin started down the block to get into the back alley access. All the buildings were attached to each other, so there was no way to get through to the alley without either going around the block or cutting through one of the other shops. Erin walked briskly despite the heat, some of Joelle's anxiety infecting her. What if something really had happened to Trenton? But that was silly. She could see him right there, kneeling over something behind the counter. Something that he was fixing. Joelle Biggs was just an insecure, hysterical girlfriend. Trenton would laugh at her for being so worried. *I was just cutting tiles, woman. What are you so worked up about?*

Erin stumbled a little over the uneven edge of a sidewalk block and continued, eyes down so that she wouldn't trip again and end up sprawled on her face. That would be a fine thing, Terry Piper coming to check out The Bake Shoppe and finding Erin there with a broken, bleeding nose from a face plant into the pavement.

Erin reached the back of The Bake Shoppe without incident and went to the door. The handle was locked. Unlike the back door on her shop, The Bake Shoppe door had a window. It was open, the screen keeping bugs out but allowing a breeze in. If there had been a breeze. It was probably pleasant during the evening but should have been kept closed during the day while the air conditioner was running.

Erin peered through the door, pressing her face against the screen and squinting. There was a direct line of sight from the back door, through the kitchen, to the front counter. The front door and back door didn't line up; the back door was closer to the center of the store. Erin could still see Trenton's feet, just beyond the edge of the counter, but she could also see farther behind the counter, where she could see that Trenton was not kneeling, but lying.

For the first few seconds, it just seemed unreal. Erin looked away, glancing around for a camera. It was obviously a hoax. A high school film project or some amateur set-up. But there was no one behind the store but her and no sign of a cameras inside the kitchen or the store. Just Erin. And Trenton lying behind the counter.

Then her brain started trying to fill in the cracks, slowly trying out scenarios and then discarding them as they didn't fit. Trenton was lying down to look under the counter for signs of rodent or bug infestation. He was having a nap. He was trying to scare his girlfriend. He was… hurt or sick. That was the only scenario that made sense. Erin couldn't discern any breathing, but she was too far away and looking through a screen that obscured details. If he were in medical distress, he might need immediate attention. How long had Joelle been knocking and pleading for someone to help her? How much time had they already wasted, walking around and peeking in windows?

Erin tried the door handle again. It was still locked. But when she yanked on it, there was some give. Erin looked down at it. There was splintering around the door frame. The door had been shut, the latch pushed into place, but it looked like it had been broken at some point and not properly repaired. Erin gave a yank and got the door halfway open. She yanked on it again, harder, and it popped free in her grasp. Erin took the opportunity and ran into the bakery. She hurried up to Trenton and grabbed his arm, shaking him.

"Trenton? Trenton, are you okay? Do you need help?" She had certified as a first aider when she was doing home care, and the approach came easily to her lips. There was no resistance from Trenton. No response. "Trenton, my name is Erin. I'm going to help you!"

He was a big man. She remembered how he had towered over her. And he had a thick, well-muscled body. All dead weight. Erin grabbed his shoulder and his belt and put all her strength into turning his torso over. She grabbed the back of one thigh, bent his leg at the knee, and used it to lever him the rest of the way over.

"Trenton? Can you hear me?"

She bent over his face, listening for breath, as she settled him flat on his back, adjusted his neck, and watched his chest. No rise or fall. No movement of air on her cheek or breath sounds in her ear. Erin started chest compressions, counting aloud to herself. Did she dare give him rescue breathing as well? Without a mask or any kind of protection? She knew nothing of his life or his lifestyle over the past twenty years since he had taken off. He could have been an intravenous drug user. A sex worker. Anything.

While she did the compressions, she studied his face and his arms. His face, while covered in a short stubble starting to show signs of gray, did not look old or like he had abused his body with hard living. He looked like an aging athlete, not someone who had lived on the streets.

On his arms, there were no tattoos, no tracks. She looked back at his face as she lowered her mouth over his. She gave his mouth a quick rub with her hand to clear away any spittle. The skin around his mouth was pale. Almost blue. She gave him two full breaths, watching his chest rise with each exhalation, and then started compressions again. One, two, three…

There was banging on the window. Erin could hear it clearly. Not the muted taps that she had predicted it sounded like from inside, but a clatter of noise. She could hear Joelle's thin voice again, followed by Terry's baritone. Erin kept pumping, considering what to do. She knew she shouldn't abandon the CPR to let Terry and Joelle into the store. She had to just keep going until someone with authority told her to stop.

Terry Piper would figure it out on his own. When he couldn't see her and she didn't come back around the front of the store again, he would go around back. He would find the back door open, and he would enter.

She could hear them calling both of their names. Demands of 'Trenton' and 'Erin.'

"Just come around the back," Erin growled, stopping compressions to give Trenton a couple more breaths. Beads of sweat slid down her back. Even though the air conditioning was running, she was sweating copiously. The CPR was far harder work than it had ever been in her classes.

Eventually, they stopped calling. After what seemed like hours, Erin heard them arrive at the back of the store. Terry commanded Joelle to stay back until he had cleared any hazards. She heard his call.

"Erin! Are you in there!"

"In here! Trenton's down! CPR!"

She could hear his movements as he opened the door the rest of the way again, and his boots snapping against the tiled floor of the back entryway and kitchen.

"Is there anyone else in here?"

"I didn't hear anyone else." Erin took a quick look around her, realizing she'd had tunnel vision and had focused only on Trenton and nothing else around him. "I don't see anyone."

In a couple more minutes, Terry was at her side. Erin could hear K9's panting and smell his doggie breath. Terry ventured out into the front of the store to check the space in front of the counter.

"I have to check downstairs," he advised. "Just like at your store."

"Yeah. Okay." Erin gave a couple more rescue breaths.

"Just keep doing what you're doing."

"I will."

Terry returned after another delay that dragged out way too long.

"Any response?"

Erin glanced at him, then back down at Trenton, still soft and unresponsive under her hands.

"No. Nothing."

"I'll call for an ambulance. But it has to be dispatched from the city. It will take a while to get here. Once I've made my calls, we can trade off. Give you a break."

"Okay. Sounds good." Erin couldn't believe how unbelievably tired she was after just a few minutes of CPR. She remembered stories she'd heard about people performing CPR for hours. How? How could a person keep it up for so long?

"Is his airway clear?"

"Airway is clear," she confirmed.

Terry left her alone while he made urgent calls to his dispatcher and to various people or departments in the city. He walked out the back and Erin could hear him arguing with Joelle, insisting that she had to stay outside. Eventually, he returned and knelt beside her.

"After your next breaths, we'll trade off. Okay?" He took something out of one of the pouches on his belt and tore the plastic wrapper off of it. He popped it out, and Erin realized it was a mouth guard for CPR. "Sorry, I only have one. You've already been kissing him, so…"

"Yeah. Protect yourself."

She saw that he had gloves on too. Blue ones like medical professionals wore. "Do you have another pair of those? I haven't checked for blood or fluids."

Terry dug out another pair. Erin gave Trenton two more breaths, moving over, and Terry took over the compressions. Erin put the gloves on and started a head-to-toe check for blood or other signs of injuries. She couldn't check his back since they had already started CPR, but she felt the back of his head and neck, his sides, and the backs of his legs, as well as everything on the front. She patted him down, checked for blood on her gloves, and kept going.

"No blood," she said. "Maybe it was a heart attack."

Terry looked around. There wasn't much either of them could see from their position on the floor behind the counter.

"I'll have to secure the scene after they come pick him up. I didn't see anything out of place. Did you touch anything?"

"The doorknob. I don't think… I don't think anything else. He was face down. I turned him over."

Terry grunted.

"The door frame was broken," Erin said. "I didn't do that. Someone had already forced the door."

"The girlfriend?"

"No, I don't think so. She seemed pretty hysterical."

Terry bent over to give a couple of breaths and went back to compressions. They stopped talking, just focusing on the rescue. When Erin detected that Terry's compressions were getting slower and less forceful, she was ready.

"Switch off again."

"I'm okay."

"We don't know how long we're going to have to keep this up. We need to switch regularly."

Terry grunted irritably. Erin waited for him to make space for her. When it was time for the breaths, Terry moved over to give them, allowing Erin to get in and start compressions again.

"How long did they say?" she asked.

"As soon as possible. They wouldn't give an ETA." His expression was guarded.

Erin considered this. "What does that mean?"

"If they had a vehicle to dispatch immediately, it would have been half an hour. Since they wouldn't give an ETA, it means they don't have a vehicle free, and they don't know how long it will take to free one up."

"Oh."

"It could be just a little over half an hour… or it could be a couple…"

Erin nodded. "Okay. Like I say, we'll have to switch regularly. Is there anyone else who can help if we get too tired?"

"I don't want more people on the scene if we can help it. If necessary, we can get the Sheriff and Tom Banks. Willie Andrews. I'm sure we have a few more CPR-certified rescuers. There's a volunteer fire department. They'll have a list of which volunteers are current in their certifications."

"I don't know if I'm current," Erin said with sudden realization.

"I'd say you're already committed." The dimple appeared in Terry's cheek. "You seem to know what you're doing. My dispatcher is also calling around to see if anyone else can send an ambulance. We'll get one sooner or later."

"Hopefully sooner."

"Uh-huh."

K9 had been watching them attentively but, apparently, he decided they weren't going to do anything more interesting, or maybe their voices told him it was going to be a long haul, and he lay down noisily beside his partner.

"K9!" Erin had never heard Terry speak sharply to the dog before. Not even when he had frightened Orange Blossom that first day, barking his head off. Terry pointed firmly to the far wall. "Over there!"

K9 immediately got up and relocated himself, lying down precisely where Terry's outstretched finger pointed.

"Don't want him getting his fur near… Mr. Plaint," Terry said to Erin, his voice normal again. "If it's a crime scene, we don't want to contaminate anything needlessly."

Erin felt her phone vibrating in her pocket. Alton Summers again? Or Vic wondering where she had disappeared to? How long before the whole town realized that there was something unusual going down at The Bake Shoppe? She ignored the call, continuing the rhythmic compressions.

"You don't think it's a crime scene, do you? He just… had a heart attack or a stroke…?"

"Probably. The chances that we'd have another murder in Bald Eagle Falls is extremely low. Extremely low," he repeated with emphasis. "But… we can't be sure without more information. We have to assume it is, and protect its integrity the best we can."

Erin's shoulders ached. She knew she should be completely focused on the rescue and counting her compressions, but her brain was ticking them off in her head in the background, and she was too amped up not to talk about what was happening.

"Do you know anything about Trenton?" she asked. "About when he disappeared the first time? His history?"

"It's an open investigation. Or at least, it was open until he showed up in town. I'm not sure whether I can just close it now, or if I need more details about why he disappeared and what he's been doing while he was gone. I've seen his identification… but IDs can be faked. I need verification that he really is who he said he is. Especially with him coming here to collect on an inheritance."

Terry looked away from her, and Erin realized that the situation was remarkably familiar. Like Erin suddenly showing up to claim her inheritance from Clementine. The police hadn't been involved in the case, but Terry knew the basics. And he had informed her that he knew she hadn't been going by the name Erin Price when Alton Summers had initially tracked her down. He hadn't given any indication since making the arrest in Angela Plaint's murder that he had any suspicions about her, but maybe it was still in the back of his head. Some tiny suspicion that maybe Alton Summers hadn't done his due diligence to make sure she was who she claimed to be.

"How will you verify who he is?"

"Now…?" Terry looked down at the unmoving man. "Now it will be up to someone other than me."

"Who?"

"The coroner."

Erin faltered in her compressions, then picked up the rhythm again. "You don't think… he'll survive?"

Terry shook his head. "You started CPR, so we need to continue it. But we don't know how long he was lying here before you started. Long enough for Miss Biggs to get upset and come find me. The statistics say that CPR will only save four percent of people with an unattended heart attack. Less than that without brain damage."

Erin was aware that her compressions were slowing. "Then why are we doing this?"

"Because once you start a rescue, you have to see it through. I'll take over on your next breaths."

Erin's arms felt like lead. She kept pumping until he could take his turn. "Okay."

CHAPTER 5

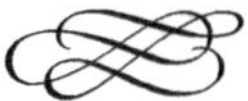

$\mathcal{E}$rin stood there watching the ambulance drive away, red cherry lights rotating slowly, and shivered, though it was still hot even in the shade. Terry put his hand on her shoulder, his touch tentative.

"You did good, Erin. That wasn't easy."

"I don't know if I would have started if I'd realized how long it would take. I'm so sore!"

"Me too. And probably for naught. But we did our best. That's all that can be expected."

The Sheriff and Tom Banks, neither of whom Erin knew well, had taken over the scene. It was probably the right thing for them to do, giving Terry a break after all the work of trying to keep Trenton Plaint's blood oxygenated and circulating, but Terry stood there looking back at the shop as if lost. He clearly didn't know what to do when it would normally have been his job to secure the scene and conduct the initial investigation.

"Why don't you come over to the shop for a bite to eat and some ice tea?" Erin suggested. "We could probably both use something to boost our blood sugar."

Terry nodded. "Yeah, that would be good… just a few more minutes."

Tom Banks wound yellow tape around the fence posts. He moved slowly and deliberately. He was an older man, his skin leathery and cheeks cavernous. Erin knew him to be a kind man, but not, she didn't think, a particularly bright one.

Erin's phone gave a short vibration, and this time she took it out and looked at it. Ignoring any of the previous notifications, she just looked at the last one, a text from Vic. *Are you okay? When are you coming back?*

She quickly thumbed a message back. *Just a couple of minutes. Need some sugar.*

Her phone vibrated in her hand with a return message. *Not my department. Talk to Officer Handsome.*

"Not *that* kind of sugar," Erin said aloud.

Terry turned and looked at her, head cocked. "What?"

"Just Vic," Erin held up her phone, "being silly."

"Oh." Terry snapped his fingers and called K9 to him. "Let's head over there."

They walked back slowly. Erin pulled her clothes away from her skin. No point in trying to pretend that she wasn't soaked right through. She was sure that Terry was just as uncomfortable as she was. They had both been through the wringer. "I might close up early today. I'm beat."

"I'm sure everyone would understand."

As Erin drew up to The Book Nook, she realized she hadn't retrieved her serving trays yet. And she never had gotten down to The General Store to get the case of jams.

"Just give me a sec. Or meet me there. I need to grab something here."

Terry waited patiently for her, K9 at his side eyeing the birds wheeling high in the sky. K9 liked to be out and about, not staying in one place. He always seemed to find some way to complain to Terry when he had to sit still for longer than he liked.

Erin went into The Book Nook and waved to Naomi. "Sorry I was so long getting over here."

"Sorry? You can't exactly leave in the middle of giving someone CPR, can you? I would have brought them over to the bakery. You didn't have to come in."

"It was on the way," Erin said with a tired smile. "How did Book Club go?"

"It's amazing how many more people come when they know there are going to be treats," Naomi said, handing Erin the trays.

It had taken some talking to get Naomi on-side to start with. She hadn't wanted anything in her store that could get crumbs or greasy fingerprints in her books. But the Book Club ladies had, as far as Erin knew, been good about it, and any books that did get marked were purchased by the culprit, so Naomi didn't have to eat the costs. What she paid for in treats she made back in higher attendance and sales.

"We should try a few themed days," Erin suggested. It was something she had come up with a few days before, not that she had just pulled out of her exhausted brain. "Like... death by chocolate, Hannah Swensen cookie varieties, stuff like that. What do you think?"

Naomi nodded eagerly. "That sounds like fun! I'll look over the shelves and see what stock I need to move that we could tie into."

"Great. Just let me know. You know where to find me!"

"Take it easy tonight. You deserve a rest."

Erin agreed, and with her trays in hand, headed back outside. Terry walked her to the door of Auntie Clem's Bakery, held the door for her, and followed her in.

"Erin!" Vic hurried around the counter and hugged Erin. The two of them weren't usually huggy, and Erin pulled back and tried to extricate herself, feeling sweaty and grubby and embarrassed about having someone hug her in that state.

"It's okay. It's okay; I'm fine."

Vic released her, but stood there searching her eyes for the truth. "Are you sure?"

"I'm good too," Terry offered, eyebrows raised and the dimple in his cheek prominent.

"I'm not hugging you," Vic retorted.

Erin laughed. "Okay, back to work. I just need to change into a fresh apron, and—"

"No, you don't." Vic stopped her, hands on hips. "You go sit down, and I'll bring the two of you something to eat. And some iced tea. You need to take a break."

"There's work to do," Erin pointed out. "Things might be winding down because of Trenton... but I still need to get things ready for tomorrow morning. We can probably close early, but we can't skip prepping for tomorrow."

"Go sit down," Vic repeated firmly. "You're on temporary leave. I'll take care of the prep. I've got your checklists; I know what to do."

"Vic—"

"No. Go sit down. Go on."

Vic gave no sign of backing down. Erin sighed, and she and Terry went over to the small tables and wrought-iron chairs to sit down. K9 sat down at Terry's side but kept looking toward Vic and making irritated snuffling sounds. Erin looked over at Vic, sniffing the air and trying to figure out what K9 was so restless about. Was something burning in the oven, but only the dog could smell it? Or was there some other danger that he could detect that no one else could? Erin felt a little jumpy after working over what was basically a corpse for a couple of hours. Maybe K9 could smell death, and that was what was bothering him.

Vic bussed a plate of assorted goodies over to the table. Erin noted that Vic knew which delicacies were her particular favorites and which were Terry's. She was a bright kid. She brought the iced tea and glasses over separately, and then looked at them. "Anything else?"

Erin was going to say they had everything they needed, but before she had the chance, K9 nudged Vic's bare calf with his cold, wet nose, making Vic yelp and jump back.

"Maybe the dog would like something," Erin laughed.

"Oh, you know, he probably would," Terry said, looking down at his watch. He reached over and scratched K9's head. "I'm sorry, buddy. Could you bring him a bowl of water, Vic? He's probably dying of thirst."

Vic nodded and went back to the kitchen.

"Dogs perspire through their mouths, by panting," Terry told Erin. "His fur helps to keep him insulated from the heat, but it still affects him. He needs to keep hydrated when it's hot out, just like we do."

Erin nodded. She took a sip of her cold, sweet tea. So cold it made her teeth hurt, but she ignored the pain and took a few swallows anyway. She hadn't realized how dry she was. Vic returned with a bowl of water and put it down in front of K9. He plunged his snout into it immediately, then started lapping the water up noisily. Vic put a biscuit on the table.

"There's a treat for him when he's done drinking."

Erin tried to ignore the slurping noises while she nibbled at a muffin. Terry wasn't eating but was turned slightly, staring into the display case a few feet away.

"Is there something else you wanted?" Erin asked him. "I'll get you whatever you like."

"No. It's just… those cupcakes…" Terry pointed at the chocolate chip cupcakes with sprinkles. "There were some that looked just like that at the —at The Bake Shoppe. Were those yours, or was he copying your recipe…?"

"Oh, no!" Erin laughed. "Joelle bought those. Gluten-free, vegan…" Erin trailed off. "Why…?"

"And there were some of those ones too, weren't there?"

"The red velvet," Erin agreed. "Yes. She took six of each. Bought, I mean. She bought six of each. The chocolate chip for herself, because she's vegan. And the red velvet for Trenton."

"And took them to The Bake Shoppe."

"Yes… well, that's where they were, wasn't it? That's where they were working. Where else would she have taken them?"

"Did she have any? Did she say what she thought about them?"

"I don't know. She didn't mention anything." Erin tried to recall what she had seen at The Bake Shoppe. She had seen her cupcakes out. On a plate, not the boxes she had packaged them into for Joelle. How many of each had been left? "I think… there were three or four of each left, weren't there? What did you see? I wasn't looking at anything other than Trenton. He's really all I paid any attention to."

"I walked around to clear the building," Terry said slowly. "I looked at everything."

She could tell that he was trying to play it back in his mind. Trying to replay each impression in his mind to answer the question.

"Yes… three or four of each." He cleared his throat, frowning and staring at the empty air between them. K9 was still drinking noisily. "If you sold them six of each, and there were three of each left, then there were six eaten."

"According to my first-grade math skills, yes. If Joelle had twelve cupcakes, and there were six cupcakes left—"

"That's too many for just one of them to have eaten," Terry went on as if Erin weren't even talking. "Both of them ate some of the cupcakes."

"I suppose," Erin agreed. "I can't see Joelle having more than one or two. Even though six of them were for her."

"So, Miss Biggs had one of the chocolate chip, and Mr. Plaint had two, or else Miss Biggs had two, and Mr. Plaint had one."

"Right."

"And he had all three of the red velvet because they were not vegan."

"Right. Joelle wouldn't have touched those."

Terry didn't say anything. He just sat there, eyes unfocused, running through it in his mind.

"What is it?" Erin prompted. "Why does that matter?"

"What did you see when you went into The Bake Shoppe? Describe everything in detail."

"I already told you everything."

"Mr. Plaint. He was lying face-up or face-down?"

"Face-down, I told you."

"Did he have anything in his hands? Had he been eating? Was there anything on the floor? Crumbs?"

"No, no, nothing that I noticed. Why? You don't think..." Erin's brows drew down, and a headache started in the middle of her forehead. "You don't think he choked on one of my cupcakes, do you?"

"Choked... maybe he had allergies like his mother..."

"His air passage was clear, and I didn't see anything on the floor. I think one of us would have noticed if he'd choked on a big lump of muffin and then dislodged it when he fell."

Terry nodded his agreement. "Did he have any allergies?"

"I have no idea. He said that he was going to bake normal stuff and leave all the gluten-free to me. He never said he would eat it. I got the feeling that he looked down on the special diets. A lot of people act that way, men in particular. That they're too big and strong to have allergies, and anyone who does must be weak or effeminate..."

"So, he probably wouldn't have told anyone if he did have allergies."

Erin didn't like the way the conversation was turning. "If he did have any allergies, I have no idea what they are. Joelle didn't mention any before buying him those red velvet cupcakes. She checked all the ingredients in the chocolate chip cupcakes and the icing and sprinkles. But she didn't check anything on the red velvet."

"Tell me what his face looked like when you turned him over."

Erin closed her eyes. "Very pale. I don't know... he might have been blue from lack of oxygen. I started on CPR and rescue breathing right away. I didn't think there was any time to spare."

"No. Of course not. Did he have any... fluids on his face?"

Erin shook her head slowly. "I… I wiped his mouth before I started breathing. So… if there was any evidence, I might have wiped it away."

"If you wiped his mouth, then it must not have been dry."

"I don't remember… he wasn't frothing at the mouth if that's what you mean. He hadn't bit his tongue during a seizure and bled. There wasn't… I don't know… no nosebleed or cuts that I noticed."

"But you must have noticed moisture, or you wouldn't have wiped it."

"I… don't know. Maybe I would have anyway. You know… because of germs."

"It's so hot, any saliva would have evaporated pretty quickly."

"I guess. Yeah."

Terry sighed. He took a long drink of his iced tea. K9 had finally stopped drinking, so Erin offered him the dog biscuit. K9 took it from her and lay down with it between his paws, as usual.

"We'll just have to wait for the coroner's report," Terry said. "I'm sure it was probably nothing related to the cupcakes. This is *not* Angela's death all over again."

"Angela wasn't killed by my cupcakes," Erin reminded him firmly. "It was nothing to do with my baking."

"And I'm sure this one wasn't either."

Erin dragged herself in the door and flopped down on the couch.

"I can't believe how exhausted I am," she moaned. "And how sore! My arms feel like they belong to someone else, they're so heavy and swollen." She shifted her position. "Except I know they're mine because they hurt every time I move!"

Orange Blossom, yowling for attention, jumped up onto the couch, and then into Erin's lap. When she didn't start cuddling and scratching him, he stood his front paws on her chest, bumping his head insistently against Erin's chin.

Erin laughed. "I'd give you attention if I could, Mr. Blossom, I'm just too beat."

Vic swooped over and picked up Orange Blossom. "That's enough, leave Erin alone. Why don't you go get into the bath, and I'll feed the baby and warm up some dinner?"

"After all the treats and iced tea, I'm going to have to pass. I really couldn't eat anything else."

"Okay. But if you change your mind, let me know. Just go have a warm bath, it will help those sore muscles."

"I'm afraid that if I got into the bathtub, I wouldn't be able to get back out without help," Erin said. "And I don't think either of us wants you to have to drag my naked self out of the bathtub."

Vic looked at Erin, brows raised. "I'm strong," she pointed out. "I could help you."

"Yes, but…" Erin was proud of the way that she and Vic had been able to settle in together as housemates without a bunch of awkwardness between them over Vic's background and gender identity. Most of the time, she didn't think twice about Vic's female identity or her former life as James Victor Jackson, Angela's nephew. They both were modest and carefully preserved their privacy. Neither had seen the other in the altogether, and that was the way Erin intended to keep it. "I think I'm just going to head straight to bed. The heating pad will be easier to manage than getting in and out of the tub in this condition."

Vic nodded. "Okay," she agreed. But she looked at Erin for a minute longer than was comfortable, and Erin was pretty sure that Vic had understood far more about Erin's discomfort than she intended. Erin would never have done anything to draw attention to the physical differences between their bodies, but she was afraid she just had.

"Good night, then," Erin said softly.

"Good night. Give me a shout if you need anything. If you've got the heating pad on, I'm sure this guy will be snuggling with you tonight."

"For sure," Erin agreed.

Erin had thought that would be the last she saw of Vic for the night. But Vic checked in a few hours later as she got ready for bed.

"Are you awake?" she whispered.

Erin had been in and out of sleep. Exhausted, but too sore and anxious to stay asleep. She had tried to read. She had written several lists. She would fall asleep for what seemed like five minutes and then wake up again, her brain too restless to get any REM sleep.

"Yeah. You can come in."

Vic crept into the room and sat on the edge of Erin's bed. She looked around for a minute like she hadn't seen the room before. Which of course she had.

"What's wrong?" Erin asked.

"I don't know. Nothing. Everything. My brain is going a mile a minute, and I don't think I can settle in."

"Tell me about it," Erin sympathized. "I might have to take something tonight, and I never take anything to sleep. I don't want to be in a fog tomorrow."

Vic nodded.

"Tell me what you're worrying about the most," Erin prompted. She looked at the paper and pencil on her bedside table. "We could make a list if you like."

"I don't need a list for what I'm worried about. It's you."

"Me? What about me? I keep telling you I'm just fine."

"You have to ask? I'm worried about you getting caught up in another murder investigation."

Erin was surprised at that.

"Trenton? It wasn't murder, Vic. It was a heart attack or stroke. These athletes who put on a lot of weight later in life and end up with sedentary lives; you hear about the dangers all the time. They think they can do everything they could as kids, but their bodies just aren't up to it anymore. They sit too much, eat too much, and then work too much in the heat when their bodies aren't used to it…"

"Maybe." Vic sat there, her face bleak. "Or maybe it was poison. Or another allergic reaction. Or maybe he was hit over the head."

"I don't think he was hit over the head. I looked for any injuries. Everything seemed to be just fine. He wasn't stabbed or shot or hit over the head. He wasn't strangled."

"Poison."

"What makes you think he was poisoned? Nobody else was there. Who could have poisoned him?"

"You." Before Erin could protest, Vic held up her hand and pressed on. "I don't mean you did it, just that you *could* have, and that's what Officer Piper is going to think and what everyone else is going to think. That Trenton was in your way, he was going to take your business, so you… took care of it."

"I did not poison Trenton Plaint."

"I know. You couldn't have without me knowing about it. I was there when you made the cupcakes and when you sold them to Joelle. You couldn't have put anything in them. Especially in just those six. But that's what other people are going to think. That you killed him."

"I don't think anyone is going to think that. If I poisoned him, why would I give him CPR? Why would I get involved at all?"

Vic looked down and didn't answer, but Erin could see the scenarios herself. The perpetrator often went back to the scene of the crime. They had to make sure. They inserted themselves into the investigation to keep track of it. They wanted to see other people's reactions. To make sure the body was found. To make themselves look heroic.

"No one has accused me of murder, and no one is going to," Erin assured Vic. "Now you go to bed and don't worry about it anymore. We both need to get a good night's sleep to be effective tomorrow. If you need something to help you sleep, you can check the medicine cabinet in the bathroom. I have a few herbs—"

"I have Ambien."

Erin looked at Vic, startled. There were still a lot of things that she didn't know about Vic. Erin had tried to give Vic her privacy. She'd never searched through Vic's possessions for drugs, prescription or otherwise. That was Vic's own business. Erin didn't even know who Vic's doctor was, whether she had gotten a prescription from someone in town or if she had had the Ambien from the time she ran away from home. They didn't have a lot of time apart, but sometimes Vic did take an evening or Sunday afternoon to run errands on her own.

"Okay, then," Erin tried to keep her tone casual. "If you need one, go ahead and take it. Tomorrow's a new day, and everything will be fine. Don't you worry about me."

Vic nodded, standing up from the bed. "I'll try not to."

CHAPTER 6

When they opened in the morning, Erin was braced for the increase in traffic and gossip that was going to run through the bakery. Everyone would have heard about Trenton, and they would all want to share their speculations and get the inside scoop from Erin. The only other person who could tell them anything was Terry Piper, and everyone knew he couldn't share anything about his investigation with civilians.

So, she was pleasantly surprised when she saw that the first person into the bakery was Bertie Braceling. Erin had yet to find anything she could sell to him, but it was a challenge she was determined to succeed at.

Bertie gave her a wide smile, toddling up to the counter. He was a short man, stout with a round face. It certainly didn't appear that his multiple allergies and intolerances kept him from getting enough calories. Or maybe it was all just a joke, and he was able to eat whatever he wanted to and just liked to tease Erin about not being able to bake for him.

He scanned the display case in front of him but knew that there was no point in asking about what he saw there. If there were anything he could eat, Erin would point it out to him.

"What's new, pumpkin?" he asked genially.

"I'm working on it!" Erin grabbed a folder of recipes from under the cash register. "Now, you said you couldn't have flours made from any grains."

"Right."

"But buckwheat is okay because it's not from the grass family."

He nodded. "It's a pseudocereal. Not actually related to wheat and corn."

"So, I wondered about this…" Erin pulled the first recipe out of her folder and placed it in front of him. Bertie's eyes went back and forth over the ingredients, and he was shaking his head almost immediately.

"No tapioca flour," he said. "Cassava gives me neurological symptoms. Did you know that cassava is actually poisonous? It can kill you if not properly prepared?"

"But not tapioca flour. All of the toxins have been removed in commercial flours."

He shrugged. "But something about it still bothers my body, unfortunately."

"Okay." Erin circled the ingredient on the recipe. "We would need to substitute another starch in this recipe. How about…" She flipped to the next recipe. "I was thinking about some no-cook raw treats. Now, a lot of them rely on nut butters, which are out, but I could use a seed butter that you were able to tolerate…" She slid the recipe in front of him. "There are lots of variations once you have the basic recipe down…"

Bertie laughed. "Dates."

"Dates?" Erin's heart sank. All the recipes were a combination of two base ingredients. A nut butter and dates.

"Used to be able to eat them when I was young. And I even got my hands on fresh dates a time or two going to markets in the city. But… now they give me an anaphylactic reaction."

Erin sighed. "So, no dates. Maybe I can figure something out with another kind of dried fruit." She looked at him, eyebrow raised.

"As long as I'm not allergic to the fruit it's made from. And there are sulphites, you know. And a lot of dried fruits like raisins are coated with cottonseed oil to keep them from clumping together…"

"Oh, Bertie…!"

"I know, dear." He patted her hand. "I warned you not to even try! It's a moving target. Even something that's safe today, I could start reacting to tomorrow."

"Just like Trenton," a woman said.

Erin looked over at the next customer, shocked at the suggestion. She hadn't seen Melissa come in, too focused on her conversation with Bertie. Vic froze, taking a muffin out of the case for Melissa. She looked at Erin, eyes wide.

"I'm sure the coroner hasn't had time to determine cause of death yet," Erin said to Melissa, gritting her teeth but forcing a smile. "He probably hasn't even had time to look at the body. Last I saw Mr. Plaint, they hadn't even declared him yet."

But she knew in her heart that Trenton had been dead when they loaded him into the ambulance. He'd been dead for hours, despite all that Erin and Terry had done.

"Well, he's been declared now," Melissa advised. She gave Erin a big smile. "That's the second person to die right after eating one of your cupcakes."

Bertie gave Erin an uncertain smile. "I'll check in again another day. Unless you're ready to give up on me..."

"Not a chance." Erin tore her eyes away from Melissa and tried to give Bertie her full attention. "I'll see you later."

He smiled and went on his way. Erin sighed and looked back at Melissa, who now had her muffins and was ready to check out.

"So, what's this about Trenton? It wasn't obvious it was an allergy; not like with Angela."

"Your cupcakes were on the scene," Melissa said. "He'd obviously eaten recently. His girlfriend said that she didn't think he had allergies, but she didn't really know for sure."

"She didn't know?"

"They apparently... haven't known each other for that long."

Erin frowned as she made change for Melissa. "What do you mean by that? Did they just meet? She wasn't a hitchhiker that he just happened to pick up."

"Well, no." Melissa giggled. "Nothing like that. They have only been dating for a couple of months. Not very long, but not... she wasn't someone he just picked up on his drive here." She laughed again.

Erin nodded. "Some people don't like to share their allergies. Because they're too macho or anxious about fitting in. But the same applies to other conditions as well. He probably wouldn't tell Miss Joelle Biggs if he had a heart condition either, would he? Something like that might scare her off."

"He didn't have a heart condition."

"According to who?"

Melissa opened her mouth to respond, then realized that she was just confirming what Erin had said. Even if Trenton did have a heart condition, he wasn't going to be entrusting it to his short-term girlfriend. The peacock was not a reliable witness as to his health issues.

"Why don't we just wait until the coroner has something to report?" Erin suggested. "I think that would be best, don't you?"

While Vic and Erin were eating their early lunch, there was banging on the front door of the shop. They looked at each other. Normally, the residents of the town were very polite, and if the 'closed' or 'back at ______________' signs were up in the window, they did not make a fuss, but just returned later when they were open again.

"Just ignore it," Erin advised when Vic stood up to answer it. "If we answer once when the closed sign is up, people will expect us to answer all the time."

Vic sat slowly back down again. "I suppose… but isn't that… inhospitable? We are still here…"

"Even a southern girl has to know her limits on hospitality. We need our lunch break. We can't function without it. It's rude for customers to think they can interrupt us when we take a break."

Vic considered that, taking another bite of her sandwich. The knocking persisted for a minute or two and then stopped.

"You see?"

But a couple of minutes later, there was a louder knock on the back door. And unlike the door at The Bake Shoppe, they didn't have a window or peephole to check through. Erin looked at the door, her heart thumping hard.

"Who do you think it is? They're certainly impatient."

"What if it's Officer Piper?"

"No… Terry wouldn't keep knocking; he'd just call me on the phone or ask me to make an appointment. You know how he is."

Erin stood up slowly. The hammering on the door continued. She crossed the kitchen and opened the door.

"Oh. It's you."

Alton Summers gave her a smile.

"Miss Price. Or should I say, Miss Albertson." That was the name that she had been using when he had tracked her down. "Or is it… Miss Landers?"

Erin winced. She gave Alton Summers a hard look. He was not a young man, though he tried to look like one. Probably in his forties. He had carefully-groomed blond hair, getting a little spare in the temples, and a quarter-inch scruff that looked more like he hadn't shaved for a week than something that he was intentionally maintaining. He wore heavy gold jewelry and had an old tattoo on his arm.

"What can I do for you, Mr. Summers?"

"You're a hard lady to get ahold of."

"I didn't think we had any business left to conduct. You got your payment from the estate, didn't you?"

He shrugged, showing yellow-stained teeth in a displeased smile. "I got some money from the estate for finding you," he confirmed. "But it wasn't as much as I had hoped it would be."

"I'm sorry about that. I wasn't the one who hired you. If you have a problem with the fees, you'll need to talk to the lawyer, not me."

"But I was thinking…" he pressed in closer to her, trying to crowd her through the doorway so that he could get into the shop. "That maybe I could get some more money from you, since you made a tidy sum on your inheritance. You wouldn't have collected anything without me."

"You've already been paid for finding me. You're not going to get more from me. Thanks." Erin tried to shut the door in his face. Summers moved quickly to put a pointy-shoed foot in the door to keep it from closing.

"I wouldn't suggest taking that tactic if I was you," he growled.

"I don't owe you anything."

"I'm thinking that maybe you wouldn't like everyone here to know the details of your past."

Erin hesitated. She looked at Summers's shoe, preventing the door from closing. There were a lot of things she would rather that Vic and Terry Piper and others in her new hometown didn't know about. But she couldn't afford to be paying some lowlife who wanted to blackmail her, either.

"You're trespassing, Mr. Summers. I'll ask you one more time to leave, and then I'm going to call the police."

"You would call the police on me? But then you might not like what I had to tell them about you. People might not come to your quaint little bakery if they knew what kind of a person you really were."

Erin dug into her pocket to pull out her phone. She knew Terry Piper's number. She didn't even have to go through the dispatcher. He was on duty, and he and K9 would be on patrol somewhere close. Erin had a pretty good idea that K9 wouldn't like the stench of the man once he got close. K9 was a good judge of character. And Erin would hope that in choosing between trusting the woman he'd come to know over the past few months and the unshaven, creepy-looking out-of-towner, Terry would take her side as well.

Summers withdrew his foot, though still protesting. Erin shut the door and locked it. She turned around and saw that Vic was out of her chair, watching Erin through the kitchen doorway. Her eyes were wide.

"What was that about?" Vic asked. "Who was that?"

"Somebody you want to stay away from," Erin sighed. She went back to her sandwich but didn't have much appetite for it.

"But who was it?" Vic persisted.

"He's a private detective named Alton Summers. He was hired by Clementine's estate to see if he could find me. Because Clementine lost track of me when I went into foster care and no one knew where I was. He's a good detective. He found me."

"What's he doing here, then, if he already found you?"

"Looking for trouble."

"Oh." Vic sat back down and picked up her sandwich. "Is he going to cause problems for you, then?"

"He's apparently going to try."

Vic nodded, chewing on a thumbnail.

"Try not to worry about it," Erin advised, saying to herself as much as to Vic. "Worrying won't help anything."

After lunch, they got back into the swing of things. There were a number of gossip seekers who came along on the prowl for information, but they told Erin more than she revealed to them.

Erin looked up to see Mary Lou walk in with a cardboard flat of jam jars. Erin struck her forehead with the heel of her hand.

"Oh, I forgot, Mary Lou, with everything that happened yesterday…"

"Don't you worry," Mary Lou assured her. "I just had a break, so I thought I would run them over. It's not out of my way. Not when I'm looking for a mid-afternoon pick-me-up!"

She approached the till and put the flat down.

"How much do I owe you?"

Mary Lou gave her the details and Erin opened the till to settle up.

"And a chocolate biscotti," Mary Lou requested.

Erin got it herself while Vic served another customer. Mary Lou was always restrained in her snack choices. She wasn't one to go with the rich, high-calorie desserts. She took care to maintain her svelte figure.

"Thanks so much for bringing the jams over. You're sure you won't tell me who The Jam Lady is?"

Mary Lou gave a secretive smile. "No, afraid not. The Jam Lady does not wish to be revealed."

Erin leaned forward. "Is it you?"

The neat blond woman shook her head. "No, I swear it's not me."

Erin studied her for a moment, but couldn't see any sign that Mary Lou was lying. She turned the mystery over in her mind. She didn't know everyone in town, and even those she did know, she hadn't spent a lot of time with, getting to know their foibles and quirks. The Jam Lady could be practically anyone.

Most of the women she knew had other jobs, though. If they were making jam, especially at the rate that the Jam Lady jars seemed to be spreading around town, she would have to be spending a lot of evening hours cooking up batches of jam. In a town where everyone knew everyone else's business, how would anyone keep hours spent on jam-making a secret?

CHAPTER 7

It had been such a disrupted week that Erin was a little surprised when Sunday rolled around and they needed to pack the car with their caving gear so that they could head straight out after the church ladies' post-service tea.

"Are you sure you want to go ahead with it this week?" Erin asked Vic. "It's been sort of a rough week, neither of us sleeping well, and I thought maybe you'd like just to take a break this week. Go home and have a nap…"

"No," Vic said flatly. "I want to go out and do something interesting, not stay at home and do nothing. Don't you think it's better to work off the stress?"

Erin shrugged. "If that's what you want. I'm just making sure."

"Are your arms recovered enough to go?"

Erin rubbed her shoulders and biceps. "Yes. As long as I don't have to do any rope climbing. If we're just walking or hiking, I can do that. Climbing… that would be pretty hard."

"We'll keep it to walking," Vic agreed. She bounced a little. "I'm excited about it. I know you're not, but I really want to try it again!"

Smiling, Erin nodded. "I'm sure we'll have a really good time," she agreed. "I'm a little anxious, but I'm sure once we get on our way, we're all going to have a really good time."

"And you forgive me for inviting Terry? I mean Officer Piper?"

"I'm sure it will be fine," Erin said, not committing. She was still mildly irritated about Vic inviting Terry along without asking first, but she knew Vic had just been being polite and hadn't intended to make it an uncomfortable situation.

The ladies' tea went well, and before long, they were on their way. Vic had the coordinates of the cave Willie had selected, and she gave Erin directions to get there. A knot grew in Erin's stomach. It had been several months since her last disastrous attempt at spelunking, which had ended up with her in hospital. She had thought that she had let enough time pass to get over her nervousness about it, but as they got farther away from Bald Eagle Falls, she found herself getting increasingly anxious.

She was relieved to see that Willie had arrived there ahead of them. Of course, Gema Reed was in prison now, so she wasn't waiting there to attack Erin, but Erin's body was still reacting as if she might be. Vic bounded out of the car before Erin had even put it into park and was immediately pulling out their gear, chattering away to Willie.

Erin got out more slowly. She looked around at the beautiful scenery, her gut cramping painfully.

"How are you doing?" Willie asked quietly.

She hadn't seen much of him. He was always busy with one job or another in town, or else out at a mine doing what he liked best, prospecting for precious ores. His skin always appeared to be ingrained with dirt from prospecting or smelting. Erin didn't know much about the processes he used to find or to refine ores, but whatever he did always seemed to leave him blackened. Though she'd initially been turned off by his grubby appearance, she had largely gotten over that. He smelled more often of soap than of sweat, had a myriad of skills that he put to use in odd jobs around town, and he'd been one of the two people to save her from her previous encounter with caving. It was probably shallow of her to find him more attractive after the rescue, but she couldn't resist her own psychological response.

"I'm fine," Erin said immediately.

It sounded too chirpy and cheerful even to her own ears, and Willie didn't believe her for a minute. He took off his ball cap and scratched his head, not voicing his doubts.

"Okay, maybe not fine," Erin admitted.

Vic stopped fiddling with the caving equipment and looked at Erin, disappointment written in her features.

"I'm still going," Erin told her firmly. "I'm just... sort of having a difficult time with it."

"If you can't go..." Vic started.

"I can. I'm not saying that. I'm just saying... no, I'm not just fine. I'm going to need some help."

"That's what I'm here for," Willie confirmed. "And you'll probably feel a lot better once we're under way, instead of everything you are dreading could happen in advance. Why don't we run through safety equipment and what we're going to do? Maybe that will help..."

Erin nodded. "Yeah. That sounds good." Although what she wanted to hear was that the cave they were going to explore was so shallow and innocuous that they really didn't need any safety equipment just to pop in and out again. And then they could all go back to town and have a cold RC together before going back home to bed.

Willie gave her a slight smile, and Erin knew he had a pretty good idea what was going through her head. But he didn't tell her what she wanted to hear and instead started getting her and Vic geared up for their exploration.

They'd been there about twenty minutes when Officer Piper showed up. He pulled in behind Erin's car and climbed out. He was pretty much ready to go, and just pulled a pack on over his shoulders as he walked over to the little group. K9 sat down beside him, and Terry scratched his ears and exchanged greetings with everyone.

At that point, Erin's mind went from being anxious about what was going to happen underground to being anxious about the social construct. She had asked Willie to guide them, and Vic had invited Terry along, so if it was a double date, then Willie was Erin's date, and Terry was Vic's. But both men were significantly older than Vic, and Erin didn't think that either of them saw her as a potential partner. More like a tagalong little sister. Vic seemed oblivious to any awkwardness, but Erin caught looks from both Willie and Terry. Evaluating looks toward each other and directed at Erin. Everyone trying to feel out their roles and relationships.

"Okay," Willie said. "Are we all ready to go, then?"

Erin held her breath. She wanted someone else to say no. To come up with some other delay. To break a boot lace or get a nosebleed or something else that would make them reschedule the exploration for another day. But no one objected.

"Let's go, then," Willie said. "I'll head in first, then Erin, Vic, and Terry can bring up the rear. That meet with everyone's approval?"

Vic opened her mouth and looked at Erin, and then at Terry, but when neither of them had anything to say about it, she shrugged.

"Okay, then," she said with a sigh. "I wish I was in the front, but I guess it should be someone who knows the system down there."

"You should have someone experienced in the lead," Willie agreed. "And I want Erin nice and close to me, so I know if she has any trouble."

"Fine, I'll take the third position, then, and Officer Piper can bring up the rear."

Everyone was right about it being better once they were inside the caves and on their way. Erin was able to relax about all the things that might go wrong, and just concentrate on what she was seeing in front of her. Her eyes adjusted to seeing everything by the dim light of her headlamp and, with Willie in front of her, she wasn't so afraid of stepping off a cliff or smacking into an overhang. They moved slowly but steadily. It was nothing like when Erin had been dragged and left underground, bound and helpless.

After a few hours, they were done, back out of the caves into the tear-inducing sunshine and the safety of their cars. And they did drive into town to the barbecue place to have some wings and cold RCs.

"Thank you so much for being our guide, Mr. Andrews," Vic gushed.

"I thought we were all on first names," Willie said. "It's Willie. Okay, Miss Victoria?"

"Vic!" She laughed. "Okay, first names, then." She patted his arm. "Willie."

"How did you enjoy it?" Willie looked from Vic to Erin and smiled at her. "You seemed like you settled down and were getting into it after the first little while."

"I did," Erin agreed. "It's different than I thought it would be. Different than last time. It really is beautiful down there, in its own way."

"You bet it is. We didn't see a lot of formations, but sometimes the crystals or veins you can discover are brilliant. Just… spectacular. People don't usually go spelunking just to see dark passageways and blind fish. They want to see cave paintings, beautiful formations, gemstones, and precious ores. They want to lay eyes on something that few other people have ever set eyes on before."

Erin smiled at his loquacity. Usually, Willie was a quiet man who spared few words. "That must be an amazing experience."

"One of the best I've ever had." He took a sip of his cola. "So why don't you tell me something about your life? What do you like to do, aside from baking?"

"She likes to make lists," Vic contributed. "And lists of lists."

"Important to be prepared," Willie said. When Erin didn't offer anything else, he prompted her. "Is baking all you have done, then? That's what you did before you came here?"

"No… actually I hadn't done any baking before. I mean, not on a large scale like at the shop. I had only baked for friends, little gatherings. I remember working with Clementine at the tea room, way back when, but that was just as a child. Serving tables, not doing any baking."

"So, what did you do up north?"

All eyes were on her. Erin shifted uncomfortably and gave a little laugh. "A little of this, a little of that."

Terry was staring at her intently. He shook his head at her answer. "Woman of mystery."

"It's nothing mysterious. Just… boring. You don't want to know all of the stupid, mundane jobs I had."

"You must have done something interesting."

Vic scratched at a dried-up spot of ketchup on the table. "That detective said you had other names."

Erin gave her a sharp look. "So did you!"

Vic closed her lips tightly. Erin knew it had been sort of a dirty move. But if Vic was going to force Erin to reveal information about her past, especially in front of other people, she'd better be ready to reveal her own.

Willie looked from one to the other, looking mildly interested. Terry leaned back, saying nothing. He didn't know their complete histories, but he did know that both had used other names. He knew why Vic had changed her name from the masculine form. Erin wasn't sure how much

Terry knew about her own background. She had been one of the main suspects in Angela's murder, so he had investigated her then. But she didn't know how much he had found. He'd never shown her all his cards, and she hadn't wanted to know.

"I was in the foster care system," Erin told Willie. "I took the name of the family I was with sometimes, to try to blend in better." She shrugged. "That never really worked the way I thought it would."

This seemed to satisfy Vic's curiosity about the matter, and she didn't explain her own name change to Willie. She hadn't come out as transgender to the general populace of Bald Eagle Falls, and she didn't jump in to take the opportunity to tell Willie and Officer Piper about it. Terry gave her no sign that he already knew.

"What other kind of things have you done?" Willie asked. It wasn't a demand. And he didn't ask about everything she had done. Just a background question. The kind of thing friends asked as they got to know one another.

Erin sighed. "I was doing some accounting before I came here. I'm not certified or anything, just bookkeeping. And I've been in retail… home care… wherever I can find work, really. I didn't have the opportunity to get a university degree…" she trailed off, feeling inadequate.

"I never went to university," Willie said with a shrug. "And if there was ever someone not prejudiced about doing odd jobs to survive, it's me!"

Erin chuckled. "I guess so. You do a lot of different things."

"I'm a restless spirit. Don't like to be tied down to one thing. My real passion is prospecting, but that doesn't bring in enough of an income to live on. A good cash-in every now and then, but not steadily enough to survive."

"You seem like… you have knowledge in a lot of areas. Not just the caves in the area, but survival and medical treatment too…"

"It's all part of spending time underground. Not something to take lightly."

"I guess not," Erin agreed. She sucked down a few swallows of her drink. "You do everything on your own, though? Isn't it dangerous to be in mines and caves all by yourself? What if something happened to you? Do you file a plan with anyone, like a solo pilot would?"

"It's always good to let someone know where you are going to be and when you'll be back…" Willie tapped the side of his glass. "But I admit that I don't. I don't actually… have many friends around Bald Eagle Falls."

"You could file it with the police department," Terry suggested. "We always recommend that hikers and other travelers and adventurers let someone know. If you don't have any family or friends who would follow up on it, just give the office a call. Then at least we'd know where to start looking if you didn't report back."

Willie nodded. "Yeah. Thanks. I might just do that."

When Erin and Vic got back home from the restaurant, Erin was strangely restless and not ready for sleep. She knew that she should head to bed before it got too late, or she would be too tired when she got up in the morning. But she didn't want to lie down yet. She pulled down the attic stairs in the hallway and climbed to her little attic retreat. She could snuggle up in the little reading nook under the window. Or sit down to write out lists or letters or a journal entry at her writing desk. Or just sit there and daydream. It was a bright, cozy little room, and she loved it.

But she was too restless to read or write. She just kept bouncing from one place to the other, looking for something to satisfy her mood.

Orange Blossom started to cry. He let out a few mournful howls, and Erin heard Vic call him.

"Kitty, kitty? Come in here!"

But the cat continued to caterwaul, his voice getting raucous. Most of the time, he was pretty quiet and didn't cry unless he was locked up, like when Erin accidentally shut him in the pantry. But sometimes he got it into his head that he'd been abandoned and yowled like his little kitty heart was broken.

"Blossom! Come for snuggles, Blossom!" Vic called.

When the cat continued to make noise, Erin got up to see to him, but Vic beat her there. Erin heard Vic pick him up and mutter to him about being so noisy. She carried him back to her bedroom, talking baby talk to him. For a few minutes, everything was quiet. And then he started up again.

Erin walked over and looked down the stairs at him. He stood with his front paws on the bottom step, looking up and obviously calling to her.

"Come up the stairs," Erin encouraged.

But he didn't. So far, he had never climbed the stairs. Erin had carried him up to the attic a couple of times, but each time he had run back down the stairs and cowered like she had done something to hurt him.

"Come up!"

He yowled again. Erin sighed. She turned off the light and descended the stairs.

"Got him?" Vic called.

"I got him. He should be quiet now."

"I don't know why he gets so upset about you going into the attic sometimes."

"Sooner or later he'll figure out how to come up the stairs to see me. Silly cat."

Erin cuddled Orange Blossom, kissed him on top of his fuzzy head, and put him down again. She went into the sewing room, still restless for something else to occupy herself with. He followed behind her like a dog.

Clementine's sewing room was a fun little room, with rolls of fabric and wrapping paper mounted to the walls, little drawers full of notions, and various other craft supplies and projects. Erin picked up one of the other projects that she had seen before but not paid much attention to. One of several genealogical books, with long family tree pages mounted on posts to bind them all together. It was obvious that Clementine had spent a lot of time and effort researching her family tree and making copies of those records. Erin looked through the books. She ignored the ones that started a century or more earlier, and looked for something current. She found one that started with Clementine's four-generation family tree, and sat down with it. She turned the page, expecting to see another family tree that went further back in town, but instead saw a family group sheet, with Clementine's and her brothers' names listed in the children's box, and their parents listed above. Erin read through them. Her father. Clementine's younger brother. And there was an older brother, Owen. Erin wasn't sure what had happened to him, but there was a death date beside each of their names. Owen had died shortly after Erin's father. Leaving Clementine and Erin the end of the Price line. She turned the page to find a family group sheet with her father's and mother's names at the top. Erin's name alone in the box for children. She'd had no brothers or sisters, though she had always wanted them. Always wanted a baby brother or sister to help take care of. Or an older sibling to play games with. She fantasized about having a big family like some of her friends so that she would never be lonely.

She hadn't known how lonely she would become. Things had been good when it was her and her mother and father, but she hadn't realized it. She'd constantly been wishing for something when she should have been treasuring what she had.

When she was seven, both of her parents had been killed in a car accident. She'd been taken into care. There had been no one else to take her. Erin didn't know if anyone had ever contacted Clementine to see if she wanted to take Erin. Erin liked to think that Clementine would have said, 'yes,' given a chance, but she had no idea if it were true.

Erin touched the names of her parents. She traced the lines across to their death dates.

She stared. The dates weren't right. They were several weeks apart. And they were *after* Erin's eighth birthday. She shook her head. She wasn't sure where Clementine had gotten her dates from, but there was something wrong with them. Maybe they were funeral dates, though Erin couldn't remember there being funerals. Everything was fuzzy so many years later. There might have been funerals that she just didn't remember with all the disruption and trauma in her life. But wouldn't they have had a joint funeral, both on the same day?

Her parents had been killed instantly. She remembered being told that. They hadn't suffered. It had seemed important to the social worker. She'd repeated it several times. "At least we know they didn't suffer. They were killed before they knew there was anything wrong. They didn't suffer any pain."

Now Erin wondered. Had the social worker protested too much, knowing that it wasn't the truth? *Had* her parents lingered after the car accident? Each slowly failing until they died weeks or months afterward?

She chewed on her lip.

In the end, what did it matter? Her parents had died. Erin had gone into foster care. And when she aged out of foster care, she took care of herself. She had always been strong and independent. She didn't need her parents, or any siblings, or even her surviving aunt. There was certainly no point in fussing about it so many years later.

Erin turned the page and studied a family tree that went back several more generations. When she had first come to Bald Eagle Falls, someone had told her, 'if you were kin to Clementine, you're kin to half the mountain.' Erin hadn't really thought much about it at the time. She had never had any family connections to rely upon. No shared history or family reunions or traditions. But looking over the family tree, Erin saw lots of familiar names. Last names of friends and customers who frequented Auntie Clem's Bakery. Even Piper, Cox, and Reed.

She'd made her home in Bald Eagle Falls because that was where the house and store that Clementine had left her were. But she hadn't thought herself part of the history of the place. A puzzle piece that belonged there. That had just been removed and was now returned, rather than supplanted.

There was a movement in the doorway, and Erin looked up to see Vic in her nightgown.

"Are you heading to bed soon?" Vic asked.

Erin looked at her watch and realized it was getting late. "Oh… yes, I'd better."

"What have you got there?"

Erin closed the cover of the book. "Just a puzzle," she said and put it back where she had gotten it.

CHAPTER 8

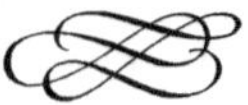

$\mathcal{E}$rin had been dealing with the whispers and rumors for several days. She knew there was no point in trying to squelch the gossip. It would be like a game of whack-a-mole. Every time she tried to talk to one person, it would just pop up somewhere else. Or people would look knowingly at each other and suggest that she was protesting too much, a sure sign of guilt. So, she and Vic tried just to keep the bakery running smoothly and welcomed any gossip as free marketing that would bring more people in to gawk and buy a few cookies. Luckily, the rumors that Erin's baked goods had killed a second person didn't seem to dissuade the populace from buying her food.

She was pleased to see Terry, who had not been able to stop by for a visit since their cave exploration. He had a tall water bottle that Vic refilled for him and he chose pizza cheese bread for his lunch. The shop was busy, but Erin went over to talk with him anyway while he ate, taking with her a biscuit for K9.

Terry brushed crumbs from his uniform and looked her in the eye. "I've got good news and bad news."

"Good news and bad news? For me?"

He nodded. Erin searched his face for clues. There was no dimple in his cheek or twinkle in his eye, so she had to assume that it was more bad news than good.

"Okay, shoot," Erin told him, holding on to the back of an unoccupied chair for support. She thought maybe she should sit down. But he didn't tell her to sit down, so maybe it wasn't too bad.

"The coroner's preliminary findings came in. Trenton Plaint did have a fatal allergic reaction."

"Oh!" The room spun around Erin, and she was glad she was holding on to the chair. She slipped around it and sat down with a thump. "So, then… it was the cupcakes?"

"It's looking that way. Yes."

"How is that good news? Or is there something else?"

"An allergic reaction means that it wasn't poison," Terry offered. "Whatever the gossips say, you didn't poison him to eliminate the competition."

Erin just stared at Terry and shook her head.

"Are you okay?" he asked belatedly. "I thought you'd be glad to hear… that it wasn't foul play."

"No. I mean, I'm glad to hear that it wasn't murder, but… my food killed a man? That's horrible. The whole point of me running this bakery is to provide people with safe food to eat!" Tears sprang to her eyes. "I can't believe… I just feel sick about it!"

Terry grasped her hand, his eyes wide. "Hey… it's okay, Erin. Don't be upset. It wasn't intentional. It was just a freak thing; it could have happened at any time. We don't even know if he knew he had an allergy. He wasn't carrying an autoinjector, like his mother."

"Not that you know of," Erin pointed out, trying not to let the lump in her throat show in her voice. "Someone could have taken it, just like with Angela."

"We don't think that's what happened. We think that he just didn't know he was allergic. He had a cupcake and never knew what happened."

Erin swiped at tears leaking from the corners of her eyes. "That doesn't change the fact that I made the food that killed him!"

Terry squeezed her hand, his forehead wrinkled. "You weren't this upset when we thought Angela Plaint had an allergic reaction to your food."

"You weren't holding my hand when we were talking about Angela." Erin sniffled. "You don't know how I was feeling back then. You were interrogating me."

He frowned but didn't argue the point. The hours and days after Angela's murder seemed like a distant memory to Erin. She had tried to forget them, to block them out. She had been in an unfamiliar place, being questioned by unfamiliar people. She'd been in survival mode, trying to show no weakness. It was different now, talking to someone she considered a friend. She could allow herself to feel.

"It could still be murder."

Erin looked quickly to her right, where Melissa had appeared. Her cheeks were a ruddy red, hair a little wild, and she was smiling. She gave Erin a friendly pat on the shoulder.

"It could," he insisted. "Maybe Joelle intentionally gave him something he was allergic to. Or someone else did. It doesn't have to be your cupcakes. Even if it was the cupcakes, someone else might have had a hand in it. *You* didn't give them to him."

Terry scowled. "Miss Lee, is there something I could help you with?"

She put a small stack of papers on the table with a flourish. "You were in such a hurry to get over here and talk to Erin that you forgot to sign off on your reports. And you know the Sheriff is waiting for them."

A slight flush rose to Terry's cheeks. "That really isn't your job," he pointed out. But he pulled a pen from his uniform pocket and began to flip through the reports.

"Clara was busy, so I offered to run them over. I knew where you would be."

His flush deepened. Erin watched him search out the signature lines in the report and sign them with quick, angular strokes.

"You don't think someone gave Trenton something he was allergic to on purpose?" Erin asked. "Not like with Angela. This *was* just an accident, wasn't it?"

"Are you confessing?" he asked, without looking up.

Erin swallowed. It had been a stupid thing to say. If anyone had killed Trenton on purpose, then she was, again, the prime suspect. She was the one who had something to gain if Trenton was out of the way and not reopening the rival bakery. No one else would have anything else to gain from his death.

Terry handed Melissa the reports and looked at Erin. His brows drew down. "I'm sorry… that was supposed to be funny. But it wasn't."

"Murder isn't something to joke around about," Melissa told him sternly. She leaned down to put her arm around Erin's shoulders and give her a quick squeeze. "Are you okay, honey? I mean really? This is such a shock for you, I'm sure. Even more than being the one to find Trenton."

Erin looked at Melissa, frowning. She remembered how Melissa had acted the day Trenton had returned to town and Lottie had burst into the bakery to spread the news. From what Erin could understand, Trenton had been in Melissa's grade in school and had somehow bullied her. Erin seemed to remember the words 'sadistic' and 'demon.' That wasn't how you usually referred to someone you knew in school. That wasn't just a casual acquaintanceship. Melissa had never wanted to see or hear from him again. Would *she* have intentionally hurt him? Killed him? She seemed very cheerful; was she gloating over his death?

And Erin had already discovered that the people who killed over secrets were the ones who were the best at pretending, at hiding what was going on behind the mask.

"Yes," Erin finally agreed, aware that Melissa's and Terry's eyes were on her, waiting for a response. "I'm… I'm fine. It's a shock, but… I'll be okay. I couldn't ever have known he had an allergy if no one told me. It sounds like he didn't even know it himself."

"Oh yes, he did," Melissa countered. "I remember. I told you, didn't I? When we were talking about him? I told you he was allergic to soy."

Terry's eyes went from Melissa back to Erin, waiting for her answer.

"Soy." Erin's heart sank even further. "No… nobody told me. Those vegan cupcakes definitely had soy in them. A lot of vegan food does, it's a quick substitute for dairy. You never said that he had an allergy, or I would have warned Joelle. And besides, the chocolate chip ones were for Joelle; the red velvet ones were for Trenton. I packaged them separately so that they wouldn't touch."

"Why would you do that?" Terry asked, frowning.

"Because she was very staunch vegan, so I figured she wouldn't want any cross-contamination from animal products. If someone is worried about shellac in sprinkles or honey, you have to figure that they're pretty strict and wouldn't want even a crumb…"

"But she bought non-vegan cupcakes as well."

"For Trenton. Not for her."

"If she was really strict, would she even buy them for someone else? If she's worried about ethics…" Terry trailed off, raising his brows.

"I don't know." Erin shook her head. "We didn't talk to Joelle any more than we had to. She was going on and on… we just wanted to get her out of here."

Terry looked at Melissa. "When did you think you told Erin about this allergy?"

"Oh…" Melissa looked around. "When…? We were talking about Trenton… I don't remember…"

Erin shook her head. "The only time we talked about Trenton was when we were grocery shopping that day, after Angela died. You were talking about how you knew him in school. We didn't talk about allergies or anything like that. And then here, when you found out that he was back in town, from Lottie… but we didn't talk, then. You were just… upset."

"Why were you upset about Trenton being back in town?" Terry looked at Melissa, putting down what was left of his pizza cheese bread.

"Because I hate him! I hated him. I didn't ever want to see him again."

"Hated him. Why? From what I've heard from the older residents who remember him, Mr. Plaint was quite charming."

"He always was. To the people he wanted to impress. But to other people… he could be really nasty."

"Like Angela was?" he suggested.

"No. Much worse than her. She was… verbally bullying and abusive. But Trenton took it to a whole new level. With him, it wasn't just talk."

"He physically assaulted you?"

Melissa shrugged, not answering him directly. "I suppose Angela probably physically abused Trenton and Davis," she said. "That's what they say about bullies. They are that way because of how they have been treated. Angela was never physically abusive in public, but maybe in private…"

Terry refused to be sidetracked. "Trenton hurt you when you went to school together?"

"You never knew what he might do when no one was looking."

Before Terry could ask anything else, Melissa swept up the papers from the table. "Got to run. Clara will be wondering where these are. The Sheriff wanted them ASAP."

Erin and Terry watched her go. Neither said anything at first. Erin took a few deep breaths.

"Well, I guess I'd better get back to work. Can't just leave Vic to get run off of her feet."

Terry put his hand over hers for a moment. "I'm sorry about the news," he said. "I would rather have told you that he just had a coronary. But I knew you'd hear the truth sooner or later anyway."

"It's okay. It's not your fault." She raised her shoulders and let them fall again, feeling helpless. "I'll get over it. It isn't like he was someone I knew. He didn't matter to me. And I didn't do it on purpose. If I'd known he was allergic to soy... I would never have allowed Joelle to take those cupcakes..."

She stood up. Terry picked up what was left of his pizza cheese bread. "What would you have done?"

Erin paused. "What do you mean?"

"What would you have done when she came in to buy something vegan, and you knew that her boyfriend was allergic to soy? What would you have done?"

"Well, I would have told her!"

"And what if she still wanted to buy the cupcakes? Just for herself? Would you have still have sold them to her?"

"I suppose."

"Would you have done anything differently at all?"

"I guess not... I already packaged them separately. She bought one kind for herself and one kind for him; I didn't think they'd be sharing them..."

"You wouldn't have done anything differently."

"No."

"Did she know they had soy in them?"

"Yes, of course, she looked at the ingredients."

"So, you didn't need to give her any separate warnings. She knew what was in them."

"A lot of good that did if she didn't know he was allergic to it!"

"But that's not your problem, is it? How could you be expected to facilitate communication between them, so that Miss Biggs would know that Mr. Plaint was allergic?"

Erin let out her breath. "I couldn't. That's not my job."

He nodded, looking satisfied. "Darn right it's not. There's only one person who was responsible for telling Miss Biggs that he had an allergy. And that was Mr. Plaint himself. It wasn't your job, or mine, or Melissa's. He knew he was allergic. It was his responsibility to tell her and to be careful of what he ate."

~

Vic moved away from the cash register to allow Erin to take her position again. She watched Terry and K9 head out the door again to get started on their patrol.

"What did he have to say?"

Erin figured Vic already had a pretty good idea, but she filled her in on the details anyway. Vic looked appropriately shocked at the news that Trenton had had an allergic reaction to the cupcakes, but her shock turned to anger.

"I can't believe it! Why would he do that?"

Erin frowned at her, surprised. "Who are you mad at? Terry? He didn't accuse me. It wasn't like with Angela, where I was the prime suspect. It was just an accident."

Vic shook her head. "I'm still mad. I don't know. I don't think he should even have told you. Isn't he supposed to keep stuff like that confidential? He just made you feel bad."

"I know, but he didn't want to. He didn't do it to upset me. What else could he do? Lie about it?"

"Just not tell you. Keep it to himself," Vic repeated.

They served the next few customers in silence. Erin had made some tiny raspberry tarts that sparkled like little gemstones, and they were going fast. The lunchtime rush had slowed, and it would be quieter until school let out.

Vic watched Mrs. Marshall, a black woman Erin recognized from the after-church teas, go out the door. Vic still had a scowl on her face, which was unusual for her. She was usually so pleasant and cheerful.

"Even if Terry hadn't told me, Melissa would have," Erin told her.

Vic looked over at her, appearing confused for a moment like she couldn't remember what they had been talking about. Both were pretty proficient at conversations that were broken up over long periods of time by customer orders, the phone, kitchen timers, and other interruptions.

"Yeah, she would," Vic agreed. She still looked peeved.

Erin decided to ignore Vic's moodiness. They were all under stress with Trenton's recent demise. Vic would take it personally that he had reacted to one of their cupcakes just as much as Erin. Best to just buckle down and focus on work and not talk about it.

But as the after-school rush picked up, it seemed like Vic was just getting more and more irritable. She banged her head when she bent down to get the last few tarts out of the display case. She kept knocking against the edge of the case with the tongs and put the orders down on the counter next to Erin with much more force than was necessary. Erin looked over at her.

"Are you okay?" she asked in a low tone.

"Don't you see the way that they're looking at us and talking about us?" Vic demanded in a harsh whisper.

Erin looked toward the waiting customers. There had been a lot of covert looks and whispered comments the last few days. But Erin just put it down to curiosity about Trenton's death and Erin's involvement. She had been the one giving him CPR. Now they knew that she was also the one who had unintentionally poisoned him. It made sense for them to look.

"It will blow over. It's just morbid curiosity."

"No, it's not. It's something else."

Erin shook her head. "Don't worry about what other people are saying. Small towns are gossip mills. You should know that from home."

"I know that. And that's why I know what those looks are. People aren't looking at us because of your involvement in Trenton's... accident. That's not what this is about."

Erin shot another look at the people waiting in line. They all looked away, avoiding her gaze. Lottie Sturm was there with her twelve-year-old, a diminutive, dark-haired girl who looked as different from Lottie as a cuckoo in a crow's nest. Lottie spoke quickly and nervously to little Sarah, discussing dinner options.

"Something is going on," Vic insisted.

Erin just shook her head, waiting for Lottie to make her choice and get a move on. She gave Vic a look, one which she knew Vic would interpret properly as 'put on your customer face and stop being silly.' Erin felt a bit bad about it. She wasn't Vic's mother, and she wasn't usually too bad as a boss. Vic was more of a partner to Erin than an employee. But if Vic were going to be sulky, people were not going to come as often. Without even knowing why, they would avoid visiting.

Vic pasted a smile back on her face and faced the customers like a firing squad.

"Did you have a good day at school today?" she asked Sarah.

Sarah opened her mouth to answer, but Lottie cut right across her. "Don't talk to strangers," she snapped.

Sarah and Vic both stared at her with their mouths open. Erin was going to step in, but decided that would be one too many people involved in the conversation, which had already taken a weird turn.

"But Mama, we know Vic," Sarah protested. "She's not a stranger."

"We *don't* know her," Lottie insisted. "We have no idea what kind of *person* she is. What kind of *morals* she has."

Vic's face went sheet white. She just stood there, staring at Lottie. Lottie indicated what cookies she wanted and Vic got them out and handed them off to Erin, moving robotically. Erin didn't know what to say. She knew that she should say something to defend Vic, but she had no idea what to say. Vic hadn't done anything wrong. But they were essentially eavesdropping on a private conversation, too. Lottie had been talking to Sarah, not to Vic or Erin. They were intended to overhear, for sure, but that didn't make it right to barge into the conversation.

Sarah looked at her mother and then at Erin, opening her mouth half way, but not knowing whether it was okay to talk to Erin. Erin was in the same boat, afraid to even smile or say hello to Sarah for fear of getting attacked. What was going on with everyone all of the sudden?

"Not her either," Lottie said firmly. "And I don't want you coming over here with your friends or alone. Only with me. The rest of the time you stay away from here. Understood?"

Sarah nodded, blinking, releasing tears from the corner of her eyes and letting them slide down her face. Erin couldn't understand what was going on.

"Do you have some concern about my store, Lottie?" she asked. "If you do, you really should talk to me. Maybe I can address it. I know there are a lot of rumors going around about Trenton, but what happened to him was unavoidable. No one knew that he was allergic…" Erin petered out, recognizing from the look in Lottie's eyes that she couldn't care less about Trenton.

There was something else going on. But Erin had no idea what.

"Thank you," Lottie said archly, "but I wasn't talking to you. I was having a private conversation with my daughter. I'd appreciate it if you'd stay out of it."

"You're talking about us, though," Vic cut in. "You can't very well say that it has nothing to do with us when you're talking *about* us! Just tell us what the problem is."

"I haven't said anything to you or about you," Lottie said. "You have the right to live your own lifestyle and I will live mine." She raised her chin, looking down her nose at them as if they were dirty children who had just tracked mud into the house. Erin felt humiliated and had no idea why.

Vic turned and gave her a look.

I told you so.

Vic had said that people were talking about them. That she had seen those looks before.

We don't know what kind of morals she has. What exactly had Lottie been talking about? All in a rush, Erin realized that she must have figured out about Vic being transgender. Terry had said that they wouldn't be able to keep it a secret forever. Not in such a small town. Now Lottie had figured it out, or someone else had figured it out and told Lottie, and she was afraid that her daughter was going to be tempted into some kind of unrighteous thoughts or behavior just by talking to Vic.

"I don't know what you're talking about," she said to Lottie. "We're all living the same lifestyle. We are all women living in Bald Eagle Falls. Part of this community. No one is living some wild, dangerous lifestyle. There's no reason to be worried about us."

"I am a good, Christian woman. I don't have anything in common with two women living in a… an unnatural relationship."

"What?" Erin was flummoxed.

"It's unnatural. Paul warned against unnatural affections. And you two…" Lottie made a motion to include Vic and Erin and gave a little self-righteous shudder.

Erin handed Lottie her change. Lottie grabbed her daughter by the hand and hauled her out the door. Erin and Vic looked at each other.

"What the hell was that?" Erin demanded.

Vic just shook her head, her eyes wide, close to tears. Erin moved over and motioned Vic toward the kitchen.

"Take a break. Go splash some water on your face and calm down," she said quietly. "I don't know what the heck that was, but you don't need to worry about it. Just take a break and take a few deep breaths."

Vic looked for a moment like she was going to argue, but then she nodded and turned away, disappearing into the back. Erin faced the rest of the waiting customers, giving them an anemic smile.

"Well, then, let's see if we can get this line moving, shall we? What does everyone want for supper?"

They were stone-faced rather than empathetic. Erin couldn't help feeling that they all agreed with Lottie, whatever it was she thought. Erin thought it was mostly aimed at Vic, and must have to do with her gender identity, but some of it seemed to be aimed at Erin as well, and she didn't understand why. Because she had taken Vic in? Both as an employee and to give her a home? Wasn't that one of those Christian duties that people were expected to do? Feed the hungry and clothe the naked and all of that? Why should it make any difference what gender the person in need was?

Erin rang the next few orders through in silence. She tried to keep her smile up, but it wasn't easy. Unnatural affections? Because they thought that Vic was unnatural? Not a real woman? Erin wanted to argue the point, but she was afraid to raise it with any of them, especially if she were misinterpreting the archaic expression.

The last few customers skittered away and no one else entered the shop. Erin went into the kitchen to check on Vic. The bells on the door would alert her if anyone else came in. She found Vic sitting on a stool beside the sink, a damp, folded-up washcloth on the counter that she had obviously been holding over her teary eyes to try to make them less bloodshot. Erin tried to hug her, but Vic pulled away from her.

"Are you okay?" Erin asked, though the answer was obvious. "I'm sorry about… whatever that was. I guess… does that mean they found out that you are transgender?"

Vic shook her head. She rolled her eyes. "You didn't get what they were saying?" she demanded.

"I… I guess not."

Vic laughed bitterly. "I thought *I* was supposed to be the naive country cousin!"

"What? Exactly what was she trying to say?"

"They think we're gay!"

Erin just stared at Vic blankly. "What?"

"You and me. They think we're lovers."

"Because we live together?"

"Your guess is as good as mine!"

"But..." Erin was at a loss for words. "They really... how could anyone think that?"

"I don't know! Just this weekend, we were off adventuring with two men. And went for drinks at the restaurant afterward. How people could see us there and still think..."

Erin, who was always worried that people were looking at her when Terry flirted with her, felt herself blushing furiously.

"You and me...?" She spluttered. "Why? It's not like we hug and kiss in public! We work together and we share the house, that's all!"

"I would guess it's sharing the house that's the problem," Vic said. She dabbed at her eyes with the wet washcloth. "I can't believe this!"

Near-hysterical laughter bubbled up in Erin's throat. She swore. "I'm going to close up. I don't want anyone walking in..."

She went to the front of the store, flipped over the sign, shot the bolt, and turned off the lights. She returned to the kitchen. Vic appeared to be recovering from the shock, starting to smile a little at the ridiculousness of the situation herself.

"Like I don't have enough to worry about being transgender," she said. "I don't have the first clue about how to deal with a boyfriend and explain the situation to him. And now... we have to deal with this!"

Erin let out a high giggle. She gasped for breath. "Well, why don't we just tell them your birth name is James? Then they wouldn't think we were gay!"

Vic just shook her head, laughing and not able to respond.

Erin giggled until she could barely breathe, and then borrowed Vic's cloth to put over her own eyes and try to calm herself down. "I think... I'm a little... hysterical..."

"With all that you've been through lately, it's no wonder. We'd better get everything settled here, and get you home to bed."

Her words sent Erin into another fit of hysteria and she half-laughed and half-cried into the cold washcloth.

CHAPTER 9

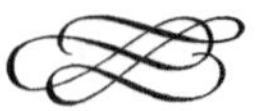

$\mathcal{E}$rin got up in the morning, determined to make a fresh start.

"I don't care what anyone has to say," she told Vic. "If they don't like our living arrangements, they can do their shopping at the grocery store or go into the city. I'm not going to apologize or explain. I thought Christians were not supposed to judge."

"Christians aren't supposed to do a lot of things," Vic agreed. "But no one is perfect. Everyone is going to fall short in some areas."

"I think it's ridiculous. What does it matter to them what other people do? Shouldn't they just be worried about themselves and what they're doing that's right or wrong?"

Vic nodded. "Yup."

"Well, I'm not going to worry about it. You and I know the truth, and anyone who prefers to read something else into it, that's their own problem."

"Yeah. You're right." Vic too displayed new resolve. "It isn't our problem what anyone else says or thinks."

Erin fed the cat, and they finished getting themselves ready for work. Erin was determined to stay upbeat. She would just laugh at anyone who gave her doubtful looks. There she was, attracted to two different men, and the town thought she was having an affair with Vic, who she'd never felt anything but friendship and motherly affection for.

They worked together efficiently, both putting the energy from their leftover anger into the morning's baking and getting everything done in record time. Vic lingered over the labels and price board, adding extra flourishes and doodles to fill the time, and Erin worked in her office trying to catch up on her filing before opening time.

When the first few customers trickled in, Vic and Erin went into action, handling the orders with unparalleled enthusiasm and efficiency. There were some surprised and confused expressions from the customers, but before long it seemed like everything was falling back into place, flowing as naturally as it ever had.

Mrs. Foster was there with the children before school began, glancing several times at her watch to make sure that she didn't run too long and make Peter late for school. Traci crowed for her "cook-kie" and then proceeded to slobber all over it as Mrs. Foster carefully made her other choices and paid at the register.

"Everything has been so crazy around here lately," Mrs. Foster said. "I just wish everything would settle down again, back to normal."

Erin wasn't sure what, in particular, she was referring to. There was plenty in her life that had been disrupted recently, but none of those things might have had any impact on Mrs. Foster. She could be talking about completely different worries. Potty training. Meal planning. Too much homework or after-school activities. So, Erin just smiled pleasantly. "Yes, I hope they do," she agreed.

"They've set a date for Trenton's funeral, did you hear?" Mrs. Foster asked.

"What?" Erin looked up at her, surprised. "Why would they have a funeral here? He didn't live here. Won't his girlfriend want to take... uh... *him* back home?"

"No, she's having it here," Mrs. Foster said. "He does still have family here, even if none of us are close. I thought it was a nice gesture... I mean, he's been away from home for so long... all of his friends must be up north... but she wants to have it here. She says that was what Trenton would have wanted."

"Are you related?" Erin asked tentatively, trying to tease apart the various lines of Mrs. Foster's explanation.

"Cousins. Not close. Uh, second I think. And once removed. Maybe? I can never keep track, but his grandfather was my—"

"Oh." Erin blanked the rest of the explanation out. "I see. Yes, I guess everyone around here is related when you get down to it."

Mrs. Foster nodded.

"I don't understand why Joelle is having it here," Erin said again, shaking her head. "I mean, maybe a memorial if his extended family wanted it, but…"

Vic was listening in. "How would she even know what he would have wanted? She didn't know about his allergy, but she knew his funeral wishes?"

"Yeah. It just seems odd."

"Well…" Mrs. Foster shifted Traci in her sling and tried to wipe some of the slobbery cookie off of her shirt. "I thought it was real sweet of Joelle. I like that girl, even if she is a vegan."

Erin laughed. "Well, I'm sure she appreciates that. There certainly are not a lot of vegans in this part of the country."

"Vegans are almost as bad as atheists," Vic declared, throwing a sideways glance at Erin.

There were several nods from the waiting customers. Mrs. Foster started to nod, then caught herself, looking at Erin. "I… wouldn't know," she temporized.

Erin finished ringing her up, chuckling. "Have a nice day, Mrs. Foster."

She waved at each of the children, especially an enthusiastic Peter, who was already demanding to know, "What's an atheist, Mommy?"

Erin shook her head at Vic. "You're incorrigible."

Vic grinned. "Who's going to go to this funeral?" she asked. "Nobody around here even knew Uncle Trenton."

"Will you?"

"I suppose," Vic admitted. "You want to come as my date?"

There was a gasp from one of the customers, but when Erin looked over at them, she couldn't tell who it had been. "We're *not* a couple!" she said firmly, but she couldn't help smiling at Vic's mischievous expression. Vic had come a complete one-eighty from the previous day, choosing to tease the gossips instead of being upset by them. "I didn't know him at all, so I don't think I'll go."

"But you tried to save his life. Maybe Joelle will want to thank you."

Erin refrained from pointing out that even if she had tried to save Trenton's life, she had been the unwitting cause of his death. It probably wouldn't be a good idea for her to show her face at the funeral. If Joelle wanted to thank Erin, Joelle knew where to find her.

"I wonder if anyone else will be there," Vic said.

"Anyone else?"

"From Trenton's family."

Erin tried to remember all of the details. "His brother?"

"There was Sophie, but she… committed suicide. And Davis. I don't know if anyone even knows where he is anymore. But no one knew where Trenton was either, and *he* came back. Someone must have told him that Angela had died. And what about their dad?"

"Isn't he dead? I thought he disappeared years ago."

"Yes… but that doesn't mean he's dead. He'd only be sixty. He could still be around, like Trenton, and come back."

"Somebody would have to know where he was, to let him know about the funeral."

Late in the day, as Erin went to the door to flip the sign over to 'closed,' she spotted William Andrews through the door, putting flyers on car windshields. She waved and managed to catch his attention. Rather than just waving back, he walked up to her door. Erin stepped back, allowing him in.

"Come cool off for a minute," she invited. "You want a drink?"

"A refill would be great," he acknowledged, pulling his water bottle from the loop on his belt.

Erin refilled it and returned it to him. "You want any baking? End of the day, I need to clear stuff out. Whatever you want is yours."

Willie took a swig from his bottle and looked into the display case. "I'm rather partial to ginger cookies."

"Sure! Let me get you a couple."

He didn't object.

"What's the sale?" Erin asked him as she picked up a couple of cookies with the tongs.

"Hmm?"

"Your flyers. What's up?"

"Oh," Willie moved closer to the counter and held one up for her. A sale on the Jam Lady jams at The General Store.

"Ah. Aren't they just so good? I can't get over how much better home-made jams taste than store-bought. Or I guess these are store-bought, but so much better than the big commercial brands.

Willie nodded his agreement. "I'd never get a commercial brand. They're just sugar. Hardly any taste, just sickly sweet."

"Exactly. Having Jam Lady jams is more like… having pancakes or a jelly donut for breakfast, instead of just toast. It makes it an event."

Willie nodded, smiling. His eyes twinkled.

Erin bent forward to hand him his cookies. "Do you have any idea who The Jam Lady is?" she asked in a low voice.

He shrugged. "I couldn't tell you if I did."

"Why not?"

"Because I would have been sworn to secrecy. If I knew."

"Somebody must know. Everybody knows everything in this town!"

"Not everything. But you've got to be pretty good to keep a secret around here."

Vic finished washing down the counters and returned to the front to start retrieving the unsold food from the display case. She saw Willie and her eyes lit up.

"I didn't know it was you! Did you get—" she saw the cookies in his hand. "You got something. Good. I hate to throw food out, and Erin and I can't eat everything that doesn't get sold. I wish there was some other way to put it to good use. Besides feeding the birds and raccoons."

"If we were in the city, you could take them to a homeless shelter. But here… no homeless," Willie agreed.

Vic had been homeless in Bald Eagle Falls, so the assertion might not be entirely true. But Vic lived with Erin now, and Erin didn't know of any other homeless people living in town.

"We could put some in the freezer for the next time we go into the city," she suggested. "We can't store that much, but we could put up a bit for each time we go there."

"Yeah," Vic nodded. "That would be good."

"I always hate to see people go hungry," Erin said.

"Yes, you do!"

"Did you… want to do something later, after I'm finished with my flyers?" Willie was looking at Erin, then turned his gaze to include Vic. "Both of you? Either of you? Some dinner? A game of cards? Pictionary?"

Vic eyed Erin. She didn't know whether she felt like Vic was a third wheel or the bratty little sister, but it was awkward. Did Willie just want to spend time with Erin? Or both of them? Was he just looking for a little company, an escape from boredom? Or something more?

"We head to bed pretty early," she said. "Getting up for the bakery as early as we do."

"Right." Willie nodded. "Another time, maybe."

"We could do something tonight," Vic inserted. "I don't need to go to bed *that* early. We could still have dinner or a drink. We still have to eat."

Willie looked at Vic, then back at Erin. "You do need to eat," he pointed out.

"Well… yes. Of course, we need to eat, as long as it isn't too late. We have the cat to feed too."

"Blossom will be fine for a couple of hours," Vic insisted. "It's not like he's a baby. He's got bowls of food and water."

"He might start yowling."

"We can't be home all the time," Vic said sensibly. "He'll have to get used to us being away sometimes." She raised an eyebrow. "Do you want to go home and take care of the cat, and Willie and I…"

Erin shook her head and quickly made up her mind. "No, no. You're right, of course. There's no reason we can't take a couple of hours for dinner. Orange Blossom will be all right."

Vic looked at Erin, lips pursed. "Okay, then," she agreed. "We'll all go together. You don't think Terry could get off, do you? As long as he's on call, he might be able to come too, make it a foursome."

"No. He's on patrol for a couple more hours. It will have to just be the three of us this time."

"Dinner, then?" Willie asked. "What do you feel like? Chinese?"

They all looked at each other, uncertain at first and then nodding more certainly.

"Chinese, it is."

CHAPTER 10

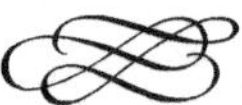

*E*rin was just thinking about dinner the night before, an odd mixture of awkwardness and fun, when the bells on the door rang. She looked up and saw a face she had hoped not to see again. Joelle Biggs. There was a man with her, sticking close to her side. Not quite holding her arm, but close to it. He was taller than Joelle and was gaunt. His face seemed familiar, but Erin was sure she hadn't met him before.

Joelle didn't walk to the display case, but directly to Erin at the cash register.

"Hi."

Erin gave a friendly nod of greeting. "Hello. What can I help you with today?"

"This is Erin. She's the one who helped with Trenton," Joelle told her companion. "Gave him CPR and everything. Her and the policeman."

"I wanted to thank you in person," the man said, putting out a calloused, cigarette-yellowed hand to shake Erin's. "And to invite you to the funeral."

Erin shook his hand uncertainly.

"This is Davis," Joelle told her. "Trenton's brother."

"Oh! Oh, I'm sorry for your loss, Davis. Both Trenton and your mother."

Davis made a motion that was half shrug, half head-shake. "Yeah, thanks," he agreed. "Appreciate it."

"To lose both of them so close together…"

His lips pressed together. "I hadn't seen either of them for a long time. They haven't been in my life."

Erin nodded understandingly, but she wasn't sure what to say to him. "I lost both of my parents when I was young."

"Sometimes I wonder if that wouldn't have been better."

Erin was surprised at his words, but even more surprised at the tone. He didn't sound bitter or sad. Just flat. There was no emotion. She didn't have any response to that. After hearing what Angela had been like as a parent, she couldn't argue with how Davis must have felt about her.

"So, you'll come to the funeral?" Davis asked.

Erin cleared her throat. "Well, I didn't really know Trenton…"

And he hadn't been particularly nice to her. He'd been the competition.

"But you were with him at the end," Davis said. "I want you to be at the funeral."

"Umm, okay. I suppose," Erin reluctantly agreed. "Tomorrow afternoon…?"

"Yes. Two o'clock. At First Baptist. I suppose you go there?"

Erin shook her head. "No, I… I'm not a religious person."

He gave her a long, appraising look. "You're not one of them."

"One of the First Baptists? No."

Joelle spoke in an undertone to Davis, as if Erin couldn't hear her. "I heard that she and her assistant…" Joelle jerked her head to indicate Vic, the innuendo clear.

"No," Erin said. "We're friends. We both have… other interests."

Davis gave a sharp bark of a laugh. "That's good. You're both too cute to be out of circulation."

Erin's cheeks burned. "I'm sorry, but I've got customers…" The Potters clearly hadn't finalized their choices yet, but Erin was desperate to get Joelle and Davis moving on their way. "So, unless you're buying something…"

Davis looked over at the baked goods, but Joelle shook her head. "No. We still have arrangements to finalize. We'd better be getting on our way. We'll see you tomorrow, Erin."

"See you tomorrow, Miss Biggs."

~

Erin picked up a couple of Clementine's big genealogical books and hauled them out to the living room with her. Vic had been playing with Orange Blossom with a piece of string and looked up to see what Erin was doing.

"What's that?"

"These are family trees and other genealogical records."

"Really?" Vic shook her head. "Those are huge. Did you borrow them from the library?"

"No. They were Clementine's."

Vic left Orange Blossom and sat down beside Erin, looking over the book that Erin opened up on the coffee table.

"Wow. Did she write all of that?"

Erin flipped a few pages. They were almost all in the same handwriting. "Yeah, it looks like she did."

"That must have taken a lot of hours to do."

"Years, probably. You can see different inks as you go back. Some of them are pretty faded."

"I thought you were an orphan! You've got all of this family?"

"You do too, probably."

"No." Vic shook her head. "Like this? No way."

"How long has your family lived in Tennessee?"

"Well… forever. I don't know how far back. Great, great grandparents… more than that."

"Then I'll bet you anything some of this is your family too."

"No. I know folks are always making jokes about all of the intermarrying, but it isn't really that bad. There are plenty of people who got married to non-Tennesseans."

"Not all of them. Not if your family has been living here that far back. Look." Erin flipped to the pages she had been looking at before. "Look at all of the family names of people who live here and shop at the bakery. Here's a Potter. And a Cox." Erin ran her finger under some of the names. "They're all related. To each other. And to us."

"Not to me," Vic said. "I didn't know anyone in Bald Eagle Falls except for Aunt Angela. My people didn't come this far…"

"I wanted to see if the Plaints were in here," Erin said. "Everybody knows everybody, and I know at the funeral tomorrow everyone is going to be talking about how everyone is related to who. Third cousins once removed. My sister-in-law's uncle. Everyone is going to know everyone else and how they all fit in, and I just wanted to see… to figure out how I fit in. If I do."

"It looks like you do," Vic said, looking over the long sheets of names. She picked up the string and dangled it for Orange Blossom to chase. "Catch it, Blossom! Catch it!"

Erin continued to scan through the pages. "I don't see any Plaints here. Or Websters."

"Webster isn't my family's name," Vic said, without looking at her. "Well, it's a grandma's family name. My family name is Jackson."

"Jackson!" Erin turned and looked at her. "Well, there's a southern name. I'll bet there are a ton of Jacksons in here." She slowed down and went back a couple of pages. "Here. Are you related to this one?"

"Who?" Vic looked at it. "Obadiah? Who knows. There are a lot of Jacksons. They probably aren't even all really Jacksons, just people who needed something to go by."

Erin followed the paternal line up and down, looking for any branches off to Plaints. She shook her head. "I'm going to go bug-eyed trying to make any sense of this. How am I going to do this?"

"What?"

"How am I going to know if I'm related to anyone at the funeral tomorrow."

"You just know you are. I don't think you can figure out and memorize all of the relationships in one night."

"No," Erin admitted. Her head was already whirling with all of the familiar and unfamiliar names. Her aunt's handwriting was neat, but after looking at it for a few minutes, Erin wanted just to close her eyes. "I guess it was a ridiculous idea."

"Why don't you just write down one name from each family you want to remember the name of?" Vic suggested. "Not too far back. A grandfather or great-grandfather. So, if you want to talk to Mary Lou about her family, you ask her if she's related to…"

Erin flipped back toward the beginning of the book and found the Cox line. Vic looked at it.

"So, you ask her if she's related to Alexander Cox. And maybe write down the year he was born. Right? You might not be able to tell them what your relationship is, but you can say, 'I'm related to Alexander Cox,' with confidence."

"Yeah. Good idea!" Erin went to the side table drawer and rifled through it for paper and a pen. "I'll have to be careful not to go overboard, but if I pick out ten different families… I'll bet almost everybody is related to one of those ten."

"Uh-huh. Probably."

Vic dragged the string along the floor and then up the front of the couch and onto the seat cushion. Orange Blossom sat there for a moment, haunches quivering, ears pointed forward, looking for it to reappear. Then he rocketed forward and ran up the couch to pounce on the string. Vic let out a shriek, trying to get away from the needle-sharp claws in time. She laughed.

"Wear him out," Erin encouraged. "Last night he kept pouncing on my toes every time I moved. I would just be getting to sleep, and he would attack!"

"Then don't wiggle your toes when you're going to sleep," Vic returned. She continued to tease the cat with the fraying string.

~

They started early as usual and kept the bakery open until noon, then closed to eat their lunches and clean up. A quick trip home to get dressed up, and they would be ready for the funeral.

"How should I dress?" Erin asked. "I've never been to a funeral before."

Vic frowned at her. "How could you never have been to a funeral before? I've been to dozens."

"Well, you have a family. I haven't had anyone. If someone dies, you don't take your foster kids with you to the funeral; that's just for real family. And if a foster parent dies, they take you to another home. Even if another foster child dies… If they have a funeral, it's done by the birth family, not the foster family. Social Services doesn't pay anything for them, and most foster families aren't rich enough to afford an expense like that themselves. The body either goes back to the birth family, or they go wherever Social Services sends bodies no one cares about. To be cremated or buried in some public plot. I don't know."

"And as an adult? You've *never* been to a funeral?"

"Whose? I don't have any family, and I moved around so much I was never in one place for more than a year or two. Not long enough to get that close to anyone."

"That's just bizarre to me." Vic looked Erin over critically. "I'll bet they do funerals pretty formal here in Bald Eagle Falls. A dress. Something dark and plain. Knee length. Shoes that aren't going to kill your feet if you have to stand for a while because we'll probably be standing around visiting after it's over. Some jewelry. Nothing distracting, but I think all of yours is pretty simple, isn't it?"

Erin nodded. "I only have a few pieces. They have to be able to go with anything."

"Right. Any of them should be fine. Nothing too showy in the makeup department, but you don't usually anyway. Classic works anywhere."

"Okay. I can do that. What are you going to wear?"

"I'm going to check Clementine's closet. I didn't bring any dresses."

"You're too tall for anything of Clementine's."

"Yeah. But I'll make something work."

They didn't have a long time to get ready, so Erin went to her room and pulled together an outfit. When she had moved to Bald Eagle Falls, she hadn't brought much with her in the clothing department. More than Vic, who had ended up having to live on the street, but less than she would have liked. She wore mostly pants at the bakery, and the town had seen her in all of her 'Sunday dresses' at the after-church teas.

She emerged from her room and went to see what Vic had managed.

Vic was in slacks because, as Erin had pointed out, Clementine was much shorter than Vic, but she had found a pretty purple blouse that was shimmery and fit her nicely. Vic had put her blond hair up in a bun, fastened with a piece from Clementine's jewelry box.

"Here, I have just the thing for you," she told Erin. She delved into a drawer and came out with a filmy green scarf. "What do you think?"

"I don't know. Do you think it will look good?"

"Stand still." Vic wrapped it loosely around Erin's shoulders and tied it into a neat knot that lay flat like it was supposed to instead of twisting around like Erin's knots always did. "There. Look in the mirror. What do you think?"

Erin had to admit that she liked the effect. "Good. I just hope it isn't too hot. I don't know about wearing another layer on such a warm day."

"That's why you need this," Vic said, giving her a handheld fan. Erin flipped it open and fanned herself.

"You don't think it looks pretentious?"

"Not when it's hot out! It only looks silly if you use it when you don't need to."

Erin folded it back away. "Okay. I'll put it in my purse. But I'm not using it if I'm the only one."

"You won't be!" Vic promised.

~

And Vic was right, of course. The chapel at First Baptist was packed, and although big ceiling fans whirred lazily overhead and air conditioning hummed in the background, it was too warm and still. There was no need for Erin to consider whether a handheld fan was appropriate, as just about every lady in the place had one out and was fanning herself.

"Do you see anyone you know?" Erin whispered to Vic.

Vic gave her a questioning look. Of course, most of the faces were familiar from around town.

"I mean, do you know anyone from the Plaint side of the family? Anyone else from Angela's extended family?"

Vic nodded. "Yes. A few."

"There are Davis and Joelle," Erin pointed out, nodding toward the two of them. Davis was in a worn, dark suit and limp blue tie. Joelle was wearing a leather jacket with faux fur trim over a shape-hugging black dress cut lower than anything Erin would have dared to wear.

"Uh-huh. And the fat lady sitting next to Davis is an aunt or cousin. Most of the row is related... but not immediate."

Vic fell silent. Erin took another quick glance around to make sure it wasn't because the service was about to start or someone was giving them a dirty look. But most of the rest of the congregation, seated early and still waiting for the pastor to begin the service, were whispering to each other like Vic and Erin.

Erin looked over the congregation, focusing on those who were unfamiliar. As Vic had said, the extended family was seated with Davis and Joelle along the front row.

"Is there anyone here you *don't* know?" she asked Vic.

Vic sat looking at the front and didn't turn her head to look at Erin. "A few."

Erin waited for details, but Vic didn't look at her or expand on this. "Well...?"

"What?"

"Who don't you recognize?"

Vic finally turned her head. She blinked at Erin. "Not now, Erin, okay?"

Erin was taken aback. Vic was obviously upset, but Erin had missed whatever or whoever it was that had upset her. She put her hand on Vic's arm. "What is it? What's going on?"

Vic shook her head. "I shouldn't have come here. But it's too late now. Just... just let me be. After the service is over... I need to go home. Right away."

"Okay. If you like. Are you not feeling well? Do you want to go now? It hasn't started yet; we could probably sneak back out."

"Not without people seeing. I don't want to draw any attention."

"Sure. Fine. Whatever you want. I'm sorry... I'm not sure... can I help somehow?"

"Shh. Just leave it alone for now."

Erin obeyed. As much as she wanted to discuss people and puzzles, she didn't want to upset Vic any more. She studied people on her own, trying to divine who the unfamiliar parties were. She looked for family similarities. She tried to analyze their body language and their facial expressions. She was good at reading people. She'd had to get good at it, with the life she had led.

The service began, and everyone else stopped whispering and appeared to be attending to the pastor. Erin's mind wandered. It didn't sound like the pastor knew Trenton or anything about his family. He was more interested in preaching a sermon on death and the Baptist beliefs surrounding it. Not something that Erin was interested in hearing. She had no curiosity about the beliefs of the various religions. She had lived with families of many different faiths before finally aging out of foster care. They had all tried to tell her that their beliefs were the correct ones. That she could only get to heaven for her final reward if she were converted to their faiths. But she had never bought it. She knew that the foster care rules said her foster families were not allowed to try to convert her, but it never seemed to stop them. Even the less pushy ones still seemed to manage to work it into conversations somehow.

Erin studied the building's architecture. The tall windows. The ceiling fans and their slight wobble over the congregation's heads. She wondered how many people would be hurt if one of the fans broke free and fell into the sleepy congregation. It was morbid, but at least it kept her awake. She glanced over at Vic, hoping to find her dozing so that Erin would be justified in poking her. But Vic was sitting up straight, staring straight ahead, not looking the least bit sleepy. Erin fanned herself, wondering how much longer the pastor could go on with his fire and brimstone. Sooner or later he'd have to wrap it up, say something nice about the deceased, and get on with the burial.

From what Erin understood, only the immediate family and closest friends would be going to the burial, which would be a very small number, but there would be a reception at the church with lots of visiting and swapping tales. Which of course meant gossiping. Erin was sure there would be plenty of speculation about where Trenton had been for the previous two decades. Where had he gone? Why had he left before school even let out, when he was on track to be his class valedictorian? Was it something that Angela had done? A fight he'd had with someone? Some other shady situation that had forced him to leave town without a word?

Mary Lou had said that someone would know something. But who? Who had seen Trenton leave that day? Or who else had known the reasons? Maybe his brother, Davis? It would be logical to ask him. Wasn't it what everyone was wondering? Surely he'd have to come up with some story. Something that would satisfy people.

Erin woke up for a musical number. Then there was a eulogy. By Joelle, rather than by Davis. She was very sweet but didn't have a lot to say when it came right down to it. Just the kind of things you could say about anybody. Or would be expected to say at their funeral, whether it were true or not. It wasn't exactly like the funerals Erin had seen on TV. But those were always in the middle of some thriller or comedy. And Trenton's funeral was not a thriller or a comedy.

There wasn't a lot of crying. Joelle choked up a couple of times, but stopped to breathe for a moment and then went on again. There was a woman on the front row who was crying. Erin wanted to ask who she was, but Vic was decidedly non-talkative, so Erin didn't say anything that might bother her.

Erin fanned herself. It helped to chase away the drowsiness only a little.

The fan would probably be more helpful if she folded it back up and slapped it across her leg where no one could see.

There was another song. Davis got up to speak. The focus of his talk was highlights of Trenton's life. But it was obvious that they hadn't seen each other for a long time. All of the memories were of their boyhood years, with a few dates thrown in for good measure. Birth date, a couple of significant events in his childhood, and his death date. No mention of disappearing from town and walking out of his family's life forever. No mention of his abrupt return after Angela's death to claim her estate.

Erin rubbed her eyes.

Trenton had been the one to claim his mother's estate.

He was the one who should have been harder to find. He was the one who had disappeared, and yet he was the one to reappear upon her death. Did that mean that someone in town had known where to reach him? And was he the only one mentioned in the will? What about Davis's portion of the estate? What about her husband? If they had never divorced and he had never been declared dead, had she left anything to him in her will?

She was more awake, itching to pose the questions to Vic to see what her thoughts were. Erin wasn't sure how she was going to get any of them answered. She didn't know who Angela's estate lawyer was, if she had left a will, or who would have any knowledge of it. Besides Davis. He must have known something, or he wouldn't have returned to town. Erin was pretty sure that it hadn't been just to go to his brother's funeral. He hadn't bothered to show up for his mother's.

Poking around in her purse for a moment, Erin located the sheet of paper on which she had written the various family names she had planned to inquire about when visiting after the funeral. Because of Vic's reaction, they wouldn't be staying after the funeral, and it all seemed a little silly to Erin in retrospect. Pretending to know who her ancestors were and that she had some kind of connection with the other members of the town? Why bother? Why was that even important to her?

She scribbled down a list. She could see Vic looking at her out the corner of her eye. Not down at the paper to see what she had written, just over at her to see what she was doing.

A scriptural passage. Another musical number. A long-winded prayer with a chorus of amens throughout. Then the pastor was finally giving his closing remarks and instructions, letting everyone know where to go. Then the congregation was standing and watching the casket and the row of family members parade out of the chapel. Once they were gone, people started to murmur and whisper to each other. Erin turned to Vic, relieved to be able to talk once more.

"You need to go home?" she prompted. "Or have you changed your mind?"

"Home. Let's get out of here."

Vic made her way toward the closest door, even though they were parked around the other side of the building. They worked their way through the other people streaming into the foyers, smiling and greeting friends and acquaintances, making non-specific comments about how lovely it had been. It had been long and tedious. Erin didn't have any real-life funeral experience to compare it to, so it might have been lovely. But it was certainly a lot less interesting than funerals on TV.

One of the ladies tried to stop Erin to talk to her. Vic grabbed Erin's hand and pulled her on so that she couldn't slow or stop to talk. They burst out of the building before slowing. Erin pulled Vic to a stop.

"Okay. We're out. Are you okay? What's wrong?"

"Shouldn't have come here." Vic started walking again, around the church toward the car.

"Why not? You're the one who wanted to come. I only came because Davis insisted."

"You can stay if you want to." Vic looked at her. "You wanted to talk to people about their families, from Clementine's book. I forgot."

"No, it's okay. That was just curiosity. A way to talk to people if I had to. I can always ask them about their ancestors when they come into the bakery if I want to start getting to know how everyone is related."

"You sure?"

Erin nodded. "Yeah. Don't worry about it."

They walked in silence for a few minutes. "So…" She looked for a way to change the subject and distract Vic from whatever was bothering her. "Was there anyone you didn't recognize? I was wondering who was there from out of town."

"My parents," Vic said bleakly. "My mom and dad were there."

"Oh." Erin suddenly understood. "Oh, my goodness. No wonder you wanted to get out of there! Did they see you?"

"No. I don't think so. They were up near the front. But I couldn't stay around there and let them see me."

"No. I get it. You couldn't stay."

"Stupid. I never even thought about them coming to the funeral. They weren't that close to Aunt Angela. I guess they were curious about Trenton and Davis. Like everyone else. It's the spectacle. I should have known they'd want a look."

Erin gave Vic an awkward little back rub, wishing she could do something else to comfort her. While she hoped that Vic would be reconciled with her parents at some point, it was still too early. The wounds were still too fresh, and her parents hadn't had long enough to get used to the new facts of life as far as Vic was concerned.

"Thanks. I know I shouldn't care so much what they say or think. I shouldn't run away from them. They're not going to change me, so they may as well see me for who I really am."

"You'll get there at some point. You're just not ready yet. Give yourself time to get comfortable."

Vic nodded. "Yeah."

They got into the car. Erin started the engine and got the air conditioning going immediately.

"So why do you want to know who I didn't recognize?"

"I just wondered…" Erin was hesitant. It seemed so silly in the face of Vic's problems. "I wondered whether Angela's husband would put in an appearance. You know. If he's still alive."

Vic thought about it, her forehead wrinkling.

"If he showed up, somebody would have recognized him."

"Maybe. He could make himself look different. It's been how long? Longer than Trenton, and he was gone for twenty years. How old were the boys when he disappeared?"

"I don't know. Teenagers, I guess. It was a few years between Uncle Adam disappearing and Trenton. He would have been thirteen or fifteen or something." She clasped and twisted her hands in her lap. "I didn't see anyone I thought was Uncle Adam… but I wasn't looking for him, and I've only seen pictures."

"I was looking for anyone who was in the right age range, but I don't know what he looked like. So, I don't know… he could have been hanging around the back of the chapel or in the foyer, too, and we wouldn't have seen him."

"But why would he come? If he disappeared all of those years ago, why come back now?"

"Trenton was his son. He might not have cared about Angela dying, but you would think that if he knew about Trenton, he would have been there."

"But how would he know?"

Erin turned on her turn signal and waited for the light to change. Why Bald Eagle Falls even needed any traffic signals, she wasn't sure. She didn't exactly drive around in rush hour, so maybe they were needed during that time. If Bald Eagle Falls had a rush hour.

"How did Trenton know about Angela? How did Davis know about Trenton? They both got the word somehow, even though neither one had been here for years."

"Yeah, I guess."

Erin saw Terry and K9 patrolling up ahead. She tapped her horn and waved at him when he turned to look. He cocked his head to the side and motioned for her to pull over. Erin did so, and Terry walked around the car so he could talk to her on the driver's side instead of having to shout across Vic.

"Hey. I wasn't expecting to see you back here so soon. There's not much point in opening the bakery back up, everyone is still at the church."

"I know," Erin agreed. "We just left there."

He leaned on the side of the car. "I suppose you got out of there as quickly as you could. I'm surprised you went in the first place."

"No, it was me," Vic interrupted. "She would have stayed. I wanted to get out of there."

"Oh." Terry raised his brows. "That's the opposite of what I would have predicted."

Erin leaned back, readjusting one of the air vents to blow at her. Having the window open to talk to Terry was letting the hot air from outside in. She knew she shouldn't be idling with the air conditioner going. Not for long.

"I was wondering…" Erin patted her pockets for the note, then remembered she was wearing a dress, not pants, and no apron. She didn't have any pockets. She reached for her purse, then shook her head. "I was wondering about The Bake Shoppe. Who the new owner will be now."

Terry pushed his hat back and wiped his forehead, thinking about it. "I haven't heard anything yet. But why would I? The police are not involved."

"I just thought you might have heard rumors. Or maybe you found out after Trenton died, before they decided it was just an accidental allergy exposure."

"I would assume that after Trenton died, it would go to Davis. The next child in line."

"Because it was a family business?"

He nodded and readjusted his hat again. "Sure. Seems only fair it would go to the surviving child."

"I'm kind of surprised that Angela left it to Trenton in the first place. Wouldn't a parent normally split their estate evenly between their children?"

"Maybe she did," Vic suggested. "But Trenton was the only one who wanted to claim it."

Terry shook his head. "The terms of Angela's will are a matter of public record. Everything was left to Trenton."

Erin was shocked. "Everything? I assumed that she left the business to Trenton and something else, maybe the house or her bank account, to Davis. She cut Davis out completely?"

"Those are the terms of the will."

"Wow." Erin looked at Vic. Vic was the one who really knew Angela. In spite of Angela's innate nastiness, she had been Vic's favorite aunt, until she had turned on Vic. "Can you believe that?"

"Does that mean she knew he was still alive?"

Erin looked back at Terry. "I guess. Do you think so?"

He had stepped back from the car a little and was reaching down to scratch K9's ears.

"I'm not sure why you care about it. Why are you so interested in the terms of the will?"

Erin thought back to Clementine's genealogical records. To discovering details about her parents' deaths that were different from what she had always been told. She disliked the feeling of not knowing the truth. Had it been an accident? Had something happened to her parents other than what she had been told? She hated the feeling of a door being shut in her face, keeping her from the truth.

And she saw the same thing in Angela's family. Secrets. Lies. People who disappeared and reappeared. People who were supposed to be proper Christians but who were just hiding behind a mask of sainthood, while everyone ignored the hypocrisy. Erin felt sorry for Davis. He had been lied to. He'd lost everyone in his family. He'd been shunned by Angela, written out of her life and out of her death. Like he had meant nothing to her.

"Is it because of the competition?" Terry asked, bringing Erin back to earth. "You're worried about the business you're going to lose if Davis reopens The Bake Shoppe?"

"What?" Erin ran back through the conversation in her mind, trying to pick up the threads of where she had left off. "No. Honestly, I don't care if anyone reopens The Bake Shoppe. Ever since I got to town, everyone has acted like I can't survive the competition. That there's only enough business in town for one baker. And it's just not true. There's plenty to go around." She raised both hands in a challenge. "Bring it on!"

Vic laughed. "Why don't you tell us how you really feel, Erin," she teased.

"I don't care who inherits The Bake Shoppe, or if they auction it off, or sell out to a big chain. I was just... curious. That's all. I didn't poison Angela. Or Trenton. And I'm not going to knock off Davis."

"No one had better try that," Terry declared. "There have been enough sudden deaths in the Plaint family. I don't want to be investigating any more of them."

"Exactly," Erin agreed.

She revved her engine, looking at the temperature gauge. "I have to get moving again and park this baby in the shade. Do you want to come over later, when you're off shift?"

Terry grimaced. "I'm not sure. I've got a lot to do. I might not be able to get over tonight."

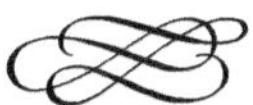

$\mathcal{E}$rin dropped Vic at home and decided to head into the city to do a big grocery shopping run while she had the chance. It was rare for her to get an afternoon—or part of an afternoon—off in which she could do something like that. Normally she had to squeeze it into the evening or the weekend. And working most of Saturday meant it had to be a Sunday after the post-service ladies' tea. Her going into the city to shop on a Sunday was even worse in the church ladies' eyes than the sin of being an atheist. They could almost forgive her being an atheist, but they could not abide her breaking the Sabbath, both by running errands and by doing things like exploring caves on Sunday. They believed that she was only an atheist because she hadn't yet learned the truth. Even though she had explained that she wasn't searching for any supernatural truth. But breaking the Sabbath… that was just wanton hedonism.

The drive to the city was only forty-five minutes if the highways were clear and there was no one to slow her down or pull her over. And usually, everyone was in just as much of a hurry to cover the ground as she was. In her old life, she would have considered forty-five minutes an unmanageable distance to travel to get to a grocery store. But she had learned not to mind it. It gave her a chance to unwind and just let her mind wander, rocking out to the stereo. Provided she played her own music, since the radio stations were few, fuzzy, and far between.

She made a list in her mind as she drove, thinking about all of the things that she might need before she got to the city again. It wasn't so much things like eggs and milk that were a problem to get in Bald Eagle Falls—though the prices were higher—but the more specialized baking ingredients, alternative grains and flours, and fun-shaped decorating sprinkles were just not carried by the stores in Bald Eagle Falls.

Erin parked the Challenger and headed for the main doors of the grocer.

"Erin! Erin Price!"

She stopped and turned around, frowning. She hadn't recognized the male voice. But then she saw who it belonged to.

Alton Summers.

Erin pressed her lips together, irritated. He apparently hadn't gotten the message the last time he had approached her. She didn't have anything to talk to him about. Erin turned back toward the store.

"You don't want to make me chase you, Erin," he warned. "I really don't think you want all of the attention you would get if I had to go in there, shouting after you. It could be very embarrassing for you."

Erin looked back at him, stopping again. "If you are going to harass me, I will call the police. Did you follow me here?" She'd barely glanced in the rear-view mirror after leaving Bald Eagle Falls. Did he just happen to be at the grocery store at the same time as Erin? While it was the closest big store to Bald Eagle Falls and where most of the residents would go for their big shopping days, she just didn't think that matched Alton Summers's personality. She didn't picture him shopping at the grocery store and eating his own meals. She imagined that he ate mostly fast food out of boxes in his hotel room. He wasn't the domestic type.

"Don't you think you'd better hear what I have to say before you call the police and start throwing around accusations?" he demanded.

"No. I've got nothing to say to you and you don't have anything to say that I want to hear."

He looked at her for a moment, smiling. "Really." He looked like the cat that ate the canary. "Maybe you'd better rethink that. Do you really want everyone to hear about your life as Erica Landers? Or under one of your other aliases? You do seem to have a lot of them."

"Just leave me alone," Erin snapped back. But there was a lump in her throat. She wasn't about to walk into the grocery store and have him throwing wild accusations around about things that she had never done. There were bound to be shoppers from Bald Eagle Falls there, or shoppers that would make their way back to Bald Eagle Falls at some point. Or call their friends in Bald Eagle Falls to discuss all of the juicy gossip about that new lady baker. Mud slinging was practically an official sport in the region.

Summers waited and saw that Erin wasn't going to go barging into the store after all. He nodded his approval.

"You've had a very checkered past, my dear," he said in a soft, smooth voice. "I think that now that you're trying to earn a reputation as a good, law-abiding member of the community, that you probably don't want to hear certain ugly rumors about you spread around."

"I don't want you spreading lies about me, no. And if you're going to, then I'll sue you. Defamation of character. It's still against the law in Tennessee, you know."

"I wouldn't have to tell any lies. Just repeat certain accusations that were made. Whether they were ever proven or not is beside the point. All people need to hear is the suggestion that something illegal was done. They'll assume that where there's smoke, there's fire, and that you wouldn't be accused if you weren't doing something wrong. Especially not accused more than once. You know that once people hear that, you'll be convicted in their minds. There's no need to wait for a trial."

"Just what is it you want from me?"

Alton Summers's face brightened noticeably. "What do I want? Just what's rightfully mine. Nothing more."

"You've already collected your fee where I'm concerned. You were hired by Clementine's estate to find her heir, and you did that. For that, you got a percentage of the estate. Don't tell me you spent it already."

But she could tell from the desperation in his eyes that it was all gone. She could have lived off of what he had been given by the executors of Clementine's estate for a couple of years, and Alton Summers had already blown through it in a few months. He obviously had some expensive tastes. He had to be either an addict or a gambler.

"I got what the executors of the estate owed me," he said slowly. "But I would think that the heir of the estate would be able to match it. To keep everything quiet and peaceful."

"Match it?" Erin repeated. "You've got to be kidding! There wasn't that much liquidity in the estate. It's all tied up in the business and the house. I don't have cash to pay you off. I don't owe you anything, and you're not blackmailing me into giving you something you don't deserve."

"Blackmail?" He shook his head, pursing his lips. "What an ugly word. It's not blackmail. It's just you… showing your appreciation for what I got you. One hand washes the other, right?"

"I don't owe you anything."

"If I hadn't found you, you wouldn't have inherited anything. Isn't that true?"

Erin nodded, conceding the point. Summers had been the only one who had succeeded in tracking her down. She hadn't left a very broad trail, orphaned young, buried in the foster care system, moving around and changing her name as often as she did once she aged out of the system.

"I chose you," Summers said, leaning closer to her. She was sweating in the heat, but she could smell him, a mixture of garlic and cheap cologne, of unwashed clothes and oily hair. It turned her stomach. "I chose you to inherit all of that money. Don't you think you should show a little appreciation for that?"

"You *chose* me? You didn't choose me. I was the person you were hired to find."

"I think we both know that isn't true," he said in a hoarse whisper. "Erin Price was just one of your names. And you were just one of the Erin Prices living in the country. I could just as easily have picked one of the others and presented her to the executors as Clementine's heir. Any of those other Erin Prices."

"Well, you could have picked one of them, but that wouldn't have made them the heir."

"I would have *made* them the heir. It wouldn't have been any harder than cleaning up your documentation. Sanitize everything. A little spritz here, a little there. I did you a favor." He shrugged. "When someone does you a favor, you should do something for them. A little payback."

"I don't owe you anything," Erin insisted, getting angrier and more desperate to get rid of him once and for all. "You were hired to find me. You did. You were paid. Get the hell out of here."

"Fine." He stood there with his hands in his pockets. "Then I'll just go back to the executors, and explain to them how a mistake was made. You assumed someone else's identity. You're a con artist. You have a long history of duping people out of their money. You especially like pulling one over on old ladies. Old people trust you. They give you their money. And then you can have all the money you need to do anything you want."

"You know it's a lie. Nothing like that ever happened."

"No? Tell that to Ebony Greer's son. Or ask... what was her name... Cheryl Mason? I'm sure her family would jump right to your defense, wouldn't they?"

"Those people were mistaken. I never took anything from anyone. I never asked anyone to give me anything. They did that on their own."

"They weren't competent to realize how much they were giving to you. They couldn't just give away their money and their jewelry that way. The money and jewelry that was supposed to go to their children when they died. You were paid to be their caretaker, and you took what wasn't due to you. You took advantage of senile old ladies."

"No, I didn't!"

Erin raised her voice so much that everyone around her stopped what they were doing and looked at her. Erin shook her head. She poked her finger into Alton Summers's chest.

"If you start repeating those accusations, I'm going to sue you. I'll do it. And you know I'll win and you'll lose. You'll lose everything, even what you don't have yet."

There was fear in his eyes. Erin knew that fear. The fear of being out of money and out on the street, without a person in the world who cared. She had lived that life for years. Living from one paycheck to another and one gift to another, never sure where she would be in another week, another month. Alton Summers had dug himself in too deep. He needed money, and he needed it right away. But he wasn't going to get it from Erin.

His jaw tightened. He was like a bulldog, sure that if he just held on, he would get what he wanted. But he wasn't going to get what he wanted from Erin.

"I'm not giving you anything. You can just get the hell out of Bald Eagle Falls because you're not getting anything from me."

His eyes were shuttered. He drew a step back from her. She thought he was going to make another threat. But he didn't. He just stood there, jaw clenched tightly, staring at her with angry, intense eyes.

Erin went into the grocery store. He didn't follow her.

∽

When the doorbell rang in the evening, Erin's first thought was that it was Terry, and he had been able to get rid of his other responsibilities in order to relax and visit with her. She closed Clementine's book. Her second thought was that it was going to be Alton Summers again, trying for the third time to blackmail her. She didn't open the door immediately, but checked through the peephole first.

"Who is it?" Vic asked.

Erin opened the door. "Hi!"

Mary Lou gave her a reserved smile. "Good evening."

"Come on in."

Mary Lou entered. She looked around and sat down on the couch. Orange Blossom was lying on the couch. He raised his head to look at Mary Lou, then laid it back down again. Erin sat down on one of the chairs, and Vic stayed on the floor, where she had been alternately working on a crossword puzzle and teasing Orange Blossom with the eraser-end of her pencil.

"What can we do for you?" Erin asked. Mary Lou didn't often come over to visit. When she came by the house, there was a reason.

Mary Lou rubbed the back of her neck slowly. "You know there have been rumors going around," she started out, feeling her way along.

"Rumors about what?" Vic asked sharply. "About Erin and me?"

Mary Lou looked at Vic for a long, appraising moment, and then turned back to Erin. "Yes. About the two of you."

"There is nothing to those rumors," Erin said firmly. "You should know better than to listen to gossip. Vic and I are friends."

"I didn't believe those rumors," Mary Lou agreed. "I think I know you better than that. After all, you and Terry Piper…"

Erin was glad that Mary Lou was being sensible about it. "Right," she agreed. "Vic and I are just housemates."

"But now, I think you should know… I've heard something else."

Erin wondered whether Alton Summers had been that quick to start spreading lies and half truths about her past. She had thought that she had gotten through to him. But apparently not.

"What else?" Vic questioned, reaching over to pat Orange Blossom. He flicked his head around quickly as if to nip her, but she pulled back quickly enough to avoid the intent of his teeth. "Hey, settle down. I'm just saying hi." He sniffed at her fingers and then let her pat him.

"About you," Mary Lou said. "James."

Erin and Vic both looked at Mary Lou, no longer distracted by the cat or other things. Erin looked at Vic, her eyes wide. Vic's face was white.

"I don't go by that anymore," Vic said evenly.

Mary Lou couldn't keep her eyes on Vic. She looked over at Orange Blossom. "Then it's true."

"That I changed my name? Yes."

"And that you are… a boy."

"No."

Mary Lou looked confused by this. "You are," she asserted. Her eyes went back to Vic. "Even if you don't look like one anymore."

"I am a girl."

"You're a transvestite. A boy who likes to dress as a girl."

"No. I am a girl. Who dresses as a girl."

There were a few more seconds as Mary Lou tried to sort that out. "Then what were you before?"

"I was a girl. But one who had been labeled at birth as a boy and tried to live as a boy to please everyone else."

"Because biologically, you are a boy."

"I am a girl," Vic repeated.

Mary Lou sighed. "I don't understand all of the new ways. Why people would accept this nonsense. A person can't change their gender just by deciding that they are something other than they are. You are what God made you. A boy. No matter what you choose to call yourself."

"Mary Lou," Erin stood up. "It's getting to be time for us to head to bed. You know we have to be up pretty early to get the bread baked before the bakery opens."

"I'm not trying to be rude," Mary Lou said. "I don't know the politically correct thing to say. You know that's not the type of person that I am. I've raised my boys to be boys, and I believe what my faith teaches about God making men and women different. They are supposed to be different, not interchangeable. This new idea that you can just choose what you want to be, without regard to biology, it's just a fad. And a silly one. I can no more change my gender than I can change the color of my skin. Or my height. I am what I am, and there's no point in denying it."

Vic stood up as well. "You could tan or bleach your skin. Or tattoo it. And there are surgeries to change your height if wearing heels wasn't good enough. People have been altering their physical appearances for thousands of years. Is that against God?"

"I think it is."

"You have pierced ears? You dye your hair?"

Mary Lou touched her blond, bobbed hair. "That's different. It is vanity… but it's not the same as trying to change who you are. Or who people think you are."

"I'm not trying to fool anyone. I'm just trying to be who I really am."

With Vic and Erin both standing, and Erin's comment that they had to go to bed still hanging in the air, Mary Lou rose to her feet.

"I won't change the way that I treat you," she said. "That wouldn't be Christian. But it will change how I think of you. I know that you are a boy, physically, no matter how you dress and act and talk. I can't change my thoughts about you. And neither can you." She stepped toward the door.

"If you can't change your thoughts about me, then why would you expect me to change the way I think of myself in order to please you? I've known I was a girl ever since I could remember."

Mary Lou shook her head. "I'm sorry, Vic. But you've allowed people to mislead and confuse you."

Erin opened the door. She didn't say anything. Mary Lou stood there for a moment longer, then walked out of the house.

Erin watched Mary Lou walk back to her car. She closed the door and turned to look at Vic.

"Are you okay?"

Vic took a big breath in and breathed it back out again. She was still pale, but her face was composed.

"I guess I'd better get used to it. I've been spoiled, with the way that you've treated me. But *that's* what everyone else is going to be like. They're all going to be trying to convince or convert me. Cure me."

"I'm sorry."

"It was bound to happen sooner or later. It was only a matter of time. I knew when I saw my parents at the funeral…"

"If they don't approve, why would they want to spread it around?"

"I don't know. Maybe I didn't run away far enough, and they want to push me further."

Erin shook her head. "Sometimes… I wonder if it's better that I didn't have any parents who cared about me or what I did once I was an adult."

~

They got ready and headed for bed, even though Erin was sure that neither one of them had any notion of being able to get to sleep in good time. They were both too wound up to even think about sleep. But the visit from Mary Lou hung between them. Neither one wanted to talk about it or to put any weight or importance on it. But they couldn't just forget about it, either. Erin was afraid that talking about it or trying to console Vic too much was just going to make the girl feel worse. It would make things more awkward between them, and Erin was already feeling enough uncertainty over her feelings toward Terry and Willie.

While Vic was in the bath, Erin went up to the attic. Even in her attic retreat, there was no respite from her restless thoughts. She kept going over the visit from Mary Lou in her mind. She should have said more. She should have been more vocal in her defense of Vic. She couldn't help feeling like she had just let Mary Lou into her house to run all over Vic. What a train wreck.

She sat in her little reading nook with one of the big genealogical books open, trying to focus on the pages. On anything but Mary Lou attacking Vic, while Erin just stood by.

She had picked up the book that had her family in it. Her parents' birth and death dates.

Had the social worker intentionally kept the truth from Erin? Why would she lie about when and how they had died? The one foundational fact that Erin had relied on for so many years couldn't be in question. How could that happen? Erin knew what had happened. She could remember it clearly.

Except that she couldn't. When she tried to conjure up a picture in her mind, it was muddy and confused. She heard the words. She remembered the social worker and the first family she had been taken to. But she couldn't remember what had happened to her parents. Why would she? She hadn't been in the car with them when they had the accident.

Where had she been? She'd only been a child. Had she been at school? A friend's house? A babysitter? Why wasn't she with them? It seemed like the social worker, a tall, thin, dry woman, had come to get her in the night. The foster care transfer had been after dark. After Erin's bedtime. She must have been with a babysitter, then. Her mom and dad had been out on a date when they met with tragedy. Bad traffic conditions, a drunk driver; Erin had imagined a lot of different scenarios over the years. She'd had a particularly vivid imagination as a child. After they had died, Social Services had come for Erin. With no family to go to, she had entered the system.

But if she were to believe the information in Clementine's book, that was wrong. She had been taken into care prior to their deaths. They had not died that first night but had lingered on for weeks or months. The details were so fuzzy after all of the years that had passed. Erin couldn't pin down the date that she thought they had died. There had never been an anniversary date marked each year. It was usually on her birthday that she thought about it the most, because she knew that she had been seven when they died. Each advancing year marked another she had lived without them. Had the accident been on her birthday? The threshold between seven and eight?

But she couldn't make that fit, either. The dates of her parents' deaths according to Clementine's records were not Erin's birthday. They were afterward. Significantly.

Then the social worker had lied to her. All of the crap about them dying instantly. That had been a lie. Told to her to make her feel less traumatized, she supposed. So that she would think that they had just stepped peacefully out of their earthly sphere into some peaceful, heavenly existence. Mrs. Jayman, her foster mother, had insisted that they were with God. Even back then, Erin hadn't believed it. God? In heaven? She was sure, after the accident, that neither existed. No one could convince her otherwise. And many people had tried.

Erin jumped when her phone rang. She picked it up and glanced at the caller ID. Melissa. Did she want to gossip about the funeral? Or had she too heard the rumors of Vic's transgender identity and wanted to be the one to inform Erin, thinking that she didn't know.

Even though she was too tired and scatterbrained to talk, Erin answered the call. It seemed like the best idea to just get it all over with. Better to deal with Melissa over the phone than in front of half a dozen other customers at the bakery. And if Erin didn't answer her call, Melissa would probably move on to Vic next, confronting her directly. Erin didn't want Vic to have to deal with two such confrontations in one day.

She swiped the screen to answer the call, and realized too late that it was a video call, not just a voice call. She swore under her breath, too quietly for Melissa to make out over the speakerphone setting. She considered *accidentally* ending the call, and then calling Melissa back with voice-only. If Erin called right back, Melissa wouldn't think that she was avoiding her call. And she would just assume that Erin hadn't noticed that the original call was a video call, or that her phone was malfunctioning. But Erin took too long to react, and found herself looking at Melissa's face. A bit too close, at a low angle that looked up into her nostrils. Erin looked for a way to set her phone down for the call, somewhere with a higher, more flattering angle.

"Hi, Melissa," she greeted, with a forced smile and cheer in her voice.

"I didn't wake you up, did I?" Melissa asked. She was in pajamas herself, but would undoubtedly be up hours past the time that Erin and Vic would be in bed. Erin propped the phone on a bookshelf, carefully adjusting her framing in the smaller picture in the corner of the screen.

"No, I'm still up," she acknowledged. "I need to hit the sack before too long, though." That would warn Melissa that it would have to be a short call, and gave Erin an automatic retreat point if things got too sticky.

"Okay. I won't be too long. I was just wondering how you were doing."

Erin waited for a moment for the other shoe to drop. But if Melissa were approaching her about Vic, she was doing it gradually.

"I'm okay," she said tentatively.

"I saw you and Vic at the funeral, but then you left so quickly. I had been planning to talk to you after. I thought maybe you were sick."

"Vic had to leave. I drove her home. Went into the city to do some shopping."

"Oh, okay." Melissa nodded and smiled. Her movements on the screen were jerky, making Erin feel like it was all just a show. Melissa was putting on an act for her. "I'm glad everything is okay, then."

Did she or didn't she know about Vic? Erin couldn't decide. If Mary Lou knew, then Melissa couldn't be that far behind. Surely whoever had shared it with Mary Lou had spread it far and wide.

"Officer Piper was at the department late," Melissa offered. "Doing a bunch of research."

"Yeah. He said he had a bunch of work to do."

"What did you say to him?"

Erin frowned. "What did I say to him?"

"It was something you said that triggered this flurry of research."

"Something *I* said?"

"Is there an echo in here?" Melissa smacked the side of her phone playfully.

Erin thought about her discussion with Terry on the way back from the funeral. It seemed like it had been a week ago, obscured as it was by her confrontations with Alton Summers and Mary Lou Cox.

"I don't know. I asked about who would own The Bake Shoppe now. I don't remember what else."

"The Bake Shoppe. Not looking at knocking off the next owner now, are you?"

"Melissa!"

"I'm just joking. I'm sorry, I get a morbid sense of humor working at the department."

Erin knew that Melissa didn't work at the police department full-time. Not even part time; she just contracted to do some occasional transcription and filing for them. But Melissa liked to make it sound like she was a fully qualified member of the police department.

"I feel really badly about Trenton's death," Erin explained. "It just tears me up that he was killed by an allergic reaction to something I made. The whole point of my baking is to provide food that is safe for people who have special dietary needs."

"I'm sorry." Melissa's smile disappeared, and she sounded truly repentant. "I didn't mean to make you feel bad."

"I know. But it did. It isn't funny."

"No. You're right. I should be more sensitive. I do put my foot in my mouth sometimes. My mom always told me to think before I open my mouth."

Erin nodded and shrugged. At least with a video call, Melissa could see her response, and she didn't need to verbalize. She decided it was time to change the subject.

"So… you knew Trenton before he disappeared, right?"

"Yes." Caution entered Melissa's tone for the first time. She looked at Erin warily.

"Did you know Davis too?"

Melissa seemed to be waiting for more. It was a few seconds before she nodded. "Yes. Not as well, but I knew all of those kids."

"What was he like? Was he as nasty as Trenton?"

"He wasn't a pleasant person to be around," Melissa hedged. She bit her lip and looked off-camera, thinking about it. "He was pretty messed up."

"In what way?"

"He was a pot head. Always stoned. Trenton was the good brother, good marks, loved by all of his teachers, and Davis was the screw-up. No one would have been surprised if Davis had been the one to disappear."

Erin thought about that. That was all she had ever heard about Davis. He was an addict. It seemed to be the only identity that had stuck to him since his youth in Bald Eagle Falls. She didn't know if she would have immediately classified him as an addict on meeting him without knowing his history, but he was a rough-looking individual. It was obvious from his cadaverous face and yellowed teeth that he had not taken care of himself. He had probably spent at least some of his life living on the street. His yellowed fingers and teeth and stale breath clearly indicated that he was a smoker, even if he had beaten his other addictions.

"So, is he still…?"

Melissa gave an exaggerated shrug. "Talking to him after the funeral, he mentioned 'his recovery' more than once. That's usually an ongoing process. Lots of ups and downs and setbacks. He doesn't look like he's been living life on easy street."

"No, you're right. He doesn't."

"Joelle seems taken with him, though."

Erin sensed disapproval. "I guess that's natural, with him being Trenton's only surviving relative. Or the only one available, at least. She needs someone to share her grief with."

"Her grief." Melissa snorted. "Even by her own account, she was only together with Trenton for a couple of months. Probably just long enough to figure out that she wanted out of it. She's lucky he died and saved her an ugly break-up."

"Maybe so." Erin didn't want to argue the point. Melissa had known Trenton, and Erin hadn't. Melissa had a much better picture of the kind of person he was, even if it had been twenty years. People could change but, in Erin's experience, few of them did. And from her brief encounter with Trenton, he hadn't changed from a jerk into a super-sweet guy.

"Weird, Joelle taking up with Davis," Melissa persisted. "He and Trenton weren't alike. They didn't usually attract the same kind of girls. Why would she want to go from a hard-headed businessman like Trenton to an on-the-skids loser like Davis? I figure she likes money; that's why she was with Trenton in the first place."

Erin frowned at her phone screen. "What makes you think that?"

"Have you seen the clothes she wears? Thrift store chic if I ever saw it. Go to the thrift stores that get donations from the upscale neighborhoods. Grab all of the big brand names. But you can tell, can't you? I mean, nothing really fits her right, or it's worn, or she's tried to cover a stain with a broach or scarf. She wants to look like she shops all the fancy stores when she can hardly get from one paycheck to the next. It's a scam. Look better, so people will treat you better. Trust you more."

"You think she's gone from one brother to the other just because of the money?"

"Davis doesn't have any money."

"He does if he inherited The Bake Shoppe after Trenton."

Melissa cocked her head, considering that. "Maybe. But they aren't going to know that until Trenton's estate is sorted out. They don't even know yet if he had a will. Someone will have to go back to Chicago and go through his papers, contact his lawyer, all that stuff."

"Joelle?"

"I guess so. She's the only one who knows him and anything about his life these past two decades."

"Chicago? Is that where he went?"

"That's where he came from. I don't know if that's where he went from here. No one from here ever found him."

"It's weird, isn't it?" Erin shifted her position and stretched out a bit in her reading nook. She was starting to get drowsy. In spite of how hyped up she had been after Mary Lou's visit, it had been a long day, and her body was starting to insist that she get some rest. She smothered a yawn. "I mean, it must be really weird for you. You knew them both twenty years ago, and then they were gone. And now... whoever thought that either of them would ever come back here, let alone both of them."

"I wish they'd both just stayed away."

"Davis too?"

"Yes. Both of them. Davis wasn't the same as Trenton, with his out-and-out meanness. He was different. Trenton was the outgoing guy who knew and controlled everyone around him. Like Angela. Davis was different. He was darker. Depressed. He was just… there was so much going on under the surface. Tortured."

"You sound like he was more your type."

"My type?" Melissa snapped. "What makes you think I like the moody, depressive type? Does that sound like me?"

Erin bit her lip. She was tired, and she was making mistakes. "Opposites attract? I don't know. It was just the tone of your voice. Like maybe you liked him, back then. It doesn't mean anything. Who can predict who a teenager will crush on?"

Melissa scowled and didn't answer.

"You clearly knew the family. There weren't a lot of prospects around here. Maybe you liked the younger brother better."

"I didn't like either of them. So, you can just put that right out of your mind. I had plenty of prospects. There were lots better than the likes of the Plaint boys."

"Prom King and valedictorian rolled into one? I guess not everyone aspires to that. Some of us like someone more down-to-earth."

"That's right," Melissa agreed. "There were plenty of other boys around Bald Eagle Falls. I didn't need Davis."

And yet, she never had married, and Erin never even heard her talk about dating anyone.

CHAPTER 12

There was a soft noise on the stairs, and Erin turned her head to identify it. She had thought that maybe it was Orange Blossom creeping up to investigate the attic, finally getting over his fear of the stairs, but it was Vic. Though she was holding an alert and anxious-looking Orange Blossom in her arms as her head and shoulders appeared through the access hold.

"Are you done?" Vic asked. "I could hear you talking to someone…"

"Just on the phone with Melissa Lee," Erin motioned with her phone. "Just… talking about Trenton and Davis."

Vic stood on the stairs, only halfway up, scratching the kitten's ears. "What about them?"

"Just about… how weird it was, both of them showing up here when no one knew where either one of them was. How different they were from each other. About Joelle and who gets the bakery now. Just…"

"Trying to solve the case?" Vic prompted.

"No, there is no case. I'm just curious about it, that's all. I should just mind my own business, I know. Curiosity killed the cat."

"Shh," Vic covered up Orange Blossom's ears, making him look cross and owly. "Don't say that around him!"

Erin chuckled. "It's not like it's up to me to decide who gets the bakery or what they do with it. I just… would like to know."

"You're curious," Vic summed up.

"Yes."

"You're going to be dead tired in the morning."

Erin pressed the button on her phone to bring it back to life. She grimaced at the time on the lock screen.

"Shoot. I didn't realize how long I was on. I'd better get moving."

Vic descended the stairs and Erin shut off the light and was close behind her.

"I get the feeling people know what's going on," she told Vic with a sigh. "I feel like everyone knows everything about everyone else, and I'm the only one who doesn't know all of the connections. Like they're all shutting me out."

"Well, I imagine they are, to some degree."

"Somebody knows what happened to Trenton and where he went. Someone kept in touch with him. And someone knew where to find Davis, too. I want to know… if someone knows what happened to their father. And where to find him."

Vic shifted uneasily. She put Orange Blossom down. The cat wrapped itself around Erin's ankles, purring and coating her pant legs with orange and white fur.

"Who needs to buy furs when you've got a cat," Erin said ruefully.

"Erin…"

"Mmm-hmm?"

"I think… you should be careful about asking people questions."

"I am," Erin said. "Trust me, I don't want another situation where someone thinks I'm a threat and that they have to take me out. No more of that."

"It's just that… you don't know who is or isn't dangerous. Or what the truth is. You could stir up a hornet's nest. And those suckers sting."

Erin laughed, but Vic's expression was earnest. Erin tried to read her eyes. What it was she wasn't saying.

"Vic… do *you* know what happened to Angela's husband?"

"That was long before my time," Vic said. "I wasn't even born yet. I wasn't even born yet when Trenton disappeared."

"No. But your parents were. You grew up in that family, and you know what their secrets are."

"We didn't have any family secrets. The biggest secret my parents had was that their little boy liked to wear dresses."

Erin didn't let herself be distracted.

"Vic. Do you know? Or have you guessed? Things are said, people hint around… until you know the truth without having to be told."

"You already know. It's just like Melissa told you before. Aunt Angela would say, 'before I got rid of my husband' and stuff like that. Sort of a joke. But everybody sort of believed it, too. That she had just gotten rid of her husband when he got in her way one too many times. It was always sort of the family joke, how Angela would take care of someone if they got in her way. But too often, it was true. People who crossed her… didn't stay around long. Things happened to them, and they decided to leave."

"Do you think she killed him? Or gave him an ultimatum about leaving town?"

"I don't know. But like I said… don't stir things up. I don't want you getting hurt."

Erin went to bed, but her mind was whirling with all that had happened during the day. It had been full of new experiences and information, and her brain wouldn't settle down, trying to process it all. She got up after an hour to take a few of the herbs that she had that were supposed to promote sleep. It always felt like a bit of a cheat, taking something to help herself sleep.

But it didn't seem to help. Erin continued to move around, trying to find a comfortable position and just turn her brain off so that she could get some rest. She considered checking if Vic was still awake and asking for one of her Ambien. She'd never taken anything that strong before. She needed to get some sleep. But when she looked at the clock, she realized there were only three hours before she had to get up, and she didn't want to be dopey driving to the shop or managing the equipment after taking a sleeping pill. She turned on her lamp and sat up with a book, waiting for her eyes to get drowsy and close of their own accord. Orange Blossom didn't know why she was up when she was supposed to be sleeping, and walked all over her, sniffing her and trying to figure it out.

Her head hurt. She closed her eyes to rest and found herself drifting.

She tried to remain in that dozy, floaty space, and not let any real thoughts or worries creep into the free-flowing nonsensical dream-state thoughts swirling around in her head.

It seemed like she had just finally slipped into real sleep when the alarm went off. Erin didn't let herself rest for even a second, forcing her feet over the side of the bed and going to the bathroom to splash water on her face. If she let herself go back to sleep, just for one more minute of rest or to reconnect with the end of a dream, she'd still be there in bed when it was time for the bakery to open.

Orange Blossom yowled and chirped as Erin made her way into the kitchen, turning on the lights. Erin cocked her head but didn't hear any signs of Vic getting out of bed. Erin determined to give her ten minutes, and then she'd go wake Vic up. Vic probably hadn't slept any better than Erin. She was the one who had to face the gossips and self-righteous know-it-alls who would be flocking to the bakery to preach hell-fire and call her down to repentance. Erin's brain had been more occupied with the mystery of her parents' death, and Angela's husband's disappearance, and how everyone in town knew more about the Plaints than she did. Even Vic, who wasn't even from Bald Eagle Falls.

Erin started the coffee, fed the cat, and popped some muffins into the microwave to defrost. She put some Jam Lady jars out on the table and looked at the clock on the wall. She couldn't let Vic sleep much longer, or they would be late getting to the bakery.

She knocked on the door, open just a couple of inches, but there was no response. She opened the door and knocked again, poking her head in.

"Vic. Vic, you slept through. It's time to get up."

There was a groan from the dark depths of the room. Erin hesitated. She had always respected Vic's privacy and never entered the room while she was sleeping or when the door had been shut.

"Vic!"

Erin took a few steps into the room. The air was close, sweaty, and stale. Vic shifted around in her sleep, but didn't sit up or answer Erin. Erin tiptoed over to the bed, and tentatively gave Vic's arm a shake. She was always surprised by Vic's muscles. She didn't look muscular, but they lay under the surface of her pale skin like iron.

"Vic."

Vic groaned louder.

"It's time to get up. We have to get to the bakery," Erin said firmly. She could remember doing this with foster siblings. Trying to get them out of bed when she was told to. She always danced between being persistent enough to wake them up, but not obnoxious enough to get smashed in the nose for it.

Vic cleared her throat a few times. Erin saw her push up to look at the clock. Vic groaned again. "I can't."

"Come on. Rise and shine. You'll feel better once you're up."

"No. I can't today."

"I know you probably didn't sleep very well. I didn't either. But we still need to—"

"I can't," Vic insisted. "I'm calling in sick."

Erin stood there. It had never occurred to her that there would be days when Vic wouldn't be available to help her. She'd always been a faithful worker.

"Are you sure?"

"You'll have to cover," Vic insisted. "I can't."

"Okay… Go back to sleep, then."

"Uh-huh." Vic turned over and started snoring almost immediately. Erin stood there listening to the low rumble for a few seconds, then sighed and left Vic alone, closing the door again, just far enough ajar that Orange Blossom could squeeze through. If he knew that Vic was home and he couldn't get in to cuddle with her, he would howl loudly enough to wake the whole neighborhood, and it was still before dawn.

"You'll have to take care of Vicky today," she told Orange Blossom as she ate her muffin over the sink. "She's not feeling well, so she'll need lots of cuddles."

Orange Blossom stopped his morning wash to regard Erin with round, serious eyes.

"I don't know if she's actually sick, or if it's just the dread of putting up with everyone knowing about her… the whole transgender thing. But either way, kitty cuddles always help."

Orange Blossom sneezed and went back to washing. Erin ate the rest of the muffin too quickly. It felt like a big lump of it lodged in her esophagus. But she knew she had to get to the bakery as quickly as possible to have time to set up without Vic. She could eat later if she needed to, having a little nibble between orders, but she had to get there and get to work to open on time. People might forgive her for Vic being away, but not for opening late.

~

William Andrews wasn't one of the usual early-morning rush. Erin didn't usually see him until partway through the day. More often in the afternoon, washing windows, delivering flyers, or a dozen other odd jobs that he was contracted to do by the various town residents. He wasn't usually one of those who stood outside her door with a cup of coffee, waiting for her to flip over her sign and open the door. Erin gave him a smile of greeting. On one hand, she wondered how he could manage to look so grubby that early in the morning, but she knew that his mining activities left him almost permanently blackened. He would probably have to scrub off three layers of skin to reveal a clean, pink layer. He was more stained than dirty.

"Come on in," she invited. "What can I get for you today?"

His eyes went to the counter, but Vic wasn't there. No one was there but Erin. She waited expectantly. The other early-morning customers filed in behind him. Erin stood waiting for him to make a comment or decide what it was he wanted to buy.

"Where is Vic?" he asked, eventually turning his gaze to Erin.

"She wasn't feeling up to it today. I'm sure after an extra day in bed she'll be raring to go."

"I wanted…" He wasn't sure what to say to fill the silence. "I wanted to be here to help her… give her some support."

By which Erin assumed he meant that he had heard the latest juicy tidbits spread by her angry parents, and knew how the majority of the town was going to react.

"That's very sweet of you. I'm sure she'd appreciate it. But she didn't manage to make it in today. Maybe tomorrow."

"Well… it's probably for the best. Let things… cool down a little."

"You can give her a call later on. I'm sure she'll be too restless by mid-morning to sleep any longer; we're so used to getting up early. I'm sure she'll be happy to know that there's someone else in town who isn't going to turn on her."

Willie cast a glance back at the other customers who were waiting to be served and spoke in a slightly lower tone. "I know what it's like to be an outcast around here. Have people look down on you. I can't say I understand exactly what she's going through, but... I'll be there for her."

Erin wondered if Willie's attitude would be any different if he realized that Vic might have romantic feelings toward him. It was one thing to say that he supported her when she was just a friend going through a tough time, but things would be a lot more tangled if he knew that she was transgender *and* had feelings for him. It was a lot to ask of a guy. And Erin herself felt traitorous for her own attraction to Willie. Why couldn't she just have feelings for Terry and leave Willie to Vic? It would be a lot neater and more logical than the two of them competing for Willie, especially when Willie wasn't Erin's only prospect.

"Would you like a muffin to go with your coffee?"

"Uh..." he looked over the products in the display case. "Sure. Are those blueberry?"

They were clearly labeled blueberry. Not as clearly as Vic would have labeled them, maybe. Erin's handwriting left a little to be desired. But she had printed it as best she could. And he could see blueberries speckling the muffin.

"Blueberry is one of my favorites," Erin said. "I make them pretty often."

"I've always liked blueberries," he said, as Erin retrieved one for him. "We used to go picking blueberries when I was a little tyke. There are a few really good places to pick around here."

Erin rang up the purchase for him. "I appreciate you coming by. Thanks for being there for Vic. We'll have to talk more later, okay?"

Willie smiled at her, his teeth very white against his darkened skin. "You bet."

Erin didn't feel like having lunch alone in the kitchen. It seemed too quiet and empty without Vic. She wondered whether Willie had called Vic or gone over to see her, or whether Vic was out of bed yet. Was she sick, or just tired and anxious about facing the townspeople now that they knew what she had hoped to keep a secret?

She decided to go over to the family restaurant for lunch instead of staying in. Vic usually wanted Chinese or hot chicken when they went out to eat, so Erin hadn't been to the family restaurant before. It was too early for the lunch rush, so the restaurant was nearly empty, and the young hostess showed her immediately to a table. Erin checked her messages, emails, and neglected social networks while she waited for her meal.

A figure approached in Erin's peripheral vision, and she looked up, expecting to see the waitress who had brought her coffee, returning with a plate of dinner.

But it wasn't. It was Davis.

He gave her a stiff smile and dropped into the chair across the table from her without invitation.

"Bit early for lunch, isn't it?" he asked. "Or late for breakfast?"

"Early lunch. There's a lunch hour rush at the bakery, so we take our lunch before that. And we're up so early, it's a long time between breakfast and lunch otherwise."

"We? I don't see your friend today."

"No." Erin looked around the restaurant as if Vic might show up at any moment. "She's not feeling well today, so it's just me."

"You eat here often?"

"No. Never been here. Thought I would try it out."

The waitress returned at that moment and settled the plate in front of Erin. Erin nodded at Davis and picked up her cutlery, waiting for him to leave.

"Okay, well… it was nice to see you again," she tried. But he didn't budge.

"What's that?" he questioned, looking at the roll on the edge of the plate, pushed into the mashed potatoes and gravy, his nose wrinkled. "Commercial brand rolls? When I get The Bake Shoppe reopened, I'll make sure they use *our* rolls."

Erin nodded. "That would be nice. Homemade—or handcrafted—is always better than the factory-produced stuff." The roll was rather limp and anemic-looking. She should have taken the opportunity to market her baked goods to the restaurant, and any of the other restaurants and shops in town that sold commercial breads, before Davis had come back to town. She'd missed an opportunity to get in ahead of him.

But her business had been pretty brisk. She hadn't had a lot of time to market anything outside of the shop. She'd said before that there was enough business in Bald Eagle Falls for two bakeries. The fact that the restaurants were using store-bought rolls was just further evidence of that. There were other niches and opportunities to be explored that Erin hadn't even considered.

She cut into her roast beef and glanced up at Davis, waiting for him to leave. But he leaned back against the chair and stretched, settling himself in rather than making any sign that he intended to leave. Erin wasn't sure how else to indicate to him that she would prefer to eat alone.

"I missed you after the funeral," Davis said. "I know you were there; I saw you and your friend come in. But afterward… I looked for you, and you weren't there. I wanted to introduce you to some of the out-of-town guests. And thank you again, for everything you did for Trenton."

"I'm sorry. Vic—my assistant—she wasn't feeling very well after the funeral, so we left pretty quickly." She tried to shift the conversation away from herself. "It was a very nice service though. Good attendance. You must have been pleased."

He gave an uncaring shrug. "Everyone just wanted to come and have a look. It was more about seeing the boy who disappeared twenty years ago than it was about paying their respects. He didn't have any friends left."

"Well, there must have been some of his old school friends there. And the family members who came. Joelle. And you, of course."

Davis opened his mouth, his expression twisted, ready to shoot something sarcastic at her. Then he closed it again. He started fiddling with the salt shaker. He wasn't leaving, and he wasn't pursuing the conversation. Erin felt more and more uncomfortable as the silence drew out.

"So, you're taking over The Bake Shoppe now?" she asked.

"Yeah, of course. I'm Trenton's only surviving relative. Everything he owned comes to me. The lawyer says I have to apply to have my father declared dead, and then I can pursue the estate. He said it isn't difficult, but it will take a while." Davis sighed. "Not like I want to hang around here with nothing to do while I wait. 'A while' could be weeks or months. Stuck in this one-horse town without being able to access what's rightfully mine."

"That's too bad." Erin decided that eating quickly was her only hope. Get the food down and get back to Auntie Clem's, away from Davis.

Davis had fallen silent again. Erin could see what Melissa had meant about him being dark and depressive. He sat there brooding, negativity rolling off of him like heat waves.

"I'm so sorry about you losing your mother and brother," Erin offered.

"It must be very difficult for you, losing them both so close together. I lost both of my parents—"

"That's what you said before," David cut in. "But I don't think that means you have any idea the kind of pain I'm in. The kind of life that I've led."

"No, I didn't mean that. I just meant... I know what it's like to be left without a family... and to have a couple of members of my family killed tragically, so close together."

"You don't have any idea the crap I've had to go through."

"No. I can't imagine what it must have been like for you, losing your father like that."

He looked at her sharply. "What do you mean?" he snapped.

"I'm not prying. I'm sorry. I just knew... I mean, I heard about how your father disappeared, all of those years ago. I was thinking how hard it must have been, not knowing what had ever happened to him."

He stared at her, eyes sharp and intense. What did he see when he looked at her? A stranger who was sympathetic? A busybody prying into his business? A potential enemy, just looking for a way to cheat him out of his rightful business? She tried to smile reassuringly, all the while shoveling the bland meal into her mouth so she could get back to the bakery. She wanted to salt the food, but Davis was still playing with the salt shaker and she didn't want to ask him for it.

"What do you know about my father?" Davis demanded. "He hasn't been around here for years."

"No. I know. I didn't know him. Obviously. And I've only heard that he disappeared, and no one knew what had happened to him..."

"He abandoned us. There's no *mystery* to it. People made a lot bigger deal of it than it ever was."

"I didn't know. I guess there's been a lot of speculation about what happened. But if you know he just abandoned you, then won't you have to conduct a search for him, rather than having him declared dead? I mean, you don't know, he could still be around, living on his own or with another family."

He glared at her. "I've already searched. He's gone. Probably died years ago. There's no point in wasting more money on detectives or advertising for him. He's long since gone."

Erin nodded. "Okay. Of course. You know what's been done and what's best."

"Yeah."

"How old were you and Trenton when he… disappeared?" She quickly corrected himself. "I mean, when he abandoned you? When he… left?"

His eyes were suspicious. Maybe he was regretting approaching her now. She hadn't meant to upset him, but he was the one who had sat down with her and brought up his father.

"I was thirteen." He turned away from her, looking out the window at the street. She could see his Adam's apple working up and down. In spite of the face and body of the grown man sitting in front of her, she saw the young teenager he had been. The heartbreak of being abandoned as a young man by the person who was supposed to be his best example and mentor. Yes, he had lived a hard life as the result of his own choices. But he hadn't chosen to be abandoned like that. The trauma was not his fault. "Do you know how young that is?" Davis said accusingly. "My mother said we were old enough to act like men and not whine about it. That she expected us to act like grown-ups. Stop being such babies. And I thought she was right. I thought that I was just weak."

Erin laid down her fork. Her instinct was to put her hand over his to convey her sincerity, but she was afraid he would misinterpret the gesture. So, she kept her hands by her plate.

"She shouldn't have done that," she said. "Thirteen is not an adult, and she shouldn't have expected you to be one. Thirteen-year-olds' brains are still developing. Their hormones are all over the place. They're just figuring out who they are."

"And I didn't much like who I found out I was." Davis's voice was low and bitter. He turned his gaze back away from the window and looked Erin in the face. "But we can't change who we are, even if we don't like it. You can't hide from yourself. I should know. I spent over two decades trying. And so did Trenton. Just in different ways."

Erin nodded.

He blinked. She thought from the roughness in his voice that he was close to crying, but his eyes were dry and tearless. Davis got slowly to his feet.

"You seem like a nice lady. I'm not sure what I expected you to be like. Maybe I expected you to be like *her*. I want you to know that I don't blame you for Trenton's death. The cupcakes weren't your fault. And it wasn't your fault that you couldn't save him. It was just time for him to go… for the last time."

Erin nodded. "Thank you. It's been hard, knowing that something I made, something that was supposed to be safe, was what killed him."

"That's not what killed him."

Erin raised her eyes to Davis's, startled. She knew the cupcakes, and his allergy to them were Trenton's cause of death.

"*She* killed him," Davis said. Erin knew he was speaking of his mother, and the way she had treated him at thirteen years old, expecting him and fifteen-year-old Trenton to be mature men when they were still on the cusp of childhood.

Angela had killed their spirits, had driven them both away. Was she responsible for her son's death in her bakery so many years later? Erin wasn't sure Angela could be blamed for the actions they had taken decades later. But she wasn't going to argue with Davis over how he felt about it.

"I'm sorry," she said. "I really am."

CHAPTER 13

*E*rin was physically and emotionally exhausted when she got home. She hadn't realized just how hard it was to run the bakery herself without her assistant. Vic had become a part of the business, and Erin just couldn't do it without her. The lunchtime discussion with Davis and the various customers who came through the bakery wanting to catch a glimpse of Vic or who talked to Erin about her had all worn her out emotionally so that she could barely put two thoughts together and felt like either going to sleep or bursting into tears. Or both.

She made the quick trip home, and for a few minutes, just sat in the car in front of the house, looking at it. Lights were on. Vic was up and out of bed, or the only light would have been in her room. So, she must be feeling better and was hopefully prepared to work at the bakery the next day. As long as she wasn't going to run away to somewhere else where she could keep the details of her gender identity secret. Erin didn't know how she would handle it if Vic decided to leave town. And the possibility had to be considered.

Erin took several long, even breaths. She wanted her body to be completely calm and relaxed. Breathe away all of the tension she had been storing in her muscles all day. Loosen up and just be relaxed for her evening with Vic, whatever it was going to bring.

Then she went in.

Vic wasn't in the living room and didn't run out to see her when she entered the house, but Orange Blossom did. He made several long howls and a series of short yips of greeting like he couldn't decide whether to be upset that she had been away for so long or happy that she had finally returned. She knew she was putting her own thoughts into the head of an animal who probably didn't think anything like she did. But she couldn't help assigning him human thoughts and feelings.

"Hello, cuddles," Erin greeted, scooping the cat up and holding him against her face. He was so soft and silky, and he immediately started purring as soon as he was in her arms. He kept making little *mrrrow* noises, showing his pleasure at her being home and the ear scratches and cuddles she gave him.

"Yes, Mommy's home," Vic said, coming out of the kitchen, wiping her hands on her apron. "You would think I had been neglecting him all day, rather than indulging His Majesty's every whim," Vic complained. "But no, when Mom comes home, forget about anything I did for him."

"He appreciates you too," Erin assured her. She walked up to Vic and hugged her around the shoulders, allowed her to scratch Orange Blossom's ears, and then they walked into the kitchen together. The house was filled with wonderful smells, and Erin tried to sort them all out, even though most of the dishes were covered so she couldn't see them.

"Everything smells heavenly in here. Did you spend all day cooking?"

"No, just the last little while. It does smell good, doesn't it?" Vic took a deep inhale.

"It sure does. Is that… lasagna? And glazed carrots? And…"

Vic laughed. "No one could ever doubt your nose! Yes! Now, why don't you go shower off, change into some comfy jammies, and then come back and we'll eat?"

"You don't want to eat first? It looks like everything is ready. You don't want it to dry out."

"It will keep for that long. I know what it's like at the end of a long day at work, and you had to do both of our jobs today. Wash out the sweat and the flour and get some hot water on those muscles. Then you can put up your feet and relax."

"Okay," Erin agreed. "I'm not going to argue." She flipped the cat over in her arms so that he was lying on his back with his feet and belly in the air. "And would kitty like a shower too?" she crooned to him.

Orange Blossom purred away, oblivious to the meaning of her words. Erin put him down in the hallway before going into the bathroom to follow Vic's suggestion and get herself nice and relaxed and sparkling clean for supper.

She was glad Vic was apparently feeling better. She was up, dressed, makeup expertly applied, and a smile on her face. She hadn't sat around all day feeling sorry for herself but had thought about what kind of a day that Erin would be having and had made them something special.

Vic was going to be okay.

Erin was probably under the hot water in the shower way too long. For sure the lasagna would be getting dried out before they could eat it. The water was starting to cool off, which meant she had emptied the hot water tank. Erin got out, toweled off, and was dressed in her flannels and ready for supper in ten minutes.

"I hope this tastes as good as it smells," Vic said. "I've helped make lasagna before, but this is my first time doing it all by myself."

"I'm thinking you did something right." Erin took a big bite of the too-hot lasagna, searing the inside of her mouth. But she smiled and swallowed it anyway. "Best thing I've put in my mouth in my life," she proclaimed.

"Good thing you're not prone to exaggeration."

"It is seriously good. I'm thinking I'm wasting your talents at the bakery. You should have your own full-blown restaurant. Where did you get the recipe? Don't tell me that you just remembered it all off the top of your head from making it with your mom."

"No! Clementine's recipe books."

Erin vaguely remembered having seen recipe books in the kitchen. One of the cupboards, but she wasn't sure which one. She usually got her recipes for the bakery off the internet and didn't own a lot of recipe books. Clementine's recipe books had only vaguely interested her since she knew they wouldn't have the specialty recipes she would need for the bakery.

"Oh. I guess there are." Erin ate for a few minutes in silence. But it wasn't like the silence at the restaurant with Davis. It was a friendly, companionable silence. Just two friends enjoying a great meal together. "So how was your day?"

"I couldn't sleep much past seven," Vic said. "Maybe I should have gotten myself together and gone to join you at the bakery, but I just…

didn't feel up to it. I needed to get my head together and figure out what I was going to do."

Erin nodded. "It's not going to be easy to face people," she said. "They're not all going to be polite about it like Mary Lou was. And that was bad enough."

"I know. But I'm ready now. It will be okay."

"Good. I sure missed you today. I really need you there to help me. Running a bakery is not a one-person job. And we've got the Founder's Day celebration to prepare for."

"Sorry for abandoning you."

"Everyone is entitled to a sick day. And you've more than repaid me for all of the extra work. This is all just divine."

"It is pretty good," Vic agreed. "So, who did you see today?"

Erin reached back. It seemed more like three days than just one. She told Vic the names of the regulars who had come through. She kept mum on the people who had come through just to look at Vic or harangue her about her life. Vic didn't need to hear any of that.

"Did you hear from William Andrews at all?" she asked. "I told him to give you a call or stop by to see you mid-morning. I didn't figure you'd be able to stay in bed all day."

"Good call. Uh… he did call… I saw his name on the Caller ID. But… I didn't answer it."

Erin rested her fork. Orange Blossom was complaining and nipping at Erin's calves, and she pushed him away with her foot. "Why wouldn't you answer it? You like Willie."

Vic's face flushed. "I know I do. But I didn't know how he would react to the news, and I didn't want… I just didn't want to face whatever he might have to say. If he talked about it like Mary Lou, or if he was disgusted that I'd ever been near him… that we might have… gotten close…"

"No, no. He was really nice about it. He said that he didn't understand everything, but that he knew what it was like to be ostracized, and he wanted to be there to support you. He was very nice about it."

Vic's expression was still worried. Erin had expected her to brighten up at this news.

"But he didn't say… that he was okay with it." Vic stepped awkwardly around the issue. "About… him being a guy… and me… not being… me being transgender. It's not something a lot of guys will accept. They don't want to... get involved."

"Well, no," Erin admitted. Her face was burning, and she couldn't pretend that it was the heat of the day or the oven. While she was fully supportive of Vic and would defend her to her dying breath, she couldn't predict how men were going to feel about having a relationship with a transgender girl. She didn't imagine it would be smooth sailing. "I don't know how he's going to feel about any of that. But he said he wanted you to know that you had his support and that he wouldn't exclude you. So... that's good."

Vic nodded. She crossed her arms in front of her, looking vulnerable and alone. "I guess I'll call him back, then. There's no way to know how it's going to go if I avoid him."

"That's right. Maybe the two of you could go out somewhere. Just have a drink and a talk. I mean, you could be here. I would stay out of the way. But if you wanted to go somewhere else, that would be okay too."

"Are you sure?"

"Why wouldn't I be sure?"

"Because... you like him. You don't want me to get involved with him because you like him."

"We don't know if you're ever going to get involved with him. For now, we're just talking about a friend. A couple of friends having a drink together. So, yes. I'm okay with that."

"What if it gets to be more?"

Erin bit her lip and refrained from pointing out that Vic was only eighteen. Still practically a baby. Willie wasn't going to pursue someone so much younger than he was. Erin was much closer to his age. At some point, Vic was going to have to start mixing with the kids her own age. How much could an eighteen-year old have in common with a man almost twenty years her senior?

"How about we just cross that bridge when we come to it. I don't want to be competing with you, but I don't want to say I'm going to limit my options either... because I do like him."

Vic considered this, biting her lip and staring down at her plate. She had eaten a few bites of the lasagna and vegetable sides, but she seemed to have lost her appetite.

"Okay," she said finally.

Erin could tell that Vic had hoped Erin would give her a wide berth, promising that she wouldn't pursue Willie romantically.

"Give him a call." Erin took another bite of her lasagna. It was sweet and spicy and tasted just the way lasagna should. "Let me know whether you want to invite him over here or go out. I'll stay out of your way in the attic if you want to talk here."

Vic nodded. "Okay. Thanks." She took her plate over to the garbage and proceeded to scrape it into the garbage. Orange Blossom complained and stood up with his paws on the garbage can, trying to get at the food. Vic gave in and put a spoonful into his dish. He proceeded to gobble it down, allowing her to scrape the rest into the garbage.

An hour later, Erin was upstairs in her attic hideaway, and Vic and Willie were in the living room talking. Erin had relocated all of Clementine's genealogy books and some of her research files to the attic. She was hoping that if she went through the research files, she could find out where Clementine had gotten the information about Erin's parents and their death dates. She obviously hadn't just made it up. She had seen or been told the wrong information, and Erin wanted to see the source material.

There didn't seem to be much order to the research files. They were organized loosely into families, but the folder that held the Price family research was bulging with dog-eared notes, letters, and clippings. Erin went through the first few pages, looking for some sort of order so that she would know where to start. But they didn't seem to be in any kind of chronological order, with material from the 1850s mixed in with obituaries from the 1980s and a letter from a cousin that was undated.

"Come on, Clementine," Erin muttered. "What kind of record-keeping is this?"

Everything in the genealogy books was so carefully documented and filed that she had expected to find the research in the same state. But obviously, Clementine had only organized the end result. All of the research was just put randomly into the folder once she had noted the details contained in the family trees.

So, Erin did the only thing she could and started going through the Price research file one page at a time. She scrutinized each clipping carefully, then turned it over and placed it face-down on the other side of the folder and picked up the next.

They were names that she didn't recognize. She knew they would be in the book that held her family tree, and that if she were diligent, she would be able to find each of the names on the charts, all of them tracing back to her somehow. But she wasn't interested in all of the other names. She wanted to find her parents' names.

Even so, some of the clippings pulled her in. Stories of her ancestors who had lived on the mountain. Or relatives who had gone off to war or sea or to follow the railway or pursue other adventures. Some had returned, and some hadn't. It was fascinating to see the color that wove through her family's past. And every one of Clementine's bulging research folders held more information like that, different branches of the family, all coming and going and marrying and having children. And dying. There were a lot of obituaries. Some of them revealed fascinating details about the deceased or their families, and some of them were sparse, with next to no information other than a birth and death date.

There were sheets of ruled paper with Clementine's careful handwriting. Items she was researching or notes she made from books or microfilm she had borrowed. The copies of old letters interspersed between the pages were strangely compelling windows into the past. She found it hard not to keep flipping through them, even though she knew that the ancient letters had nothing to do with her parents' deaths. They were much too old.

There was a movement nearby, and Erin looked at the stairs to see if Vic were coming up to talk to her. There was no sign of her. Just the noise of the house settling. Maybe a wind was picking up outside, a branch rubbing against the house. She strained her ears and could still hear Vic's and Willie's voices from the living room. They sounded light, laughter interspersed through their conversation. Erin looked back down at her folder.

Erin was afraid that she was going to skip over something important. She couldn't stop to read everything, but she was also worried that she was going to skim over something too quickly and miss an important clue. She didn't want to have to go through the file more than once. Maybe she would return to it just to browse through family stories for entertainment, but she didn't want to have to keep combing it for details about her parents.

"Come on, Clementine. It was important. How far is it buried in here?"

She leafed ahead through the folder, delving farther and farther down to see if she could tell how long it was since Clementine had collected the clippings. Clementine's lined notes had dates on them, and if the order of the collection had been maintained then, as if it were an archeological dig, all she should have to do was to find the approximate placement of notes that Clementine had made around the time of Erin's parents' deaths. Then she could look more carefully for anything relevant. Looking for those lined papers, Erin dug down to the beginning of the research folder. The notes didn't start until after Clementine's retirement. Which made perfect sense. Only then would she have had the time to devote to her hobby. But that was ten years after Erin's parents' death. Which meant that Erin was either looking for a different folder which held information Clementine had collected or noted around the time of their deaths, or she hadn't searched out their death dates until after her retirement, and it *was* buried somewhere in the thick pile of papers Erin held, and she needed to continue to search out the information one page at a time.

Erin sighed.

There was another muffled noise. Erin looked toward the stairs again. There was a stealthy movement. But she could still hear Vic's and Willie's voices in the distance, not close to the stairs. Erin put a paperweight on top of each stack of papers in the folder, the ones she had looked through and the larger pile of papers still to be reviewed, to make sure that they wouldn't drift or be carelessly bumped, disturbing her order. She moved around the desk and tiptoed over to the stairs to peer down.

Orange Blossom was on the stairs. Still only two steps from the bottom. He had something in his mouth that he was dragging up the stairs. His body was partially blocking it, so Erin couldn't tell what it was.

"Kitty, kitty?"

Orange Blossom startled and looked up at her, dropping whatever he was holding. He looked up at her for a moment, his mouth slightly open, like he held it when he smelled something funky. He let out a yowl.

"Shh. I'm right here. No howling."

He bent down again to pick up his toy, whatever it was he was trying to bring to her. Erin supposed that Vic was busy with her visit with Willie and wouldn't play with him. She made a clicking noise with her tongue and watched Orange Blossom to see whether he was actually going to make it the rest of the way up the stairs, and not just start crying for her like he usually did. The kitten continued to work his way up the steps, placing his paws tentatively as if testing whether each platform would hold his weight, moving up it nearly turned backward as he dragged his toy up with him.

Erin caught a glimpse of the gray fur. Her stomach lurched. She let out a yelp.

"Vic?"

The voices in the living room quieted. There were a few seconds of silence.

"Vic?" Erin called again, trying to keep her voice steady. "Can you come here a sec?"

In a moment, Vic appeared at the bottom of the stairs.

"Hey, he's climbing!" Vic observed, delighted.

"Can you see what he's got? I think… he's caught a rat."

"A rat?" Vic leaned closer to Orange Blossom, not wanting to scare him off of the stairs after he'd been brave enough to start up them. "Ugh. Really, Blossom?"

Orange Blossom worked his way up another step. Vic moved back and forth for a better look, then laughed.

"It's not a rat, Erin. It's okay."

"Is it a mouse? A bat? What? It's so big!"

"No, I think it's just a bit of fur he found in the sewing room."

Erin remembered the leopard-spotted faux fur she had put into the kitten's nesting basket the first night she had brought him home, trying to find a way to comfort him so that he would stop crying. Whatever Orange Blossom had, it wasn't leopard-spotted, but he might have dug through Clementine's scraps and found something else that interested him.

She clicked her tongue again for the kitten. He looked up at her, the fur piece still hanging out of his mouth, and continued to work his way up the steps. Finally, he was at the top. He set his piece of fur down, sat on his haunches, and started to wash. Erin could confirm for the first time that it was, in fact, fake gray fur, the piece a little curled to give the appearance of a long, thin body.

"You're right. It's just a piece of fur," Erin told Vic, feeling her face flushing with embarrassment. "I'm sorry, I didn't mean to interrupt you and Willie."

"It's okay," Vic assured her. "I'm just happy to see he finally figured out how to get up there."

"Backward," Erin laughed. "Hopefully, he'll figure out how to do it forward at some point!"

"He will." Vic yawned. She held her hand in front of her mouth. "I guess… we should probably be heading to bed soon. I don't want to jam you up in the morning again. I'll say goodbye to Willie."

"I didn't mean to interrupt you. If you want longer…"

"No. I know you didn't mean to. You just needed to be rescued from a mouse."

"From a rat," Erin protested. "That's way too big for a mouse."

The piece of fur was almost ferret-sized. It would have freaked anyone out.

Vic chuckled as she withdrew, headed back toward the living room again. Erin crouched down on her heels, watching Orange Blossom.

"You're feeling quite proud of yourself, aren't you?" she asked him. "Catching yourself a big ol' mouse and bringing it all the way upstairs to me. Is this supposed to be dinner?"

She reached out to pick up the piece of fur, the end a little wet from the kitten's mouth. As she picked it up and pulled it away, Orange Blossom pounced, grabbing the piece of fur back and wrestling it ferociously to the ground. He bit it repeatedly, rolled over onto his back and kicked at it with his powerful back legs, and let out wild snuffling noises as if it were fighting back against him. Erin was tempted to give the fur a little twitch to wind him up even further, but she was mindful of his pointy bits. She didn't want to get all scratched up. It seemed like she always had long kitten-claw marks on her hands and arms since Orange Blossom's arrival.

"Now that you got up here… it's time to go to bed."

The kitten ignored her. Erin made lip-smacking noises. "Blossom. Kitty, kitty?"

He stopped and looked at her, ears pricking up. He flipped back over and sat up, looking more dignified. "I'll get you a treat before bed. How would you like that?"

Erin turned the light off and started down the stairs. Orange Blossom tumbled down behind her, and then past her. By the time he got to the bottom of the stairs, he had regained his feet and raced down the hall ahead of her into the kitchen. She was always amazed at how much he seemed to understand from her, whether it was from her words or just her body language or usual habits.

"I'm just getting Orange Blossom a treat," Erin called out as she headed past the living room without looking in. "Do you want anything?"

"Not kitty treats," Vic teased.

Erin followed Orange Blossom into the kitchen and got him a couple of soft treats from the can in the pantry. The cat danced around her feet when he heard the shaking of the canister. He chirped and purred and rubbed up against her leg. When she held the treats in her hand, he tried to jump up to reach them. At least he no longer tried to climb her legs like a tree. Usually. She tossed one of the treats, and he dove after it and pounced on it. He batted it across the slippery floor, careening around behind it like some crazed stock-car driver. Eventually, he trapped the treat under one paw and gobbled it up. He looked over at Erin expectantly. She tossed him a second treat, and the fun was repeated. Erin had one last treat for him and then shut off the lights.

She heard Vic shut the front door.

"You can leave the light on," Vic called out. "I'm going to get a cup of tea before bed."

Erin flipped the switch back on again. Orange Blossom ran by her and raced toward the sound of Vic's approaching feet.

"Look out!" Erin called.

But the warning came too late. Vic yelped as Orange Blossom attacked her feet in a frenzy of play. Erin looked around the corner and watched Vic tumble the kitten onto his back and scrub his belly with her fingertips. Orange Blossom tried to grasp Vic's hand with all four paws and bit at her hand. Vic rubbed his face with her other hand, pushing his biting teeth back. She picked Orange Blossom up and held the furry bundle against her chest, trapping him there with both hands and holding him still until he calmed and stopped struggling.

"Sh, now. It's bedtime," she crooned.

Orange Blossom looked at Erin, his eyes still wide, pupils huge and black.

"No, I'm not rescuing you. She's right. It's time for sleep. Not play."

Erin went to the bathroom to brush her teeth and get ready for bed. When she got out, Vic put the kitten down on the floor, releasing him slowly. Orange Blossom got his legs under him, and stalked off down the hall to Erin's bedroom. He jumped up onto her bed, ignoring his own little nest, and waited for her.

"Night, Vic," Erin called.

"Good night." Vic's voice floated back from the kitchen. Erin slid under her covers and waited while Orange Blossom kneaded the blankets, cuddled his body against hers, and washed himself thoroughly. Then he was finally still, and she could go to sleep.

Vic had been quiet all morning as they first prepared for the day and then made their way over to the bakery to get everything ready for the first phalanx of customers. Erin vacillated between prodding Vic to find out what was wrong and giving her time to just work it through on her own.

Vic looked up from the labels she was printing to catch Erin staring at her. Instead of looking away, Erin raised an eyebrow in question. Vic looked back down at the labels and printed a couple more.

"Glad you're doing that today," Erin told her. "I can't tell you how many times yesterday I had to clarify what something was or how much it cost because the customers couldn't read them."

"We should keep them from one day to the next, instead of rewriting them every day."

"I suppose. Anything we have regularly, we could just keep the label for next time. I just like the way they look when they're fresh and new each day."

Vic nodded. Erin puttered around putting everything straight. It was much faster to get everything ready when the two of them were there.

"I sure missed you yesterday."

"How am I ever going to find someone who will be interested in me?" Vic demanded.

"Uh, sorry?"

"I thought maybe… we've done things with Willie a few times, and I've always gotten on with him, so I thought… maybe he would be interested. But he's not. He's friendly, but he's not… he's not any *closer*. And not… going to get closer."

Erin bit the inside of her cheek, thinking about it. She was relieved to hear that Willie wasn't interested in pursuing a romantic relationship with Vic. But at the same time, she felt bad for her friend. Vic deserved to have someone. Erin felt guilty about being interested in two men, when Vic didn't have anyone. She was such a pretty, lovely girl; she should have a whole flock of boys around her. Young men around her age who were interested in spending time with her. But Vic was in bed early every night, not hanging out at the bar or any night spot either in Bald Eagle Falls or in the city. They had to be up early, so she just couldn't. Even on weekends. Erin should hire someone who could at least help on weekends so that Vic could go out and have a bit of a social life.

Only, going to bed early wasn't the only problem. Now that Vic's background was out in the open, it was going to be a lot harder for her to find anyone who was interested in a romantic relationship. Between the backwoods rednecks and the Bible-Belt Christians, there wasn't much tolerance for someone who was transgender. Or anyone else with questionable moral standing in the community.

"I'm not that bad-looking," Vic insisted, bringing Erin back out of her own contemplation of the matter.

"No! You're very pretty. I certainly don't think it's anything to do with your looks. It's just that… people around here aren't very accepting of differences. If you were a different race or religion, it would be just the same."

"Not quite *just* the same."

"Well, maybe not. But you would have trouble then, too."

"I really thought… I had a chance with Willie. He's the only one who has been interested in doing anything together. And we both like caves, unlike *you*. I thought that would help. There can't be a lot of girls who would share his interest in caves and minerals and all."

"There's a big age gap, though. He's old enough to be your dad. He likes you; I know he does. He cares. But more from a fatherly perspective."

Vic wrinkled her nose. "I don't care about age, so why should he?"

Erin shrugged. "It matters to some people. Or it might not be age. It might just be that he doesn't feel like the two of you click. That he's not attracted to you that way."

Vic busied herself attaching labels to the different products in the display case.

"Mrs. Potter was asking about the Founder's Day Fair. About what we're going to bring."

Erin leaned on the counter and rubbed her temples.

"Yes. I'll make a list. I'm thinking… some muffins, chocolate chip cookies, some loaves of quick bread, and some cheese rolls. What do you think? Does that sound pretty good? Are people going to want other things?"

"Well, it's a country fair, so you probably want a few pies too. Tarts, maybe. And there's going to be a Jam Lady booth, so maybe you should see if they want some plain bread for people to sample the jams."

"Who's in charge of it?" Erin demanded, her pulse quickening.

Vic smiled. "The General Store is going to be managing it."

"Dang."

"I think it's Mary Lou, don't you? She's the person who's handling all of the sales and distribution. She's the only one who knows where they're coming from."

"She swore it's not her."

"She's lying."

Erin shook her head slowly. "No… I don't think so. I don't think she was lying."

Vic squinted at Erin thoughtfully. "Hm. But she knows who it is. It can't be that hard to find out."

Erin laughed. "Well, you let me know when you find out."

Vic shrugged. "I bet I can."

"This town is sort of weird," Erin said, heading over to the door to flip over the sign and open up. "There's all of this gossip, and it seems like everybody knows everything about everyone else. Like there's no way you could keep a secret around here."

"Yeah." Vic's tone was bitter. Erin realized she was going to have to be a lot more careful not to hit Vic's sore spots. The girl was obviously feeling vulnerable.

"But then there are these secrets that everyone is keeping."

"Like who the Jam Lady is?"

"No, I mean about things like Angela's family. Her husband disappearing and no one ever knowing what happened to him. I don't think… I don't see how he could have disappeared without a trace, and Trenton too. Someone must have known something. But they've buried it. And everyone acted like Angela was an upstanding member of the church and of the community… when everyone was scared of her. She was mean and nasty to everyone, including her own kids, but when I moved here, everyone acted all loyal to her, like she was one of their best friends. And then after she died, everything else started coming out."

"She was a good Christian lady," Vic summed up, "except she wasn't very good and Christian after all."

"I guess. And Gema too. She was so determined to keep everyone thinking she had followed all of the teachings of her church when she hadn't. But protecting the lie was more important than actually aligning herself to the teachings of the church."

"People are more concerned about outer appearances than what's on the inside."

"Yes." Vic had put her finger on it. "That's it exactly. What's outside has become the most important thing. Not what's inside."

She opened the door, and the day's first customers streamed in.

Erin took a couple of trays of goodies over to the Book Nook for the Book Club.

"I've got cookies, brownies, some tartlets, and mini-muffins." She showed the tray to Naomi.

"That should keep everyone happy for a while." Naomi smiled. "Everyone sure enjoys your goodies on Book Club day. It's my best day for sales every week."

"Good to hear it!" Erin took a look around. "What are you reading today?"

"Digging Up Your Roots."

"Gardening?"

"Family history," Naomi laughed. "A lot of the ladies around here are interested in genealogy and the history of the area."

"That's funny; I've been going through a bunch of Clementine's genealogical records. She has all of these big books, and then fat research files full of all of the backup for what's on the family trees. It's just massive. When I think of the hours that she must have spent on it…!"

"I remember her working on that," Naomi agreed. "She was very interested in researching family history. She said it helped her to feel grounded. Knowing where she came from."

Erin nodded.

"Maybe you could bring some of her work around as an example. Except… I suppose you're not going to be going home before Book Club. You still have a few hours to put in at the bakery."

"Yeah. Sorry, I should have asked what you were doing this week. I could have brought stuff with me this morning."

"Don't worry about it. I never thought to ask, even though I knew how much Clementine was into it. I'd love to see some of it sometime, though. Just whenever you have a few minutes. I love to read history about the area. If you rely on oral history, all of the gossip and ghost stories, you don't really get a good picture of how this area grew up. But reading some of those original sources… there's some really interesting stuff. And it all intertwines, all of the old families in the area."

"You know…" Erin considered how much she wanted to share about her research. "I've been trying to find out some details of my parents' deaths. Clementine has the dates on the genealogical records that she compiled, but they don't match what I remembered. I wanted to find her source documentation. But so far… I haven't been able to lay my hands on it. It looks like she didn't start on the genealogy until after she retired, and my parents died ten years before that."

"Hmm." Naomi considered. "Well, you could try going to the library and looking at the archived newspapers for that period. They've kept a lot of stuff."

"That's a good idea. I'll have to do that… sometime when I can get some time off during library hours."

"That's the trouble with running your own business. You're always busy, and it's hard to get to banks and other businesses that run the same hours as you do. It's a pain." But Naomi's voice was cheerful. The inconvenience obviously didn't bother her that much.

"Yeah. I'll have to see when I can get over there. Maybe I'll sneak over during my lunch one of these days."

"Sure. That would work."

Erin headed for the door.

"What about her journals?" Naomi asked.

"Hmm?" Erin looked back. "Journals?"

"Didn't your aunt keep a journal? Those types tend to be record keepers. She seems like the type, especially if she was interested in family history."

"Uh…" Erin thought about it. She hadn't fully explored Clementine's room, which was now Vic's, or the sewing room where the genealogical books and files had been stored. Either one of them could have held stacks of journals. Thinking about it, she thought she might have seen them in the sewing room closet at one point. But since she hadn't been looking for them, she hadn't paid any attention or registered their location. "Yes. I think she did."

"See if you can find her journal for the time period when your parents died. She's bound to have written about it when it happened. Or as soon as she found out about it. She might have even kept a copy of the obituaries glued into her journal."

"Great idea! I am definitely going to look."

Naomi gave her a broad smile. "Great! Let me know how it goes. And any time you want to bring some of Clementine's books by… I'd love to sneak a peek."

"Sure, I'll do that."

Erin popped out of the Book Nook to go back to the bakery, and nearly collided with Officer Piper. She stumbled, trying to stop herself from tripping over K9, and Terry reached out his hand to grab her arm and steady her.

"Careful there, Miss Price."

Erin raised her brows. "Are we back to Miss Price? How did that happen?"

He held her gaze for a moment, then looked away. He looked down at K9 and scratched his ears. "Right. Erin, I mean."

"Is everything okay?"

She took in his demeanor. In spite of the fact that he had caught her by the arm, he didn't linger, letting her go immediately. He didn't seem to want to look at her face or take the opportunity to chat like he usually did.

"Terry?"

He took a breath and looked toward her. But not right at her. She could tell that he was focused somewhere beyond her right ear, rather than at her face.

"Yes. Everything is fine. But I'm on duty, afraid I have to focus on my work."

"Oh. Sure. Of course. So, you didn't want to come in for anything?"

"No. Not today. Sorry."

K9 whined, making a little movement toward Auntie Clem's. But Terry caught hold of his collar and pulled him back firmly. "Work to do," he repeated to the dog.

K9 tried to nose at Erin. She reached out to pat him, then changed her mind. He was on duty. A working dog. And she knew enough to leave a working dog alone. Just let him do his job.

"Okay. Maybe I'll see you after work sometime this week. You've been busy the last few days."

"Yes. I have." He made no promise to go by to visit her, and his dimple did not make an appearance as he spoke to her.

Erin nodded and turned away from him. She went back into her shop and focused on her work.

Both Erin and Vic were more subdued than usual as they cleaned up the bakery and headed for home. While Vic had avoided some of the town's curiosity about her gender identity by lying low the first day, people were persistent, and there had been a lot of looks, comments, and questions throughout the day. Some of them thought that they were clever in the way they posed their questions or made their comments, but it was pretty obvious to Erin and Vic what they were talking about. Erin sent Vic into the kitchen or storeroom several times to complete jobs Erin didn't need her to do, at those times when Vic started to get red or teary-eyed and needed a short reprieve from being on display out front. Vic had not once argued or expressed irritation at being sent back and forth.

Erin had been fussing around about Terry most of the afternoon. She had mentioned his distracted behavior to Vic, but the girl had no patience to worry about anyone else's problems.

"He's just got other things on his mind," she told Erin. "You know he likes you. He just has something else he needs to do. He'll probably stop by the house tonight."

"There aren't any big new cases that he needs to put extra hours in on," Erin pointed out. "If Trenton died by accidental exposure to soy, then there's nothing for him to investigate around Trenton's death. And there haven't been any big robberies or drug deals or anything like that."

"Nothing that has made the papers," Vic said. "You don't know what's going on because you can't ask him and he can't tell you."

Erin loaded some premixed muffin batters into the fridge for the morning. "Do you think I should call Melissa? She might know something."

"No. You should just stay out of it. If he said he's been busy with work, then he's been busy with work. He does have things to do other than flirt with you."

Erin felt her cheeks flush. Vic always made the two of them sound like lovesick teenagers. When all Terry and Erin did was talk. It wasn't like they got all gooey with each other. Erin still wasn't one hundred percent sure what his feelings toward her were.

Especially when he stopped talking to her. Because of work.

"I guess… we'll just have a quiet night, then," Erin said.

"Yeah. Probably a good thing. We're both still trying to catch up on sleep."

Vic was quiet in the car on the way home. Erin didn't know what else to say to her. She decided that Vic just needed some quiet time to think for herself, and didn't try to start another conversation.

At least Orange Blossom was happy to see her. Erin picked up the orange furball and held him up to her face. He purred like a tiger and rubbed the top of his head against her cheek. He started to knead her with his paws, and Erin ignored the sharp pricks of his claws and just enjoyed his attentions.

She heated up a couple of servings of leftover lasagna and poured bottle dressing over a bag of premixed salad for their supper. Neither of them had much to say, and they just headed their different directions after finishing the meal.

CHAPTER 15

*E*rin started in the sewing room. She looked through the desk that held the genealogical records. No journals there. She checked through the closet and the various storage boxes and other nooks and crannies, but couldn't find them there. She hesitated about bothering Vic with a search of Clementine's room. Vic usually spent time in the living room after supper, but she had gone to her room and shut the door. Erin stood in the hallway for a moment looking at the door, trying to decide whether to bother her. Then she turned to go up to the attic. The door opened and Vic looked at her.

"What did you want?"

"Sorry, I didn't want to bother you…"

"No, it's fine. What is it?"

"I'm trying to find Clementine's old journals. If she had any. Have you seen anything in her room?"

"Uh, yeah." Vic opened the door the rest of the way for Erin to enter. The room was in need of a good airing-out. The bed was rumpled but had been made. There were clothes hung over the furniture, but nothing was scattered on the floors. While it wasn't the tidiest room, it certainly had nothing on some of the teenager rooms Erin had seen growing up. Vic ran her fingers through her silky blond hair, looking around. "Under the bed, I saw some boxes there. And maybe in the closet too."

Erin knelt down on the floor and lifted up the bed skirt to look. She stirred up dust that made her nose tickle, and she held her nose, trying not to sneeze. Orange Blossom wandered into the room and started making inquisitive noises, wanting to know what everyone was up to without him. Erin dragged a few heavy boxes out from under the bed. Diaries. The boxes were not dated, so she had to open up each of the small, hardcover books to have a look at the dates that they covered.

"These are all too recent," she said, after looking through a few books in each box.

"What year are you looking for?" Vic asked, bending over to look at some boxes in the closet.

"Back before you were born."

"Oh. Okay."

Vic started going through the boxes in the closet, while Erin shuffled around the boxes under the bed, looking at some of them more than once thinking that she had missed one.

"Does she have journals from when you used to come here?" Vic asked, flipping through books.

"I don't know. I didn't really stay here, so I don't know what she did. I would just spend the day with her in the shop. It was a tea shop then."

"Right."

Erin shoved the journal boxes back under the bed. "These are all too recent. Are you having any luck over there?"

"Yeah. Not bad." Vic pointed to a couple that she had pulled out of the closet. "Those ones are the oldest I've found so far. Maybe not as old as you're looking for…"

Erin opened a few and started to flip through them. She looked at the dates. She would have been eight or nine. But Clementine went through several journals a year, and each box held about twenty of them. She sat down on the bed and started pulling out stacks of journals.

"This looks good. I think maybe this is the right one."

Vic put her hands into her kangaroo-pouch hoodie. "What exactly are you looking for?"

Erin wasn't sure how much she wanted to reveal. It was private, close to her heart. The death of her parents was a wound that had never healed but had continued to fester throughout her childhood, and even into her adult life. She didn't spend as much time obsessing over it as she had when she was younger, but it was still the biggest thing that had ever happened in her life.

"Um… just family records when I was younger. Things that I was too young to remember about."

"Like family reunions? That kind of thing?"

Erin hesitated, then nodded. Orange Blossom jumped up on the bed and started to nose through the dusty books with interest, pushing them around. Erin grabbed at a small pile before it could fall off the bed. "I think I'd better take these upstairs. Thanks for your help."

"Sure, no problem," Vic agreed. "It is your house."

"It's yours too, and this is your room. I don't want to infringe on your privacy."

"I probably won't be here for much longer."

Erin looked up. "Are you going out? I thought you were tired."

"No, I mean… I should find my own place. I'm working now, so I should see what I can find that is within my means. Get out on my own."

"Oh." Erin stared at Vic. It had never occurred to her that Vic would be striking out on her own so soon. They had a good relationship. They had a routine that worked. They didn't smother each other, even though they lived and worked the same place. "I didn't know you were thinking about it. I'm happy having you live here."

Vic didn't look convinced.

"I'm glad to have someone else here, so I'm not just kicking around on my own. It's nice, having someone to share the space with. And we get along." Then it occurred to her. "Is it because of Willie? Because you don't like feeling like we're…" Erin struggled to put it into words without sounding silly. "I don't know. Competing."

"It's not Willie. Not just that. I just think… it would be better for you if you had your own place. And I'm old enough. I should be more independent."

Erin slotted all of the diaries back into the box. "Then who is going to make lasagna for me?"

Vic laughed. It was good to hear her genuine laughter. Not something that was forced or faked. "That was a one-time deal. I'm not making lasagna every week."

"Maybe once a month?" Erin coaxed.

Vic shook her head, her smile disappearing again. "I just don't know what I'm going to do. I really should find a place of my own."

～

Erin took the box of journals up to the attic room, and she put it beside her reading nook, moving slowly. The announcement from Vic was a shock, and she didn't know how to deal with it. She hadn't foreseen any changes in the near future. She had just assumed that things would remain the same, with her and Vic living together and working together every day, just as they were.

Why did that have to change?

She had finally settled down and found her home. Somewhere she didn't have to think about leaving again in a few weeks or months. She had everything she needed, including her own business. It was everything she had ever dreamed she might have. At least Vic wasn't talking about quitting the bakery and leaving town as well. Or was that next? Was she trying to break it to Erin gently that things were not going to last? Maybe it was too much for her, everyone knowing all about her, looking at her and whispering about her. She could go farther away, somewhere no one knew her. Somewhere no one knew her family. And somewhere where the population was large enough that she'd be able to find people to date. People who were open-minded enough not just to turn her away.

Erin started to pull books out of the box and put them carefully into order. It was a job that didn't require much input from her reeling brain. She opened each book, checked the date, and put it into the appropriate stack so she would be able to find the journal that dealt with her parents' deaths.

But why did she want to read about that? It had been enough of a tragedy when she'd lived through it. Why would she want to put herself through it again? She'd lost everyone in her life that was important to her, and now she was going to lose Vic too. It wasn't fair. It just wasn't fair that she couldn't have that normal, happy life everyone else had. Why did she have to always end up alone?

Eventually, she had all of the journals neatly stacked in order. They covered approximately three years, from when she was six to when she was nine. The accident and her eighth birthday would fall right in the middle.

But she didn't pick up the middle journals. Instead, she picked up the earliest ones, from when she was six.

She remembered little of her life from that long ago. She knew that it was possible to remember things from earlier than that. People could remember as far back as when they were two or three. Some people. But Erin had little memory of being that young. She could remember coming to Bald Eagle Falls for a visit. Her parents leaving her with Clementine at the tea shop. Erin had enjoyed working with her. Carrying plates of cookies to the ladies sitting around talking with each other. Lively conversations. The smells of different kinds of teas so pungent, one of the clearest things in her mind. Erin could identify many of the teas by smell alone, something that had amused Clementine and her hens. They would test her, letting Erin smell their teas and then try to identify the boxes they had come from.

Who left a five- or six-year-old child with an old woman in a tea shop? It was one thing to leave her with a babysitter, someone who could give Erin her full attention. But that wasn't what they had done. Clementine wasn't retired and living at home where she could watch a child. She was working. Erin knew now what it was like, trying to take care of all of the customers on her own the day that Vic had stayed home. Running the shop as a one-person show was difficult. She couldn't imagine how much harder it would be with a young child underfoot. Erin had tried to help out and do what she was instructed to, but she had still been a child. Distractible. Clumsy. Underfoot. Erin couldn't imagine trying to run the bakery with a five-year-old underfoot and no Vic to help her out.

Erin didn't remember them discussing it in front of her, but they must have had a conversation at some point, Clementine taking Erin's parents aside and explaining that they couldn't just dump Erin on her. That she couldn't run the tea room properly with Erin underfoot. That they would have to find some other arrangement.

Erin leafed slowly through the book. She didn't stop to read it; she just let her eyes flow over the writing already familiar to her from reading the genealogical records and files. She picked up words and phrases here and there. The names of Bald Eagle Falls residents, the surnames familiar, but Clementine and most of her friends now gone. But the younger generations were still there. Places like Bald Eagle Falls had long memories.

She watched for her own name, even though she didn't want to see it. She had dug out the journals for one purpose only, and that was to find out what had happened to her family. To read about the accident. But she wasn't sure she could read it.

How much information would Clementine have had? Just a newspaper clipping? The obituaries? Or would she recount the entire story in painstaking detail?

Erin knew she was reading the journals written before the accident, and that was okay. She could read all of the details of life in Bald Eagle Files when she was a little girl. All of the secrets of the sleepy little town that Clementine had been inspired to share. Births and deaths. Politics. Happenings at and around the little shop. Erin put each book down in turn. Keeping them in order. Drawing closer to the date of her parents' accident.

Then she sat with the journal in her hands. It would be in that one. She had gotten a feel for the rhythm of the dates in the journals, and she knew the accident would fall between the two covers of that book.

Orange Blossom started to yowl. It was getting late, and he was looking for her company. She could hear him start to come up the stairs. Still slowly and awkwardly, like he was climbing a mountain instead of just stepping up the stairs smoothly.

Erin opened up the journal and started paging through it. She read the first few words of each entry, knowing that sooner or later she would hit the one that announced her parents' deaths.

Then she read the words. *Who would believe such a thing could happen to one of our Bald Eagle Falls families?*

Erin closed the book.

CHAPTER 16

*E*rin looked over the boxes, running through her checklists and making sure they had everything she had planned to take to the Founders' Day Fair. The whole town was buzzing with excitement. School was out. There would be a midway, popcorn, cotton candy, snow cones, and all of the other trappings of a traditional, small-town country fair. Baked goods and canned goods would be judged. There were events involving sheep and goats that Erin didn't understand.

"Did we miss anything?" Vic asked, looking over Erin's shoulder.

"No, I don't think so. Everything is here."

"Is that enough bread for the Jam Lady sample booth?"

Erin nodded. "I think so. If it's not, one of us can come back here for more. But I didn't want the bread to be sitting out in the heat all day. Even in plastic, it's going to get dry."

"Yeah, okay. Don't want that!"

"No. It's hard enough to get a nice texture on gluten-free bread. We want to be able to present our best product. People are already prejudiced against anything that says gluten-free."

Vic looked at Erin, amusement in her eyes.

"Maybe *prejudiced* isn't the right word," Erin amended.

"No, prejudiced is just fine. It just hit me funny. I just had a vision of myself labeled gluten-free. People do start with certain… expectations."

"Yes." Erin studied her friend. But Vic didn't seem upset by her wording, so Erin moved on. "Let's get these loaded into the car, then."

Erin took one box. Vic stacked up two and carried both at the same time. In a couple of minutes, they had everything ready to go. Erin drove over to the school parking lot. Already, tents and awnings had sprung up all over the field. Erin checked in with Mrs. Potter at the participants' registration table and studied the map of the field to figure out which tent she was supposed to report to.

Most of the food venues were under one huge tent, with fans and air conditioning units running inside to keep it a few degrees cooler than outside. Erin had been worried about standing out in the heat for so long and was thankful for whoever had had the foresight to ensure that the food vendors' tent was air conditioned.

"This is cool," Vic said, looking around.

"That it is," Erin agreed. She looked at the time on her phone. "We'd better get to work, though; I don't want to be late getting everything arranged."

But Vic was quick with the arrangement of their goods and setting up the display to the best advantage. She had pre-printed her labels, and they were all ready to go quite a while before the fair was scheduled to open.

Erin watched the other vendors get set up and, before long, the early birds started to trickle in. It was much the same crowd as was always first at Auntie Clem's on a regular weekday. Erin supposed it was in the nature of an early bird to be early no matter what the day or event.

She could smell the popcorn and the cotton candy over the smells of her own baking. The midway music was playing, and there was a loudspeaker announcing events and results of some of the pre-fair events. The crowds started to fill out, and it wasn't long before everything was in full swing.

Erin looked around during a lull. There was plenty for the fairgoers to do, so people were not lingering long over her baked goods. There were lemonade and sweet tea as well as all of the high-calorie fair goodies to fill up on; people could buy Erin's baking any day of the week, so it was less of a draw.

The faces were mostly familiar. She had been in Bald Eagle Falls for long enough to recognize most of the residents. But there were a few unfamiliar people. Out-of-towners who had come to take part in the fun. Hopefully,

Vic's parents hadn't felt the need to return to town to see the Founders' Day Fair. She'd had enough disruption in her life.

Erin spotted Alton Summers and her stomach clenched. She had figured that after their last confrontation, he would leave town. She had threatened to expose him; why would he stick around? As the crowds shifted, she had a better view of him and realized that he was arguing with someone. His face was red, and so was Joelle's. She talked with her hands; short, angry movements punctuated the conversation. Alton shook his head and stepped in closer to her. Threatening, deliberately in her personal space, trying to intimidate her. But Joelle wasn't any shrinking violet. She placed one hand on his chest and gave him a violent shove. Alton was forced to step back. He stood there long enough to utter one more threat, emphasized with a pointing finger, and then he turned on his heel and stalked away, pushing through the happy crowds to get out of there.

Erin grinned. *You tell him, Joelle!*

"Hi, Erin!"

Erin turned at the familiar voice and focused on her newest customer. One of her favorites, young Peter Foster.

"Hi, Peter. What would you like today?"

His eyes roved over the goods that Vic had put out on display.

"Hmm…"

"Did you have some popcorn and cotton candy?" Erin asked.

"Yes. But I still have room!"

"I don't doubt it."

He waved a bill at her. "Mom gave me money and said to get something for everyone. She's sitting on a blanket over there." He gestured to the picnic area.

"What did she want you to get? Something to go along with your lunch?"

"Uh-huh. We have salads and hot chicken."

"How about some cheese rolls or pretzels, then? You guys have already had lots of sugar."

He nodded. "How about the pizza pretzels?"

"One of my favorites," Erin agreed.

"Okay. So… five of those. Maybe four, I don't know if the little girls can eat a full one…"

"I'll give you six," Erin said. "You can take the extra home if you don't eat them all."

"Okay."

As Vic packaged the pretzels up for Peter and Erin made change, Erin saw Joelle approaching.

"Hi, Joelle. Let's see, the vegan products I have available today—"

"No, I don't want anything. I wondered if you wanted this." Joelle offered an ice cream cone to Peter.

He shook his head. "I can't," he said automatically, "I have allergies."

"Oh, right." Joelle caught Erin staring at the confection. "Davis bought it for me," she said. "I don't know why. He knows I'm vegan. He just doesn't think about it. He's always doing stupid stuff like that."

She waved the cone a little as she talked. With the heat of the day, it was already starting to melt, and a glob of ice cream fell onto her sandals. Joelle swore and bent down to wipe it off with a napkin. "I just got these!" She swore a second time, moving her foot to look at the strappy little sandals from several angles. "Can you still see it? Are they wrecked?" She tossed her ice cream cone at the nearest garbage can and missed, splattering it inside and outside the can.

"No, it looks fine," Erin assured her. "I don't think it's going to be stained." She remembered what Melissa had said about Joelle buying high-end thrift store finds, and wondered if Joelle were trying to show off the brand to her. "They're very cute." And they were; a far cry from the clunky, wide-strapped sandals Erin could remember her mother wearing for hiking.

"They are, aren't they?" Joelle cooed, admiring them. "I just had to have them."

"Yeah."

Vic handed Peter his bag of pretzels. Erin gave him his change. "Say, 'hi' to your mom and sisters for me, Peter," she told him.

Peter grinned and told her 'thank you,' then walked away. Joelle watched him go. "Cute kid. I'm sorry about swearing in front of him. I have to watch my sailor's mouth."

Erin nodded. "So, you didn't want anything, then?" she asked, with a significant look at the display of baked goods.

"No, no. I just wanted to get rid of the ice cream cone. Stupid. I went for the nearest kid, didn't even think that if he's buying something here, he obviously can't have *normal* food."

"It's probably not the best idea to give treats to children you don't know anyway."

"Why not?" Joelle thought about it for an instant and swore again. "Somebody will think I'm trying to poison or lure them? In a small town like this in the middle of a crowd?"

"Crowds are good places to lose kids. If you have a way to lure them away without people noticing."

"I wouldn't do that! You know that, don't you? I'm not some sicko!"

"I'm sure you're not," Erin said. She couldn't help catching Vic's eye, though, and Vic made a face that Joelle couldn't see. "But you don't want to get people uptight. And you don't want to end up giving something to a kid like Peter who's allergic but might not be mature enough to ask if the food is safe for him."

"What a world we live in," Joelle huffed. "Honestly, do kids have to be bubble-wrapped?"

Since there were no customers hovering to buy something, Erin decided to take the opportunity to shut Joelle down and to see Naomi. She'd been watching for her chance all morning, and it seemed like the best time.

"I'm just going over to the Book Nook display," she told Vic. "Won't be long."

Vic nodded. "Sure. Take your time." With a look at Joelle, she chuckled quietly.

Erin headed over to the tent she had noted Naomi setting up earlier in the day. She took a couple of glances back over her shoulder to make sure that Joelle didn't follow her. She didn't need to get into a heated discussion with someone over how serious allergies and intolerances could be. People who thought that it was just being overprotective had another think coming to them. How could Joelle think that after Trenton had died from his allergy?

"Erin!" Naomi's cheerful voice rang out the minute Erin stepped under the awning. "I'm glad you came by!"

Erin looked over the well-appointed display of Digging Up Your Roots, some pictures and old newspaper clippings, and one of Clementine's genealogy books lying open. The tent was quiet. Apparently, genealogy was not a big attraction at a fair, even on Founders' Day. A couple of older folks browsed over the handouts that Naomi had arranged giving tips on how to get started on their own family history, including blank journal pages and four-generation family trees.

Erin went up to the display to look at Clementine's book. She stared at the page of names. None of them meant anything to her. Familiar, but not people she had known or had yet come to know through the stories and clippings that Clementine had kept.

"It all looks really professional," she told Naomi. "This was a great idea for a display at Founders' Day. Everyone can come in and start thinking about who the founders were in their family."

Naomi nodded. "There hasn't been a lot of traffic, but we only need a few people to get started, and when they start sharing with their friends, everyone is going to want to know something about the stock that they came from. Especially in a town like Bald Eagle Falls, where everyone tends to be so closely related."

"Yeah. It's amazing how everyone is related."

"So how are you coming along in your search? Did you find any journals?"

"Boxes of them."

Naomi laughed. "I should have known. Clementine was just that kind of lady. Every family should have a historian!"

Erin flipped through a couple of pages in the big genealogy book.

"I suppose with that many, it's going to take you some time to find what it is you're looking for...?"

Erin looked around, not wanting anyone to overhear the conversation. But in the chaos of the fair, the Book Nook tent was an oasis. A few people browsed, but no one was close enough to listen in on Erin's private conversation.

"No... I don't think it will take me long. I found the right years. And I was skimming through them. But..."

Naomi straightened the Digging For Your Roots book and looked at Erin curiously. "Well, what?"

Erin told her about the entry that had begun 'Who would believe such a thing could happen to one of our Bald Eagle Falls families?' "It was the right year. May first. I'm not sure what day my parents' accident was... but it seemed about right. I know it was before my eighth birthday."

"Well... what did it say? Was it about your parents?"

"I don't know."

"How can you not know? What was it about?"

Erin bit her lip, staring down at the family tree. "I couldn't read it. I shut the journal, and I went to bed."

Naomi's brows rose high, and she laughed in disbelief. "You saw that, and you just closed the book and went to bed?"

"Yes." Erin was shaky just thinking about it. "I just went to bed. I couldn't... I couldn't read what she had to say."

"Erin, you're as white as a ghost! Sit down." Naomi moved a chair closer to Erin and directed her into it. "Are you okay?"

"I don't know if I can read it."

"Ever?"

"Yes. I mean, no. Never. When I think about reading Clementine's description of what happened to them... I just can't face it."

Naomi rubbed Erin's back between her shoulder blades. "But you can't just ignore it. You're going to have to read it sooner or later."

"It's..." Erin closed her eyes and shook her head. "It's so awful, Naomi. You don't know what it was like. Losing both of my parents like that... so suddenly, to just be on my own. It was... like everything that happened in my life before that... was just gone."

"It must have been very traumatic. You were just a little girl at the time; very young to lose your parents."

"It was the defining moment in my life. The moment that defined who I was and would be for the rest of my life. And... it just makes me sick, thinking about reading about it, even something written by Clementine. How can I do it?"

There was quiet in the tent as Naomi considered this. Erin could hear a man's voice on the other side of the tent discussing the sheep in one of the upcoming events. Erin had no idea what any of his jargon meant.

"Well... I guess you don't have to," Naomi admitted, pushing her hair back over her ears and fiddling with the glasses she wore on a chain around her neck. "No one is going to force you. But I thought you wanted to know what had happened. I thought that's why you decided to go looking."

"Yes. And no. I thought it was what I wanted, but faced with it now, I'm not so sure."

"What do you already know about what happened? They must have told you something."

"You know the crazy thing? I can't remember any details. Even whether they were hit or whether they hit someone else. I don't remember being told. The only thing I can remember is being told over and over again that they died instantly. That's all."

"They wanted to reassure you. To let you know that they hadn't suffered."

"I guess. But the death dates Clementine had down… that's why I started. That's why I was looking for the details. According to Clementine, they died weeks apart. They couldn't have died instantly."

There was no reason that Vic and Erin should be more tired after the Founders' Day Fair than they were any other full day they had worked at the bakery. The hours were pretty much the same. The traffic was less. They were standing and walking on springy turf rather than hard, unforgiving tile floors. But Erin felt sweaty and gritty and like she'd just worked two back-to-back shifts. Looking at Vic, who wiped her face and stretched her long limbs stiffly, Erin could tell she felt pretty much the same way.

"Weird, huh?" Erin said. "It shouldn't have been any harder than any other day."

"Less. You would think. I don't know. Maybe it's the noise or the heat. I feel like I've been chewed up and spit out."

Erin grinned. "Yup. Me too."

Vic packed the last few things into boxes. "We'll take these to the car, and then we're done."

Erin sighed. "I really should get over to the bakery and start a few batters, so we can start putting them in the oven as soon as we get in."

"I can't face it tonight," Vic declared. "And neither can you. You look as bad as I feel. Let's hit the sack. We'll go to bed early and will make up for it with how much more energy we have in the morning."

Erin had to admit it sounded tempting. And if she went to bed early and ended up tossing and turning and unable to get to sleep, she could always run over to the bakery and whip up a few batters, and then return home to sleep knowing that she was all set for the morning.

"Okay, you talked me into it. Point me toward my bed."

"Drive first," Vic advised. "Then sleep."

Bald Eagle Falls being as small as it was, they were home in a few minutes. They just left everything in the car and went into the house. Erin gave Orange Blossom cuddles and fed him. She'd had enough fair food that she didn't want anything else. "Now I'm going to bed early," she told the cat. "I don't want you howling about how lonely you are because nobody is staying up to play with you. Just come and cuddle up and go to sleep with me."

Orange Blossom made a small noise around his food. Sometimes he acted just like a human being. Erin waited until he was done eating before turning off the kitchen lights. Orange Blossom's eyes shone in the dark. He looked at her for a minute, then started to wash. Erin headed to the commode to wash up herself. After giving her teeth a quick scrub, she was headed for bed.

"Goodnight, Vic!"

"Night!" Vic was already in her room with the door shut. Erin hoped it wasn't a sign that she was upset about something or was going to be too tired to get up in the morning again. She hadn't acted like she was upset during the day. In fact, she had acted more cheerful than Erin had felt. More like her old self again.

Erin left her door open a few inches for Orange Blossom, and was shortly in bed. No reading. No lists. Just putting her tired self to bed. It felt wonderful to be able to stretch out on the soft bed and just wait for sleep to come.

~

At first, Erin slept heavily. She was exhausted and just conked out. *Sayonara.* And she was sure, far away in that dream state, that she'd been asleep for a number of hours. But the quality of her sleep had changed, and she was dreaming. One of those frantic dreams where she was trying to get up and ready to go in the morning, but couldn't find the bathroom or change her clothes or any of the other things that had to be done before she could go to work. The kind of dream that she often had just before her alarm went off in the morning. Yet she knew it wasn't time to get up yet.

Orange Blossom started to yowl. For a long time, it was just part of Erin's dream. She was trying to get ready for work, and the cat was crying, and she just couldn't get it all together.

Then she finally roused from sleep enough to call Orange Blossom. "Here, kitty, kitty. Come in here. Come cuddle."

He came to the door of her room, pushing his face through the opening of the door, and meowed loudly. The cat was as loud as an air raid siren sometimes. Erin had never known that cats could make that much noise. She had always thought the cartoons of people throwing boots at cats singing on the fence were an exaggeration. Until she got Orange Blossom and people started complaining about him being so noisy if she left him alone or shut him out of her room.

"Blossom! Cut it out!" she snapped.

He was quiet only for a few seconds and then started meowing again. Erin sat up, rubbing her eyes. Her brain was still thick with sleep, but she was starting to become more aware. Was there something wrong? She had come to recognize some of his different meows. And sometimes when he cried like that, it was because there was water on the floor. A leak in the roof or a drippy valve on the commode, and he would act like the whole house was being flooded.

"What is it? Is there water?" She listened for the patter of rain on the roof or a dripping faucet, but couldn't hear anything. Just the usual night noises. The house settling. A sort of static that filled the night for her that her doctor said was probably tinnitus. Too much loud music as a teenager. "Come on, kitty. Come get into bed. It's time for sleep."

He stubbornly refused to enter the room. She heard his claws ripping at the rug. A bad behavior he had developed that she put down to wanting more attention.

"Blossom! Stop that! No claws!"

She had meant to get some claw clippers when she went into the city last. The special safety clippers for cats that kept them from getting cut to the quick, but helped to keep the furniture and rug from being shredded.

Erin dragged herself out of bed to chase him, even though she knew that was probably exactly what he wanted. He was as bad as a three-year-old who squealed with delight when his mother tried to catch him after misbehaving.

"Blossom!"

Erin started coughing. Her lungs burned. She just about fell to her knees; she was suddenly so dizzy and lightheaded from getting up so fast. She tried to get after him again, but she couldn't stop coughing.

Something was wrong.

Something was really wrong.

Bent over, it was easier to breathe. As soon as she tried to straighten up again, her lungs burned and her eyes teared up, and her head spun. She kept down, dropping to her hands and knees. At first, all she could think of was chasing Orange Blossom to keep him from clawing the rug. But she gradually realized that the cat clawing the rug wasn't the biggest problem she had. Something was wrong. There was a noise, a sort of a crackling. And something that made her lungs hurt. And her eyes.

Finally, it all connected.

Fire.

Erin swore.

She was already partway down the hallway, and hadn't seen any flames or felt the heat of a fire, but she knew the feeling of smoke in her lungs, worse than any girl scout campfire she'd ever sat around, and the smells of combustion. Not just wood, but the rank smell of burning plastics and synthetics as well. Those fumes could be toxic.

Erin realized she had followed the cat as far as Vic's door. She raised her fist and started to bang on it.

"Vic! Vic! Fire! Wake up, Vic!"

She felt the door handle and laid one hand on the flat, vertical surface of the door. It wasn't hot. She tried turning the handle. It wasn't locked. The door swung into the room.

"Vic! Vic, get up now!"

There was a murmur of protest from Vic.

"Get up now!" Erin insisted. She put all of the force she could into her voice. "Vic! Get up! There's a fire!"

Vic woke abruptly, the words finally getting through to her brain. She sat up, as Erin had, looking around her in confusion.

"It's smoky. Get down on the floor," Erin told her. "We'll crawl to the front door."

"Where's the fire?"

"I don't know. We'll find out. We have to move."

Vic slid out of bed to the floor, and she and Erin moved together out of the room. Erin's eyes were streaming. She tried to see Orange Blossom. Where had the cat gone? He could cram himself into such tiny spaces, and there was no way they could search for him if he'd tried to hide from the fire.

"Kitty, kitty?" Erin coughed. She tried to cover her mouth and nose to prevent more smoke getting in.

"Forget about the cat," Vic insisted.

Erin knew she was right. She kept crawling. They stayed close together, like a couple of kids playing trains on their hands and knees. Vic grabbed Erin.

"Wrong way. The door is this way."

Erin tried to pull away from her. "No, the door is—"

"Come on." Vic was too strong, and Erin eventually complied, following her again.

"I don't think this is the right way."

"It's the smoke. Trust me."

Erin coughed. Her lungs were on fire and all she wanted to do was get outside and breathe clean, fresh air.

She hadn't been able to see the fire before, only to hear the distant crackle of the flames and to smell the smoke. But in the living room, there were flames. She forced herself to stick with Vic and not to do what every instinct told her to do, to withdraw from where the flames were and curl up in a ball, hiding from the monster.

"Erin? Are you there?" Vic felt behind her and encountered Erin's arm. She drew Erin forward, her grip like steel.

"Are we there? Where's the door?"

"Here. I think." Vic stood on her knees, patting at the door like Orange Blossom did when he wanted into or out of a room. It seemed like an eternity before Vic sorted out the locks and door handle and pulled the door open. There was a suctioning feeling, and then the door opened, and there was a whoosh from the fire in the room as outside air flooded into the room. Vic grabbed Erin again and pulled her out of the house.

They both sprawled on the doorstep, coughing violently and trying to breathe in the fresh, oxygen-rich air.

"Erin! Vic!"

They were surrounded by neighbors wrapping them with blankets and pulling them away from the house.

It's okay. The fire department is on its way.

They'll have this put out in no time.

Thank goodness the two of you are safe!

What happened?

Erin was overwhelmed. She coughed and couldn't answer any of the questions. She just held the blanket that had been wrapped around her, cuddled inside it, trying to sort out in her brain what had happened. An electrical fault? A light left on? They didn't use candles. Whenever she tried to talk, she was racked with more coughing. Vic seemed to be more under control. Erin could hear her answering questions. Every now and then, she tugged on Erin and asked her if she was all right.

The fire truck arrived, manned by volunteers, their faces obscured by their protective gear. The flashing light hurt Erin's eyes, and the siren bounced off of all of the buildings, filling her ears even after it was shut off.

As much as she wanted to, she couldn't watch them fight the fire in Clementine's house. In her house. She covered her face, crying. Still coughing and feeling like she wasn't getting enough air. Like maybe there wasn't enough air in the world, and she would never get enough again.

"Erin. Here. Sit down."

Someone forced her to sit and, in a few minutes, pressed an oxygen mask over her face. Erin tried to gulp the oxygen down.

"Just take long, slow breaths... Nice and even and regular... Just normal, even breaths..."

She tried to obey the soothing voice, but it was difficult. Time passed. There was a lot of activity around her.

"Erin, are you okay?"

Erin looked up, trying to follow the familiar voice to its owner. Erin eventually homed in on the figure speaking to her. Vic.

"Yes. Yes, I'm fine. Thank you for getting us out of there."

"Wouldn't have been able to if you hadn't woken me up."

Erin rubbed her eyes and blinked at Vic. She too was wrapped in a blanket, but it hung more loosely around her. Erin studied it, eventually realizing that Vic was holding something beneath the blanket.

"What's that? Do you have...?"

Vic opened up the blanket a little, to show Erin Orange Blossom nestled in her arms.

Erin's eyes streamed tears. "Thank goodness he's all right! He's the one who woke me up."

"Good kitty," Vic crooned to the cat. Erin thought she could hear him purring, even with all of the noise and chaos going on around them.

CHAPTER 18

$\mathcal{I}$t was a long time before everything was quiet again. Erin found that she was sitting on the steps of the fire engine. Terry was there, asking her questions and trying to get a coherent story out of her. Erin patted K9, his warmth soothing.

"I know it's just a house," Erin said, wiping her tears away. "But is the fire out? Is it… salvageable?"

"The fire is out. The firefighters will continue to monitor it, make sure there are no hot spots that will reignite. And we'll have an investigator from the city come and take a look and see if they can tell how it started. You have no idea?"

Erin wiped away more tears. They just wouldn't stop coming. She told herself it was just because of the smoke in the air.

"Is it a write-off? The house? What's going to happen?"

"They'll look at it and get in touch with you, let you know what needs to be done. I'm not an expert, but… it looks like it was fairly localized. It didn't go through the whole house. Ceilings still intact. Though everything will be smoke damaged."

"Clementine's little house…"

"*Your* little house," Terry amended. "I know you haven't been there very long, but it is still yours. That's your home. It's okay to be sad about it."

Erin nodded and sniffled. She had the oxygen mask off so that she could talk to Terry. She was able to breathe without coughing. The smell of smoke still hung in the air, but it wasn't so overwhelming.

"What is that?" Erin demanded.

"What is what?" Terry frowned at her, his brows drawn down.

"That... smell..." Erin made a face and tried to identify it. "Is it... gasoline? Kerosene?"

Terry gestured to the fire truck. "Diesel."

She could smell the exhaust and the diesel coming from the fire truck, but there was something else too. Erin got up and walked closer to the house. She wandered the yard, looking at the shrubs and neglected garden along the front of the house. It was sharper there, more insistent.

"There is something here," she told Terry. "Can't you smell that?"

"All I can smell is smoke," he confessed. "What are you smelling?"

"Gasoline, I think. Or something close to it." Erin sniffed at the breeze as it shifted the directions the smell was coming from. "But that doesn't make sense."

"It does if it was arson."

"Why would it be arson?" Erin shook her head. "It must have been an accident. No one would intentionally light a fire when two people were inside sleeping!"

"You might be surprised what people will intentionally do. I think you'd better move farther away from the house. I'll put up crime scene tape, try to preserve the scene for the investigator."

"I just don't see... I don't think it could be intentional. Who would do that?"

Terry motioned Erin back, and she obligingly went back toward the fire truck. Vic approached, still holding the cat under her blanket. She and Erin gave each other a sideways hug.

"You okay now?" Vic asked.

"Bit better. Yeah. Thanks."

"It will be okay. Won't it?"

"We'll get it sorted out. Terry says there will be smoke damage..."

Vic nodded. "But it doesn't look too bad, does it? I mean, the whole house didn't burn down."

"Someone will let us know."

They both stood around, watching the firefighters walk back and forth and Terry string up yellow crime scene tape, K9 faithfully at his side. Erin felt separate from everything that was happening around her. Like she was in a bubble.

Terry walked back over to Erin, holding something white in is hand, held gingerly by one corner.

"What's that?"

"That's what I'm trying to figure out." Terry gave Erin a frown.

Erin turned her eyes to the piece of paper. Generic, white, lined paper. But it had her handwriting on it. Erin leaned closer and tried to make it out.

"Oh. I wrote that before the funeral," she explained. "It was just a list of names."

Terry looked at her. "What names?"

"Just names of people who show up in my family tree. I wanted to be able to ask people who they were related to." It sounded silly when she said it aloud. "It's nothing. I ended up not even using it, because we went straight home after the funeral."

"With this? It was in one of the flower beds."

"What was it doing there?" Erin shook her head. "It must have fallen out. I remember looking for it in my purse after the funeral... but I must have left it in my pocket. And dropped it."

"There is more on here than just names."

Erin studied it, trying to read her own handwriting in the dimness of the night, the note flapping in the breeze.

Inheritance?

Adam Plaint dead?

Trenton and Davis?

There was also a year scribbled down. The year that Erin's parents had died. She looked up at Terry, shrugging. "Just questions I thought of while I was at the funeral. I didn't want to forget what I was thinking. I'm a list maker."

Vic nodded her agreement at this. "So many lists!" she said melodramatically.

Terry tapped the paper with the back of his fingernail, careful not to get prints on it. "What were you doing investigating Trenton's death?" His voice was flinty.

"I... wasn't..." Erin shook her head. He looked thoroughly unconvinced. "I was just wondering about the store, who the new owner would be. That's all. Curiosity about my competition."

"Who did you ask?"

"Just… you. Remember, after the funeral when we stopped to talk…?"

"I remember."

Erin was increasingly confused by his hard tone. "I just don't understand what you are so upset about."

"Somebody just tried to roast the two of you alive. And I think this is why." He rattled the paper in front of her face. "Because you've been poking around asking questions and stirring things up instead of leaving the investigating to the professionals. I thought you learned your lesson after Angela's death. Why would you go getting mixed up in this?"

"The only thing I've been stirring up is cake batter. I haven't been investigating anything!"

He indicated the note. "Yeah? What does Adam Plaint's death have to do with cake batter?"

"I wondered whether he was dead or had just made himself disappear, like Trenton. If he was still alive, then I thought *he* should have inherited The Bake Shoppe after Angela's death."

"No. Her will specifically left her estate to Trenton. Everything went to him."

"Yeah, that's what you told me. *After* I wrote the list."

Terry's eyes went back and forth over Erin's face as if he were reading something written there. "And as far as we know, Trenton died intestate. What does that mean to you?"

Erin licked her lips. The smoke and breathing through the oxygen mask had left her mouth as dry as cotton. She needed a drink to moisten her mouth. She swallowed and tried to speak calmly. "Well, Davis said he had to have his father declared dead. To inherit the store."

"When did you talk to *Davis* about it?" Terry sounded exasperated.

Erin shifted anxiously. He made it sound like he had been chasing after Davis asking him questions. Like some amateur detective on TV. "I didn't. I mean, I wasn't the one who went and asked him questions. He came up to me. When I was eating at the restaurant. I was eating by myself, not bothering anyone. He came up to me and started talking to me and asking me questions."

"What was he asking you about?"

"Why I left the funeral instead of staying to visit afterward… he said he wanted to introduce me to some people." Erin tried to remember the other aspects of their conversation. "He wanted to know… what I knew about his father, his disappearance."

She knew by Terry's expression that he had interpreted her words the wrong way.

"Not in a creepy way. It didn't come out like that. Just in the course of the conversation… what did I know about his father's death, anyway? That I couldn't know what it was like for Davis to be abandoned like that when he was so young." Erin sighed. "But I don't know about that… I know what it's like to feel abandoned at a pretty young age."

"Davis said that his father abandoned them? Not that he died?"

"Yes. He was very definite about that."

Terry was looking at the piece of paper. "Then why did you question on this list whether he was dead?"

"That was *before* I talked to Davis. It was just what I was thinking about when I was at the funeral. When he came and talked to me, it was after that."

"Did he see this piece of paper?" Terry stared Erin in the eye. She felt like she was caught in the crosshairs of a gun sight. "Erin, I need you to be sure of this. Did Davis ever see this piece of paper? Did you have it on the table while you were eating? Did you pull it out to write a phone number on or this date reference? I need to know where it was from the time you wrote it until now."

Erin's legs were wobbly. She grasped his arm to steady herself. Terry took her back over to the fire truck, where she had been sitting before, and settled her into place.

"Are you okay? Feeling lightheaded?"

"A little," Erin admitted. "I don't know what came over me. The smoke, I guess."

"It can leave you feeling a little queasy. You've had lots of excitement."

He stood there looking at her, and Erin knew he expected her to answer his question.

"Uh… I wish I could tell you what you want to know… I didn't give that paper to Davis, or to anyone else. I didn't have it on the table when I talked to him. I'm pretty sure, anyway. I had it at the funeral…" Erin shook her head and looked at Vic, who had followed her back to the fire truck and was hovering close by, pretending not to listen to the conversation, but clearly drawn in by it. "Vic... you saw I had it at the funeral."

"Yeah, sure. You were writing down a list. I saw that, but I didn't see what you wrote."

Erin looked at the note Terry still held in his hand, pinched by the very corner of the piece of paper. He was trying to preserve it as evidence. There could be fingerprints on it. She went over each of the lines in her mind. She should have written down a more detailed list of questions when she had gotten home. But things had gone off the rails when Vic's parents started spreading the word about her history. Erin had forgotten she even had questions about The Bake Shoppe. Without the list to refer to, it had all just faded from her mind.

"I had it then, at the funeral," she told Terry. "Then when we stopped to talk to you, I was looking for it... but I couldn't find it in my purse. So, I just asked you..."

"And when did you see the note again after that?"

"I don't remember. I don't know if I did. It wasn't important. I didn't look for it again. It might have been in my purse, or in a pocket." She looked over at the bushes where Terry had picked it up. "It might have fallen out when I took my keys out of my purse. Just because it was in the bushes... I don't think that necessarily means that whoever lit the fire had it."

"The last time you remember seeing it was at the funeral."

"Yes."

"It hasn't been outside for that long."

"But it might have been in my purse until today. Or yesterday. There's no proof anyone else had it."

"Unless it has their fingerprints on it."

Erin nodded. "You really think this has something to do with the fire? You think that someone lit my house on fire because of what was written on that note?"

"Yes. It's too big of a coincidence."

But what was on it that was important? Erin thought back to the notes she had scratched down quickly.

Adam Plaint dead?

Trenton and Davis?

"Do you think…" Erin stared at the note. "Do you think someone thought I was accusing Trenton and Davis of killing their father?"

"It could certainly be taken that way."

Erin was glad she was already sitting down. She leaned her head against the fire truck and tried to breathe normally. Not to hyperventilate. Not to panic about Terry thinking that she had been the victim of an attempted murder. Because someone thought that she had accused him of murder.

"Davis."

"He's the only one around to be concerned about this theory of yours."

"It wasn't my theory!"

"Your apparent theory."

"Should I tell him that I don't suspect him?" Erin asked. "I can explain the note to him… so he doesn't think I'm trying to put him in jail?"

"No! You shouldn't talk to him at all. Especially if he is our arsonist. That's going to be my job."

His mouth had a grim set to it. He walked away from Erin and Vic for a minute, going over to talk to the police chief, who had just come out of the house. Then he went to his car to retrieve an evidence bag. After putting the note in it, smoothing it all out flat, so there was no extra air in the bag, he went back to Erin.

K9's nose quivered as he sniffed in Vic's direction, where she still held Orange Blossom under her blanket.

"The thing is…" Vic said slowly. "If Davis came after you because he thought you were accusing him of murdering his father… then wouldn't that mean… he thought you could prove that he had?"

Erin's stomach flipped over. Her head was still whirling, and Vic's suggestion didn't help matters.

"No! How would I be able to prove anything? I'm not a witness. No one came forward when his father disappeared in the first place. The case is cold, now. There's no way for anyone to prove that Davis or Trenton had anything to do with Adam's death or disappearance."

Terry was looking down at the note. "Except maybe this interview list."

"That's not an interview list! Most of those people are dead. They don't know anything, or they would have come forward when Adam died."

"Davis has been gone from Bald Eagle Falls for almost as long as Trenton. How would he know who was alive and who was dead?"

Erin shook her head. "It was a list of relatives of people in town. Who to ask them about if we got into a conversation after the funeral. Just a way to be more comfortable around people and get a better idea of how everyone was related. It's not a witness list!"

Terry shrugged. Erin heard the echo of his words. *How would Davis know that?*

"You wrote down the year that Adam Plaint disappeared. Or died. Why?"

Erin shook her head. "No. I wrote down the year that my parents died. Davis was talking about Trenton's life… when he had done different things. I wrote down the year that my parents died because I wanted to remember to follow up on some… discrepancies."

"What discrepancies?"

Erin rubbed her forehead. "I don't see how that matters…"

"Erin. This is my investigation. You need to answer my questions. Even if you think they aren't relevant."

Erin looked over at Vic, who shrugged and nodded. "It's not anything to do with the Plaints."

Terry waited.

"I remember when my parents died," Erin said. "Not the date… but I remember about when it was. And that it was before my eighth birthday."

"Uh-huh."

"But the dates that Clementine has down in her genealogy book were after my birthday. And not both the same day."

Terry squeezed his brows together and shook his head. "You're right. That doesn't seem relevant. Except that you wrote it down on this piece of paper. This piece of paper that reads like an accusation that the Plaint boys killed their father."

"That wasn't what I meant."

"But whoever read it didn't know that."

"Davis said his father had abandoned them. I believed him. Why would he come after me after that? I mean, if I started trying to blackmail him, sure." Erin thought about Alton Summers and the way he had tried to blackmail Erin into giving him money. There was a connection in her brain, something that was just beyond her reach. She tried to follow it for a few seconds, but couldn't figure out what it was, and focused back on the conversation with Terry. "But I didn't. I didn't do anything that would make him think I believed he'd killed his father. I accepted what he told me, and I never talked to him again."

"Something obviously made him believe otherwise."

"Maybe he was just being extra cautious," Vic suggested. "Maybe he didn't care whether Erin believed him or not, he just wanted to… tidy up all of the loose ends."

It was late. Or it was early. Erin's usual wake-up time was approaching, and she felt rotten. The only sleep she had gotten was the couple of hours before the fire. Her throat hurt. Her head ached. She was so tired she wanted to just lie down and sleep for three days.

"Erin."

Erin forced herself to sit up and open her eyes. It was Terry. He had to have been up all night too, but he looked better than she felt.

"Yes?" It came out as a croak. Erin cleared her throat. "What is it?"

"The fire chief would like to walk you through the house. You can point out if anything is out of place, ask him any questions you have about the damage. You'll want to contact your insurer and this way you'll have some idea of what to say to them."

"I thought someone was coming from the city…?"

"I don't know when that will be. Maybe not for another day or two. Are you up to it? Do you want to walk through?"

"If it's safe."

"He won't take you anywhere that's unsafe. Come on, then."

Terry led her to the door of Clementine's house and introduced her to the fire chief, Ben Mackie. Erin was pretty sure she had sold baked goods to a Mrs. Mackie. She must have been Ben's wife.

"Chief Mackie," Erin greeted, with a nervous nod.

"Just Ben. We're going to be walking through your house, so we may as well be friends."

"Can we come along?" Vic asked.

'We' had to refer to her and Orange Blossom, who against all odds was still cradled in Vic's arms. Erin had figured the cat would have insisted on being released hours before. Or else Vic would have to find somewhere he could be shut away or kenneled safely.

"Only one of you," Chief Mackie said crisply. "I want to be sure that nothing gets touched. I can't watch more than one person."

Erin gave Vic an apologetic smile and wave and went into the house with Mackie. It was still before sunrise, so the only light in the house came from the few streetlights outside. Mackie had a powerful flashlight that lit up the whole room. He played it around the living room when they walked in the door. That was where the fire had seemed to center, so Erin was prepared for the worst. But there seemed to be surprisingly little damage. The furniture was in a bad state, the walls burned and blackened with smoke. But the ceiling hadn't collapsed and seemed relatively undamaged. Erin took courage that perhaps the rest of the house wouldn't be too bad.

"Is it a total write-off?" she asked Mackie. "Will they have to knock it down and rebuild? Or is it salvageable?"

"I've seen worse. It will be the insurer's call."

"But what do you think? Is there damage to the structure of the house? Load-bearing walls and all that?"

"If I thought there was, I wouldn't be walking you through it."

He took her into the kitchen, then down the hall into each of the bedrooms and the commode.

"What about the attic?" Erin asked.

"Is it developed?"

Erin nodded. She pulled down the attic stairs. They appeared to be undamaged. Chief Mackie played his flashlight over them, then examined one step at a time, mounting them only after assuring himself that each one was safe. Erin was reminded of Orange Blossom's cautious ascent of the stairs. She followed Mackie up. He shone the flashlight around the attic room.

Erin could still smell the smoke. But the attic room seemed to be in pretty good shape. The fire hadn't made it all the way up there. The walls were not scorched. There were no holes in the floor.

"I only want you to step where I do," Mackie instructed. "Even though the floor looks sound, I only want you to walk where I do. Single file. One step at a time."

Erin obeyed him. They moved across the room and looked at the genealogy books and journals Erin had been studying. In spite of their flammability, they had been protected by being left in the attic. Some of the boxes and books in the other rooms had been damaged, but the ones in the attic looked pristine. Erin reached for the journal. The one that contained the information about her parents' deaths.

"Leave it there," Mackie ordered. "Don't move anything."

"I can't take it with me? It looks okay. It hasn't been damaged."

"Leave it there. It will keep until the scene has been released. Until then, we can't let you touch or remove anything."

Erin nodded and withdrew her hand. They headed back to the stairs. Mackie swept the flashlight toward the stairs, and Erin jumped when she saw an animal lying beside them.

"Oh!" She laughed. "The cat's fur."

"What?" Mackie looked at it closely. "The cat's…?"

"It's fake fur. He found it in the sewing room and dragged it up here," Erin said. "Scared the heck out of me because I thought he caught a rat. Or a weasel."

Mackie chuckled. "I can see why."

They left it there, and Erin followed Mackie's lead back out of the house to where Vic was waiting. Terry was a short distance away, leaning tiredly against his car, writing down whatever notes or statements he had to file.

"It's not too bad," Erin told Vic. "I think we'll be able to move back in there, once it's been cleaned up a bit. There's damage, but I think… I don't think we have to knock the whole thing down. And we'll be able to save most of the important things. The living room and kitchen are the worst."

Orange Blossom stuck his head out of Vic's blanket and meowed plaintively at Erin.

"Oh, I know," Erin said. She held her hands out, and Vic transferred the warm, furry body into her arms. "I know, you want to go back into the house and go to sleep now that it's almost morning. But you can't." She cuddled him against her cheek, and he started to purr like a motor. "You were a good kitty to wake me up. Better than a watchdog."

"He woke you up?" Mackie repeated.

"Yeah. He did. And then I got Vic up, and we all got out of the house without getting hurt. I don't know if either of us would have woken up if it wasn't for him."

"Can we get some things out of the house for him?" Vic asked. "And for us? Clothes? Toothbrushes?" She scratched Orange Blossom's ears. "Toys?"

Erin thought of the piece of fur up in the attic. She would have picked it up for the cat if she'd been allowed to take anything. But Mackie had said she couldn't touch anything, and she assumed that applied even to a random piece of fur.

"Holy crap!"

Everyone looked at Erin in surprise. Mackie, Vic, even Terry looked up from his writing.

"What?" Vic asked.

"Joelle!"

"Joelle?"

"Joelle! She wasn't... Terry! I think you need to... I should have noticed!"

Terry walked over. Vic and Mackie tried to make sense of Erin's incoherent exclamations.

"What is it?" Terry was frowning. "What about Miss Biggs?"

"She's a fake!"

"Okay... a fake what?"

"She's not a vegan."

Vic and Terry just stared.

"She was wearing leather at the funeral. And fur. And her sandals at the Founders' Day Fair. Leather again."

"So...?"

"If she's vegan for ethical reasons, she wouldn't wear leather and fur. She'd avoid anything that came from animals. Not just food, but her clothes too."

"Maybe it's nothing to do with ethics," Vic said. "Sometimes it's just for health. Not animal rights."

"No," Erin shook her head. "She was talking about the bees, remember? She was concerned about animal-based food colorings and coatings. Someone who's just avoiding meat, eggs, and dairy for health reasons doesn't worry about all of those little things. She was only pretending to be vegan. She's running some kind of con."

Terry shrugged. "It's not illegal to pretend to be vegan. Annoying, maybe, but not illegal."

"But murder is."

He raised his brows. "Murder?"

"If she was only vegan for her health, then she wouldn't care about every last ingredient. She would just accept that something labeled vegan didn't have any eggs or dairy in it and not need to look at the other ingredients."

They still didn't get it. Erin took a deep breath in and released it slowly.

"Unless there was another ingredient she was looking for."

Terry's eyes riveted on her, suddenly connecting to her train of thought. "You mean like soy products?"

Erin nodded.

Vic stared at Erin wide-eyed. "You're saying that she was looking for something that had soy in it?"

"And the best bet was to ask for something dairy-free or vegan."

"Why would she want to kill Trenton?" Terry demanded. "She was his girlfriend."

Erin closed her eyes and saw Joelle arm in arm with Davis at the funeral, coming with him to the bakery, and Joelle and Alton Summers arguing at the Founders' Day fair.

"No, she wasn't. She's Davis's girlfriend." She opened her eyes and looked at them.

"Davis's!" Terry looked at her like she was crazy.

Vic shook her head and opened her mouth to speak.

"She was," Erin said firmly. "They must have planned the whole thing. Davis knew he wasn't getting anything under his mother's will. It was all going to Trenton. If he wanted to get anything, he had to get Trenton out of the way. He knew about Trenton's allergy. They arranged for Trenton and Joelle to meet and get involved."

"They've only known each other for a couple of months," Vic mused. "The timing is right."

"Joelle arranges for Trenton to 'accidentally' eat something with soy in it. He didn't carry an auto-injector, so she didn't have to worry that he was going to be able to inject himself and recover."

"It's a pretty big jump," Terry said. "From deciding she's not an ethical vegan because she wears leather and fur to fingering her for the murder of her boyfriend. There's no proof. One of them would have to confess, and there's not even an open investigation into Trenton's death."

"Talk to Alton Summers."

"Alton Summers," Terry echoed.

"Who's he?" Vic demanded.

"That guy who came by the bakery."

"The one who was trying to—" Vic cut herself off suddenly, looking at Terry.

Erin licked her lips and swallowed hard. With her teeth gritted, she filled Terry in with the vital information. "The one who was trying to blackmail me," she said. "He even followed me all the way to the city and tried again."

"Trying to blackmail you? Why didn't you come to me with this?"

"I don't know… I didn't want to have to talk to you about it. I told him to get lost. Told him I would report him if he kept it up."

"How do you know Alton Summers? How did he know anything about you to try to blackmail you with? Was it something to do with Angela's death?"

Erin cuddled Orange Blossom and scratched his ears and chin. K9 sat beside Terry, his eyes on the lump under Erin's blanket.

"Summers was the detective who tracked me down after Clementine died. He was hired by her estate lawyers. That must be how he knew Davis and Joelle too. Angela's estate lawyers hired him to find Trenton. He tracked down Davis first and set everything in motion. So, he knew that Joelle was Davis's girlfriend, not Trenton's."

Terry turned away from Erin abruptly. He went over to his car and leaned in to pick up his radio. Erin heard him snapping out orders to the dispatcher. He gave instructions for Tom Banks to find Alton Summers right away and bring him in for questioning. No, it couldn't wait until Tom was up. He needed to be paged immediately.

When Terry returned to where Erin and Vic were standing, his face looked tired and worn. Like he'd aged ten years in a few minutes.

"Why would they try to burn your house down?" he asked. "If nobody guessed about Joelle poisoning Trenton, and you believed Davis when he told you that his father abandoned them, then why come after you now? Is there something you're not telling me? What happened since Davis approached you at the restaurant?"

Erin shook her head. "I don't know… Nothing."

"You haven't talked to him since then?"

"No."

"Or Joelle?"

"I talked to her at the Founders' Day Fair. But only for a minute, and it wasn't anything about Adam Plaint."

"Did you talk to anyone about him while you were at the Founders' Day Fair? Anybody at all?"

"No. I didn't."

"Somebody could have overheard you. A place like that, things get so chaotic, you don't know who might have heard what."

Erin remembered looking around in Naomi's tent to make sure they couldn't be overheard. But she'd been able to hear someone else talking about sheep through the tent wall, which meant someone outside the tent might be able to hear her. Erin shook her head. She hadn't talked to Naomi about Trenton or Davis or their father. She had only been talking about Clementine and her own family.

"Something must have happened," Terry said, his voice low. "But maybe it wasn't something you did. Maybe it was Alton Summers approaching Joelle. Maybe they decided at that point to wipe out any threats." He licked his lips. "I just hope we don't find Summers dead and Joelle and Davis gone."

CHAPTER 19

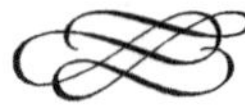

*E*rin and Vic had both doubled their usual coffee intake by the time they opened the bakery, and they each had RC colas under the counter as they worked.

"We should work in shifts," Erin had suggested. "You could go sleep while I work, and then we could switch."

Vic shook her head. "I can manage." She studied Erin. "Do you really want to?"

"No," Erin admitted. "I want to know that we're all here, safe and sound."

Orange Blossom was shut in Erin's office, a tiny room, which he didn't like, but he had quieted after a while and gone to sleep. It had been a tiring night for him, too.

So, they agreed they would both work together as usual, and if they had to close early, they would pack up and go back to the Inn. While the hotel didn't technically allow pets, Erin got the impression that they would look the other way for a few days.

Mary Lou came by mid-morning with a new case of Jam Lady jars. Erin accepted them with thanks.

"The sample table seemed to be keeping up a pretty brisk business at the fair," Erin observed. "I think everybody knows how good the Jam Lady products are by now. You must be keeping busy with them."

"Yes, it's going really well," Mary Lou agreed. "And thank you for doing your part and carrying them here."

"They pair so well with artisan breads. It's a good up-sell."

"It works well for us both," Mary Lou agreed.

Vic took another sip of her RC and put it down again. "I know who The Jam Lady is," she offered.

Mary Lou looked at her sharply. Erin perked up. "You do? How did you figure it out?"

"Well, like I said, Mary Lou is the only distributor, the only one who knows where they come from."

"Right...?"

Mary Lou took a quick look around the store. The last customer had left, and they were alone for the moment. "That doesn't mean anything," she dismissed.

"It does," Vic insisted. "You're not getting them from the city. They're coming from somewhere in town."

Mary Lou didn't answer.

"Mary Lou said it isn't her," Erin reminded Vic.

"I'm not saying it is. The amount of product that she's selling, it would take someone working almost full-time to produce. And she couldn't do that and work at the General Store."

Mary Lou nodded. "That's right. It isn't me."

"But they come from your house."

There was silence in the bakery.

"You buy the jars and take them home."

"I..."

Erin looked at Vic. She hadn't thought anything of it when Vic had said that she could find out who The Jam Lady was. Erin hadn't been aware of any investigating that Vic had been doing but, obviously, she had been subtly watching and asking questions, below Erin's radar. She looked back at Mary Lou, whose face was growing pink. Mary Lou again turned and looked toward the door, worried another customer would walk into the conversation.

"Okay," she said in a low voice. "But you have to swear secrecy. I don't want word getting around. The Jam Lady is anonymous. The mystery is part of why it is selling. Everyone wants to taste it and speculate on who is making it."

Erin nodded. "I won't say a word. I have a vested interest in it selling too."

Mary Lou looked over at Vic. "Fine. Tell her."

"It's her husband! Mr. Mary Lou."

"Roger," Mary Lou amended. She dabbed at her forehead with the back of her wrist. "Swear you won't tell anyone. He would be so embarrassed, and The Jam Man just wouldn't sell as well!"

"Your husband makes these?" Erin demanded, her voice rising a few notes. "Really?"

"It's the first thing he's had any interest in since… he got sick. He enjoys doing it, and it's the first time he's felt productive and capable. You can't take that away from him."

"No," Vic and Erin both said simultaneously. They looked at each other, grinning.

"We won't," Erin declared. "I won't say a word. The pronoun 'he' will never leave my mouth. I promise you."

Vic nodded.

Mary Lou looked at Vic and then down at the floor. "Trust the other man masquerading as a lady in this town to be the one to figure it out."

A few seconds of uncomfortable silence ticked by. Erin had no idea how to respond to the comment. Mary Lou wouldn't raise her eyes to look at Vic. Vic stood with her mouth open, no words coming out. It was some minutes before she spoke.

"Your husband is no less of a man for making jams," Vic said in a slow, measured way. "And I'm still a woman, no matter how I was raised or how society labeled me."

"Can we just call a truce?" Erin begged. "Mary Lou, you don't have to agree with Vic, but does that mean you have to argue with her? Can't you just call her by the name and pronoun she prefers, and let it go at that? If one of your boys decided to… dye his hair bright pink or get a tattoo, you wouldn't want people to shun him, would you?"

"I don't know how you can make the comparison. We're not talking about Vic's hair."

"You'd still love him, wouldn't you? Isn't the whole Christianity thing supposed to be about showing people love? The sinners, the lepers, the outcasts?"

Mary Lou nodded at this. "Yes," she admitted, finally raising her eyes to look at Vic.

"But you're not. You wouldn't want to be on the same side as people who threaten to kill people like Vic, would you? There is all kinds of violence against them in the name of Christianity."

"No. I don't agree with that. Violence is not the answer."

"Then maybe love is."

Erin was feeling a little more human after having had a nap. A knock on the hotel door woke her up, and she knew even before Vic answered it who it would be. Vic opened the door and let Terry Piper into the room. K9 stuck to his side. The dog's nose quivered as he looked around and spotted Orange Blossom sleeping on one of the twin beds. Terry laid a hand on his head just as he started to bark, and K9 quieted obediently. Orange Blossom opened one eyelid to stare at the dog but didn't twitch another muscle.

"Come sit down." Erin motioned to one of the chairs and sat in the other. Vic sat down on the nearest bed.

Erin knew that Terry had taken a break after his all-nighter at Clementine's house, but he still looked exhausted. He had probably been unable to get any sleep, still worried about the case and the happenings in his town.

"How did it go?" Erin asked eagerly. "Did Alton Summers talk? Did you get Joelle and Davis?"

"Summers wasn't particularly inclined to be cooperative, but he admitted that Joelle was Davis's girlfriend originally, not Trenton's. That's not enough in itself to charge either of them with anything. But it was enough to bring them in for questioning."

"And they hadn't run?" Vic demanded. "They all just sat around waiting to be arrested?"

"I guess they were pretty confident we wouldn't tie them to the arson. I'm sure they probably had a plan to get rid of Summers, but they hadn't put anything in motion yet. I need to know whether you are willing to charge him with blackmail."

Erin shook her head. "I just want him to get out of here. Leave me alone."

"You want to just let him walk?"

"He's not the one who killed Trenton. Unless you think he was in on it too."

"There's no love lost between them. If he was ever part of the plan, I suspect they cut him out. They wanted the whole pot for themselves."

Erin dreaded what was coming. "You're charging them with murder, aren't you? And arson?"

"Unless Joelle turns on Davis, I don't think I'm going to be able to pin anything on him. Joelle was the one who took up with Trenton, knew about his allergy, looked at the ingredients, and bought the cupcakes. We'll charge her with murder, but she'll contend that it was an accident. Even if she admits to knowing about his allergy, she bought him cupcakes that were safe. She's the only one who knows whether she offered him hers, or he just had a couple while she was gone."

"You can't charge Davis?"

"Davis wasn't even in town until after Trenton's death. His story is that Joelle left him. She was a gold digger and switched allegiance when she heard that Trenton had inherited substantial assets and Davis was getting nothing."

"What about his father's death and the arson?"

"There's nothing to implicate him in Adam Plaint's disappearance or possible death except for your note. And even if he took your note as an accusation, we both know it was never intended as one. You didn't have any evidence the boys were involved in their father's death. You didn't have any witnesses to question."

"And the arson?"

"Still gathering evidence. It will take time to process. We're chasing down search warrants for the car and house, but we can't hold Davis for long without evidence."

Erin shook her head and rubbed her temples.

"He's the one behind all of this. And we can't get him?"

"Not if we don't have any proof."

"And we don't," Vic said. "It all fits… but we don't have the proof."

"Unless Joelle turns on him on Trenton's death—and can prove he was involved and it wasn't all just her own doing—he'll walk. We'll never even charge him, let alone get a conviction."

CHAPTER 20

The arson investigation had taken several days, but Erin and Vic were finally allowed back into the house to retrieve what possessions they would need as the house was cleaned up, repaired, and repainted. The insurance company had recommended a crew from the city who were good with fire and water damage, and arrangements were being made. Erin and Vic needed somewhere else to stay during the renovations, and Mrs. Potter had agreed to lease them a little cottage that she owned on the outskirts of town. That solved the problem of what to do with Orange Blossom, who was wearing out his welcome at the Inn.

Erin packed a suitcase. It wasn't that long since she had been living out of one, so she didn't have that many possessions to choose from. Vic was in the same situation, only more so. She had run away from home with only a backpack, and it hadn't held very much. She borrowed a suitcase from Clementine's closet and got her things together.

Erin went up to the attic. She picked up Orange Blossom's piece of fur at the top of the stairs and shoved it into her pocket.

The journal had been on her mind in the days since the Founders' Day Fair. She knew it had been silly to close it and not read the journal entry when she had found it. No matter how much it scared her, she needed to find out the truth of her past. The secrets that had been kept from her could be just as damaging to her as they had been to Trenton and Davis. She had to know what had happened.

"Are you going to be a few minutes?" she called down to Vic.

"Yeah. Are you in a hurry?"

"No, take as long as you need."

Erin sat down in the reading nook and picked up the journal. Red. Hardcover. Nondescript. No hint that it held the key to the secret past that had been haunting her since she found the wrong dates in Clementine's family tree. She opened the book, and flipped the pages slowly to May 1.

~

Who would believe such a thing could happen to one of our Bald Eagle Falls families?

Adam Plaint has disappeared, and I fear the worst. Angela says that he is not missing and she won't file a missing persons report or initiate a search for him. She is such a pillar of the community that no one dares contradict her. But I know she is lying about it. Adam was a devoted father, and he would never leave his boys behind. I could see him taking the boys and leaving Angela, the mean-spirited bully that she is, but he would never leave those two precious sons of his behind.

But could Angela really have done anything to harm him? And if she had, would her sons stand beside her and lie about it?

In spite of it all, the boys were over to work on the garage today. I told them that they didn't need to do it today, but they both stared down at their feet and said that their mother had told them they had to. Men don't back out of their responsibilities just because of an inconvenience. To her, that's all that Adam's disappearance is, an inconvenience. It wouldn't be Christian of me to say that it was convenient for her rather than inconvenient... but I can't help thinking it.

I left the boys to it. Adam had supervised the digging of the foundation and had shown the boys how to mix and pour the concrete, so they promised me they knew what they were doing and would have the pad completed today. Bless their precious little hearts. There were so many sacks of concrete for them to lug from the car. Trenton is a big boy, but Davis is so slight; more like his father. Even so, he kept up with his brother. I took sweet tea out to them mid-morning to keep them hydrated, but I'm afraid it wasn't enough. Davis in particular looked so ill. His eyes were dark and sunken, and he would barely touch the tea and cookies.

At the end of the day, they had done a beautiful job, and I now have a concrete pad for the garage to be built on. The boys don't have the skill to do the building themselves, but several of the men in town have offered to help get it up, and I'm sure Trenton and Davis will do what they can to help.

~

Erin swallowed and closed the journal again.

It hadn't been her own secret that she had discovered, but the Plaint family's. She looked out the window by her reading nook. It looked down at the back yard, where the garage she never used stood, overgrown with ivy and weeds. Clementine's old Volkswagen was still housed in it.

She knew why Davis had tried to burn down her house. She pulled out her phone and dialed Terry's number.

"Erin."

"Terry. I think I have evidence in a cold case."

"A cold case?" Terry's voice was puzzled.

"I think… Davis overheard me talking to Naomi at the Founders' Day fair. I know why he set the fire, and I think I know where you can find Adam Plaint's body."

ALLERGEN-FREE ASSIGNATION

AUNTIE CLEM'S BAKERY 3

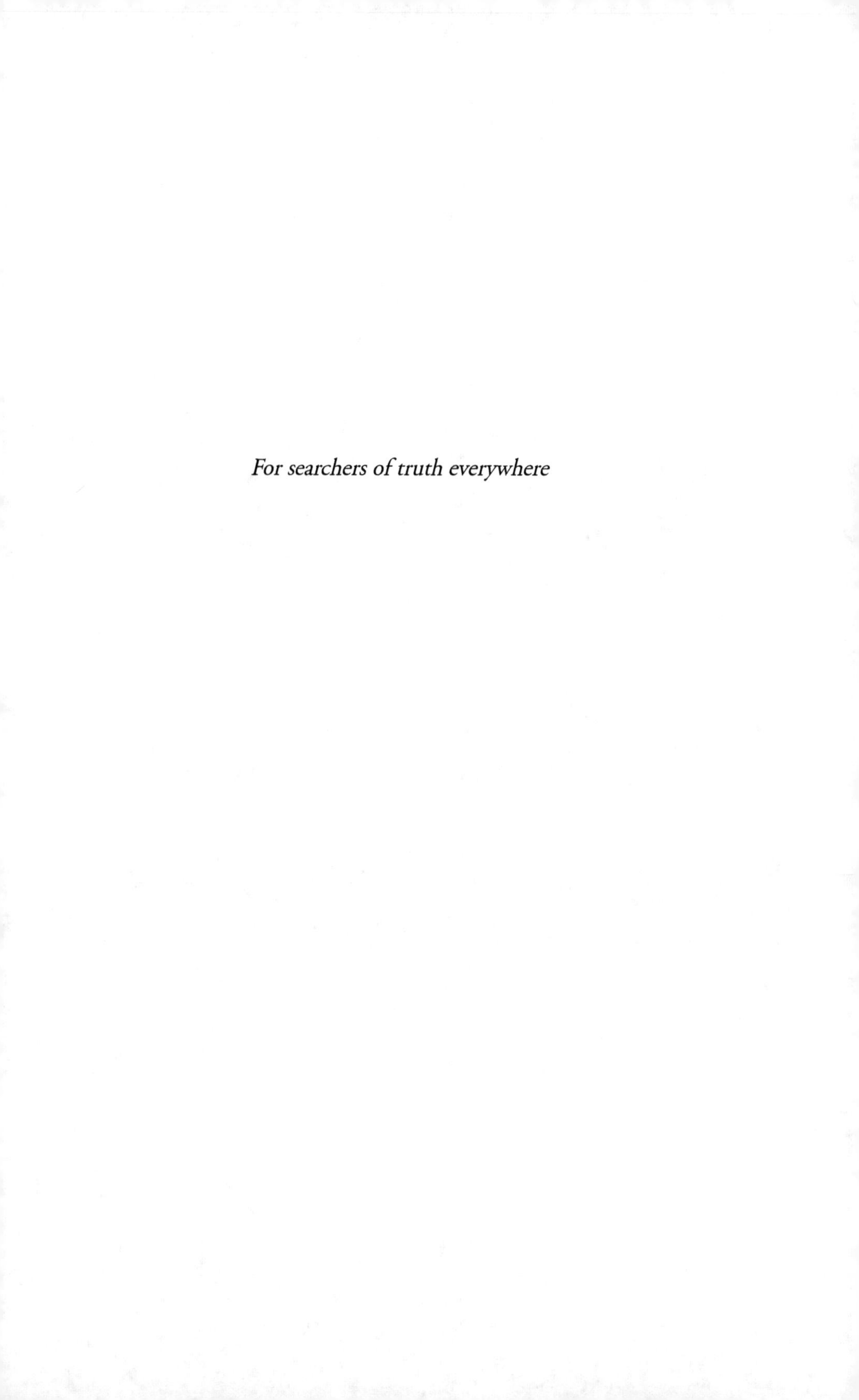

For searchers of truth everywhere

CHAPTER 1

Erin stood watching the heavy machinery close in on the little ivy-covered garage in the back yard of the white and green house. Over the weekend, she and Vic had moved the assorted storage boxes, tools, and other bits and pieces into a mobile storage pod for temporary safekeeping and Erin had moved Clementine's Volkswagen out of the garage for the first time.

Officer Terry Piper moved up beside her, his German shepherd, K9, at his side. He touched the small of Erin's back, fingers tentative.

"Are you okay?"

Erin nodded. Her throat was suspiciously tight, but she couldn't explain why.

"It's just a garage," she said. "And I never even used it. No reason I should feel attached to it."

Terry let his hand rest there for a minute, warm and comforting. "It's part of Clementine's property... I guess that means something to you."

"It's silly. It wasn't even built yet when I was here as a little girl. It wasn't built until I was seven. No reason for me to get all sentimental about it." She pressed her lips together tightly for a moment, trying to convince her body that what she said was true. There was no reason to feel bad about them knocking the garage down. There was no reason for sadness or tears or the tight, hot feeling in her throat. "This is a murder investigation," she said sternly. "We have to do it."

He rubbed her back. "I know. But we don't have to like it."

Erin just shook her head. Terry didn't discuss it any further. The sheriff was there, wearing a hard hat, and he gave the signal to the bulldozer. Its engine revved and it slammed into the garage.

It wasn't fast work. Erin had expected the demolition to be quick. Instantaneous. On TV, she had seen huge buildings, business towers and hospitals and the like, imploded with explosives and razed to the ground in seconds. Knocking down the garage wasn't like that. It was excruciatingly slow. Her legs got tired, standing there watching. The sun climbed the sky and Erin wiped her sweaty forehead with the back of her arm and looked around for a drink. The demolition team had brought in a cooler full of bottled water, and after getting the nod from the supervisor, Erin grabbed one and cracked it open. She sat down on the grass in the shade of the tree. Terry stood for a few minutes longer, then conceded and sat down as well. K9 lay down between them. When Erin was just about done her water, she held it out to K9. She dribbled the last of the water into her palm and he lapped it up.

Eventually, the walls and the roof were down, and the bulldozers and bobcats pushed the rubble out of the way. They were left looking at the cement pad that had been poured before the garage was built. Erin stood up again to look at it. Terry walked up to it for a closer look, as did the sheriff. Tom Banks, the part-time police officer who was on call when Terry was not available was there too. The whole police department out in force. They walked around the pad, looking down at the cement. They took pictures and had low-pitched discussions, scratching their heads, wiping away sweat, and settling their hats again. Terry returned to stand beside Erin.

"There it is," Erin said. "The concrete pad and foundations that the Plaint brothers poured."

"And under it somewhere… the body of Adam Plaint."

"If we're right about what happened."

"I think we are," Terry said. "I think *you* are. Mr. Plaint disappeared without a trace, and the next day the boys came over here to finish pouring the foundations. Why would they be here the next day? There wasn't any rush. Your aunt would have understood that with their family tragedy they couldn't be here that day. She told them they didn't have to be there."

Erin nodded.

"But wouldn't she have seen something suspicious? I mean... two teenagers hauling a grown man's body into the yard...? That wouldn't have been obvious?"

Terry scratched at the back of his neck. "If it was me... if I was Angela, looking for a way to dispose of that body... I would have brought him the night before and dumped him into one of the trenches dug for the foundations. Covered the body with a tarp or a thin layer of dirt. Then all the boys had to do the next day was mix the concrete and pour it in."

"She and the boys moved the body together?"

"That seems most likely. I don't know if the two boys could have done it without her help. Davis was only thirteen, and from what everyone has said, he was scrawny. Not built like Trenton."

"What's the next step? What are they going to do? Start breaking the concrete up with a jackhammer?"

"I'm worried that if we do that, we're going to damage the body. Whatever is left of it. We need to do this carefully to preserve as much evidence as we can."

"So...?"

"We've talked to a company in the city with ground-penetrating radar. That seems like the best solution. See if we can locate the body before we start breaking the concrete up. So we know how to proceed."

"How long before they get the machinery here?"

"I'm hoping tomorrow."

"So, you're done for today?"

"Pretty much. Other than cleaning up the rubble. I'd like to get as much of this cleared out of the way as possible."

Erin sighed and nodded. The back yard looked empty without the garage there. The concrete pad was like a big scar. She walked closer for a look. Terry made a movement as if to stop her, but didn't say anything. What was he going to say? Not to touch the evidence? That she might trip and hurt herself? She couldn't do any damage to the investigation, and it was her own yard.

There was a movement under a bush, and Erin glanced over, expecting to see a bird, or maybe a stray cat. But the shape was not right. She got a little closer. A kitten? It was bigger than Orange Blossom had been when she had rescued him. He'd barely even been weaned. But the shape was chunkier, not the slim, lithe shape of a cat.

"Terry...?"

Terry moved toward her, hearing the concern in her voice.

"What is it?"

"I think... I think something got hurt by the machinery..."

Terry got close enough to see the tufts of fur. K9 was sniffing eagerly, moving in. Erin grabbed his collar and held him back. Normally she wouldn't interfere with a working dog, but she was afraid of what would happen if she let K9 get too close to the injured animal. Terry took a couple of steps forward and took hold of his collar.

"He won't cause any trouble. It's a rabbit." He was close enough to make out the shape. "You're right, I think it's hurt."

Erin moved in. She hadn't wanted to get too close in case it was a dog or a skunk or something that might attack a human when cornered. But she wasn't worried about being attacked by a rabbit.

It eyed her as she got closer. Erin could see its back feet kicking out, but there was blood matting the fur and things obviously weren't working the right way, the rabbit couldn't run away.

"It's just a baby," Erin said. "Its leg is hurt."

"Older than a baby," Terry disagreed. "Unfortunately, rabbits don't do well when injured. It will probably die of shock."

"No..." Erin was too soft-hearted. She didn't like to see any creature hurt or killed. "We have to take it to the vet."

"Get a blanket or a towel to wrap it up. It might bite or scratch. We can take it to the doc, but don't get your hopes up. The kindest thing is probably just to have him put it down."

She was glad that Terry hadn't offered to do the job himself with his police firearm. Death might be a fact of life for a farm boy or small-town boy who had been through a number of pets, but Erin wasn't used to animals dying. She suspected Terry was probably more worried about her than he was about the rabbit.

She took off her jacket and got in close, trying to slide it carefully under the injured animal. The rabbit kept squirming away, its eyes wide with panic. Erin was too tentative, too worried about hurting it further to catch it.

"Throw the coat over top so it can't see you," Terry advised. "Then wrap it around and pick it up inside the coat."

"Okay." Erin tried doing as he said. She was still worried about hurting the rabbit, but it was easier when he couldn't see her coming and was trapped by the fabric around him. She did her best to wrap the coat around it and bundle it up, like Terry had wrapped up Orange Blossom the day that she had first brought the kitten home. She turned the jacket over and looked at the rabbit. She could just see its nose twitching through an opening. "Okay, I've got it."

"I'll drive you over to Doc's," Terry said. "But don't get your hopes up too much. This is a wild animal, and it's injured. Just the stress can kill them."

Erin sniffled and nodded. "Yeah, okay. I'll try not to."

It was the first time she had ridden in Terry's police cruiser, and despite her worry about the rabbit, Erin looked around the interior with bright interest. Bars over the back windows, CB radio, onboard computer, a number of knobs and switches she didn't know the purpose of. Lights and siren, she supposed. Maybe a loudspeaker.

K9 seemed confused about what Erin was doing in the front seat and whined when Terry made a sharp movement for him to get into the back.

"Is this where he usually sits?" Erin asked as Terry slid in beside her.

"Yes. But he'll be okay back there for a couple of minutes. His friends won't make fun of him for riding in back."

Erin looked over at Terry and saw the familiar dimple in his cheek.

Nothing was very far away in Bald Eagle Falls, Tennessee, so they were at the vet's office within a couple of minutes. There were a couple of people in the waiting room, one with a cat and one with a dog.

Sarah Lawson, the pretty young receptionist and vet's assistant, smiled when Erin and Terry entered, her eyes alive with curiosity.

"What have you got?" she asked, standing up and walking out from behind the counter so she could look down at Erin's bundle.

Erin pushed the coat away from the rabbit's face the best she could. "A rabbit. He has an injured leg, or maybe two."

"What happened? Did you hit it with your car?" Sarah looked sympathetic toward Erin, but not hopeful.

"No. One of the vehicles that was knocking down my garage must have gotten it." As Erin thought about the bulldozers that had razed her garage to the ground, she felt nauseated. They could do so much damage to a little creature like the rabbit. What did she think the vet was going to be able to do?

Sarah shook her head, pressing her lips together. "Doc's with a patient right now, but I'll get him to look at your bunny as soon as possible. Let's get you into an exam room."

Doc only had one and a half exam rooms. It wasn't like a big city vet hospital. He would be in the main exam room with a family dog or cat, and Sarah took Erin to the overflow examination table in the corner of Doc's supply room. Terry stayed with K9 in the waiting room.

Unlike the main exam room, there were no seats or other amenities.

"Let's just have a little peek," Sarah said, easing the bundle out of Erin's hands. She laid it on the table. She first opened up the end with the rabbit's head. Its eyes were still wild and rolled back. Its mouth was slightly open and Erin could see its long rodent-like teeth between parted lips. Sarah worked open the other end of the bundle, keeping one hand pressed to the rabbit's middle to keep it from squirming away. Erin wasn't sure what Sarah could see when she looked at the bloody back legs. The rabbit kicked a couple of times. "Okay. We're going to need x-rays, so he'll have to be sedated. Can I get you to hold him again?"

Erin took over holding the rabbit down on the examination table, murmuring to it in a soft voice that was usually reserved for Orange Blossom. Sarah prepared an injection.

"We have to do this in order to get x-rays and examine him properly." She tapped the needle to break loose the air bubbles. "But you should know that sedation will depress his vital functions, and together with the shock he's already in, we could lose him. Okay? We have to do it, but it's risky."

Erin nodded and tried to swallow the lump in her throat. "Okay."

Sarah grimaced at her. "Sorry." She pulled the jacket back once more, and injected the sedative. It took effect almost immediately, and Sarah unwrapped the jacket completely, returning it to Erin. "Baking soda works best on bloodstains," she advised. "Soak it in cold water while it's still wet."

The rabbit looked tiny and vulnerable laying on the examination table. Though Terry was right, and it was bigger than Orange Blossom had been, it was still not full-grown.

"It's a domesticated breed," Sarah observed. "Not a cottontail. Is it someone's pet?"

Erin shook her head. "I don't know. It was outside. I suppose it could belong to a neighbor and just got away from them…"

"Maybe. Or someone might have released a previous generation. People think they're doing a kindness by releasing pet rabbits into the wild when they're not wanted anymore. Born free and all that. But they're not doing any favors to their pets or the environment. A pet isn't equipped to survive in the wild, but if they do, rabbits are notorious for overpopulating. This one's pretty young, I can't see anyone releasing it at this age. It's probably feral."

Erin cleared her throat and swallowed again. She could see the rabbit's rapid respirations as it lay there. But other than that tiny movement, it looked as though it were already dead.

"I'll get some x-rays and get Doc to have a look as soon as he's done. Why don't you wait with Officer Piper in the waiting room?"

"Okay. Thanks."

She retreated to the waiting room and sat down in the chair next to Terry's. K9 was watching the cat and dog across the room, his tail sweeping back and forth in a wide, slow arc, and he paid no attention to her.

"Are you okay?"

"Yeah. She's going to take some x-rays."

He nodded. Erin took a couple of deep breaths and tried to steady her nerves. She was shaking and still felt sick.

"I should touch base with Vic and see how she's doing."

"If it's busy, she won't be able to talk."

Erin worked her phone out of her pocket and checked the time. "She should be having her lunch."

CHAPTER 2

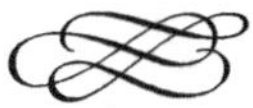

Vic sounded slightly out of breath when she answered the phone. "Erin? What did they find?"

For a moment, Erin was confused. Then she realized that Vic was wondering about the police investigation. If they had found Adam Plaint's body.

"Oh… well, nothing yet. They knocked down the garage, but they're talking about how to locate the body… if there is one… without breaking all of the concrete up and maybe destroying evidence. They want to see if they can find it using x-ray equipment, so they can get it out with as little damage as possible."

"Yeah, that makes sense. So how long is that going to take?"

"I don't think it will be today."

"Are you coming in, then?"

"Uh… yes… but I may be a little while yet."

There was a moment of silence. "Are you and Terry going out for lunch, then?"

"No. We had… we found… there was a little rabbit that was injured by some of the machinery. We brought it to the vet. We're still finding out what they are going to do about it. If they can do anything."

"Oh…" Vic drew the word out in a long crooning noise. "What happened? You don't know if it is going to be okay?"

"No. I don't know. Terry said not to get our hopes up. And Sarah said even the sedation could kill it. I guess rabbits don't make very good patients."

"Okay. Well, I'll hold down the fort, and you get in when you can. Or let me know what's going on."

"Is everything okay? Are you managing all right? I know it's crazy busy when it's just one person… we really do need to get someone in there part-time who can cover when one of us has something else going on or is sick."

"It's busy," Vic admitted. "And people… behave differently when you're not here."

Erin bit the inside of her lip. "What do you mean? How are they acting?" Erin had hoped that they were past everyone being shocked that Vic was transgender and could just accept it and move on. But she could tell by the familiar note in Vic's voice that the 'behavior' she was talking about was probably something to do with her gender identity.

"More… preachy… than usual," Vic said eventually. "When you're here, they don't generally bring out the scriptures and what God thinks of me."

They knew that Erin, as an atheist, wouldn't put up with that kind of crap. Vic tended to take their words to heart, but Erin would throw their religion back at them. Didn't Christianity say they were supposed to be loving and accepting?

Erin sighed heavily. "Don't listen to them," she said. "You have my permission to refuse to serve anyone who thinks they can come into my shop to preach. They pay for the baking, not for the privilege of harassing my employees."

Vic gave a short laugh. "Uh—yeah."

"I mean it. Don't take it. They don't have any right to tell you what to do or what to be."

"Okay. Thanks, Erin."

"I'll be in just as soon as I can get this sorted out. Hang in there."

Vic hung up. Terry raised his eyebrows. "Who is bothering her?"

"I have my suspicions. Why is it the most religious who are the least tolerant? Shouldn't they be the most loving and accepting? Isn't that the whole idea of Christianity? God is love and all that?"

He raised his hands, palms out. "Don't ask me. You can't paint us all with the same brush. Everyone has their own faults."

Erin took a deep breath and let it out. She was furious that people thought it was okay to bug Vic just because Erin wasn't there. Her heart pounded and her blood boiled. But that wasn't Terry Piper's fault. He didn't have anything to do with it. And he had never treated Vic with anything but respect, even when she was a murder suspect and he first found out that she was transgender. He had never suggested that she was more likely to be the murderer because she was some kind of deviant. Not like others in town would have, if they had known back then. But the townspeople had only recently found out, and were still all in a tizzy over it.

"You're right. I'm sorry. I won't take it out on you."

"If you want to vent, I'm here. Just don't think I condone it. And if either of you ever wants to lay charges for hate speech or harassment, you let me know."

"I hope it won't ever go that far."

"So do I."

Erin busied herself playing with her phone and waiting for Sarah or the doctor to come out.

Time passed slowly, but Erin knew it wasn't even noon yet when Doc came out to the waiting room, walking beside Sarah as they spoke in low tones. Sarah went back to the reception desk and sat down. Doc turned to Erin.

"Why don't you join me, Miss Price?"

Erin stood up. She looked at Terry, but he just nodded for her to go ahead. The exam room was small, and maybe he thought it would be too much to have him and K9 squeezed in there with Erin and Doc and the rabbit. If K9 decided to bark at the rabbit, he might scare it right to death.

Erin had met Doc Edmunds before, getting Orange Blossom's vaccinations and other necessary medical procedures taken care of. She was afraid he was going to say the same thing as Terry had, that the kindest thing would just be to put the rabbit down. She couldn't bear to make that decision.

The rabbit was not in the exam room. Doc put a file folder down on the table and looked at Erin over the rim of his glasses.

"I've had a look at your little friend and the x-rays that Sarah ran."

Erin nodded.

"He has a fracture in one of his back legs. Clean. The other one has only superficial injuries, nothing broken. Spinal cord injuries are always a concern with rabbits, but everything seems to be okay with its back in this case."

"Does that mean it will be okay? All you have to do is fix the broken leg?"

"That's about all I can do." Doc hesitated and gave a little grimace. "But that's not the only issue with cases like this. Wild animals can't always be rehabilitated and in this case, we're looking at an invasive species that cannot be returned to the wild. There is a risk that it won't be able to cope with the trauma it has already experienced, or with being caged or in close proximity to people. There are problems associated with sedation, feeding, risk of infection…"

Erin rubbed at her eyes and swallowed, trying not to let the lump in her throat grow and take over her emotions.

"You sound like you're saying we shouldn't try."

"I have concerns. I don't think a positive outcome is impossible… but we have a lot of factors working against us. I don't know if you want to risk it."

"I do."

He didn't respond immediately, studying her face, looking into her eyes, trying to read everything he could from her expression.

"Okay." He nodded. "I'll do what I can. I'll set the broken bone, give it IV fluids and antibiotics, and try to keep it calm and relaxed when it comes out of sedation. The rest will depend on the critter himself. I can't promise a positive result, but I'll give it a try."

"Thanks."

"I have your numbers on file; Sarah or I will give you a call later on today before we lock up and let you know how things went."

Erin had a heavy heart as Terry dropped her off at the cottage. She drove her car over to Auntie Clem's Bakery on Main and parked in her private parking stall behind the building. She forced herself to put on a cheerful face for Vic, who would need her support and attention after her challenging morning. Vic's head turned to look at her as she walked into the kitchen, but she didn't stop to visit. Things were usually too busy with just one person manning the counter.

"Hi, Erin."

"Hi! I'll be right with you!" Erin quickly washed up, made sure that her hair was all tucked neatly into place, and pulled on one of her aprons. It was strange to spend a morning away from the bakery. She was usually there seven days a week, with only Sunday afternoon off to relax or pursue other interests.

There were only a couple of customers in the shop, and they were strangely quiet as Erin joined Vic at the service counter. Erin glanced at Vic, wondering whether they had been bothering her. Vic gave her a determined smile and didn't give anything away.

The afternoon swept by quickly, and it seemed like it hadn't been nearly long enough before Vic and Erin were cleaning up and putting things away for the evening. Erin told all that she knew of the police investigation into her garage and the tale of the little rabbit. Vic related little of her day. She looked tired and ready to go home.

"You know, I've been thinking about the garage," Erin said.

Vic pulled the plug in the sink to let the soapy water out. "What about the garage? I mean… it's not there anymore… so what is there to think about?"

"Well, once they're all done with their investigation, I'm going to need to rebuild it."

"I would think you could probably use the same contractors as have been working on the house," Vic suggested.

Erin had been thinking that as well. The various parties who had been working on fixing her house after the fire had all seemed very competent. They showed up, got stuff done on time, and Erin hoped that in a couple of weeks, the house would again be habitable so she and Vic and Orange Blossom could go home.

"Yeah, I think so," she agreed. "But I've been thinking about the specifications. Size and style and functionality…"

"Uh-huh." Vic's mind seemed far from the discussion.

"Vic…"

"What? Yeah, I think that all sounds good. It will be nice to get everything fixed up."

"I was thinking about having a second floor over the garage."

"Hm?" Vic looked up from the cutlery she was drying and putting away. "A second floor for what? Storage?"

"No. I thought maybe a separate suite. Like… guest quarters. Or… a rented space…"

Vic blinked, suddenly becoming interested in the conversation. "A separate living space over the garage?"

"Yes. What do you think?" Erin couldn't help grinning at Vic.

"Do you mean you'd be looking for someone to rent it?"

"I know you've been looking elsewhere for an apartment… do you think you might be interested? It would save me having to advertise to find someone to rent it…"

"Of course I'd be interested!" The words came out of Vic in an explosion. Her smile far outstripped Erin's. "I could pay rent for my own space, but still be close by. I could still come over and see Orange Blossom and we could go to work together. But if I wanted to have someone over, or do things on my own, I'd have my own apartment…"

Erin nodded. "Are you sure you don't want to go to the city, though?" she asked. "I've been worried that you might go to the city… to get away from all of the busybodies and to access…" Erin cleared her throat uncomfortably, "…er… the larger dating pool."

Vic paused for a moment before answering. "I can't say that I haven't thought about it," she admitted. "But if I've got a place of my own here, I can always drive into the city. It's not that far away."

"And you're not worried about what the church ladies have to say? That they're going to make it too uncomfortable for you here?"

"Just give me some time… I'll learn how to handle them."

Erin was relieved. "Good. I was hoping that it might be something that would work for you. And if I have a paying tenant, I'm thinking I might be able to hire some part-time help so that each of us can get some time off each week. Before we end up burning out."

～

Just as they were shutting off the lights to leave, Erin's phone buzzed. She looked at the caller ID and picked it up immediately.

"Yes?"

"Erin, Doctor Edmunds here. I told you I'd give you a call to let you know how your rabbit was doing."

"Yes?" Erin's voice came out in a squeak. Vic turned and looked at her.

"He's come out of sedation okay and seems to be resting comfortably. No alarm bells. These little guys don't handle trauma well, but he seems to be pretty tough. If he makes it through the night okay, I think we can have hope for his recovery."

"Oh, that's good news. Will you call me again in the morning, then? Let me know how he's doing?"

"I'll have Sarah give you a call. Keep your fingers crossed or say a little prayer, whatever you've been doing up until now. He's beaten the odds so far."

"Thanks, Doc. I will."

She hung up and nodded at Vic, who was eagerly waiting for the details. "He's doing okay. Doc says if he makes it through the night, he'll probably be okay."

"Good! Can we go see him tomorrow, then? I want to see him. Is he cute?"

"Well… he wasn't in very good shape when I rescued him. But hopefully he'll be looking and feeling better tomorrow."

"I just love bunnies."

Erin smiled. Everyone else had been pretty negative toward her rescue attempt, so she was happy to hear Vic's encouragement.

"I've never had one, but I've always through they were pretty cute."

"We'll have to think of a name for him. Are you going to release him when he's all better?"

"Apparently not a good idea. He's not a wild rabbit. Probably the baby of a pet someone released. You can think about names, but let's not actually give him one until we're sure he's actually going to survive."

Erin drove by the house, but all of the equipment was sitting idle and there were no policemen or other workers around doing anything, so she didn't stop. Vic gaped at how empty the yard was without the garage.

"I can hardly even believe that's our yard," she said, shaking her head. "That's so weird."

"Hopefully they'll get it all fixed up in the next couple of days," Erin said. "I just want everything out of there, so we can start rebuilding. I don't like the idea of Adam Plaint's body buried back there."

"At least we don't have to sleep in the house while it's there. That would be creepy."

"We did sleep in the house while the body was there. It's been there since we moved in. Unless I'm wrong and they didn't dispose of his body there."

Vic gave a shudder. "Don't tell me that. Now I'm going to have nightmares."

Erin shrugged with one shoulder while she pulled back into the back lane to head for their temporary residence in Mrs. Potter's cottage. "I don't think you need to worry about it. It isn't like you saw his body."

"Ew. You're making it worse. I can't help imagining it, and my imagination is probably way worse than if I actually did see it. Too many zombie and forensic TV shows…"

Erin laughed. "Stop thinking about it. Think about going home to Orange Blossom instead."

Vic looked much happier about this. "Yeah."

Though the cottage was on the other side of town, it only took a few minutes for them to get there. Erin let them into the house, and Orange Blossom was immediately under their feet, scolding them with strident yowls.

"You'd think we abandoned you!" Vic said, scooping him up so that Erin could get in and close the door again. "You know we come home again every day. We're not going to abandon you!"

His purr sounded almost as loud as the bulldozers that morning and he pushed his head against Vic's chin. Erin reached over and scratched his ears.

"Silly cat!"

They both cooed over him as if he were a baby. After a minute, Vic handed him over to Erin. "I'm starving. You take him so I can put something on."

While Vic made her way to the diminutive kitchen, Erin cuddled the cat up to her face, closing her eyes and breathing in his familiar smell. She tried to just let the worries of the day flow away. She couldn't control what happened to the rabbit or the police investigation. She couldn't stop people from being prejudiced against Vic. She might as well just let those things go, and focus on the things she did have control over.

Erin felt more like herself after dinner. She had a couple of hours to relax, and then she needed to hit the sack so she wouldn't be too tired to get up again in the morning. While Vic played with Orange Blossom, Erin pulled out Clementine's journal, and a similar hard-backed notebook that she had started keeping notes about her own family in. Vic looked up from the game with Orange Blossom.

"Are you reading that again? Isn't that sort of morbid?"

"No," Erin protested. "I'm not reading about the Plaints. I'm looking for anything on my parents."

Vic's eyes didn't move away from her, trying to discern whether she was telling the truth.

"I have the bit about the Plaints memorized anyway," Erin said. "I've read it so many times already." She smoothed the pages with her fingertips. "Whenever I read about it, I feel so sorry for those boys."

"For Uncle Trenton and Davis?" Vic shook her head. "I don't know why you would feel bad for them, they're nasty people. The way Trenton was bullying you? And I'm sure Davis was the one who set the fire."

"I know… I don't feel sorry for them now, as adults, but I can feel bad for the way they were treated when they were boys. Trenton was fifteen and Davis was only thirteen. Thirteen!"

Vic nodded. She dragged a feather along the ground, waiting for

Orange Blossom to pounce on it. "That is really young," she admitted. "But not as young as you were when you lost your parents. And you lost both of them."

"But my father wasn't murdered. I don't know whether they had anything to do with him being killed or not, but it sure looks like they were the ones who had to dispose of the body. Can you imagine a thirteen-year-old being forced to dispose of his own father's body? Can you imagine what kind of damage that must have done to him?"

"Yeah… if it was something he was forced into, and he wasn't the one who killed him in the first place. We don't actually know that it was Aunt Angela."

"Well… no," Erin admitted. She had assumed all along that it was the only other adult in the family. Especially having met Angela a couple of times, before the woman ended up being the victim of murder herself. "But Angela always said that she was the one who had gotten rid of Adam. Everyone thought it was just a joke, but that doesn't mean it was. I think she enjoyed making people wonder."

Orange Blossom made his move, pouncing on Vic's hand instead of on the feather, making her yelp and jump back, too late to avoid the kitten's sharp claws. "Oh! Ow! Ouch, Blossom, that hurt!" She sucked on the worst of the scratches before continuing with the conversation. "If she was the one who did it, and she forced her sons to help her… then I guess I can feel sorry for them too. But I'm not sure that's what happened. She might have just been covering for them. Keeping the police or anyone else from finding out what really happened to her husband. Or maybe she never knew. Maybe the boys killed him, and she never knew what had happened, and thought he had just left, like she said. We don't have any way of knowing what really happened."

"The only one who really knows what happened is Davis. And he's not talking. But why would he or Trenton kill Adam? Clementine says in her journal that he was a devoted father, and would never have left the boys behind. That doesn't make it sound like there were any problems between the father and the sons."

"How would Clementine know? It's just like with everybody you've gone up against with these cases. The bad guys don't advertise themselves. Everybody thinks they are upstanding members of the community. You never know what's going on behind closed doors. Clementine wouldn't know what kind of relationship Adam really had with his sons. He could have been abusive."

Erin stared down at the words in the journal. They were her key to solving all of the mysteries surrounding the Plaints, and she didn't want to admit that they might not be gospel. If she could just rely on what Clementine had said, she could unravel everything and solve the cold case. But if Clementine didn't really know what was going on between Adam Plaint and his boys… then she would be right back where she started.

"Well, never mind," she said. "I said I'm not reading that part again. I'm looking for more information about my parents."

Vic patted Orange Blossom, trying to settle him down so that he wouldn't keep attacking her. She pulled him onto her lap and stroked him gently.

"Have you found anything new?"

"No… not really. I need to go look through some of the other journals. The accident must have happened after May, and that's when this one ends." But all of the other journals that hadn't been damaged in the fire were in storage, out of the way so that they would be safe while the contractors finished fixing the fire and smoke damage.

"You don't remember what month it was?"

"No. I was only seven. I don't have any idea what month it was, except that it was before my birthday. That was July, so I'm guessing the accident must have been in June."

"Even though Clementine's genealogy stuff says they died after that."

"That's what I'm trying to figure out," Erin sighed. "I'm going to ask DHS for a copy of my records. And see if I can somehow track down and get a copy of my parents' medical records."

"Wouldn't you be better off just finding an obituary? That would give you the dates."

"I'll need to go to the library, see if they have those newspapers. But I want more than the date… I want to know… that it really happened the way I remembered. The way the social worker told me."

"Why would she lie?"

Erin looked down at the book in her hand. "I don't know."

❧

Having already taken one morning off to supervise the destruction of her garage, Erin couldn't leave Vic in the lurch another day, so they were up in the wee hours of the morning as usual, baking bread and muffins in the bakery and arranging them in the display case. Vic penned the labels, as usual, and they stopped for their own breakfast break before opening the store.

"I can't believe how hot it is already," Erin complained, fanning herself. She wasn't used to the Tennessee summer heat, and even though they had air conditioning and it was early, it was already uncomfortable in the kitchen with the combination of the weather and the ovens.

Vic nodded. "That's why we invented iced tea," she offered, putting a glass on the counter at Erin's side. Erin sipped it and wiped her forehead.

"It's going to be a long day."

A few minutes later, Erin flipped the front door sign to 'Open,' and they let in the small clump of early-morning shoppers. Most of them were regular customers, there to pick up a muffin or other treat for breakfast before work. They would be followed by the before-school crowd, and then a few more who did their weekly or semi-weekly bakery runs Tuesday mornings. Then Vic and Erin would take a break to have their sandwiches before the lunchtime rush.

"Always smells so good in here!" Bertie Braceling declared.

Erin was surprised to see his round, smiling face so early. When he stopped by, it was usually later in the day.

Bertie was one of her challenges. His unique and extensive list of allergies and intolerances made him practically impossible to bake for. But Erin was determined to do it. She had succeeded in developing a properly flexible tortilla recipe that worked for him—at least it would until he developed a new allergy to one of the ingredients—and a just-add-water pancake mix so he could make pancakes for himself at home, but so far, she had not been able to come up with a quick bread that wasn't mushy or a yeast-risen bread that wouldn't collapse on cooling. It seemed like it should be a simple matter of swapping in a flour that he could tolerate for one that he couldn't, but each one had different properties and she hadn't found a recipe that would work consistently.

"Hi, Bertie. Hey, I was thinking about egg substitutes. Have you ever heard of aquafaba? It's kind of the new big thing in eggless cooking…"

"Otherwise known as chickpea brine?" he asked. "Yes, I've tried it, but…"

"Doesn't it work like they say?"

"Oh, it seems to work just fine. Nice properties. But it gives me terrible heartburn."

"Oh." Erin sighed. "I should have known."

"It's funny," Bertie mused, "since I am fine with chickpeas themselves, and with chickpea flour, if it is properly soaked and fermented… but I don't think our bodies were designed to consume the cooking water…" He gave a low chuckle. "I am enjoying the pancakes, though, and I thought I'd pick up some more mix."

"Sure," Erin agreed, giving him a smile. She ducked into the kitchen to retrieve a batch of 'Bertie's Batter' stored in one of the lower cupboards. "Anything else?" she asked, before she could stop herself. She knew there was nothing else that he could actually eat.

"No, not today, pumpkin. I still have tortillas in the freezer."

As she rang up the purchase for him, he leaned in closer to her.

"What exactly is going on at your house today?" he asked. "The town is buzzing about this hush-hush police investigation going on. First knocking down your garage, and now… with all the new equipment there today…" he trailed off, waiting for her to fill in the details.

"I really can't talk about it," Erin said. "The police department wants it kept quiet until they have something ready to report to the public. Right now, it is just all speculation."

"Well, there is a lot of speculating going on! What exactly do they expect to find? I assume there wasn't any Confederate gold in the walls of the garage?"

"No, no treasure!" Erin laughed. "Really, Bertie, I can't talk about it. But if they find anything, they're sure to do a press release right away."

"The usual sources are mighty quiet."

Which Erin assumed meant Melissa Lee and Clara Jones, two rather indiscreet members of the support staff who normally kept the public well-informed about what was going on in the police department. Terry had intentionally kept the women in the dark about the investigation until they actually had something to report, which hadn't been easy.

"I'm afraid I can't help you. They are trying to keep it out of the public until they know something for sure."

He shook his head. His face was still wreathed with smiles, but there was something else in his eyes. Disappointment that she wouldn't spill the beans? Just curiosity?

"Well, I suppose it can't be too long before they either find something or don't find something. They're not going to knock down your house if they can't find anything in the yard, are they?"

"Oh, no," Erin rushed to assure him. "It wouldn't be in the house. The garage was built—" She cut herself off, not finishing the thought.

Bertie nodded. She hadn't told him anything, and yet she had. He now knew something about the timeline, at least, of the police case. The era the garage was built in.

"You get out of here," Erin said sternly. "I'm not telling you anything else."

With a laugh, Bertie retreated. "Toodle-oo, then. We'll talk about it later!"

He left the shop. Vic looked over at Erin. "What a scamp."

Erin laughed. She looked at her phone to check the time, wondering how things were proceeding at the house. If Bertie was right, and she had no doubt that he was, the police department was apparently hard at work looking for any sign of Adam Plaint's body. Terry would call her when they found anything. Or would he? She wasn't actually privy to what was going on with the police investigation, but she was the one who had provided them with the tip that Adam Plaint's body might be under the garage. He would at least tell her whether they had found anything, even if he couldn't give her any details.

The phone rang while she was looking at it, and Erin nearly dropped the phone. Vic giggled.

"Is it Terry?"

Erin shook her head. She tapped to answer the call. "Hello?"

"Erin, it's Sarah, from the vet's office."

"Yes...?" Erin was afraid to ask how the rabbit was doing. She didn't want to jinx it, or to make Sarah feel bad if the rabbit had not made it through the night.

"Just called to let you know that your rabbit is still doing well. In fact, he's pretty perky this morning. I think he's going to make a quick recovery."

Erin's smile stretched wide. "That's great news! Thanks for calling."

"You bet," Sarah's voice was warm. "Probably Doc will call you later on today to plan out his recovery, or you can come over here after work to visit your friend and talk to the doctor."

"We'll probably come by. What time are you open until?"

"Officially six, but we're usually here a while after that, so just ring the bell if it's later."

"Great! Thanks again."

Erin hung up and beamed at Vic. "The rabbit. Looks like he's going to be okay."

"Yay! Good news." Vic stepped over and gave Erin a quick hug. "I'm glad he's okay."

They both went back to serving the customers. Erin saw looks exchanged among them, and her stomach tightened. They had been dealing with people thinking that she and Vic had an intimate relationship for a while, and any action or word that could be misconstrued by them was. And the word spreading that Vic was transgender just seemed to spur rumors on. Erin looked over at Vic, rolling her eyes, and they went on with serving customers without comment.

It wasn't until mid-afternoon that Terry called. Erin took the opportunity to duck into the kitchen for privacy, and applied a damp towel to the back of her neck.

"Terry, what's up?"

"We were successful in recovering human remains."

Erin took a deep breath and let it out slowly. She tried to keep her mind focused on Terry's words rather than letting it rabbit off in other directions. She opened one of the ovens to check on a batch of cookies, even though there were still two minutes left on the timer.

"Are you there?" Terry asked. "You okay?"

"Yeah. Just trying to process that. It has to be Adam Plaint, doesn't it? There's no question of that?"

"Officially, the remains have to be identified. We can't just make that assumption. But taking your Aunt Clementine's journal into account... we know that the Plaint boys filled in the concrete the day after their father disappeared. So, it's pretty certain that it's his body. Too much of a coincidence for it to be someone else."

"Yeah. Oh, those poor boys. I just can't fathom. What it must have been like for them to be forced to bury their own father." She thought of her discussion with Vic the night before. "Assuming they were forced to do it."

"I think we can assume that it was under duress," Terry said dryly.

"Unless one of them killed him. If it was one of the boys, Angela might not have even known."

"What motive would they have to kill their father?"

"We don't really know. People keep secrets."

"They do," Terry agreed.

"Okay. So, what's next?"

"Your property is now officially a crime scene. You won't be able to live there for a few days. But you weren't anyway, so that's not a problem. Your contractors will be forced to take a few days off. We'll finish our scene investigation, and then you're free to rebuild."

Erin nodded. "That doesn't sound too bad."

"We're going to have to issue a press release right away. People have been rubbernecking all day, and now that they've seen evidence being removed from the site, there will be a clamor to know what happened. So, expect a lot of questions."

"Right. We already had Bertie Braceling and a couple of others here asking questions."

"I'll have Davis in for questioning, since he's the only one left in the family to ask any questions of. But having dealt with him before on the arson rap... I'm not expecting to get anything out of him. Unless he wants to unburden himself about what his mother did."

"I can't imagine... knowing that one of your parents killed the other."

"Usually when it goes that far... it doesn't come out of the blue. Chances are, there had been fighting and abuse going on for years before it came to a head. So, it may not have come as a shock to the boys, but it would still have been traumatic."

"You think Angela was abusing her husband all those years?"

"From what I've heard about her since her death, she certainly had the personality for it."

Erin thought back to the couple of times that she had faced Angela Plaint. She had been a formidable woman. Angry and bitter, not willing to listen to anything Erin had to say. And Melissa had described her as bullying and publicly humiliating her children. Not the kind of woman Erin would choose to be around. "If the way her kids turned out is any indication, she wasn't a very easy person to live with."

Terry made a choked sound. "One commits suicide, one disappears, and one is a drug addict, and as far as we can tell, a murderer and an arsonist. Yeah. I think that might reflect a rough upbringing."

"Will you be able to come by tonight? Let me know how it all goes?"

"I don't know. Depends how long it takes. And I won't be able to tell you much about the case. Can't be leaking details of an active investigation, even if it is a cold case."

"Okay. Well, come by tonight if you can. Otherwise, tomorrow?"

Terry cleared his throat. Erin waited for him to reiterate that he wasn't going to be able to give her any details. But he apparently decided against it. "Tomorrow, then."

Erin said goodbye, and hung up the phone. She took a few more long breaths, took the cookies out of the oven, and then returned to the front of the shop. Vic looked sideways at her.

"Everything okay?"

"Yes."

"You look kind of pale. Was it…?"

"It was Terry." Erin lowered her voice to avoid being overheard by the customers poring over the display case.

"And…?"

No matter how low she chose to speak, it was going to get out. Lottie Sturm was there, and she liked to spread news at least as much as Melissa Lee and Clara Jones. She was watching Erin like a hawk, her girlish blond pigtails flopping ridiculously behind her head. It was an absurd style for a mature woman, and Erin didn't know why no one bothered to tell her so. But she wasn't going to be the one to do it. Erin had a suspicion, looking at Lottie's intent expression, that even if she whispered, Lottie would be able to read her lips. She *was* a professional gossip.

Erin abandoned any attempt to be discreet. The police department was doing a press release. There would be a special run of the town paper. But before the print hit the streets, everyone would already have spread the news far and wide.

"He confirmed they found human remains."

There was a shocked gasp from Lottie. The other customers looked on with wide eyes. Vic nodded. She was unruffled. It was, after all, what they had both been expecting. She turned back to the customers.

"Who was next, then? Mrs. Sturm, have you decided what you want…?"

Lottie ignored Vic, staring at Erin. "Human remains? Who found human remains? Where?"

"The police department has been conducting an investigation," Erin told her calmly. "They'll be making a statement."

"An investigation into what? Where? Under the garage on your property? They knocked it down yesterday and didn't find anything!"

"That's because it was under the concrete."

She looked further shocked and horrified at this. "Who was buried under the concrete? How did they find this out?"

Erin supposed she should be grateful that they weren't accusing Clementine of foul play, since it had been her property at the time. Erin's thoughts veered off to an Arsenic and Old Lace scenario of Aunt Clementine entertaining gentlemen callers. She had to suppress an inappropriate smile at the thought.

"They haven't yet identified the remains," Erin said. "They have to go through that procedure now."

"But they must know! They must have some idea what happened, or how would they know to look for a body there? How did they know?"

Erin looked at Vic. Vic didn't give any indication of what Erin should say, or if she should just stop and let Terry Piper handle all of the questions.

"Did you want some cookies, Lottie? There are people waiting…"

"No. I want to know what happened, that's what I want. Whose body? How did they know to look under the cement for a body? Explain it to me!" Lottie's round face was growing red. Erin wasn't sure why she was acting like Erin owed her an explanation. It didn't have anything to do with Lottie, she was just being a busybody.

"That garage was built twenty years ago," Erin said. "I wasn't around way back then. I can't tell you what happened. You'll have to wait for the police investigation."

"They must have told you something! They couldn't just knock your garage over and dig it all up without telling you something!"

Erin opened her mouth to answer, and Mary Lou Cox came in the door. She was a regular customer of Auntie Clem's, but it wasn't her usual time to come, and she stepped into the bakery just a little bit faster than she normally would. She looked her usual professional self, with a well-tailored suit and her smooth, ash-blond hair in a short bob. Not a hair out of place. And yet she seemed just a little distressed. Something in the way that she moved more than in her smooth, mild expression. Her eyes went around the bakery and she smiled pleasantly.

"Good afternoon," she greeted, and she got in line, focused on the display case in front of her.

"Twenty years ago," Lottie repeated. She looked around at the other ladies, scowling. "What happened twenty years ago?"

"What do you mean?" Mary Lou asked.

"Clementine's garage was built twenty years ago. How could there be a body underneath it? Was it an old burial site? Indian graves? Early pioneers or Civil War casualties? Bald Eagle Falls has a rich history, you know. People are finding arrowheads and gold coins and other kinds of artifacts all the time. Why not human remains?"

There was silence in the bakery for a few minutes. Erin looked helplessly at Vic. There was nothing they could do to hurry the women along in their purchases. They were going to stand around and discuss the breaking news, and they were not going to be deterred.

"Oh, my," Mary Lou said. She reached out to steady herself, but there was nothing to hold on to. Erin stood rooted to the floor, afraid Mary Lou was going to faint and knowing she wouldn't be able to get there in time to catch her.

But Mary Lou didn't faint. She looked at Erin with wide eyes, and again repeated, "Oh, my."

Erin took a deep breath and let it out. *Oh, my indeed.*

"Adam Plaint," Mary Lou said. She continued to stare at Erin, waiting for confirmation. "Adam Plaint disappeared twenty years ago."

"No…" Lottie said in a low, horrified tone. "You don't think…?"

Mary Lou shook her head in disbelief. "I always thought he had left her. I know Angela was fond of saying that she had gotten rid of him, but I never thought… I always believed that he left her. He just couldn't stand to live with her and her ways anymore, and he took off. I always pictured him… happy somewhere else, in a new life, maybe with a new family. I never thought… that she had killed him."

"Don't jump to conclusions," Erin warned. Though, of course, that was what she had done in the first place. That was how they had found Adam Plaint's body. Because Erin had jumped to conclusions. From reading about Adam Plaint's disappearance and his sons faithfully filling in the concrete of Clementine's garage foundations and pad the next day.

"But that's it, isn't it?" Mary Lou said. "That's why he never came back. Not when his son disappeared, or his daughter died, or anything. He disappeared without a trace twenty years ago, and never made contact with his children again."

"We don't know for sure," Erin reiterated. "They haven't officially identified the remains. That will take time."

"Incredible. All this time. Under Clementine's garage."

"It's a wonder he didn't haunt her," Lottie said. "Maybe that's what killed Clementine. He appeared to her and she had a heart attack."

That was going too far. "Clementine wasn't haunted," Erin said flatly. "And she didn't see a ghost and have a heart attack. She was unwell for some time before she died. She had to close up her shop and retire, because she wasn't well. And it wasn't because she was being haunted. I've read her journals, and she was *not* haunted."

"Not that she said," Lottie said in a sullen tone.

"Not at all."

Lottie looked over her audience and decided to let it go at that.

"But that means…" Mary Lou trailed off.

Erin knew that Mary Lou had realized that Angela had not been the one to dispose of the body under the foundations. She couldn't have carried a man's body there, and she wasn't the one who had poured the cement.

And Mary Lou had teenage boys at home. Erin had heard from more than one source what great boys they were. Like Trenton, they did well at school, were athletic, and they worked to help support their family. Davis had not been on the fast track for success, but he had still been part of it, working with his brother to install the concrete pad for Clementine. Mary Lou shook her head slowly, and Erin knew that she was thinking about her two teenage boys, and how awful it was that the Plaint boys had been involved in such a sordid, senseless thing. Erin nodded her agreement.

"I know," she said softly. "I know."

Mary Lou took a deep breath. She stepped past the other customers who were not making any move to make their purchases and looked at the baked goods in front of her. "I think I would like some of those marshmallow peanut butter bars," she declared. "My boys have always been partial to peanut butter bars, and I think they deserve a treat." She nodded for emphasis. "I was just going to ask you how your inventory of Jam Lady was holding up, but I think I owe them something sweet, to show them how much I appreciate them."

"Of course," Erin agreed.

Vic leaned down and used a pair of tongs to count out twelve of the peanut butter bars for Mary Lou. Mary Lou always got twelve, never a baker's dozen, so that the treats would divide up evenly among the family members. Two boys and her husband, Roger. Mary Lou got the rare blueberry muffin for herself, but would probably never consume anything as calorie-laden as the rich peanut butter bars.

"Our jam supply is good," Erin said, nodding her head to indicate the small pyramid of jam jars on top of the display case. The Jam Lady jams were a great up-sell for the bakery fresh bread, and Erin and Vic had been true to their word and never even hinted at the fact that they knew who the Jam Lady was. Not a lady at all, in fact, but Roger Cox, Mary Lou's husband. Though proud of his new venture, Roger preferred to remain anonymous and leave everyone guessing as to who the Jam Lady really was.

"What? Oh, good. Very good." Mary Lou received the box of dessert bars from Vic, and paid Erin at the till. "Well, I expect we'll be hearing all of the details of this whole affair very shortly. Is the police department making a release?"

"They're working on it right now."

"Good. What a shocking thing. Whoever would have thought that he was right there, under Clementine's garage, the whole time. I wondered… when he didn't show up after Angela's death. Or after Trenton's. I just always thought… he had left."

Mary Lou paid for her treats and left, still shaking her head in shock and dismay.

There was silence in the bakery for a few seconds following Mary Lou's departure. Erin could feel the tension in the air. People trying to decide whether to just make their purchases or to keep talking about the grisly discovery.

"I always thought he ran away with a woman," Lottie broke the silence. "Everyone including his wife knew he was having an affair. When he disappeared…" Lottie gave a shrug. "It just made sense that he'd gone away with her. After all, who would stay with Angela Plaint?" Lottie paused "Not to speak ill of the dead, of course, it's not like she didn't have reason to be bitter."

"He was having an affair?" Erin repeated. Why was this the first time she had heard this? Adam Plaint's disappearance had been discussed numerous times, but she'd never heard this tidbit. Lottie looked around at the other customers, but they avoided her eyes.

"I'm not one to spread gossip," Lottie said. Erin struggled to keep her face expressionless. "But everybody knew it at the time. He weren't worth a plug nickel as a husband."

No one came to Adam Plaint's defense, but they weren't going to participate in Lottie's slander, either.

CHAPTER 4

*E*rin did her best to close up in good time, but with people hearing the news of the body found under Clementine's garage floor, everyone wanted to come in and gossip about the horrible goings-on with the person most affected by the news. Erin supposed that Davis was probably the person most affected by it, but he was not available to the public like Erin was, as he happened to be occupied with the police. She eventually just had to flip the sign to 'closed' and ignore the subsequent knocks on the door so that she and Vic could tidy up and prep for the next day.

So, it was later than she had planned when they finally got to the vet's office. There were still lights on; Erin rang the bell as Sarah had instructed. Sarah came to the door a few minutes later and peeked out at them. She smiled and nodded and unlocked the door to usher them inside.

"I wasn't sure whether you were going to make it," she commented. "A few more minutes, and you would have missed me."

"Thanks for letting us in," Erin said. "We just wanted to have a peek at him…"

"Have things been pretty crazy over at Auntie Clem's?"

Erin looked at Vic, an eyebrow cocked for her response.

"Like an asylum on a full moon," Vic drawled, getting a laugh out of both of them.

"I figured, when I heard the news, that you might not be able to make it over. I'm glad you did."

She didn't delay in taking them to the back rooms of the vet's office, where several cats and dogs languished in cages built into the wall. Erin looked eagerly for the rabbit and found him on one end, on the top tier of the cages.

"Oh, ain't he the sweetest thing…" Vic poked her fingers through the bars at the rabbit. "Oh, Erin, you have to keep him! You are, right? You're going to take him home once he's all better?"

Erin felt like she was dealing with a ten-year-old.

"I've never had a rabbit before. I don't know the first thing about taking care of them…"

"You didn't ever have a cat before, either, and you've picked up on that pretty quickly."

Erin had to give her that. Orange Blossom had become such an integral part of Erin's life so quickly, it was hard to imagine living in Bald Eagle Falls without him. She felt like she had always had him.

"But a rabbit is totally different than a cat…"

"Not so much," Vic said. "They're easy to take care of. You said you can't release him, right? He's not native, so it's bad to release him into the environment." The rabbit hopped to the front of the cage to sniff at Vic's finger protruding through the bars. Erin wanted to warn Vic that she could get bitten, but the rabbit didn't seem inclined to do anything like that. "Just look at him," Vic cooed in a voice that was usually reserved for Orange Blossom. "He's just as sweet as sugar. Come on, Erin, you have to keep him…"

"Well, I suppose I have time to think about it," Erin conceded. She wasn't promising to take the rabbit. She already felt guilty for leaving Orange Blossom alone for so much of the day. She wasn't sure about taking on another pet as well.

"Not so much," Sarah said apologetically. "He's going to need a new home pretty quick. He doesn't need to stay here until the bone is all healed. He can go home with a cast. There's no special care required, other than making sure it doesn't get wet. He doesn't seem inclined to chew on it, and he's getting around all right. The other foot only has superficial wounds. The bandages can come off in a couple of days."

"He's going to be out in a couple of days?" Erin repeated in alarm.

"He can go home tomorrow, if you're ready. There's no need to have him taking up a kennel here."

"Oh, boy. I'm not ready for that…"

"I'll help," Vic offered. "We just need to get a cage. And food. And bedding. He's practically tame already."

"He's not, though. He was probably born wild. He hasn't had any contact with humans before this."

But she had to admit that the rabbit didn't seem too disturbed by the people gathered around his cage. And he didn't bite or run away from Vic.

"Maybe," Erin finally conceded. "Let me think about it…"

The next evening, Officer Piper dropped in on Erin and Vic to hear their news about the new rabbit and to give them what details he could, few though they were, about the investigation into the human remains that had been recovered.

Orange Blossom was cuddled up on Erin's lap, so she let Vic answer the door. The cat looked up as Terry entered with K9 at his side. He gave them a glare, but apparently decided not to move from his warm, comfy spot, so he didn't hiss or stalk off as he usually did, but put his head back down, curling his tail around his nose, and kept one eye on the intruder.

"Good boy," Erin praised, patting him and giving his ears a rub. "You know that K9 isn't going to bother you, don't you?"

Terry smiled and sat down on the easy chair rather than on the couch where Erin was sitting, to give Orange Blossom a bit of space.

"He's starting to get used to us."

"I think he's fine with *you*. It's just your partner he has a problem with."

"Species discrimination," Vic contributed.

Erin could see the dimple in Terry's cheek, even though he pretended stern disapproval at Orange Blossom. He settled back into the easy chair like he hadn't been able to sit down all day. K9 lay down at his feet, sighing noisily.

"You two look like you've had a long day," Erin observed.

"I'm used to long hours. And even disagreeable citizens. But interrogations of murder suspects is a little out of my wheelhouse. It's really not like you see on TV. That always makes it look like a picnic. Like improv. The cops threaten, wheedle, or trap suspects into confessing in a five or ten minute scene. Bang, bang, boom, they're done and the case is solved. And of course, the suspect is convicted and gets a nice long sentence."

"Not the way it happens in real life?" Erin guessed.

"Not by a long shot. If you watch some of the news magazine shows, you hear about nine-hour interrogations, but you don't actually see how that works. You see the thirty seconds before the suspect confesses. It's like magic."

Vic sat down on the couch beside Erin. "Whenever I hear about those nine-hour interrogations, it's always about whether they coerced a confession."

Terry nodded. "At that point, it's all about wearing the suspect down. Breaking them. And what comes out then… isn't always the truth."

"Were you talking to Davis all day?" Erin asked.

There was a pause while Terry considered what he should say. "I talked with him for quite a while… but we don't have anything to hold him on. Once he decides he's done, he's free to go. And guys like Davis… they know their rights. They know they can just walk out. He's not afraid it will make him look bad. His goal is just to get out of there."

"He didn't say anything?" Vic cocked her head and pushed a lock of long, blond hair over her ear. "Confirming it was Uncle Adam, or that it was Aunt Angela who killed him… or anything?"

"No. He's better off just keeping his mouth shut, and he's experienced enough to know it."

"But if he said his mother did it, he couldn't be charged with anything, could he?"

"He could be charged as an accessory."

"When he was a child?" Erin objected. "If his mother forced him into it —" Erin looked at Vic. "*If* she did, they can't hold him accountable for it, can they?"

"It all depends on the circumstances," Terry said. "Are there thirteen-year-olds who are guilty of premeditated murder? Who are culpable? You bet there are. But if it was Angela who killed him, and she forced the boys to help her, that becomes less clear. They could have gone to someone else for help. They could have called the police or confessed to your aunt. But Davis especially was young and in a difficult position, still under his brother's control even once they were away from Angela."

"There's no one left to dispute his story," Vic pointed out. "Why doesn't he just admit to it? Say that it was his mother, and that she and Trenton forced him to help dispose of the body. That would leave him in the clear, wouldn't it?"

"It might. But right now, we don't have any proof that he had anything to do with it, just the circumstantial evidence that he was there when the concrete was poured. He could argue that he didn't know there was a body there. Someone else had covered it with a layer of gravel and he didn't ever see it. Trenton and Angela did it and he didn't know. No one would be inclined to believe him, but he could argue it."

"So, why doesn't he? Why doesn't he just get his story out there, so people can see he is being forthcoming, instead of looking like he's guilty?"

Terry raised his eyebrows, and his mouth quirked slightly. "Ever hear the line 'anything you say can and will be used against you'? As soon as he opens his mouth, he locks himself into a story. If we find anything that contradicts his story, we can show he lied. And that points to guilt more than anything else. A guilty mind."

"But how is it better to say nothing? Everybody is just going to assume he's guilty."

"It doesn't matter what everyone in town thinks. Everyone in town thought that Angela ran her husband off twenty years ago, and apparently, they were wrong. What matters is whether he can be charged and convicted. And Davis has lived out there in the real world long enough to know how the system works. Better to be gossiped about than to be in prison doing hard time."

K9 let out a grumble and shifted positions. Orange Blossom's claws dug into Erin's leg in response.

"Ouch," Erin protested, lifting the cat up to detach his claws. "No claws! He's not doing anything to hurt you."

"I wonder how he's going to behave with the rabbit," Vic said.

Erin blinked at her. She hadn't even thought about how the two animals were going to get along together. She had a hard enough time wrapping her mind around the idea that she was going to have to take care of a rabbit as well as a cat. Would it be in a cage? Hopping around the house? In a pen in the back yard? She'd never owned a rabbit before, but she'd also never had any friends who owned rabbits, so she had no idea what they were like as pets.

"How do cats and rabbits usually get along?" she asked Vic. "Would you have to keep them separate?"

"I don't think so. The rabbit is little right now, but he'll be almost as big as Blossom once he's grown. He'll be able to defend himself."

"Would Blossom attack him? I don't want them fighting."

"I don't think so." Vic looked at Terry. "You don't think he would, do you? You've had pets."

"Generally, if they're raised together, you don't really have to worry about it. Orange Blossom is still hardly more than a kitten, and the rabbit is juvenile too. They'll probably be curious, but I think the rabbit is too big for him to consider prey. Little pink newborns, that would be another story, but the rabbit is tougher than you think. He's already on his own."

"This is getting complicated. I never even planned to have a pet and now I'm going to have two."

"It will all work out," Vic said. "I'm sure it will be no problem."

William Andrews stopped in at the bakery during the afternoon lull. He didn't like it when it was crowded, and the townspeople tended to shun him, so he was pretty adept at judging when it would be safe to drop by the shop.

"I hear you're adopting another little one," he commented to Erin, as Vic took his water bottle back into the kitchen to refill it for him.

"Can't keep anything a secret around here," Erin laughed, rolling her eyes.

Willie raised his eyebrows. "You'd be surprised. This town is full of secrets."

"Well… I guess I'm starting to find that out too. Things aren't always as they appear on the surface, are they?"

Willie gazed at her, his eyes serious. She had the feeling that he had something important to say to her. But Vic returned with the water bottle and handed it across the counter to him, and Willie broke eye contact and gave a smile that encompassed them both.

"Just make sure you don't get in the way of any of those secrets," he said lightly. "People can be very sensitive about having their dirty laundry aired."

"Like I haven't learned that," Erin agreed. That lesson had been drilled into her head and had left her with a severe concussion. She had been lucky to get out of it alive. She was alive thanks, in part, to Willie. "Don't worry, I'm not poking around."

He gave her an assessing stare, and then turned to look at Vic. "Is she?" he demanded.

"She's letting the police department do the investigating," Vic said, but her eyes wandered over to Erin as she said it. It was a conspiratorial look, like they were pulling something over on Willie.

"I am!" Erin insisted. "Do you think Terry would let me have anything to do with a police investigation?"

"He hasn't been able to keep you out of them before. Just… I don't want to see you getting hurt, Erin. I'm serious. There is more… there are things going on here… you've only scratched the surface, and I don't want you getting hurt."

Erin rubbed at a smear of chocolate icing on the counter, unable to look him in the eye. She wasn't investigating. She had asked questions, but Terry wasn't going to tell her anything that was confidential. All they had talked about was whether Davis might have had something to do with his father's death, and whether there was any way he could be convinced to talk or prosecuted for whatever part he might have played. She wasn't even sure how anyone would know that they had been talking about the case. Other than perhaps noting Terry's squad car parked in front of her rented cottage and deducing that they might be talking about the body found in her yard.

"I don't know what other secrets this town might have to hide. I'm not the one digging anything up. I'm leaving that all to the police. I promise."

She could feel him looking at her still, the whites of his eyes contrasting so sharply with his black-stained skin, and she couldn't look up.

"I remember Adam Plaint," he said slowly. "I'm sure everyone has different memories of him. People have romanticized him over the years. The man who disappeared. Out there somewhere, living a completely new life, finally free of his harpy wife's influences. The handsome, mysterious man."

"That does sound sort of romantic," Vic admitted, her voice soft. He'd been her uncle. She'd probably seen pictures of him. Heard the story told at family get-togethers. She'd probably heard plenty of speculation about where he had gone and why.

"Don't believe it." Willie's words were sharp and biting. He didn't raise his voice at all. But he clearly had a message for both of them. "It's been twenty years, and people's memories get fuzzy. They make things up. Change the old stories. There was nothing romantic about Adam disappearing. And if his wife had something to do with it, maybe she had provocation."

Erin looked up at Willie, surprised at the sharpness of his tone. Had Adam been abusive? Maybe one of the boys had killed him, or there had been a fight and he was killed accidentally. Was it possible that Angela had actually been justified? Maybe protecting her children from her husband?

"What kind of provocation?" Vic asked. "You mean an affair?"

Willie took a quick glance behind himself to make sure that he was the only customer, and that there was no one approaching the door. "Didn't I just say to stay out of it? Digging into people's secrets is dangerous."

"How can it be dangerous?" Erin disagreed. "They're all dead, other than Davis. And he's got everybody's eyes on him right now. I don't think he can take two steps without people watching him."

"He's not the only one left. Adam had friends. Other family. So did Angela and the kids. You don't know how far people will go to protect the memories of their loved ones. And Davis Plaint has not been neutralized. He's still a threat. He tried to kill you once. Don't forget that."

Erin had been trying to forget it. She kept telling herself that there was nothing to be worried about. She wasn't a threat to Davis, so he was no longer a threat to her. She didn't know anything that could put him behind bars, despite what he had thought. Even now that Adam's body had been discovered, she still didn't know anything that could put him behind bars.

Terry had said not to worry about Davis. He kept a close watch on her and Vic, making sure they were safe, driving by the house for random checks. Keeping on top of Davis and making sure he knew he was being watched.

But it wasn't enough. Terry was there to protect the whole town. He couldn't be worrying about her all the time. He wasn't her personal bodyguard. How was Erin to protect herself from Davis? He had tried using fire the first time. What if he moved to a more direct or lethal approach? What if he tried to shoot her or run her over with his car? Terry wouldn't necessarily be there to help.

"Do you own a gun?" Willie asked, reading her expression.

"No. I don't think I ever could. Even if I had one, I don't think I could fire it. It's just not in my nature."

"I can shoot," Vic offered.

Erin glanced at her in surprise. Vic always seemed so gentle and kind, Erin couldn't imagine her ever taking a gun in hand, let alone learning how to use it. "You can?"

"Sure. I grew up 'round here. Shooting squirrels and any other varmints that my mom didn't want around. I'm pretty handy, actually."

Erin shook her head. "I can't imagine you hurting any living thing."

Vic gave a wide shrug. "There's a difference between a pet and a critter that's going to wreck your house or your livelihood. You have to be able to keep them separate in your mind. And as far as shooting people goes… I've never done it, but if someone was coming after me or you, you can bet I wouldn't hesitate."

"Good." Willie nodded his approval. "Then you need to get a gun. You girls are almost always together, so that puts my mind at ease a bit more about Erin. But most of all… stay out of other people's business." He looked Erin in the eye. "You understand me? Don't take any chances. Just stay out of it."

Erin nodded. "I am," she agreed faintly.

The bells on the door rang, and Willie nodded his thanks for the water and for the cookies he had purchased, and slipped out the door.

CHAPTER 5

Far too soon for Erin's comfort, Doc told her that the rabbit was ready to come home and he needed to free up space in the kennels. There was no point in her paying extra to have the rabbit boarded there when she could just as easily have him at home. He didn't need any medical care that she couldn't manage, and he needed to get used to them and his new home.

They had a cat carrier for Orange Blossom. The rabbit didn't seem to mind it like the cat did. He kicked out once or twice with his hind legs, rapping on the side of the carrier, but then he settled in and just crouched there, waiting.

"It's just like a little burrow," Vic said. Erin didn't know whether she was trying to convince the rabbit, or Erin, or herself. "He feels all nice and comfy and safe in there, because it's like a burrow. Cats don't like it because they don't live in burrows. They like to be out in the open."

Erin didn't know about that, but she did know that Orange Blossom didn't like the carrier. She should have listened to Terry, who said from the beginning that the best way to take a cat to the vet was wrapped up in a towel. It was much easier than trying to stuff a cat into a cage or carrier.

Vic held the bunny carrier in her lap in the car, trying to make the rabbit feel as safe and unthreatened as possible. She kept it steady, not letting it tip as the car went around corners or to bump against the inside of the car.

"I'm sure he feels very safe," Erin told Vic, peeking in at the rabbit. He seemed placid and unconcerned by the trip or the new surroundings. Erin, who kept hearing about how easily rabbits could be frightened to death, was happy her rabbit seemed to be of a hardier disposition.

"Are we going to introduce him to Orange Blossom?" Vic asked, as they walked up the sidewalk to the cottage.

"I don't know. Don't you have to keep them apart for a few days?"

"I think that's when you're introducing two cats to each other."

"What are you supposed to do with a cat and a rabbit, then?"

"I have no idea. I guess we leave the rabbit in the carrier and let Orange Blossom smell around it? Just see what he thinks and how he reacts while the rabbit is safe inside?"

"Okay. That sounds all right."

As soon as Erin opened the door, Orange Blossom was yowling and winding his way around their legs. Vic didn't pick him up like she usually did, already holding on to the rabbit carrier. Orange Blossom put his front paws on Erin's legs, reaching up and batting at her in a bid for attention. Erin put down her purse and picked the cat up.

"Hello, kitty," she whispered. She held Orange Blossom up to her face and breathed in his familiar scent. "We have a surprise for you today."

"Do we ever!"

Orange Blossom paid no attention to the visitor to start with. He was too busy getting loves and cuddles from Erin. He purred loudly and bumped his head up under her chin. Erin scratched his ears and under his chin, murmuring to him. But eventually, she put him down on the floor next to the rabbit carrier.

"There. What do you think of that?"

Orange Blossom turned away from the carrier with disdain. His previous experiences had not endeared him to the carrier. But then the rabbit moved inside the carrier, and the cat's ears riveted on it. He sat, staring at it intently, ears forward, every inch of his body alert. He didn't look at Vic or at Erin, just kept staring at the carrier.

Vic giggled. Orange Blossom's ear flicked in irritation, and then it was pointed back at the carrier again. He crouched low, his tail snaking back and forth, irises big and black. Erin could see his nose quivering as he sniffed the air, getting the rabbit's scent. He had to know by now that it wasn't just one of them making the noise, as they sometimes did when they played with him. It was independent of Erin and Vic, with a smell all its own. Even Erin could smell the musky scent of the rabbit, something new that they hadn't ever had in their house before.

Orange Blossom crept slowly closer to the carrier.

"The mighty hunter," Vic whispered.

Again, Orange Blossom's ear gave one irritated twitch, and he remained focused on his new discovery. He approached the carrier and smelled it around the outside, pushing his nose in close against it. But he couldn't see into the covered carrier and had to go around the end in order to peer in.

When he reached the end and looked inside, his eyes got even wider. Vic broke into a fit of giggles. "Just look at him," she said. "He can't believe it."

Orange Blossom finally looked away from the carrier at Vic, his body language clearly projecting *what have you done?*

"It's just a rabbit," Erin found herself explaining to him. "It's not like it's anything that's going to hurt you."

"And you're not going to hurt him," Vic inserted sternly. "Neither of you is going to hurt the other one."

"I don't think he can understand you," Erin pointed out.

"But he could understand you saying it wouldn't hurt him?"

"Uh…"

Vic had proven her point and didn't bother to push it any further.

Blossom sniffed around the end of the carrier with great attention, as if he might miss something. Erin wondered how much more sensitive his nose was than hers, and what information he was getting from his investigation. Could he smell certain chemicals in the rabbit's scent, telling him what kind of creature it was, its sex, or its age? Was there a scent that indicated that it was hurt? Erin imagined Orange Blossom could still smell the vet's office on the carrier and the rabbit. The place was full of harsh cleaners and antiseptics that carried a strong smell. And there were other animals there, cats and dogs and other pets. Could Orange Blossom smell each of the other animals that had been close to the rabbit, or only the rabbit himself? She'd love to know exactly what Orange Blossom could smell. But on the other hand, she often found her own sensitive nose to be an inconvenience, making her leave the room because of smoke, perfume, markers, or other strongly offensive smells. And it kept her from being able to try sushi or other seafood, gagging at the smell even if it were someone else's order. At least there wasn't a lot of sushi in Bald Eagle Falls. Beef, pork chops, or hot chicken, even Chinese takeout, but not sushi.

Orange Blossom looked around both sides of the cat carrier, and then back inside again. He tried to snake his paw in between the bars of the front to touch the rabbit. But the rabbit remained at the back of the carrier, out of reach.

"Come out and play-ay," Vic sing-songed to the rabbit.

Orange Blossom put his ears back and turned to look at Vic.

"Sorry!" Vic laughed. She looked at Erin. "Should we open it up? Let them meet each other face-to-face?"

"I don't know. What if he attacks it?"

"He's not going to do that," Vic said. "Are you, Blossom? Blossom wouldn't do anything to hurt it."

She picked Orange Blossom up to cuddle him and talk to him some more, but the cat struggled to be put down, and Vic complied, setting him back on the floor to continue his explorations.

"We need a name for the rabbit," Vic said.

"Here it comes."

"What?"

"Do you have something in mind?"

"Well… yeah, I do… unless you were thinking about something…"

"No. I don't know what to call him. What's a good rabbit name?" Erin was thinking about Beatrix Potter. Flopsy, Mopsy, Cottontail, and Peter. Any of those would be a good name. Even if the rabbit wasn't a cottontail, he still had a tail that looked like cotton.

"I was thinking… Marshmallow."

"Marshmallow?" Erin frowned. "But he's not white… not all white. He's got a lot of brown…"

"Like a toasted marshmallow," Vic maintained.

"A toasted marshmallow. But we're not going to call him toasted, right? Just Marshmallow?"

"You don't like it? What was your idea?"

But Erin didn't have any intention of arguing for a different name. She hadn't been so sure about Orange Blossom's name, but it had stuck. She couldn't imagine him with any different name. If Vic thought that Marshmallow was a good name, Erin was okay with it.

"No, I don't have any," she assured Vic. "If you think he's a Marshmallow, I'll go with that. As long as you're sure."

Vic nodded. "I think it's a really good name, don't you? He's so nice and fluffy and round, and the white and the brown… just like a toasted marshmallow…"

"Okay. Sure. Marshmallow it is."

Vic smiled broadly. She crouched down to look into the carrier with Orange Blossom.

"How do you like that, little guy?" she asked. "Do you want to be called Marshmallow? This is Orange Blossom and you guys are going to be great friends! Do you want to say 'hi' to him, Orange Blossom?"

Despite the fact that they hadn't agreed to let the rabbit out of the carrier or the cat in, Vic undid the latch on the carrier and swung the little door open. Orange Blossom pushed his head into the carrier, but didn't go all the way in. The coarser hairs on his back twitched as he investigated the new visitor. In a moment, he was reversing, pulling his head back out and backing up quickly. The little rabbit hopped placidly out of the carrier. He gave a little jerk of his back foot, making the cast snap against the floor, and Orange Blossom took a leap backward.

Erin couldn't help laughing along with Vic. Orange Blossom gave them both a haughty look, and retreated, jumping up onto the couch. He perched on the arm of the couch and looked down at Marshmallow as he hopped around, exploring the room.

"He's not tame," Erin pointed out. "How are we going to catch him again? Rabbits are fast."

"We'll catch him."

"What if he pees on the rug? Mrs. Potter will not be impressed."

"He won't," Vic assured her. "They like to have just one place where they poop and pee."

"What if that place is here?" Erin pointed at the rug beneath her feet.

"Well, keep him off of the rug, then. We can clean up the floor easily enough."

Erin moved over slightly to block Marshmallow from moving onto the rug. He stopped, and while he didn't look directly at her, Erin was sure he was examining her, trying to figure out what she was and if she were a threat. He nibbled at the fringe of the rug.

"No, don't do that," Erin protested. She stepped forward and made shooing motions with her hands. "Get back. Leave the rug alone."

Marshmallow turned and hopped in the other direction. Not in a hurry, like he was scared. Just a leisurely place, exploring his new environment. Erin and Vic stood watching him, and Orange Blossom continued to watch from his perch up on the couch.

Erin hung up the phone, frustrated, and sat with it on her lap, staring at it.

"Are you trying to explode it with your eyes?" Vic inquired, looking up from the slim newspaper she was reading in the easy chair opposite Erin.

Erin gave a short laugh. "That doesn't sound like such a bad idea right now actually," she admitted. "Why does it have to be so hard to get ahold of my records? Shouldn't I automatically be allowed access to my own information? And I'm my parents' only living relative, so shouldn't I be entitled to their information? Who else can act on their behalf? It seems to me their next of kin should be able to get access to it without having to call the President of the United States."

"They won't give you anything?"

"There is so much red tape… no one has come out and said I can't get it, but I have to find the right person in the right department in the right town… the files are only available in paper form, wherever they are… stored in a warehouse somewhere, so once I do find the right person, I'm still going to have to wait for them to be retrieved, assuming they haven't already been destroyed."

"Can they do that? Destroy your files?"

"Sure. They're only required by law to hold them for a certain length of time, and they have record destruction plans. Who knows, I may be chasing ghosts. Files that don't even exist anymore."

"But somebody knows what happened. What about contacting the social worker who handled your case after your parents' accident? They'd remember."

"But to find out who that was, I have to have access to the records. I don't remember the name of the social worker. Or even the first foster family I was with. It was so long ago and I went through so many different homes."

Vic thought about this, staring off into the distance. After a while, she turned her eyes back to Erin.

"Maybe it's better you don't know what happened. Maybe DHS is just protecting your interests. If you don't remember what happened to you when you were seven or eight, maybe it's because it was so traumatic. I can remember a lot of what happened to me when I was that age. Lots of details. I remember the names of all of my school teachers, so why don't you remember the names of your foster parents? Or when it was that your parents died?"

"You're younger than I am," Erin pointed out. "I've had ten more years to forget. And I went to new homes more often than you got a new teacher. You probably went to the same school your whole life, didn't you?"

"Well... yeah..."

"So you knew all the teachers in the school, even before you had them. You knew them for twelve years and you just barely graduated. For me, it's different. It's twenty years since I was in that home, and I was in completely different places every year or so."

Vic nodded her understanding. "You didn't find anything at the library?"

"No... it's a good thing it's a weekly paper instead of a daily. My eyes still hurt from looking at all of that microfilm. But... nothing. No obituary. I checked all the way from May to September. No obituary. No mention of the accident. I did find a couple of articles that mentioned Adam Plaint's disappearance..."

"Anything juicy?"

"It was all pretty barebones. There has been concern over the abrupt departure of Adam Plaint... no missing persons report has been filed... no police investigation..."

"How could the police never have investigated when he just disappeared like that?"

"Because his wife told them not to."

Vic's forehead wrinkled. "But wouldn't she have been a suspect in his disappearance? They'd have to get corroboration from someone else, wouldn't they? Maybe even track down Uncle Adam and talk to him to confirm he wasn't the victim of foul play?"

"I don't know. Small town police department. Maybe they figured Angela was an upstanding citizen and there was nothing to be concerned about. People do abandon their families. Just take off and start a new life somewhere else. If they figured that was what had happened…" She shrugged. "Who knows? They must have been satisfied that he was okay, for one reason or another."

Vic tilted her head, looking down the hallway for Orange Blossom. It was strange not to have him there in the living room, cuddling with them or playing games. But since they had settled the rabbit in his cage, Orange Blossom had been sitting watching him, and hadn't returned to the living room to socialize.

"So what are you going to do?"

"It's not anything to do with me," Erin said. "I'm leaving it to the professionals."

"No, I mean about your files. Are you going to be able to get them?"

Erin sighed and looked down at her phone. "Yes… I've got some more calls to make. If they're out there, I'm going to find them!"

Friday was just a normal day at the bakery. Erin felt like she had been holding her breath all week, and had finally been returned to normal. She'd barely thought about the body that had been buried in her back yard, the rabbit, or Vic's problems being accepted by the community. It was just a normal day focusing on baking and serving her customers. Mrs. Foster, the mother of Peter, her favorite customer, came by for cupcakes and some bread to get them through the weekend and, as always, was full of praise.

"You don't know how nice it is not to have to bake bread all the time, or to go into the city to stock up on frozen gluten-free bread that really isn't very good. Peter is always so happy to have nice, soft bread like his sisters. And real baking." She beamed. "I'm just so glad to have you here in town, Erin."

"Thank you," Erin couldn't help smiling back. "I'm so glad to be able to provide a service. I know how hard it is for kids like Peter to try to fit in with their friends, when they can't eat what everyone else is eating. If there is ever anything particular that he needs that I'm not selling, just ask me. I'll see what I can do."

"You're just the cat's pajamas," Mrs. Foster declared. "Truly, you are."

Erin laughed a little as Mrs. Foster left. She looked at Vic. "Did you hear that? The cat's pajamas."

Vic was staring out the window, not paying any attention to Erin. Erin looked at her for a minute.

"Earth to Vic… earth to Vic…"

"What? Oh. Sorry. What were you saying?"

"What's wrong? What are you thinking about?" Erin refrained from pointing out that she thought it had been a pretty good day for Vic, without a lot of people pushing back and telling her how she ought to live her life. Vic did not need Erin bringing it up. If something that someone had said was what was bothering Vic, she'd let Erin know. She was pretty open about it.

"Uh… Willie. He was going to call me last night, and he didn't. And I haven't seen him around today. It's been so hot, I was sure he'd at least need a water bottle refill, but I haven't seen him anywhere today."

Erin glanced out the front window. It wasn't the most logical thing to do. She knew that Vic had just been looking out, trying to spot Willie Andrews. Erin wasn't going to turn around and see him standing there.

"Maybe he's doing something that took him out of town today. Just about anywhere would be cooler than the town square. Maybe he's couriering evidence on the Adam Plaint case today. Taking it into the city for analysis."

"They already sent everything."

"They might have found something else. Or he might be working for someone else. You know how he is. He's always doing something new."

"Yeah… but he didn't call me."

Erin had to admit that was unusual. Willie knew that Vic had feelings for him, and while he wasn't interested in her romantically, he was always considerate and a good friend. If he said he was going to call, he called.

"You're right. That is strange. Well… hopefully, he just got a rush job, and maybe he didn't have cell coverage when he tried to get ahold of you. Or dropped his phone in the lake." Erin laughed. "It happens!"

"Yeah, maybe." Vic gave a wan smile, trying to look like she wasn't going to worry about it anymore, but Erin knew better. Vic had such a tender heart. She was easily hurt by slights, even though she tried to tough it out and pretend she wasn't. And she attracted a lot of disapproval from the Bald Eagle Falls residents.

So they both continued to work as if there weren't anything to be worried about. Erin had already been splitting her attention between digging into her own history and worrying over her house and the discovery of Adam Plaint's body, she wasn't sure she could fracture it one more time. But William Andrews's failure to call Vic or put in an appearance wasn't something that had happened twenty years before. It wasn't a comfortable old mystery to dig into. It was really worrying, because if something had happened to him, they might only have a limited amount of time to figure out what it was and help him…

"Can we close early?" Vic asked, casting another glance at her phone. They had both been covertly checking the time every few minutes since Vic had expressed her worries about Willie.

"Will it be any better if we go home? We're just going to be worried there instead of here."

"I want to talk to Officer Piper. I'm really worried."

"Okay," Erin nodded. "You go ahead. Flip the sign over and go see where you can get with Terry. I'll finish up here and catch up with you later on."

Vic breathed out and didn't even try arguing that she should stay and help Erin until everything was taken care of. She just headed for the door to turn over the closed sign, and started untying her apron before she was even back to the kitchen. She murmured her thanks and goodbye to Erin, and was gone.

"She really is worried about him," Erin said to the empty room.

Erin caught up with Vic while she was still at the police department, sitting at a desk with Officer Piper. K9 lifted his head to look at Erin and sniff in her direction, and then he put his head back down. Erin realized with a pang that she should have brought him a doggie biscuit from the bakery. He was always disappointed when he didn't get one either at the house or at Auntie Clem's. Terry looked up at Erin as she came into the room, and rubbed the space between his eyebrows.

"Erin. Thanks for coming."

"Is it okay? Do you want to talk to us separately?"

"You aren't witnesses to anything as far as I'm aware. I don't need to get your stories separately." He shuffled some papers in front of him. "How long has it been since you have seen Willie?"

"Not that long... he was at the bakery the other day... Wednesday, I guess...?" Erin looked at Vic for confirmation. Vic nodded.

"And did he say anything about what his plans were? Whether he was going out of town, or out to one of his mines?"

"No, not to me. He was just talking to me about..." Erin felt heat rising to her cheeks. "About not getting involved in the Adam Plaint investigation. And I haven't! I've stayed out of it."

Terry nodded, his mouth twitching slightly.

"So, that was all. But he told Vicky that he was going to call her..."

"I already told him," Vic said flatly.

Erin glanced at her and then back at Terry. "I know it hasn't been a long time, but he always calls back. You know how he is. When he says he's going to do something, he's reliable."

"He usually is," Terry agreed. "But he has a lot of commitments and can be called out on a job on a moment's notice, too. Or, like any man, he can get wrapped up in what he's doing and forget that he was supposed to make a call. I'm not sure it's anything to be concerned about at this point."

"You called him, Vic?" Erin asked. "No answer?"

Vic nodded. She looked away from them, staring at the blank wall and blinking. "Yes. I called yesterday and it just rang through to voicemail. I called a couple of times today..." Probably more than a couple, Erin suspected. "And it's just going straight to voicemail now without ringing. Like the battery is dead."

"Or the phone is off. Or doesn't have a signal," Terry suggested. "If he's in a mine, he won't be able to get a signal."

"He didn't say he was going to be. He said he'd call me."

"I know. But even Willie Andrews can make a mistake. We don't want to get into a panic over nothing. It's been twenty-four hours since you expected to hear from him. I haven't noticed him around town on my rounds today. I'll make a few calls to see whether anyone else has him out on a job and I'll knock on his door. Then we'll see. I may start the ball rolling then."

Vic opened her mouth to protest, then looked at Erin. She let out her breath. "Thank you."

Terry waited for more, then nodded. "I know you want me to get out a search party, but we can't jump straight into search and rescue, when we don't even know whether he is missing or where he was last seen. I have to take it one step at a time. The first step is to establish whether he's really missing or not."

Erin could see Vic's Adam's apple bob up and down as she swallowed.

"How long do you think that's going to take?" Erin asked.

"Longer than you would like. I can't promise any timelines."

"Can you search his credit card or his phone? See when and where they were last used?"

"Not before I establish that he actually is missing and open a case. He has his right to privacy. He could just be… working or out of town."

Erin tried to read Terry's expression. She knew him pretty well, but when he had his police face on, she couldn't always tell what he was thinking.

"Do you think he's on a job? Or seeing someone else?"

Terry gave her a long blink and gave nothing away.

"I couldn't tell you. I have no way of knowing before I start investigating."

"Maybe he went to see family," Erin said to Vic. "I don't know anything about his family. Are his parents still around? His grandparents? There could have been a family emergency."

"He doesn't have any family around here. Not that he associates with. And he would have called me."

Erin could think of plenty of circumstances under which Willie wouldn't have been able to call Vic to let her know what was going on. "What if he had to leave in the middle of the night? Or was so distracted by an emergency call that he completely forgot he was going to call you?"

"I thought you would be on my side, not his," Vic indicated Terry with her eyes.

"Nobody is taking sides. Just pointing out there are logical reasons he might not have answered his phone or have forgotten to call you."

"It's just as likely that he's sick or hurt. Or murdered! He wouldn't be the first one in this town to be murdered!" Vic's voice was getting louder and gruffer. A pink flush was rising to her cheeks.

"He hasn't been murdered." Erin tried to calm Vic.

"You're jumping to unwarranted conclusions," Terry said. "There's no reason to think that anything has happened to him. I understand that you are off-balance because of the murders that have taken place, but none of those have anything to do with William Andrews. He didn't even know the Plaints. He's only been in town for a few years."

"That's not true," Erin disagreed, turning back to Terry with a frown. "He knew Adam Plaint. He said he did."

"I remember him moving to town four or five years ago."

"Then he must have moved *back*. Because he knew Adam Plaint and his family. That's one of the reasons he was warning me off."

Terry leaned back in his chair, making it creak alarmingly loudly. He rubbed his chin, his half-day-old whiskers rasping under his fingers.

"He knew Adam Plaint."

"Yes."

"And didn't want you near the investigation."

Erin nodded impatiently.

"And then at some point after he tells you to stay away from the case, he goes missing."

"Right."

Terry stared up at the ceiling for a few minutes, considering. "Maybe I'll ask Davis if he remembers Willie. Or if he's seen him the last couple of days."

"He's not *involved* in Uncle Adam's death," Vic objected. "He didn't have anything to do with that. That's not what he was saying. Just that people could get upset if Erin went around turning up people's secrets again."

"Again?" Erin challenged.

"Did he say whether he knew Angela Plaint?" Terry asked, bringing his chair back down to level.

"No, he didn't say anything like that," Vic snapped.

"He just said… that maybe if Angela had been involved in his death, she'd had plenty of provocation," Erin said reluctantly. Vic shot her a dark look. But Erin couldn't help it. That *was* what Willie had said. She wasn't going to lie about it.

"What kind of provocation?"

"He didn't say. I don't know. I thought maybe he meant another woman. Or, I don't know, maybe Adam was abusive, and she or one of the boys was just defending themselves… Honestly, he was telling me to stay out of it, so I couldn't exactly demand to know details. He just said… that Adam was no saint. People's memories might have become colored over the years. Distorted. They might be making him into a romantic figure… when he really wasn't."

Terry pulled a different file over to himself, and opened it up to jot some notes inside. It was a pretty thin file for a murder investigation. Erin had always thought that murders took up big thick binders, and boxes of papers. But it was only the beginning. The investigation was not even a week old. The file would surely grow over time.

"That's all I think I need from you tonight," Terry told Vic. "Unless there is anything else you can think of that I should know. I know you'd like me to move faster and with more vigor on this. If there's anything you know that you are holding back, you should let me know…"

"No." Vic shook her head. "I don't have anything else. I've told you everything I could think of that might affect your decision. I don't have anything else to tell you."

"Okay. Thanks for letting me know. I'll start making those phone calls right away. And… I'll let you know what I can. Tell me if you hear anything from him. Phone, email, text, anything. Even a word. I want to know about it."

Erin and Vic both nodded. They got up and headed for the door. K9 got up, looking like he would follow them, then stopped when he saw that Terry wasn't going out with them. He lay back down, making a grumbling noise.

Erin could relate. She knew how he felt.

CHAPTER 6

It took Erin a long time to get to sleep, with all of the week's worries and stresses weighing down on her. She knew that most of it was beyond her control, and she should just try to relax and sleep, or she would be groggy in the morning when it was time to get to work.

But that was more easily said than done.

Orange Blossom jumped up onto the bed in front of her face with a querulous *mrrow*, making Erin jump in surprise. The cat had been lurking around the rabbit cage so much since Marshmallow's arrival, Erin hadn't expected him. He circled around Erin and sniffed at her. He nudged her chin with his forehead, expecting pats and attention. Erin scratched his ears and chin.

"You need to settle in and go to sleep," Erin whispered to him. "It isn't playtime. It's time for sleep."

He took another circuit around her, then eventually stopped at her belly and started to knead the blankets, making a sleeping nest for himself.

"Okay," Erin murmured. "Now go to sleep."

She said it as much to her own brain as to the cat. She needed to do the same thing. Dig down, get comfy, and put herself to sleep. The next day would come far too early if she didn't.

She tried to slow her breaths and her heartbeat. She counted Orange Blossom's breaths as he made little old-man wheezes in his sleep.

And then she was dreaming. To begin with, she knew it was a dream, but as she got pulled further into it, the dream became more vivid and she forgot that it wasn't the truth.

It was raining. She was in a car. It was dark. Erin was frightened. She was watching the rain come down outside her window, trying to focus on what was outside the car instead of what was inside.

"You owe it to me," a woman's voice said. Erin thought that it must be her mother. But she couldn't remember what her mother sounded like or looked like.

She formed the word 'Mommy' on her lips, but the sound didn't come out. Nothing came out. The other two people in the car might as well have been there alone. They paid her no attention. And maybe that was all Erin was. A ghost of the past. Or of the future. Just an observer of what had taken place twenty years before.

"I owe you?" the man's voice was harsh. "I did what I did for you. I think you're the one who owes me. Don't you think?"

Erin didn't know what they were talking about, and that made the loud voices seem even more threatening and frightening. She tried again to call to her mother, but she couldn't. She just sat there in the back of the car, watching the rain pour down outside and run in streams down the other side of her window. That was all she could do. On the other side of the car, the other back window was not rolled up all the way, or was not sealed properly, because rain was getting into the car and making a wet spot on the other seat. Erin looked away from it, not wanting to get into trouble for pointing out the problem. Her mother would just get angry at her.

But even when she didn't look at it, she could still smell the rain and the wet upholstery, so strongly that it amazed her that no one else did.

"And what do you think we're going to do now?" The woman was speaking again. "Just carry on as if nothing has happened? Hope that no one will figure it out? Come on. You know that's not going to work. You can't just pretend that it didn't happen."

"No one knows anything." The man tried to soothe Erin's mother. To make her feel better so she would stop shouting at him and be happy again. Erin knew how he felt. She didn't like it when Mommy yelled either. She only liked it when Mommy was happy. And that wasn't very often anymore. When she had initially picked him up in the car, she had been happy, but then they had started to argue, their moods getting darker and darker, until it was as nightmarishly dark inside the car as it was outside. At least outside, there were streetlights. Inside the car the darkness was so thick she could almost feel it.

～

Erin awoke gasping for breath. She sat up, disrupting Orange Blossom, taking in gulps of air as if she were drowning.

"No!" she said aloud. "No, no, no!"

She reached over, knocking things off of her bedside table, fumbling to find the switch on the lamp and to fill the room with light. She had to be able to see. She had to be able to see everything around her in order to know that it had just been a dream. She had only been imagining it. That thick, inky blackness could not reach her.

"Erin?" She heard Vic's voice outside her door. "Are you okay?"

"Vicky?" The name caught in Erin's throat, and she coughed and sobbed and tried to get control of her emotions.

Vic turned the handle and pushed the door open cautiously. They didn't go into each other's rooms. The last time Erin had opened Vic's door uninvited and gone in to where she slept, it had been when the house was on fire. When she had good reason for breaching the privacy of Vic's bedroom.

"It's okay," Erin told her, snuffling and trying to stifle further sobs. "It's okay, come in."

Vic opened the door the rest of the way. She squinted into the lamplight. "I heard you calling. Are you sick? What's wrong?"

Erin tried in vain to slow the wild beating of her heart and the sobs that kept welling up in her throat.

"A dream. I just had…"

"Wow. That must have been one humdinger of a nightmare." Vic walked the rest of the way to Erin's bed, her white nightgown fluttering around her. She sat on the edge of the bed, picking Orange Blossom up and holding him in her lap to make space. "You okay?"

She rubbed Erin's shoulder to soothe her. It felt good, and Erin was glad that she wasn't the only one in the house. She didn't have nightmares often, but it was nice to have someone there to tell her that it had just been a dream and everything was going to be okay.

"It was… I don't know if it was just a dream, or a memory. I haven't ever had one quite like that before…"

"What happened? Do you remember?"

"I was in the car. With my mom and my dad. They were fighting, and I was scared."

Vic nodded. "It's really scary for kids when their parents fight. Parents are supposed to get along and make them feel safe. When they start fighting with each other… it's like the child's world might collapse."

Erin tilted her head to the side slightly.

"Did your parents fight a lot?"

"Not a lot. I don't know. How do you compare it to someone else's parents? Everyone is different. Did yours?"

"I don't ever remember them fighting. I mean… except for this dream. To tell the truth, I don't really remember them at all. I think that's who I dreamed about, but it could have been any foster parents. I was the only kid in the car, and I think all of my foster families had other kids… so it must have been my real parents, right?"

Vic nodded. "Must have been. What did they look like?"

"I don't know. They were in the front seat of the car, and I was in the back. So I couldn't see them, I could only hear them. It was… really dark."

"The dark can't hurt you. And dreams and memories can't hurt you. Just try to relax and you can go back to sleep and have a nicer dream. One about… kittens and bunnies and puppies…"

"We're not getting a puppy."

"Little roly-poly, fuzzy puppies. So cute you can't wait to pick them up and cuddle them."

"I'm serious, Vic, we have enough animals to look after…"

"Just imagine it. To help you have nice dreams. Here's Blossom." Vic put Orange Blossom back down on the bed, very close to Erin's face. "He'll help you to go back to sleep again and not have any more nightmares, won't you, Blossom?"

Hearing his name, Orange Blossom started to purr loudly. Erin laughed and cuddled him close. She had always wanted a pet while growing up, being shuttled from one foster home to another. She had never been allowed to have one, but she had spent many lonely nights wishing that she had something warm and alive to hold instead of a lifeless pillow. Or wishing that she had a dog to guard her when bad things happened.

"He's so nice and fluffy," Erin said into Blossom's fur. She got tickles of fur up her nose and sneezed. At least Orange Blossom was used to this reaction now and didn't jump down and leave in a huff.

"Yeah," Vic agreed. "You just hold him and think of how nice and soft he is, and the bunny, and have nice dreams now."

"Okay."

Vic stood up. "Do you want me to shut the lamp off?"

"No."

"You want to sleep with it on?"

Erin nodded, settling back in to sleep. "Yes."

"I could never sleep with it on." But Vic left it as it was and didn't try to persuade Erin to turn it off to go to sleep. None of Erin's foster parents would have allowed such a thing. But then, she had usually been sharing a bedroom with at least one other foster sister, and the light would have kept them awake.

Vic shut the door quietly behind her and went back to her own bed. Erin closed her eyes and tried to go back to sleep, but at the same time was worried about falling back into the same dream again.

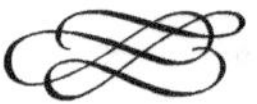

CHAPTER 7

It was never easy getting through the morning after a rough night. Erin couldn't take the luxury of sleeping in even for a couple of minutes. She had to be up and get things rolling, so that she could be at the bakery in time and get bread and muffins baking before the morning rush began.

Vic was tired as well, complaining about having to get up, but she rolled out of bed too and, after a cup of coffee and feeding the animals, they were both on their way.

The morning rush came and went and they were able to relax a little. The Potters came in for their weekly purchase and, as usual, the old couple dithered over the choices and took an inordinate length of time to decide what they wanted. Even though, by now, they had tested most of what Erin made, and could make an informed choice. Vic made faces at Erin while they weren't looking, and Erin was hard-pressed to keep up the small talk with the Potters while they tried to decide what to get.

When the Potters left, Vic headed toward the door to turn over the sign for their lunch break and Erin turned around to go into the kitchen, looking forward to the caffeine kick from another cup of coffee and a nice thick tomato and avocado sandwich.

"Uh—Erin?"

Erin turned back toward Vic. The younger girl had stopped before reaching the door. Before Erin had a chance to ask what was wrong, a figure reached the door and pushed it open, jangling the bells at the top. Erin was shocked to see Davis Plaint. He sauntered toward the display case, ignoring their reactions. Or maybe he didn't even see the effect he had on them.

"Excuse me," Davis sneered, as he bumped against Vic in his walk toward the baked goods.

"Hey—" Erin started to protest.

But Vic responded in a way that Erin had never seen her act before. She turned toward Davis and gave him a shove in return.

Vic might give the impression of frailty with her tall, willowy figure, but Erin knew from experience that her looks belied her sinewy strength. She was no pushover.

"Who the hell do you think you are?" Davis challenged, facing her with the ferocity of a bulldog.

"Oh, excuse me," Vic said in her most southern drawl. "I'm so sorry, Uncle Davis. How very clumsy of me."

"Uncle…?" Davis's eyes took on a new light. "Oh, you're that one. The —" his eyes flicked over to Erin, and he apparently thought better of calling her anything offensive in front of witnesses. "The Jackson girl."

"Your cousin," Vic agreed. "Your mama was my aunt."

They drew apart, and Erin breathed a sigh of relief that there wasn't going to be a fist fight in the middle of her bakery.

"I always liked working for her when I was younger," Vic went on. "She'd pay me for doing jobs for her. And give me cookies."

None of them pointed out that that had been while Vic presented as a boy, and Angela had not been nearly as nice when Vic had made an appearance as Angela's niece rather than as her nephew.

"She made good cookies," Davis admitted. He looked toward the cookies in the display case. "Not gluten-free crap like that," he sneered. "Real cookies."

"You've never even tasted Erin's cookies," Vic objected. She went back around the counter and bent down to grab a chocolate chip oatmeal cookie with a pair of tongs. She knew they were still warm from the oven. She put it in a paper sleeve and held it out toward Davis. He stepped forward, but didn't take it immediately. "First sample," Vic said, "on the house."

Davis took it from her with some reluctance. He looked it over like it was something gross on the bottom of his shoe. But Erin could smell the cloyingly sweet scent of the cookie and chocolate chips, still melted from the oven, and he must have also been able to. He brought it up to his mouth and took a bite. Surprise flooded over his features, and he chewed the first bite slowly, his eyes closing momentarily while he savored it.

"Real cookies," Vic said, her voice hard and pleased at the same time.

"Okay…" Davis opened his eyes and took another big bite. "These are good," he admitted around the mouthful.

"You'd better believe it. Erin knows how to bake."

Davis continued to chew, intent on the cookie. "I did wonder how a place like this could get so much business, even if it is the only bakery in town that is open right now."

Erin and Vic were both silent, not sure where to take the conversation next. The silence drew out as he ate the cookie, looking around.

"Are you still planning on reopening The Bake Shoppe?" Erin asked eventually. That's what he had told her, the last time they had talked.

Davis shifted his gaze slightly to look Erin in the eye, and she felt a chill. He hadn't just come into Auntie Clem's for a cookie, and all of the surprise and softness over her gooey chocolate chip oatmeal confection was gone. He was, once again, Angela Plaint's son. A murderer. One who had already tried to kill Erin once. They had never expected him to come straight into the shop like that. But he had obviously come gunning for her. Not literally, she hoped.

"You'd better believe I am."

Erin had a disconcerting moment of disorientation, not sure what he was talking about. And then she remembered. Opening The Bake Shoppe. He was still planning on reopening The Bake Shoppe. Last she'd heard, in order for him to make any decisions about the asset on his own, he had been told that he would have to find his father or prove that he was dead.

Had Erin done that work for him? With the human remains being unearthed from under her garage, everybody now knew that Adam Plaint had not just left his family behind. He was dead. And that made Davis the full owner of The Bake Shoppe.

"But I'm not here about that," Davis said. "Or to buy cookies." Though he spat the words out with distaste, Erin noted that he didn't make any show of throwing out what was left of the cookie.

Vic shifted into a closed stance, her arms folded in front of her.

"What is it, then?" Erin asked, when he didn't offer it himself.

"That boyfriend of yours," Davis said.

Erin thought first of Willie Andrews, and opened her mouth to challenge him, to ask where he had seen Willie, or what he had done to him. But Davis barreled on.

"Don't try telling me that the cop isn't your boyfriend. I've seen the two of you together. You've got him under your thumb. So I'm here to tell you. Back off. Get out of my business. Stop trying to block me with your stupid tricks. I know what you're up to."

Erin's mouth dropped open. She breathed in a few times, trying to compose words in an order that made sense, but she couldn't gather her wits.

"Erin hasn't done anything. What are you talking about?" Vic demanded.

"She's trying to ruin my reputation. Run me out of town. Prevent me from reopening The Bake Shoppe. She's so worried about losing her little empire here that she'll stoop to anything to stop me."

"No! I haven't done anything to you," Erin protested. She'd been careful to stay away from Davis. She'd never said anything about him in public. She was confident—or pretty sure, anyway—that she'd be able to keep Auntie Clem's Bakery running, even if Davis did reopen his mother's bakery.

"I haven't done anything," Davis repeated, taunting her in a snide falsetto. "I don't have any idea what you're talking about." Then he dropped back to his usual low voice. "You accuse me of trying to burn your house down. Of killing my own father. You tear up your own yard looking for some kind of proof of wrongdoing. Now you've got your cop boyfriend asking me questions about my father again, poking around my house and my place of business. How is a guy supposed to get a business up and running when there's someone like you around, doing your best to chase me out of town!"

He took a deep breath and Erin gulped, bracing herself for the next onslaught. But it didn't come. Davis just stood there, his eyes smoldering, staring at her.

"Officer Piper's searching your house?" Vic asked, grasping at the new information.

"You know he is. You two are the ones who sent him there!" Adam broadened his targeting, including Vic in the accusations. "You think the inept police department in this town would ever be there otherwise?"

"Neither of us sent the police to your house," Erin told him calmly. "Neither of us has anything to do with the police investigation. If he's there, it's because that's where his investigation has led him."

"I know it's you. You're the one that sent him to harass me, because you want me out of town."

"No," Erin shook her head. "I don't know what makes you think that. I haven't done anything against you. You decided out of the blue that I was trying to harm you, but I'm not. You can stay in Bald Eagle Falls and reopen The Bake Shoppe. I don't care. Go ahead. It's not going to hurt my business. I know what I'm doing," Erin motioned to the last bit of cookie still in Davis's hand, "and I'm going to continue to operate my business whether you're here or not."

"I didn't have anything to do with my father's disappearance," Davis snarled. "And I didn't have anything to do with Willie Andrews's disappearance. Nothing! You got it?"

Vic went rapidly pale at the mention of Willie.

"Who said anything about Willie Andrews disappearing?" Erin asked. "As far as I know, there hasn't been any missing persons case opened."

"Terry blasted Piper!" Davis exploded. "Don't pretend you don't know all about it. Don't pretend you didn't put him up to it. Andrews takes off all the time. Who's cared about it before now? No one. There's a reason people around here don't like him; did you ever think of that?"

Erin ventured a glance at Vic. "I don't know what you're talking about. We like Willie just fine."

Davis snorted. "Like I said."

Erin drew in a long breath. "Well, did you want to get anything? If not, I think it's time for you to leave."

"Think you can just kick me out of here and I'll leave you alone? Think again!"

Davis walked up to the counter and made a show of looking over the goods in the display case. "Been living on store-bought baked goods all this time," he grumbled. "But I don't suppose any of this is any better."

"You don't have to buy anything. You're welcome to leave."

"A dozen of the oatmeal cookies." He'd already tasted those, and he wasn't going to walk out empty-handed. "And what about these cheese stick and pizza pretzels…?"

Erin raised her brows. "What about them? Did you want some?"

"Is that real cheese? Or some over-processed vegan petroleum product?"

"It's cheese."

"Then I'll take… three each, of the cheese sticks and the pizza pretzels."

"Which pretzels do you want? These ones are just basic sauce and cheese, and those are deluxe, they have olives and garlic and some goat cheese…"

"Yeah, the deluxe. I don't follow any low-fat diet."

Vic counted out and packaged the goods and Erin rang them up on the till. "Can we do anything else for you?"

"Like I said, just stay out of my way—"

The bells jangled with the opening of the door, and Erin looked up as Davis handed her his payment.

Melissa Lee strode in with a broad smile that meant she had gossip to share, her wild brown curls bouncing frenetically. Davis turned quickly to see who had come in, his muscles tensing for confrontation. Melissa's smile disappeared and her generous mouth dropped open.

Erin didn't say anything aloud, but inwardly, she swore. She didn't know all of the details of the relationship between Melissa and Davis twenty years before, but she knew that Melissa had some very definite opinions on the Plaint family, and she had not wanted to ever see Davis again. Erin expected Melissa to turn and run back out of the shop, but she didn't. She just stood there, feet frozen to the floor, mouth open, eyes wide like a deer in the headlights.

There was a shocked silence while everyone took in the scene and tried to figure out what to do. Erin looked in Vic's direction without turning her head. Vic was always gracious and knew exactly what to do to put people at ease. It seemed like magic to Erin, who always felt like she was fumbling around in the dark as far as relationships were concerned. But Vic didn't step in with any magic words. She didn't say anything at all. And neither did Erin. Davis had told her to stay out of his business, so that's what she was doing. Just staying out of it.

"Melissa," Davis said, in a soft, stunned voice.

Melissa didn't answer at first. She ran her fingers through her curls. "I don't… I didn't know you were here," she said. But she didn't turn to leave.

"Just picking up some baking," Davis said, indicating the bag that Vic still held in her hand.

Vic looked down at it, then put it on the counter beside the till. Woodenly, Erin put the cash in the draw and made the appropriate change, reaching out to hand it to Davis.

He put her off balance. When they had first met, he had pretended to be friendly, as if he appreciated what she had done for his brother. He'd said she was a nice lady. And then he'd tried to burn her house down with her in it. The way that he had been ranting and raving—had that been the real Davis? Or another mask, this one designed to make her defensive and afraid? Was it all an act, or was he letting his true colors show? The man who stood frozen and somewhat bashful in Melissa's gaze was different again, not like either of the personas he had shown her.

"How are you?" he asked.

"Just fine." Melissa's mouth was a thin, straight line, and her voice was hard. "I'm just fine, thank you very much."

Erin had suggested once that Melissa must have been attracted to Davis. That she sounded like she liked him. Melissa had instantly protested the suggestion and said that she hadn't liked either one of them. Trenton had been a bully, smarmy to the teachers and cruel to other students—to people like Melissa, Erin assumed. Davis had been sadder, brooding. Erin could see that side of him. Tortured by whatever had happened in the past. He'd never recovered from whatever it was.

Erin again looked at Vic, hoping for some relief from the high-tension atmosphere. But Vic seemed at a loss as to what to do.

"You look good. Just like I remember. You haven't changed a bit," Davis said.

Melissa gave a fake laugh. "You've got to be kidding. With all of these wrinkles? I look like my mother."

"That's not such a bad thing. You look nice."

Was he just going to stay there, chatting her up in Erin's bakery, after the scene he had made? He seemed completely oblivious to where he was or that there was anyone in the room besides him and Melissa.

"I left messages for you," Davis offered.

"I know you did."

"You didn't return them. So I guess that means… you don't want to talk to me. You don't want to… have dinner… or anything."

Melissa shook her head.

"It wouldn't have to mean anything," Davis said. "It wouldn't be a date. Just two people getting together… for old time's sake."

"I don't want to remember old times. Things are different now. Back then… it's too painful. I don't want to get back together."

Davis nodded slowly. He must have realized that. Realized that there was a reason she hadn't been returning his calls.

"People aren't exactly lining up to welcome me back," Davis complained. "No one wants anything to do with me." He gave a bitter laugh. "It's like high school all over again."

"People have their reasons."

"People should get over the past. All of their talk about being Christian. Loving the sinner. Welcoming back the prodigal. Where's the forgiveness now?"

"Davis…" Melissa started, then stopped. She shook her head. Her eyes were wide. "They think… they think you killed your father. And Trenton. And tried to kill Erin and Vic." Melissa's eyes went to Erin. "They're my friends. People aren't just shunning you for things that happened back in high school. They're afraid of you."

He stared at Melissa as if this had never occurred to him. Being back in the town where he had grown up, he had reverted to old grievances. The outcast. The boy who couldn't make friends. How early had his drug use started? After his father had been killed, had he rolled up into himself, pushing everybody away? Not allowing himself to love anyone again? Or had he loved Melissa and she had pushed him away?

"Are *you* afraid of me?"

Melissa looked as surprised by the question as Davis had at the thought that people were afraid of him. She shook her head slowly. "I don't know. Maybe. I hadn't really thought about it."

"But you still don't want to see me. So you are just avoiding me for what happened in the past."

Melissa's lips pursed, then flattened into a line again. She fought some kind of internal battle, her cheeks getting pink. Finally, she nodded.

"Yes. I can't go through all that again. I just couldn't. I don't think you realize… how much it hurt me. How much it took out of me. I couldn't go through it all again."

"*You* didn't have to go through anything. It was hard for you to watch? It was hard for you to see my life swirling down the crapper? It didn't happen to you. It happened to me."

"I can't get involved. I told you before… we're not good for each other. It wasn't good for me, and it wasn't good for you."

"You don't know what it was like for me. You were the only one I had. And then you abandoned me too."

Erin felt like she was intruding by standing there listening to Davis and Melissa. But what was she supposed to do? Fade back into the kitchen? Remind them that they weren't alone? That they were standing in her bakery having an intimate discussion, not somewhere private?

"You were… you weren't ever going to be able to give me any emotional support," Melissa said. "I tried to give you what you needed, but you weren't ever going to be able to give me anything back."

"I was too damaged?" Davis sneered. "Sorry to disappoint you by being an emotional cripple."

Melissa just gave a helpless shrug.

Davis finally picked up his baking from the counter. He looked at Erin, and she thought at first that he was going to warn her again to stay out of his business. But he didn't. He looked at her without connecting, his eyes far away and full of pain. Erin wasn't even sure he saw her.

Then he headed for the door and walked out, making the bells on the door jingle, followed by silence.

~

"Well."

Vic finally broke the silence. She looked at Erin and then at Melissa.

"I didn't expect him to be here," Melissa reiterated. She seemed to be in a daze, lost somewhere in the past.

"So you two *were* friends," Erin observed. "The way you kept saying you didn't want to see either of them again, you made it sound like they were both your enemies. But only Trenton was. Davis was…?"

"Erin…" Vic gave her a warning look, and a slight shake of her head.

Melissa didn't appear to notice. "We were… acquaintances," she said. "I knew him. But… you heard…" She shrugged again. "He was… he wasn't someone who was easy to know. He didn't let people get close to him. And those who did… you wouldn't want to get sucked into it all. Like drowning in a whirlpool. Pulled into a black hole."

"And that's what happened to you? That's why you don't want to see him again? Because you don't want to get pulled down again?"

"You don't know what it's like to be around someone like that. Someone who is always down, negative, depressed. Someone who is so needy they'll suck the life out of you, and never say thank you, and never give anything back. You can't just keep pouring everything into someone like that."

"It sounds really difficult," Vic agreed. "Sounds like you need chocolate."

Melissa laughed, showing a real smile for the first time since she had walked in the door. "You might be right."

"Secret elixir for those who have been sucked dry," Vic declared. "I'm thinking cookies. Something that would go nice with a pint of Ben and Jerry's."

"The girl's on a roll."

Vic looked into the display case. Erin noted that she didn't suggest the chocolate chip oatmeal cookies. That wouldn't seem appropriate after selling a dozen of them to Davis. She needed something that had not been tainted by his mood and his accusations.

"Marshmallow chocolate fudge," Vic finally decided. She looked back up at Melissa. "How does that sound?"

"Like the perfect night. Give me a half pound."

Vic nodded, and weighed the fudge out for Melissa. "So… what's new?"

"Oh!" Melissa perked up. "I completely forgot when I saw Davis. The coroner hasn't confirmed the identity of the remains yet, but he's said it is a man in his forties. The approximate height matches up. They still need to get dental records or DNA to make a positive match. But it looks like we're on the right track."

Erin was amazed that she could talk about Adam Plaint as if she hadn't just been talking to his son. Melissa seemed to be able to completely separate the two ideas. To compartmentalize the emotionally distressing meeting with Davis and talk about the human remains as if it were a case that had nothing more to do with her than a TV show murder.

"How long will that take?" Vic asked. "And what would they compare the DNA to?"

"They can compare it to Trenton's. They have enough tissue samples to run a comparison. It's not conclusive, of course, but they should be able to tell if they are father and son. That way, we don't have to compel a DNA sample from Davis."

Erin glanced toward the door. Of course, Davis was long gone, out of sight. "He was pretty upset about the investigation. He thinks it's my fault Terry is searching his house."

"You heard?" Melissa was disappointed. "I was going to tell you that part too. Because we have three possible murders connected with the old Plaint house, Terry—excuse me, Officer Piper—was able to get a warrant to search the house. Davis didn't have to give permission and couldn't do anything about it. And believe me, he wasn't happy about it. The sheriff was there, and he said Davis 'bout blew a gasket. He was worried Davis was going to barricade himself in and we were going to end up with an armed standoff!"

"I'm glad that didn't happen," Erin said. "We don't need any more excitement around here."

Melissa's eyes shone. That was not the way she saw it. It was obvious that she thrived on the attention she got over any news from the police department.

"That's why he was in here, right before you came in," Erin said. "He thought I had put Terry up to it. And he wanted me to stay out of it and leave him alone."

"Well, I have to admit, we have had a lot more excitement than usual since you moved into town," Melissa teased. "Murder and mayhem."

"It's just a coincidence. I didn't put Terry up to anything."

"I know that." Melissa smiled. "But you *are* the one who suggested we might find Adam Plaint's remains in the foundations of your garage."

"That was just… that wasn't my doing. That was just a guess… after reading Clementine's journal and putting two and two together. And Terry could have said that it wasn't anything. That it wasn't worth pursuing. He was the one who made the decision to follow up and see if I was right."

"And you were."

Erin nodded uncomfortably. She rang up Melissa's purchase and settled up with her. Melissa took the little bag of fudge.

"Did Davis ever talk to you about his dad?" Erin asked, reluctant to let Melissa go without discovering a few more details first. "Back when you were teenagers? Did he ever talk about what had happened? Or what kind of a person his dad was?"

"He didn't have to tell me. I could see what kind of a person he was."

Erin wondered about that. So many people in Bald Eagle Falls were not exactly who they had seemed to be. Despite being a sleepy little town where everyone knew everyone else's business, there were an awful lot of buried secrets.

"What kind of a person did you think he was?" Erin asked.

She fully expected to get the answer that Adam Plaint had been a devoted husband and father. That he wasn't the type to leave his wife, or to abandon his children.

"He was... sneaky," Melissa said slowly. "I don't know a ton about his past; about how many people he had seen... whether he had been sneaking around on Angela for years... but I can tell you, he was a player. He wasn't the type of man who stayed home."

Erin frowned. "He had affairs, you mean."

"I don't know if he had a lot, or just one. But I know he was seeing someone else before he disappeared... before he died."

"How?"

"For one thing, the way Angela reacted when her sons wanted to date. If she ever caught scent of them dating or wanting to date... I heard her accuse them more than once of being... unchaste. Saying that they were like their father. They always hated it. Got really embarrassed by her."

"They weren't allowed to have girlfriends?"

"No. Not around home. They could get away with it at school, and no one thought anything of it, because that's what was expected of boys, especially Trenton. Big, strong, handsome guy. Of course he always had a cheerleader on his arm. But when he went home, he'd better not smell like perfume or have lipstick on his collar. Or Angela would be on the warpath about him dogging around. Just like his father. She would get out the Bible and start quoting scriptures to him about unchaste women and David and adultery... she could go on for hours..."

Erin shook her head. "Who was it his father was seeing before he died?"

"I don't know." Melissa spread her hands. "You'd have to ask someone older than I was. I was only fifteen at the time, I don't know who was seeing who. And it was all a big secret. No one was supposed to know about it. You may not have noticed, but people around here tend to be very judgmental. If you're not following the commandments. The big ones, anyway..." Melissa trailed off, looking at Erin and Vic and getting a darker red as she remembered who she was dealing with. "People get judgmental," she repeated lamely. "If you don't want to be judged, you have to keep it a pretty close secret."

"Why is it that appearances are so much more important here?" Erin asked. "Why does it matter more what it looks like than what's really true? Shouldn't the truth be the most important thing?"

"Well, yes, of course it is, dear. But appearances are important too… refraining from the very appearance of evil…"

"But isn't it more important to refrain from evil?"

Melissa hesitated. "I don't think you understand…"

Erin shook her head briskly. "Maybe I'm the only one who does."

Vic wanted to go straight home and to find out whether Terry had found anything out about William Andrews, but Erin had been putting off a trip to their storage unit for a few days, and she really needed to retrieve a few things. Not the least of which was Clementine's next diary. She knew it must have the details in it of Erin's parents' accident and deaths. She wasn't having a lot of success in getting any information from DFS and the hospital where she assumed her parents had been treated, or where their bodies had been taken after the accident. She had filled out more forms, but she had little confidence that she would be successful. They would call or write her back, telling her she had to go to a different department, or fill out a different form, or to look into another line of inquiry.

"It sounds like he spent a lot of the day searching the Plaint house anyway," Erin said. "I don't know that he's had any time to look into where Willie might have gone."

"Don't you care? I thought he was your friend too. Don't you care that he could be lying injured somewhere? Something terrible might have happened to him, and I'm the only one who seems to care about it."

"I care," Erin protested. "I just think… he's used to being a loner. He probably just went off to one of his mines and forgot that he had promised to call. I don't think that anything has happened to him. Just him… being a man."

She didn't confess her secret fear that Willie might be off seeing another woman. Especially not after all of the talk of the afternoon.

Vic shook her head, scowling. "He came and looked for you when you were in the cave," she pointed out. "He saved your life, helping Terry to search the caves for you."

She was right, of course. And it did make Erin feel bad for not being concerned. But when he had come to search for Erin in the caves, he had known where she was and that she was in trouble. With him, she had no idea whether he was in any danger or where to start.

"We'll go see Terry after this," she promised. "But I have to get this journal before the storage place closes for the night. They're not open that late."

Vic sighed in exasperation and folded her arms across her chest.

"It won't take long," Erin promised.

The man at the security desk for the storage unit was in his fifties, sloppily dressed, with what seemed to be a permanent leer. He looked Erin over slowly, his eyes raking her body, and then looked over at Vic. He licked his lips.

"Help you, ladies?"

"Erin Price. I have a storage unit here."

He was staring openly at Vic. "You got ID?" he asked Erin, not bothering to look in her direction.

"Yes." Erin took out her wallet and slapped it down on the desk in front of the man, trying to bring his attention back to business.

The man finally looked away from Vic, back down at Erin's driver's license. "Erin Price." He tapped her information into the computer, and waited for it to bring up the details of her unit. "This way."

As they walked down a row of closed, locked doors, the man inserted himself into Vic's space, walking as close beside her as he could without actually putting his arm around her.

"And what's your name, sweetheart? I don't think I've seen you around town before."

"Victoria Webster," Vic said politely, not looking at him. "I work at the bakery."

"At the bakery," he repeated slowly, brows drawing down. "The new one?"

"Yes."

He looked at Erin, and then back at Vic. His lip curled. "Then you're the…" He looked at her in the light of this new revelation. "You don't look like a boy."

"I'm not." Vic's voice was flat, her pronunciation precise.

"You're the assistant at the new bakery. I know all about you. You're a guy, dressed up as a girl." He looked again over her willowy figured, shaking his head. "You sure don't look like one."

Erin tried to catch Vic's eye, wondering what she should do or say. Vic was perfectly capable of answering for herself and handling the man, but Erin thought she should say something too, to show her solidarity with Vic. The man had to know that what he was doing was harassment, and couldn't be allowed.

"I am who I am," Vic said. "I look like myself. I don't see why it should make any difference to you what I look like."

"It matters to me if there are people like you walking around pretending to be girls when they're not. You're misleading people. Making them think you're something you're not. People should know when they look at you…" the man's lip curled up, "…what package they're getting."

Vic opened her mouth to defend herself.

"Leave her alone," Erin snapped.

The man turned back to her, looking astonished that she had jumped in. "Leave her alone? Leave *him* alone, you mean. Leave *it* alone. And no, I'm not going to leave it alone. What kind of an establishment do you think you're running? You can't run that kind of place in Bald Eagle Falls. You can't hire people like that. You can't be serving unsuspecting customers who have no idea what kind of… perversions… are serving them. You let *it* touch their food? Little kids go in there after school, and you let *it* stare at them? Talk to them? I don't know why you haven't been run out of town."

Erin stared at him, unable to think of what to say in answer to this vitriol. She shook her head, horrified.

"I don't know what they're thinking, letting your rent a storage unit here. You shouldn't be allowed to rent anything. It's a good thing someone tried to burn your house down. It's too bad they didn't succeed. Maybe then you would have left."

Erin ground her teeth. The shock was leaving, and in its place, anger was starting to swell and grow inside her. "I would not have left town," she said. "I would have built a new house. No one is going to chase me away.

This is where I live now. And this is where Vic lives. And if you don't like it, you can just take your business somewhere else."

"I do. I wouldn't set a foot inside your establishment. Not one foot. It makes me sick that I even have to talk to this… this *thing*." He looked at Vic, his proximity no longer just intrusive, but threatening. "People like you should be killed and displayed in the public square."

"That's enough!" Erin shouted. "You are a hateful person. If there's anyone who should be run out of town, it's you. If you say one more thing that is threatening or even rude, I'm going to call the police, and you can explain to them why you're behaving like this."

"Oooh, the police, I'm *scared*," the man mocked. But as he led the way down the hall, he kept his mouth shut. So maybe what Erin had said had had some effect on him after all.

He marched up to Erin's storage unit and unlocked the top lock. Erin had her key out at the ready and unlocked hers. "Thank you," she told him pointedly, and waited for him to go.

He stood there as if waiting to see what was in her unit. Exactly what did he expect to find? A room full of BDSM props or pornography? She couldn't understand why people thought that just because she was friends with a transgender woman, that meant she must be a predator or mentally ill, out to corrupt or hurt their children. She was the same person she had always been, and she couldn't even imagine doing something to intentionally hurt someone else or to lead them into some kind of evil practices.

She and Vic both stood there, waiting, and eventually the man could no longer pretend he had a legitimate reason to be standing there. He shook his head and reversed direction, walking back to his security desk.

Erin looked at Vic. "I'm *so* sorry, Vic."

Vic's eyes welled with tears. "Sorry for what? You didn't do anything wrong. You can't help it that there are people like him in the world. Even in Bald Eagle Falls. That's just a fact of life."

"But he's wrong. He's so wrong. You're a good person. You're not out to hurt or deceive anyone. I know that. I know you."

"I know," Vic agreed.

Erin opened up the storage locker door. It was a small room. Not really big enough for them both to get into at the same time, as tightly packed as it was with the contents of her house. Erin looked over everything slowly. She had promised that it would just take a few minutes to get in and out with the journal, but she had a sinking feeling that it was going to be a lot longer than that.

"Do you know which box it's in?" Vic asked.

"I know which box it is… I just don't know where that box is in all of this."

From Vic's expression, neither did she. Erin slid along the wall to the nearest set of boxes. The journals had been stored in boxes in Vic's closet, so she was looking for old boxes, not anything with the storage company's name on it or any of the plastic bins that had stored Clementine's sewing room supplies. Erin started going through the stacks of boxes, looking for something familiar.

"It will just take a few minutes to find…"

Without comment, Vic started around the other side of the unit, aiming for another stack of cardboard boxes.

Erin realized they should have labeled things better. She had Vic had put labels on the new boxes they had packed, indicating which room they were from and the general class of contents… books, dishes, ornaments, videotapes… But as for the boxes that had already been stored under beds and in closets, they hadn't bothered going through them and trying to label the contents.

She sighed and pulled an unmarked box down from the stack. She opened it up, saw hardcover books, and pushed it in beside the stack. She grabbed the next box in the stack, opened it up, and did the same. She moved on to the next box in the stack. Vic was doing the same thing on the opposite side of the room, both of them going through boxes as quickly as they could to narrow down where the journals were in the storage room. Vic was the one to find the first box.

"Journals!" she announced.

"Great, let's have a look!" Erin pushed the boxes she had been working with out of the way and squeezed around to the other side of the room. She looked down at the journals in the box, and could tell immediately that they were too recent. "Not that one, but it's bound to be in one that's close by."

Vic lifted another down from the pile and put it down. Erin opened it up and shook her head.

It was a few more boxes before they got to the right one, and Erin started lifting journals out and scanning the dates to see which was the time period she needed. She and Vic went through the box silently, and then looked at each other.

"Not there?" Vic asked.

"Maybe we missed it."

They went through the journals more carefully, announcing the dates and putting them back in the box as each was ruled out. Eventually, they had gone through them all, filling the box back up.

"It should have been in that box," Erin said.

"It should have been. But maybe it's in another one close by. She could have pulled it out to read it, and put it back into the wrong one. Who knows, there could be a lot of reasons. Let's go through the others that are closest on the timeline."

Erin looked at her watch. "I'm sorry; I said we would only be five minutes. It's going to be hard to talk to Terry before going to bed."

Vic sighed. "We're here now, we may as well finish the job."

Erin grimaced. "I'm sorry. I thought we would just be in and out."

"It's okay. I'm going to talk to Terry no matter how late it is. Let's just finish up here so we don't have to come back. I don't want to have to deal with Mr. God-complex out there again unless it's to move everything out of here."

Erin looked toward the door. The security man wasn't there, but she understood Vic's sentiment. She didn't want to have to see him again either, if she could help it. And his vitriol hadn't even been aimed at her. Not directly, anyway.

"Yeah. Okay. Let's find it."

They each grabbed a separate box, the one before and the one after the one that journal should have been in. They went methodically through the journals as they had with the last box. They took each journal out and checked the date, stacking them on the floor as they went. Then they looked at each other.

"No luck?" Vic asked.

"No."

"Let's switch boxes and check once more as we put them back in."

Erin nodded her agreement, and they squeezed around each other to do one final check. Erin wiped her sweating forehead with the back of her hand. The building was air conditioned, but she had been working hard and was sweating freely. She finished putting journals back in the box, and lifted her box onto the stack without a word. Vic did the same. It was obvious that neither of them had found what they were looking for.

"Sorry," Vic said. "I don't know what to suggest. I guess we can come back and look through the rest of the boxes another time. Or maybe when the house is done, and we take them back, we can go through them each one at a time."

It was a big job, they both knew. There were a lot of places the book could have been stashed. Erin didn't have a clue what she was going to find in all of the boxes that had been stored in the garage.

"I guess so. Weird that it's that particular one that is gone."

They both stretched and headed for the door of the unit. "Is it?" Vic asked. "I mean… maybe she didn't write one during that period because she was so upset. Or maybe she kept it somewhere else to look at it again when she was missing them. To remember their last visit or their memorial."

"Or maybe someone took it."

"From here?" Vic demanded, as Erin pulled the door shut and engaged the locks. "It's pretty secure."

"No, not here… before… when they were at the house."

"When?" Vic's brows drew down in a frown as they made their way out of the building. "When he tried to burn the house down?"

"I don't know. Maybe then. Maybe some other time. Any time in the last twenty years. Clementine must have had company over hundreds of times during that period. Or, there is the chance someone just broke in— picked the lock or just walked in through an open door—without Clementine ever realizing that someone had been in the house. She didn't even have a burglar alarm. Or a cat or dog. Nothing to warn her if someone had been in her house. They could just have taken that journal without her ever knowing it."

"Why would someone steal the journal?"

"Maybe… they got the wrong one. Maybe they meant to get the one that covered the period when Adam Plaint was killed. Or maybe Clementine said something even more incriminating in the later one. She could have found out, you know. One of the boys might have confessed to her. And then later, regretted it, or told the other brother about it… and they had to take it to protect themselves."

They got out to the car without another encounter with the security man, and Erin slid into the Challenger's seat with a sigh of relief.

"Can you believe Melissa and Davis…?" They hadn't had a chance to discuss it while at the bakery, and Erin's mind had been occupied with other things afterward.

"That they were friends back then, or that she won't even talk to him now?"

"I don't know. I just… can't believe any of it. It's like watching a play, I have a hard time believing it is real. I thought she hated him, but she really doesn't, does she?"

Vic didn't answer immediately, staring out the window. "I think she'd like to. Or she likes to think that she does. But no… I think she feels guilty for breaking up with him when they were kids. Or whatever it is that happened. She thinks… she could have saved him." She looked at Erin. "Do you think that's right…?"

Erin nodded. "Yeah, I think you're right on the button. But she couldn't have. With all that he went through… She couldn't have stopped him from drinking and getting into drugs, and living whatever life he's lived."

"But she never found someone else. Do you think they'll get back together again?"

"No, no," Erin said immediately, a little louder than she had intended. "I think she's right not to get involved. To stay as far away from him as possible. If he's a killer, like we think he is, she wouldn't want to be close to him. Or to know that he's going to end up in prison sooner or later. I know there are women who like to be in relationships with men in prison, but I don't think she's one of them."

"No." When Erin glanced away from the road to look at Vic's face, Vic's eyes were wide. "I don't think she's the type."

CHAPTER 8

Terry wasn't at the police department when Erin swung by, but she hadn't been sure he would be. He was often out on foot patrol, making sure that everything was running smoothly in Bald Eagle Falls, just keeping an eye on things. But with the excavation of Erin's yard and the discovery of the remains, Erin suspected he was pretty busy on other fronts. Davis had complained that Terry was searching his house, and Erin didn't know how long that would take. With just one person, or the handful who were involved with the town's police department, searching an entire house thoroughly would surely take all day. Maybe two or three. It wasn't just a matter of looking through drawers. Any evidence of Adam Plaint's murder would be well-hidden. Maybe buried, painted over, or covered up in some other way. Angela's and Trenton's murders were far more recent, but Erin wasn't sure what they would be looking for in those cases. There wasn't likely to be anything in the house.

"Should we just go to Aunt Angela's house?" Vic asked.

"No, I'll give him a call. He could be somewhere else, and if he's at the house, he might want us to stay away. I'm... not too sure I would want to be around there. Or be seen around there."

Vic nodded in agreement. "You don't want Uncle Davis thinking that you're involved in the investigation. Any more than he already does."

"Exactly. I'm staying well out of all of it."

She dialed Terry Piper's number and waited while it rang. She scanned the street idly to see who was around. It was the end of the work day, so people were headed for home. Picking up last-minute groceries for supper or having a meal at one of the restaurants. Running errands before the shops all closed. She didn't see Terry out on the street. But then, she didn't expect to.

"Erin?"

"Hi, Terry." Erin paused for a minute and just smiled, thinking of his dimple and his boyish face. "What are you up to? Vic and I were hoping we could talk."

"What is this about?"

The question was rather formal, and Erin wondered if there were someone else in the room with Terry. She lowered her voice, even though she knew that anyone eavesdropping on the conversation wouldn't actually be able to hear her side of it.

"About Willie Andrews. We're really starting to get worried about him. I know you were busy with the Plaint house today, but we wondered whether you had gotten anywhere on finding Willie."

"How did you know I was at the Plaint house today?" Terry's voice was suspicious.

"Because Davis came by the bakery. Just about blew a gasket over you being there. He's convinced that I put you up to it. He was not a happy camper."

"He was madder than a wet hen," Vic put in, though too quietly for Terry to hear.

"He came by the bakery and threatened you?" Terry demanded.

"Well… yes. He was…" Erin looked at Vic and repeated her words, "… madder than a wet hen."

Terry chuckled. "Hello to Vic too. I'll warn Davis to stay away from you. I don't want him causing any trouble."

"It might cause more trouble if you talk to him. Like a kid whose mom goes to the school over bullying. He already thinks you're under my control. If you warn him off, it might just make things worse."

"I don't like him confronting you. We'll see."

"So can we see you? About Willie? If you want, you can come by the house. But we thought you would want us to come to you. Do you want us to meet you at the department? To fill out forms?"

"I don't need you to fill out any forms." Terry sighed. Erin could picture him looking tiredly at his watch. And she was tired too. But she'd promised Vic to follow through and see what they could find out about Willie. "I got the key from his landlord. Do you want to meet me at his place?"

"Oh. Sure, we could do that. Where is it?"

Terry gave her directions to Willie's house, and Erin put the car in gear.

"Okay. We'll see you there."

"Where are we going?" Vic asked, as soon as Erin had hung up.

"Willie's house."

"Is he there?" Vic asked hopefully.

"No. Terry says he got the key. I guess he's going to go in and check it out."

"Good. Finally, he's doing something."

When they reached the house, Terry was standing in the front yard letting K9 sniff around. Erin wasn't sure whether the dog was supposed to be hunting for Willie' scent, or someone else's, or if he just needed to relieve himself.

"Just give me a minute," Terry said, "then we'll go in."

After more sniffing, K9 lifted his leg by a tree, and Erin looked away, waiting.

"Did you say *we'll* go in?" Vic asked. "Are Erin and me allowed to go in too?"

"I'll take a quick look first," Terry said. "Make sure everything is okay. Then… it's not really usual procedure, but you can come in if you don't touch anything. I'm really wiped and could use another set of eyes. If we can figure out what his schedule is, where he was headed, that would be the best use of our time."

Erin didn't say anything. She accepted his explanation on its face, but it seemed odd that he would allow them into what could be a crime scene. They weren't police officers, not even deputized to help him, and she felt a little uncomfortable intruding in Willie's house.

She and Vic waited anxiously outside while Terry went in to clear the house before allowing them entrance.

"You know what he's doing, don't you?" Vic asked. Her face was pale and drawn, but her expression flat like she was wearing a mask. "He's making sure that Willie's body isn't in there. That's why we have to wait."

Erin opened her mouth to object. She was sure Willie was just fine. But it had been a few days, and he had promised to call Vic. Erin was just starting to feel anxious about it herself. Even though she was sure he was just off visiting another woman or working in a mine, Erin thought that Terry was right to take action. If Willie had planned to be away for that long, surely he would have told one of them.

In a few long minutes that seemed like an eternity, Terry came out the door and motioned to them.

"All clear. Now remember, I don't want you touching anything. Don't even turn the page in a book or pull a curtain straight. Leave everything as it is. Just look, and we'll try to determine what his plans were."

They followed him into the little house.

It was smaller than Clementine's place. Not as decorative, a boxy little bungalow with stuccoed exterior and little by way of landscaping outside. The little tree K9 had watered appeared to be a recent addition, standing off by itself in the front yard.

Terry turned on a couple of lights as they walked into the house. He was wearing gloves.

It was a bachelor's house. But it wasn't too bad. Erin had seen a lot worse in the foster homes she'd grown up in and the homes of the seniors that she acted as an aide for when they were no longer able to keep things up by themselves. The furniture was sparse and well-used. There weren't a lot of fast food wrappers lying around, but there were enough on the table and sticking out of the garbage can to divine what his usual diet consisted of. The house was too warm and the air was stale. Shut up for too long. It had obviously been a few days since anyone had been there opening doors and windows and stirring the air around.

"No notes on the fridge," Vic said. "That's where people leave itineraries and emergency numbers."

Erin hadn't thought about that. She nodded. She looked around for a telephone. Sometimes people wrote notes beside the phone. But there didn't appear to be a landline, and Erin couldn't identify any place that he typically sat to make notes for himself. She and Vic left the kitchen, not touching anything, and checked out the rest of the house.

"There's a laptop," Erin announced, when she saw the slim silver form on a desk in what was obviously Willie's home office.

"Don't touch it," Terry responded from wherever he was.

Erin rolled her eyes and waited for him. She had no intention of touching anything. Did he really think she would open up the laptop and start tapping away on the keys?

Terry came into the room, followed by Vic. With a gloved hand, Terry opened the laptop. They all watched the screen light up. It was, of course, a login screen.

"I don't suppose either of you knows his password," Terry said.

Erin and Vic both shook their heads. "No."

He made a couple of guesses, then switched tactics and logged in as a guest user. The desktop loaded.

"What I'm hoping is that the calendar is shared to all users…"

Terry clicked on a calendar icon, and they all watched it come up… blank. Vic swore under her breath.

"Give it a minute," Terry said. "If no one has ever logged in as guest before, it might take the calendar a few minutes to populate."

They waited, but there was no change to the screen.

"Come on," Erin begged.

But there was still no change. Terry shook his head and clicked the browser. Like the calendar, there were no favorites or bookmarks loaded. Terry tried Google calendar and Microsoft.com, and a few other common websites, but none loaded Willie's account automatically. Terry logged back out of the guest account. He lifted the laptop to look underneath and at the bottom.

"Look for anything that could be a password," he instructed. "A sticky note with one word on it. An email address with another word. Most people keep a reminder or a hint for a family member somewhere close by."

Vic and Erin wandered around the room. Erin didn't touch anything, but noted that there were a lot of loose papers, filing drawers, and other places where the information could be stashed. Terry put the laptop back down and took a glance around the office.

"What's your best guess?" he asked Erin.

"My guess? About where the password is written down?"

"Yes."

She motioned to the filing cabinet. "In there."

He considered. "Not on a sticky note."

"No. He was an experienced spelunker. He knew that he had to leave information for someone if he disappeared. Somewhere it could logically be found, but not be right out in the open… he wouldn't want to take the chance that a sticky note would fall down and blow away."

Terry went to the filing cabinet and opened the first drawer. It was filled with neatly labeled, orderly folders. He fingered the first few folders.

"Not at the front," he said.

"Try P."

"For password?"

Erin nodded and waited. Terry moved down to the second file drawer, then the third. He reached for the middle of the drawer, and flipped through the folders, then drew one out. Erin held her breath.

"Passwords," Terry announced.

He returned to the computer and sat down in the chair. Opening the clamshell again, he waited for the login screen. There were several pieces of paper in the folder, and he took out the front one. There was a column of single words, all but the last neatly struck-through. He apparently had good password hygiene, changing them regularly. Terry tapped in the last word on the list, and the machine hummed into action. They all watched with bated breath as the desktop came up, and then a line of icons at the bottom of the screen. Terry clicked the calendar, and this time, as the month view appeared on the screen, the squares were populated with appointments and notes.

As they all huddled around the computer, they could see the entry two days before to call Vic.

"You see?" Vic reached out and almost touched the screen in her eagerness to show it to Terry. "I told you."

The entry before the call to Vic was hyperlinked to a location. Terry clicked it, and was jumped to a map with a pinned GPS location.

"He must have a mine there, or some other cave he wanted to check out," Vic said. "We have to go find him."

Terry looked at his watch. "It's going to be dark soon."

"It's already been two days. If he's bleeding or in shock, even if he's just dehydrated, he could die."

"I know. I'm not saying we can't go check it out. But we're going to have to be properly equipped and get support." Terry reached for his phone. "It's going to be a long night."

Vic and Erin had a hurried supper while Terry called for the town's volunteer firefighters, search and rescue from the state, and whatever personnel he could raise from the city, giving everyone the GPS coordinates to get them to the cave Willie was supposed to have been visiting before he missed calling Vic. Erin could barely swallow her burger and fries and worried that it was going to be that much harder for Vic. She was younger than Erin, and although she did her best to appear tough in the face of bullying and abuse, had a tender heart. Erin knew she had feelings for Willie that went deeper than just friendship. He might not be willing to take the relationship any further, but Vic certainly was.

"I told you he was missing," Vic told Erin, not for the first time. "I knew something was wrong. I told you something was wrong."

"I know. And now we know where to look. It will be okay. We'll find him. We'll figure out what happened. He'll be okay."

"You almost died when you were in that cave. If something happened to Willie... if he's hurt and laying in a cold cave way underground somewhere..."

Erin gave a shudder. She couldn't help it. Caves were not her favorite place to be, and when she thought back to being trapped in the pitch-black as she had been, she felt a pressure around her heart, squeezing it until it hurt.

"I know. And now it's time to return the favor. We'll find him, Vic. We'll figure it out."

"I was so scared when you were in the cave. I knew something awful had happened to you. And I couldn't do anything about it."

"You did, though. You got help, and they found me and got me out of there. It all worked out okay. No permanent damage, just a bit of anxiety over close, dark spaces."

Vic shook her head.

"Try to eat," Erin advised. "We don't know how long it will be until we get a warm meal again. Things could be pretty disrupted over the next little while."

Vic looked down at her meal, barely touched. She dragged a couple of fries through a splotch of ketchup and put them in her mouth. "I'm trying."

"I know."

They stopped by the house to feed Orange Blossom and Marshmallow, and then they were back out the door. Erin could hear Orange Blossom starting to yowl as she shut the door.

"He'll be fine," Vic told her. "He's got Marshmallow to keep him company."

"Do you really think that will help? It's not like they can play together, with Marshmallow in his cage."

Vic was silent. Erin knew she was worrying over nothing. It didn't matter whether Orange Blossom yowled all night while they were gone. They needed to be thinking of Willie. Something that Erin was really trying to avoid.

They met up with Terry and followed his police cruiser with its lights flashing. They left the town limits and were soon in wild back country. Rolling hills, dense trees, no houses to be seen. Erin guessed from her brief look at the mapped location that it was about an hour out but, keeping her foot on the gas to stay with Terry, they got there much faster. It was dark as they approached the location. Terry used the spot light on the police car to scan for a break in the trees, then slowly drove the rough track that was little more than tire tracks worn into the grass, until they reached the end.

It wasn't far off the highway. There was a small clearing. Willie's truck was parked there, but Erin didn't see any sign of him.

Vic jumped out of the car before it came to a full stop, and ran toward the entrance of the cave or mine. Erin parked the car and hurried after Vic.

The three of them converged on the cave entrance. There were warning signs indicating that it was private property and that it was a hazardous area.

"We have to go in," Vic said, shining her flashlight into the hole. "He's in there somewhere, hurt."

"We need to wait for assistance," Terry told her.

Vic gave him an incredulous look.

"You can take a look inside," Terry said. "See what kind of a job this is going to be. They're going to need a heads-up on what kind of terrain it is and what kind of equipment they will need. But you're to stay within sight of the entrance. No exploring. Just take a look, see what we're up against."

"Okay," Vic agreed, and practically dove into the hole.

Erin followed, but not too closely or eagerly. "Vic? Slow down. You don't know what you're facing."

The cave was dark. Erin had brought the best flashlight she could, and a hardhat with a light on top for spelunking, but the dark still felt oppressive. The lights cut little paths through it, but didn't do much to light up the entire cave. Vic shone her flashlight around, moving it from one place to another very quickly. Erin tried to be more methodical, doing a complete circle around the entrance.

There was only one direction to go. It was a steep downward track that seemed to lead into pitch blackness. Erin tried to steady her breathing. She remembered what it felt like to be lost and alone in the dark, hurt and not sure if anyone would ever find her and get her out of there. But Willie and Terry had come. And K9. And with their aid, she was able to get out and recover in the hospital.

Terry entered behind Erin. It was crowded with the three of them.

"That's the only way to go." Vic shone her flashlight into the downward track. "I can't tell how far it goes, but it's steep."

All three of them shone their flashlights into the cave, but even with all of the flashlights together, they couldn't see how far it went.

"Okay. Stay here or come out. I need to pass the information along." Terry left the cave.

Erin looked at Vic, hoping that she too would go back to the surface for some air. But Vic stayed there, biting her lip and staring down into the darkness. "Willie? Willie, are you down there?"

They both strained their ears for some response, but there was nothing but silence. Not even the drip of water or a whisper of wind.

"We should get our equipment," Erin suggested. Vic had thrown all of their spelunking gear into the car. Erin hoped that Vic would agree to get it all sorted into packs and divided between them. Anything to get Erin back out of the cave for a few more minutes. But Vic didn't immediately take her up on it.

"I doubt they'll let us go down. They wouldn't let me do anything when you were lost."

"It will take all of the rescuers time to get here. Aren't we going to do some reconnaissance first?"

"This is it," Vic said bleakly. "Standing here in the entrance. That's our recon. We're not going to see anything else, and it will be hours before anyone else is here to help." Vic cupped her hands over her mouth and shouted down the hole again. "Willie!" She looked back at Vic, her expression anguished. If Willie was down there, seconds mattered.

"Did you hear that?" Erin asked, though it was silent as a tomb in response.

In the light thrown by Erin's headlamp, Vic's eyes widened. "No, what?"

"I thought I heard something," Erin lied. "We'd better check it out."

"But..." Vic made a motion toward the opening of the cave, where Terry had stepped out and was now making whatever radio or phone updates he could. Then she caught on. "Yeah. We'd better check."

"There's only one way to go," Erin pointed out. "It's not like we're going to get lost. We'll just go a few steps... see if we can figure out what that noise was."

Vic threw one more glance in Terry's direction, but she didn't need to be talked into it. Her whole body was bunched, coiled like a spring ready to launch into action. She led the way into the tunnel.

Erin kept close behind Vic. Inside her head, she was battling the fear. Not fear for Willie, which was what she *should* have been feeling, but fear for herself. What if she hit her head? What if she were attacked? What if the tunnel branched out in three directions, and they chose the wrong direction? What if whatever or whoever had prevented Willie from returning home and making that call to Vic hurt them and prevented them from leaving the cave again?

"Vic...?" She tried to get the girl to slow down.

It wasn't steep enough that they needed climbing equipment, but Erin was having a hard time placing her feet on the dark, downhill slope. She didn't want to slip, to trip, to skid on loose gravel. A sense of vertigo made her want to slow down. To sit and wait until she felt steady again. But Vic kept going. She was like a mountain goat, seemingly having no problem at all figuring out where to put her feet. Erin knew they couldn't have gone far, but she felt isolated from the cave entrance. What if the track had branched off, and she and Vic hadn't even realized it? What if they couldn't find their way back when they turned around?

"Vicky, slow down. Please."

Vic turned her head to look back at Erin.

"Come on," she encouraged. "There's nothing to be scared of. We're only a few feet in."

"Do you see anything?"

"No. Of course not. We need to go farther."

Erin caught up with Vic, breathing harder than expected. Vic touched her arm briefly, reassuring. "It's okay. Do you want to go back? I can do this by myself, and you can tell Terry that I went on my own. That you told me not to."

"I don't want you to be down here by yourself. There could be..." Erin couldn't finish the thought. She didn't want to voice all of her fears. She didn't believe in the supernatural, but couldn't help feeling like if she said what she was thinking, she would jinx them or bring her fears into being.

"Come on, then." Vic held on to Erin as she led the way farther into the cave, and even though it was more awkward to move holding on to each other that way, Erin felt comforted and wasn't willing to give up the physical contact.

Then Vic stopped abruptly. Erin shone her light to see why Vic had stopped, and saw that the passage was blocked by a large gate. It filled up the whole tunnel, there was no way to squeeze around it. It was locked, padlocked shut. No way to go any farther and no other branches to explore. It was a dead end. Willie had blocked off his mine to prevent access by trespassers.

Vic's flashlight traced the outline of the gate, looking for any points of weakness or access. She examined the latch and the lock.

"Did he go in and lock it behind him?" Erin asked.

"No... it doesn't look like it can be locked once you're inside. And that wouldn't make sense, he'd need someone to be able to get in after him if he was hurt. You wouldn't want to lock out any chance of rescue. He knows about cave safety. He wouldn't do that."

Erin played her flashlight around the walls, looking for another exit, but there was nothing.

She shone her flashlight at a darker spot on the floor of the tunnel and everything changed.

~

"I told you to stay in the entrance!" Terry's voice was tight and angry. "I was very clear about that. I don't want to have a secondary emergency to deal with and I don't want you contaminating the scene!"

"It was my fault," Erin told him, trying to take the heat off of Vic. "I thought if we could just go a little farther down… see what we were up against…"

"You knew better. Both of you knew better, but you're a grown woman, not a teenager. You should be the voice of reason, keeping Vic out of trouble, not the one suggesting stupid exploration when the police officer on the scene has told you to stay put!"

There was a hot lump in Erin's throat. She nodded and blinked, trying to keep her emotions from taking over. "I'm sorry."

"You've contaminated the scene!"

She nodded. She and Vic had both walked right through the evidence before noticing it. Flashing back to the sight of the dried dark blood on the rock floor of the tunnel, Erin again felt her stomach revolting and the head rush of an impending faint. Vic grabbed her arm to hold her steady. Erin was already sitting on the ground, so she didn't have far to fall, but she really didn't want to completely black out in front of Terry.

"Leave her alone," Vic barked. "Can't you see how upset she is? She just about took a header down there when she saw the blood. She's sick. Just back off!"

Erin closed her eyes and covered them up with her hands. "Where did he go?" she asked. "If he *was* down there and hurt himself, where did he go? He didn't go into the mine, because the gate is still locked. So, where is he?"

Terry put one hand on the back of Erin's neck, and the other on her forehead, checking her temperature. His hand went down to her wrist to check her pulse. "His truck is still here, so he didn't drive away. We don't know whether he was hurt, or whether someone else was. Maybe it was someone else, and he took them to hospital in their car. We don't know how long the blood has been there, or if it is even blood. It could just be a warning to make sure that people pay attention to his no trespassing signs. You're jumping to conclusions."

"Like I jumped to the conclusion that Willie was missing?" Vic challenged. "Sometimes things are exactly what they seem to be. He was here two days ago. He got hurt. And then… what? Did he wander out in a daze and get lost in the forest? Did someone drag him out by his ankles? What?"

"There's no proof there was anyone else here. The simplest explanation is that he tripped and fell on that downward slope. He hit his head. Scalp wounds bleed like the dickens. And then…" Terry trailed off.

"What about footprint analysis?" Vic asked. "Can't you tell from the footprints how many people were there? Rule out Willie's footprints and see how many other footprints there are…?"

"It's mostly rock, and you can't get impressions from rock. And as far as the tracks through the blood… both you and Erin walked through it and scuffed it up. So we're up to three sets of footprints, I'm not going to be able to figure out if there are four. Not without a lot of luck."

"Footprints," Erin said weakly.

"What?"

"You said we didn't know how long the blood has been there. But you can tell… it was dry."

"Yes, it's dry now," Terry said with exaggerated patience. "If it was wet, there would be transfer. But you and Vic didn't track the blood. Just scuffed up the dried blood."

"But there *were* bloody prints."

"From earlier, when it was wet," Terry agreed.

"Then he didn't just put the blood—or paint—there as a warning to keep people away. The bloody footprints would have worn away if he was walking through there regularly."

Terry looked at her for a minute, then nodded. "Okay. Yes. But we don't know how often he's here. It could be an old mine that he just came by to check on. He might not have been here for years."

"Then the grass would have grown up over the tire tracks."

Vic was nodding. "Erin's right. You know he was here regularly because he's worn a path through the grass. That would go back to natural in one season, if he hadn't been by. When you hear hoof prints, think horses, not zebras."

Terry answered a call on his radio and gave the caller the most recent information. That it appeared that William Andrews had been injured, and had possibly left on foot. It was no longer a cave search, it was a ground search. And in two days, he could have covered a big area on foot.

"Why wouldn't he stay with the car?" Vic asked. "Why didn't he wait in his car, or drive out to the highway for help, or make a call for help? He has a radio, doesn't he?"

"He might have been dazed," Erin said. "Didn't even know what he was doing."

Terry went over to Willie's truck for a look inside. The door was unlocked, and Terry shone his light around the interior, not touching anything, but examining it as closely as he could by light of the flashlight. He returned to where Erin was sitting.

"He does have a two-way radio in the truck," he confirmed to Vic. "As far as I can see, there is no blood in there. Not on the handles, radio, or floor. I don't think he went back to the truck after getting hurt. If he was the one who was hurt. We're only assuming that; we have no way of knowing whether it was him or someone else."

"I don't think there was anyone else here," Vic said.

Terry chewed on his lip. "I don't either," he admitted. "We'll have to examine the tire tracks into the clearing in the morning, but like with the blood... we've already driven two vehicles in here over the evidence. I'll tell the other searchers to leave their cars at the highway and walk in, but I don't know if we'll be able to tell anything."

"Poor Willie," Erin said. "I wish we had come out here sooner... Do you think...?"

"No way of knowing where he is. Or what condition he's in. All we know for sure is that he is not at home, and he is not in that mine or his truck. He might have called for someone to come pick him up after getting hurt. Or..."

"He might be out there wandering, lost. Or lying hurt or dead in the trees somewhere."

"We'll do our best," Terry promised. "We'll get searchers out here, and we'll do our best to find him."

CHAPTER 10

A search was being organized in the morning when the sun started to come up. As soon as it was light enough, they would send people out to conduct a grid search. Erin's eyes were gritty and sore. She was both tired and wired. Even though she and Vic had gone back to Erin's car for a nap while waiting for the rest of the searchers, neither had gotten a wink of sleep. It didn't help that they couldn't stop talking to each other, going over the same ground again and again.

Terry was looking rather red-eyed himself. At least he had calmed down and stopped being so angry at Vic and Erin for disobeying and going farther down the tunnel. He wiped his forehead as if he could rub away the fatigue, and just shook his head.

"I doubt if there was anything we could have told from the blood evidence before you stepped in it," he said. "We can still DNA test it, but that will take time. I don't think it gives us any more clues to what happened to Willie."

Erin nodded, grateful for these words. Terry turned away from her as he answered a call on his radio. Terry's voice got louder as he spoke into his mic, and he raised a hand to quiet the chatter around him. His face was a picture of concentration as he decoded the voice behind the crackles of static. "The hospital?" he asked. "Say again?"

There was another burst of staticky noise from the radio.

"Are they sure?" Terry demanded. "We've got everybody ready to go up here, and if they're not sure…"

There was a brief response from the other party.

"Ten-four. We'll be in to check ASAP."

Terry released the button on his radio and turned to face Erin and the other assembled searchers.

"The search is called off," he said.

There were squawks of protest from the search teams.

"William Andrews has been found," Terry said. "They were unable to identify him before, but when our picture went out over the wire, they were able to make a positive identification."

There was a buzz of response. Erin realized that Vic was swaying on her feet, and grabbed her arm to steady her. The girl's face was as white as a sheet. She hadn't had anything to eat since the burger and fries, and she really hadn't eaten more than a bite or two of that meal.

"Vic! Are you okay?"

Terry took a step toward them. "What's wrong?"

"Willie," Vic said faintly. "They identified his body?"

"No!" Terry gripped Vic's other arm, and he helped to direct her to sit down on a weather-worn log. "No, Vic. He's alive." Terry raised his voice so that the other helpers assembled could hear as well. "He's alive. He's at the hospital with a head injury, but it isn't life-threatening. He's going to be okay."

Vic covered her face and started to cry. Erin hugged her and sat down beside her on the log, pulling her close. "It's okay. There, there. He's going to be okay, Vicky. It's okay."

"I thought he was dead." Vic wiped at her face with her arm and looked up at Terry, eyes still streaming. "Why couldn't they identify him? Couldn't he tell them who he was?"

"I can't tell you all of the details yet. It's hard to have a good, cogent conversation over the radio. We'll go to the hospital to confirm the identity, and find out the story there."

"Maybe he's unconscious," Erin said. "That would explain why they couldn't identify him."

Vic covered her face again, still sobbing.

"I'm sorry," Erin said. "I'm sure he's fine. He'll be okay, Vicky. Terry said it wasn't life-threatening. He'll recover."

"I know."

"Then why are you crying?"

"Because... I'm so happy he's okay. I'm just so relieved!"

~

Terry dispatched the various groups of searchers as quickly as he was able, filling out forms and making reports as necessary and seeing them on their way. Erin and Vic were eager to go see Willie, but they waited as patiently as they could for Terry to finish up. They had, after all, been the ones to put the whole operation into action.

By the time everyone was on their way back home, Vic had managed to calm her tears. She wiped her face and blew her nose and did her best to put on a cheerful face again. It took time to get to the hospital, and then for Terry to cut through the red tape and locate William Andrews, but eventually they were talking to a doctor about his case. He was a dark-haired, short man, a little rotund. He had the hurried, distracted air of many doctors, looking like he would rather be somewhere else than talking to them.

"Our John Doe—your Mr. Andrews—is a very lucky man. He took quite a blow to his head, came in here looking like he'd been the victim of some back-alley thuggery, but he doesn't appear to have any permanent damage."

"How was he a John Doe?" Terry asked. "Was he unconscious? How did he get here? I know he left his own vehicle behind."

"He is suffering some retrograde amnesia," the doctor admitted. "From the blow to his head. He couldn't tell us his name, even once he started to get over some of the confusion. A trucker picked him up, but didn't know what had happened to him."

"He must have wandered out to the highway after he got hurt," Terry suggested. "When was he admitted?"

"A day and a half ago."

"Thank goodness for small miracles," Vic said softly. "Can we see him now?"

"He can have visitors. But don't stay for too long, he'll tire quickly. He needs rest to heal."

Vic started down the hall before Terry and Erin even turned around.

They hurried after her. Terry touched the small of Erin's back as they walked down the hall.

"I'm sorry."

Erin looked at him, frowning. "For what?"

"For being so upset when the two of you went down the tunnel. I should have... controlled myself a bit better."

"You did tell us not to. We should have stayed by the entrance like you told us to."

"I guess it turned out that the blood evidence wasn't that important. But it could have been."

"I know."

"But I'm sorry anyway."

"Okay."

Vic veered into a hospital room up ahead, and Erin and Terry picked up their pace a little to follow her. They turned into the doorway just in time to see Vic rush up to Willie in his hospital bed, and give him a big hug.

"Willie! I'm so glad to see you!"

After Vic pulled back, Willie touched her on the shoulder, looking up at her with a frown.

"Do you know who I am?" Vic asked.

Willie nodded slowly. He looked at the doorway to see Erin and Terry walk in. Then he looked back at Vic again, his hand still lightly on her shoulder.

"Victoria," he said softly. "And do you know who I am?"

"Willie Andrews," Vic told him. "Remember?"

"No." He considered her answer for a minute. Erin and Terry joined Vic at the bedside, through they didn't offer hugs. Willie looked at them for a minute.

"Terry," he said with a little nod. "And... Clementine?"

Erin laughed. "No, Clementine was my aunt. Erin."

"Oh." His expression cleared and he nodded. "Right. Right, sorry."

Erin looked over the bandage wrapped around his head. He was dressed in a hospital gown, and Erin assumed the nurses had given him a good scrubbing, but his skin was still dark from his mining activities. "I guess you got a good bump on your noggin."

"I guess I did." Willie reached up and touched the bandage with gentle fingers.

"Do you remember what happened?"

"No… do you?"

"It looks like you fell in one of your mines," Terry said. "There's a steep downhill slope, and a pool of blood at the bottom. Apparently, you wandered back out, but were pretty confused."

Willie shook his head, looking puzzled at this. "Which mine?"

Terry described the location the best he could, and pulled up the GPS on his phone to show it to him. Willie pinched and zoomed and scrolled around the map. "I can't remember going there," he said, shaking his head. "I don't know what happened."

"The doctor doesn't think it's anything to be worried about. He thinks you'll heal up just fine."

"I don't like not remembering."

"What *do* you remember?" Vic asked. She sat on the edge of the bed and took his hand. "You couldn't remember your name?"

"It's kind of weird." Willie spoke slowly, weighing each word. "I feel like I remember everything. I know who I am and all about my life… but when I try to remember certain things, like my name, or how I got hurt, it's like it's just on the tip of my tongue… but I can't quite reach it." He let out a breath. "Willie. It feels right. You don't know what it's like… not to remember what you are called. It's not like you normally go around referring to yourself in third person in your head… but I wouldn't know how to respond if someone called me by name. Only now, I do."

"You don't remember why you went out to the mine?" Erin asked.

"I have work to be done out there. I'm usually there once or twice a week." His lips twisted into a little grimace before revealing, "It's a good mine. You won't tell anyone where it is…?"

Erin looked at Terry, not sure what to say.

"I'm afraid a good number of people know where it is now," Terry admitted. "We called in the fire department and search and rescue to help find you. I suspect… everyone in town knows where it is now."

Willie swore.

"Sorry," Terry said. "We were more concerned about your life and well-being than keeping the location of the mine confidential."

"Of course," Willie said. "I'm just used to keeping secrets. If people don't know where the mines are, they can't steal from them…"

"It looked like you had it locked up pretty good," Terry pointed out. "No one is going to get in there."

"Anyone with a pair of bolt cutters can get in that gate," Willie dismissed. "Are you telling me you wouldn't have cut the lock to see what was on the other side of the door?"

"We might have."

K9 grumbled about Terry standing around talking, and lay down at his feet. Erin resisted the impulse to bend down and scratch his ears. He was a working dog, and she knew she wasn't supposed to interfere or distract him.

"What's done is done," Willie said. He gave Vic's hand a squeeze. "Sorry about making you worry."

"Oh, I'm okay." Vic spoke breezily, brushing off his concern.

"Your eyes are red."

Vic let go of his hand to cover her eyes for a moment, then gave a little laugh. "Okay, you caught me. They're a little red from staying up all night worrying that you might be lying dead in the woods somewhere. But mostly, they're red from crying when I found out you were okay."

"Why did you cry *then?*"

"I don't know. I just did. I was so relieved, it all just came pouring out. It was pretty ugly. I'm not a quiet crier."

"You weren't that bad," Erin said.

Vic shook her head ruefully and rubbed the space between her eyebrows. Terry shifted restlessly. Erin looked at his face and was surprised at the concern she saw in his expression. After finding Willie and talking to him so that they knew he was okay, she expected him to be more relaxed. Vic caught Erin's look and also looked at Terry. Pretty soon, he became aware that he was the center of everyone's attention. There was no further conversation as they waited for him to speak.

"Why didn't anybody know who you were?"

"I couldn't remember."

"But what about your identification? What happened to your wallet?"

Willie blinked at him. "I don't know. I didn't have it?"

"You couldn't have, or they would have been able to identify you."

"I guess so… but I wouldn't have left it anywhere else…"

"You didn't leave it in the car or at home?" Erin asked, before realizing that Terry would have found it if it had been in one of those two places.

"No, I wouldn't do that. I always have my wallet in my pocket. I wouldn't leave it anywhere else."

Terry frowned. Erin shook her head. "It wasn't in the cave. I didn't see it in the clearing anywhere. Maybe you lost it in the truck that picked you up."

"Maybe," Willie agreed. But he looked just as baffled by it as Terry. "I… I can't remember anything that happened before I got here. I just remember… being in hospital. And even more than that… why I would fall down in my own mine. I've been down that tunnel hundreds of times before and never tripped or fallen."

"Well, don't worry about it," Vic said, patting Willie's hand. "We should probably let you rest now."

Erin fell into bed, exhausted. There was no point in going to the bakery so late in the day. She knew she would be useless on so little sleep. Even just driving home had been a challenge and, in retrospect, she probably shouldn't have done it, but she wasn't sure what other options she'd had. She and Vic parted ways when they got into the cottage, yawning and stumbling into their bedrooms.

Erin didn't bother to change. She just pulled the blanket over herself and curled up, closing her eyes. Orange Blossom followed her into the room, yowling to inform her of his displeasure over being abandoned all night. He sat in the middle of the braided rug, looking at her and waiting for some kind of response, but Erin was too tired to do more than murmur his name. He stopped complaining and jumped up onto the bed, where he sniffed her and padded around her, circling to investigate every inch of her. She wondered how much he could read about what had happened and how she was feeling by her scent. He started to make little crooning, mother-cat noises, and eventually curled up against her back and purred, soothing Erin into sleep.

Quickly the vestiges of awareness dissolved, and she was there, immersed in the moment, living it again.

She was wrapped in a blanket in the back seat of the car. She was drowsy, heavy with sleep. Her lids were sticky and hard to open, and when she did pry them open just a crack, she could see only darkness outside and rain tracking down the window. No lights except those of the car, lighting up the markers at the side of the road to keep them safe.

They were arguing again. Voices raised too loudly for Erin to go back to sleep. She didn't understand all of the words. But she knew that it was her fault they were fighting. She had done something to make them angry, and she didn't know how to fix it.

"Mommy..."

"Now you've woken her up." Her mother's voice dropped to a harsh whisper. As if she hadn't been loud too. "Go back to sleep, Erin. It's not time to wake up yet."

"Mommy, what's wrong?"

"Nothing is wrong. We're just talking."

"I want to go home," Erin whined. She wanted her bed. She wanted everything to be right again. She didn't like their arguing. It made her feel scared and all tight and sick inside.

"You can't go back home!" It was the man's voice, harsh and unrelenting. "Can't you get that through your stupid head?"

Sobs bubbled out of Erin. She rubbed the fuzzy blanket against her face.

"Don't talk to her like that. How is she supposed to understand what's going on? She's just a baby."

"She's a baby because of the way you treat her. She's old enough to be able to understand what I tell her. If you'd quit babying her and making excuses for her, she'd be better behaved."

Erin cried into the blanket. She didn't like his voice when it got all hard and mean. Mommy hit him on the arm, making the car veer into the other lane and making him swear and cuss.

"You just leave her alone! None of this is her fault," Mommy snapped.

"Do that again, and you're going to cause an accident. Keep your hands off of me."

"Mommy," Erin cried. "I'm scared."

"You see? You scared her," Mommy accused.

But it wasn't just him. Erin wanted desperately to stop the fighting. To make it like it had been before, when they were both happy and purred at her and spoiled her. She knew it was her fault that they were fighting. Erin choked for breath.

Mommy turned around in her seat, reaching around to catch Erin's knee. Her fingers were hard and Erin tried to pull away from her.

"You stop that now," Mommy said. "No more blubbering. I need you to be a big girl. Go back to sleep and leave the grown-ups to talk."

Erin flailed, trying to loose herself from her mother's unyielding grip.

Erin awoke with a start, shaking herself out of the dream with her violent thrashing. Orange Blossom jumped off the bed, complaining.

Erin gasped for breath, still sobbing, her heart racing. She tried to slow her heart and breathing down and to unclench her muscles. The sun was still bright outside, still afternoon, not night. That was probably why her sleep was so disrupted. She always dreamed more when she slept during the day. She decided she might as well get up so that she would be able to sleep when her regular bedtime rolled around. She splashed water on her face and, when she came out of the bathroom, almost bumped into Vic in the hallway.

"Are you okay?" Vic asked.

Erin wiped at the dampness remaining on her face. "I had a dream."

"A nightmare?"

Erin shrugged. She didn't like to admit to being scared. She had grown up in homes where any sign of weakness was immediately targeted by foster kids who were older or tougher than she was. "It was weird. Like, maybe a memory. I was in the car and my parents were arguing."

"Is that… when they had their accident?" Vic's voice was tentative, and she checked Erin's face for her reaction.

"I don't know." Erin remembered her mother hitting him in the arm, making him swerve. Had the accident been caused by their fighting? Had Erin caused it by crying and causing more trouble between them? She put her hand out to steady herself, and Vic grabbed it, then put an arm around Erin's waist to support her.

"You got up too fast. Why don't you come sit down?"

Erin tried to protest that it wasn't from getting up too fast, but there was no point. What difference did it make? She was embarrassed by Vic's attention, but allowed herself to be guided to the living room to sit down. Orange Blossom, apparently forgiving her, followed her and sat at her feet.

"Do you remember it?" Vic asked. "I always thought that you weren't in the car when it happened. You never said that *you* were in an accident, just them."

"I…" Erin tried to remember. All that she could bring to mind was the social worker telling her that her parents had been killed instantly. Which, if

Clementine's genealogical records were accurate, was incorrect. Why would she tell Erin that they had died instantly if they had languished for weeks or months afterward? "I don't remember. I didn't think so, but… maybe I was. If this dream was a memory…"

"Or you could be remembering another time. Your parents probably argued more than once. It doesn't necessarily have anything to do with the accident they were killed in."

"Maybe not," Erin agreed, though she was unconvinced. Why would the memory surface now, when she was trying to find out what had happened all those years ago, if it wasn't to do with the accident? These memories of a car ride had to mean something. They had to be significant.

"I always have weird dreams when I fall asleep during the day," Vic confided. "I'm sure that's all it is."

"But what if…" Erin swallowed. "What if I caused the accident? What if it was because I was crying? It was too distracting, or she hit him while they were fighting about me, or she grabbed me and I was kicking and one of us bumped him or distracted him…"

Vic rubbed Erin's back soothingly. Orange Blossom got up and rubbed against Erin's legs.

"It's not your fault," Vic said. "It doesn't matter if you were crying. If it was unsafe, they should have pulled off the road. They were the adults, not you. You were just a little girl, and if you were upset by them fighting, that's not your fault. It's theirs. They were already distracted by their own emotions and whatever was going on between them."

"Why would the social worker tell me they died instantly? Why would she lie about something like that? They didn't die right away. I don't know what their injuries were, but what if one of them had gotten better instead of dying? How would they explain that to me?"

"It's weird," Vic admitted. "Are you sure they're dead now?"

Erin considered that. She didn't let her hope rise at the suggestion. After all these years, was it possible that one of her parents was still alive? She shook her head. It was unfathomable.

"Clementine's book says they're both dead. The social worker said they were both dead. It has to be true."

"Okay. It just seems to me that there are a lot of open questions… it might help to figure out what are assumptions and what are facts."

"They're both dead. I'm sure of that."

"What do you remember about them?"

"Not much… I was pretty young… And I don't know how many of the memories are contaminated by memories of other parents in other homes. After a while, everything just starts to run together."

"What do you remember for sure?"

Erin closed her eyes and tried to picture them. "Dark hair. Both of them. I don't know how tall, they were both bigger than me!"

"What do you remember doing with them? You remember working with Clementine at The Tea Room. You must remember doing other things."

"I don't know. Playing baby dolls with my mom. Going for walks with my dad." Erin warmed to that, remembering, envisioning the sights and smells. "Nature walks. I don't think we were ever in the wild, just in a park in town… or wherever I lived. Picking up pinecones and rocks and leaves. Junk. But I thought they were treasures. He'd complain about having to walk home with his pockets weighed down with all of the rocks and things. But… I don't think he really minded." She remembered the amusement in his voice. Not the anger she heard from the man in her dream. That hurt her. When she had gone on walks with him, her father was always kind and patient.

"And you went into foster care after the accident, that's what you remember."

"Yes."

"There isn't any reason you would have been put into foster care before the accident? They weren't… having trouble taking care of you, or having problems with a CPS investigation…?"

Erin shook her head slowly. She would remember if any of that were true, wouldn't she? But it was true that the timeline was confused. She knew she had been in foster care for her eighth birthday, but according to Clementine's genealogical records, her parents hadn't died until some time after her birthday. The time lapse could be explained if she had been placed into foster care before the accident. "No… I remember the social worker saying that I had to go to another family because my parents had been killed in an accident."

"And they wouldn't lie about that…"

"No. Why would they?"

"Why would they tell you that they had died instantly if they didn't?"

"I don't know." Erin sighed. "I need to bake something. I can't think straight. I just want to relax and bake."

Vic held up her hands. "I'm not going to stop you! What are you going to make? Do you want me to make some supper? Before we have sweets?"

"No. I'll bake bread. We can have sandwiches. I want to really get my hands into some dough. Really knead it."

"You're not making gluten-free?" Vic asked, her voice higher than usual. She had learned in her time with Erin that bread batters for gluten-free bread were still fairly liquid, not kneadable dough like wheat bread.

"Nope. Regular bread."

"It seems sort of sacrilegious! Are you sure you're allowed?" Vic teased.

Erin allowed herself a smile. It felt good after the vestiges of the fear following her dream. "I think it will be okay as long as we don't tell anyone."

They had spent most of the day together, but Terry still came over at the end of the day. His eyes were red. Even K9 seemed to be more fatigued than usual, though he had been sitting around most of the day instead of on foot patrol with Terry as he usually was. Erin gave Terry a brief hug at the door, something she didn't normally do. But she just felt like she needed it, and he probably did too.

Terry looked down at her for a moment, startled, their faces close together, and then he smiled and gave her a little squeeze before slowly letting her go.

"Hi."

Erin smiled, her face warming a little. "Come into the kitchen," she ordered. "There's fresh bread."

"Yes, ma'am," Terry agreed, his southern accent exaggerated. "I always do what I'm told where fresh bread is concerned."

She motioned for him to sit down and, as he had promised, he obeyed. Erin pulled the towel off of the warm loaf of bread she had set aside for him. She sliced it with a long, serrated knife, into perfectly straight, even slices, or at least as close as she could get to perfectly straight, even slices. At least they were better than what she had been able to cut as a child. She put a couple of warm slices on a plate for Terry, and a stack on another plate in the middle of the table so he could help himself. Vic pulled several Jam Lady jars out of the fridge.

"I've died and gone to heaven," Terry declared.

K9 put his nose down on his paws with a noisy sigh. Erin caught Vic's questioning glance. "Why don't you get him a biscuit, and then we'll get the bunny out."

Vic presented K9 with a homemade doggie biscuit, which he took delicately from her hand and then consumed with noisy vigor. When he was done, he lay back down and licked his chops a few times, making sure that he got every last crumb.

"How is the bunny?" Terry asked.

"He's doing really well," Vic offered. "He still has the cast, of course, but his cuts are healing, and he's pretty frisky."

"He's a lot more brave than I thought a rabbit would be," Erin said. "I always thought they were shy, scared of everything. But they're not. At least, Marshmallow isn't."

"Marshmallow?" Terry raised his eyebrows.

"Vic named him. Although… it seems to work for him. I can't actually complain."

Vic went to get the rabbit. Orange Blossom was sitting in the middle of the kitchen doorway, watching K9 with disapproval. He didn't budge, making Vic go around him. He started to wash, staring at the dog like every lick was an insult aimed in his direction. When Vic returned with Marshmallow, the cat seemed even more disgusted, and slunk off into the living room, refusing to have anything to do with the other animals, at least to begin with.

"He's such a drama queen," Vic observed. "Prima donna. Thinks he should be the center of attention all the time."

"I like having another animal around to keep him company," Erin said. "I think secretly he likes Marshmallow. But he doesn't want us to know it."

Terry chuckled. "Well, let's have a look at this little guy."

Vic bent over and put the rabbit down on the kitchen floor. Marshmallow kicked up his heels and thumped on the floor a few times with his cast before sitting down and observing Terry and K9, his head turned to the side.

"The way their eyes are set, they don't watch things straight on like a person or a dog does," Vic said. "Or like a cat. They watch you out the side instead."

Terry didn't move, careful not to scare the rabbit. K9 snuffled the air and inched toward the animal, eager to get a closer look.

"Stay," Terry warned him in a low voice.

K9 stopped moving and lay flat again, his ears pricked toward the rabbit, watching it intently. He whined in the back of his throat. The rabbit continued to sit tall, watching the dog sideways. His ears flicked a few times while the rest of his body remained frozen in place.

"What do you think, K9?" Erin asked the dog in a low voice. "What do you think of our new bunny?" She looked at Vic. "He probably thinks it's a mighty strange looking dog."

"He knows it's not a dog," Terry corrected. "He's chased plenty of squirrels and rabbits in his day. He wants to know what it's doing in the house and why he can't chase it now."

They watched the animals, both frozen in place, for a few more minutes.

"He's looking pretty good," Terry said. "I honestly didn't think he'd survive. But he's acting like nothing ever happened."

"Yeah. That's what the vet said too. It's like he's always lived with us. He's not even shy about being picked up."

"Maybe he was someone's pet and somehow escaped."

"No one has said anything. We've asked around. Apparently, there have been rabbits around here for a long time. Several generations of them. They're just treated like any other pest."

Marshmallow decided he was done being cautious and that the dog wasn't going to do anything to him. He started lolloping around the kitchen, snuffling along the baseboards for any fallen treats. But Erin noted that he kept one eye toward the dog all the time. He hopped over to the fridge and stood up on his haunches, flicking at the door with his front paws.

"You want a treat?" Erin asked. K9's ears followed her, but she disappointed him by going to the fridge instead of the cookie jar. Erin opened the fridge door and the rabbit stood up, nosing at the drawers and standing up tall to see what he could find. Erin opened one of the drawers and pulled out a fresh carrot for him, then pushed him out of the way of the fridge so that she could close the door again. She held the carrot out for him, and he pulled it away with his teeth, then crouched on the floor, eating it. K9 tried again to get up and go over to the rabbit, wanting to investigate further and see what the rabbit was eating. Terry grabbed his collar and pushed him back down. K9 stayed put, whining.

"You already had your treat," Erin told him.

"Can I give him another one?" Vic asked.

They both looked at Terry for his decision. "I suppose. Give him one so that he doesn't go after the rabbit for his."

Vic got another cookie out of the jar, and K9 sat up eagerly to take it from her. Erin turned her head at a movement in the kitchen door. Orange Blossom was slinking there, pouting about the rest of the animals getting treats, when no one had offered him one.

"Come on, then, if you want one," Erin told him. "If you're going to pout in the living room, you're not going to get a treat like everyone else."

He opened his mouth and meowed at her silently.

Erin laughed. "Come on," she insisted, and made kissy noises to call him. "Come on in, if you want something."

Orange Blossom finally entered the kitchen, ignoring the other two animals and heading straight for Erin. She got out a can of kitty treats and shook it, which sped him up. Erin poured a few onto her palm. He stood up and patted her leg, begging.

"Am I forgiven, now?" Erin asked him. "You're going to talk to me now, because I have treats?"

He made a couple of yipping noises, and Erin put the treats down on the floor. Orange Blossom dug in eagerly.

"Well," Terry wiped his mouth with the back of his hand. "If everyone else's treats are as good as the fresh bread and Jam Lady jams, I can understand why they are so excited about them."

"It's so good," Vic agreed. She grabbed a piece of bread from the stack and swiped Terry's knife for a moment to smear it with wildberry jam.

"You'd better be planning on sweeping the floor if you're not going to use a plate," Erin warned.

"Yes, Mom."

Erin smiled at both her two-legged and furry friends. There was a warm, communal spirit in the kitchen. Something that she had longed for through many long years of foster care, transferring from one family to the next, never really feeling like she had a place of her own. Now, even though she was only in a temporary residence while she waited for her house to be fixed, she had the feeling that she belonged. She had finally found her own place in life.

"Did you find anything else out about Willie?" she asked Terry. "Anything about the trucker who found him, or where his wallet might have disappeared to?"

"I put traces on his credit cards, but so far, no one has used them for anything in the last two days. I can only assume that means that he lost it, rather than it being stolen."

Vic started to speak around her mouth full of bread and jam. She covered her mouth and finished eating before trying again. "'Scuse me. Do you really think that he just tripped and hit his head in the cave?"

"He could have. The floor was uneven. It's quite a steep grade. Anyone could trip and fall at any time. I don't claim to be the most well-coordinated person in the world, but I still trip over nothing. A crack in the sidewalk or a loose pebble. Step off of a curb the wrong way and turn my ankle. Anyone can have one slip-up. It's just magnified in an environment like that."

Vic scratched behind her ear. "But do you really think that's what happened?"

Terry was silent, considering. He looked down at K9, who was finished his second biscuit, and scratched his ears. The dog was once again staring at the rabbit, though alternating his attention with Orange Blossom as well.

"I couldn't really say," he admitted finally. "It might have happened just like that. And it might not have. I can't say there is any indication of foul play. There's no sign that anyone else was there. Not until we analyze Willie's shoes and make sure he is the one who left the bloody footprints."

"You think someone pushed him?" Erin asked Vic. "Or hit him over the head with something?"

"We've seen him in caves before," Vic said. "He's careful. He doesn't hurry. He's always aware of the hazards. I know anyone can make a mistake, and maybe he got distracted walking down a tunnel that he's walked down hundreds of times before. But... I just don't think so. I think there was someone else there."

CHAPTER 11

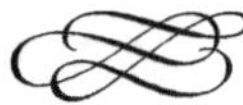

$\mathcal{I}$t was a busy day. Not only because the bakery had been unexpectedly closed during the search for and discovery of William Andrews, but also because it was Erin's first day training a new employee.

Bella Prost was a seventeen-year-old who was only carrying a half-load for her last year of school, so she had enough time on her hands to take up a part-time job, and she was interested in becoming a baker or a cook. There hadn't been hundreds of applications to go through, but a fair number of the high-school and graduated-but-not-yet-employed students had been interested in the position. Erin hoped that Bella would work out. She seemed like a nice girl and Erin thought that her sunny personality would be a good complement to hers and Vic's. Bella was slightly overweight, with a head full of blond curls that bounced around her face.

"What do you want me to do first?" she asked Erin. She looked around the kitchen, where Vic and Erin had already been busy for a few hours. "I can sweep up or wash dishes if you want."

"No, let's get you out front to start with," Erin told her. "Throw on an apron and a cap, and I'll get you oriented there."

"Okay." Bella beamed. "Wherever you want me." She obediently dressed herself, and joined Erin at the front of the shop.

Erin ran through the day's goodies in the display case. "Now, our customers are all repeat buyers, so they'll probably know more about the products than you will to begin with. You'll get to know what their special dietary needs are, so that you can point them in the right direction when we have something new on offer. This is our Bible." She pulled out a three-inch black binder from under the cash register. It was filled with recipes in plastic sleeves. "These are all of the ingredients for all of the products. If someone asks you what is in a muffin or a cookie, they are just in alphabetical order, so you can check the list." Erin opened it to chocolate chip oatmeal cookies. "As well as a list of ingredients, there is a key beside each recipe. Gluten-free, dairy-free, egg-free, vegan, nut-free, and so on. Everything is gluten-free and nut-free. But not everything is vegan. There are a lot of eggs and dairy in some of the recipes."

Bella nodded attentively.

"And in the second section," Erin turned the pages over to the last one-third of the plastic page protectors. "These are the labels for the different products we use. So if someone wants to check the ingredients for the chocolate chips, or to see where the rice flour comes from, or whatever, you shouldn't have to run back to the kitchen to check packages."

"That's smart."

"Saves a lot of time. You never know what questions people are going to ask, but you should be able to answer most of them with the Bible. Of course, Vic or I will always be here with you and can answer a lot of the questions from memory, but the book is here for you when you need it."

"Great. I'll use it. And everything is gluten-free and nut-free."

"Right," Erin agreed. She looked around. "Now, what else do I need to show you? I'll walk you through the cash register, but it's pretty intuitive, you'll pick it up in a few minutes. Um… we have the Jam Lady jams. They are a good up-sell for bread or rolls, so any time someone buys them, just ask if they want jam to go with it. About half will say yes. Pretty much everybody knows Jam Lady—"

"Uh-huh," Bella agreed, patting her stomach. "I've had them."

"Good. You can recommend them, then!"

"Yeah. For sure."

"We also have doggie biscuits," Erin pointed to the cookie jar. "Make sure people know they're buying dog biscuits and not cookies. Not that they'll get sick from them or anything, but they're not terribly palatable for humans."

Bella giggled. "Do you sell a lot of those?"

"Not a lot. But people do like their pets, and some of them want to get a treat for their dogs when they get one for themselves. And Officer Piper's dog, K9, he gets one for free when he comes by on patrol."

"Isn't that considered bribing a police officer?"

"Not in Bald Eagle Falls. Officer Piper and some of the others who do public works or are outside a lot sometimes come by with their water bottles, which we refill at no cost. It's so hot here, we don't want people getting dehydrated.

"That's nice of you." Bella looked up at the chalk board behind them. "And you offer beverages?"

"Coffee in the morning. Iced tea all day. Just a little something to go along with muffins or cookies when people eat in." Erin nodded toward the small tables at the front of the shop. "Most people don't, but we have a few who do from time to time. And we have the after-church ladies' tea on Sunday. I'll probably get you to help with that whenever you can. It would be nice if Vic and I could take alternate Sundays off. Right now we're pretty much working six and a half days a week."

"That's why you need me," Bella said cheerfully. "You'll just burn out if you keep that up."

"You're right. It can be really hard to get up some mornings and right now we don't have anyone to cover if one of us gets sick. Or anyone to help if we want to get off for a day or even just an afternoon now and then." Erin shook her head. "I don't know how my aunt ran the tea room all by herself."

"She must have loved it."

"I think she really did. But eventually, she had to retire. You can't just keep at it for years without a break."

"Show her the loo," Vic called from the kitchen, "and then we'd better get the last of these cookies into the display and open back up."

Erin looked at the clock. Their early lunch hour was almost over, and she hadn't yet stopped for anything to eat.

"Okay," she agreed. "Would you make me a sandwich, Vic—"

"Already did," Vic said placidly. "And you don't need to rush to eat it. Bella and I will take care of things while you have a break."

Erin motioned to the door that led down the stairs and to the commode. "I'll show you the basement."

Bella paled. "I don't really think I need to go down there," she said.

"It will only take a minute…"

"No, I'm okay. I'm not going to need it."

"Well, you're going to at some point," Erin laughed.

Bella still didn't budge. Erin stopped and looked at her, trying to figure out what was wrong. Bella was no longer laughing and smiling. Her expression was strained.

"Is it the stairs?" Erin guessed. "Do you have mobility issues?"

It was an old building, and each of the shops had adapted to its limitations the best it could, but that meant that the facilities weren't always accessible like they had to be in modern buildings. If Bella couldn't get up and down the stairs, she would have to go to one of the other shops nearby, and that could be a problem.

"No…"

"What is it, then?"

Bella's eyes went up to the ceiling and she blinked a couple of times. Vic could apparently hear or see that something was wrong and stood in the doorway to the kitchen, trying to help.

"Bella?"

Bella looked back at Erin. "I was hoping I could avoid going down there," she said. "I could go somewhere else, if I needed to…"

"Why?"

She should have been able to figure it out herself, but for some reason Erin didn't clue in.

"Because… that's where Angela Plaint died," Bella finally confessed. "I don't want to see it. Or to have to be down there by myself."

"There's nothing scary about it," Erin reassured her. "There's no blood or any sign that something happened there. People use it all the time and no one is bothered by it."

"And it's not haunted," Vic offered.

Bella looked at Vic, then back at Erin. "I really don't think I can."

That was going to be a problem. "Just come see," Erin urged. "You've just built it up in your mind to be something it's not. Really. You can't tell anything happened downstairs."

Not only would Bella have to leave the building to go somewhere else if she ever needed to use the commode, but she wouldn't be able to go down to the storeroom to fetch anything they needed, either. Erin couldn't just brush off Bella's feelings. The girl was as white as a ghost; it was obviously a genuine fear, not just affectation.

"Just go down; you'll see," Vic agreed. "The worst thing you can do with anxiety is give in to it. You have to face it down."

"You really need to be able to go down there if you want to work here," Erin agreed.

Bella shook her head. "I can't."

"It's just a basement. I'll bet you've been plenty of places where people have died, and don't even know it. It's a small town and a lot of people have died here over the generations. Probably even in your house."

"Not helping, Erin," Vic warned.

Erin bit her lip and quit trying to talk Bella into it with logic. "All right," she said eventually, "well, I need to eat my lunch, so you and Vic are on duty. Give me a shout if you need anything."

Vic got out of the middle of the doorway so that Erin could get by. Vic gave her a nod. "We'll work it out," she agreed. "Give it a little while."

Erin could hear Bella's deep sigh of relief as she ducked into the kitchen to have her lunch. She sat down with her lunch and tried to put all of her troubles out of her mind.

Erin got an automated email from DHS that her request had been approved, and to allow six to eight weeks for delivery of the records she had requested. She showed the email to Vic on her phone as they sat in the living room recuperating after a long day at the bakery.

"Six to eight weeks! Doesn't that seem like a long time to you? If they have the records, does it really take more than a few days to copy them and mail them off? Six to eight weeks?"

"Maybe they won't actually take that long. Maybe it will only be a few days. But they have to cover themselves, you know, in case it takes longer."

"How long could it take to photocopy a few documents and put them in the mail?" Erin griped again.

"You don't know how much is involved. They have to dig them out of storage somewhere. Probably offsite. They might not be cataloged very well, and they have to go through a bunch of dusty boxes." Vic's words brought back to mind looking through the boxes in the storage locker for Clementine's missing journal. "And you don't know how much documentation there is going to be to copy. I mean, you were in foster care for how many years?"

"From just before I turned eight until I aged out. Ten years."

"You don't know how many documents that is. How many times did you move? And how thick were the reports they had to write every time you went somewhere new? And then if you had any problems or there were any investigations, then they'd have to have more reports. I bet it's pretty thick."

"But all I want is the initial intake papers. The documents that show what happened to my parents. And if the social worker lied to me."

"Still…" Vic shrugged widely. "You don't know how much paperwork may be involved or how long it will take to go through it all. You'll probably get it sooner, but they have to say six to eight weeks to cover themselves off."

"I sure hope it doesn't take that long."

"Well, you've waited this long. You can wait a little longer."

Erin had been hoping for a little more sympathy than that. But deep down, she knew that Vic was right. She was just venting. It didn't really matter if it took six to eight weeks. She just wanted her answers faster than they were coming. She sighed, and turned off her phone.

"At least you got an answer," Vic said. "That's good news, after all of the hoops you've had to jump through."

"I'm just afraid it's only an automated computer answer, and when they actually look at the request, they're going to come back again and tell me that they don't have what I want. They're going to say that they were lost or destroyed or I have to go to another department again."

"Be happy with the answer you got."

Erin hit the wake up button on her phone to double-check the time. "I'd better be heading off to bed. You're going soon?"

"Yes. I just want a few more minutes to read." Vic held up the heavy library book she had been reading. A Stephen King. Erin shuddered. She'd had enough of murders and horror stories the last little while. Quite enough.

"Okay. Don't be up too late, or you'll regret it in the morning." Erin forced herself to yawn, trying to convince herself that she was actually sleepier than she was. She knew she should be tired, but she was wound up after receiving the confirmation from DHS that they were going to send her what she had asked for.

But six to eight weeks!

Erin trudged off toward the bathroom. Orange Blossom, who had appeared to be sound asleep on Vic's lap, lifted his head and then quickly followed her to the bathroom door, where he sat patiently waiting until Erin was finished her oblations and headed to bed. He settled himself more quickly than usual, and in a few minutes, was lying against Erin's neck, purring up a storm. Erin closed her eyes and tried to relax.

In spite of Erin thinking she was too hyped up to get to sleep, it wasn't long before her brain drifted and she began to dream.

She was sitting in a hospital room, on a tall gurney that she was a little afraid to try to get off of. She'd been left alone and was lonely and scared. It had been a really long time, and she wanted her mommy and daddy. She wanted her bed in her house. She wanted someone to hold her and to tell her that everything was okay now.

She pulled her fuzzy blanket around her more tightly. She knew she was behaving like a baby. A big girl of almost eight shouldn't act like such a baby. But she couldn't help it. She couldn't be grown up when she was all alone there. She was confused, and the blanket was the only thing she had for comfort. It was a good thing the boys at school couldn't see her.

A woman came in, and with her was the policeman that had brought Erin to the hospital hours earlier. He had held her close like her daddy, so she felt warm and protected even in the midst of everything else that was going on.

"Hi, Erin," he said softly. "I thought you'd be asleep by now."

Erin shook her head. He came and stood by her bedside, stroking a lock of hair that had fallen in front of her face and tucking it behind her ear.

"I want to introduce you to someone. This is Mrs. Flack. She's going to help you out."

Erin looked at the woman. She had dark hair like Erin's, twisted into a smooth bun that was pinned behind her head. She had a buttoned-up blouse and a dark blue, pleated skirt. She smiled at Erin, but all of the lines around her mouth and eyes made it look unnatural, like she was lying about how she felt.

"Hi, Erin. How are you doing? This must all be pretty scary for you, huh?"

Erin clutched her blanket and resisted rubbing it against her face or hiding behind it. She didn't want this new, disapproving woman to think that she was a baby. To know how scared she really was.

"I'm Mrs. Flack, and I'm going to be taking you to a family who can help take care of you tonight."

Erin resisted a strong urge to put her thumb in her mouth. "I want my mommy."

"I know you do, honey. But…" the social worker glanced at the policeman, "your mommy died in the accident. She can't take care of you anymore."

Erin sniffled, the fear and loneliness bubbling up inside of her.

"My mommy," she repeated, unable to squeeze any other words out through her tight, hot throat.

"I'm sorry. But I've got someone who will take care of you tonight. And we'll find someone you can stay with permanently. So you'll have a new mommy."

"I don't want a new mommy."

"I know, honey."

Erin held her blanket in front of her face and started to cry. "I want my mommy!"

"Shh, shh…" Someone was shaking Erin. "Sh, it's okay. It's a dream, Erin. Wake up."

Erin tried to pull away from the hand shaking her, then gradually started to comprehend the words, and sought out the contact.

"Open your eyes. Wake up."

It was a long time before Erin could completely break free of the dream and open her eyes to see the real world. Vic sat on the edge of the bed, shaking her gently and studying her with intense eyes.

"Vic."

"Yeah. You okay? You were really deep."

"Yeah."

Vic rubbed her shoulder. "Were you dreaming about the accident again?"

"No… sort of… I was dreaming about after. When the social worker came."

"It must be because you were thinking about your file when you went to sleep. Do you remember what happened?"

"I don't know… I was in hospital, but I don't think that really happened. I don't remember being in hospital."

"What were you there for? Or did it make that much sense?"

"I don't know why I was there… that's where they took me after the accident, I guess. They must have needed to make sure that I wasn't injured. I don't think I was hurt at all."

"So you *were* in the car when the accident happened."

Erin struggled with the idea. She had always told herself that she hadn't been there when it happened. She'd been at home or with a babysitter, and they had come to the house to tell her and to take her away. She didn't know why that was important to her.

"I don't know… if the dream was a memory, and it was accurate. But dreams are usually something that your mind just conjures up. I don't know that it was a real memory."

"But if it was, then that means you were in the car with them when it happened. So maybe your other dreams were memories too. Memories of what happened before the accident." Vic paused. "You don't remember the accident, do you? None of the dreams have actually been about the accident?"

Erin shook her head. She wiped sweat and tears from her face, and found herself choking up again. She couldn't explain why, but she couldn't stop the hot tears from escaping and the sobs from making her breathing ragged. Her heart hurt. She missed her parents so keenly, she didn't know what to do to stop it.

Vic hugged her close, trying to comfort her.

"It's okay, Erin. It's all right. It was just a dream. And if it was a memory… it happened a long time ago. You're okay now. Everything is okay."

Erin couldn't cry about her mommy and daddy to Vic. She wasn't an eight-year-old anymore. She was a grown woman, and her loss was long behind her. She stifled the sobs the best she could, shaking in Vic's arms.

"Shh," Vic soothed again. "It's okay." Vic hugged her and rubbed her back and, when Erin eventually drew back, pushed the sweaty locks of hair back from her face, much as the policeman in the dream had. "You're getting all stirred up with this. Maybe... maybe it would be better if you didn't try to find out what happened."

Erin grabbed a tissue from the box on her bedside table and dabbed at the tears.

"I need to know. I need to know what happened." She swallowed hard. "It's my mom and dad. If they were yours, you'd want to know what happened to them, wouldn't you?"

Vic didn't have a very close relationship with her parents, who did not approve of her transgender identity. But Vic's expression softened at the question.

"Yes... I'd want to know what happened."

Erin blew her nose. "Sometimes it's better to know, even if it's bad."

It was nice to get together with Terry again in a normal, relaxed setting—not because Terry had questions or they were worried about Willie, but just to get together to enjoy each other's company.

It was the first time that Erin and Terry had had dinner together, just the two of them. They had gotten together with Vic, maybe Willie, sometimes with a larger group. But it had never been just Erin and Terry. And K9. Erin felt self-conscious and worried that everyone in the restaurant was watching them. After all, in a town like Bald Eagle Falls, everyone knew everyone else's business. She knew she was on display, and that they would study her like a fish in an aquarium.

The waitress approached and took their drink order. Both of them ordered soft drinks. No alcohol, and Erin had had enough iced tea for the day.

"Do you want to share an appetizer?" Terry asked.

Erin demurred. "Whatever you want. I'm good either way."

"An order of onion rings?" Terry asked the waitress.

She paused, her pencil hovering over the order form pad. "The onion rings are not gluten-free," she warned.

Obviously, she knew who Erin was, even though Erin didn't know her by name.

"I don't have any allergies or intolerances myself," Erin said. "I just have a specialty bakery. I'm okay with gluten."

The waitress stood there for a moment looking at her, eyeing her as if she had been dishonest

"You don't eat gluten-free," she said in a flat, disbelieving tone.

"No. That's just how I cook at the bakery. Because I enjoy providing a service to people who can't have regular baking."

"Then why don't you just have a few things that are gluten-free, and make everything else the normal way?"

"To avoid cross-contamination. Some people are very sensitive. But there is no wheat or gluten in my kitchen, so there's no cross-contamination. And people who have to eat a gluten-free diet, they're not used to having very much choice. To being able to eat all of the things that we take for granted. So I want to provide that experience for them... a whole bakery, where they can eat whatever they want. Like little Peter Foster. You should see his eyes light up when he can choose anything he wants."

The waitress gave a smile. "He is a cutie, that little one," she admitted. "I always feel bad when he can't have mac and cheese like any other kid. Or pizzas, or tacos, or even a sandwich. He always has to get something like a baked potato, or salad, or roast beef. Not even a hot dog wiener."

Erin grinned as a new idea worked its way into her brain. "Can you give me a copy of your kiddie menu?"

"Uh... okay...?"

The waitress retreated for a moment to fetch a single-sheet children's menu, with the dishes on offer on one side and a maze, word search, and picture to color on the other.

"So, just the onion rings to start?"

"Yes. Thanks."

Terry looked at the menu when the waitress walked away again.

"What are you up to?"

"I'm thinking of a care package for Peter. If I provide the restaurant with a few of these things—tortilla, pizza shell, burger bun—then they can have them available for Peter or another child who has to eat gluten-free. They don't need to keep a lot on hand, I can just supply single servings for when they need them. Then Peter can have something fun and safe when he comes in."

Terry nodded, looking approving.

"You sure like that little boy."

"He's such a sweetie. And I want him to have a good experience. I don't want him to be like Caroline."

She had told him about her foster sister before. How she had insisted on sneaking gluten, until her body just couldn't recover from the damage. She had wanted so badly to fit in. To be just like all of the other kids. Erin didn't want any other child to have to go through that. Or for their siblings to have to watch them waste away and die from something that could have been prevented.

Terry's eyes slid away from Erin's again and he frowned. Something was obviously distracting him.

"What?" Erin asked. "What is it?"

His eyes returned to her. He rubbed his hand over his face, considering what to tell her. "We got the initial word back on the identification of the remains," he said reluctantly.

"Oh!" Erin nodded eagerly. "So they've confirmed that it's Adam Plaint? I know it's not certain until they get back the DNA, but..."

Terry shook his head. "It isn't Adam Plaint."

Erin stared at him, stunned. "What? How could—?"

"The dental records are not a match. Not even close."

"Then... who is it?"

"I wish I could tell you. I'm told it was a Caucasian male, thirties to forties. Six feet. The clothing is degraded, but blue jeans and t-shirt. Sneakers."

"Holy crap."

They sat there staring at each other, both trying to make sense of the bizarre revelation.

"We matched up the date of Adam Plaint's disappearance with the date that Clementine's garage foundation was poured," Erin stated.

"Right."

"We thought we might find his body under the concrete and we did. Or we found a body." She cocked her head at Terry. "How long had it been there? Maybe this was previous a burial ground, only no one knew..."

"T-shirt and blue jeans," Terry said. "This was no ancient burial ground. It's modern. The time frame is right. But it's the wrong body."

"Then... I can't wrap my mind around it. What happened?"

"We have to start looking at some other scenarios. We thought Angela or, on a long shot Trenton or even Davis, could have killed Adam Plaint. Well, somebody died, but it wasn't him. So maybe *he* killed the unidentified male, and he dumped the body where he knew it would be buried the next day, then got out of Dodge."

"Not because he was running away from his family or having an affair, but because he was afraid of being discovered to be a murderer."

"It's a little shaky," Terry admitted. "We don't have any evidence. But it fits the facts that we know to date."

"But who was the man?"

"I'll have to do some research... see who else might have disappeared around the same time. Working on the assumption that it was somebody he knew, and not just a drifter."

"What reason would he have to kill someone he didn't know?"

"That's my thinking. He had to have a motive. And not just someone knocking on his door and asking for a handout."

"Trenton and Davis... do you think they knew?"

Terry considered. "They must have. It's possible that the killer... Adam Plaint, if that's who it was... placed the body and covered it with a thin layer of dirt or gravel, so that the boys didn't notice when they were pouring the concrete over top of that. But... it's a stretch. I think they must have known."

They sat looking at each other. "It's very strange," Erin said. "Everything is turned on its head. I just can't believe it wasn't Adam Plaint."

"I imagine word will be out tomorrow. Can't keep anything confidential in this town. I'm lucky I got the report before anyone else. Sometimes I feel like I'm running to keep up instead of leading the charge."

"It's your administrative staff. They can't keep their mouths shut."

"I know. Want to come work for the PD?"

Erin shook her head. "Not a chance." She picked up her drink and took a sip. "I'm more than happy where I am. Though if Davis opens up The Bake Shoppe, it's going to make things that much more difficult for me."

"Well, up until now, I thought you had paved the way for him. Finding his father's body would mean that the estate could call off any search for him and Davis would own the whole store and everything else himself. But since the body isn't Adam Plaint, then it's back up in the air again. We still don't know what happened to Adam Plaint and if he's alive or dead."

"After Trenton's funeral, Davis said that their father just took off. That he abandoned them. He said there was no mystery; they knew at that time that he had just left them."

"Maybe it's true."

"But he said he knows that his father is dead now. That he's searched before, and he's sure that he's dead now."

Terry touched Erin's hand tentatively for a moment, then put his hand over hers when she didn't object. "I don't see how he could know that."

"Unless he killed him. If he intentionally killed Trenton to get his hands on the estate, he could have killed Adam at some point as well."

"Yes… it's possible."

The waitress came over with a large basket of onion rings. Erin leaned over, inhaling the savory, sweet onion smell. They looked deep fried to perfection, golden brown batter clinging to the onion.

"Those look great," she enthused.

The waitress took their dinner orders, and disappeared into the kitchen to pass them on.

"Do you think Adam Plaint is dead?" Erin asked. "Or do you think he's still out there somewhere, hiding? Afraid to let anyone know he's still alive, for fear that he'd be charged with murder. Or just that he'd have to face his family again. I can't see him going back to Angela. Can you imagine her taking him back after all those years?"

"No. So that leaves it open. Maybe he just ran away, and maybe he was killed. He could have died from something innocuous over the last few years. Cancer. Heart disease. Not necessarily anything violent. Not necessarily anything to do with his family or what happened twenty years ago."

"And unless Davis can prove it, the estate has to conduct a search to prove there are no more beneficiaries."

"I don't imagine he's any too happy about that."

"I don't get the feeling Davis is any too happy about anything."

"No. I don't think he's had a very happy life. I don't know what his formative years were like, but from what I can tell, thirteen onward sucked big time."

Erin laughed. She ate a couple of onion rings. It felt good to talk about the case. Good to sit with Terry Piper where she was safe, and not worry about what Davis was up to. And not to worry about what had happened to her parents twenty years ago. Just to laugh and act as if neither of them had a care in the world.

"So... I don't really know a lot about you," Erin said.

"What are you talking about? You know everything there is to know about me."

"I know your job. And that you're good with animals. And with people. You're good at what you do. I gather you grew up around here, somewhere in Tennessee. But you don't talk much about your family or your childhood."

Terry looked off across the restaurant, eyes unfocused. "If I talk to you about my life, does that mean you're going to talk to me about yours?"

Erin's heart gave an extra beat that made her chest hurt. She looked down at the onion rings, dipping a couple in the pool of ketchup Terry had poured onto a plate.

"You already know about mine," she said. "More than I know about yours. You know I grew up in foster care. That my aunt Clementine lived here and ran The Tea Room and made me her sole heir. You know that my parents were killed in a car accident. What else is there for me to tell you?"

Terry grunted. He didn't try answering right away. Then he looked back at Erin and focused on her. "The facts don't add up to a whole story," he said. "I know bits and pieces about you, but there are big gaps. Things that are more... mysterious."

"There's no mystery," Erin declared. "I'm just what I told you. The details are just... details. Nothing of any importance." She carefully directed the conversation. "So are your parents still alive?"

Terry sat back in his seat. He scratched the back of his neck. "My mother is."

"Your father isn't? How old was he when he died? You're not that old; most of my friends up north still had their parents."

"I was a teenager. It was quite sudden."

"Oh." Erin proceeded with caution. 'Sudden,' she had discovered over the years, usually meant either suicide or some other kind of violence. Not a disease. Not in his sleep. Unexpected. Sudden. "I'm sorry. Do you remember him?"

"Sure. Of course. I was old enough to remember him quite clearly." For a few minutes he didn't offer anything. Then, "He was a policeman."

"Just like you. Or, you are just like him. That's neat that you followed in his footsteps. He'd be really proud of you."

Terry picked apart an onion ring. "I hope so."

"You're a good cop. I don't know what this town would do without you."

"They'd find someone else, I guess."

"Not someone as good as you."

"How do you think Davis and Trenton felt about their father?" Terry asked, flipping the conversation back to the Plaint family.

"I don't know… You need to talk to people who knew them, and knew him. I don't know whether to believe the people who say he was a great guy, or the people who say he wasn't really that nice."

"Since no one is perfect, I would assume he was flawed. A normal person. Not a superhero, but not a villain either."

"Yeah. I suppose. So they probably loved him, like everybody loves their parents. They might fight with them sometimes, especially as teenagers, but they still love them."

"I haven't found any evidence that any of them kept in touch with him. I've been through all of Angela Plaint's papers. Through The Bake Shoppe and the house. Through whatever old possessions she kept of the children's when they left home. Through all of Davis's things. It doesn't look like any of them kept in touch with him. Not even in secret."

"Which up until now we thought meant they knew he was dead."

"And maybe even now. Why else wouldn't any of them ever try to contact him again? The daughter's things are still at the house, too. Angela never got rid of them, just closed up her room and left it as it was. No sign that she ever tried to contact her daddy. Not even when she knew she was going to die."

"You think she knew he was dead."

"I think she did. And I think she wanted to be with him. There wasn't anyone to write a letter to, because she knew he was dead and she wanted to rest with him."

Erin nodded. "That makes sense."

"Then where did he go? Did he leave here through his own choice? Run away? Or is he dead? Maybe he never left town at all."

"But if he killed the man who was under the garage foundations…"

"There's no evidence of that. Only coincidences connect them."

"I don't believe in coincidences. There has to be a reason. There has to be a logical connection between the two of them. You don't have two men just die or disappear at the same time without any explanation. There has to be a connection."

The waitress brought their entrees. K9 sat up, sniffing the air and looking interested, but Terry made a motion, commanding him to lie down again. "Sorry, bud, no table scraps." He looked across the table at Erin. "I think there's a connection too. I just don't know what it is or how to prove it."

CHAPTER 12

*E*rin settled in front of the microfiche reader and looked at her watch. It was strange not being at the bakery in the morning, after growing accustomed to being there every day. Bella was taking a shift and Vic had shooed Erin away.

"I'll take a break on Sunday, go into the city to see Willie in hospital. Everything in town will be closed on Sunday, so you won't be able to do anything."

Erin had wanted to get back to the library, which, as Vic said, was not open on Sundays, and it gave her the perfect opportunity. But Erin was still reluctant to leave the bakery in the hands of someone so inexperienced so soon.

"I know what to do and Bella will learn," Vic promised. "And you have a phone. We can reach you if we need you for anything."

"Are you sure? I could train Bella for one more day…"

"It's not that complicated. Trust me. Take your day off."

So Vic was supervising Bella's first full shift and Erin had time to do what she wanted. She had a long list, but she settled on reviewing microfiche at the library. When she had looked through it before, she had been looking for her parents' obituaries sometime after Adam Plaint's disappearance. She had read a few articles about him vanishing, but she hadn't absorbed anything else that had been happening in the community at the time. With the discovery that the body under her garage was not Adam Plaint, Erin thought it wise to see what else had been going on before that time. To see if she could connect up the dots and figure out what had happened to Adam and who the mysterious stranger who had ended up buried in her yard was.

The articles in the town's weekly newspaper were humdrum. Rummage sales. What students had earned honors at the high school. An effort to clean up the neighborhood. Erin couldn't see any of the reported events causing enough friction between two members of the community to result in someone's death.

She had to remain open to the possibility that it wasn't Adam who had killed the stranger; it could be anyone in the community. His wife or sons. A best friend. Someone he had a misunderstanding with. Willie had suggested that Adam might be having an affair. So there might be another woman involved. Or her husband or family. If it had been a young woman, her father or brothers might have had something to say about Adam dallying with her.

"Oh, hey Erin."

Erin looked up from the backlit screen. It was Melissa Lee. Erin was momentarily disconcerted to see her at the library in the middle of the day but, on reflection, there was no reason Melissa shouldn't be. She only worked part time at the police department. Erin didn't know whether she had other part time ventures as well.

"Hi, Melissa." Erin looked around to see what books Melissa was browsing through. But she was in the reference section, so chances were she wasn't picking up any beach reads. "What's up?"

"Doing some research," Melissa explained, sitting down at the other microfiche machine. "Just like you, I gather."

"Uh… yeah. What are you looking for?"

Melissa looked at the archives Erin had out. "Any unusual activity twenty years ago."

"Ah. For the police?"

She nodded. "Seems we've got a mystery on our hands! I take it Terry told you about our strange body."

"Yes. Pretty weird. I was so sure it was going to be Adam Plaint."

"So were we all."

"I haven't found anything interesting yet," Erin said, indicating the microfiche records she had gone through already. "I'm working backward from the time that the garage foundation was poured. I don't think I'm going to find anything, though. I've gotten a couple of months back without any alarm bells. No mysterious strangers or disappearances other than Adam's. But you lived here back then; maybe when you read something it will trigger a memory of something else that happened."

Melissa nodded. "I was only fifteen at the time, but you never know. I've got a pretty good memory."

Erin continued to skim over the text of the newspaper in front of her. "Do you think... I mean, you knew Trenton at the time. And Davis too, I guess. Do you think that either of them could have killed someone? They're the ones who ended up hiding the body."

Melissa considered while she put a sheet of microfilm into the machine. "I don't know. I can't imagine either of them doing it... But Trenton was cruel... if the right opportunity presented itself, I suppose so."

"And Davis?"

Melissa drummed her fingers on the table. "He was so withdrawn, even back then. Folded in on himself. Thirteen-year-old boys, you expect them to be rambunctious, rude, dare-devil... but he was quiet... dark... I don't think he had many friends, if any. He was a loner. Unlike Trenton, who always had a pack of admirers around him. Trenton was the show-off, the bright light."

"He didn't look after his little brother?"

Melissa swore. "No, not at all. Davis was the butt of his jokes, his cruelty. If there was no one else around to torture, then Davis was his favorite target."

"Trenton is lucky *he* didn't end up under the garage."

Melissa laughed. "I wish he had. It was a relief when he disappeared. For all of us."

"But his mother looked for him. She did file a missing persons report for him, unlike with Adam."

"Yes. Maybe she did have some motherly feelings for him... buried way, deep down. As far as I know, he never contacted her to let her know he was alive."

"Yet she left her estate to him," a male voice contributed.

Erin and Melissa both startled and turned to see who had spoken. Erin saw a scruffy, blond-haired man, his hairline receding. Alton Summers, private investigator.

"What are you doing here?" Erin demanded, hearing her voice go up several notes. She did *not* like Alton Summers. He had caused her enough grief.

"The same as you," Alton said, gesturing to the microfiche readers. "A little background research."

Melissa and Erin were using the only two microfiche readers. Erin didn't plan on giving up hers, and Melissa had barely started. Summers was going to be out of luck.

"Why?" Melissa wanted to know. "What's it got to do with you?"

Erin could have explained it before Summers did. But she let him answer for himself. "I'm acting on behalf of Trenton Plaint's estate. They need to establish who his next of kin were. Who inherits from him."

Melissa frowned. "I thought that was pretty clear. Davis."

"Davis is one of his potential beneficiaries. But clearly not the only one."

"Who else?"

"Intestacy laws say that a parent ranks ahead of a sibling. So if Adam Plaint is still alive, he ranks ahead of Davis as Trenton's beneficiary."

"So Davis has to share The Bake Shoppe with him?"

"No, Davis doesn't get anything if Adam Plaint is still alive."

"Nothing?"

"Adam Plaint inherits ahead of Davis. Everything, not a split."

Melissa shook her head. "That doesn't seem right."

"So what are you researching?" Erin asked. "I don't think you're going to find anything here that tells you whether Adam Plaint is still alive."

"You'd be surprised what I can find." Summers's eyes settled on Erin for a few seconds longer. "Or maybe you wouldn't. I did find *you*, after all."

Erin's face got warm. "Yes, you did," she agreed.

"I'm good at what I do. And I need access to one of those machines."

Erin wasn't inclined to give up her microfiche on her only day off. Alton Summers could use one any day of the week. Melissa was on police business, and she wasn't likely to give hers up just because Summers said he needed one.

"I just got here," Melissa said.

"We're probably looking at the same fiches. I could just pull up beside you."

Melissa looked at Erin as if looking for her advice. Erin shrugged. She wouldn't want to be sitting that close to Alton Summers, but Melissa would have to make her own decision.

"Well... I suppose so," Melissa said reluctantly. Summers didn't wait for her to change her mind, immediately grabbing a nearby chair and wedging it in beside Melissa. Melissa was looking at Erin again, but for rescue rather than advice. Erin couldn't do anything about it; Melissa was the one who had said yes.

"Where are you starting?" Summers questioned, leaning in. Erin could smell his body odor, and he wasn't right beside her. She could only hope that Melissa's sense of smell was not as good as Erin's, because even from a few feet away, it made Erin gag.

"I'm starting at the time that Adam Plaint disappeared, and then I guess I'll work my way backward." The same as Erin was doing.

"Why would you go backward? You're looking for something that happened after he disappeared, not before."

"Something could have happened before. Something did—someone killed the man who was found under Clementine's garage. If he was killed before the foundations were poured, then he was killed the same day as Adam disappeared."

"And if there was something in the paper describing a stranger having an altercation with Adam Plaint, then that would have come out at the time that he disappeared. But there wasn't. So we're looking for any evidence he was still alive after the date that he disappeared. I need to see whether I can pick up his trail."

"Well, then, how about the week before he disappeared, to start with. Then we can work our way forward."

Erin admired Melissa for sticking to her guns. Melissa pushed wild curls away from her face. She used the knobs on the reader to find the newspaper she was looking for.

"Nothing much happening," she murmured, as she scrolled through the stories. "Community clean-up. Ladies' tea. There's your auntie, Erin."

Erin glanced over at the screen and nodded. She too had seen Clementine's advertisement for the weekly ladies' tea that took place at The Tea Room after church services. A tradition that Erin had reinstituted at Auntie Clem's Bakery.

"I doubt if Adam Plaint's disappearance had anything to do with the ladies' tea," Alton Summers scoffed.

"I didn't say it did. I'm just thinking. Remembering."

"If you wanted to do something without your wife noticing, the ladies' tea would be a good time to do it," Erin suggested. "She'd be out of the way the same time every week."

"Only Adam Plaint didn't disappear on a Sunday," Summers pointed out.

"No, but this other man could have been killed on Sunday," Melissa inserted her opinion. "We don't know what day he was killed, just what day he was buried. He could have been killed a day or two before that."

"Why would Adam Plaint want to meet him in secret?" Summers made a note in his notepad. "And remember, Angela said he wasn't missing, that he'd just left. Or she'd made him go. If she was keeping something he'd done a secret, that means she knew about it. If she didn't know where he had gone or why, she would have wanted a police investigation."

Erin's head was starting to spin trying to think through the points of logic. She nodded her head slowly.

"We need to know what happened after the disappearance." Summers waited for Melissa to get with it and navigate to the newspaper after Adam Plaint had disappeared.

Erin looked back at her own screen, paging through the newspapers before the disappearance. She didn't like to agree with Summers on anything, but she had to admit he was right. She hadn't found anything in the papers leading up to the disappearance that mentioned a mysterious stranger, or disappearance, or contention between the Plaints and someone else.

Melissa sighed and put in another sheet of microfiche. Erin took the next one after that. For a while, they were each lost in their own newspapers, catching up on the news of Bald Eagle Falls from twenty years before.

Melissa sat back, covering her eyes. "I'm going to go blind staring at this stuff. Whose idea was it to archive anything on microfiche, anyway? It's practically unreadable! Why haven't they computerized it?"

"This was the technology at the time," Summers said. "Be glad that it was microfiched and that you're not having to go through dusty old newspapers by hand. That's a lot worse."

"I don't see how it could be," Melissa griped.

Summers scratched his belly through his t-shirt. "It's a weekly paper, so we don't have nearly as much to go through as looking through a big city daily. It's pretty quick to read through."

"I've read as much as I'm going to." Melissa pushed herself away from the table. "I'll let the PD know that there isn't anything suspicious around the time that that man was murdered and Adam Plaint disappeared. There's no mention of anything that seems to be related, nothing suspicious, and no mention of the Plaint family or Clementine's property anywhere."

"You should read at least a year's worth of papers," Summers told her.

"A year? I've read a couple of months, and that's plenty. I have other work to do. If you want to keep going, have at it." Melissa made an expansive gesture toward the microfiche machine, inviting him to do just that.

Summers slid into the seat that Melissa had just vacated and, with his eyes trained on the screen, started to manipulate the controls. Melissa rolled her eyes and shook her head at Erin, expressing her disgust, but Summers said nothing and gave no sign that he realized that she was exasperated with him.

Erin swapped her microfiche for a newer one. Melissa stormed off.

"A year?" Erin asked. "That's how far you're going to go forward looking for some clue of what happened to Adam Plaint?"

"No, that's how far I told Miss Lee she should look."

"Oh. Well, why should she read that far but you don't need to?"

"You misunderstand. I'm not stopping after a year. I'm reading after that."

Erin turned her head to look at him, raising an eyebrow. "How far are you reading?"

"All the way."

"Twenty years' worth of newspapers?" Erin couldn't keep the incredulity out of her voice.

"No. Only ten. After that, they started to digitize, so I can use search terms to get through those years much faster. But the first ten years, those I'll have to go through on microfiche."

"That's over five hundred papers."

"Yes. It is."

"Won't your eyes get tired?"

"Yes. I won't do it all today. But I'll break in the first chunk. And this is probably the most important. If he was going to reappear or make contact, it would be within two years after, or else after Angela Plaint's death. Those are the two most likely times for him to make an appearance. That doesn't mean I'll find any mention in the papers. But I need to exhaust all possible avenues."

"That's a lot of work."

"Tracking down heirs isn't easy. Ever. If it was easy, the lawyers wouldn't need to hire me. They'd do a Google search, find the person, and make contact. When Google fails, that's when they call me."

Erin nodded and went back to skimming her pages. She wasn't sure what she was looking for anymore. Any mention of the Plaint or Price names. Anything that sounded like a crime. Anything that showed a map or a picture of Clementine's neighborhood.

At the familiar sound of a dog panting and a whiff of his scent, Erin looked up from her research. She smiled at Officer Piper and K9.

"Hi," she greeted with a happy smile. "I didn't think I'd run into you here."

"Well, you didn't. Not exactly." His head swiveled toward Alton Summers. "Miss Lee mentioned seeing you here, Mr. Summers."

"And I hope she told you that I waited until she was finished with her microfiche machine before I took it over," Summers answered evenly. "I didn't bully her into giving it up. In fact, I told her she should do more research than she did."

"I'm not sure she came up with anything helpful. Reading further wouldn't necessarily have produced any results."

"Well, not reading any further certainly doesn't."

"I'm not here to talk to you about Miss Lee's research methodology. Or to accuse you of stealing the microfiche machine away from her."

"What then?" Summers returned. Though his eyes were on Erin, a little quirk in the corner of his mouth that said he knew exactly why Terry was there.

"Because I wanted to warn you to leave Erin alone."

Erin didn't know whether reverting to the use of her first name instead of 'Miss Price' was intentional, or if it had just been automatic to him. Did he intend to indicate to Summers that he had a personal relationship with Erin? That he wasn't going to put up with any nonsense because she meant something to him?

Summers leaned back in his chair, tipping it back on two legs and making it let out a long creak. He didn't even seem to notice it. He folded his arms across his chest in a closed-off, belligerent gesture.

"What makes you think I would do anything to bother Miss Price?" he demanded. His careful enunciation of 'Miss Price' told both of them that he had noticed Terry's slip into the familiarity of her first name.

"Because in the past, you have attempted to blackmail her. And you attempted to blackmail Joelle Biggs. And I'm pretty sure that you were complicit in the plot to kill Trenton Plaint for his inheritance. That's what makes me think you're going to bother her."

"If you could prove any of that, I'd be in jail right now."

"Obviously, there's not much I can do without their cooperation. But you might want to watch out, because I know what you've been doing, and if at any point Erin does decide she wants to charge you... I will be more than happy to do so."

"More than happy," Summers mocked, mimicking him like a ten-year-old.

"You leave Erin alone. Are we clear?"

"Yes, sir, Officer."

Terry's eyes went to Erin. "You going to be here much longer?"

"No... I don't think so. I don't quite have Mr. Summers' staying power. Just a few more pages."

"All right. You let me know if you run into any problems." Terry looked at Summers. "Call me, text me, I'll be back here faster than a cat with its tail in a mousetrap."

Erin laughed. "Charming."

"Let me know."

"Okay."

Terry favored Alton Summers with one more long glare, and then walked K9 back off at a brisk pace. He was barely out of earshot when Summers spoke to Erin.

"Do you really think it would do you any good to have one single policeman on your side if I decided to attack your reputation?" He said it in a low hiss, like a snake.

Erin looked over at him without speaking.

"Do you think the police department can stop gossip? You know how things spread around here. All the ladies in the town need are some juicy little tidbits about your past life, and they'll tear you apart like a pool full of piranhas. You won't have any friends here anymore."

"Should I tell Terry that you're threatening me again?"

"Not unless you're willing to lay charges."

Erin pressed her lips together. She had no desire to bring charges against Summers. If she did, the secrets that he kept threatening to share would be all over the police reports, and subsequently all over town. And she had no way to combat them.

"Then how about you leave me alone, and I'll leave you alone?" Erin suggested.

"I don't really want to leave you alone." He held her gaze for a moment, but then looked back at the work at hand. "But I don't have the time for you right now. I have other things to do."

Erin waited for the other shoe to drop, but he let it go at that. She looked back at her own glowing screen and tried to focus on the words.

Her eyes caught on Trenton Plaint's name, and she slowed down to read what it had to say about him. He had won some kind of scholarship. The article detailed his success in various teams he had played on since childhood.

"You know when the other time he'd be most likely to show up would be?" Erin asked, flipping eagerly through the microfiche for the right month.

Summers looked over at her. His mouth pursed like he'd bitten a lemon. "When?"

"When his son disappeared."

Summers nodded, slowly at first and then with more vigor. "Yes, definitely. In fact, that in itself might be a clue that he had returned."

"He came back to take his son out of here? Got him away from the home and Angela. Introduced him to whatever new life he had established. Trenton was the one who was the most successful. Maybe Adam Plaint figured that was reason enough to get him out of Bald Eagle Falls and set him up somewhere else."

Erin put the microfiche into the reader and searched for news of Trenton Plaint's disappearance. It had to have made a big splash. Even if Angela had been able to talk the police out of searching for her suddenly missing husband, she hadn't been able to prevent a report being made when her son disappeared a couple of years later.

She became aware that Summers was no longer looking at his microfiche, but at hers. He had beady eyes. Small, dark, animal-like eyes that gave Erin the creeps. The more time she spent around the man, the less she liked him and wanted to spend time around him.

"Do you mind?" she growled.

"Finding anything?"

"There's a lot to read through."

He blinked a couple of times and looked back at his own screen. "What year did his daughter die, do you know?"

"No. She was young. Early twenties, I think."

He pulled out his phone and started tapping on it busily. Apparently finding what he was looking for, he browsed through the sheets of microfiche and pulled one out, putting it into his reader. Erin had to admit that it seemed likely that Adam would have come home when he heard about his daughter's death, even if it was just to go to the graveyard, avoiding any public appearances. If he had returned to Bald Eagle Falls for Trenton, how callous would he have to be to not even give his daughter a moment of consideration when she committed suicide?

They were both intent on their screens for some time. Erin sighed.

"I'm not finding anything. You?"

"No." Summers's voice was little more than a grunt. "Everything has been… sanitized. No mention that the daughter killed herself. No mention of the disappearances of her father and brother. Nothing that suggests any friction with anyone else in town. It's like she just died in her sleep. And Adam and Trenton never existed."

Erin shook her head. She got the same feeling when she read through the newspaper articles. Everything was normal and above-board. There was no significant crime in Bald Eagle Falls. No problem families or parts of town. No concerns expressed over anything except untidy yards or graffiti.

"Nothing here, either."

~

Erin had dinner ready for Vic when she got home from work. She was restless, eager for all of the details from Vic on how the day had gone. All of the little problems or concerns. The personalities. The gossip. How Bella had done, and whether she'd had to go to the commode.

It wasn't lasagna like Vic had made for her when she'd been home sick another day, but she managed a nice pork roast with gravy, fresh rolls, Jam Lady jam, and the necessary vegetables to round the meal out.

"Someone's been cooking!" Vic called out as soon as she walked in the door. "It smells heavenly!"

Erin couldn't help giving her a big grin. "Hungry?"

"Starving."

"You want to change and have a bath before dinner?"

"No. I want to inhale everything that smells good in the house."

Erin laughed. She had anticipated that Vic would want to eat right away, and she was glad she had called it right, because she wouldn't have wanted the roast to dry out while they were waiting for Vic to get ready. She opened the oven, and immediately Orange Blossom was winding his way around her feet, tripping her up.

"Shoo! Get out of the way!" Erin tried to push him aside with her foot. "Don't get in the way of hot dishes!"

Vic swooped in and picked the cat up to get him out of the way. "Behave yourself," she told the cat. "You want to get burned? Or for Erin to get burned? You have to stay out of the way when we're getting stuff out of the oven."

Erin moved quickly to get everything ready, sure that the cat would not allow himself to be held for long. Then he'd be squirming and kicking to be put down, and be underfoot again.

She was right, and in a minute, Vic had to release Orange Blossom. He stalked into one corner of the kitchen to sulk, though, rather than getting in Erin's way again, so it was a good result.

Vic washed her hands and helped to set the table and transfer the serving dishes over to it.

"So how did it go?" Erin demanded. "I want all of the details. I feel like I was away for a week!"

"It was just a normal day…"

"Don't tell me that! Tell me what happened?"

"Bella met Bertie Braceling."

"Oh…" Erin sat down and started to serve up. "And how did that go?"

"He strung her along for a while, trying to get her to find something he could eat, before breaking the news to her."

"What an old devil. And you let him?"

"She needed some kind of initiation. She did very well. In the end, I showed her where to find the tortilla shells and the pancake mix and Bertie went home happy. I think he was tickled to be able to tease a newbie. You know how he gets a kick out of being impossible to cook for."

"It's funny." Erin stared off into the distance. "Isn't it? How some people can just take it in stride, and they don't care that you can't cook anything special for them, and they're just willing to work with the limited diet they got, and other people… even those who just have one ingredient they have to avoid, find it so restricting and just pine for the foods they can't have and the social eating that they used to be able to do, and can't anymore."

"Let's keep this positive," Vic directed, not wanting Erin to let herself be distracted by thoughts of Caroline. "It was a good day. And you had a good rest?"

"I didn't exactly rest," Erin said. "I did sleep in, but I did research at the library, and I cooked, and got a little bit of cleaning done and playing with the animals."

"Find anything at the library?"

Erin described meeting Melissa and Alton Summers, but there wasn't much to say, as all of their speculation had just led to dead ends.

"If I murdered someone, I would run away and never come back," Vic said. "Why do we expect Adam Plaint to be any different?"

"It's just that with Trenton later disappearing… and Sophie dying, it seems like he might have been back once or twice. But neither of us came up with any leads."

"And nothing on the identity of the mysterious man?"

"Not a speck. I'm still glad I went. Now I know there aren't any leads in the paper. But it wasn't very productive."

Vic nodded. She pushed herself back from the table slightly, turning away from the rolls and jam. "Anything in the mail today?"

"I don't think I checked."

Vic got up and went to the door to see if there was anything in the box. She returned to the kitchen examining a large manila envelope. "Erin… I think this is…"

Erin's stomach instantly tied in knots. She had kept herself so busy with the research at the library, she had forgotten her own mystery for a few hours. "It's not… it isn't my file, is it?"

"I think it is."

"It's probably just a letter saying I need to fill in other forms. Deal with another department."

"I don't think so. It's too thick. It's not just a letter."

Erin put out her hand and took it from Vic, handling it by the edges as if it were evidence in a murder. She almost expected it to burn her hands when she touched it.

"I'm afraid to open it."

"How are you going to read it, then?"

Erin laughed helplessly. "I don't know. I don't think I can read it now."

"After all of that work? All of the research and forms and complaining? You'd darn well better read it."

"Okay, okay… maybe tomorrow."

"Today. Don't put it off any longer."

"Why not? I'm feeling kind of tired. I'll leave it until I'm feeling up to it tomorrow."

Vic reached for the envelope. "I'm going to open it."

Erin yanked it back. "No, you can't do that! It's mine!"

"Then open it."

Erin took a minute, fumbling, to get her finger under the flap of the envelope and tear it. She took a deep breath and reached inside for the thick wad of papers.

"What if it doesn't answer any questions?"

"Open it."

She pulled them out. On top was a letter on official DHS letterhead, releasing the documents to her under privacy and freedom of information laws. She studied her own name and file number on the letter. She had been waiting for so long, it seemed impossible that she was about to finally get the answers to her questions of when and how the accident had happened. An explanation why her parents' death dates were so different from her recollection.

And she was suddenly sick. She ran to the bathroom, sure she was going to throw up.

"Erin? Are you okay? What's wrong?"

Erin really didn't want to throw up the meal she had worked so hard at. It had been delicious, but it wouldn't be the second time around. Erin steadied herself on the counter and tried to breathe slowly and get her body under control.

"I'm okay," she said rapidly, under her voice. "I'm okay, I'm okay, I'm okay."

"You're fine," Vic agreed. "You're just having a bit of a panic attack. Everything is going to be okay. This happened years ago. It's not happening now. You know it was years ago."

"It's okay. It's going to be okay."

"That's right. Now just sit down and look at the papers, and you'll feel a lot better."

They were still in her hands. Erin had forgotten she was holding them. Her hands were numb. She looked down at them.

"Sit down," Vic repeated, steering Erin toward the commode. The bathroom was crowded with both of them in there. Erin perched on the toilet seat and stared down at the bundle of papers in her hands. Vic nudged the cover page. "Just look at it. You want to know what happened, right?"

"No."

Vic chuckled. "Yes, you do. Turn the page."

Erin obeyed, moving like an automaton, with no real will of her own. The photocopied pages were twenty years old. An intake report that was dated before her eighth birthday. That was what she remembered. Her first birthday in foster care. The accident had been before her birthday, not after, like Clementine's records indicated.

Erin breathed a sigh of relief. She was right, then. Clementine had just led her on a wild goose chase. The papers verified what Erin recalled.

"You see, it's okay," Vic said softly. She was watching Erin's face, not reading the papers. She knew that the papers were private. Something for Erin's eyes only, unless she decided to share them. "Everything is going to be okay."

"Yes." Erin nodded. The nausea was starting to pass. She was feeling steadier. What had she thought she was going to discover? She focused on the words on the page, trying to make sense of them. It was like reading Chinese symbols. She could see them, but they didn't have any meaning for her.

She started at the top. Intake report. Date. Her name, Erin Price. Her birthdate, just a few days out. 'F' for female. Then the narrative began. Erin Price's parents were in a devastating car accident that rendered them both incapable of caring for her. She had no known next of kin and was in need of care on an emergency basis.

Erin stared at the individual letters of the words, waiting for it to sink in. The social worker had a broad, wide hand, the letters as perfectly round as a kindergarten teacher's printing.

Incapable of caring for her.

Erin blinked at the words. Incapable of caring for her; not 'dead.' Why didn't the intake papers say they were dead?

She forced herself to continue down the form. Past the summary paragraph and into the details.

"This…" Erin licked her lips, her mouth suddenly dry. Vic was looking at her, waiting for her to finish her sentence. "This isn't right."

"What is it?" Vic asked. She picked up Erin's cup from the side of the sink and filled it with cold water. Erin could smell the water in the closeness of the room. It was all she could think about. The only thing that made any sense.

"The social worker said my parents died instantly. I remember that clearly. She kept repeating it."

"But the paperwork says something different?"

Erin took the cup from Vic and took a few swallows of water. Her mouth was a desert. It was like she hadn't drunk in days. She put the cup back down and touched her finger to the page, trying to pin the words down and keep them from swimming on the page. By touching them, she tried to convince herself that they were real. It was talking about her. Not someone else. It was what had happened to her.

"It says that my mother sustained… massive head trauma." Erin swallowed. "And my father had spinal cord injuries and internal bleeding." She breathed through her mouth. "It's present-tense. Not that they died from it. They were still living."

"But they still couldn't take care of you. They still needed to take you into foster care so that there was someone who could take care of you."

"But… yes. But… they lied to me."

"Maybe they thought you were too young to understand. That it would be easier for you if they just told you they were dead."

"How is that easier?" Erin demanded. She was angry at Vic, as if it had been her choice.

"Because you could carry on with your life without all of the uncertainty of what was going to happen to you next."

"How could I? How could it be better to think they were dead when they were still alive?" Erin rubbed her forehead, trying to disperse the tension and growing pain. "I never got to say good-bye. I could have said good-bye."

"They probably went straight into surgery," Vic said. "And you don't know if they even survived that."

Erin looked down at the papers. "How could they do that to me? Tell me they were dead, when they weren't?"

"Does it say… when they did die?" Vic said the words delicately, like a cat picking its way through a puddle.

Erin turned the page. More official gobbledygook. Court papers with her name on them. The minor child. A profile sheet of the foster parents she was first turned over to. People whose names were unfamiliar to her. She didn't remember them. They had probably only been emergency respite. Looking after her needs for a day or two until the social worker could identify a long-term guardian.

Had they contacted Clementine? Had they even known about her?

Erin turned over the page, but there was still nothing about her parents dying. For a moment, Erin imagined that they were still alive. That after they had woken up, they'd been unable to get her back. That they had spent years trying to cut through the bureaucratic red tape to find her and bring her home again. But Clementine had listed death dates beside both of their names. They had each died, without Erin ever seeing them or saying good-bye to them.

There was a progress report. Dry, clinical words and phrases indicating that she was adapting well. A new family profile sheet. A more familiar name. Erin thought she might vaguely remember them. The family she had been with for her birthday.

Erin wiped at her cheeks, wet with tears she hadn't even been aware of shedding.

Vic waited for more information, not wanting to push Erin. Letting her find her own pathway to the truth.

Another progress report. Lots of negative words about transition difficulties. Bedwetting. Fighting with siblings. Lack of attention. What had they expected? That she would be unmoved by her parents' reported deaths and quickly adjust to living with new people? That after her life was turned upside down, she would be able to just continue on without any kind of damage?

She might not have been injured in the car accident, but she had been changed forever.

Erin forced herself to turn pages. To swim through the pages detailing the consequences of the accident without knowing what had happened. Were her parents still fighting for life while the social worker worried about how long it was going to take Erin to adapt to her new family? It seemed ridiculous to even call them her family when her parents were still alive. If they recovered, what would they tell her? Would they tell her that they had lied? Or would they just keep her away, pretending nothing had happened?

Erin drew in a shuddering breath and continued to turn pages.

Then came an update report noting her father's death. A date and time. Dry, clinical words stating that he'd been paralyzed in the accident with no hope of recovering use of his arms and legs. He hadn't been able to communicate. And then he'd developed sepsis.

Erin came dangerously close to getting sick. She picked up her cup and pressed it to her forehead, trying to cool her burning, sweating face. Erin noted with one removed, logical portion of her brain, that Clementine had gotten the date right.

"Erin?" Vic's voice was soft.

"My dad died," Erin told her. Her words were choked. After so long, why would knowing the details be so painful? She had known he'd died. He'd been gone for twenty years. She'd mourned him long ago.

"I'm sorry."

"I never got to say good-bye. He was alone in the hospital. Paralyzed and septic. And there was no one there to hold his hand or tell him good-bye."

Vic moved closer. She pulled Erin's face against her in a hug. "I'm so sorry."

"It's not fair. Why did they lie to me?"

"They knew he would never be able to take care of you," Vic suggested. "If he was paralyzed, they knew that he'd never be able to look after you, even if he recovered from his other injuries. So they tried to spare you."

"They didn't have any right."

"I know."

"And my mom? What happened to her?" Erin pulled away from Vic and looked down at the papers. So far, she had come across no reports on her mother, other than the mention of head injuries in the intake report. "She was in a coma? What if she woke up? People do wake up, and then she could recover, and she could take care of me."

"I don't know, sweetie."

Erin felt frozen. Unable to continue looking through the twenty-year-old papers. She knew what Clementine's genealogical records indicated. If Clementine had been right about Erin's father's death date, would she be likely to be wrong about Erin's mother's? That meant that if Erin kept flipping pages, sooner or later she would come across the page informing her that her mother had died a couple of months down the line. Had she ever woken up? Had she been aware of the deception? How DFS had lied to Erin while her parents both languished in hospital beds, alone?

"Are you done?" Vic nodded toward the papers.

They both knew that Erin hadn't gone through all of them. But maybe Vic sensed that it was too much and Erin couldn't go on.

"Yes."

It was too much for her. As much as she had thought that she wanted to know what had happened to her parents and why the dates on Clementine's family tree were different, she really couldn't handle any more in one day.

Erin straightened the papers and got to her feet.

Vic put her arm around Erin to support her. Her arms were strong and capable. "You're wobbly as a newborn calf. Take it slow."

The bathroom was really too small for both of them to walk abreast, but they turned toward each other and manage to squeeze past the counter, and then sideways through the door.

"Do you want to lie down?"

Erin wasn't sure what she wanted, but she nodded. Vic helped guide her to her bedroom and to her bed without collapsing. The muscles in Erin's thighs were quivering and her knees kept threatening to bend when she didn't mean them to. She stretched out on her bed. Vic took the papers from her hand.

"I'll just put these on your desk for when you want them."

She pulled Erin's blankets up and fussed over her.

"Do you need anything else?" She brushed Erin's hair out of her face. "More water? A sleeping pill?"

Erin shook her head. "No, thanks, I just want…" She closed her eyes and sought the blankness of sleep. "I just want to forget everything."

"Okay. Give me a shout if you need anything."

Erin just kept her eyes closed and didn't answer. She tried to block out all of the thoughts. She didn't want to think. She didn't want to imagine. She didn't want to remember.

But her mind wouldn't stop working. Trying to make sense of all of the new information, she started to dream before she even realized she was falling asleep.

She wasn't in the car this time, but in bed. An uncomfortable bed with hard bars under the mattress and scratchy blankets. Her parents were in the same room as she was, their voices close at hand, their bigger bed a blacker shape in the dark room.

"Can't we work it out?" Mommy begged. "Please…"

"I'm just supposed to forget this?" Her father's voice was a low growl like an animal's. "Just forget how my wife made a fool of me and put it behind me? That's convenient for you, isn't it? No consequences for your actions?"

"I made a mistake."

"This isn't just a slip! You didn't trip and fall into this guy's arms! How can you expect me to just get over that?"

"I need you. We're a family. I can't do this without you."

Erin could hear them moving. She could imagine her hand on his arm, him jerking away, pushing her back. She'd seen the gestures repeated enough times.

"I'm not raising another man's child."

"But we don't know—"

"I know. Do you really want to make a public issue of it? Fight me in court?"

Mommy started to cry. Erin clenched her fists and hid her head under the pillow. Crying was worse than fighting. She felt the fear welling up in her. What was going to happen to them? She had friends whose parents had split up. She didn't want them to. She wanted them to stay together. But why was her father saying she was another man's? He was her daddy. He'd always been her daddy. There was no other daddy, like there was in other families. Just him.

Erin couldn't help crying, even though she knew if she was caught, the tears would make everything worse. She cried silently, head buried under the pillow. Trying not to make a sound that would let them know she was awake.

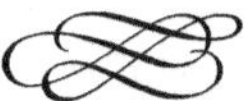

CHAPTER 13

*E*rin woke up, disoriented. She wasn't sure at first what had awakened her. Gradually, awareness seeped in, and she realized that her phone, still in her pocket, was vibrating. She squinted at the clock to see what time it was, but couldn't clear her vision enough to make it out. The room was dark and still.

Eventually, she managed to slide the phone out of her pocket to look at it. Unknown caller.

When she lived up north, she never would have answered a phone call without a proper caller ID. But Terry's cell phone had a blocked caller ID on it, and sometimes the telephone interchanges around the town were unreliable, forgetting to relay caller ID numbers or even showing the wrong call information. It was something that Erin was just learning to live with. Sometimes answering a call was like Russian Roulette.

She tapped the screen to answer the call and put it up to her ear before realizing that she had been sound asleep and didn't really have her voice yet. She cleared her throat a couple of times, trying to wake up her vocal cords.

"Uh—hello?"

"Leave the past alone." The voice in her ear was harsh and robotic, making Erin wince and pull it away from her ear. "Just let sleeping dogs lie."

"But—" Erin's brain was not operating quickly enough to give a cogent answer. That she wasn't investigating anything. Or, she had been doing a little research, just out of curiosity, but she hadn't found anything and was still just as much in the dark as everyone else.

All she could think of was how Davis had tried to burn her house down when he thought she had turned up information about him and Trenton killing their father. At least, that was why they had thought Davis had tried to burn the house down. But if the man who had been killed hadn't been Adam Plaint, then what had Davis been worried about? "I'm not," she sputtered, but was able to get nothing else out when the background buzz on the call went dead, and she knew the call had been disconnected. She looked down at her screen.

What the hell was that?

Was it Davis again? Worrying that she was, once again, digging too close to his secrets? Adam Plaint himself, not wanting to be found? Someone else whose guilty secret Erin was too close to exposing, not even realizing it? She wasn't much of a sleuth if the only truths she could ever expose were the ones she had come upon accidentally.

To begin with, Erin put her phone down on the bedside table and plugged it in to charge. She closed her eyes and waited for sleep to come. But it didn't. Erin turned over and pummeled her pillow and tried again. She considered getting out of bed and putting on her pajamas, having climbed into bed in her clothes after the shock of receiving the file from DFS. Maybe if she had her proper pajamas on, she'd be able to get back to sleep again. But getting up and changing might also just wake her up further, completely ruining any chance of getting back to sleep again. And she needed to be up early in the morning to get to the bakery. No matter what had happened twenty years ago, real life continued to march forward, and she needed to run her business and earn the money to feed herself and her animals.

Erin cuddled under the blanket, closing her eyes and striving to relax every muscle in her body. But she was too twitchy, and her brain was going like a hamster on a wheel.

It was Davis. It had to be. He had seen her at the library, or someone had told him she was there. Looking at old newspaper articles and talking to a private detective and a representative of the police department. She could see how that would look to him, all of the investigative forces in the town gathering in one place, talking the case over. It didn't matter that they hadn't found anything. All that mattered was that Davis thought they had found something. Or might soon find something.

He had come after her once before. Tried to burn her house down around her for discovering that Trenton and Davis had something to do with their father's death. Or with something. Her cryptic shorthand notes could be construed by someone with a guilty mind as her having made a discovery. Davis Plaint. Or Adam Plaint. Or someone else. They had never been able to prove that it was Davis, however much they believe it was him.

Erin sat up in bed. She knew she wasn't going to be able to get back to sleep again. That ship had sailed. The phone call had banished every vestige of sleep from her brain.

What if he tried again? What if he decided Erin wasn't going to do as she was told, and he had to finish what he had started?

They weren't safe there, two women and their pets. No burglar alarm. The world's smallest police force. No 9-1-1 service.

Erin turned on her lamp and started to write a list. But she couldn't focus on it. She couldn't shake the words of the caller from her mind. What if she didn't do what he had told her to? What if he thought that she was investigating the mysterious stranger's death, or Adam Plaint's disappearance? Or some other secret that they didn't want revealed? What would happen then?

Erin sighed. With a lead weight in her gut, she picked her phone up and dialed Officer Terry Piper's phone number. She could have gone through the police department's emergency department. Then she might get the Sheriff or Tom Banks rather than Terry, if it was his turn to sleep rather than to be on call.

But Erin didn't want one of the others. She knew it was selfish, but even if Terry wasn't on call, she only wanted him.

In only a couple of rings, Terry had picked up, so fast that Erin thought he couldn't possibly have been asleep.

"Piper," he snapped out.

"Terry, it's Erin." She knew he must have picked up his phone too fast to look at the caller ID.

"Erin…? What's wrong?"

"I don't know. I probably shouldn't be calling you about this, but…"

"What? What is it?"

"I had a phone call. A few minutes ago. It was a blocked number, but I picked it up anyway. You know…"

"Who was it?"

"I couldn't tell. A computer voice. Altered. It said… to stop digging around in the past. To let sleeping dogs lie."

There was silence for a few moments. Erin closed her eyes, picturing Terry's face. Waiting for him to look at the problem from all angles.

"I'm coming over."

Erin was too relieved to put on a show of protesting. "Okay. Thanks."

"Erin."

"Yes?"

"Don't open the door to just anyone. Make sure it's me first. Look and be sure before you open the door."

"Okay."

He hung up. Erin looked down at herself. She didn't know whether to comb her hair and change to make herself more presentable. Or whether to put on her pajamas so that she didn't look like such a lunatic, in clothes all wrinkled from sleep. But if he wanted them to move, to go somewhere more safe, she'd have to change back into day clothes again. There wasn't any winning solution.

Orange Blossom crawled out from underneath the blankets she had inadvertently flipped over top of him. He gave a wide yawn with an adorable little squeak, and then rolled over onto his back, offering his tummy to be rubbed.

Erin knew that was often just a ploy to get her fingers close enough for attack, so she was cautious in reaching out to give him a scratch. He was warm and soft from sleep and just closed his eyes when she scratched him, his rumbling purr filling the room. "You're a suck, you know that?" Erin murmured to him. "You just want all the attention."

He lay there purring.

Erin heard a vehicle pulling up to the house, and flicked her curtain back for a peek out the window. It was Terry's marked police car. She watched him get out and watched K9 follow him out and heel as Terry headed up the sidewalk.

She did as she was told, turning on the porch light and staring at him through the peephole before unlocking and opening the door, even though she had just seen him walk up to the house.

"You're okay?" he said in a low voice.

"Yes."

"Okay. Shut and lock the door again. I'm just going to take K9 and walk around the property, make sure there's no one lurking around. I'll knock when I come back. But again... don't open the door unless you're sure it's me."

"Do you really think someone else is going to come to the door expecting me to let them in?" Erin challenged.

"Not the time to argue, Erin," he snapped.

Erin realized he was right. She closed the door and locked it. She sat down on the couch to wait for him. She was wide awake and listened alertly to every creak and groan of the house. She could hear Marshmallow moving around in his pen and wondered whether he was awake or having a dream. Did rabbits dream?

She heard his footsteps on the sidewalk again, and went to the door. Her hand was on the lock before she remembered to check that it was really Terry. It was, and she let him in.

They sat down on the couch and Terry flipped open his notebook.

"This call came to your cell phone?"

"Yes."

He didn't ask her what her number was. He already knew that. "What time?"

Erin took out her phone and went to the recent calls list. "One thirty-seven."

"And it was just a short call? A minute or two?"

Erin nodded. "Probably not even that. Just a few sentences. Then he hung up before I had a chance to say anything. Not that I knew what to say..."

"You say 'he.' Was it a male voice?"

"I don't know. It was altered. Like you hear on stalker movies. So it could have been a man or a woman."

"Was there anything about the speech patterns that you might have noticed? A familiar turn of phrase? The spacing between the words? Something pronounced in a unique way?"

Erin closed her eyes and tried to play back the scene in her mind. "I don't know. It woke me up. I wasn't very alert. Just... 'let sleeping dogs lie.' That's not really helpful. Anyone could say that."

"Yes." Terry sighed. "What was he talking about, do you think? You haven't been part of the police investigation. You haven't been doing any sleuthing on the side, have you?"

"No." Erin's cheeks burned and she looked away from him. "Uh… no, not really. Just… just looking at the microfiche. I had looked through them before when I was trying to find out information about my parents and I wanted to see if there was anything in there that might give us a clue to the identity of the man…"

Terry frowned. K9 moved from sitting to lying, giving a wheezy sigh. "I thought you were there looking for more information on your parents. Why did you go back to the papers? Had you seen something that you thought might help to identify the remains?"

"No." Erin tried to put it into words. "I just thought… if something happened before this man died and Adam Plaint disappeared… well, there might have been something in the paper. Something that no one had realized meant anything at the time, because they didn't know there had been a murder."

"But you didn't remember anything specific. And you didn't have the feeling you had missed something."

"No. I was just… indulging my curiosity."

"Who else knew you were looking for information about Adam Plaint's disappearance and John Doe's remains?"

"Well… everybody, I suppose. Melissa was there. Alton Summers. The librarian and anyone else who happened to wander through. Anyone that Vic told at the bakery. They all knew I was at the library. They didn't all know I was interested in the Plaints, I guess… but Melissa and Alton did. And Vic."

"And with all of those jaws going, anyone in town could have heard that Erin Price was on the case."

"Or just have guessed what I was looking up when they saw me at the library. Most people would probably assume I was still looking for information on my parents, but…" Erin trailed off, her mind jumping to the DFS file and the disturbing dream.

"What?" Terry asked. "What else happened?"

"No… nothing else to do with the Plaints. Just… about my parents."

Erin heard footsteps, and looked up to see Vic padding down the hallway toward them. Vic covered a wide yawn.

"Erin? What's wrong? Is everything okay?" She got far enough into the room to see Terry, and folded her arms over her chest, uncomfortable with him seeing her in her nightgown. "Terry? What is it? What happened?"

"It's okay," Erin assured her. "I just got a phone call. It kind of scared me, so I called Terry."

"You should have woken me up. What kind of phone call? What did they say?"

"Just the usual," Erin said lightly. "Keep my nose out of everybody else's business."

"Did you tell anyone what Erin was doing at the library today?" Terry asked. "That she was looking for information on Adam Plaint or our John Doe, rather than research on her own family?"

"Me? No!" Vic's face was pink. "I wouldn't do that. I said you were at the library doing research, but I never told anyone it was about the body." Vic looked at Erin and glanced sideways at Terry. "I didn't think you wanted anyone to know that."

"No," Erin agreed. "I wasn't planning on sharing it."

Terry shook his head at this. "You really *do* need to stop poking your nose into things. People can be dangerous if they think you could harm them. Or their reputations."

"But it wasn't real investigating," Erin insisted. "Anyone could look at newspapers. I wasn't going around asking people questions. Looking for alibis. I'm not a detective, I was just curious about whether I could find anything. I didn't know you were going to send Melissa to look it up."

"I'm not incompetent. With a murder that happened twenty years ago, of course I'm going to look back at the papers at the time."

Erin shrugged. "I was just trying to satisfy my own curiosity."

Vic sat down in the arm chair. She pulled her long legs up and curled them under her, and pulled a throw pillow in front of her, where she clutched it to her like a teddy bear.

Terry looked at Erin. "You were going to tell me something."

"I was?"

"Something unrelated. About your parents."

"Oh. Yeah."

Vic nodded, but she didn't cut in with details about the DFS file. Erin took a deep breath and let it go. "I got my file today. From when I was put into foster care. I wanted to know why there were discrepancies between what I remembered and what actually happened. Or if Clementine just got it all wrong."

"But I gather she didn't."

"No. They told me my parents had died when they put me into foster care. I remember that. I clearly remember them telling me that my parents had died instantly. I didn't have anyone else, so they had to put me into foster care."

"They didn't know about Clementine?"

"I doubt Clementine could have taken care of me anyway. Or maybe they did know about her and she said no. I haven't looked at all of the information on the file yet, so I can't tell you."

He gave a slow nod, considering what she had told him. "So why would they tell you your parents had been killed when they hadn't? That seems… rather unethical, to say the least."

"I think they were trying to spare my feelings… somehow. My parents were badly injured, but it took a long time after the accident for them to die."

"That's pretty horrific." He reached over and gave her shoulder a consoling rub. "I'm sorry. That must have been hard to find out about."

"It was," Erin agreed. She looked over at Vic. "I had another dream, too."

Vic sat up a little straighter and leaned forward. "Really? In the car again? Another dream about the accident?"

"No. I was sleeping in a cot. My parents were sleeping in the same room, arguing with each other. It must have been a hotel, or someone's guest room."

"What did they say?"

Terry said nothing, sitting back and listening.

"I…" Erin choked up, and took a minute to swallow and get her voice under control. "I guess they were talking about me. My dad said that he wasn't going to raise another man's child."

Vic put her hand over her mouth, eyes widening. "No!"

Erin nodded. "Do you think I'm just making it all up? My mind is trying to figure out what happened to my parents and what happened to the Plaint family and this other man, and it just came out of my subconscious?"

"Well… what do you think? It was your dream; how did it make you feel?"

"It wasn't like a dream where bizarre things happen and things shift, or where I dream that I can fly or breathe underwater. It doesn't have that 'unreal' feeling. But then… not all dreams do."

"You think it was a memory," Terry said.

"I don't really want to think that. I don't want to think… that my father didn't love me, or that he wasn't really my father, or that my mother was… unfaithful."

"Of course not. And you don't have any evidence to back it up. So you don't necessarily have to worry that it is true. You have a good imagination. It was a clear dream, but that doesn't mean it was anything other than a dream."

"No," Erin agreed. But she didn't really believe it. Terry saying that it wasn't a memory just further solidified in her mind the certainty that it was. It had really happened. She'd been suppressing it, suppressing all of her memories of what happened around the time of the accident. But it was still there, stored in her brain. Waiting for the time that she would acknowledge it.

Vic looked at the clock on the wall. "Are you going to go back to sleep?"

"I don't think I can. We have to be up in a couple of hours anyway. But you should go back to bed, if you think you can get back to sleep."

"Yeah." Vic yawned widely. "I think I probably can. Are you going to stay here?" she asked Terry.

He looked at Erin. "I think it would probably be a good idea. Are you okay with that?"

Erin was relieved to know that he would stay there and watch over her. The phone call was probably nothing. The caller would at least have to wait for a day to see if she were going to heed his demands before he took any action. He wasn't going to come to her house and set it on fire again. Unless the only reason he had called was to make sure that she was home, so that he could silence her once and for all. She shuddered.

"Yes. Please."

"Okay. You go back to sleep, Vic. I'll keep an eye on things here."

Vic nodded. "Okay. See you in a couple of hours." She got back up from the chair and headed back to the warmth and comfort of her bed.

"Are you okay?" Terry asked Erin.

"Yes. It was just a phone call."

"After all that has happened, neither of us can afford to ignore a call like that. Maybe it's nothing. Maybe it's just a prank, or it's as far as the caller is willing to go. But we can't be sure that it isn't Davis, or someone else who will do violence to protect their own interests."

Erin hugged her arms around herself.

She was glad that Terry was staying with her.

CHAPTER 14

 rin pressed a hand over her eyes, trying to ease the gritty, burning
feeling that was getting worse as the day progressed. Staying up
half the night was not conducive to running a business the next day. The
warmth of her hand helped the pain a little, and helped her tear ducts to
produce some soothing moisture.

The bells on the front door rang, and Erin dropped her hand away from
her face, putting on a smile to greet her customers.

A couple of women came in and went to the display case to view what
was on offer. Erin's smile tightened as she saw who her customers were.
Lottie Sturm, her blond pigtails bouncing, along with Clara Jones, a woman
with brassy, bottle-red hair and chunky jewelry who had never set foot in
the bakery before. Clara worked at the police department, doing computer
and administrative work and keeping things running. Erin knew from experience that she wasn't afraid to share her opinions. And one of those opinions had been that gluten-free baking or any special diet baking was crap,
and she would never eat it. Erin wasn't sure what had compelled Clara to
darken Erin's doorstep.

"Afternoon, ladies," Vic greeted pleasantly. She was, luckily, not looking
as tired and worn as Erin felt. She hadn't been up for half the night, but had
fallen quickly back to sleep after getting up to talk to Erin and Terry. "What
can I help you with today?"

Erin wasn't sure if Vic knew who Clara Jones was, but in any case, she was not likely accustomed to the sharp side of Clara's tongue.

"Um," Lottie cast her eyes over the items in the display case. "Some cookies," she said offhandedly, as if she hadn't really come there for baking at all.

Clara Jones barely even made a show of looking at the baking. "I was happy to see that you have Bella Prost working here now."

Erin was thrown a bit off-balance by the remark. Vic looked at Erin, giving a little frown that indicated she was puzzled as well. But she turned back to Clara and Lottie with a steady smile.

"She's putting in some part-time hours to give Erin and I a little time off a couple of days a week," she agreed.

"I'm not sure her mother would approve if she knew..." Lottie's lip curled and her nostrils flared, "... what *kind* of people she was working with here."

Erin thought they had gotten through all of the hate aimed at Vic for being transgender.

"Lottie—"

Clara Jones cut in. "I thought that maybe you had decided to hire Bella instead of..." she trailed off with a lingering look at Vic.

Erin cleared her throat. "If you're not here to buy something..."

"I suppose I'll take some cookies too," Clara said.

Vic didn't move to serve either woman. Erin moved closer, not because she planned to serve them herself, but in order to stand in solidarity with Vic.

"What kind of cookies did you want?"

"You should be ashamed," Lottie said, and Erin wasn't sure at first which one of them she was addressing. "Walking around town dressed like that. Pretending to be a girl when you're not. It's against nature—"

"Lottie!" Erin tried again to stop her.

Bells jingled at the door, but nobody looked to see who it was, frozen in a tableau.

Erin cleared her throat. "I think it's time for you ladies to leave."

They glared back at her. Bullies. Not budging.

"You haven't given us our cookies yet," Clara pointed out.

"And I'm not."

"We're here as paying customers."

"You've been asked to leave," a male voice said.

As one, they turned to look at the newest customer. Willie Andrews. Erin let out a breath of relief. Not only was she happy to have him there to intervene, but she was also happy to see that he was out of hospital, apparently recovering and himself once more.

"You don't have any right to kick us out," Clara argued.

"Do you want me to call the Sheriff and ask him?"

Since the Sheriff was Clara's boss, she probably didn't want to get on his bad side. Allegations of trespass and hate speech probably wouldn't go over too well with him.

"Or do you just want to leave?" Willie suggested.

Lottie and Clara looked at each other. Eventually, they moved silently toward the door, past Willie, and were gone. Willie watched through the door until they were a suitable distance away before turning his attention to Vic and Erin.

"What was all that about?"

Erin sighed. "Vic."

Vic didn't say anything.

Erin touched her arm uncertainly. "Are you okay?"

Vic nodded. Willie walked up to the counter. "Vicky?"

"Yeah, I'm fine," Vic said. Her voice was a little shaky, but she was holding it together.

"What makes people think they have any right to attack people just because they are different?" Erin fumed. "I hate that they think they can come into my shop and act that way!"

"You didn't let them," Vic said. "I know you wouldn't ever just stand by."

"I didn't do enough. I should have just…" Erin shook her head in frustration. "I don't know! Got them out of here faster."

"You did fine," Willie said. "You would have gotten them out of here without my help."

"They're more scared of you than they are me. They don't think they have to listen to me."

"You would have gotten them out," he repeated.

"Maybe. But thank you. How are you doing? Are you feeling better?"

The bandages that had previously swathed his head had been replaced by smaller gauze pads and tape. He looked much more like himself.

"Yes. I'm doing a lot better. Especially now that I'm out of the hospital. I despise hospitals."

"And your memory?" Vic asked. Her voice was stronger now that she could focus on someone else. "Did everything come back?"

"Well, not everything. But the important stuff. Who I am. The details of my life. Or most of them, anyway. The people I care about."

Vic turned a little pink and looked studiously down at the display case between them.

"Something for our rescuer?" Erin suggested. "On the house."

"Hmm..." Willie looked down at the baking thoughtfully. Erin was pleased that he didn't protest the token of their appreciation. Willie Andrews wasn't the kind of man who put on a fake front to get people's approval. "No gumdrop cookies today?"

Vic's eyes danced. "I've got some in the oven right now, if you don't mind waiting around for a few minutes."

Willie smiled. "I don't mind at all. Why don't you catch me up on all the latest news?"

Erin decided to take some gumdrop cookies to Officer Piper as well. After all, he'd rescued her too. Not only had he come to her immediately when she called him about the threatening phone call, but he had also dropped what he was doing and gone to the library when he heard that Alton Summers was there with Erin, to make sure that Summers knew he'd better behave himself.

Vic said she could manage the bakery on her own for a few minutes, and Willie agreed to hang out and visit with her while he had a couple of cookies, just to be sure that nobody came by and harassed her.

It was a rare cool day in Bald Eagle Falls, so for once Erin didn't have to worry about sweating through her clothes just walking down to the police department. She didn't see Terry patrolling on her way there, and hoped to find him in his office. She could leave the cookies there for when he got back, and hopefully everyone else wouldn't eat them all, but she preferred to present them to him in person.

Clara Jones was not seated at the desk Erin had previously seen her at, and Erin breathed a sigh of relief at avoiding that awkward situation. She peeked around the doorway into Terry's office.

He was sitting at his desk, shuffling through a file and a stack of large photos.

"Terry…?"

He looked up and smiled. "Erin! Everything okay?"

She reached around the door with the plate of cookies.

"Oooh, come in, come in!"

Erin entered his office, buoyed up by his eagerness. She set the cookies on a bare spot on his desk. Terry helped himself to one, and put his hand under it to catch any crumbs as he took his first bite.

"Gumdrop! I haven't had gumdrop cookies in years. Mmm." He glanced around his office and picked up his coffee cup. "I'm going to get milk from the vending machine. You?"

Erin laughed. "Sure. Sounds great."

He walked past her to get it. Erin sat down in his guest chair and waited for him, smiling to herself. She was glad that she had taken a break from the bakery to bring him the cookies. Things would be quiet at the bakery until school let out. Vic could handle everything. Seeing Terry and having a cookie with him was better than a jolt of coffee.

As she waited for his return, her eyes were drawn to the photos on the desk. She avoided reading the papers in the file he had left out, but she couldn't help looking at the pictures. They were evidence photos. Keys. Pocket change. A round, flat river stone with a slight indent in the center. She didn't move the top pictures to see what was underneath. For all she knew, the innocuous items could be covering a gruesome picture of the human remains found in her yard, or Angela or Trenton Plaint's dead faces. She had no desire to see any of those things. She looked away, staring at the calendar on Terry's wall like she was fascinated by it.

He took longer than she expected, and when he returned, had two glasses of milk in his hands. She had expected to drink straight out of the carton and was touched that he had taken the extra time to make it presentable.

"Thank you!"

"All I'm providing is the milk. You brought the real magic."

Terry put his glass down on the desk and gathered his photos together.

"What are those?" Erin asked.

His lips pressed together while he decided whether to answer her or not. Then he gave a little shrug. "John Doe. Your human remains. Contents of his pockets."

Erin nodded. "No wallet?" she guessed. He obviously couldn't have been carrying identification, or they would have a name for him.

"No. Anything that could identify him was removed. Our killer didn't want the victim to be identified if he was discovered. Or not immediately, anyway. It doesn't mean we won't be able to identify him, but it's going to be a lot harder."

Erin took a few bites of a cookie, enjoying the intense sweetness and the stickiness of the gumdrops. She chased it down with a couple of swallows of milk. "Do you have cause of death yet? You know it was murder?"

"Murder is manner of death, not cause of death. And no, an official determination has not yet been made. But there were several obvious injuries to the body, and the way it was disposed of suggests foul play, not an accident or natural causes. You don't generally bury someone in concrete when they have a heart attack."

"No. What injuries?"

Again, there was a delay as he considered what he was going to share with her. "The most obvious was a fractured skull. Occipital," Terry gestured to the back of his own head. "Of course he could have taken a fall and struck something on landing… there's no guarantee he was hit by someone else… but under the circumstances…"

"Yeah. Probably not," Erin agreed. "Poor guy…" She had another sip of milk, trying to talk herself out of eating another cookie. Too many of her own baked goods, and she'd be as round as a ball. With her height, any weight she put on would show up immediately. She caved and took one more cookie. "We should share these around, before I end up eating them all."

"I'm not sure I want to share."

Erin looked back at the closed file on his desk. "The thing that bothers me the most is that no one has any idea who John Doe might be. Nobody missed him? Nobody remembers a drifter or stranger in town? It's like he just appeared there, out of nowhere."

"It's very puzzling," Terry agreed.

"It's crazy. You're sure there wasn't any mix-up in the dental records? The records that the coroner got were Adam Plaint's records, and not someone else's? Because if he was just Adam, it would all make sense."

"It's all been checked and double-checked. It's not Adam Plaint."

"Are we sure Adam Plaint is who he said he was?"

Terry laughed. "What?"

"I just mean… maybe he was an impostor. He said that he was…" Erin trailed off.

"And exactly when did this switch occur? When did the impostor Adam Plaint take the place of the real Adam Plaint? And how did he do it without anyone noticing? Was he an identical twin? Someone who'd had plastic surgery to make him look like Adam Plaint? And then he just stepped in and took over, without his wife, children, or coworkers noticing?"

"No. I guess not. That doesn't make any sense. I'm just grasping at straws."

Terry nodded. He drained the rest of the milk in his glass, put it down on the desk, and looked at it dubiously, as if wishing it were something stronger. "We've been through all of the scenarios," he said. "Trust me. The Sheriff and I have been on the phone with the coroner, spitballing every crazy idea we could think of. And unless you're willing to accept the idea of a changeling, twin, or time-travel, those remains are not Adam Plaint's. Adam Plaint is still missing. Just like he has been for twenty years."

"Alton Summers is on the case. He's pretty dogged. It wasn't just luck that he was able to find me and Trenton. If Adam Plaint is still out there, my money is on Summers to find him."

"The trouble is, he may not be out there. He may be buried underneath someone else's garage."

Erin blinked at him. She pursed her lips, thinking.

"What?" Terry asked.

"What about other building sites? Were there other garages or houses that were put up the week he disappeared? Excavation sites? Gardens? If the Plaint boys disposed of one body, maybe they disposed of another."

"Suppose I can have Melissa check what building permits were approved before then. It's always a possibility… but it's a pretty long shot."

~

Erin drove her car home, but Vic insisted that she and Willie, who was still hanging around the store, would walk home.

"It's all the way across town," Erin protested.

"That would be a valid reason not to walk if the town was bigger," Vic said dryly. "But since it's hardly a wart on a bear's behind, I don't think it's going to hurt us to walk."

"It's too hot to walk. You'll get heatstroke."

"It's the coolest day since I came to town. And you too. And don't forget, I was raised in these parts, so I'm used to the heat. Not like a poor northerner here for her first summer. For me, this is balmy. And Willie and I are going to walk."

Erin looked helplessly at William Andrews, expecting him to be the voice of reason. He was twice Vic's age. He should tell her that it was a silly idea and they should just drive home with Erin in an air-conditioned car. But he didn't try to dissuade Vic.

"We'll be fine, Erin. I'll look after Victoria."

"But..." Erin raised her hands in a gesture of surrender. "Fine. Walk home. Enjoy yourselves. Just don't complain to me when you're all dehydrated and sick."

"We won't," Vic assured her.

"Fine." Erin grabbed the bags she needed to take home with her, and walked out the door to her car. "See you later tonight."

As she left, she could hear Vic laughing. Erin supposed she was being silly. Vic was pretty good at looking after herself. She'd been homeless before Erin had taken her in, and she hadn't been kidnapped and murdered then. And she wasn't alone, she was with Willie. He would take care of her if there were any trouble. Though he was the one just out of the hospital...

When she reached the house, Orange Blossom ran to meet her, yowling and telling her all about his day, or how his dry food was stale, or wanting to know where Vic was. Erin stooped and picked him up. She cuddled him close to her face.

"There now, hush. Everything is fine. No need for you to get all worked up over nothing."

She was aware that she was trying to talk herself out of her own uneasiness. The cat had no clue what she was talking about. He wasn't crying because he missed Vic, she was just labeling him with her own uneasiness.

Anthropomorphizing him. He yowled and complained every day, whether Vic was there or not.

But it was still comforting to have someone to talk to. He rubbed his head against her and she immersed herself in the silkiness of his fur. He was so warm and cuddly. Cats had the reputation of being aloof, but Orange Blossom had always been affectionate and social.

"Well, let's have a look at the state of your dishes, then, shall we?"

She carried him into the kitchen and checked his dishes. A few bits of his dry food were at the bottom of his water dish, all bloated and falling apart. The sight always made her gag a little. She didn't know how he managed to always get food into his water dish. She was careful never to get any in the water when she poured out his food. And she placed the bowls as far apart on the mat as she could. But somehow Orange Blossom always managed to get a few pieces of food into his water. Erin put him down to dump the defiled water into the toilet and run cold water for him. He liked it better when it was cold than when it was room temperature, and she didn't think she was spoiling him by making sure that he got fresh, cold water a couple of times a day.

Erin warmed up a frozen dinner in the microwave, looking at the wall clock and wondering how long it would take Vic and Willie to walk to the house. Less than an hour. As Vic had said, it wasn't a big town.

She had just put her warmed-up dinner on the table and was getting a fork from the drawer when there was a loud crash and the sound of breaking glass from the living room.

Erin let out a shriek, and stood there in the kitchen, frozen, staring toward the front of the house. She didn't know whether to go see what the noise was, or to cower under the table like Orange Blossom.

"Who's there?" she shouted. She strained her ears for an answer, but there wasn't one. She couldn't hear any more footsteps. There was not a second crash. Had it been gunfire? Would she get shot if she went to investigate?

If someone had shot into the house through the front window, there was nothing to stop them from circling to the back of the house where she made a nice big target standing in the middle of the kitchen trying to figure out what was going on. Erin decided that Orange Blossom had the right idea, and she crouched low and scooted across the floor to join him under the shelter of the table. She looked nervously at the big kitchen windows, but couldn't see anyone in the back yard. Even so, she pressed herself all the way against the back wall and positioned a chair in front of her as a barrier.

For the second time in as many days, she dialed Terry's cell phone instead of the dedicated emergency line.

"Hi, Erin." His voice was mellow and relaxed. Erin hated to bother him. He'd already been up most of the night talking with her and making sure she was safe. He deserved to go home at the end of his shift and have a break. Just to relax and not worry about anything. "Erin?"

"Terry… there was a loud noise." Erin tried to keep her voice from wobbling, but didn't seem to have any control over her vocal cords. "Something broke the living room window. Crashed into the house. I don't know whether it was a shot…"

Terry swore. "Are you safe? Is there anyone with you?"

"I'm home alone. I don't know… who is outside. Or how many. Or what they…" Erin's voice choked off and she couldn't complete the thought. What did they want from her? Was it Davis, intent on killing her for certain this time?

"Stay where you are. Get down low and take shelter. Make yourself small. I'm coming, but I have to call the others. I can't approach alone against an armed assailant. I need someone to back me up."

"Yes," Erin squeaked. "I know."

"I have to hang up. I don't have two lines. If there are any new developments, call the emergency operator. Do you have the number?"

"It's in my phone."

"Call it now. Don't wait until something happens."

"Okay." Erin swallowed hard, trying to get rid of the lump in her throat. "Bye."

She didn't know if he would be able to hang up on her, so she ended the call herself and navigated to her contacts list. Her hands were shaking. Her whole body was shaking, vibrating with tension. Orange Blossom rubbed against her, oblivious to the danger they might be in. If he thought it was strange that she was hiding under the table, he didn't give any indication of it. Erin whispered to him.

"Don't worry. Everything is okay. I'm sure I'm just being a ninny over all of this. It was a bird. Or a lamp fell over. It's nothing to worry about. I'll get the whole police department descending on the house, and then they'll all laugh at me."

After several tries, she managed to get the emergency dispatcher number up on her screen and tapped it until the phone decided to cooperate and dial out. Erin waited, her body quivering, as it rang.

"Bald Eagle Falls dispatch."

"It's Erin Price. I already called Officer Piper, but he said to call you… in case something happens before he gets here." Erin's voice rose in pitch for the last phrase.

"Yes, Miss Price. What is your location, please?"

Erin gave her address and phone number, and again explained her uncertainty as to what had happened and whether she was in any danger.

"Stay on the line," the dispatcher told her. Erin could hear computer keys clicking. "I show Officer Piper, the sheriff and Tom Banks all en route to your location. They will be there in a minute, but I want you to stay where you are until I tell you otherwise. Don't go out to meet them, do you understand?"

"Yes. I don't know whether the door is locked or unlocked."

"Don't worry about that."

"Okay."

"I don't want you to go check. You just stay down and stay away from any windows or doors."

"Okay."

There was radio noise in the background, the operator's microphone picking up the officers' reports into their shoulder-mounted mics. It wasn't clear enough for Erin to pick out their words, but she knew their voices. She could tell whenever Terry spoke, his sentences terse barks of instruction or acknowledgment.

"They're on site," the dispatcher told Erin, confirming what she had already guessed.

She listened for any sound over the phone or outside the house that would signal that they had spotted an intruder. There was no yelling. No confrontation. Erin tried to slow her breathing. It was okay. Everything was going to be all right. Whoever or whatever had broken her window was gone. They must have had a pretty good idea of what the response time of the Bald Eagle Falls police department would be. They knew how much time they had to get in and get out. Erin had probably never been in any real danger. They only wanted to scare her.

But last time, Davis had tried to kill her.

"Have you seen or heard any sign that there is someone in the house with you?"

Erin breathed shallowly, listening for a breath other than her own. She hadn't heard any more footsteps. No doors or windows opening.

"No. No, I don't think so."

"Do you feel safe to go to the door? Or do you want the officers to breach and clear it for you?"

To breach her door? Erin didn't want them breaking it down. There would be no way to get it fixed that night, and she would again be required to seek shelter somewhere else.

"I'm okay. I'll open the door."

"I'll stay on the phone with you. If at any time you think there might be someone in the house with you…"

"Okay," Erin whispered. She crawled out from under the table, and listened. She could hear the voices outside, but nothing in the house. Standing up took a lot more willpower than she expected; her body seemed to have its own sense of self-preservation and didn't want her to make herself a bigger target, to make herself vulnerable out in the open. Her legs wobbled and shook as she forced herself to straighten up. Out of consideration for this sense of self-preservation, she flattened herself against the wall, and crept along it instead of stepping into the middle of the room. It had never taken so long to get to the door before. Then Erin was finally there. She looked through the peephole, but couldn't see anyone. She knew that they were out there, but she couldn't see where.

Erin twisted the bolt to unlock the door. She turned the handle and pushed the door open.

A man grabbed her and pulled her to the side. Erin fought back against him as the sheriff and Tom Banks rushed into the house, sidearms drawn, swiveling this way and that like Navy Seals on TV.

"It's okay, Erin. It's me. You're okay."

Erin melted into Terry's arms. Her legs collapsed and he had to catch her. He held her tightly until the other two officers came out of the house to report that it was secure. Then he helped her to sit down on the front steps.

"Just breathe," he told her. "It's okay, Erin. Just breathe, and then you can tell me what happened."

She was hyperventilating, gulping down air as fast as she could, her head spinning. She closed her eyes and tried to slow everything down. She tried to just breathe normally like Terry suggested. He was right. They had cleared the grounds and cleared the house. There was no one lurking around trying to hurt her. Whatever had smashed the front window as gone again. Erin's body shuddered as she tried to take a long breath in and then to push it out slowly until her lungs were empty. Her heart started to slow down a little. She turned and looked at the living room window.

She was afraid that there wasn't going to be a mark on it. That a random noise had sent her into a panic without reason, and the police would be irritated by the call. But there was a large hole in the middle of the plate glass. It wasn't small, like Erin imagined a bullet hole would be. It was larger than her fist. Nearly the size of a dinner plate.

"What was it?" she asked. "Not a bullet? Not a gun?"

Terry looked at it and shook his head. "No. Sheriff's gone back in to see what it was. A brick maybe."

"It wasn't just a bird, was it? Am I being silly?"

"No. A bird wouldn't make a hole like that. In an airplane windshield, maybe, but it wouldn't fly into your house window that hard."

It wasn't long before the sheriff was back outside, displaying a rock with a paper rubber-banded to it. The Sheriff's hands were gloved in blue, stretched tight around his thick fingers. She and Terry looked at the rock. But there was nothing special about it. Just a roundish, softball-sized river or garden rock.

"What does the note say?" Terry asked.

The sheriff teased the rubber band away from the rock and slid the note out. He released the rubber band, letting it snap back against the rock. He fumbled with the note, maybe because of the gloves he was unaccustomed to wearing. He unfolded it three times. His eyes traveled back and forth as he read it over. He then turned it for Terry to look at, keeping it shielded from Erin's view. Terry gave it a quick review and nodded at Erin, so the sheriff turned it for Erin to read.

Keep to baking or get out of town. Keep your nose out of everyone else's business. This is your last warning.

Erin sighed and put her face in her hands. "I didn't do anything," she insisted. "I am minding my own business."

Terry didn't say anything.

"You know I didn't. All I did was work in the bakery yesterday. I didn't go to the library. I didn't ask anybody questions about anything. I don't understand why he's targeting me when I'm not doing anything!"

"You did come to the police department yesterday."

Erin shook her head, not looking up at him. "To bring you cookies. I wasn't doing anything else. Not investigating."

"An outside observer wouldn't know what you were there for. They wouldn't know what you and I had to say to each other. They wouldn't know if we… discussed the case in passing."

Terry's voice was cautious. Erin supposed it was due to the presence of the Sheriff. He might not be pleased to find out how freely Terry and Erin had discussed the John Doe case and the Adam Plaint disappearance.

"I just want it to stop," Erin said, trying to keep the sob out of her voice.

"Erin!" there was a call from the sidewalk, and Erin pulled her hands away from her face and looked up to see Vic and Willie on the edge of the property, prevented from getting any close by Tom Banks and his yellow crime scene tape.

"They can come over," she told Terry.

"No, I don't want any prints obscured if your stalker stepped on the lawn when he threw the rock. We don't know yet what evidence we might be able to recover. No one can enter the crime scene unless it is to recover evidence."

"Can I go talk to them, then?"

"If you're okay. I don't want you fainting on me."

Erin rubbed her thighs, still quivering with adrenaline. "I… I'm fine. I think." She got to her feet. Terry kept his hand on her for a moment, then let her arm go. Erin was stable enough on her own to shuffle down the sidewalk, watching carefully for anything that might be construed as evidence to ensure that she didn't contaminate the crime scene.

"What happened?" Vic demanded, as soon as Erin was within a few steps.

"It's nothing. Someone threw a rock through the window. Threatening me, telling me to keep quiet."

Vic swore under her breath. "Oh, I'm so sorry, Erin. I should have been here."

"No. It's probably better that you weren't. More targets… I don't know if the guy has a gun. Better it was just me."

"You must have been scared to death." Vic reached across the yellow tape to give Erin a hug. "I'm so sorry."

Erin gave Vic a squeeze in return. "Please, don't worry. It wasn't anything… the police department got here right away. Obviously, or they wouldn't have beaten you here. I wasn't alone. I had Orange Blossom, and then Terry was here."

"Orange Blossom." Vic laughed. "I'm sure he was a great help in a crisis like this. Good ol' attack cat. If someone came into the house, he would just trip them up. And then lick their faces."

Erin laughed, her voice high-pitched. "No, it was just… good to have someone there who wasn't worried about anything. Just… like everything was normal and there was nothing to worry about."

Vic and Willie nodded. Willie reached over and squeezed Erin's arm. "So you're okay? Do you guys need somewhere to spend the night? Do they want you out of here?"

"I don't know yet," Erin said. "There's not really anything for them to investigate. Someone threw a rock through the window. There's not anything to look at inside."

"If you need somewhere… I'll stick around. We can sort it out."

Erin nodded. "Okay. Thanks." She turned and looked at Terry and the other police officers. She'd never seen them all in one place before. It was the equivalent of a five-alarm fire for Bald Eagle Falls. They were talking seriously, looking around, making motions to each other. Erin didn't know if she should walk back to Terry to talk to him, or stay out of the way. She imagined they wanted to focus on gathering evidence, so she should stay out of the way.

The window was boarded up, and Terry cleared Vic and Erin to stay. There was no guarantee they would be any safer anywhere else in town. Everyone would know where they went to stay. And no one had burglar alarms that provided any amount of security if someone really wanted to harm them.

"I'll stay the night," Willie offered. "I'll make sure they're safe."

Terry looked uncertain about this. He had probably intended to make the same offer. But he had stayed after the phone call, and he needed to get as much rest as he could before he was on shift again. Willie was his own boss and could sleep in and determine his own work schedule, so it made more sense for him to be the one to take protection duty this time.

"I want a call if there is anything suspicious," he warned. "Even if it's just noises in the night. Cars idling in front of the house. Another phone call. Anything at all suspicious."

Willie nodded seriously. "I'll call," he agreed. He shifted his belt, lifting it and snugging it into place. "I have a concealed carry," he advised.

Terry raised an eyebrow and looked Willie over, reevaluating. "I don't want any gunfire," he warned. "If you're too quick with a gun, I'm going to be arresting you, and I'd rather not do that."

"I'll be careful. I won't be firing unless someone else pulls a weapon on us. I'm not one to spook at cats."

"I hope not," Terry said with a wry smile. "Since the ladies would be crushed if something happened to Orange Blossom."

"Not going to happen. But I will protect them if someone comes after them."

Terry nodded. "Right, then. Lock up tight after me, and we'll talk in the morning. Call to give me the all-clear once they're at the bakery." Terry looked at his watch. "I'll go on shift early to make sure that everything is quiet once they get there."

Then Terry and the rest of the police department were gone, and the house seemed strangely quiet and still. Orange Blossom meowed a couple of times from one of the bedrooms.

"Come on, Blossom," Vic called out to him. "We're still here. Come for cuddles."

Erin heard the cat jump down from the bed and, in a few moments, he was strolling down the hall to see them. He stopped when he saw Willie there, putting his ears back.

"It's okay, baby," Vic assured him, picking him up. "Willie is a friend. You've met him before. He's just going to stay and make sure nothing happens to us. So we can all sleep easy tonight."

Willie reached out to pat the cat, but Orange Blossom jerked back to avoid his touch, folding his ears all the way back and snarling, raising a paw to strike. Willie laughed and pulled back. "Looks like he's a mama's boy."

"He's probably just freaked out by all of the strangers in the house," Vic said, patting Orange Blossom to calm him down. "Cats don't like changes in routine or strangers in their territory. He'll be okay."

Erin fetched some bedding from the linen closet and looked over the couch in the living room. They had cleaned up the broken glass, but she was afraid there might still be shards they had missed, and didn't want William Andrews lying down on them. She put the linens down and ran her hands slowly over the couch, checking all of the crevices carefully, making sure there were no slivers of glass snagged in the upholstery.

"It looks okay," she said. "I just hope I haven't missed any glass. You know how it is when you just drop a dish on the floor, and you're still finding shards of it months later."

"I'm sure it will be fine," Willie said. "I'll be careful, and if anything sticks me, I'll find it and throw it out. Don't worry."

Erin nodded and spread a sheet over the couch. She neatly made up the couch into a bed, hoping it would be comfortable enough for Willie to at least get a little sleep, though she figured it was going to be a disrupted night for all of them. She tidied up a few other things that were out in the living room but should have been put away.

Willie sat down on the couch. He nodded in satisfaction. "This will be just fine. More than adequate." He looked at the papers on the coffee table and picked them up, his eyes curious. Erin reached to take them from him. "What's all this?"

Erin's face warmed. "It's just… personal information."

He didn't hand it back as quickly as Erin had expected. His eyes moved across the cover page, and he used a finger to flip a couple of corners to see the papers underneath.

"It's personal," Erin said, taking hold of it and firmly tugging the sheaf of papers out of his hand. "Information about my parents. About…" She couldn't finish the sentence, to tell him about how they had died. She held the papers against her chest.

Willie shrugged and didn't ask her any more about them.

She awoke a couple of times in the night and lay there listening, ears pricked for her phone, or cars or footsteps outside, broken glass or crackling flames. Anything that might suggest she wasn't safe. But there was nothing. The house was quiet, other than its usual creaks and groans. She closed her eyes and pulled the blankets closer and went back to sleep.

Morning came too quickly, as had so often been the case lately. Erin thought fleetingly that it would have been better to set up shop in a town that didn't have so many murders and threats to keep her up at night. Getting up in the morning wasn't so hard if she could get to sleep in good time and not lie awake worrying for a couple of hours before dropping off to sleep. It was draining her.

Willie sat in the back of the Challenger; a tight squeeze, but he insisted the ladies sit in the front. He went into the bakery first and took a look around before deeming it safe for them to enter and start in on their daily routine. Erin opened the fridge and remembered with a sinking feeling that she had intended to go out to buy butter and a couple of other ingredients that she was getting low on. It had all left her mind completely with the rock sailing in through her window. Everything but the immediate threat had flown from her mind.

The store wouldn't be open so early, so they started with the recipes she could make with the ingredients they had on hand. Once everything was in the ovens, she looked at her watch and figured the owner would be there and would help her out even if they weren't officially open yet.

"I'll have to make a run to the grocery store," she told Vic and Willie. "You'll be okay here?"

"What do you need?" Willie asked. "I'll pick it up for you."

"I've got a list. I'd rather you were here with Vic. I won't be long."

"You don't want to wait until there are more people around, so it will be safer?"

"No. I want to get it done before the morning rush. It will be fine."

"Terry said he was going to be on duty early. Give him a call and he can escort you over…"

Erin shook her head. "He'll be keeping an eye on things. I don't need door-to-door service."

Willie's mouth was a grim line. He looked at Vic, but she shrugged and didn't express any concern. "There's no one up this early to make any trouble."

"Okay, then… just be careful. Be aware of your surroundings, and if anything worries you, even if it just niggles at you… give me or Officer Piper a call."

Erin nodded. He was as bad as a foster mother letting her teenage daughter go out on a date. Nothing untoward was going to happen on the way to the grocery store a few blocks away.

She left quickly, before he could think of any reason to keep her from going and before it got any later. She wouldn't be there to open up, but if she hurried, she should still be back before things got too busy for Vic to handle alone.

There was no traffic on the street. Sleepy little town. She saw Terry and K9 walking down Main Street in the cool of the morning, and gave them a little wave. Her phone didn't ring after she passed, so Terry didn't have any concerns, any reason to stop her from going to the store.

Hers was only the third car in the parking lot. She could see Mr. Cooper, the elderly gentleman who owned the grocery store, moving around, checking the doors, opening the tills, putting out signs for the fresh produce. She wasn't sure whose the other car was. A stock boy or cashier getting ready to start their shift.

The door was unlocked, so Erin just went in. Cooper looked up and saw who it was. He gave her a big smile.

"Morning, Miss Price. Emergency grocery run?"

"Yes. So sorry to bother you before opening. I intended to come last night, but things happened… and I forgot I had planned to."

Cooper nodded slowly, his fine white hair forming a sort of a halo around his head in the morning sunshine. "I heard about your trouble," he said seriously. "A rock through your window? Deplorable. I don't know what this world is coming to."

Erin nodded. "It was pretty scary. But no one was hurt. So we're just moving on."

"You girls are very brave. I don't know what I would do if someone did that to me. Close up shop and move out of town, maybe."

And maybe that was exactly what her stalker was hoping she would do. Just get out of town and stay away from any buried secrets. Erin held up her list.

"I'll be quick. Thanks so much."

He nodded and went back to setting up displays. Erin grabbed a cart and headed to the dairy case. After a few months in town, she knew where everything was and was pretty efficient picking everything up quickly.

So she was focused on getting from the dairy case to the baking aisle and didn't even see Davis until she nearly ran into him. Erin put on the brakes and pulled her cart to a stop, her heart thumping hard. She hadn't expected to see anyone other than Mr. Cooper, and certainly hadn't thought she would see Davis Plaint there.

Davis's face was as pale as Erin's must have been. He looked at her from deeply-set eye sockets. It didn't take long for his expression to change from surprise to anger.

"What are you doing here?"

Erin swallowed and licked her lips. "Picking up some groceries for the bakery." She cleared her throat. "I was supposed to get them last night, but *something* prevented me."

"That wasn't me," Davis protested immediately. "I haven't been anywhere near your house."

"You've threatened me before. You tried to burn my house down. Why would I believe you?"

"I didn't say I wouldn't," he said nastily. "But I didn't. Looks like you've made a few enemies in Bald Eagle Falls, Miss Price."

"What are *you* doing here?" Erin looked around. "Did you follow me?"

"Don't flatter yourself. I have other things to be concerned about. Like making enough money to survive until I can get the inheritance that is rightfully mine. A person has to eat, you know. It might be months before I can get anything out of the estate. I can't go that long without eating, and I don't have any savings to speak of."

Erin supposed that made sense. She had been able to claim Clementine's estate right away, since they had been looking for her and all she had to do was show her ID and prove who she was. She had gotten the bakery up and running within a couple of weeks, so she hadn't burned through all of her savings. But if she were unemployed in Bald Eagle Falls, things would be different. There were no homeless shelters, no soup kitchens. No way for someone who was indigent to survive until the money started coming in.

"So you're working here? What are you doing?"

"Stocking. Carry out. Whatever needs to be done. When you're hungry, it doesn't really matter what it is."

Erin looked down at her list. "Well, I have things I need to get before the morning rush."

He stayed in front of her, blocking her way. Erin supposed she could retreat or go around him, but she waited instead for him to step out of her way.

"It wasn't me," he told her again.

"It wasn't you who threw the rock through the window, or who killed that poor man?"

Davis looked taken aback by the question. "Neither one," he asserted. "I didn't have anything to do with killing anyone. And I wasn't the one who threw that rock through you window. I have an alibi."

Erin made a face at that. She doubted his alibi was anything to speak of. He was the most likely suspect for having thrown the rock through her window. Where there was smoke, there was fire. And around Davis, there was billowing smoke.

"I do. You can check. I was at the doctor's office. They can confirm it."

"That's not up to me. I'm not an investigator. Tell the police."

"I will. I already have. I'm telling you, it wasn't me. And you can tell that cop boyfriend of yours. Tell him to just leave me alone. I'm just minding my own business. Unlike *some* people around here, who can't leave other people's business well enough alone."

"If you didn't do anything, why are you so worried about what I might be doing?" Erin asked. "What do you have to hide?"

"Anyone who thinks an innocent person can't be convicted by circumstantial evidence knows nothing about the justice system."

Erin stood there facing Davis, the shopping cart between them creating a buffer. Was this the man who had tried to burn her house down? Was he now intent on scaring her off and, if words didn't work, would he move into action again?

"Who was the man you buried under Clementine's garage?"

His face was little more than a skull. White face, deep-set eyes, the planes of his face narrow and spare. His Adam's apple bobbed up and down.

"You don't know what you're stirring up," he said in a low growl. "You don't have any idea how this is going to blow up in your face."

Erin bit her lip and strove to keep her breathing slow and even. "I'm not stirring anything up. I'm not investigating anything. This has got nothing to do with me."

He gave a short, humorless laugh. "You just keep saying that."

Erin finally decided that he wasn't going to let her by, and she didn't care. She pulled back and went around him, going up the next aisle instead. She parked her cart at the front end of the aisle, then walked without it back to the baking aisle to grab the other ingredients she needed. She expected to still see Davis standing at the other end of it, staring at her with those dark, sunken eyes.

But he had vanished.

Erin drove back to Auntie Clem's somewhat shakily. Nothing had happened. At least, that was what she told herself. Nothing had happened to her and she didn't have any reason to be upset. She imagined Davis as the big villain in the drama that was her life, and yet every time she saw him, he seemed small and petty and incapable of the things that he had been accused of. Murder? Arson and attempted murder? She could see him making the threatening phone call. Even the note thrown through her plate glass window. But he seemed small and inconsequential when she saw him. Always acting like he expected people to feel sorry for him. And it was hard not to.

But no matter what she thought of him, her body still reacted to his presence as if he were a danger, and she knew she needed to honor and respect the signals her body was sending her. Her intuition was not likely to lead her the wrong direction.

She pulled into the parking space behind the bakery and carried her groceries in. The shop was open and she could hear Vic serving customers out at the front. She quickly put the ingredients where they belonged, checked on the ovens, put on her apron, and headed out to help.

They were all regulars. No one who needed any special care. They all knew what she sold and what they liked or needed for the evening's meal. Erin gave Vic a smile and went to the cash register, where she helped the next couple of customers check out. Willie was sitting in one of the wrought-iron chairs at the front of the shop, and he stood up and approached Erin when she was free between customers.

"Everything okay, Erin?"

Erin smiled and nodded and didn't explain to him about running into Davis at the grocery store. There was no point in getting Willie or Terry on Davis's case. If he was working at the grocery store now, then it was inevitable that Erin would run into him at some point. He hadn't threatened her. Not exactly. He had professed his innocence, but that was not threatening in and of itself. Was it possible that he had not been the one sending the threats? That there was someone else close to her who was angry about her curiosity and wanted her out of the way?

"If everything is all right, then, I'm going to take off for a while. Things are busy here, and that means you're safe. No one is going to attack you while you're surrounded by people."

"Yes. I'm fine here. Thank you for everything last night and today. I really appreciate it." She looked at Vic. "We both appreciate it." She wasn't sure whether the friendship between Vic and Willie had shifted to a deeper level, as the evening walk to the house and staying over to protect them suggested.

Willie gave a quick nod. "I'll check back in later."

CHAPTER 16

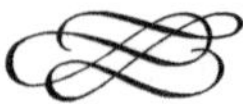

Treating William Andrews and Officer Terry Piper to dinner seemed like a good start in thanking them for what they had done for Erin and Vic over the previous few days. The Chinese restaurant was just across the street from the police department and, since Terry had the tightest time constraints, they decided to eat in the restaurant most convenient to him.

Erin had worried before about the four of them looking like a double-date, which she didn't want, but as they had continued to get together occasionally for dinner or other activities, it had stopped bothering her. She felt like they were just a group of friends getting together for dinner, and they didn't need to feel like they were paired off in any configuration.

"So, these threats you've been getting…" Willie said. "They're related to Adam Plaint's disappearance or the human remains you found under Erin's garage?" He looked at Terry for his input.

"Not my garage," Erin said. "Clementine's garage. I never used it for anything, and now it's knocked down. It was her garage, not mine."

"Okay…"

"Yes," Terry agreed. "We're working on that assumption. Let sleeping dogs lie. Keep your nose out of other people's business. It all sounds like it's related to the old business of Adam Plaint's disappearance and apparently, the murder of John Doe." He looked at Erin. "No, they haven't ruled it a homicide yet. I'm just trying to shortcut the discussion."

Erin laughed at the way that he anticipated her question, and stirred the ice cubes in her soft drink.

"So you think it's Davis?"

Terry pursed his lips. "Yes and no. I do think he's behind it… but he has an alibi for the rock through the window. I don't know if that means he hired someone, or someone else also has a gripe with Erin."

"He said it was someone else," Erin said. "That somebody else in town didn't like me stirring up trouble. Do you think everyone keeps saying 'stirring up' because I cook? Or is it just coincidence?"

Terry studied Erin. "Davis said that when…?"

"I saw him at the grocery store. Apparently, he's working there until he can get the money from Angela's estate."

"And… you didn't tell me this, why…?"

"I didn't want to bother you with it. I've been calling you about everything, and he didn't *really* make any threats. There wasn't any point in you going over there to tell him to stay away from me. He was in his own place of work. You can't ban him from there."

"Do you not realize how dangerous it is to be talking to him?"

"What's he going to do in the middle of the grocery store? Mr. Cooper had already seen me there. Other people knew that I was there. If something happened to me, everybody would know where to look. He'd never get away with it."

"I want you to stay away from him."

"I can't stay away from the grocery store. I need to be there more often than anybody else in town. I need to pick up ingredients every few days."

Terry didn't look happy about this answer. Erin looked away from him, tracing her finger through the condensation on the outside of her glass.

Terry turned his attention from Erin to Willie. "I could really use your insight. None of the rest of us were here when Adam Plaint disappeared. Some of us weren't even born yet." He flashed a smile at Vic. "But you lived here back then. What do you remember from that time?"

Willie frowned and rubbed the stubble on his chin. "I was here," he admitted. "But you have to understand…" He licked his lips, looking awkward. "I wasn't friends with the Plaint boys. They weren't my type of people and I wasn't theirs. And I was older than them. We didn't hang out."

"But you were around. You can provide a little background for what was happening. You were… late teens when Adam disappeared…?"

"Yes."

"So you would have heard a lot about it. There must have been a lot of buzz around town."

Willie nodded. "I suppose. Not that I was ever hooked into the grapevine. I didn't hear all of the rumors."

"But enough to know what most of them were. What was your feeling at the time? That Adam Plaint had run off and abandoned his family? Or that he had been killed?"

"Hmm. I don't know. I didn't really care… I remember thinking that Trenton and Davis would have been better off if their mother had been the one to leave. So I guess I thought he left."

"Was there anyone else who disappeared around the same time?" Erin asked. "A man, I mean?"

"There weren't any other disappearances. I would remember. That would have been something to talk about, if two men had both disappeared. That just doesn't happen."

"Just a drifter?" Terry asked. "I just can't make it fit the picture. Why would anyone kill a stranger? Or bother to hide the body?"

"Stranger things have happened." Willie shrugged.

"Of course they do. But I don't like them to mess up my case. I want to make sense of this. Where is Adam Plaint, and who was the man who was buried?"

"If you want to find out what happened to Adam Plaint, why don't you talk to one of his old friends? They'd be far more likely to know what happened than I am."

Terry leaned back.

"You're right. But it doesn't seem like he had a lot of friends. Maybe his wife didn't want him to have any outside interests. Some women are like that. They get married, and there's no more guys' night out. No more poker games or football or drinks at the bar after work."

"She *was* the controlling type. I'm not sure who all of his old friends would be. You might check with Bertie Braceling. He and Adam Plaint were close. Old school chums. Went out together sometimes for golf or drinks."

"Bertie?" Erin was surprised. "I didn't realize they were friends."

Willie nodded.

"Willie," Vic ventured. "You said before that if Aunt Angela killed Uncle Adam, that maybe she had good reason. What did you mean by that?"

Their dishes arrived, and their discussion was interrupted by serving up the various different dishes, passing things back and forth, and trying to use their chopsticks to chase the food down. Erin caught Vic's significant look at Willie, and knew she was still waiting for an answer to her question.

"Was he abusive?" Vic demanded. "Physically? Mentally? You said he wasn't the great guy that everybody is remembering him to be."

Terry leaned forward to hear the answer. It was obvious to everyone at the table that Willie knew something he was holding back.

Willie was silent as he ate a few bites of his Chinese food.

"Well... sometimes kids see things that adults don't. Or maybe adults don't want to see them."

"Like...?"

"Like... flirting with other women. He wasn't faithful to Angela. You'd be pretty resentful too..."

"You bet I would," Vic agreed, so vehemently that everyone laughed.

"And did Angela know?" Terry asked.

Willie's shoulders lifted and fell. "I don't know why you would ask me. I didn't know the Plaints, I was far below their station. They wouldn't have had anything to do with me."

"I'll ask around, see if I can shake anything loose," Terry said. He had his notepad out, and made a brief note before picking up his chopsticks again.

"Just make sure everybody knows that it didn't come from me," Erin said. "I don't know why Davis thinks I'm behind all of his woes, but I wish he'd figure out that I'm not the one investigating it."

"Well, you just stick to your own family history, and let me deal with that."

Willie opened his mouth as if to say something else, then changed his mind and just worked on getting food into his mouth using the chopsticks. Erin frowned.

"What were you going to say?"

"I just think... it's best if we live in the present. Lots of bad has happened in the past... but you can't live in the past."

"I know... but I really want to understand... what happened to my parents. How I ended up where I did."

"But you know. They were in a car accident and they died. Why do you need more than that?"

"I just do," Erin insisted. "I have to know what happened."

❧

At the house, a movement out the kitchen window caught Erin's eye, and she looked out sharply to see what it was, still nervous about the rock being thrown in through the living room window. She didn't need a matching hole out in the back. But it wasn't someone creeping about in the back yard. It was Bertie, out walking a small white dog. Erin wasn't sure what breed it was. It had rather a square build and face, with wispy white fur going every which-way. She stepped out the door and waved at him.

"Hi, Bertie!"

Bertie's face was wreathed in smiles. "Erin! That's right, I had forgotten that you are renting the Potters' cottage while your house is being fixed up. I guess we're neighbors."

Erin already knew the people on either side of the house, but she wasn't sure who was across the back lane. "Where do you live?"

He gestured farther down the back lane. "Other side, about three doors down." He looked down at the dog. "Just taking Miss Marjorie out for a bit of fresh air."

"I'm surprised you have a dog."

"Why is that?"

"I just assumed you'd be allergic." Erin laughed. Of course having food allergies didn't automatically mean he would also have airborne animal dander allergies.

"Well, you would be right," he said. "This is actually my neighbor's dog. I said I would walk her for a few days. I can manage ten minutes at a time. I wouldn't be able to live in the same house as her."

"Oh." Erin nodded. "Well, I'm sorry. It must suck not to be able to have any animals. I have a cat and a rabbit… it's the first time I've had pets."

"I remember having pets when I was young, but by the time I was a teenager, my allergies were asserting themselves and I couldn't have anything. I had a snake for a while… but that didn't last."

"Can I walk with you?" Erin suggested.

Bertie raised his eyebrows. He looked down at the white dog. "Well, I can't speak for the company and we won't be going far, but if you'd like to walk with me…"

Erin fell into step beside him as he continued on down the alley, the dog stopping to sniff every light pole or tuft of grass.

"Not very quick progress, I'm afraid," Bertie said. "Neither of us is particularly fast anymore."

He wasn't elderly. In spite of his allergies he'd always been independent and active. He didn't use a cane.

"Oh, that's fine," Erin said.

"You'll be wanting your supper before long."

"We'll only be a few minutes." For half a minute, they walked in silence. Erin thought through half a dozen different ways to approach the topic, but wasn't sure if any one was better than the other. "I understand that you and Adam Plaint were friends, back in the day."

Bertie looked at her, his eyes widening. "Well, that's going back a long way."

"I know. But you were?"

Bertie nodded slowly. "Yes… we went to school together. We kept in touch after we graduated. A lot of people moved out of town after they graduated; there weren't a lot of us who stayed. It's the same every year. The movers and the shakers move to the city, and the homebodies stick around here, try to keep the town alive."

"So you kept in touch after he got married?"

Bertie walked with deliberation, lifting and putting down his foot as if he had to calculate the length of each step.

"Of course. It's a small town, you see each other as you go about your daily business. We went to the same social events. But we both had work. Other responsibilities."

"Right." Erin looked at the sky, just starting to darken. "What was it like? I moved around a lot, so I don't have any friends from school. Or from my foster families."

"That sounds very lonely. It's nice, having someone who knows you like that, from the old days…" He chuckled and shook his head. "And sometimes, you wish there wasn't someone who knew you like that."

"No fresh starts?" Erin suggested. That was one thing that she liked from a rambling lifestyle. If she made a mistake, it didn't really matter, because she could just reset her life, start fresh somewhere else.

"Yes, exactly," he agreed.

"What was Adam like?"

Bertie gave a wide shrug. "Like anyone. Family man. Set up his own business. The bakery, that was his. That's what he was in charge of, to begin with. So he was up early in the mornings. Kept himself busy. Like you do."

"Somebody said that he might not have been faithful to his wife," Erin said tentatively. "Did he… have an affair?"

Bertie's expression closed. He shook his head, looking angry. "Who is trying to darken his name? He's been gone for twenty years. What's the point in smearing his reputation?"

"I'm not trying to smear his reputation. I just want to know what happened."

"You don't need to know about his private life."

"I do! How else can we figure out what happened to him?"

"What happened to Adam was tragic. There's nothing that anyone can do about it now."

"What is it you think happened to him?"

Bertie looked at her sideways and didn't answer. He clucked at the dog, trying to call its attention away from a clump of weeds.

"You said it was tragic," Erin persisted. "That sounds like you know what happened. Like he didn't just leave his family. What happened to him?"

"Why does it matter?" Bertie protested. "Why can't you just leave it alone? You have your whole life ahead of you. Look forward instead of back."

"Because what happened is important. To Adam, to whoever was buried in my back yard, to me—it's all important. The past affects the future. You can't lay it to rest if you don't know what happened."

"But why do you care about Adam Plaint or a stranger?" Bertie shot back. "What does it matter to you?"

"Whether he is alive or dead affects who inherits The Bake Shoppe. And who inherits The Bake Shoppe affects me and my business. If Trenton and Davis killed their father, then don't you think they—Davis—should have to face the consequences? Or if it was Angela, then maybe we could take some of the burden off of Davis's shoulders. Give him a little peace and let him go on with his life. Leaving it all unresolved… it doesn't serve anyone."

"How is maligning Adam Plaint going to help anything?" Bertie walked along, watching the dog. "Let the past rest, Erin. Let it all go." His voice was pleading. She almost felt sorry for him. He'd been keeping secrets for the past twenty years.

"Don't you think you'll feel better if you tell the truth?" she urged him. "How can any of it rest if you don't tell what happened?"

"No." Bertie's voice hardened. It was so sharp that the dog looked up from piddling on a weed, checking to see if she were in trouble. "No, Erin. Please. Let it go. No one will benefit from knowing the truth. Least of all you."

Erin stared at him. "What do you mean, least of all me? You just finished saying that none of this affects me."

"Oh—" He shook his head in anger or confusion. "Can't you just let it go? Can't you just understand that the past is best left in the past? It's just not worth digging up all of these old secrets."

"Bertie." Erin put her hand on Bertie's hand to stop him and hold him still. "Please. What happened?"

He pushed her hand violently away, a motion that made Erin start back in alarm and set the dog off yapping. He was strong. Not a soft old man.

Erin looked at Bertie uneasily. He'd always shown her a friendly face, cheerful and teasing, easygoing in spite of his physical health issues. She had left the house to talk to him without considering any risk to herself.

What if *he* had thrown the rock through her window? What if he, Adam's best friend, had a stake in not allowing the details of what had happened to come to light?

His eyes were flaming.

"Why couldn't you just leave it well enough alone?" he demanded. "Before you came to town, everything was fine. Everyone had forgotten about the past. And then you… parading into town, dragging it all with you. Reminding everyone. Stirring it all up all over again."

"I haven't!" Erin protested. "I didn't have anything to do with Angela's death. Or Trenton's. Can I help it if Davis thought I knew what had happened twenty years ago? I don't. Is it my fault that there was a body buried under the garage—"

"You're the one who had to dig it up!"

She stared into his eyes, baffled.

"Why couldn't you just let him rest in peace?" Bertie demanded.

"But I… I thought Adam Plaint was buried there. I thought Trenton and Davis had—"

"No. No, no, no."

"Then what? Explain to me what happened."

Bertie put his hand over his face. "No, Erin. Just let them all rest."

"All? All of who?" Erin had a sudden vision of a mass grave beneath her ancestral ground. "What are you talking about?"

Bertie had pushed her hand away before, but now he grabbed her arm. His fingers squeezed it tightly. She could feel his muscles shaking.

"Your mother," he hissed.

Erin froze. She stared into his face. "What?" Barely any sound came out.

"Adam Plaint was having an affair with *your mother.*"

Erin could barely breathe. Bertie squeezed her arm even more tightly, pushing in so close to her that their noses were almost touching.

"Is that what you wanted to hear?" he demanded.

"No…"

She tried to sort out the consequences of this knowledge. The dominoes began to fall, each one hitting the next. Adam Plaint's disappearance. Her parents' car accident. A stranger buried in the yard, a smooth river stone in his pocket.

"Daddy."

She remembered putting the treasure into his hand. A perfectly round, smooth stone with a slight indentation in the middle that he slid his thumb into and rubbed.

Carry it for me, Daddy.

"My father died in the hospital," Erin said. "After the car accident."

"The man in the car with your mother died," Bertie corrected. "Neither of them ever woke up."

"It was my father."

"He had the same general build and appearance as your father. But he had extensive injuries and swelling. He would have been difficult for anyone to identify on sight."

Erin felt nauseated. "No."

"The little girl in the car was crying for her mommy and daddy. No one had any reason to doubt that the man in the car *wasn't* her daddy."

"He was."

Bertie shook his head. "He wasn't." He shook her arm, which was going numb in his grip. "I told you to leave it alone. To stop digging. To leave the past to the past."

"You didn't want me to look at my parents' death. It wasn't just the Plaints and the John Doe you didn't want me investigating. You didn't want me finding out about my parents."

"You just wouldn't listen!"

"Who killed my father?"

"Does it matter?" he shot back, exasperated.

"Yes. It matters. Who killed him? You knew all this time and you didn't tell anyone?"

"I wasn't there." Bertie swallowed. "Adam was my best friend. I don't know how many times I told him to quit fooling around. Just to… stay home and take care of business there. But he always had an eye for the girls, and that didn't stop when he got married. He embarrassed his wife. His children." Bertie sniffled loudly. "It was only a matter of time before a husband or father caught on and decided to take matters into his own hands."

"My father."

Bertie nodded. "It was Davis who called me. Hysterical. Hiding in the closet with the wireless phone. Sobbing so hard I could hardly understand him. Your father had confronted Adam. There was a fight. The poor boy could barely speak…"

"So you went to help. And you and Adam took my father's body to Clementine's house. Put it in the foundations they had dug. Left him to be buried when they poured the concrete the next day."

"Not Adam," Bertie snapped. "Adam had already fled, coward he was. Left his wife and his children to deal with his mess. So I helped. Angela and I took… the body. Davis and Trenton could never have moved it themselves. Everything was already dug and ready to go, just like it had been planned."

"And she said he'd left them. That she'd made him leave."

"It was the truth. The truth is always preferable to a lie."

"Like the lie that it was my father who died in that accident."

"*After* the accident," Bertie corrected. "The weeks that we had to wait, fearing the misidentification would be discovered… What a relief it was when Adam finally died."

Erin shook her head, her eyes hot with tears. "I can't believe you were involved in this. That you let them pull you into it."

"It was twenty years ago, Erin. Everyone was in a panic. We weren't thinking straight. We've had plenty of time to regret it since. Look at how everyone has suffered as a result. Don't you think I would go back in time and change it if I could? But I don't have a time machine and there's no way to change those decisions that were made in panic and desperation."

Erin wrenched out of his grip and held her hands over her eyes. "I can't… I just can't believe it."

The revving of the car engine didn't enter either of their consciousnesses, not until it was practically on top of them.

They were both too overwhelmed with the drama of the past to be aware of anything but each other. Erin finally looked up and saw the big car racing straight toward them. She and Bertie sought each other, each trying to pull or push the other out of the path of the onrushing vehicle.

Erin tripped and fell backward, landing on her back and her elbows with a blow that left her dizzy and breathless. Erin heard the thump and the terrified yipping of the little white dog as the car collided with something large and solid.

CHAPTER 17

*E*rin! What happened? Erin, are you okay?"

Vic's shrieks pierced Erin's consciousness. She opened her eyes, though bright flashes and dark spots still mobbed her vision, making it impossible to see more than fragments of the scene around her.

She knew Bertie was there and tried to crawl to him. The dog was yipping around them.

"Bertie. Is Bertie okay?"

Vic tried to prevent her from moving any closer. "You're both hurt, Erin. You shouldn't be moving. You should wait for help."

Erin found Bertie in the lowest point of the alley. She held his hand and stared into his face, nose bloodied and face cut up from the collision.

"Bertie. Hey." She didn't know what to say to him. Whether to thank him for finally telling her the truth or for pushing her out of the way of the car. Or whether to tell him something else. Something that he needed to hear.

"Erin." His voice was raspy, his breaths shallow and liquid. She leaned closer to hear him better. "Erin, there's one other thing…"

"What?"

But that was the end of his words. He groaned and wheezed, and even while Vic and neighbors gathered around and tried to help somehow, Erin knew he was ebbing away.

"Bertie."

She pressed her palm to her forehead, trying to see him clearly. Trying to sort out what to do. Stop the bleeding? Start rescue breathing? Move him to recovery position with his feet higher than his head? It was all jumbled in her brain and she knew that it was all hopeless. Because he was already gone.

When Terry got there, Vic was holding on to Erin, crying. Terry shone a little flashlight into Erin's eyes, the flashes painfully bright in the gathering darkness of the night.

"Erin, can you give me a description of the car? Did you see the license plate?"

"She's hurt, Terry," Vic protested. "She can't answer questions now."

But Erin grasped at Terry's hand, trying to hold him there, and hold herself there. "The driver," she whispered. "I saw the driver."

It had been the one person who could still be hurt by Bertie and Erin standing together, sharing what had happened twenty years before.

The man with the haunted eyes.

The boy who had hidden in the closet twenty years earlier and begged for help.

Davis.

~

"You need to be still, Erin," Vic said, trying to persuade her to lie quietly. "You don't know how badly you might be injured. You need to wait until the doctor can look at you, do x-rays, and make sure your back isn't hurt."

"I wasn't hit," Erin protested. "The car didn't hit me. I just tripped."

"You still might have hurt yourself. You're as white as a ghost. Please, don't try to get up."

"Bertie. He pushed me out of the way, and now…"

"I know. I know, Erin. I don't understand what happened."

Vic was holding Erin's hand. Erin squeezed it. "Bertie knew. He was the one, he knew all along."

"It wasn't Bertie who threatened you," Vic protested.

"It was. He didn't want me to find out about Adam. About my mother."

"Your mother…?"

"That she was the one he was having an affair with. The man that Adam killed…"

Vic's mouth opened into a wide 'O.' She stared at Erin.

"No."

"The man buried under Clementine's garage was my father. He didn't die in the accident. From the accident. Adam Plaint killed him. *Adam* was the one in the car with my mother. Not Daddy."

Vic's eyes and mouth were wide and round.

There were sirens and voices, competing with each other so that Erin couldn't continue the conversation. The first responders checked out Bertie and then moved on to Erin, immobilizing her, wrapping her like a mummy to strap her to a backboard. She'd been on a backboard before, after the incident in the cave. But she knew she wasn't that badly injured this time.

She felt numb. Overwhelmed by all of the new information and everything that had happened at once.

Willie appeared over her and patted her on the head, staying out of the way of the paramedics.

"Hey, Erin. How are you doing, there?"

"Good. I'm good, really. They're just being overly cautious."

"Better that than not cautious enough. When you're talking about motor vehicle versus pedestrian…"

"The car didn't hit me. Bertie pushed me away. It hit him."

"Oh." Willie looked over toward Bertie. "I'm so sorry, Erin."

"He was trying to protect me, all along. From finding out the truth. From Davis…" Erin couldn't turn her head to look around. "Where's Terry? Where did he go?"

"He's coordinating a manhunt for Davis," Vic said from somewhere close by. Her voice was low and teary. "He's getting roadblocks set up on the highway. Not going to let him get away."

They started to move the gurney back to the ambulance. Erin saw Willie go to Vic and give her a hug.

"It will be okay. She's all right."

"I know. I'm just…"

Willie nodded. He looked toward Erin. "We'll see you at the hospital, okay, Erin? We'll be right behind you."

Erin's automatic reaction was to nod, but she couldn't move at all.

"Okay," she agreed, trying to sound cheerful. "I'll see you there."

~

She was at the hospital for quite a while before Willie and Vic caught up with her. They had probably been kept away in the waiting room. By the time they were shown to her bedside, Erin had been released from her backboard and restraints and allowed to lie in a normal hospital bed in a flimsy hospital johnny.

"Erin! We're here. Are you all right?"

Erin sat up a little, trying to look normal and unhurt. "I skinned my elbows," she offered, lifting up her arms to show them. "That's about my worst injury."

Vic laughed. She leaned over Erin to give her a hug. "I was so scared. You looked so bad."

"Scared to death, but I'm okay."

Vic stayed leaning in close to Erin. "They got him."

Erin felt her eyes go wide. She hadn't expected to hear that news. Not so quickly, anyway. "Davis? They caught him?"

"At the roadblock. He was doing his best to get as far away from here as fast as possible."

Erin shook her head slowly. "But he wanted so badly to reopen the bakery. He wanted to keep us from finding out what had happened so that he could have the bakery and reopen it."

"Well, he screwed that up," Willie said flatly. "You can't go running people down with your car and think you're just going to go back home and no one will notice!"

"I don't think he really thought that through," Erin said. "He must just have seen us together, talking, and panicked. He knew that Bertie was the one person who could tell me the truth. He could probably tell, just looking at us, that Bertie was talking to me about it."

"I'm so glad he didn't hurt you," Vic declared. "I've never been more relieved."

"I'm just glad that everything can finally go back to normal," Willie said. He took Vic's hand and gave it a squeeze. Looking at them, Erin could see that she no longer had a choice between Terry and Willie. She wouldn't risk ruining all of her friendships by getting between Vic and Willie.

~

Later, when Vic left to get clothes for Erin to change into, it was just Willie and Erin.

"You knew about my mother, didn't you?" Erin asked.

He looked at her, eyes hooded. "What?"

"You knew that's who Adam Plaint was having an affair with."

Willie looked away. His darkened skin didn't show a flush, but Erin was sure it was there anyway.

"What makes you think I knew?"

"A few times when you've looked at me… when you've started to tell me something. And you kept telling me not to go digging into the past. Just to look forward. You didn't want me to find out, did you?"

"I couldn't see how it would do you any good." Willie shook his head. "Are you happier knowing?"

"Not happier, no…" Erin thought about how to describe it. "I do feel… like I know more about who she was, though. As a real person, not just my mother. I don't regret finding out. I wish someone had told me sooner."

"I'm sure I'm not the only one who knew," Willie said. "There must be others."

"Did Davis know you knew?"

He shook his head. "I don't see how he could. I didn't have anything to do with him back then. Not twenty years ago and not now. I doubt if he would even remember me from back then."

Erin remembered Davis's slurs about Willie, but didn't feel the need to enlighten him.

"Did Bertie, then? Did he know you knew?"

Willie's brow wrinkled in concentration. "I don't think I ever told him. But we did talk occasionally, around town, coming and going from the bakery, doing odd jobs for him around the house." He gazed at Erin. "I did mention how much you look like your mother. So he knew I remembered her from twenty years ago."

"So maybe he put two and two together. He knew you remembered her. That you were around when Adam Plaint disappeared. He knew that you were friends with Vic and me, that you might tell me things about my mother."

"Might have." Willie scratched his head. "But what does that matter…?"

"I just wonder… if he followed you out to the mine. If he could have hit you or pushed you to keep you from saying anything to me."

"You think it was that important to him? You think he cared that much about you not finding out Adam was having an affair with your mother?"

"And connecting everything up. That they had an affair. That Adam killed my father. That he and my mother died because they were fighting in the car, trying to run away from what he had done."

Willie pondered this.

"He was always so sweet to me," Erin said. "I never would have thought he could do something like that."

"Something like what? Helping to cover up a murder?"

"Threatening me and scaring me half to death. Hurting you. He was so desperate to keep it from coming to light."

"He liked you. Maybe because you are so much like your mother."

Erin raised her eyes to him. "He liked her too?"

"Oh, yes. She was like you in some ways. Kind to people. Not looking down her nose and sneering. People loved her. At least, those who weren't jealous of her. Maybe he thought that by preserving your innocent memories of her, he was protecting her, like he hadn't been able to twenty years ago."

Erin shook her head, thinking back to the few scraps of memory she had of her mother.

IT HAD, OF COURSE, taken the contractors longer than planned to get the house all fixed up for them to move back into, and the new garage built in the back yard. Erin stared across at it from her little attic hideaway. Vic was incredibly excited to have a place of her very own in the little suite over the garage. Erin was glad that she would still be close by, so that they could share meals, drives to the bakery, and other good times together. Vic could have her own space whenever she wanted it, to entertain Willie or other company or just to retreat to on her own. Erin knew it was important for Vic to have her own space. Erin had spent a lot of years on her own and was more than happy to have a roommate to keep her company. But Vic was just starting out and she hadn't experienced true independence before.

Erin felt all kinds of conflicting emotions looking at the new garage. Missing her father, who had been buried there. Her mother. Clementine. And now Bertie. Each of their deaths hurt her in a different way.

But she didn't want to run. For so much of her life, that's what she had done whenever things got too tough. Whenever she felt like she was getting pulled into things. She just left and started over.

She was, in a sense, starting over yet again, but in the same place. It was a good place, and she didn't feel that old urge. She had friends in Bald Eagle Falls, and she wasn't going to run away.

~

The doorbell rang. Erin's evenings often brought visitors; Vic, Terry, Willie, sometimes the church ladies, or others. She opened the door without checking to see who it was, no longer worried about finding herself face-to-face with Davis Plaint or some other malevolent force.

And there was Alton Summers.

Erin took a deep breath.

"Mr. Summers. What can I do for you?"

He looked her over. Made a slight sideways motion like he was going to slide in through the doorway without being invited. But Erin blocked the opening and put her foot on the other side of the door to prevent him from opening it any farther.

"What do you want?"

"I have some information for you. I thought you might want to receive this information in the privacy of your home. It is something that... you might not want to be spread around. Not want your neighbors to overhear."

"What?"

She knew the way that he worked and she wasn't budging an inch. No matter how many times he came back to her asking her for money to keep his information quiet, she wasn't going to give it to him. He could threaten to expose her past all he liked, she wasn't going to be talked into it.

"This is information about your mother."

Erin clenched her teeth, but otherwise strove to remain as unmoved and impassive as she could. "Yes?"

"I have information..." He displayed papers she could not see. "Information that shows that before your mother's death, she was pregnant."

Erin breathed in a deep breath. She remembered her father's voice in her dream. The one that took place in the hotel, not in the car. Her father's voice, not Adam Plaint's.

I am not raising another man's child.

She had thought he was referring to her. That he had discovered somehow that she was not his child, so he didn't want to be her daddy anymore. Her heart rose at the news that he had not been talking about her. He had not been rejecting her and turning her out of his life. He meant the new baby. The one in her mother's belly.

"I see," Erin said to Summers. "Yes, thank you for letting me know that."

"If you don't want the rest of the town knowing about her infidelity…"

"Alton… it's already all out there," Erin said. "You're a bit late to prevent that news from circulating around Bald Eagle Falls."

"But she was *pregnant.*"

"Yes. It's very tragic. Thank you for letting me know."

He stood there a moment longer, his jaw tightening. How many attempts was it going to take before he realized that he simply couldn't blackmail Erin? She wasn't going to pay for his silence. Bald Eagle Falls had too many secrets already. She wasn't going to pay to keep any more of them quiet. It was better to know the truth.

Erin sat down on the couch and picked up the little sheaf of papers that she hadn't been able to continue reading. She had stopped when she reached the papers reporting her father's death. Or the man who they had thought was her father. It was no longer painful to read. The man who was paralyzed and couldn't communicate with the doctors had not been her father. Her father had already been dead at that point, buried by the Plaint boys under the concrete foundations of Aunt Clementine's garage.

For her own peace of mind, she knew she had to read the details of her mother's death. She knew everything there was to know about the circumstances of the accident.

Why the interval of months between the accident and her mother's death? Had it taken that long for her to succumb to the brain trauma she had sustained? Or had they kept her alive, hoping for some miracle? The hope that she would one day wake up and be able to return to her life. To be Erin's mother again. To be alive and vibrant and live a full and satisfying life.

There could be no more secrets.

Erin turned past the pages that she had already read. To where she knew she would find the documents confirming her mother's death.

But there, in cold, clinical words, she didn't find what she had been expecting. On the day of the accident:

Apnea test performed. No brainstem reflexes. Brain death confirmed.

She had been declared brain dead the day of the accident. Why would they keep her hooked up to machines after that? Were they looking for the permission of the next of kin? Did others of the doctors disagree with the diagnosis?

Patient to remain on life support until fetus can be safely delivered or is no longer viable.

Erin swallowed hard and kept reading. A date, and then the words, *healthy baby girl delivered. Five pounds, four ounces. Sixteen inches long. Patient's life support terminated.* And then, a time of death notation.

Erin sat there staring at the paper. Her mother had been kept alive to deliver a healthy baby girl. Small, but viable.

Erin had a sister out there somewhere.

Not a foster sister, but a real blood relative.

She had a sister.

~

There are two holiday shorts that fit into the timeline after Allergen-Free Assignation. They are available on pdworkman.com

Witch-Free Halloween

Dog-Free Dinner

Did you enjoy this book? Reviews and recommendations are vital to making a book successful.

Please leave a review at your favorite book store or review site and share it with your friends.

Don't miss the following bonus material:
Sign up for mailing list to get a free ebook
Read a sneak preview chapter
Other books by P.D. Workman
Learn more about the author

Sign up for my mailing list at pdworkman.com and get Gluten-Free Murder for free!

PREVIEW OF STIRRING UP MURDER

AUNTIE CLEM'S BAKERY #4

CHAPTER 1

$\mathcal{E}$rin managed to block Orange Blossom from getting out the door as she took out the garbage. She drew in a deep breath of fresh air and enjoyed the stillness of the early morning. There would be plenty of action at Auntie Clem's Bakery. It was good to cherish the quiet for a moment at the beginning of her day. Adele told her that she needed to take more time for herself and be at one with nature and the universe. It probably wouldn't hurt, but Erin's mind was always racing ahead, already working on the next thing.

She held her breath when she opened the garbage bin and threw her bag in. Even though she washed it out regularly, it still made her gag if she caught a whiff of it from a few feet away. Erin glanced up and down the street for any sign of activity and then went around to the back of the house.

There was a light on in Vic's loft over the garage, so Erin knew she was up and around and would be joining Erin before long to start their day at the bakery.

As soon as she was in the door, Orange Blossom was winding around her legs, *mrrowing* for food and attention. Erin bent down to pat him and then to pick him up and give his ears and chin a good scratch.

"Hey, Blossom. How was your night?"

The orange and white cat yowled and yipped chattily, telling her all about it. Even after having had him for a few months, it still made Erin laugh at how vocal he was. She'd never known any cat to be so noisy and interested in carrying on a conversation with his two-legged companions.

"I see. Well, that all sounds very interesting," Erin told him. She put him down on the floor and washed up, then went about getting his breakfast ready while her coffee brewed. Blossom stood up on hind legs and batted at her with soft paws while she opened a smelly can of cat food and scooped it into a dish for him. When she put it down on the floor, he immediately pushed his nose into the bowl and began to chow down, his loud purr rumbling through the kitchen.

The coffee finished brewing just as Vic tapped at the back door and entered. Erin wasn't sure how she managed to look fresh and polished so effortlessly first thing. Erin always felt so awkward and plain beside her young bakery assistant. Vic's height was the only aspect of her appearance that hinted at her transgender identity, and her height only increased her poised, willowy air.

"Morning," Vic drawled. "If it isn't just as crisp as a new dollar bill out there this morning. I do love this time of the year!"

Erin smiled at her Tennessee twang. "It really is lovely," she agreed. "If it could only stay like this all year instead of getting so blasted hot."

"We had such a mild summer, you don't know hot."

Erin shook her head. "Ugh. Don't tell me that."

Erin poured them each a cup of coffee.

"Now that the holidays are over, we need to be thinking about what else we can do to draw customers." Erin studied her coffee as if the answer might be there. "We don't want to go through a big slump because people aren't buying gingerbread men and pumpkin pies."

"We don't exactly have a big pool to draw customers from. Bald Eagle Falls isn't the biggest place."

"I know, but I think we still have untapped resources. Not everyone comes to Auntie Clem's. What are people buying in the city? What are they getting at the grocery store that they should be buying at the bakery? And why aren't they coming to the bakery for it?"

Vic sipped her coffee. Orange Blossom, having finished gobbling down his breakfast, sat back on his haunches and stared at them as he applied tongue to paw and washed his face.

"People who can eat gluten buy bread and baking at the grocery store because it is cheaper and convenient. Easier than making a separate trip to Auntie Clem's. And because of the stigma of gluten-free food being inferior."

Kicked into a higher gear by the caffeine, Erin's mind was already whirring, thinking about all the factors involved. "What if we sold bread to the grocery store? They could sell it off the shelves with their commercially produced stuff. People wouldn't have to make an extra trip. It would be right there."

Vic pursed her lips. "I'm not sure about that. If people don't come into the bakery, we can't up-sell. If they pick up a loaf of bread from the shelf at the grocer, how are we going to sell them cookies or cupcakes? Can we really stock the shelves at the grocery store too? That would be a lot of extra work."

"It would be. And we wouldn't be able to build a relationship or to up-sell... unless we sold cupcakes and cookies to the grocery store as well..."

Vic was shaking her head.

"Which would also be extra work," Erin admitted. "And if people didn't buy as much at the grocery store as we expected, Mr. Cooper would lose money. The margins are so thin, we couldn't afford to sell it to him much lower than we sell to bakery customers."

"I don't think you can be in both the bakery and the grocery store."

"No. You're right." Erin was quiet while she thought about other possibilities. Orange Blossom finished his bath and went over to Vic, rubbing up against her and yowling to be picked up.

"He's so demanding," Vic complained. But she put her coffee cup to the side to pick him up and cuddle him.

"That's because he's spoiled," Erin said.

"He is not!" Vic planted a kiss on the top of Blossom's head. "He was demanding even when you first got him. Before either of us had a chance to spoil him."

"That's true," Erin admitted. She eyed the clock on the kitchen wall. "I guess we'd better head out."

Vic gave Orange Blossom one more scratch and put him down. "Okay, Blossom, you'd better be good today. Marshmallow is here to keep you company, so no noise."

Orange Blossom stood looking at her for a minute, eyes intent and ears pointed forward. Then he turned and left the room. Erin got a carrot out of the fridge for Marshmallow and gave him his treat on her way out.

~

It wasn't long before Officer Terry Piper stopped by the bakery as he patrolled the neighborhood. Since it wasn't hot, his water bottle didn't need to be topped off yet, but Erin gave his partner, K9, a gluten-free doggie biscuit.

"How is everything today?" she asked Terry.

"Pretty quiet. Mrs. Sturm reported some vandalism last night, but I don't know if we'll be able to get anywhere on that. Kids, most likely."

"Vandalism? What happened?"

"Her car has been egged. No damage, just a mess."

Erin shook her head, thinking about the woman with the girlish blond pigtails and the people she had seen interact with Lottie. "You're probably right. Sounds like kids. Did she have any idea who it might have been?"

"Nothing too certain. Unfortunately, Lottie Sturm is... not well-liked among the younger generation."

Vic snorted. "Lottie isn't liked by a lot of people in any generation. If I had a nickel for every time she tried to stir up trouble..."

"I don't know if she tries to, or if she's just awkward," Erin said.

"She's not awkward," Vic said. "It's totally on purpose. She's a trouble-maker. That's the kind of person she is."

"We really don't know anything about what kind of person she is. Some people say the wrong things and hurt people's feelings without meaning to."

"And you think Lottie Sturm is one of those people?"

Erin considered. "No," she admitted finally. "You're probably right. She seems to get a certain amount of enjoyment out of it."

Vic nodded vigorously in agreement.

"Regardless of whether or not she brought it down on herself," Piper said, "I've taken her statement and opened a file, and if the culprits are found, they will be dealt with. Other than that, it was a quiet night, and it's shaping up to be a quiet day." His eyes met Erin's. "No bodies. No twenty-year-old mysteries. Just the normal Bald Eagle Falls stuff."

"Good. I don't think I'm up for any more bodies. I'll stick to baking. That's what I'm good at."

"Well, I can't disagree with that," Terry agreed. He was eyeing a fresh batch of chocolate chip cookies that Vic was starting to lay out in the display cabinet.

Vic and Erin exchanged a look. "Do you want one?" Vic asked, eyes twinkling.

"I don't know, I probably shouldn't…" Piper patted his belly like he might be putting on weight. But if he was, Erin certainly couldn't tell. His police uniform fit him as neatly as it ever had and didn't pull or bulge around the middle.

"Oh, come on." Vic put one into a paper sleeve for him. "With the amount of walking you do on a day of patrol? You'll walk this off easily. "

"I suppose." He took it when Vic handed it across the counter to him. "But even so, the sugar probably isn't good for me."

"It's gluten-free," Vic said with a wave of her hand. "That means it's good for you."

Erin opened her mouth to object that just because something was gluten-free, that didn't mean it was healthy. The cookies were full of refined sugar and flours, chocolate, and butter and were far from being a health food.

She saw the way that Piper was looking at her, expectant, waiting for the lecture, and closed her mouth. Was she that predictable?

"It's a dessert," she said instead. "As long as you don't go overboard, I don't think it will harm you."

"One little cookie never hurt anyone," Vic declared.

"Well…" Erin couldn't help objecting to this. Her muscles tensed up in spite of the fact that she was just talking to her friends. "If they're allergic or intolerant, then one cookie could cause damage, even an anaphylactic reaction—"

"Terry's not allergic, though."

"I know that. I mean that if he was…"

"I'm just going to eat this cookie," Terry said.

Erin looked at him. He took a bite of the warm cookie, leaving a smear of chocolate on his lip. The tension drained out of Erin and she laughed weakly.

"Okay. Good. And you two quit teasing me."

They both grinned like kids caught with their hands in the proverbial cookie jar. Erin shook her head.

The bells on the front door chimed, and Erin turned to greet the next customer.

CHAPTER 2

The fixer sat across the table from his boss. The man was physically unimposing, but if he could pay, that was the only thing that mattered.

"You found her?" the boss asked.

"Of course I found her. It wasn't hard. She's not in hiding."

"If you could find her, so can someone else."

He ran his fingers through his hair. "Sure. Anyone who is looking and has a little experience and the right tools could find her too."

"Even though you didn't know her name…"

"A name is nothing. Just one piece of the puzzle. If you have enough of the other pieces, you can figure out the solution."

The boss's eyes flicked around him, and he lowered his voice so it was almost a whisper. "Then I need for her to… disappear."

The fixer sat back in his chair considering the boss's words. "And by disappear, you mean…?"

It wasn't that he hadn't ventured over the line before. He worked outside the law at least as much as he worked within it. But if the boss was looking for a permanent solution, the fixer wasn't so sure. He would charge a much higher price, but he was also taking on a lot more risk. Was he willing to put his own tail on the line?

The boss scratched his head, twisting his face into a grimace. There was a long silence between them. He looked around to be sure no one was paying them any particular attention. Eventually, the boss wet his lips and cleared his throat. But he continued to speak in a whisper.

"I don't want her dead," he said. "That wouldn't be right. But if she disappeared, fell off the grid…"

"Why would she do that?"

"Maybe… she had to go into hiding."

The fixer thought about this, rolling it around in his mind and trying to formulate a plan. "Why would she go into hiding?"

"Why does anyone go into hiding? Maybe her boyfriend is abusive. Maybe she stole something. Maybe she was in danger. Be creative. Sometimes people leave just so they can start over again somewhere else."

"But how would I make any of those things happen? If you really do want to drive her into hiding, and you don't want her… dead… then making her decide to disappear… that's a lot more difficult than trying to warn her off or to blackmail her. I'm not sure how to work that."

"You've done well until now. I thought you were pretty competent."

The fixer was encouraged by these words. He did his best. He was willing to outwork everybody else to get the results his bosses needed. But he wasn't sure this current boss quite understood what he was getting into.

"You do know what family that boyfriend is part of, don't you?"

The boss narrowed his eyes. "Are you telling me you're afraid of some two-bit Tennessee family?"

"I didn't say I was afraid of them." But of course, any contact with organized crime made him nervous. He didn't like to be put in the line of fire of family business, big or little. "But it isn't like dealing with one person or one family. This is an organization. If we interfere with the girl or with her boyfriend, we're going to have targets on our backs and a lot of people looking for us."

"Are you saying I should be getting someone else for this job?"

The fixer chewed on his lip and ran his fingers through his hair again. "I have to think it through. We need to come up with a plan here. Something that makes sense."

"I don't need anything complicated. The fewer details I know, the better. Just make sure she goes into hiding where no one is going to find her."

"What's the payout for making her disappear permanently?"

The boss studied him carefully. "You understand that I don't want her dead. I'm not saying hide the body where it won't ever be found. I'm saying don't kill her."

"Killing her is not part of the deal. That's agreed."

"Not just that we haven't made it part of the deal. But it can't happen. I don't want her death on my conscience."

"Yes. Agreed. That's understood."

The boss looked down at the top of the table, scarred by many hands and nails. Using his body to shield anyone from seeing what he was doing, he traced invisible numbers with his index finger. The fixer watched the numbers and counted the digits. It wasn't a windfall. It wasn't the type of money he could retire on. But it would be enough to live in comfort for a while and not have to survive hand-to-mouth.

How far was he willing to go for that kind of money?

How much was he willing to put on the line?

It had been a while since Vic and Erin had gone out together to eat, just the two of them, so when Vic suggested a girls' night out, Erin accepted. She knew that Vic didn't have many other friends. Even though Vic was a fun, friendly, compassionate girl, she wasn't well-accepted in Bald Eagle Falls. The town was part of the Bible belt and, while the women there weren't any more perfect there than anywhere else, they were judgmental of the moral wrongs they saw or imagined. And Vic being a transgender girl meant that they would not have anything to do with her socially. It would have made for a lonely existence without Erin and Adele around or being able to go into the city for larger gatherings. And of course, she had Willie too, but he was out of town attending to some unnamed business. Erin wondered fleet-ingly what he was up to. But Willie was Willie, and he kept his business dealings pretty close to his chest.

They decided to go for Chinese, where they hadn't been for a while. Willie preferred the 'meat plus three' at the family restaurant, or maybe the hot chicken at the BBQ.

Erin watched Vic struggling with her chopsticks, a w-shaped wrinkle of concentration between her eyebrows. Vic looked up and saw Erin watching her, which made her drop the mouthful she had finally managed to wrangle.

"Shut up," she said sheepishly, "I can do a lot of things, but chopsticks are not my forte!"

"You're doing fine. You just need a little practice and you'll be an expert."

"At home, we always used forks when we went out for Chinese. It never even occurred to me to use chopsticks."

"You can use a fork here if you want to."

Vic always had before. But she shook her head. "No. I want to learn how to do this. Eating with chopsticks is different than eating it with a fork. I want the authentic experience."

"Okay. You're doing fine, so don't mind me."

Vic nodded and went back to work. Erin ate her meal slowly. She didn't want to be done when Vic was still trying to get her first few mouthfuls down.

"How's the research going?" Vic asked. "Did you mind being taken away from it tonight?"

"No, not really. I keep running into dead ends and I just get frustrated. Other people seem to manage to find long-lost family members, so why can't I?"

"You've just started. Sometimes those searches take years, you know. Decades, even."

"Don't tell me that!" Erin's heart sank. "That was pre-internet. Now, it should just be a matter of doing a few searches, and then... bingo, here's your new family!"

"Even when you know someone's name, it can be hard to find them on the internet. Not everybody even has email or social accounts. Some people who do still don't leave any tracks. And since you don't even know her name..."

Erin shook her head and wound noodles around her chopsticks. "How can I not even know my own sister's name? I mean... not even her birth name. How do you begin a search when you don't even have a birth name? Every time they talk about tracing adoptees on TV, they always say 'her birth name was...' Where do you start if you don't even have that?"

"I wish I could tell you. Usually there is a friend or family member who knows the history. Or hospital records. Or an attending nurse. Pretty hard when you don't have any of those things to start with.

"Everybody who knew anything is dead. The hospital only keeps five years' worth of records, and even if they did keep them longer than that, they've had black mold and a fire. Not just one or the other, but both!" Erin sighed in exasperation. "If I believed in God, I'd think he was trying to tell me not to look any further. Every time I think I found a way to track her down, it's blocked."

"God will make a way for you." Vic gave her a mischievous grin. "If there is a God."

"I can't just sit back and rely on some power of the universe to take over and direct my life." Erin used a pot sticker to wipe up juices on her plate. "If I did that, I never would have gotten anywhere in my life. I haven't gotten where I was by sitting still."

Vic gazed at her for a minute. "No... but you didn't get the bakery because you decided that was what you wanted to do and saved up and bought it."

"No," Erin admitted. "I just took the opportunity when it was presented to me. I thought this was my one chance to do what I always wanted to and make gluten-free baking for people with dietary restrictions."

"But you don't think an opportunity like that was more than just chance? Maybe fate? Or God? Or the universe?"

"It wasn't chance or God. It was Clementine. I guess she knew how much I liked it when she ran the tea shop. She didn't have any other living relatives. So she left it to me." Erin shrugged. There was nothing coincidental about that.

"I'm not convinced it wasn't by divine design. How do you explain the fact that you wanted to start a baking business and that's the opportunity that Clementine gave you?"

"I hadn't ever thought I'd be able to start a baking business. I just liked making gluten-free food for friends and clients who wanted it. I liked baking because I liked working with Clementine when I was a little girl. It's no coincidence or design. It's just history."

"Okay." Vic gave a wide shrug. "Whatever you say, Erin. It was all just you and Clementine and your history together. I just think it all fits together rather nicely. That doesn't always happen, you know. I liked hunting when I was little, but if my Uncle Archibald left me a hunting lodge, I wouldn't run it. I'd just liquidate it and get out of there."

"It's not the same."

"No. Because for *you* it was meant to be."

Stirring Up Murder, Book #4 of the *Auntie Clem's Bakery* series by P.D. Workman is available at pdworkman.com

ABOUT THE AUTHOR

Award-winning and USA Today bestselling author P.D. (Pamela) Workman writes riveting mystery/suspense and young adult books dealing with mental illness, addiction, abuse, and other real-life issues. For as long as she can remember, the blank page has held an incredible allure and from a very young age she was trying to write her own books.

Workman wrote her first complete novel at the age of twelve and continued to write as a hobby for many years. She started publishing in 2013. She has won several literary awards from Library Services for Youth in Custody for her young adult fiction. She currently has over 60 published titles and can be found at pdworkman.com.

Born and raised in Alberta, Workman has been married for over 25 years and has one son.

~

Please visit P.D. Workman at pdworkman.com to see what else she is working on, to join her mailing list, and to link to her social networks.

~

If you enjoyed this book, please take the time to recommend it to other purchasers with a review or star rating and share it with your friends!

facebook.com/pdworkmanauthor

twitter.com/pdworkmanauthor

instagram.com/pdworkmanauthor

amazon.com/author/pdworkman

bookbub.com/authors/p-d-workman

goodreads.com/pdworkman

linkedin.com/in/pdworkman

pinterest.com/pdworkmanauthor

youtube.com/pdworkman